Lindley counte̶d̶ ̶.̶.̶.̶ knelt no more than five yards from where he was standing. They were arranged in rows, with their heads towards the south.

'Who are they?'

'So-called criminals.'

Lindley's throat was dry. 'What kind of criminals?'

'Murderers, rapists, pirates, thieves – you name it.'

'Thieves?' He heard the incredulity in his own voice.

'Why not? Does it matter what they call them? The truth is that most of them are just ordinary river people suspected of helping the rebels.'

Lindley felt his scalp itching. Sweat was trickling inside his shirt. He glanced about him, looking for the executioner.

Robert Carter was born in Staffordshire and educated in England, Australia and Texas. Formerly with an American oil exploration company and then with the BBC, he has taught, worked in and travelled the wilder places of the earth. Now living in London, Robert Carter writes full time. This is his fourth novel.

Also by Robert Carter

Armada
Talwar
Courage

BARBARIANS

ROBERT CARTER

ORION

An Orion Paperback
First published in Great Britain by Orion in 1998
This paperback edition published in 1999 by
Orion Books Ltd,
Orion House, 5 Upper St Martin's Lane,
London WC2H 9EA

A CIP catalogue record for this book
is available from the British Library.

ISBN: 0 75281 696 9

Typeset by SetSystems Ltd, Saffron Walden, Essex.
Printed and bound in Great Britain by
Clays Ltd, St Ives plc.

THE TAIPING REBELLION

In 1850 China's population was 413 million, by
1862 it had fallen to 267 million.

Few in the West have ever heard of the Taiping
rebellion, and yet it was a war begun by
Westerners and finished by Westerners, a war in
which British, Americans and Frenchmen all
played their part, a war that killed four times
as many people as World War One.

And at the heart of it was an Emperor's belief
that he was the Son of Heaven, and a rebel's
belief that he was the younger brother
of Jesus Christ . . .

THE CHINESE SYSTEM OF HOURS

11pm – 1am Rat
1am – 3am Ox
3am – 5am Tiger
5am – 7am Hare
7am – 9am Dragon
9am – 11am Snake
11am – 1pm Horse
1pm – 3pm Goat
3pm – 5pm Monkey
5pm – 7pm Rooster
7pm – 9pm Dog
9pm – 11pm Pig

'The Barbarians are like beasts, and not to be ruled on the same principles as people. Were any one to attempt controlling them by the great maxims of reason, it would tend to nothing but confusion. The ancient kings well understood this, and accordingly ruled Barbarians by misrule. Therefore to rule Barbarians by misrule is the true and the best way of ruling them.'

– The Manchu maxim 'On the Intercourse with Barbarians' –

For D. R. Hurd,
an old China hand.

PROLOGUE

The Summer Palace, near Peking
27th April, 1856

The young woman's groans came again as she entered the twentieth hour of her labour.

She was exhausted. It had been a hellish night, a time of delirium and nightmare. Pain drenched her, and now the room was once again filled with leering, evil spirits. The gongs that sounded the hours drove them away, but each time they had returned, and even when the Taoist priests had chanted their stern exorcisms an hour ago they had still not left her bedside.

Nobody had told Yehonala the pain would go on and on like this. She tried to gather her strength by breathing, hating the place. It was a library, a place of reading, not the right place to give birth. It was like a temple, lit by the dismal red light of buffalo horn lamps, chilly and forbidding. Everywhere she looked there was polished cedar wood and carved dragons inlaid with mother-of-pearl. All around were shelves containing China's ancient Classics, all wisdom, all knowledge.

It was one of the Court astrologers who had suggested that she give birth in the Library of the Topaz Wu-t'ung Tree, and so the Emperor had agreed.

He's a jellyfish, she thought. Spineless. Too weak to rule even his own women.

Yehonala gripped the padded cotton quilt, then lay back, gasping as the pains in her belly died away once more. She could not quell the quickness of her breathing, nor the thumping in her ears and throat. The maid who perched on one side of the divan dared not touch her. A senior maid dabbed the sweat from her face with a paper towel. She saw grey light seeping in at the windows, heard a hawking cough

1

and the distant shrilling of peacocks. Dawn, and still the torture wasn't over.

'What's happening to me?' she muttered. 'Is the baby's head too big? Am I dying?'

'It's what all women must suffer, Lady,' First Midwife said. 'If we're lucky enough.'

She was as stolid as a dumpling. She had seen it all many times before, and that was a comfort, but twenty hours was a long time.

'I wish it was over.'

'The Heavens are awaiting the most auspicious moment, Lady.'

What if my muscles are exhausted? she thought. What if I'm not able to squeeze any more and the baby dies inside me?

She closed her eyes and breathed to gather her strength, aware of servants moving in the room. The smell of peonies was in the air now, bringing to her mind piquant images of spring. Peonies everywhere, she thought, peonies placed in vases, peonies woven in the bright gowns of the court ladies, peonies glimpsed outside in the budding gardens . . . Then the pain came again and blotted out everything from her mind.

'Why won't it come?' she asked the Chief Eunuch when the contractions abated. 'What's wrong with me?'

'Take courage and be patient, Lady Yehonala. The labours of birth are the same whether the child be worthless girl or precious boy, a rice-planter's child or heir to the Dragon Throne, but the whole Empire has been holding its breath for you tonight.'

It was true. For she was 'Little Orchid', First Concubine to Hsien-feng, Emperor of China, and all the world was offering up prayers that the baby inside her would be born alive and healthy, but – above all things – that it would be a boy-child, an heir, to carry forward the Ch'ing dynasty into the next generation.

What will happen when the auspicious moment comes? Perhaps then they will decide to cut me . . .

A maid offered her tea, but she pushed the bowl away. She heard the Emperor's retinue approaching. Heard his voice outside the birthing room. She was twenty years old. Five years ago, when she had been selected, Hsien-feng had also been twenty. The Hsien-feng Emperor, last representative of a spent family, a dying line, diluted by weakness and luxury, one from which – so it was said – the Mandate of Heaven was about to be withdrawn.

For three thousand years all China had believed that it was Heaven that conferred the right to rule on an Emperor. This was called 'the Mandate of Heaven'.

You were never fit to rule, she thought, disgusted by the thought of him. You were always more concerned with a wine glass or an opium pipe than with statecraft. If only you knew. Then you and all your ancestors should be glad I've deceived you.

Feverish questions tumbled through her mind:

Will the baby be whole?

I don't care, so long as it is a boy.

Will it be strong?

It doesn't matter – so long as it is a boy.

What name shall he be called?

Any name. But it must be a boy's name . . .

If it is a girl I promise to kill myself, she told the gods sincerely. If it's a girl, it's better born dead.

Hsien-feng's wife, Niuhuru, Empress of the Eastern Palace, had presented him with a daughter a year before. His disappointment had been profound, and he had refused to see either wife or child. After that Yehonala had whispered her own promises to the easy-to-despise weakling who was the Son of Heaven.

She remembered that night very well. A large ivory table stood outside the Emperor's bedchamber. On it were many jade tablets, each carved with the name of a consort or concubine. When Hsien-feng retired to the Chamber of Divine Repose he would select a tablet, and a special eunuch would depart to fetch the naked girl. She was naked by tradition, so that no weapon could be concealed on her. For modesty's sake she was carried through the corridors and courtyards of the Forbidden City wrapped in a coverlet of diaphanous scarlet silk.

Yehonala recalled the night she had been laid at the foot of the Emperor's bed, in a room decorated entirely in the colour of passion. She had been burning with ambition yet also frozen by terror. She had lived in the Forbidden City for three years but had never before come within a hundred paces of the Son of Heaven. Now at last, in this crimson-draped chamber, she was to lie with him, knowing that if she succeeded in pleasing him she would rise to power and influence, but that if she did not, she would henceforth be ignored and sink to a life no better than that of a maid.

But right away everything had begun to go wrong. Hsien-feng had not seemed so awe-inspiring in bed. His penis had been small and narrow, and worse, an ugly shape that reminded her of a ginseng root. His ideas about what to do with it had been primitive too. He had lain back, his mind far away, waiting. So she decided to trust her intuition and take the greatest gamble of her life.

'I know what it is you really want,' she had told him. 'And I can give it to you.'

'If you give me a son I will raise you to the title "Empress of the Western Palace",' Hsien-feng had whispered back, his voice hesitant.

'I will give you a son, but I don't mean that. I know what it is your body craves now.' And she had bitten him hard.

After that, he had selected her tablet again and again, and she had known that she had found the key to unlock his secret heart.

'Yehonala,' he had groaned one summer night, enraptured by her tantalizing touch. 'You are not like the rest.'

'No.'

'The others are all so compliant, so unresponsive. But you – you understand what I need.'

'Get down on your knees to me like a dog,' she had said, luring him, and he had done so eagerly, the Ruler of the World, to take his punishment, as usual.

They had coupled throughout the long, humid nights of early summer, and she had tied him and teased him and abused him. She had used a bamboo switch on his buttocks and thighs and back, readying him for her body, before getting astride his trussed form. And when he had released his seed in her she had faked her own pleasure, and encouraged him to believe in the tumbled aftermath of that great Imperial bed that he was the greatest lover a woman could ever know.

Yehonala looked at First Midwife. Last night had been longer and far more strenuous than any of those dutiful nights coaxing Hsien-feng's reluctant seed from him. Last night incense had burned in the great bronze urn that stood in the corner of the room. Oil lamps had lit the cool chamber of polished wood. Blood-red lanterns had hung in the branches of the four topaz wu-t'ung trees in the tranquil courtyard.

Yes, Son of Heaven, she thought. I know your secret, but you will never know mine.

Beyond the latticed window, throughout the precincts and pavilions of the Yuan Ming Yuan – the Garden of Perfect Brightness – the greatest of the summer palaces, maids and eunuchs and court ladies were mingling and talking in hushed voices. When she looked back she saw her most important ally, the shrivelled Chief Eunuch, An Te-hai.

'It will be a boy,' he told her.

'How do you know?'

'Because the court astrologers all agree. They've seen it written in the Twelve Mansions of the Heavens.' He pointed to the luo-shu chart that the astrologers had pinned up on the wall – it contained magic numbers that had the power to lessen pain. 'After all the trouble we've been to, Lady, it had better be a boy.'

The remark struck a barb of fear into her. It was a veiled threat. An Te-hai was a natural intriguer, arrogant, avaricious and capable of incredible malice. She had been at pains to guarantee his friendship – if 'friendship' was the word for what a eunuch of the Forbidden City ever gave or received.

Whatever it is, she thought, I've put myself in his hands, and maybe also in his power – because he knows the truth about those long summer nights.

She shifted to ease the ever-present ache in her back, but then the contractions overwhelmed her again, and she shut her eyes and clenched her teeth and fought.

When she came to herself again the light was brighter outside. Did I call out his name? she wondered, thinking of the baby's real father as they propped her up on goose-down pillows. Where is he now? How I wish he was here. It is a father's right and duty to greet his son as he makes his first appearance in this world.

Her thoughts went out to him as the pain gave notice that it was about to possess her once more.

'I can see the head. Push, Little Orchid. Push now.'

With a shuddering effort she clenched her teeth and pushed. When she looked down she saw a wizened face protruding from her like a strange purple fruit, covered in bloody mucus. She expected to be horrified, but she was smiling, the pain and danger magically transmuted to joy.

One of the midwives cleared the baby's mouth with her finger. She eased the blue cord of life over its head. She heard them urging her, saying, 'Again, again,' and felt the body follow out all in a rush. Then infinite relief came over her as she felt the life-force miraculously redistribute itself inside her body.

'Please, Lady, give me your hands,' First Midwife urged, lifting the tiny form.

Yehonala pulled the baby onto her breasts and cradled him momentarily. Then he was taken away from her. She saw the cord cut and tied before the baby was swathed in clothes and hurried outside to the waiting Emperor.

She felt alone as sharp, ecstatic voices came to her from outside. The word was passed. Servants whispered, eunuchs crowed. An Te-hai called out, 'It's a boy. A boy after all! He will be a great, great man!'

The gates of the library compound were opened. Across the lake a ten-thousand-strong army of Imperial servants was gathered, from the highest ministers of state to the graded mandarins who ordered the Middle Kingdom. All were drawn up in precise rank and file. All were wearing formal black and red hats and grey robes of state to honour this long anticipated moment. As the Emperor appeared everyone threw themselves down on their bellies into a full kowtow, hoping that Heaven had smiled, but fearing that it had not.

Hsien-feng's high voice was rhapsodic as he spoke to them. He held up the swaddled newborn like a hunting trophy, his long golden nail protectors like talons around the child. 'My son! My son! He shall be called Tsai-ch'un!'

And all the world rejoiced.

BOOK I

Hong Kong – November, 1859

Harry Lindley stood at the steamer's rail, looking out at the green-draped hills that dominated the island of Hong Kong. He wore a wide-brimmed hat, a white silk Singapore shirt, open at the neck, a lightweight jacket and trousers of cream linen, ruffling now in the breeze.

'Fragrant Harbour,' he murmured, savouring the words. 'China. At last.'

Three paces away the ship's first officer tapped out his pipe, and grunted. Like Lindley he was a Scot. His name was John Sutherland.

'It's been a good passage, Doctor.'

As Lindley stared out at the settlement of Victoria – traders' warehouses, the square tower of the cathedral and the white painted Governor's residence – he thought of his mother. She had died a year and a half ago, of the cholera. In all her life she had never left Scotland. She had refused to follow her preacher husband when his missionary zeal had taken him to China thirty years ago. Instead she had brought up her only son alone, and had said little about her husband that was not an accusation.

Lindley looked up at the masts. The huge P&O screw-steamer *Chusan* could spread four thousand square feet of sail in an emergency, but she had steamed via the Cape of Good Hope, Ceylon and the Straits Settlement, arriving in the swift time of four months and five days.

Sutherland turned away from the rail also. 'Can you smell that?'

'What?'

'That wind blowing out of China. This land always smells to me of dung and death. You know they fertilize their fields with human blood.'

Lindley smiled, but Sutherland's words had shocked him. 'Come now, Hong Kong looks like a pleasant place.'

'Hong Kong's not China. Don't forget that. For every living Chinaman there are thirty who have died. It's a land of ghosts.' Sutherland gestured at the mountainous island. 'Are you going ashore?'

'I thought I'd look around.'

'Do that. There's opportunity aplenty for a man in Hong Kong. You might change your mind about Shanghai.'

Lindley faced him briefly, then looked away. 'No. I came to China to answer some important questions. I can't answer them in Hong Kong.'

Sutherland glanced sidelong at him. 'What kind of questions?'

Lindley thought darkly of the collection of letters in his cabin. Letters from his father. They had been addressed to him twenty years ago, but he had only read them in the last eighteen months, after his mother's death. He had discovered a locked iron box in her bedroom. The letters had been written by a man very different to the father he had been allowed to believe in.

'I said, what kind of questions?'

'Personal ones.'

Sutherland had been trying to find out about him for most of the voyage, but all he or anyone else knew was that Lindley had studied Chinese and that fifty heavy wooden crates were in the *Chusan*'s holds, bound for Shanghai's British Concession.

Lindley looked down. Over the side and below, women were sculling with large oars thrust over the sterns of their boats, faces upturned, shouting out in sing-song pidgin to the deck hands.

'Hi ya! Massa! More bettah go shore!' Then Lindley recognized the Cantonese term, fan-kwei – 'foreign devil' – and grinned.

'Harbour women can be wild. They're born, live and die aboard their sampans. Some of them never once set foot on land.'

He gave Sutherland a sceptical glance. 'Is that so?'

'Aye, Doctor. Don't ever save the life of a Chinese or he'll consider you responsible for him for ever after.'

'What?'

'As God's my witness, you interfere with a Chinaman's destiny at your peril. Even if that destiny is to die.'

'That's absurd!'

'It's what they're taught to believe. To obey and to suffer, and then to die. There are no Christians out here, you know.'

Lindley grunted at Sutherland's bigoted ideas, but he told himself, that's the first trap. I must keep an open mind.

'Harry . . .'

He turned to see the Reverend and Mrs Chapman, the preacher and his wife. He smiled, liking her subtle flirting, and wondered again what had made a good woman like her marry a narrow prig like Alfred Chapman. He was a man full of zeal and anxious to carry the word of God among the heathen. He wore wire-rimmed spectacles, was humourless and narrow-faced, narrow-spirited too. At least Eliza Chapman had the spirit to follow her husband out East, even if she had deliberately flirted with him so that she filled his dreams in the smothering heat of tropical nights between Ceylon and Singapore. She had tempted him with her mischievous eye and her tumble of honey-coloured curls.

Chapman offered his hand. 'Well, then, Mr Lindley, since you're going on to Shanghai I suppose this is the last time we'll see one another.'

'Yes.'

Eliza's smile trembled. Her eyes were cast down, her face slightly flushed. 'Goodbye, Harry.'

He nodded, knowing how to remain controlled, but wanting to give her a last kindness. 'Goodbye, Eliza. I'm very thankful we met.'

The boat was alongside. When Eliza got into it, Lindley felt his emotions strike a minor chord. Chapman was right – they would never meet again. He knew that.

He watched the boat move away until Eliza's parasol was a tiny speck of white.

'Extremely attractive woman, Mrs Chapman,' Sutherland said.

'Yes.'

'Must have taken a great deal of self-control.'

'What do you mean by that?' he said sharply.

Sutherland softened his tone. 'I think you know exactly

9

what I mean. You could have changed her life for the better, you know.'

He absorbed the remark silently for a moment, knowing exactly what Sutherland was driving at. At last he said, 'I didn't come to China to rescue missionary's wives from unhappy marriages. As it happens, I have a mission of my own.'

He was grateful when Sutherland looked up at the smoke-stack again, and said, 'Wind's getting up, Doctor. The glass has been falling for forty-eight hours.'

'Rain coming, you think?' he said, regaining his equilibrium.

'Aye. You'd best get ashore if you're going. And if you'll take a word of advice from an old hand, besides these boats there are other boats in the harbour manned by men. Keep away from them.'

'I will,' he said.

Sutherland began to walk away. 'You'd better heed what I say, Doctor. After dark they frequently murder their passengers.'

After the cramped world of the *Chusan*, Lindley wanted to walk. He paid a dollar for a silver-capped walking stick and set out to see the town. On the main street, outside the Governor's house, stood Indian sentries in turbans, a white flagpole and a unit of soldiers in red jackets stamping up and down. Warehouses and business premises had sprung up right along the coast. It's hard to believe, he thought, looking about him, that less than twenty years ago this place was a Chinese fishing village.

A sedan ride out to Happy Valley cost him another dollar. He lingered at the racetrack, listened to the birds and let his eyes roam over the green slopes. He started to walk back as dusk began to fall and the same barefooted porters who had brought him out approached him again. They were wiry little men, limbs thin as pencils, weather-beaten, but with good humour and amazing strength. Like all Chinese they spoke to Europeans in 'pidgin', or business English.

'You want come long, massa? Me wantchee you come long.'

'One dollar you?' Lindley said.

10

The man who had spoken pointed to himself then the other porter. 'One dollar, same – same this man, ga-la?'

He shook his head and began to walk on. 'No can.'

'Hi-ya! Can do. Can do.'

'No can do.'

The porter conceded, looking hard done by. 'Waw keh! Massa you come.'

Lindley squeezed into the tiny open car, stick resting on his lap, and was lifted up. His soul rebelled against the idea of being carried by men, especially men so much less well-nourished than himself, but it had been his resolve to accept the local ways and he put his objections aside. As they headed into the Chinese town he heard a sudden riot of fire-crackers, and ordered the porters to stop. He paid them off and began to walk among the Chinese shacks and lantern-lit noodle stalls, and tried in vain to blend with the swarming crowds.

He had been prepared for hostile looks, but there were none. It's as if I was a ghost, he thought, remembering Sutherland's words. In a public place they all look straight through a person. How different to Bombay where everybody stares at you. Strange how all the men and boys here have shaved heads, except for a single, long braid that hangs down at the back. Sutherland said it was compulsory, the mark of their subservience to the Manchu Emperor. But, if that's so, why do they continue to wear it in British territory? Perhaps they've grown used to the style. Perhaps they've just forgotten what it means. Or do they think the Emperor might still take back the Colony from the fan-kwei, and punish those who gave up their pig-tails?

He watched as he walked, trying to learn. Many of the men, he saw, covered their crowns with little round, cushion-like hats. He looked out for the bound feet he had been told about, but saw none. The universal Chinese custom, he had been told, was for girls to have their feet tightly bound so they deformed as they grew, becoming like hooves, and all because Chinese men were said to find feet like that sexually stimulating. But here the unmarried girls wore bright cotton coats, black trousers and European-style shoes on properly formed feet. Their hair was plaited at the back to match the men's. They went about arm in arm, just as girls did in Edinburgh. He recalled another of John

11

Sutherland's remarks that Chinese women never cut their hair, and decided that that might easily be true.

Ahead of him now a blind street fiddler scratched an alien tune on a three-stringed instrument. Nearby an open-fronted drug shop was lined with hundreds of jars of pickled roots and other nameless fetishes. Dozens of sacks of aromatic herbs and powders filled the air with taints of ginger and dried fish and camphor and musk and aniseed. A crone begged from him, cackled at the brass coins with square holes in their centres that he put into her hand. A dozen eyes refused to watch him, and no face gave a clue to its owner's thoughts.

As he walked on, men and women wandered against him like a tide. Their movements were unpredictable and unlike people he had been among before. He felt large and obvious, and saw that this was a place Europeans never came. There seemed to be a warning now in the deliberate way everyone ignored him.

A vivid burst of light startled him and made him look skyward – just a festive firework, exploding noise and brilliance. Other rockets followed, throwing out expanding balls of green and red stars. As flat echoes came back off the hills and the sparks died he saw high up on the Peak other more mysterious flashes – Morse light passing from the signal station to unseen shipping out in the harbour. It made him think of the crates lying in the belly of the *Chusan*. It reminded him of their purpose, and the thought of the immense power of what was in them unsettled him.

One of his father's letters from twelve years ago had said of the new colony, 'The place is well appreciated by the Chinese. The whole coast for several hundred miles north and south is infested with pirates. Trading vessels have even been plundered and their crews massacred while our gun-boats lie almost within gun-shot range . . .'

Lindley gripped his stick harder, counting the turnings from the temple square.

A little further along he noted a peeling door, men arguing in the shadowy entrance. Another man arrived and rolled up his sleeve as if showing a tattoo and was admitted. One of the men noticed Lindley, stared hard at him, spat, then shut the door to his view. His sense of danger intensified.

He went into one of the booths on Chicken Bone Lane, requested a bowl of noodles from the owner in halting words, then sat down at a table to eat. The liquid was peppery and contained limp greens and pale fragments of meat in a nest of noodles. He used the chopsticks to stir his meal up in the way he had seen the laundrymen aboard the *Chusan* do. He savoured the taste and sipped at the little handleless cup of pale fragrant tea that was put down before him.

He was sure that the owner thought his presence here disastrous for trade. His neck prickled and he knew that someone – a woman – was watching him.

He looked up at her and saw a girl with a strikingly beautiful face. She stood alone in a doorway across the street. Her complexion was deep olive in the lantern light, so dark that her teeth seemed very white when she parted her lips. She was wearing dark peasant pyjamas, black canvas slippers and a rice-straw hat, but she could not have been a peasant. Her eyes were large and almond-shaped with arching brows, and her hair was combed back into a thick rope. He caught her staring.

She had such delicate features and so graceful a manner about her that he found himself reluctant to look away, and for a moment they stared at one another, neither one able to break the spell. Then, maddeningly, the stall owner moved between them carrying a crate.

Lindley tried to look past him, but when the stall owner moved aside the girl was gone. He looked along the street, but there was no sign of her, so he finished off his noodles and left.

Later Lindley arrived in a part of the colony where other Westerners were to be found. A row of gaudy drinking haunts opened out onto a European-style sidewalk. When the rain started he went into one of the sing-song halls, sat down and let the din wash over him. The liquor was hard and the crash of gongs, drums, horns, the scraping of an excruciating fiddle and the shrieking falsetto of a succession of female singers passed for entertainment. An evil-smelling herbal drink was placed in front of him and each time he sipped at it his mouth burned.

He looked around. The image of China his father's letters

had built up did not square at all with this. And what about my father? he thought. What if he turns out to be just what my mother said he was? A feckless dreamer obsessed with saving souls in faraway places, but willing to neglect his own wife and child? You've given up everything to come to Shanghai.

He took another slug of the rotgut and turned away from the thought. Apart from the singers there were no women here and he thought of Sutherland's savage comments on how the Chinese treated their womenfolk. 'They're on a par with goods and chattels, considered unworthy to mix with men in public. Except in domestic matters they're totally ignored. And it's the greatest breach of good manners for one Chinaman to ask after the health of another's wife. They think it's vulgar to talk about female relatives at all.'

From where he sat he could see the entrance lobby. The sing-song hall charged no admission, but people wishing to come in were screened by the proprietor's sons. There were dozens of patrons, almost all of them Chinese. Nearby a group of men were laughing, playing a riotous game of forfeits. One held up his fingers at the same time as the others guessed how many. The penalty for guessing wrong was for the losers to down their drinks then hold their cups bottom up over their heads. Every now and again one of them would disappear into the back with a singer.

A female singer tottered towards him on deformed feet. She was thickly powdered and daubed with paint. He let her take a seat on his knee, knowing that she had singled him out as a rich new arrival. He had noted that the etiquette was never to refuse a cup from the hand of a singer. He drank down what remained of the fierce liquor. The girl's fan contained a list of songs, and she handed it to him to select from. As he did so, a waiter refilled his cup.

'Hi-ya. I this piecee man belong numbah one. Can do so fashon? Ga la?' She pointed to a song then smiled, revealing a row of tiny teeth, yellow against crimson rosebud lips and the deadpan white of her face. She looked about wide-eyed like a conspirator, then whispered to him, 'S'pose you wantchee look see, me wantchee you come along me catchee samshoo.'

He didn't understand, but her manner persuaded him it had to be a proposition. 'No can. Go ship soon.'

'Awww! No! Engleman numbah one.'

'No Engleman! Scotsman!'

'All same-same.'

'Oh, no! Certainly not same-same.' His throat burned but he played along amiably, handing over the obligatory silver dollar, and pointing out his song. 'China gal numbah one!'

She lifted the refilled drink to his lips, to the hilarity of the other guests. 'Chin-chin, ga la!'

'Chin-chin.'

He drank again, and she hopped off his knee to begin her caterwauling. He knew she would be back.

As the cymbals clashed and the strings began twanging once more he heard a commotion at the door. He turned to see a woman dressed in black peasant pyjamas. She had her back to him and was arguing with one of the proprietors' sons. Without warning the man thrust her into the street. She went down among the mud and filth. When she got up Lindley saw that she was the same striking girl he had seen at the noodle stall.

She came back inside, arguing, pointing to her clothes, until the doorkeeper made a lightning grab for her hair. He wound it in his fist and started dragging her out again. That was far too much for Lindley.

'Hey, you!'

The girl was flailing and yelling, but her head was forced down and she could do nothing. Then the man bumped a table and it went over, spilling a paraffin lantern. The fuel that leaked from it flared up brightly, scattering people nearby. Waiters began flapping at the fire, trying to smother it. The doorman disengaged one of his hands and began slapping the side of the woman's head viciously.

'Hey – I'm warning you!'

Lindley grabbed the doorman's arm and drove him back. The doorman would not release the girl's hair. She sprawled to her knees and gasped with pain, so Lindley threw a punch that dislocated the doorman's jaw. The sound was unmistakable, and the man went down in dumb agony.

Lindley dragged the girl to her feet and pushed her behind him. As the flames were stamped out several men wreathed in smoke came forward, ready to lay hands on him. He faced them instinctively, backing away. He was bigger than any of them, but outnumbered. When he saw the enraged proprietor push forward, shouting, a revolver in his hand, he thrust a table into the path of the nearest man, grabbed the girl and leapt for the doorway.

'Come on!'

They fled together up the street, knocking people out of their path as shots rang out behind them.

The alley they dodged into was a morass of mud and cinders. Eaves dripped overhead. The controlled side of Lindley's mind cursed him for getting involved in a fight that was none of his business, but the rest of him exulted. A thrill rushed through him, and he laughed at the madness and the danger.

'That was grrreat!'

Then he looked at the rain-drenched girl and saw how the whites of her eyes glittered in the darkness.

It was almost midnight and the five-grain liquor had turned sour on Lindley's tongue. He had drunk more than he thought. The rain had stopped, but overhead wind was roaring in the trees, and low, ragged clouds were swirling out of the mainland. Lightning split the sky beyond like rumours of titanic warfare in the interior.

'So, your name is Fei,' he said, looking to her once more. The breeze had dried out her hair and it streamed behind her, catching blue light.

She nodded miserably. 'Fei-ch'ien. I come Macao. Macao no good.'

'Why Macao no good?'

'Father plenty no good.'

'Why your father no good?'

'He make me marry. But – no good.'

Waves lapped the shore somewhere below. They sat on the edge of the little park that overlooked the harbour. Nearby in a sheltered bay hundreds of sampans rode like a raft, battened down for the night, their matting roofs dark and wet. Their planks clattered as they bumped together. Further out the *Chusan*'s riding lights glimmered over the choppy waters. She would sail at first light. Behind her the bare hills on Kowloon side – China proper – stood in absolute blackness.

'What were you doing in that den, anyway?' he asked.

'Boss catchee me. Say want become singer,' she said.

'You?' He laughed shortly. 'A singer? In there? Those girls are prostitutes.'

'Boss want say me steal bottle liquor, say English soldier come cut off head.'

'The wicked old bastard,' he said, knowing she would not know the word.

'That wicky old bastard get plenty poor girl by making lie like that.'

'I bet.' He wiped his forehead with a handkerchief. 'So you came to Hong Kong to avoid being forced into an arranged marriage? Is that it?'

'No good,' she said, shuddering. 'You don't know.'

'Maybe I do.' He told her. 'My mother and father didn't like one another. You savvy?'

She made no reply, and he wondered what would happen to her stranded here alone, without means and without anyone to help her. John Sutherland's words about Chinese women haunted him: 'They're just slaves, most of them. Bought when very young and trained up to an evil life. They have no expectation of happiness, or even comfort.'

After a while he asked her, 'So, what do you intend to do here?'

She looked away, evading, then said brightly, 'What you name?'

'My name Lindley. Harry Lindley.'

'Lin-li,' she said approvingly. 'Lin-li plenty good name. Plenty good luck name.'

'Oh, you think so, do you?'

'Numbah one. Where you go?'

He decided there could be no harm in telling her. 'Shanghai.'

'Oh, Shanghai!' She became enthused. 'Shanghai plenty big. Plenty silk trade. Plenty big river. You big ship go Shanghai?'

He didn't answer her. The wind roared in the trees. He still felt wonderful. His heart was pounding but they had both escaped the sing-song hall alive and justice had been done, so he felt wonderful, far better than he had any right to feel, and yet . . .

She tugged at his sleeve. 'Lin-li, got uncle. Aunty same same. Plenty happy.'

17

'Well, why didn't you say so? Where do they live? I'll take you there.'

'You take me there?' She was suddenly full of thanks. 'Oh, you good man! Plenty good man!'

He stood up, anxious to fulfil his promise right away. It was late and he would have to get her to safety before dawn. 'Come on,' he said, gesturing at the harbour. 'Big boat sail soon. Me catchee little boat go there. First I take you uncle.'

She was on her feet and pulling his sleeve again. 'I catchee you me plenty good sampan.'

'No, Princess. I said first I take you uncle.'

She stared at him, uncomprehending but happy. 'Yes. Yes. I savvy. You take me uncle.'

'Where? Where does uncle live?'

'Uncle live Shanghai.'

The *Chusan* had steamed a thousand miles north from Hong Kong when the pilot brought her to a mooring in the Huang-pu River. It was four a.m., and first light brought a cold, grey morning, close to freezing. Mists hung over waters packed with small boats, junks, sleek Western clippers and powerful-looking steamers.

One side of the river was open mudbanks, the other was densely built up. Lindley looked to where the British Concession fronted the river. A muddy tributary joined the Huang-pu and European-style buildings hotels and commercial premises, lined the 'Bund'. Signs of new construction were everywhere. Money must be pouring into this place since the Treaty opened it up, he thought. Strange to think it's going to be my home from now on.

Further south he saw a tumbled mass of shacks and warehouses. And there in the misty distance, making him narrow his eyes, a massive ancient-looking structure rising impressively above the land. His eyes drank it in: solid, encircling walls, tapering slightly at the top, and set with square towers at intervals, each bearing an elaborate pagoda-style roof.

'The Old City,' he murmured. That wall must be fifty feet high and two or three miles around. The labour it required was stupendous. It bore comparison with anything medieval Europe had built.

He shivered, feeling the chill air keenly after so many sweltering days and nights in the tropics, and looked around the steamer's busy decks. There were now two problems to consider: the crates in the ship's hold, and now Fei.

What could I do? he thought. I had to bring her along. A promise is a promise. I did say I'd take her to her uncle.

It was going to be difficult to get her off the ship without anyone noticing. Bringing her aboard had been simple. An assortment of boat girls had embarked to service the crew, and in the confusion he and Fei had slipped aboard and below. The time they had spent together in his cabin had been harder for him. She was so utterly delicious to look at, her manner was so captivating and her bodily movements so naturally feminine, that he had had difficulty controlling himself. She had delicate wrists and ankles that exposure to the sun had tanned beautifully. When she combed out and pinned her long hair he could not stop himself appreciating the intricate movements of her fingers and the way that her shapeless black shirt did not quite hide the rise of her breasts.

They had talked superficially, but he had been aware of the undercurrent of communication between them. He had gazed at her perfect face, and realized that she was fully aware of the effect she was having on him. Periodically he had torn himself from her company, knowing that if he stayed in the cabin with her much longer he could not help taking advantage of the situation. During the walks he took on deck he could regain his detachment, but at night it was much harder to assert his willpower, and he had suffered sleepless agonies with every passing hour.

'I came to China for a reason,' he told himself now. 'And what kind of a man allows himself to be ruled by a woman's beauty?'

When he saw the boat coming out from the Customs House he decided it was time to go below. In the cabin, his trunk was packed up and ready for the porter. Behind the locked door Fei was briefed and waiting.

He gave a knock and the door opened. Her face was anxious. He draped her shoulders with his best coat, making sure her long hair was tucked inside the collar.

'Don't worry,' he said, manoeuvring the steamer trunk out into the passageway. Then he came back inside and watched from the porthole to follow the progress of the boat until it bumped alongside, then he ushered her out and sent her ahead of him up the companionway and onto the deck.

The head of the gangway down to the boat was manned by two seamen and a young purser's mate. 'Just a minute, sir. Your name?'

'Lindley.'

The mate searched down his sheet of paper, then ticked off a name. 'I see, sir. And who is this . . . woman?'

Lindley tried to sound nonchalant. 'The lady is with me.'

'I got no Chinese listed. Where did she come from?'

He met the seaman's eye coldly. 'She's just come aboard. If you don't mind we'd like to get ashore.'

The seaman stiffened, unconvinced. 'Sorry, sir. This boat is for Europeans only.'

'What?'

'Regulations, sir.'

Lindley looked down at the boat and back. 'Which is the Chinese boat?'

The mate cocked his head knowingly. 'The Chinese don't have a boat. There ain't no Chinese on the list.'

'Well, what is she supposed to do, man? Swim ashore?'

The seaman's eye moved slowly over Fei's downcast face. 'Where did you say she come aboard?'

Lindley suppressed his anger. 'Look, we're anxious to get ashore. If you'll just—'

'What's the trouble here?'

It was Sutherland, his officer's jacket and cap gleaming with braid. Fei gasped. The instant the seaman moved towards her Fei threw off the coat and circled away like a street fighter. Lindley saw a knife flash in her hand, and to his astonishment she made for the ship's rail.

'Fei! No!'

Lindley tried to stop her, but she darted a glance at Sutherland and dived headlong into the water.

'Jesus Christ!'

Lindley peered down into the cold, grey-brown waters, unable to believe what had happened. He began to throw off his jacket, but Sutherland moved to hold him.

'Don't be a fool, Doctor! She wouldn't have jumped if she couldn't swim!'

Lindley watched for her to resurface, but she did not.

Lindley checked the address in his notebook again as the Bund jostled around him. His nerves were still jangling, and now a fist of anger was forming inside his chest. After half-explaining himself to Sutherland he had come ashore. He had half expected to find Fei waiting for him, dripping wet, at the pier head, but she had not been there, and neither had his father.

The letter could not have been more exact: they were to meet at the Customs Hall. After a two-hour wait, half of him looking out for his father and the other half looking out for Fei, he decided to make his way to his father's address.

This can't be the place, he thought, looking up at the house. But it was. Number six, Yan'an Street, an impressive two-storey residence in a side road in the middle of the sprawl of Chinese dwellings that lay between the fortifications of the Old City and the British Concession. The house was built in European style, but with whimsical Oriental decoration. It stood apart from its neighbours and was set back from the property line behind an untidy garden. All the windows and doors were boarded up.

He paid off the porter, mounted the steps and stood in front of the battened door, feeling empty. He had seen the look in the Chinese girl's eyes, the way she held the knife . . . It had all been so sudden, so unexpected. There had been times during the last few days when he had felt very close to her, but then she had just turned into a wild animal and had disappeared, leaving him with a hollow feeling in the pit of his stomach. His steamer trunk stood alone at the bottom of the path, mocking him. Fifty crates in the *Chusan*'s hold were going to be following it ashore today. There was work to be done.

He looked the house over. Judging by the state of the place it's been empty for at least six months, he thought, his worries mounting. If my father's not here, then where is he? He walked around the property. At the back there were more boarded-up windows. Faded papers were scattered in the yard, along with broken glass. He saw from the markings on the boards that old opium chests had been used to secure the house. The back door was locked. He went back to the front door, took off his hat and jacket and rolled up his shirt sleeves.

He wrenched the first board free, then used it to lever out others. The door lock had been smashed, but it was secured by a chain and padlock. He kicked at it, but saw that it would not open. The window behind it proved to be intact though. He smashed the glass and was clearing the frame of broken pieces when he sensed someone watching him. He did not turn around.

'Lin-li . . .'

'What do you want?' he said, shoulders tensing but still not turning to face her.

'No father here?' she said.

'No.' He turned. She was looking up appraising the house with hands on hips. She was filthy and not yet fully dried out. He was so glad to see her his stomach turned over. 'That was a bloody stupid thing to do.'

'Captain come. Arrest. This slave plenty scare.'

'He wasn't the captain. And you're not a slave. I wouldn't have let him arrest you. You might have died jumping into the water like that.'

Her laugh was fluting but dismissive. 'Only water. No die. All swim plenty good, same-same.'

'You drew a knife. I didn't know you had a knife on you.'

She looked away, pouting. 'You not understand.'

'I not understand? Oh, that's royal!' He continued chipping at the glass and then climbed in over the sill, but he caught a piece of glass in his palm, winced and looked down at it with annoyance.

'Oh, Lin-li! I help.'

'I don't want you help. Go away.'

'Yes, yes. I help. You show me.'

He ignored her and continued inside. The gloom was pierced by dusty shafts of light that entered between the opium boards. There was a poignant smell of decay. The rooms were large and well-proportioned. Once they had been well-furnished, but the place had been ransacked.

He found a large roll-top desk overturned in the corner of the big front room. The drawers were gone.

He felt an echo of the shock of his mother's death run through him, or it might have been a sickening premonition. Papers were scattered around. He bent to pick one up. It was a tract, printed in bold Chinese characters, proclaiming the Kingdom to come. He read it.

GOAT PRINCE GIVE KINDNESS

'The Lord is a loving shepherd . . .' he muttered, translating.

Another paper, this time written in his father's hand, looked like a letter that had never been sent. He turned it over and read:

> I have revised my opinion of my task here. Great difficulties lie in the way of the Gospel in China. The good work is moving but very slowly. The people are as hard as steel. They are eaten up body and soul by the world, and do not appreciate there can be anything beyond their senses. To them our doctrine is foolishness, our talk mere jargon. My efforts fall upon them like a shower upon a sandy desert. Sometimes I am ready to think that China is doomed, but there is a promise which dissipates the gloom, that those 'from the land of Sinim' are to come . . .

A drop of blood fell from his hand. The wound was deeper than he had realized, and as he read the dusty page it became sticky with his finger prints.

He heard noises and went back into the entrance hall, his voice stern. 'Hey! Who said you could come in here? Get out!'

The girl was climbing through the frame, her slipper reached for the floor, but she withdrew it, crouching poised like a cat in the window frame, watching him.

'I said – out!'

'I help,' she said, sounding wounded.

'You no help!'

It wasn't supposed to be like this. This should have been a private moment but the Chinese girl was here, taking it away from him. During the voyage east the tension inside him had been building up. Now he wanted to be alone here in his father's house, to think, and to decide what to do next. Matters were complicated enough – nothing had gone right since she had turned up.

'You no help. I have a job to do. I brought you to Shanghai didn't I? So why don't you go find your family.'

'No can,' she said quietly. 'Family all dead.'

He looked at her, his anger suddenly disarmed. 'Dead?'

'Yes. Same-same ancestor.'

He was aghast. 'What? You mean, all of them?'

She nodded and jabbed at her face and body with a forefinger, then shrugged. 'Like this same-same.'

'Smallpox?' He walked away. At the foot of the stairs he sighed and said, 'Good God, what kind of place is this?'

She was already stepping down off the sill. 'This dirty place. Too much dark. Too much stink. We make better – you see.'

'Lord give me strength! I thought Chinese women were supposed to be obedient to men?'

'Yes, yes. Very obedient. You see.'

The upper floor was no different to the ground floor. All the furniture had been broken or stolen. The walls still showed where pictures and a large cross had once hung. Floorboards were marked where carpets had been removed. Religious pictures had been trodden underfoot. He noticed what must have been the door to his father's bedroom. There were fresh signs of disturbance in the dust outside that drew him to investigate, and the smell was oddly . . .

As he entered the room, the door creaked behind him and as he turned he reeled back.

'Jesus God!'

The sight of the raised machete and the fierce face held him, but no attack came. The machete stayed motionless in the air, and only the contorted features of the man changed, from fear to amazement.

'Who are you?' Lindley demanded, blood pounding in his head.

The young Chinese did not answer, but his machete inched lower. Lindley showed open palms to him and tried again, this time using Shanghai dialect.

The other gaped, then answered. 'My name is Shen Yu-shen.'

'Mr Shen . . . what are you doing here?'

'Guarding this house.'

'Guarding? What for?' Lindley's eyes did not move from the other's. 'Do you know the owner?'

'The Reverend Lindley is my minister.'

Lindley stared back, the shock still pulsing through him. 'Where is he?'

He saw that Shen could not have been older than twenty. He had an intelligent light in his eye, wore poor quality clothing, canvas and rope slippers, and his queue – if he had one – was wound round and tucked up inside his cap. He was pale and trembling with fear. Lindley decided to announce himself. 'How do you do, Mr Shen. My name is Harry Lindley.'

The other started at the name.

'What's the matter, Mr Shen?'

'You – you are from the Reverend Lindley's family?'

'Yes. I am his son. Didn't he say anything about me? Didn't he mention that I was on my way?'

Shen hung his head. 'Please forgive bad manners. I thank the Lord God of Heaven that you are here.'

They sat together in the gloom, sipping pale tea from dirty glass tumblers. Lindley saw the hostile way Shen regarded Fei. Maybe he has his own views about what she is and why she's with me, he thought. What's certain is that he doesn't trust her as far as he can spit.

Fei had made a fire and found a battered kettle and glasses and a tin tray. Now she swirled her tea in its glass idly. At the bottom were a few green tea leaves. She set it down in the centre of the tray. Lindley was amazed that she could pretend meekness so well. Today has revealed a lot about her I didn't know, he thought. She has a beautiful exterior, but she's a fierce creature underneath. I wish I knew what she wants from me. He sipped tea and nodded amiably at Shen, knowing it was important to put the young man at ease as far as possible. The tea was surprisingly strong and refreshing. 'So, you're a Christian, Mr Shen?'

Shen's eyes shifted. 'Oh, yes. Your father brought me to the light. I am a Christian convert.'

'Did he have many converts?'

'The Ebenezer Mission Church of Shanghai had thirty-two worshipper. We used to meet in this room for song and prayer two times every week.'

Lindley gestured at the shattered interior. 'What happened?'

Shen hesitated. 'One night some bad men come. Your father leave this house in my care, so I try to stop them. But they don't listen. Come in. Break everything. Break cross like devils. Steal everything. I am very worried. They say they are going kill me and burn the mission down.'

'What men?' he asked, but he saw Shen's eyes glaze.

'Some . . . bandits.'

'Bandits.' Lindley gauged him. 'You've stayed here ever since?'

'I put board at window. So everyone think nobody here. Then I wait your father.'

'Where did he go, Mr Shen?'

'Travelling on Son of Ocean. Six month ago.'

'You mean the Yangtze? He went up the Yangtze River? Into the interior?'

Shen slurped the hot tea and wiped his mouth. 'Your father go inland many times. Bring word of the Lord into Middle Kingdom. He say he come back by time of White Dew.'

Lindley knew that by the reckoning of the Chinese calendar 'the White Dew' was some time in early September – over two months ago. 'Do you know where he planned to go?'

'I think to Chiang-kiang. About three hundred li – one hundred Western mile.'

'What happened to his congregation?'

'They frightened. All run away.'

Lindley sat back, his forebodings deepening. Two months was a long time to be overdue. John Sutherland had painted a picture of the Chinese interior being a vastly dangerous place. Word aboard the *Chusan* was that the Manchu regime in Peking was fighting hard to keep foreigners out of China, that they feared the crumbling of their two-hundred-year overlordship.

He gestured at the bare room. 'You're a brave man to have stayed here, Mr Shen. Now tell me: who really smashed the house up?'

Shen appeared uncomfortable with the memory. He rubbed at his forehead. 'No mission house welcome outside Concession land.'

'Haven't the Jesuits had a mission in the Old City for many years?'

'In China tradition is always respected. Roman Catholic teach very quiet. Catholic priest never preach in street. Never give book to convert. Catholic priest stay many years.'

26

'Whereas my father was anything but quiet, if his letters are true.'

Shen looked away. 'Your father, his heart open. He speak loud Gospel to all people. Give out many book and tract. Hundred people hear every day. This very new. Everybody talk – in family, in teashop, every place. Your father say talk good – ask question, always to make doubt – this important for change mind. In this way people see idolatry bad, old way bad.'

'You mean the images of their own gods? Buddhas? Taoist gods?'

Shen's eyes slid away again. 'Many years ago country people near Shanghai never has rain. These people pray to idol to send. But no good. So people say idol useless. After that much more listen your father.'

Lindley put down his tea glass, thinking of the tremendous danger posed by the fifty crates being landed from the *Chusan*. 'The authorities must see his work as a threat. Are the mandarins active in Shanghai?'

'Mandarin' was the word used to describe officers of the Emperor's government, the robed and hatted officials of every degree who ran the Empire.

Shen swallowed drily. 'Chinese city ruled by very strict mayor. His name Wu Hsu. He taotai – city governor.'

Lindley knew it was a position of absolute power. Wu Hsu could not be overruled in any matter concerning Shanghai – except by a direct order from Peking.

It makes sense, Lindley thought. Shanghai's a flash point. The Emperor's bound to have appointed a tough governor here. The Chinese population are terrified of the mandarins. Wu could have sent a mob down. This place is outside British jurisdiction. But that still doesn't explain why my father hasn't returned.

Lindley stood up. 'Mr Shen, will you continue to help my father?'

Shen stood up also. He nodded and then left. Steep shafts of sunlight lanced the gloom.

'I help you, Lin-li.'

He did not look at her. 'If you want to help me you can start by telling me the truth. There never was any uncle in Shanghai, was there?'

'Uncle family die.'

She said it with such subtle slyness that he almost found himself believing her.

'I saw you acting in front of Mr Shen just now, so I know when you're lying.'

'Not lying.'

He picked up one of the battens that he had removed from the front door and began ramming out the boards that covered the window. As they fell away sunlight streamed into the room.

'You were never running away from an arranged marriage, were you? I don't even believe you're from Macao.'

'Macao plenty bad. I help you, Lin-li.'

He sighed and felt a powerful urge to take hold of her. 'By God, look at you. You'd drive me insane if you stayed here. How do you think you can possibly help me?' He put his face in hers. 'How you thinkee you help me? Eh?'

'Because, Doctor Lin-li, foreigners are always duped in business matters in China. But I'll be able to negotiate for you . . . if you'll let me.'

He stared at her. 'Well, I'll be damned!' She had spoken to him in fluent Shanghai dialect.

'Yes, you probably will be.'

He threw his head back and laughed. 'So, your family are from here after all.'

'Much nearer to Shanghai than to Hong Kong.'

He grinned. 'Well, it's good to be able to talk to you properly – even though this is going to be the last time.'

'Listen, I can bargain for you,' she said testily, then added with significance, 'I understand feng-shui.'

He knew the phrase meant 'wind and water', and referred to an ancient form of geomancy, or earth magic. Feng-shui was so widely believed that few Chinese would build a house or open business premises without consulting a scholar who could assure them of an auspicious location.

'Feng-shui is just foolish superstition,' he said.

'You may not believe in it, but in China feng-shui is very powerful. It makes prices rise and fall. For example, unless you have agreed special storage for your cargo it will be shipped from the Customs House to Soochow Creek. I would be able to negotiate warehousing for one fifth the price they will charge you.'

'One fifth? How?'

'Because I know of a warehouse that was built on the eye of a dragon. That is very bad feng-shui. Everybody fears that if their goods are stored there they will spoil or be stolen or burn. It is a bad-luck place. Therefore the owner cannot charge a high price.'

Lindley shook his head thoughtfully. 'A fifth of the price, you say?'

'Maybe less.'

'You should become comprador for one of the big traders.' A comprador was a native agent and business go-between.

She tilted her head. 'I'll be your comprador, Lin-li.'

'Maybe you will, at that.' He slapped one of the papers he had salvaged with the back of his hand. 'According to this there's a clause in the Treaty of Tientsin that says religious mission houses may exist freely in any part of China. That's backed by force of law. I'm going to show Mr Wu what he's dealing with.'

She sighed. 'Be very careful.'

'It's Mr Wu who'll have to be careful. He's going to have a fight on his hands!'

She let his bravado hang unanswered, then she looked at him strangely and asked, 'Are you a Christian?'

He turned to her. 'I don't know. Why do you ask?'

'Are you sure your cause is right?'

'Of course.'

'Are you prepared to fight for it?'

'Yes.'

'And to die for it?'

He searched her face and saw that she was wholly serious, so he gave her the answer that was in his heart. 'When people decide to fight they must be prepared to die, or they're not really fighting.'

'I'm glad you said that,' she told him.

He inclined his head and asked her, 'Fei, who are you? And what do you want with me?'

But the wall had appeared between them again, and she did not answer.

It was called the Forbidden City by all who saw it: a moated wall the colour of freshly butchered meat, rising fifty feet above the ground, a wall topped by watchtowers at each of the four corners and pierced on each side by massively defended gateways. The meaning of those vermilion walls was clear – that the city of yellow-roofed palaces enclosed within was the true and inviolate centre of the world.

Somewhere inside the Western Palace, a baby was crying. Yehonala heard the gong signifying the start of the Hour of the Goat. The twelve animals of the Chinese Zodiac stood for the twelve 'Hours' of the day and night. Each lasted two Western hours. She tried to quell the feelings inside her – pleasure touched by dread. Today, the astrologers had warned her, would be a day of extreme danger, but she had made up her mind to go ahead with her plans despite their advice.

She put down the Imperial Decree she had been reading. Her hands were delicate and the nails of the third and fourth fingers of both hands were as long as the fingers themselves. She wore conical nail protectors of gold mesh decorated with seed pearls and the blue iridescence of king-fisher feathers. It is vital to maintain appearances, she thought. Now, more than ever before.

An Te-hai, the Chief Eunuch, had dressed her in an orange silk robe, the colour of an Imperial consort. It was long, with long sleeves and cut round at the neck, trimmed at collar and cuffs with black fur, and covered all over with exquisite stitching. The court embroiderers had produced a golden dragon surrounded by a halo of violet rays that changed colour as she moved.

Her chambers were opulently furnished with couches and cabinets, lit by long-tasselled lanterns and kept warm by charcoal heaters. Beyond the latticed windows the day was cold and clear, pleasant enough in the sunshine, but she knew that once the sun sank behind the roofs of the Western Palace the courtyard cobbles would quickly give up their heat and the air would begin to freeze. She drew her silk robe closer about her, and saw her two hand maids look to one another. They were growing increasingly nervous about the crying that echoed across the courtyard of the Palace of Eternal Spring. She saw their anxiety and reminded herself that she possessed the power of life and death over all maids and eunuchs in this part of the palace complex. It was proper to put their minds at ease.

'It is good to hear young voices in such a stuffy old palace, is it not?'

'Oh, yes, Lady. Very good.' They bobbed their heads demurely in unison, agreeing with her as hard as they could.

'The child is a lusty one. Strong lungs. One needs strong lungs to live in Peking.'

'Oh, yes. Very true. Sometimes it may be a little dusty in the capital.'

'You may both finish this,' she said, passing her tray to the nearest maid. When Yehonala gave anything from her plate or cup it was a mark of high favour.

'Thank you, your Imperial Highness.' Their voices sang again in unison.

She noted the maids' gratitude. That was all as it should be.

'How is the child's mother?'

'In very good health, Lady. Very much in milk today.'

She smiled approvingly. 'Today is special. I hope Little An has not forgotten.'

'Oh, no, Lady Yehonala. How could anyone forget the tenth day?'

As if summoned by her words the Chief Eunuch appeared. He paused at the doorway before entering. He was a wizened man, slightly built and with a jaundiced pallor. His nickname among the Emperor's brothers was 'Skeleton Face'. He wore an embroidered skullcap, and a long, surcoat of brown and blue, patterned on chest, back, shoulders and sleeves with a circular device that contained the character for longevity. He was head of all the Imperial eunuchs, a position he owed to his astute alliance with the concubine who had assured the succession.

'Oh, Lady Yehonala, what can have happened to you?' he asked, his voice reedy and incredulous.

'What do you mean, Little An?'

'You are looking more radiant than ever before. Today your skin is quite perfect!'

Despite herself she smiled at his gaucherie. Neither of the two maids showed any reaction.

'You are so, so beautiful.'

'An Te-hai,' she said lightly. 'I've told you before, I never listen to flattery.'

'Flattery? Lady, you shame me. I speak only as I find. You are surely the most beautiful woman in all the world.'

'Do you really think so?'

An's skull-like face displayed innocent humility. 'Am I not wholly honest, Lady?'

What a convoluted game, she thought, amused by his antics in front of the maids. I'm glad I've let the world believe I'm vain, because vanity is a form of stupidity, and it's wise for clever people to hide some of their cleverness behind a veil. In reality I'm no more vain than you are honest, and you know that. You still flatter me for the benefit of others though, because you also know that spies are everywhere and everything that's said or done in the Forbidden City is reported to someone. You're clever, Little An, but even so, I'm much cleverer than you. And I would worry if I were not.

A red lacquer tray was in his hands. On it stood a mortar and pestle, a small lacquer dish and the familiar silver beaker. He stepped up to the threshold, bowed formally and entered, setting the tray down on a small rosewood table beside her. He then uncovered the dish and poured the contents – fifty small pearls – into the mortar.

'I'm told that Fragrant Bud is in good milk today,' she said, naming one of the Imperial wet-nurses. 'I hope there is enough for her child.'

'Oh, yes, Lady Yehonala. Beauty milk is only taken from the left breast'

She watched An Te-hai smash the pearls to glittering grey dust with the pestle, then empty the dust into a silver beaker. She downed the mixture in a series of gulps. The milk was still warm, the pearl dust gritty in her mouth.

'Mother's milk is excellent for the skin,' she said, dabbing her lips with an embroidered yellow napkin. 'And pearl dust taken every ten days improves the lustre of the eyes.'

The skin of An's face was parchment-thin and stretched tight over the bone. 'It's said that a concubine must never lose her faith in human milk, Lady, not if she wishes to remain a concubine, and there are other, quite secret reasons for your skin to look its best today.'

The remark froze her. Two maids were present.

'Hai-lung,' she said quickly. 'Sweet baby, come to me.' The dog waddled toward her obediently, a Pekingese pug, trailing long, dark brown, silky hair. He had the most liquid eyes and the finest pedigree of any dog in the Imperial kennels. His name meant 'Sea Otter'.

'He soaks up love like a sponge,' she said, allowing the dog to snuffle at her fingertips.

An nodded. 'He has great heart for such a tiny animal.'

'Isn't love strange, Little An? To give love is to receive it. Whereas to withhold it is to deprive yourself.'

'A paradox, Lady. Just like these towels.'

She looked at him quizzically. 'Towels?'

'Yes, Lady. I have noticed that the more a towel dries the wetter it becomes.'

She watched him retire, not enjoying his sarcasm, not liking the risk he had taken in front of the maids by referring, in veiled terms, to her lover.

The excitement inside her began to mount again as thoughts of Jung-lu entered her mind. He was tall and strong – every inch a horse soldier – and so utterly unlike the Emperor in every way. She felt a delicious warmth spreading in her lower belly. An Te-hai had said that the idea of her continuing to see Jung-lu was insanity. 'A wiser empress than you would have taken his head the instant you gave birth,' he had said.

But I love him, and Little An doesn't understand love. That's why I arranged through intermediaries to have the commander of the Peking garrison assign Jung-lu duties here in the capital. She looked up, noting that the crying had stopped. Her thoughts jumped to her son who was presently in the care of his two favourite eunuchs, feeding the ducks on Beihai Lake.

'Is everything in order?' she asked mildly when An Te-hai returned.

'There is nothing to report, Lady. Except that the Golden Water was frozen this morning.'

She knew he meant the artificial stream that meandered through the Forbidden City in its limestone channel. It had been designed to improve the feng-shui of the Emperor's domain, as had the artificial hill to the north made from earth that had been scooped out to form the vast moat. It protected the Emperor from the evils of the north wind.

An rubbed his hands. 'Golden Water has stayed frozen all day. This means the deep cold is coming. Maybe it will snow today.'

'When is the heir due back?'

'Before sundown, Lady. I gave instructions that he be brought to you at the start of the Hour of the Rooster.'

'Good.'

'He's such a happy child.'

'That's because he takes after me. I was a happy child too. What happens to us, An? Where does childhood go?'

An's eyes were suddenly very old. 'You are lucky to have left it behind. I am imprisoned there for ever. My father took me out one day and put an end to all my hopes of growing up – with a knife.'

After a while she said, 'It is time to renew inner peace.'

An dismissed the maids. They knew the hour had come for Lady Yehonala's private devotions. It was unthinkable that the mother of the heir could ever be left alone – she was watched over even while she slept – but once a month she herself demanded to be left alone to spend three or four hours in silent prayer and meditation, attended only by the Chief Eunuch.

An followed her unhurriedly from chamber to chamber and along the maze of passageways that made up the Western Palace. Finally they came to a private parlour where the smell of stale sandalwood incense pervaded the air. The interior was dominated by four dark wooden screens carved with a twining mass of dragons and phoenixes. Against one wall a large wooden statue of a Chinese female Buddha gazed serenely down, flanked by two green jade elephants. An erotic thanka – a devotional painting from Tibet executed by Tantric buddhists – showed the impaling of a pale goddess upon the phallus of a black god.

She saw An bow carefully before the goddess Kuan Yin before he entered. Eunuchs are always superstitious, she thought. And none more so than you, Little An. I know you're genuinely terrified of lightning, and the rumour is that you consult an expert fortune-teller near the Fu Cheng gate whenever enemies threaten.

'Quickly,' she said, letting her anticipation show. 'And don't forget the spare lantern.'

An checked the corridor outside and barred the door. He drew the heavy drape that would remain in place for the next four hours, then produced two brass keys and opened a chest of aromatic nanmu wood. Inside were items of clothing. Yehonala removed her courtly dress and donned simple garments, finishing with a hooded cloak. Meanwhile An lit a candle and started to pull up a section of floor planks that concealed the trap door.

The tunnel had been An's gift to her. He had told her that it had been there since the early days of the present dynasty, its existence wholly unsuspected for two hundred years except by the succession of Chief Eunuchs and the heads of the prosperous family who owned the inn on Tunghuamen Street. The recessed entrance had been superbly hidden by the carpenters and stone masons who had constructed it, but their skills had proved fatal. The Emperor of those days had ordered them all slaughtered as soon as their work was complete.

An reached down and felt the heavy slab of wood, finally releasing two invisible catches. The slab was so exactly counterbalanced that the lightest touch caused it to swing up on an iron lever.

Yehonala looked in. The tunnel was a thousand paces long and big enough to walk upright with arms out-stretched. It made a shallow ramp down through the white limestone base on which the palace had been constructed. Dank breath caressed her face as she entered, following the eunuch. They trudged monotonously, enclosed in an orb of light, the tunnel ahead unchanging, An's shadow bloated and sinister on the curving wall. The candle flame shivered as they passed under the eastern side of the moat. Fantastic moulds grew here in the blackness, fouling the air. The floor of the tunnel was muddy and wet, but then it dried again and began to rise, a shallow ramp of serrated marble, until it became a stair that opened into a tiny, wood-clad ante-room. An pulled aside a sliding door and she had arrived in the private room at the inn on Tunghuamen Street.

Her nerves tingled. Her crime was enormous. Just to venture outside the Forbidden City without permission was punishable under unchanging ancient law by prolonged torture followed by a humiliating death and eternal disgrace. Should her enemies ever prove a case against her, not even the Emperor would be able to save her. But it was a crime she had committed dozens of times, and would continue to commit for as long as Jung-lu lived.

He was waiting for her in the adjoining room.

'I will return in three hours,' she told An.

An pulled the sliding door back into place and she was suddenly alone in the sparsely appointed chamber. The single window was a maze-like lattice covered by thin paper. She put her eye to a place where the paper had been slit and looked out into the inner court. The door to it was shut and barred. Snowflakes flurried in the space. Five motionless guards were positioned at intervals, wearing Manchu battle armour – a helmet with neckguard and a heavy, padded and iron-studded overcoat in the colours of the Bordered Blue Banner, the military corps to which her own clan belonged. Each soldier was armed with a spear-like glaive – a pole with a razor-sharp blade on top.

This was the normal level of security when a senior army officer was temporarily resident. Five guards would ensure privacy. They would hear everything, but know nothing – this was simply a captain of the Emperor's guard taking his pleasure.

She left the window, paused as anticipation thrilled through her, then opened the door to the next room. The air inside was overheated. Lanterns glowed with a smoky, buttery light. A huge bed was set into the far wall, recessed, and Jung-lu relaxed there, naked among the heaped furs. He was twenty-five years old, with a strong, muscular body and handsome Manchurian features, a distant kinsman also of the Nala clan. They had been betrothed in childhood, a promise nullified by her selection as the Yi Concubine. He was looking at her with an unmistakable expression.

'You're late.'

'I'm sorry.'

She shrugged off her mantle and sat down on the bed. As she did so he reached an arm across her shoulder and ran his hand diagonally over her breasts, pulling her to him, his mouth coming close to her ear. His other hand clinched her. She felt her own desire flare, and also the desire in him. He was a powerful man, born in the Year of the Tiger, virile and strong, and he knew how to take a woman.

'Don't be angry with me,' she whispered, meaning the reverse. She twisted. Her mouth hungered to taste his, but he pulled away and thrust her down. He slid his hand inside her gown and tore it open, sending sensations through her that made her moan. The strength in his arms seemed incredible. Then he began to do what she craved most.

36

Her moans echoed in the bedchamber as he made love to her. Outside in the courtyard the guards stood motionlessly as the snowflakes whirled into drifts.

When it was over her fingers lay on his broad, muscular chest. Their bodies were nestled in deep furs, sated, stained and damp. A distant bell tower rang out the Hour of the Monkey – mid-afternoon. She looked up at his angular face as he lay back. He has Mongol eyes, she thought, like the Great Khan of legend. I see his looks in little Tsai-ch'un all the time. Sometimes it terrifies me that others must see it too.

'Tell me about my son,' he said, as if reading her thoughts.

It was the question she had always dreaded. She kept her voice even, 'He is very well. He plays patiently with all his nursemaids. The eunuchs treat him preciously, like fine porcelain. He says all kinds of silly things to them and laughs a lot.'

She saw the muscles move in Jung-lu's jaw. 'He is my son. One day he will know that. Until that day, the graves of my family will continue to yawn wide.' She understood what was troubling him, what was driving his possessive instincts, but there was no possible remedy.

'My father's ghost came to me again last night,' he murmured, peeling open the old wound once more. 'He wanted to know how my son would bury me, as I buried him, and he his father before him. What reply can I give to him?'

She said nothing.

He asked, the bitterness clear in his voice now, 'How will Tsai-ch'un perform the rituals a son must perform for his father if he does not know who I am?'

Still she did not answer him.

'Yehonala, this is the way it has been for eight generations, back to the time of Nurhachi the Founder. My father's ghost must have an answer, or he will never find rest.'

She withdrew her hand, her tenderness suddenly vanishing. 'I did not come here to listen to this old, old complaint. You know the situation cannot be altered now.'

He sat up, goaded by her hardness. 'There is still duty.'

'Keep your voice down. Your duty is to your oath.'

'Yes! To the Son of Heaven. He is our master. What we have done is treason.'

She twisted, facing him. 'Hsien-feng is a despicable weakling. You know that as well as I do.'

'But he is the Emperor!' He grimaced. 'And you have deceived him. You have caused me to deceive him. Together we have deceived the Son of Heaven, the Court and the whole world. Even the gods are saying—'

'I know what the gods are saying,' she said. 'The gods are with us. They know the blood of Nurhachi has run thin as water.'

'Hsien-feng is weak, but still he is the Emperor.'

'And how long do you think he would have remained Emperor if I had not propped him up? When the Yellow River changed course six years ago the whole of China was ready to say he no longer held the Mandate of Heaven. When I gave him an heir all that talk stopped.'

'Given time and enough coaxing the Emperor would have sired his own son.'

She laughed scornfully. 'The great K'ang-hsi Emperor had over 150 sons and grandsons. Hsien-feng sired nothing but a sickly girl-child. After nine generations the line of the Aisin Gioro is spent.'

Jung-lu's expression was unwavering. 'My father must have what is rightfully his!'

'What more could your father want?' A tiny sneer curled her lip. She knew exactly the effect her insolence would have on him. 'Your grave, and his too, will one day be tended by the next Emperor of China.'

He recognized the hint of promise. 'You will tell my son the truth when he becomes Emperor?'

'When he becomes Emperor. Only then.'

He brooded, weighing her words further, still not trusting her. 'You said I would see him.'

'And so you will.'

'When?'

'As soon as I can arrange it. Do you suppose it's easy?'

'Bring him through the tunnel.'

'That's impossible. He's the heir. He is watched continuously.'

Jung-lu lay back, tense as a bowstring. 'Then I must see my son soon. Before he starts to talk and make sense of the world.'

'Somehow . . .' She paused, hesitant. 'I promise you – you shall have one look at him.'

She started to put on her underclothes, examining her body in the dull light. There was a scratch on one of her breasts. 'I told you to be careful not to mark me. What if one of my maids notices and reports it?'

'Lie about it. You're very good at that.'

She bit back further words. No one else was allowed to speak to her like he did. No one else would dare. Nor could anyone else wound her as he could.

'Without you, I would be nothing,' she said, attempting to calm him.

'Tell me,' Jung-lu said stonily, staring once more up through the ceiling and into the vaults of Heaven. 'Has he learned to say "father" yet?'

'Thank the gods you've come back, Lady!'

An Te-hai's whispering voice was quaking, and his urgency alarmed her.

'What's the matter?'

An Te-hai began sealing the tunnel entrance as fast as he could. 'Someone knocked on the door.'

'Knocked?' She felt her blood freeze. 'You must have imagined it!'

'Once, perhaps, Lady. But not twice.'

'Twice? Someone knocked twice, knowing I was in meditation? Who would dare do that?'

'I don't know.'

It was as if the blood had run from her. Her arms were leaden as she hurriedly took off her clothes and put on court robes. Her mind whirled. An looks genuinely scared, she thought. Has something happened to Tsai-ch'un? He's fallen through the ice and drowned. Oh, no! Let it not be so. Those stupid eunuchs. If he has been harmed I'll have their heads. I swear it by Kuan Yin.

The serene face of the female Buddha regarded her knowingly. An asked her, 'Have you had dealings with Su-shun lately?'

The name sent an arrow of fear and loathing through her. Su-shun hated her. Since the birth of the heir he had opposed her as any political player might oppose a rival, but during the last year that opposition had hardened into a personal hatred. Su-shun was immensely rich, only an Assistant Grand Secretary as yet, but rising up as fast as spring bamboo.

'Why do you ask about Su-shun?'

'I wonder – could he have moved against you?'

'How?' She asked, full of fear and therefore impatience. 'How could he move against me? He has no leverage against my position here. What do you know, An?'

'Nothing, Lady. I only wondered—'

'Don't wonder. Think! Use your brain. And only then speak to me.'

She pushed her feet into white silk half socks and smoothed her robes, arranging her hair and make-up speedily until she was her courtly self again. When she was ready she composed herself and told An to open the door for her.

They were waiting for her outside. Snow flurried in the last sickly light of the day. A depth of new-fallen white blanketed everything. Two young eunuchs in blue coats of quilted cotton stared at her, then fell to their knees. They kowtowed, getting down on their fronts and pressing their heads into the snow as if trying to burrow beneath it.

'Make them get up,' she said, recognizing them as two of the eunuchs who had charge of her son.

'Report!' An ordered.

They stared at the Chief Eunuch's bloodless face, then one began to babble incoherently.

'Yes, yes. You were caught at Beihai Lake by the snowfall,' An said. 'Then what happened?'

'We were on the far side, Master An,' the elder eunuch blurted. 'We knew we were not to come back until the Hour of the Rooster, but then his Imperial Highness fell down into the mud at the side of the lake and began to cry, and we saw he was very wet and cold. We did what we could, but we wanted to change his clothes, so we took him across the bridge to Jade Islet when it started to snow, but some guards there would not let us enter the pavilion, not even to take shelter. They told us to go back to the Forbidden City, so there was nothing else we could do but come back early and against orders. Please forgive us, Lady Yehonala! What could we do?'

'How is my son?' she demanded. 'If you have allowed harm to come to him you'll wish you had never been born.'

'He is happily asleep, Lady. No harm has befallen him. Please – we would rather die first.'

An said, 'Who told you to interrupt her Imperial Highness's devotions?'

'No one, Master.'

'Then it was your own idea?'

'We thought it was too important an incident not to report urgently.'

'Whose guards would not let you take shelter in Jade Islet pavilion?' Yehonala demanded, her voice deadly.

They looked at one another, stricken.

'Answer her Imperial Highness!'

'Please don't ask us! The guards made us swear on our lives not to speak of it.'

'Fetch the rods and beat them until they tell you,' she told An. The terrorized eunuchs began to kowtow furiously again.

'Get up! Get up, pig excrement!' An raged. 'I order you to tell me who would not let the heir take shelter. Who offered the Emperor's son a deliberate snub? Answer!'

The eunuchs wailed miserably until An hauled the nearest one upright and slapped him to silence. 'You will die for this! You and you! Both your heads will roll in the snow before this hour is up, unless one of you answers her Imperial Highness to the best of your knowledge immediately.'

The younger eunuch's face was a mask of agony. 'They were the guards of Assistant Grand Secretary, Su-shun.'

'Did Su-shun know the heir was with you?'

Again the frightened silence.

'Did-he-know-the-heir-was-with-you?'

One nodded, and the other followed suit. 'Yes.'

It's a deliberate snub, Yehonala thought exultantly, her mind calculating the consequences. Su-shun has never before allowed his civility towards me – or the heir – to lapse. What marvellous good fortune this is! Exactly the ammunition I require. One word to the Emperor and he will lose Hsien-feng's trust.

'This is an outrage,' she said, mortifying them all. 'Master An, you will sweep this disgusting ordure out of my quarters instantly. I will consider their punishment later.' The junior eunuchs could not believe they had been dismissed so lightly. They looked to one another then vanished like hares. When they were out of earshot Yehonala said, 'Exceptionally interesting, don't you think?'

'How dare an Assistant Grand Secretary deliberately insult the heir like that?'

She permitted herself a smile. 'Su-shun did not insult the heir deliberately, An. He was angered to have been discovered in conference with his allies at Beihai Lake. What could he be up to?'

'Another plot, obviously.' An looked to her. 'Lady, if he applies himself he could bring three of the four most influential men in China, barring the Son of Heaven himself, to move against you.'

'Will they move against me? Or are they merely seeking to influence Hsien-feng for their own ends?' She knew very well what those ends were – 'squeeze'. Su-shun was now a magnate with many legitimate interests, but he had grown rich at the expense of the state. All officials from eunuchs to mandarins squeezed personal revenue from their positions, but Su-shun had been spectacularly greedy. And as an Assistant Grand Secretary, his avarice had known no limits.

She decided it would be a mistake to let An know the real extent of her fears. 'I'm not yet alone. And within the Household I can always count on you, Little An.'

'Of course, Lady.'

'And the Emperor's wife, Niuhuru, would always be sure to take my part. And there's Prince Kung.'

An made no answer. His hatred for Prince Kung was mutual. The Prince was the Emperor's twenty-seven-year-old half-brother. His mother had reared both boys, and they had been very close in childhood. His influence was formidable, but by no means at Yehonala's disposal. Niuhuru, mother of the Emperor's daughter, had been given the title 'Empress of the Eastern Palace' before Yehonala had been made 'Empress of the Western Palace'. She was a placid woman who had always been kind to Yehonala, but she lacked all ability at political manoeuvre. Taken together, they did not offer the hope of a very strong alliance.

When Yehonala arrived back at her personal residence she dismissed An. Shouts of 'Li-la!' – 'Coming!' – announced her. Eunuchs and maids, no matter what their errand, scurried out and dropped into the kowtow and remained there. Hai-lung's yapping greeted her.

'Where is the heir?' she demanded.

One of the nurse maids stood up. 'He's here, Lady Yehonala.'

A voice came from the next room. A plump woman with a face as round as the full moon cradled the three-year-old on her lap. Tsai-ch'un was grinning. All around were his toys. When he saw his mother he slid to the ground and came to hug her. She picked him up and carried him to her favourite seat.

'What a big boy you are.'

'Big boy,' he echoed happily.

'Did you see the ducks today on the Emperor's lake?'

He nodded. 'The Emperor has lots of ducks to look after.'

She laughed. 'And did you fall down in the mud?'

He nodded again, giggling. Yehonala picked up a little plaster figure of a white rabbit. It had a string in its back. When she pulled it the rabbit's eyes rolled and it shot out a little red tongue. Tsai-ch'un laughed.

When the gong signalled the Hour of the Rooster, they took the heir for his bath. Alone, Yehonala thought again about her weakling husband and the way that his grip on power was being loosened. She thought of the increasing influence of Su-shun and his allies, of the rebellion in the South, and the amazing insolence of the Outer Barbarians.

All living things are subordinate to the Emperor of China, she thought. He is Nan Mien – 'he whose face is ever turned towards the South'. Perhaps there's no solution to China's plight, she thought. There's certainly none while Hsien-feng sits on the Dragon Throne. Goddess Kuan Yin, please tell me: what must I do?

Harry Lindley arrived at the most expensive hotel on the Bund. He looked round as the noonday gun boomed out over the British Concession, then mounted the white steps.

The Grand Hotel's spacious saloon was crowded with Europeans dining and drinking. White-jacketed Chinese waiters threaded their way between the tables with silver trays loaded with champagne. It seemed to be the favourite drink among the carousing ship-owners and Treaty port entrepreneurs. He ordered himself a whisky and sat down to look at his Chinese dictionary.

Inside, a page from one of his father's letters formed an apt bookmark: 'The conquering of this difficult language is worth the struggle. It is intended by the providence of God to be a channel through which Divine truth, like a life-giving stream, shall flow into four hundred million thirsty souls.'

He had been in Shanghai a week now, and had learned no more of his father's whereabouts. He had laid out money, and repairs to the house had begun, but Fei had cautioned him that everything in China was hog-tied and corrupt – that Manchu officials had to be bribed or they would make things impossible.

Lindley savoured the heady, peaty smell of the single malt as it rinsed the bottom of his heavy octagonal glass, but as he did so he sensed something amiss and looked up. Conversation in the lobby was coming to a halt, and now he saw why. A neatly dressed man with a dark moustache was frogmarching a huge, bearded sailor down the centre aisle of the lounge.

The shorter man's hair was black and stylishly long. He had a Western moustache – long, with a tab of hair growing under his lower lip and down onto his chin. Lindley judged him to be about twenty-five years of age, maybe a year or two older.

There was fury and agony on the bigger man's face, but his arms were doubled behind him in a complicated armlock that controlled him completely. When he reached the door, the armlock was disengaged and the sailor was thrust down the steps and into the street.

'You better get back to your ship, stoker! Hear me?'

Lindley recognized the accent. The smaller man was a Yankee. He marched back, his face still set with determination, and disappeared into a side room.

Conversation started up again, but soon died as the American reappeared a second time. A different sailor was being steered towards the door. He was thrown out too.

'And don't neither of you come back!'

The American turned round, satisfied, and started back inside, adjusting his cuffs and shrugging his jacket straight as he went. He caught several men's eyes and nodded to them as if he knew them. He had almost reached the door to the side room again when the two sailors came bursting back into the lobby, wild-eyed as bulls. Lindley's glance went immediately to the second man. He had a knife in his hand and was cursing wildly. Customers gasped. A woman screamed. Furniture legs scraped the floor as tables emptied. The huge sailor bellowed and threw himself forward.

The American parried the stoker's mad rush with a superbly timed blow that crumpled his opponent. Then he took up a champagne bottle from an ice bucket. He smashed the blunt end against a pillar, and began to circle. The second sailor came on, stabbing and slashing. One sweep laid open the American's jacket arm so that he dropped the bottle. The American swept up a chair and jabbed it defensively, looking able to hold his own. He grinned, taunting the sailor, telling him to come on. The knife flashed back and forth, but there was no way around the reach of the jabbing chair legs and the sailor found himself pushed back. But now, next to Lindley's table, the stoker was on his feet again, shaking his head clear. He picked up a chair and started forward.

The odds had changed, and Lindley did not like it. Without thinking, he dashed his whisky up into the stoker's eyes, then jumped up and launched his fist as hard as he could into the man's face. The unexpected force of the blow knocked the stoker back over a trolley and his head slammed onto the black-and-white tiles of the floor. This time he showed no signs of getting up.

The knife-man continued to back away, but the American forced him against a table that overbalanced in a shower of soup-plates and cutlery. The knife-man was on his knees. A lightning move sent the knife spinning away, and an elbow blow to the side of the head laid him out cold.

With both sailors unconscious the American looked at the ruination around him. He straightened his jacket defiantly and raised his voice. 'Champagne on the house!'

The diners resumed their seats. The maître d'hotel nodded with resignation. Waiters dragged the unconscious sailors out by their heels and began to deal with the chaos.

The American examined his arm – the cut was clean and deep. He tore off the bloody lower sleeve, then looked up grinning. 'Thanks.'

Lindley nodded an acknowledgement. 'No trouble. What did those boys do to annoy you?'

The American grunted. 'Neither of them understands the meaning of good faith. A man can't do business without good faith.'

'So you're a businessman? I'm a physician. Why don't you let me take a look at your arm?'

The American made no move. 'It's nothing.'

Lindley saw a tattoo on the American's arm had been cut neatly across the middle. It was a military crest with the legend 'CRIMEA' underneath. The war there had finished three years ago. The wound was bleeding freely. 'I ought to suture that. It needs a dozen stitches.'

'Go ahead.'

'I don't carry a medical bag around with me.'

'Do you carry a calling card?'

'Harry Lindley. At least let me see if I can stop the bleeding.' He cut a piece of shirt sleeve and began to bind it around the wound. 'Where did you learn to fight like that?'

'It wasn't the Crimea.' The American raised his good arm. 'Waiter! Champagne. And two glasses.'

'I don't drink champagne. And I never drink with bar-room brawlers, especially those I don't know Mr—?'

'Ward.' The American looked at him appraisingly. 'You're pretty handy with your fists yourself – for a physician.'

'I don't suppose I have to ask what sort of business you're in?'

Ward seemed to make a decision. 'I guess you'd call me more an adventurer than a businessman, Doc. I'm originally from the port of Salem, Massachusetts. I've sailed the world, fought with William Walker's filibusters in Central America. I went to the Crimea as a volunteer in a French corps. This is my fourth trip to China. And this time I've got business in mind.' The waiter popped the champagne cork and poured. 'Secret business. Potentially very profitable – but not easy to arrange.'

'And what do you do meanwhile?'

'Meanwhile, I'm running a chartered river boat.'

Lindley made no reply as he finished the dressing. Shanghai had the stink of fast money about it. It sucked in plenty of men with gold rush minds – the hopeful and the hopeless alike – then spat them out again.

'What's the matter, Doc? You've turned awful quiet.'

Lindley looked up. 'I haven't been here too long, Mr Ward, but it seems to me that Shanghai's full of confidence tricksters and free spenders. Everyone you meet has some kind of half-baked scheme to become a millionaire.'

Ward's eyes were dark and piercing. He bridled at Lindley's attitude. 'So, why did you come to this running sewer, Doc? Too fond of the booze?'

Lindley was unsmiling. 'Why I'm here is my business.'

Ward nodded thoughtfully. He began to turn over a small disc of carved yellow jade in his fingers. 'Fair enough. But you did me a favour. I'd like to repay it. I may have need of a physician real soon.'

'If you keep picking fights with Royal Navy stokers, Mr Ward, I should think you will.'

Ward sat back, tucked the yellow jade ornament back into his watch pocket. 'You know, Doc, if I had fifty thousand taels of silver there isn't a thing I couldn't do in China.' A tael was a Chinese ounce.

They were joined by another man – tall, heavy-boned and strong-looking. He deferred to Ward. 'I heard what happened, Colonel. I come as fast as I could. You all right?'

'Yeah.' Ward turned to Lindley. 'This is Dr Lindley, he's a physician. Dr Lindley, my associate, Henry Burgevine.'

'Glad to know you, Doc.'

Lindley nodded back and took the other's hand briefly. Burgevine's accent showed he was a Southerner, but from which state of the Union Lindley could not tell.

Ward grinned good-humouredly. 'Well, excuse us, Doc. Time is money.'

'Aye, and vice-versa, Mr Ward. I advise you to get that arm stitched as soon as possible.'

Ward straightened. 'Sure. Like I say, if you were to hear of a liquor-drinking sawbones who wanted to make himself a swad of money so's he could maybe switch to drinking champagne, why I guess I'd have just the job for him.'

Lindley raised his eyebrows. 'As a matter of fact, Mr Ward, it's the sawbones that might have a job for a man with the river boat.'

Lindley secured the dressing on Ward's arm. The American had called out of the blue, bringing Burgevine with him.

'How long did you say you been here?' Ward asked.

'I didn't. But it's about a week.'

'Maybe I ought to explain a little something to you, Doc. One or two important facts about China, like the country's been held down by Manchurian invaders for over two hundred years. Like how, because of that, life is counted very cheap here. Like how it's pretty well suicide for a Westerner to travel in the interior without permission – and they don't give permission. Doc, there's no surer way of getting yourself shortened by twelve inches than trying to get to Chiang-kiang.'

Burgevine grinned and Lindley felt his annoyance rise.

'The Chinese are not savages, Mr Ward. Their country's a little down at heel, I admit, but this is a land with a civilization that was in splendour when Europeans were still living in mud huts. They invented porcelain. They invented paper and gunpowder. They have an unbroken tradition of government stretching back thirty centuries. They're not fools. With the right approach, it must be possible to obtain the necessary permits.'

'You don't have the first idea about this place, do you?' Burgevine said, shaking his head. 'This is crazy country. Set one foot wrong out there and they'll turn you into pig shit.'

Lindley looked to him coldly. 'Well, thank you for that contribution, Mr Burgevine. Your incisive analysis of the situation does you tremendous credit.'

Burgevine stared back blankly. 'Huh?'

Ward looked at his watch, snapped it shut and said, 'We just about have enough time. Henry, why don't you go over and see if Sergeant Hughes has changed his mind yet?'

'Sergeant Hughes? You mean . . .?' Burgevine made an imaginary pistol out of two fingers, then mimed putting it to his head and firing.

'That's him.'

Burgevine seemed to think about raising a query, but then recognized something meaningful in Ward's expression and did as he was told.

After Burgevine left Ward leaned in confidentially, indicating the door that his associate had just passed through. 'He's a bear, Doc. But he's my bear.'

'You certainly appear to have him well-trained.'

'Let me give you a word of advice: don't get too sarcastic

with Henry. He has a nasty side to his character that you wouldn't want to see.' Ward held his stare uncomfortably for a moment, but then he winced and flexed his arm. 'C'mon, Doc. I want to show you something. I'll pay for the ride.'

Without waiting for a reply Ward strode outside, and down the street, springing into one of the sedans that waited in line on the corner. He smiled broadly, indicating the one behind. Lindley looked it over doubtfully, but then climbed in.

'Where are we going?'

'A place that'll open your eyes some. I think it's time you knew what it is you've come to.'

Lindley watched the bearers' faces as Ward bargained the fare. They were seasoned negotiators, and either they knew Ward well or had recognized him as a man who should not be toyed with. For a moment it looked as if Ward was about to step out in disgust, but then the head bearer nodded, and the sedans were expertly lifted up on their poles and they moved off.

They headed for the southern suburbs, a little way back from the river. The four bearers trotted nimbly down crowded streets and alleys, their loads poised with amazing dexterity. They shouted for the people to make way, as they passed under the huge ramparts of the southern wall of the Chinese city, and along the river that ran parallel to it.

Shanghai's massive wall stood back from the river about a hundred yards, Lindley judged. Between the two was a maze of tumbled shacks and hovels composed, to the north and west, of small shops and dwellings. They became less and less respectable as the foreign factories fell behind.

The bearers kept up their pace until they reached a congested marketplace. People stared openly at them, some called out. The abrasive sound of Shanghai Chinese came to him, shouts and staccato argument and the calls of vendors. This part of the city was a riot of sights and smells and sounds. There were itinerant hawkers with their portable stoves, calling out, peculiar pastries, seething mysterious foods that filled the air with odd, liquorice aromas. As he passed their pitches blind fiddlers scraped bizarre wailing tunes, child dancers postured, women argued at stalls that were crammed with bolts of cloth, street barbers shaved heads and dressed queues, oil-sellers and porters boned along with absurd loads yoked to their shoulders, reeking carts fumed as they collected fresh manure. He saw iron cooking pans arranged for sale, knives, baskets, basins of live crabs, rows of unknown river fish laid out for sale, and tumbled heaps of strangely shaped fruit. Hanging up on bamboo poles as he passed beneath were smoked ducks and sucking pigs, all kinds of flesh monstrously prepared, displays of horrible offal, caged starlings and jays, and everywhere lost in the crowd glimpses of decaying brick, or the glaring red and gold-painted columns of a pagan shrine.

Lindley's mind was alert for dangers. This was a place no sane foreigner would choose to come. They went on a little further and were set down at the end of a short thoroughfare running north and south about fifty yards in length, ten yards wide at its northern end, but gradually narrowing to five at its southern. It stank worse than any street Lindley had ever visited. He brushed the creases from his trousers and straightened his jacket. Ward clapped him on the back and sidled by. 'Watch out for pickpockets,' he murmured.

Lindley could feel his trust in Ward's judgement beginning to vanish. 'What is this place?'

'Somewhere a friend of mine took me the first time I came to China.'

'Why won't you say what it is? It's not a damned brothel you're taking me to, is it?'

Ward laughed. 'You'll wish it was. I want you to see something that might educate you about China's unbroken tradition of government. But take a deep breath beforehand.'

Ahead the end of a house reduced the width of the passage to a yard and a half. It was blocked by a high wooden gate, but when Ward pushed at it it opened. He tore an official paper from a wooden post, looked it over, screwed it up and discarded it. Then he went in, and pulled Lindley after him.

'Welcome to China.'

Lindley's eyes took in the sight. A roughly triangular patch of bare ground, open to the sky and about fifty yards in length, on which several pigs were rooting. The southern side was formed by a row of workshops where coarse, unglazed earthenware was being made. Urns stood drying in the sun outside the pottery workshops. Beyond the western end was a main street, walled off by a gallery with a tiled roof. Before it fragrant sandalwood billets were smouldering in an iron brazier. Even so the stench was appalling. Lindley swatted away the flies that settled on him and held his handkerchief to his face. The piquancy of stale eau de cologne only seemed to make the smell more sickening. It's too far from the river to be the tanneries, he thought. It stinks worse than an old slaughterhouse.

He looked up to see the northern side bounded by a dead brick wall about twelve feet high that backed onto several small warehouses. Against the wall there was a wooden cross large enough to crucify a man. An iron rack stood beside it. It displayed a number of human heads in different stages of decomposition.

'Jesus God!'

Ward sucked his teeth. 'Yeah, wonderful, isn't it? This lane's no larger than the deck of a clipper ship, but above five hundred men and women have been put to death here in the past month.'

Lindley stared about, his guts chilled by Ward's matter-of-fact tone.

'It stinks so bad because the soil is saturated with blood. Human blood, Doc. The bodies stay here until the families claim them for burial. A lot of the time nobody claims them. When I first came here I saw four bodies lying right where they'd fallen.' He gestured vaguely toward the end of the execution ground. Their heads were near them, and two pigs were moving among them, feeding in the pools of blood. 'In China the dead always get far more respect than the living.'

Lindley looked with horror at a young woman who was sitting at the door of one of the pottery workshops. A two-year-old child sat on her lap. Both stared hard, not at a sight so common as pigs feeding on earth soaked by human blood, but at the strangely dressed foreigners.

'See that hole in the ground over there?' Ward said, gesturing again. Lindley looked to where the cross leaned against the wall. 'That's where they set up the cross. It's for the highest legal punishment they have – they call it ling che.'

'They crucify people here?' Lindley's voice was incredulous.

'Crucify?' Ward laughed abruptly, but it was a bitter, mirthless laugh. 'You're still thinking like a Westerner. There's much worse than crucifixion in China. Why, you said it yourself: they've had better than three thousand years of civilization to refine their methods.'

Lindley felt a shaft of pure horror run through him. 'What do you mean?'

'You'll see.' Ward cracked open his watch again, then pointed to the gallery at the western end, and the brazier that was still smoking. 'That's to sweeten the air for the mandarins – the officials. They're due here soon.'

'You intend to wait?'

'You want to learn about the real China, don't you?'

'Not this way.'

'What's the matter? Sight of a little blood disturb you? I hope you don't intend to throw up. You'll lose all face if you do that.'

Lindley straightened, feeling a spike of anger. He saw the way Ward played with the little yellow jade ornament he had taken from his vest pocket. It had a brilliant red cord on it. Why is he mocking me? he wondered. But then his thoughts were broken off by a commotion at the entrance. Manchu soldiers were massing at the gate, parting the crowd out on the street with split rattans, driving back the people and making way for a party of men all of whom were wearing the kuan, the red and black mushroom hats of Manchu officials.

The first half dozen of them entered the gateway and came into full view. They were all dressed in black silk surcoats. Each had a large square of coloured embroidery on his chest depicting a stylized bird with outspread wings set against a heavily patterned background.

'They're officials of the eighth and ninth civil ranks,' Ward said, following his eye. 'Pretty small beer. Ninth rank wears the flycatcher, eighth rank the quail. You can tell the military grades; they wear animals instead of birds. That patch of silk gives them the right to treat regular Chinese like they're sub-human.'

One of the officials approached and brusquely motioned them to leave. Lindley felt a momentary flood of relief, but Ward went to meet them, and barked a series of phrases that Lindley could not hear. The official fixed them with a despising look, but then turned and left.

'They're a bunch of bastards,' Ward murmured after him. 'The word mandarin isn't Chinese. It comes from the Portuguese word mandar, which means "to command", and that's just what they do. They kiss the asses of those set above them like their life depends on it – which it does – but they treat everyone else like dirt. The trick is to leave them in no doubt about your own high status. Then they leave you alone.'

'What did you tell him?'

'That we were sent here by the British Consul as official observers. That the taotai – he's the city mayor – has given us special permission to be here.'

'Good God. Has he?'

'Of course not. But this fellow isn't going to know that.' Ward looked up. 'Talk of the devil.'

A more impressive official had just appeared at the gate, carried shoulder high in a spectacular magisterial palanquin. He too wore the red and black hat and the black silk p'u fu, but his attire, Lindley noted, was of much finer quality. He was surrounded by lackeys and spear-carrying guards, a stocky man, in his forties, cruel-faced, and when he stepped down he showed himself to be above average height for a Chinese. He appeared to have a tremendous sense of his own power. His hat was surmounted by a coral red button, and although the badge he wore on his chest was also a kind of bird it was not like those worn by the others.

'What rank is he?' Lindley asked, watching the mandarin closely.

'A golden pheasant on his jacket and a red jewel on his hat. That makes him second rank.' Ward whistled briefly through his teeth. 'We're honoured today. This is something special.'

The red-button mandarin took his place in the gallery directly behind the iron brazier, and his retinue formed up on either side of him in strict hierarchy. There were civil and military grades there, and seats had already been set up for them. As they took their places, Lindley saw the senior mandarin look directly at them then away again instantly, noting their presence.

Lindley looked to the rest of the official procession, the

tension knotting his belly now as the victims were brought in. There were about three dozen of them, mostly walking, each with a guard, but several were carried in large bamboo baskets suspended from a pole borne by two porters. He saw that the strength of the men being carried was completely spent. Whether it was from fear or from the treatment they had received he could not judge. They fell pitifully onto the ground as they were tumbled out on the spots where they were to die.

All the prisoners were in rags, and their heads were shaved, except for a place at the back of their skulls where the long plaited queue was coiled. He watched as they were lifted to a kneeling position, and held upright by guards who stood behind them. Those who were able to walk were led to their places and also made to kneel. There they waited in silent misery as the cross was manhandled away from the wall and placed in the hole. The gate to the killing ground was closed, and a guard stationed on it. Then the victims' hands were bound behind their backs. Lindley counted thirty-three of them. The nearest knelt no more than five yards away from where he and Ward were standing. They were arranged in rows, with their heads towards the south. The narrowness of the killing ground left space for one man nearest the gate, then came a file of two, one of four, then five of five. At the back of all, twenty-five yards away, one man was bound up to the cross.

'Who are they?'

'So-called criminals.'

Lindley's throat was dry. 'What kind of criminals?'

'Murderers, rapists, pirates, thieves – you name it.'

'Thieves?' He heard the incredulity in his own voice.

'Why not? Does it matter what they call them? The truth is that most of them are just ordinary river people suspected of helping the rebels.'

Lindley felt his scalp itching. Sweat was trickling inside his shirt. His heart was beating fast. He glanced about him, looking for the executioner, and identified a well-built, vigorous-looking man with an unsheathed sword in his hand. He was pulling up the sleeves of his jacket. No, he can't be, Lindley thought. He had expected, or wanted, there to be something ferocious or brutal in the man's appearance, but this man had good features and an open, intelligent expression.

'There's no block,' Ward murmured. 'They just kneel with their necks stretched out.'

A proclamation was read out, then silence fell over the proceedings. Again, Ward spoke. 'The executioner always stands on the criminal's left-hand side. You see the swords?'

Lindley's eyes were drawn to a table that had been set up with half a dozen swords on it. Each was about three feet long and an inch and a half wide at the hilt, narrowing and curving towards the point.

Lindley swallowed. His mouth tasted foul. 'The blades seem almost . . . unequal to the task.'

'They're the sabres worn by all military officers on duty. They're as sharp as hell. Executioners are ordinary soldiers chosen from the ranks. They're required to "flesh a maiden sword" for their officers. They call it kai kow – "opening the edge". It's to imbue the weapon with the power of killing.'

Ward's words daggered him. He wished the American would put the yellow jade ornament away, instead of constantly turning it over in his fingers like he did.

The first victim was readied. He struggled soundlessly when he saw the executioner step forward, and threw back his head, panting in terror. The guard behind him grasped his wrist bindings, tilting his arms up. Then the executioner's assistant, a lad of about fifteen or sixteen Lindley judged, uncoiled the victim's plait of hair and pulled hard on it, forcing the head down.

'He'd do better to accept the inevitable,' Ward said. 'A headsman will never strike twice. It's bad luck.'

Lindley watched, at once fascinated and repulsed by what was happening. Now the executioner was looking towards the senior military officer, until he heard the word pan! – punish! Then he turned and readied himself, holding the sword out tensely with both hands, his feet apart and firmly planted. He aimed the sword, bringing it to six inches above the chosen joint, then Lindley heard him shout out sharply, 'Don't move!'

He raised the sword as high as his head, then brought it rapidly down with all his strength, at the same time dropping his body to almost a sitting posture as he struck, to give the blow extra force.

Lindley gasped, rooted by shock. The executioner had failed to sever the first victim's head completely. It fell forward with the body, and he saw the features moving in terrible contortions as blood gushed around it, attracting the pigs.

But the executioner had already moved on. He seemed possessed of a demonic energy now. The second victim's head sprang off his trunk easily, then a moment later the third. The executioner passed on without pause, coming closer, until he reached the man closest to where Lindley stood. The sound of heads hitting the ground became a regular beat, coming every six or seven seconds. It was unlike anything Lindley had ever heard. Each time the sound caused him to flinch, until he wished he could shut it out. The heads bounced and rolled, blood fountained horrifically, but not one of the victims struggled or cried out. Most of the bodies fell forward, but some remained rigidly upright until they were pushed over by the guards. Immediately the second body fell, Lindley watched an old man come forward and begin methodically dipping bunches of rushes in the blood pools. When they were fully saturated he put them by and went back for more.

Still the executioner and his assistant moved along the ranks. The only other movement came from the ghoulish old man and the flicking tails of the pigs. Nothing in his medical studies had prepared Lindley for the experience. His disbelieving eyes roamed the impassive faces of the officials, as they stared into the middle distance. It was like something from a nightmare, but it was actually happening.

The young executioner's assistant supplied his master with a fresh sword every fifth or sixth cut. He collected the used one, wiped it and returned it reverently to the table.

Lindley turned away. 'This is . . . *hideous*.'

Ward made no reply. He was watching steadily, his jaw clenched, his thoughts unknowable.

As soon as the last victim was dead, the executioner approached the cross. The man tied to it was well-muscled, in his late twenties, Lindley judged. Unlike the others his hair was plentiful and worn to shoulder length. He was quickly stripped of his rags by the assistant, who then brought his master a knife, a single-edged dagger that gleamed.

Lindley wiped his face, unsure what he was about to witness. His skin was cold and saturated with sweat. His hand was trembling. 'Dear God. What has the man done to deserve this?'

'He's a chang mao – a long-hair.'

'Long-hair?'

'A loyal subject of the Coolie King. A rebel. They call themselves Taipings. They used to control a pretty big slice of southern China. They ran it with an iron hand from their capital up at Nanking. But not so much now because they're surrounded and under siege by an Imperial army, though the siege isn't succeeding.'

'And this man is from Nanking?'

'According to the proclamation he's from Shanghai. He's a spy.'

'A spy? Look at his hair. How could he be a spy?'

'That's just the official accusation to make him sound important. My guess is he's a Taiping regular officer who came from some city recaptured by the Imperials.'

Lindley was appalled. 'He's a prisoner-of-war?'

'Not exactly. The authorities usually get hold of them by taking their parents or wives. Men will sometimes surrender to save their families from torture. And to make sure they get the reward.'

Lindley stared in amazement. 'What?'

Ward cast him an unreadable glance. 'Sure! The mandarins are clever dealers. They always think of the future. They rarely break faith because word gets around. The reward is always paid.'

'The families collect it?'

'Of course.'

Bodies were being dragged through the pools of blood, placed in coffins of unplaned wooden boards and loaded onto a cart. The severed heads were gathered up and impaled on spikes on the iron rack. Pigs were excitedly rucking the newly blood-soaked ground. The executioner's assistant picked up an old sabre. He placed one foot on the back of the first body, and lifted the head, sawing at the unsevered part of the neck until it was cut through, the muscles of the body still twitching. Oblivious to the horror the old man continued soaking up the blood with his bunches of rush pith, and putting them aside.

'It's used by the Chinese as a medicine,' Ward said. 'Not a technique you're familiar with, I guess.'

'No.' Lindley wiped his face again. The stench and the heat were sickening him, but he remained in control of himself.

Ward glanced at him and said, 'Can you believe what you're seeing? Hmm? Can you actually believe what that man's doing to a fellow human being? It's like some kind of insane invention, isn't it?'

'I don't know what I believe any more.'

'Well, you'd better figure that out. Because what you believe is important here. It makes all the difference between what you'll do – and what you won't.'

'Yes.'

'Take these fellers.' Ward gestured at the corpses. 'The Chinese believe that to be reborn you have to be buried whole. That's why the relatives of condemned men bribe the executioner to allow their victim's heads to be sewn back in place after decapitation. That's why they're so pathetically grateful when the sentence is only strangling. Strangulation is a more painful and lingering death, but what's a little pain when a whole fresh lifetime is in the equation? Let me ask you: have you heard of the "death by a thousand cuts" yet?'

'No.'

'You surprise me. People tell stories and joke about it a whole lot in Shanghai, but it's no joking matter as you'll soon see. You're very privileged. Very few Europeans have ever actually seen it performed.'

Twenty yards away the man tied to the cross was waiting motionlessly for his torture to commence. His eyes gazed on the bespattered earth, and Lindley recognized the moody stare that he knew often hid human terror. But there was more in the man's bearing than that. He had immense dignity.

Up on the official stage the mandarin of the second rank was in conversation. Several minutes passed and nothing happened.

'What's he waiting for?' Lindley asked, the tension provoking him.

'He's not waiting,' Ward said. 'Everyone else is waiting. For him. I guess you've had a bellyful of China now?'

Lindley felt totally drained. He eyed the official, hating the kind of inhumanity that did not deem all suffering to be equal. His own thoughts were in chaos. *If this is Manchu tyranny no wonder the population floods into Hong Kong and our concessions in the Treaty Ports. No wonder there are rebels. Ward said they were based at Nanking. That's 150 miles up river. Near Chiang-kiang, where my father's supposed to have gone. What if they behave to Westerners there as they do to their own here?*

'You're still in need of money,' he told Ward doggedly. 'And I still need river transport.'

Ward looked to him and seemed surprised when Lindley engaged his eye. There seemed to be a new respect there, but Ward remained cautious. 'How much money?'

'The going rate, Mr Ward. Fifty crates. Five foot by two by three. Each weighs around four hundred pounds.'

'Christ. What's in them?'

'What does it matter to you?'

'Maybe it doesn't. Why do you really want to go to Chiang-kiang?'

'Because, so far as I know, my father's there. He's a missionary. And I intend to find him.'

'Why take the crates?'

'He asked for them to be sent out. I'll tell you this much: what's in them is of no use in Shanghai. My father will be glad of them, and know what to do with them – if we can find him.'

Ward nodded slowly. 'In that case a thousand taels. Half down now – no refund. The other half on completion.'

He knew from what Fei had told him that the figure was high but fair. 'That's a deal.'

Ward pulled a little blue accounts book from his breast pocket and began to jot down figures in it. 'Agreed.'

Across the square the mandarin of the second rank nodded to a lower grade official who gave the command.

'Ling che! Pan!'

The man on the cross tensed as the executioner approached. His lips moved in silent incantation. The first strokes were two cuts across his forehead, then his left breast was cut off, then flesh was sliced from the front of each

59

thigh. One by one, Lindley watched parts of the victim pinched between finger and thumb, carved off and thrown for the pigs. The victim did not scream or make any sound, but his heaving chest and quivering limbs attested his extreme agony. He never once stopped mouthing a prayer.

Who are these Taipings? Lindley wondered, the cold sweat now pouring from him. Who are these men who can bear such a fate in silence? Even when the victim's movements stopped the carving continued, until every designated extremity had been removed. Then the bloodied remains were finally cut down from the cross and decapitated.

Ward started towards the gate, and Lindley followed. Their way was blocked by the official to whom Ward had spoken earlier. Another exchange passed between them, some of which Lindley caught, but then the man half bowed in an almost insolent way and stepped aside for them to pass.

'What was that about?'

Ward pushed open the gate and strode through. 'He says the taotai sends his respects to the honourable British Consul.'

Yehonala tried to quell her fears as her handmaids helped her put on full ceremonial dress. The problem of what to do about Su-shun's clique had become acute, and it was now vital to find allies.

I must use today, she thought. I must use this morning's ministerial presentations, and this afternoon's inspection of the guard. Su-shun has found a new way to control Hsien-feng – and opium is a way more potent than mine.

Her long winter dragon robe was warm. It was mink lined, the outside brilliant yellow silk decorated in the Five Colours – black, white, red, blue and yellow – and smothered in symbolic embroidery that showed billowing waves, clouds, twining dragons and the Twelve Womanly Symbols. Her winter boots were padded with raw silk, and the tops were lined with sable. Her hat was like all official hats, a black upturned rim, black chin-strap and cascades of crimson tassels falling over a conical crown. As consort and mother to the heir added ornament was permitted, so the central spire of her hat was crusted with gold and pearls.

A messenger knelt at the door and she took a letter from him. When she saw it had come from the South her heart began to beat faster.

Tsai-ch'un was chanting his lessons in the next room.

'Jen je chu, hsin pen shan . . .' In the beginning the heart of man was naturally good . . .

Learn, and learn well, my son, she thought, putting the letter into her sleeve unread. Because knowledge is power. One day, Tsai-ch'un, you will succeed to a line of emperors that spans eleven dynasties and two thousand years. When you climb onto the Dragon Throne you will become more than human. You will cease to be my son, and become instead the Son of Heaven.

As a divine creature, she knew, he would live a life separate from the human world. Before him, all subjects would fall to their bellies in the kowtow. In this private citadel of the Forbidden City his life would be ruled by the cycle of the seasons. He would emerge from it only on ritual occasions – to make sacrifice to Imperial ancestors, to perform the Rites, and to offer up annual prayers at the Temple of Heaven. In robes special to him alone, he would sit through ten thousand Court audiences in which he would face south, while everyone else faced north. He would devote many thousands of hours to his personal study of the Confucian Classics, and when he wrote he would write in Imperial vermilion, while everyone else wrote in black, because what he wrote would have the force of absolute and unquestionable law. The personal pronoun chen, meaning 'I', would be used only by him. No one would use – or even write – the characters of his personal name, Tsai-ch'un, on pain of death. Even the word 'Emperor' would be specially set apart from other words on whatever page they were written.

Oh, yes, little one, she thought with pride and sadness. You cannot know it now, but your life is already decided. This is to be your destiny, and my destiny is to make it so.

The child voice plucked again at her heart.

'It's thrilling to see another generation learning exactly as I did,' she said, turning to her retinue.

They absorbed her remark without comment, unable to offer an opinion of their own.

'Good education is so necessary,' an elderly eunuch agreed solemnly on their behalf.

'How wise you are,' she said, wishing that someone, some day, would dare to contradict her. 'We must all strive to attain the perfect society that our great sage, Confucius, defined for us.'

'Yes, Lady.'

'No matter what ingenious inventions the Outer Barbarians bring from across the Four Seas to plague us,' she said, 'we will continue, unchanging as the cycles of Heaven and Earth. For ever.'

She felt the letter in her sleeve then glanced at her young attendants, feeling for their precious innocence. These poor, trapped souls can have no understanding of the momentous events unfolding outside, nor any knowledge of the reports I've read during the past year. Memorial after memorial has come out of the South, telling of cities razed and productive country laid waste by rebellion and warfare, and the ever-present interference of foreigners.

There has to be a way to correct Hsien-feng's tremendous ignorance of the world, she thought, descending the steps and moving into the sunshine. Lately he has not been able to deal with state affairs, and when he tries he fails.

The last letter from the South had carried devastating news. General Tseng's tone had become increasingly desperate. He must be allowed to deliver his report in person, she thought. I will write to him and invite him to an Imperial audience, but how much will An Te-hai demand for arranging it?

Outside the morning was windless and still and cold. The smell of wood smoke was in the air and the sound of carpenters hammering in an adjoining compound. She crossed the courtyard to where an open sedan chair waited, was taken up and carried past a pair of gigantic red doors covered in fist-sized golden studs. She passed along broad, red-walled passageways, towards the central axis of the Forbidden City. The main ritual halls and throne rooms were built on a line running exactly north-south through the centre of the complex, as correct observance of feng-shui demanded.

She heard the shouts of military commanders. Hundreds of Imperial guards were already stationed along the ramparts and terraces surrounding the vast cobbled expanse, their breath coming in white plumes in the dry cold. The standards of all eight Banner corps flew there – red, blue, white and yellow, bordered and unbordered. Ministers waited in the grey outer courtyard before the Gate of Supreme Harmony, filling the space with the colours of their official robes. They stood, hatted and gowned, in silent ranks as the nobles gathered and moved toward the sombrely lit Hall of Supreme Harmony. Inside the floor was flagged with polished stone, and huge wooden pillars, blood-red and perfectly cylindrical, held up a complex of minutely decorated rafters inside the high roof. An intricately carved throne stood against the centre of the north wall – gilded, magnificent, vacant.

Yehonala watched as Niuhuru, Empress of the Eastern Palace, appeared in identical dress to her own and acknowledged her with a brief glance. Her eyes strayed to the Censors – aged adjudicators – and near them the Mongol general, Sang Ko-lin-sen, commander of the capital's garrison, dressed in a military chao fu robe, surrounded by lesser generals.

Moments later Prince Kung himself arrived, wearing boots, jacket and trousers, all of simple black silk. A single huge pearl the size of a canary's egg decorated his hat. He took his place between the Censors and Po Chun, the outspoken President of the Board of Revenue. Prince Kung hates ornament almost as much as he despises eunuchs, Yehonala thought. He always wears the minimum allowable, so that some think of him as no more than a sullen scholar, but I know better. He has a powerful mind. I must persuade him to back me in the coming struggle. And Po Chun too – they're both essential.

Other Princes of the Blood filed in. They took up their places with the other Grand Councillors. Then Su-shun took up his position. As Assistant Grand Secretary he was far away from the throne. He was in his forty-eighth year, a powerfully built man, but running to flesh now. In his youth he had been famous for riotous drinking, for hawking and hunting. Then, suddenly, at the age of forty, he had become single-minded about the acquisition of wealth.

And now he's rich he wants power, she thought. But while Po Chun remains President of the Board of Revenue, his career will remain blocked. Po Chun has even criticized his assistant in public.

A reedy eunuch's voice sang out the warning: 'Li la!' – Coming! – and, as one, the entire assembly knelt in the kowtow.

Three great studded doors were thrown open and the Hsien-feng Emperor appeared alone in the middle doorway that was exclusively his. The prime meridian of the world is dedicated to him alone, Yehonala thought, adhering to protocol by not looking directly at him. But isolated by such grand architecture he seems even less imposing than he does in private.

Hsien-feng's slight frame was hung with robes of Imperial yellow. He was thin, with an unhealthy pallor and no aura of authority about him. His Ministers called out their names as the Emperor's feet passed their heads, then Hsien-feng climbed into his sedan chair and was rifled up by bearers who transported him up the three tiers of white marble to the great hall. The bearers negotiated stairs on each side of the huge slabs of dragon-carved stone that no living foot was allowed to touch.

When the Son of Heaven got out of his sedan chair Eunuchs of the Imperial Person crowded round him. These were fanatically loyal, a select cadre responsible for His Imperial Majesty's safety and comfort within the Forbidden City. They were secretive about Hsien-feng's movements when he ventured beyond its walls on various ritual duties. They remained alert to threats, often arranging the Emperor's itinerary and transport in a way designed to confuse assassination attempts. Now they made way for him to enter the audience hall and assume his seat on the Dragon Throne.

Yehonala watched the ceremonial proceed, her mind straying to her own battles, but then her attention returned abruptly to the proceedings. A Minister was kneeling in the kowtow, knocking his head three times on the ground, before offering his memorial.

'Your Imperial Majesty has required of my office information concerning that wicked breed of foreign devil, the In-guo.' He laid a scroll of yellow paper tied up in yellow silk on the floor, and it was picked up by a Eunuch of the Imperial Person, opened and put before Hsien-feng's eyes. He took it.

'What is this?'

'A history of the In-guo, Imperial Majesty – they are the most troublesome of the various breeds of Outer Barbarian. Their island home is located in the most distant of the Four Oceans, but they come to our southern provinces in vessels of their own devising.'

Hsien-feng looked through the scroll wordlessly and the Minister's dread increased. 'These Barbarians, the In-guo, live in the remote parts of the earth, Imperial Majesty. They say they come to China for purposes of trade.'

'Trade? Are they by chance the same breed as those reputed to have visited Jehol and arrogantly refused to kowtow before my great-grandfather sixty years ago?'

The Minister's head bobbed with relief. 'Yes, indeed! The very same, Imperial Majesty.'

Yehonala felt dismay seep through her. The Minister who stood quaking before the Son of Heaven had offered the scroll at her suggestion. The presentation had revealed for all to see the depth of Hsien-feng's ignorance.

Above them all Hsien-feng smiled wanly. 'The In-guo seem to be continually at war with someone or another.' Then he let the scroll fall and his smile vanished. 'Should they persist in this wrong-thinking, our armies must mightily smite them and pledge themselves solemnly to destroy utterly these evil-doers. May they repent while yet there is time. This is my judgement. It is time to retire now.'

Fool! Yehonala thought. He's been sucking at the opium pipe again. Damn him for his despicable weakness, and damn Su-shun for his unscrupulous strength!

A shock of embarrassment paralysed all present in the bitterly cold hall. No one dared ask the Son of Heaven publicly if he felt unwell. No one would dare ask in private. In four days the winter solstice would arrive, and with it the Rites, the most important ritual of the year, in which the Emperor renewed the link between Heaven and Earth. The Rites caused the warm days of spring to emerge from the cold of winter. If the Emperor did not perform the Rites, the spring would not come.

They're destroying him, Yehonala thought. Through their

own greed and ambition and imbecility that ignorant clique are destroying the Emperor, and so destroying us all. She felt again the vital letter from the South that was nestling in her sleeve, and wondered what new disasters it would relate.

Across the Hall of Supreme Harmony, Su-shun shifted his bulk and dropped first into the kowtow at the Emperor's departure. Yehonala felt the magnate's insidious personality radiating icily in her direction. When she looked to him his smiling eyes were already upon her.

'You did *what*?' Ward said.

'I gave the Governor a copy of the New Testament,' Lindley repeated. 'And a couple of medical texts. Then I told him I wanted my father's property protected from rioters in future.'

'You didn't listen to my advice.'

'He agreed to everything.'

'Is that a fact?' Ward flashed a dark glance around Lindley's drawing room. On the table was a copy of the *North China Herald*, and the *Daily Shipping List*, both Shanghai publications printed in English. He slapped a hand on the table. 'You've lit us up like a damned illuminated target!'

'Why? According to the Treaty of Nanking, I'm already entitled to travel into the interior. And so are you.'

'How many times have I got to tell you? You're not entitled to anything here.'

'They signed a bloody treaty!'

'Under duress, so they say. Doc, they won't stick by it. They don't want interference in their internal affairs. They don't even recognize our form of diplomacy. In their view, they're the God-almighty Celestial Empire and we're just a bunch of raggedy-assed Barbarians who come here to get what they already have. And don't forget there's a civil war going on. Chiang-kiang is closer to the rebel capital of Nanking than it is to Shanghai. We'd be landing in disputed territory.' Ward shrugged. 'And you think Wu's going to give permission? Listen: there are warning posters all over the Chinese city that say in foot-tall red characters, "Never eat Christianity". What do you think of that? And more to the point who do you think's behind it? Buddha?'

'"Swallow" not "eat",' Lindley said.

'What's the difference?'

'If you translate too literally you make the Chinese seem like bloody fools. They're not.' He let a moment pass, then said, 'Tell me about the civil war. Who are the Taipings? What do they want?'

'I told you: they're rebels. They want to overthrow the Emperor, and run China their way. But they'll never do it. They're crazy. Full of crazy beliefs.'

'Like what?'

'Like . . .' Ward shook his head, unwilling or unable to explain. 'Just . . . crazy.'

'Either you don't know, or you don't want to tell me. Which is it?'

Ward shot him a hard glance. 'What's in the fifty crates, Doc?'

'I told you. That's not part of the deal, and none of your business.'

'I'm making it my business – or the deal's off.'

He realized Ward was not bluffing. 'Something my father asked me to ship from London. Something he told me not to talk about. To anyone.'

'Doc, I need to know.'

Lindley rubbed his chin, then said, 'Ten thousand Bibles.'

'*What?*' Ward exploded.

'My father's own work. For the first time a translation into the Chinese language.'

Ward showed his disgust. 'Oh, that's just tremendous! You've told the most important man in three provinces exactly what you're going to do to upset his peace. And now you're telling me you intend to load fifty cases of nitroglycerine aboard my boat and go sailing into a war zone!'

'What are you talking about – nitroglycerine?'

'I'm talking about ten thousand Chinese Bibles! Are you out of your mind? That must be Wu's worst nightmare!' Ward threw up his hands. 'Don't you understand what's going on up that river? It's the bloodiest civil war China's ever seen – damn it, it's the bloodiest war in the entire history of the world, and like everything else in China, Peking wants it to be private. Don't you see? That's why Governor Wu's been charged with keeping foreigners out of there.'

Ward seemed about to say something more, but then Fei came into the room. She picked up an empty vase, brushed back a wisp of hair and glanced suspiciously at Ward, before going back out. Lindley saw the way Ward looked at her. The look was lingering, appreciative.

'Who was that?'

'My housekeeper.'

Ward nodded slowly. 'Is that a fact?'

'Aye, that is a fact, Mr Ward.'

'Where did you find her?'

'We travelled here together from Hong Kong,' he said testily. 'Listen, Governor Wu was extremely polite to me. He took a keen interest in the books I gave him. He even discussed his interpretation of the Gospel, which wasn't precisely what a westerner would have arrived at, but he thought it carried a very moral message.'

'You're damned right his interpretation's not the same as ours. The last thing Governor Wu wants is some crazy Scot subverting his people with powerful alien ideas. And the last thing Shanghai's trade interests want is the same individual ruining it all for the rest of us. One way or another. Doc, you're going to get somebody killed. Probably yourself.'

Lindley's temper brinked. 'I can very soon find someone else with a boat who's willing to take a commission. I must tell you though, Mr Ward, I did not have you down as a coward.'

Ward stared at Lindley unblinkingly, his dark eyes lit with a sudden intensity. 'Don't ever – ever – say that again.'

Lindley knew he had touched a nerve. 'I'm sorry. I didn't intend to imply anything against you personally, Mr Ward. This is a business agreement we're discussing.'

'I'm not backing out of anything.'

'I'm pleased to hear that.' Lindley got up and moved to the window as the heat faded between them.

When he turned he saw Ward's fingers turning over his small piece of jade. His eyes were scanning an article of home news in the *North China Herald*. It mentioned the attack that had been made on the US government armoury at Harper's Ferry, Virginia. The perpetrators had been caught and hanged at Charlestown. When Ward finished reading he looked up and said quietly, 'Well, I'll be damned.'

'Anything wrong?' Lindley asked.

'Maybe. Maybe.'

Fei watched Lindley as he ate the last of the evening meal of chicken and rice. It was seven o'clock and already dark outside. Inside the house was comfortable, a fire was burning in the hearth and the room was warmly lit. So far her plan had worked well: the missionary's son was kind and good-natured, and it was not at all difficult to make him do what she wanted.

I know he wants to have me, she thought. I catch him looking at me in that way very often, and though he tries hard not to show it, he cannot hide his true thoughts very well. His head is full of knowledge and will-power and optimism, but he has no guile and no scheming business mind at all. In Shanghai every man needs a scheming business mind, or else what is there for him? The warehouse had been easy to arrange and the crates were safe. The American's arrival had worried her at first, but she had decided to take advantage of what might turn out to be a piece of good fortune.

'Fei, that was delicious. I feel much better now.' He left the table and poured a generous whisky, then went to sit on his English studded leather sofa. After looking at her strangely, he disappeared behind a newspaper. His mood had not lifted since the American had left.

'Do you want to go to bed soon?' she asked, knowing he liked his bed warmed by a copper pan filled with hearth ashes.

'No. Not for a little while.'

They had been together in the house from new moon to new moon and every night she had used the copper warming pan, and every night he had resisted laying a finger on her. Look at him, she thought wryly. What a wilful man he is. He's still controlling himself, telling himself that if he touches me he'll be deflected from his task and that his reason for coming to China will be lost. How little he yet knows. It's very good he thinks what he does, because it balances him on a knife edge, and that's where I must try to keep him.

But a deeper part of her felt differently. That part of her was disappointed he had not made any open move towards her. She watched him for a few more moments, weighed her feelings, then asked him, 'Do you want me to find a woman for you? For tonight?'

He lowered the paper, his expression unsmiling. 'What did you say?'

'I said: do you want me to bring a woman for—'

'Yes, yes. I heard what you said.' He compressed his lips – an unreadable gesture. Then the newspaper rose up between them again.

'Don't you want a woman?'

His voice came from behind the screen. 'No. I don't want a woman. And you shouldn't be asking.'

Why is he so annoyed? she wondered, mystified. It's a reasonable request. He's a physician, he must know that men make yang essence in their bodies, and must therefore expel it at convenient intervals in order to restore the balance between yin and yang and so stay healthy in body and mind.

'What about the seven emotions?' she asked.

'Hmm?' The paper came down, but his face was grudging. 'I'm sorry, Fei. I have . . . things on my mind. What do you want to know?'

'What about the seven emotions?'

'What about them?'

'You're a physician, and you don't know about the seven emotions?'

He drew a patient breath. 'No. I'm afraid not.'

'You should know that too much joy scatters the spirit and injures the heart. Too much blood makes a red face and causes anger and damages the liver. Anxiety hurts the lungs. Too much concentration and the spleen and stomach will suffer. Grief harms the heart and the lungs. Fear withers the kidneys and makes the bladder weak. And sudden frights are very bad because they give the heart sharp pain and turn the kidneys to stone.'

'Fei, that's very interesting. Now, if you don't mind . . .'

The paper rose up again and she looked at him for a long time, 'Lin-li, why did you go in the sing-song hall in Hong Kong if you don't like women?'

Down came the paper again, revealing a dark expression this time. 'I do like women. But I don't want to discuss my preferences with you – if that's quite all right.' He cleared his throat with finality.

'When did you last have a woman?'

'Fei! Did you not hear what I said?'

'You said I'm to be your housekeeper. So, I have to look after your health and happiness.'

'Yes. But not in that way.'

She sighed and fidgeted, not understanding his strange attitude. What she had been taught as a child had always stressed the virtue of chaste obedience for women, but how was she to know what men wanted? Much less foreign men. She had been prepared for him to be as different from Chinese men on the inside as he was on the outside, and so he had proved to be. But she had not been prepared to find that difference fascinating or delightful.

She looked at his fingers holding the edges of the paper. They were sensitive and expressive. His complexion and colouring and his green eyes were almost inhuman, certainly like no Chinese ever born, yet they had an undeniable handsomeness when put together as they were. Even the way he smelled was pleasant – after a little while.

She remembered the first time she had seen Europeans in Shanghai. She had been seven years old. It had been whispered that Barbarian men were gross-featured and dangerous, that all of them drank powerful liquors that would fell a horse. They often became drunk and wild, then killed people for no reason. Inside their clothes they were said to be as hairy as monkeys. She had watched them promenading in their bizarre clothing, showing their thoughts on their faces, shouting and laughing in public irrespective of the rank of others who might be present. Their chiefs wore tall black hats and heavy felt coats and sucked on evil-smelling cigars. There was an air of arrogant violence about them, as if they sensed they were inferior and their civilization unimportant. They always behaved as if they were trying to make up for being Barbarians, which of course they never could, and that was why they became so angry. In those days she had been very afraid of them. But she had found that this man was different. Christians, at least, are our brothers, she thought, recalling her lessons. We must love them. That much is an undeniable duty, and yet . . .

The silence had grown too long and she sighed. 'Lin-li, do you remember I asked if you are Christian?'

'Yes.'

'You said you didn't know.'

'That's right.'

'But . . . if you don't know, then you cannot be a Christian.'

He turned to her, his expression indulgent. 'Fei, what are you driving at?'

'If you're not a Christian what does it matter if you have a woman any time?'

He folded the newspaper and put it aside. 'Just because I can't claim to have found faith in Christ, doesn't mean that I'm bound to behave like a complete barbarian. Our social customs are different. That's all.'

She weighed his words. Aboard the big ship she had been ready for him to attack her. She had expected it. Europeans are famous for their lack of self control, aren't they? Why did he not try to rape me? Perhaps he is pledged to austerity. She went over to the fireplace, aware how his eyes followed her. He watched her as she knelt down and leaned forward to put a log on the flames. She felt his scrutiny pass from the sinews of her ankles over the normally shapeless fabric of her pyjama pants as it stretched.

'Oh, God . . .' she heard him mutter. 'Must you do that?'

'Do what?' She straightened and brushed a wisp of hair back over her ear. 'It's too cold in here.'

'Do you think so?' he said, his voice oddly throaty. 'I don't.'

She came to perch on the arm of his sofa, wanting to share one of her favourite stories. 'Have I told you the ancient tale of the Emperor Yuan-ti, of the Han dynasty?'

'No.'

She looked down demurely. 'That Emperor had so many concubines that he never even saw most of them.'

'Lucky fellow.'

She put his whisky glass into his hands. 'It's true. He only saw portraits, painted by a famous Court artist called Man Yen-shou. That was why the concubines always gave presents to Man. They knew he could make them appear beautiful to their lord.'

He smiled at her, his attention captured, and she continued.

'But the loveliest of the concubines was called Chao Chun, and she decided not to bribe Man Yen-shou, thinking it would be all right if he painted her as she really was. So Man decided to paint a portrait of her that failed to do justice to her great beauty, and because of this the Emperor never desired to have her brought to him. But then there came to the Heavenly Court the Shang-yu – the Great Khan of the Huns. He it was who reigned over the Turkomans of Hiung-mu, so Emperor Yuan-ti, wishing to bind closer the ties of friendship with his powerful neighbour, decided to offer him a wife.'

Lindley grinned at last, her storytelling melting him. 'And, of course, the girl he chose was Chao Chun?'

Fei nodded. 'How did you know? When the Khan of the Huns came to take his leave Chao Chun was at her new husband's side. The Emperor was astonished. He had not known that his harem contained one of such transcendent loveliness. And now Chao Chun was his no longer.'

Lindley's eyes had become soft in the buttery light.

Fei went on, 'Of course, as soon as the Shang-yu departed, Man Yen-shou and the concubines who had bribed him were beheaded in the market place. But for the rest of his life Emperor Yuan-ti was haunted by the memory of Chao Chun's beauty and by regrets for a happiness that might have been his.'

'She must have been a very beautiful woman.' Lindley looked over the rim of his whisky glass appreciatively.

'Lin-li, I think this is a very sad tale.'

'Yes, it is.'

'It's a tale of love, and love tales are always sad.'

'No,' he said, smiling. 'They're not proper love tales if they're sad. They're tragedies. Unrequited love is a tragedy, don't you think so?'

'What's "unrequited"?'

'When one person desires another, but is rejected. That's fine for stories, but not for real life. I like happy endings. People should be good to one another. They should be happy – if they can be.'

'Is that why you became a physician? To make people happier?'

He smiled again. 'I never thought of it before, but perhaps you're right. I'm an optimist, I suppose. I couldn't think of trying to live any other way.' He touched her hair and said, 'I want you to know that despite what I said before, I'm very glad you're here, Fei-ch'ien.'

She felt a rush of warmth at his touch and she saw with shock just how much desire he felt for her. He was resisting her with all his might. It's all right, an inner devil voice told her. This situation is different. You have permission. A special dispensation to do whatever is necessary to ensure success. Why not admit that you want him? Why else would you have been playing the temptress with him so much? And in any case who will know?

God will know, she thought. It's still not right. Even though I do admit that I want him. Maybe it's not right because I want him. Because then it's not duty and it's not necessity. It's only self-indulgent pleasure, and if I give in I will spoil all my hopes. When the war is over who will consider marrying a woman who is not a virgin? Who will respect a woman who has shamed herself with a foreigner? Never mind that, her inner devil voice said, tempting her. You have special permission. Afterwards you can always lie about it.

When she slid down off the arm of the sofa and onto the seat beside him he uncoiled her hair at the nape of her neck. She tossed her head, letting it swing to one side in a fan-like motion, then as if in a trance she moved her face up towards his. His eyes were fiery. Their mouths were very close now. His attention seemed concentrated on her lips. When he tilted his head slightly, she felt herself respond by doing the same. When their lips touched it was barely contact, but the sensation filled her with excitement. She had never done this with any man.

He took her in his arms, and she could not stop herself thrilling to the sensation. How can such a wonderful feeling be against God? she asked herself. How can it? And how can it really be that the creator of the universe is interested in so unimportant a thing as my own secret pleasure?

He pulled back and searched her face with tenderness, taking time to confirm her consent. She saw that it was not simple compliance he was looking for, but her freely-given permission. She had not expected this, and it decided her.

'You asked me a moment ago did I want to go to bed,' he said huskily. 'I do – if you do.'

'Yes.' She heard herself say.

The agreement was made. He pulled her up and led her upstairs. She sat on the bed while he undressed, then she started to take off her own clothes in the darkness. The only light was coming from downstairs. It spilled across the polished floorboards and rugs and glinted on the brass rods of the bedstead. The goose down pillows yielded. The fresh cotton sheets were exquisite against her skin. His warm hair-covered chest, unlike the chest of any Chinese, was soft and strong at the same time. Its feeling entranced her, driving from her mind all thoughts of duty to God, her father and the holy mission she had been given to accomplish.

Yehonala opened the eye-hole and looked out of her palanquin into the freezing night. Tonight was the winter solstice – midwinter, the moment when the Rites must take place.

Overhead rags of cloud streamed across the sky, and high above them the ink-black heavens hung aloof and merciless over the crisp ground. The air was too cold for snow. Instead a cruel wind was blowing straight out of the iron heart of Siberia, ghosting ice-dust across the open boulevards.

She rearranged her feet on the sealed copper pan of hot ashes that took away a little of the chill, and closed the eye-hole. Then she drew the furs closer about her, damning the intolerable delay.

The precincts of Tien-t'an were sacred and forbidden, surrounded by an outer wall twelve li in extent, all of it heavily guarded. Soldiers of the Eight Banners were stationed every three paces along the way, protecting the double-moated, triple-walled Fasting Palace with massive force. The entire route from the Forbidden City along which they had passed in silence was lined with more soldiers, and still more had driven the Common People away from the route and erected yellow screens to keep the Emperor from profane view.

She heard a knock, and damned the intrusion. The shock of the cold as the door opened was heartstopping, but seeing

An Te-hai here at the Temple of Heaven and pushing his way into her palanquin was almost too much to bear.

'Lady, the Grand Secretary is dead!'

She couldn't be sure she had heard him correctly, but then he repeated it.

'Po Chun?' The news had sickened her and filled her with fear. 'How?'

'Dragged from his mansion by troops of the Bordered Red Banner. Summarily beheaded in the middle of the street. It happened an hour ago.'

That was undoubtedly what was holding up events. She said shakily, 'The Imperial procession must have been re-routed to avoid the street where Po Chun's walled mansion stands.'

'It stands no longer. In its place is smouldering rubble and a doorway sealed up with a message, "A traitor once lived here." All of Po Chun's property has been confiscated, and his entire household – family, servants, everyone – have been banished in shame to Black Dragon River.'

'How can he have done this?' she said, meaning the Emperor. The cold seeped deep into her bones. 'How can he have let this happen?'

An's gaunt face was ghastly in the darkness. 'His Imperial Majesty is presently . . . indisposed.'

'Tonight?'

She had seen the Rite performed four times now – Hsien-feng's arrival at the Imperial Vault of Heaven to venerate his ancestors' funerary tablets, his lighting of incense and his formal prostration before the reading of the Pedigree of the Aisin Gioro bloodline:

'We offer respect to Nurhachi the Founder; to his eighth son and heir Huangtaiji; to Fu Lin, ninth son of Huangtaiji; to Hsuan Yeh, third son of Fu Lin who became the great K'ang-hsi emperor . . .'

After the dynastic roll-call came the procession down the great raised causeway that followed the north-south meridian to the open Round Altar, there to worship those same ancestors, and the sun and the moon and the stars, and the clouds and the rain, and the winds and the thunder, and then to make bloody sacrifices.

The plate of the Round Altar was the most awe-inspiring place in the world. It was the navel of the universe, where

Heaven and Earth were joined. It was a raised sacrificial platform made of nine concentric circles of white marble – always nine and multiples of nine – four hundred and five slabs in all, and the four hundred and sixth was a central boss, a convex stone also of white marble, slightly raised for the Emperor. There he stood when it was time to make his report to Shang-ti, the great God, the Creator of All Things . . .

Where is he? she wondered, frantic. He should have emerged from abstinence an hour ago. If he delays much longer this charcoal will lose its heat completely and my body will freeze solid with cold. If An is right, we can't even be sure that Hsien-feng has left the Forbidden City yet.

A huge bronze bell began to toll, and moments later a line of five closed palanquins crossed the outer moat bridge and turned into the path that led east to the vast, raised causeway. Their own bearers waited, crying silently with the cold, until the Imperial palanquins passed by. Then Yehonala felt herself lifted up and they moved off.

Five palanquins, she thought with enormous relief. Five palanquins for an Emperor, because steps must be taken to confuse assassins. We Manchurians will always be thought of as invaders by the Chinese. Two hundred years ago we came from the wilderness beyond the Wall and took the reins of power from the decadent Mings. In that two hundred years we have become more Chinese than the Chinese themselves, but still they refuse to accept us.

What a mockery, she thought, a Manchurian Emperor coming here to report the state of the Chinese Empire – which he rules over, but about which he has virtually no knowledge – to a Heaven that probably despises him as much as the Han Chinese despise us for having smashed their Ming line.

The procession moved a few yards down the causeway then stopped. Yehonala's eye went to where a tent of yellow silk had been erected. It strained on its ropes, rippling. Like the banners around it it fought the wind. The sumptuary regulations specified that the Emperor must wear a blue coloured chao pao when praying at the Altar of Heaven. It was here he must change into the sacrificial robe, and mount the chariot that would take him south along the causeway, like a god coming to earth from heaven. Wooden floor lamps had been lit all along the route, their candlelight flickering through yellow paper windows as attendants struggled to keep them all alight.

She watched the five identical palanquins, wondering which of them was occupied by Hsien-feng. They were put down, but nothing happened. There was going to be another delay. Horses stamped and snorted. She saw great elephants, gifts from the Dalai Lama, looming impatiently in the darkness, harnessed to the gilded chariot that would travel the causeway. She heard porters' feet and the jangling of harnesses. Distant thuds from the drum tower told her that the Hour of the Ox was ending and the Hour of the Tiger beginning.

So, Su-shun, she thought, her mind finally coming out of its dreadful paralysis. Po Chun is dead and the last of your adversaries at the Board of Revenue is vanquished. You have control of state finances. What can I do now to stop you?

The lowing of sacrificial cattle came to her on the wind. They were tethered by iron nose-rings frozen into their frostbitten muzzles. Their hooves skidded on frozen urine. Their moans were taken up and twisted by the wind so that they seemed ghostly and portentous. They know what their fate is to be, she thought. They set us an example by remaining placid. The copper pan under her feet was barely warm now. She cracked open her palanquin door and the blinding cold enveloped her again instantly. She got out and went immediately to Niuhuru's palanquin, looking in on her.

Niuhuru's faultless features were hidden in her furs. What a pity that such beauty of face and body is wedded to such peacefulness of mind, Yehonala thought. What formidable allies we would make if your mental skills were as excellent as the rest of you.

'Lady Niuhuru, please pardon this unexpected intrusion,' she said formally. 'But I fear we may be encountering a slight difficulty at present.'

Niuhuru blinked in confusion. 'Lady Yehonala, I too fear that may be so.'

Good, Yehonala thought. At least she understands that this is an appalling calamity. Now I must steer her carefully.

'The question is: what can be done about it?'

'Yes. That is certainly very puzzling.'

'Unfortunately, it appears to be a situation without precedent.'

Niuhuru's eyes were round. 'Who would know if there was a precedent?'

'I will make enquiries.'

Yehonala called a captain of the Plain White to her. 'You. What's the delay?'

The guardsman's flat face was screwed up against the bitterness of the night. He dropped to the ground in kowtow immediately, but still Yehonala registered his amazed reaction to her question. It was a question that could not be answered by anyone, let alone a man of his lowly rank.

'Go and tell them to do something,' Yehonala said. 'Or we'll still be here at sunrise.'

The guardsman was jolted by the command. Horrified, he lifted his head. 'Yes, Lady. Immediately.' Then he backed away on hands and knees and retired to the yellow robing tent.

After a few more minutes in the biting cold she returned to Niuhuru. 'It seems that while the Imperial palanquins remain unopened no one in particular is responsible for opening them.'

Niuhuru looked horrified. 'The Emperor will emerge when he is ready. Who may question that?'

The maroon-robed priests and officials stared, each waiting for his seniors to act, but no one considered himself senior enough. Yehonala tried to master her growing anger, but then a knot of figures came out, conferred again, and one of them, a lamaist priest, approached the line of five palanquins and prostrated himself before the first of them to pray for an emergence.

Yehonala cursed their craven stupidity under her breath. She said to the prostrate man. 'You fear too much for your head. It is possible His Imperial Majesty is unwell. It is our duty to find out. Must I do everything myself?' She stepped past the priest who shivered on the ground like a dog, and opened the first palanquin. It was empty. The door of the second palanquin would not open easily and she was forced to jerk it open. It too was empty. She passed on to the third, and the fourth. The Emperor was not inside either. Finally she faced the last palanquin. A hundred astonished eyes were on her. She had shattered formality and made a fool of herself. What if the Emperor really was ill, or dead? What would everyone do? And who would decide?

She stepped up to the last palanquin, pulled at the handle and the door came free. She flung it wide.

It was empty also.

The T'ai-he bell tolled again in the silence that followed. The open doors of the line of Imperial palanquins flapped and banged in the wind. Hsien-feng had abandoned the Rites. Heaven would now ensure that affairs on earth be rectified.

'You've allowed Su-shun to destroy you, Hsien-feng,' she whispered. 'No miraculous pregnancy can save you this time.'

Then she saw the horror on the priests' faces and could not stop herself from laughing hysterically.

Three days later Yehonala hired an enclosed palanquin and rode it from the courtyard of the inn on Tunghuamen Street. Her son sat on her lap. Twelve li beyond the walls of Peking, as she travelled north-west towards Kunming Lake, it began to snow again.

She discreetly looked out of the swaying box. The bearers were already labouring knee-deep in snow, crossing the flat landscape exactly as she had directed, when suddenly she loosed the toggles that held the wooden slat blind and called out. 'Stop here.'

The head bearer looked at her incredulously. 'Here, Madam? But it's the middle of nowhere.'

'I said here. Don't you listen?'

The palanquin went down, its legs sinking into the snow, and she struggled out. The snow came almost to the tops of her felt boots, and fresh flakes began to settle on her. The lead bearer came forward to help her, but she swept up her child and said, 'Wait for me here. I expect to be away for one hour, possibly a little longer, but even if I am six hours you will continue to wait for me. Is that understood?'

The head bearer bobbed his head. 'Yes, Madam.'

The other bearers looked at one another, reading one another's thoughts. It was very cold, and there was certainly something very dubious about this passenger and her child, but a fare was a fare, and important people were always travelling incognito, and a fat bonus like this did not happen every day.

'Please be careful, Madam. These are evil times. The street rumours say the Emperor made no report to Shang-ti this year, and—'

'What nonsense!'

'But, Madam, it's certainly true that the blizzard froze two thousand Imperial soldiers to death while they waited. I myself saw the bodies. Surely the Emperor has lost the Mandate of Heav—'

She whirled on him. 'Don't you know that kind of talk is treason?'

The lead bearer looked at her with new eyes. 'I'm only telling what I heard.'

'Don't spread rumours. Just obey orders.'

Yehonala trod through the snow, her black silk boots crunching through the whiteness. The memory of what had taken place at Tien-t'an three days ago echoed in her mind. The rest of that bitter night had turned out to be as strange as the first part. She remembered her relief at finding all the Emperor's palanquins vacant. She had laughed and then fallen to the ground, feigning a swoon. As An Te-hai had helped her back to her own palanquin the fear had begun to lift from her.

Su-shun almost made an unbelievably stupid move, she thought. Maybe he was too busy exulting at a victory over Po Chun. Maybe he actually supposed that by destroying the Emperor he would be disposing of me also. He must have realized very late that if Hsien-feng was forced to abdicate it could only be in favour of my son, and that would strengthen my position. A movement just off the causeway to the west made every head turn away from her. Another palanquin had appeared on the ramp. It had approached the five vacant ones, coming to rest just ahead of them. Almost immediately Hsien-feng had stepped out in full Imperial yellow. He had cast a momentary glance at her, never suspecting her immense disappointment that he had finally arrived.

She put the memories behind her as she reached a stand of five cypress trees and began to scan the frozen expanse of the lake beyond. Almost immediately she saw a lone horseman and knew it was Jung-lu. He urged his mount on, riding with an easy rhythm, then broke into a gallop and wheeled the horse toward the ice-bound shore. She wanted to call to him, to warn him, but his name stuck in her throat. Jung-lu danced the horse round in a reckless turn. He delighted in risking himself, testing his skill. Or was it his intention to scare her? The horse stopped and braced its legs, its hooves slipping as it sensed danger, but Jung-lu kicked it on savagely, and it sprang into a gallop.

Yehonala felt the cold eat into her face as she watched. Swirls of snow twisted across the desolate plain of ice. She clasped Tsai-ch'un closer to her.

Jung-lu was mid-way across the lake now. The thundering of hooves seemed to come from another world as the horse raced on. The spirit of his ancestors was flowing strongly in him. He carried lance, bow and quiver, and wore a helmet and full war gear, yet his exquisite balance and complete mastery of the animal gave him a fluid grace that over-powered her fears. Then suddenly horse and rider were gigantic and violent beside her, the beast snorting plumes of steam, champing and turning its head in the flurrying snow, and she pulled her son to her protectively.

He leapt down, hardly looking to her, eyes only for his son. She turned the boy to face his father, and Jung-lu took him like a war trophy, lifting him into the sky in both hands, his face enraptured.

'Tsai-ch'un!' he said. 'Tsai-ch'un, my son! At last I can raise you up!'

'You see. I kept my promise.'

Yehonala watched, saw her son's little face turn to her. He was terrified as he struggled against the monstrous soldier who had swept him up and carried him away from his mother. 'You will learn to ride and shoot and hunt.' Jung-lu strode out onto the ice. 'Come with me and I will show you how to be a soldier!'

Yehonala followed. 'Please, Jung-lu, no! It's dangerous out there!'

'He must come to hear the spirits talking.'

'What spirits? Jung-lu, the ice is not safe!'

He ignored her, carried the child away. Tsai-ch'un started to scream. The untethered horse shook itself and whinnied close by her, jangling its gear. Father and son were thirty paces away. She started out on the ice after them. 'Wait! Jung-lu!'

He stopped until she caught up. Tsai-ch'un had stopped trying to wrest himself free. A stare and a sharp word from his father had called for obedient silence.

'Listen!'

For a while there was nothing. She strained her ears. Still nothing. When she relaxed he hissed at her to keep still.

'There! Did you hear that?'

She had felt it through her feet. A dull, groaning sound reverberating all around in the stillness. She listened for it again, hoping it would repeat, but it did not.

'What was that?' she asked. She listened, and the groaning came again.

'Spirit voices,' he said, his own voice full of wonder. He turned to Tsai-ch'un. 'Listen to the voices of your ancestors, my son. Hear what they say, and do not forget their words.'

'It's an ice-quake,' she said, alerted. 'The sound of cracking ice. I heard it once at Beihai Lake.'

She reached for her child, but Jung-lu pulled him away. His fierceness met her eye. 'Are you scared, woman? Scared that we'll all fall through the ice and die? Life's an illusion anyway. Isn't that what the learned monks say? So what's death? At least we'd be a family in death. Together. Man and wife and son. As it was meant to be.'

'I want to go back.'

'It's safe enough here,' he said. 'This ice is thick enough to march an army across.'

'Please let go of my son.'

'Look down there.' Jung-lu knelt and dusted the snow off the semi-transparent surface. She could see that here the ice was thick, full of beautiful greenish light and trapped air bubbles and so veined with fractures that it looked as if it had been hit by a giant hammer. She feared that Tsai-ch'un should keep looking in case he began to see the spirits of the dead writhing in the cold black water beneath.

'An Te-hai says I should have you killed!' she shouted, breaking the spell. Jung-lu stood up.

'An Te-hai's a treacherous little piece of turtle shit.'

'He was thinking of me. He has my best interests at heart.'

Jung-lu towered over her, magnificent and threatening. 'You can't depend on any man without balls.'

'I can control him.'

'Can you? I'd sooner skewer him on my lance and roast him alive.'

'In the coming fight against Su-shun I'll need all my allies. I need you both now that Po Chun is dead.'

The wind ruffled the long hairs of his fur-fringed helmet. He looked at her, his eyes wild. 'Why don't I make a decisive strike at Su-shun? Fifty picked men, one hellish rush at his jugular. I could obliterate him.'

'Su-shun's protected by seasoned guards at all times. You'd die wastefully.'

'Maybe. But think of the glory!'

'I can't afford to think of glory. It's my job to win a throne for my son.' She looked back across the open, snow-covered fields to where the palanquin bearers waited. It was growing dark, and there was more snow coming. 'We have to go back now.'

'Remember what I have told you.'

'I will. And I pray you will do the same.' She gathered Tsai-ch'un to her and started back towards the palanquin.

'I cannot make her open the gate of the Western Palace, your Imperial Majesty.'

The throbbing at An's temple intensified as he tried to devise an answer to the Emperor's question. The headaches had been getting worse lately, and kneeling in the kowtow made the pain almost unbearable. It was not helped by the presence of so many august councillors, among them Su-shun and Prince Kung.

Hsien-feng's voice took on a petulant edge, echoing in the high wooden cavern of the private audience hall. 'My consort defies me. But I am her Emperor.' He glanced at Su-shun. 'She must do as I wish.'

'Yes, your Imperial Majesty.'

The Western Palace was Yehonala's private domain, walled and self-contained, a palace within the Forbidden City that could be locked at her pleasure. In fact, it had been An who had ordered the gates barred. And they would stay that way until he gave the code word to open them. Yehonala's own staff had been told that she was at her devotions. That for the first time she had taken her son to sit before the Buddha. That she was not to be disturbed under any circumstances.

'Perhaps, if your Imperial Majesty were to explain to the Lady Yehonala the reason for the summons, she would become easier to persuade.'

'Incredible impudence! Go back and insist she present herself now!'

'Of course, your Imperial Majesty. Immediately. But there is one small difficulty.' An could feel Su-shun's eyes on him. It was hard to intrigue efficiently while being watched by so loathsome and perceptive an enemy. He decided his best course was a display of cringing humility.

'What difficulty?' Hsien-feng said.

'It is hard to explain – your Imperial Majesty must know that the Lady Yehonala fears for the safety of the heir!'

He had blurted it out, and there was a moment of shocked silence. 'Why? Is my son unwell?'

'Oh, no, your Imperial Majesty! The heir is in wonderful good health, and very happy. However the Lady Yehonala is concerned that someone at Court wishes him harm.' The attack was delivered like a smooth blade slipping between a man's ribs, and Su-shun tensed exactly as if the blade had been of steel.

'Who?' The Emperor demanded. 'Who wishes to harm my son?'

'The Lady Yehonala does not say.' An kept his head down. Out of the corner of his eye he could see servants lighting lanterns outside. The reflection of snow filtering down dappled the polished cedar wood floor. How long can I stall them? he wondered. Already half the Imperial staff are running about like excited ants. I told you, Lady, that it was madness to keep your promise to Jung-lu. I don't know why the Emperor's decided to call you to him, but I wouldn't be surprised if your absence has been reported. And if that's so then I wouldn't be in your boots now. No, not for all the tea in China.

'What is the cause of the Lady Yehonala's worries?' the Emperor asked. 'Answer.'

An paused, correctly showing extreme hand-wringing reluctance to venture an opinion before superiors.

'What is the matter with you, Chief Eunuch? Answer!'

'Who am I, Imperial Majesty, to give voice to opinions. They would only be lowly—'

'I am ordering you to speak! Are you stupid? You must do as I say, or I will have you whipped!'

The Emperor broke off ominously. The pounding in An's head became intolerable. He wondered what to say next. Then he saw a long shadow falling across the brightly reflecting floor, and looked up to see the figure that stood alone in the entrance way.

Yehonala was calm and composed, and appeared utterly demure.

'You wish to see me, Imperial Majesty?' she asked.

Hsien-feng threw up his hands. His tone completely changed. 'Yehonala! Why did you not come at my first calling?'

'I was bathing when your summons came.'

Hsien-feng pointed a slipper at An Te-hai. 'This fatherless creature said you had barred the Western Palace against me. Is that true?'

She looked at An's prostrate form with an expression of pity. 'The Palace was barred at my order. But not against my Emperor – nor my husband.'

'Then, why?'

'I closed the gates against those who would harm our son. I ordered that from now on the Western Palace is to be barred at all times when I am not personally with Tsai-ch'un. His attendants and nurses been told not to venture outside.'

Hsien-feng tried to act his ordained part – Emperor talking to subject, man talking to woman. He puffed himself up. 'I order you to tell me what danger there is? The eunuchs? The maidservants? From whom does the danger come?'

She glanced fleetingly at Su-shun. 'It's too hard to say.'

Prince Kung had been sitting in silence, but he noted the glance, and said, 'Majesty, we believe that Councillor Su-shun prides himself on knowing how women think. Perhaps he will offer us his interpretation of what fears might afflict the Lady Yehonala.'

Hsien-feng turned to him. 'Councillor?'

Su-shun smiled, suddenly master of the game. 'Lady Yehonala, I believe his Imperial Majesty wishes to know why – specifically – you feel it was necessary to take such precautions. Are you making an accusation?'

Yehonala kept her eyes downcast. 'Tsai-ch'un is the most precious child in the Empire. I am his mother. And mothers sometimes have ... feelings. Feelings they know they should not ignore.'

'Ah – then there is no specific threat to the heir?'

Yehonala drew a shuddering breath and looked up. 'Oh, yes. Yes, indeed. Very specific.'

Su-shun held her gaze, his voice also steady. 'Please explain what you mean, Lady Yehonala.'

'Simply that I have consulted my astrologer, and the indications are quite clear. Apparently, a rising star is to be feared. Which star my astrologer could not say.'

Su-shun's laugh was short and dismissive. 'Majesty, what your consort, the Lady Yehonala, did was merely to take a sensible precaution: to bar the doors of the Western Palace against unwanted visitors from the spirit realm.' He moved smilingly onto the offensive. 'But, Lady, surely a bath did not require a whole hour. If I may be so bold as to enquire, what were you doing that prevented you leaving your barred Western Palace when the Emperor summoned you?'

'With respect, how does the Grand Councillor know how long it takes an Emperor's consort to bathe? An Emperor's consort must always be mindful of her appearance. But you are quite right, there was something else.' She paused, timing the stab exquisitely. 'I was making arrangements for a petition that there should be an award to succour Po Chun's widow.'

Hsien-feng's forehead creased. 'Yehonala, you speak the name of a traitor.'

'I apologize, Imperial Majesty, but Po Chun's widow was certainly not to blame for his wickedness. She had no idea what a monster he really was under that faultlessly dignified exterior. She was deceived by his wickedness into believing him to be a sober and reliable man – honest and forthright.'

Hsien-feng seemed to feel the cold. He gathered his robe about him like a man with a fever. 'I want you to know why I called you here, Lady Yehonala.'

'Imperial Majesty?'

'I should like you to accept a gift.'

Hsien-feng ordered his attendants to unveil an exquisite

87

piece of green jade carved in the likeness of a dragon and a phoenix sporting together. It was clearly priceless. Yehonala's blood had run cold at the word 'gift', now the enormous value of the gift made her light-headed with fear.

The sending of gifts was the usual means of control over the princes and princesses of the Imperial family. Each time a gift arrived, the eunuchs who brought it received cumsha. The eunuchs acted as intermediaries between members of the Court and dealt with tribute-bearers from the provinces. Cumsha was the commission paid for a eunuch's trouble. Since gifts could not be refused without a terrible breach of Court etiquette, and since cumsha was calculated to one-tenth the value of the gift, a 'gift' was in reality an inescapable fine.

Yehonala fought to control her composure. Had she fatally misread the extent of Su-shun's growing power over the Emperor? Had she finally pushed her insolence too far? She told herself there could be nothing to worry about: she had been summoned to accept the gift. The gift had not been sent to her. Therefore the gift was truly a gift, and not an award of costs against her. 'Imperial Majesty, surely there has been some mistake?'

'No mistake. I wish to show my appreciation, Yehonala.'

Prince Kung said, 'At Tien-t'an your devotion to my brother was there for all to see. You did the unthinkable – but you did it brilliantly.'

'Oh, surely I am not worthy of any gift, Imperial Majesty,' she said, using the phrase expected of her. She blinked back invisible tears, also as was expected of her, only now the tears were almost real: Hsien-feng's mumbled words had produced relief beyond measure. She looked at the gift again and saw that the symbolism of the jade shouted loudly: Hsien-feng was the Imperial dragon, and the phoenix was Yehonala. In itself it was worth a great many thousands of taels of silver – as a political gesture it had saved her life.

'It's quite exquisite. I can never offer enough thanks to his Imperial Majesty. Anything I may have done was merely my duty.'

'Your husband thanks you with his heart,' Hsien-feng said. 'And the Emperor thanks you with this piece of jade. Prince Kung helped me choose it.'

Joy surged in her at that, but she let nothing show on the

outside. Be careful, she cautioned herself. This might be Prince Kung's overture to me – an overt offer of alliance – or it might be something else. It might simply be a way Prince Kung has found of snubbing Su-shun and implicating me at the same time. I must know which before rejoicing.

'Imperial Majesty, I think you should not have gone to Tien-t'an in the first place.'

Su-shun erupted. 'How could His Imperial Majesty not have attended Tien-t'an? The state of the realm always has to be reported annually to Shang-ti.'

'Always – until now.'

'What do you mean "until now"? It's mandatory. It has always been mandatory. What you're suggesting is ludicrous!'

'Excuse me, Councillor, but nothing has always been mandatory. Traditions are started by great men. Then, after an interval of time, ended by other great men. Certain parties are now wondering if Shang-ti is the appropriate deity for the Emperor to consult in these troubled times.'

'Shang-ti is the god who created the whole universe,' Su-shun scoffed. 'Which god could be more appropriate than He?'

'In the South Shang-ti is also identified with the God of the Christians – the one they call "God the Father".'

Su-shun's face had begun to colour. 'How can they say that? The two are not the same. They have been infected by Barbarians!'

'I'm only reporting what is believed in the South, and what certain parties in Peking are now saying. They insist that Shang-ti and the Christian God are identical.'

'Misguided ideas!' Su-shun cried. 'Who are these "certain parties"?'

'Certain religious authorities,' Prince Kung said, with unexpected directness. 'Also elements of the military and civil administration. And that's not all they're saying, because if Shang-ti is the Christian God then He is also the deity of the Taiping rebels. The question being asked all over China is why does his Imperial Majesty report the state of the empire to the God of the rebels each year? Who is responsible for advising him thus?'

As the Prince's words echoed away in silence, Yehonala spoke, her words breathy but decisive. 'Imperial Majesty, I request permission to share this wonderful jade with your first wife, the Lady Niuhuru? My conscience tells me it is not appropriate that I should possess such a work of art, while that lady whose concern for you was equal to my own should have nothing.'

She saw Hsien-feng's eyes flicker, 'You might both have feared for me, Yehonala. But it was you who acted.'

'Then let us share the jade, but grant me a minor additional favour.'

'What is it you desire?'

'Only that your Imperial Majesty will allow me to serve you further in whatever capacity he chooses. Also, I wish to be allowed to classify your memorials in the Hall of Records.'

Hsien-feng's slow eyes blinked. 'A curious request. But if it is your desire, so be it.' A Eunuch of the Imperial Person bent to whisper to Hsien-feng, who gratefully signalled the end of the audience.

As the gathering broke up Yehonala marvelled at Prince Kung's declaration. Events had begun to move fast. She thought again of the horrifying letter that had come from the South. I must write urgently to General Tseng and have An Te-hai arrange for him to be granted an Imperial audience to report on the Taiping menace.

I must act. For if I do not China will fall.

The air was cold and mist hung over the river like a sickness. The surface of Soochow Creek was laced with froth moving slowly towards the Huang-pu river. The stink of river mud was pungent in Lindley's nostrils and John Sutherland's words about the fields of China being fertilized with human blood came to his mind and chilled him.

Lindley stood with Ward and Burgevine, watching as the loading continued. Ten crates still stood on the quay, the rest had been carried aboard by a gang of coolies.

The *Hyson* was a ninety-foot iron-hulled stern paddle steamer. She had been built to operate on American rivers, and was ideal for navigating the network of muddy rivers and shallow canals of the Yangtze valley. 'She only draws four feet of water,' Ward told him proudly. 'She mounts one thirty-two pounder on a moving platform at her bow. And there's a twelve-pound howitzer at the stern.' Stout planks had been lashed round the bulwarks to a height of six feet –

deck protection, loopholed for rifles. The steam chests were also protected by timbers.

'Expecting trouble?'

Ward shrugged. 'We'll outrun it. She'll make eight knots.'

'Upstream or down?'

'Don't worry.'

'I'm not worried. How many crew?'

'Six. An engineer and two hands below. One deck hand, a cook and Ningpo Sam.'

'Who?'

'Our river pilot.'

An alarm bell sounded inside Lindley's mind. There had been too many stories of vessels pirated after being betrayed by members of their Chinese crew. Two days ago he had read a report in the *Herald* about the brig *North Star*. She had sailed from Hong Kong bound for Japan with seventeen crew and 12,000 dollars in silver aboard. She had been becalmed seven miles from her anchorage and attacked by a native junk. Dozens of axe-carrying pirates had swarmed aboard and everyone had been hacked to pieces – everyone except the Chinese steward, who two hours beforehand had asked to clean the captain's revolver. He had filled the nipple of every musket aboard with clay.

'Do you trust your crew?'

'I don't trust anybody.'

Lindley watched the coolies dragging the crates aboard. 'What's the risk from pirates?'

Ward shrugged, but like a man in possession of privileged information. He took out his piece of yellow jade and began fingering it. 'We're not carrying bullion.'

'They're not going to know that.'

Ward's dark eyebrows rose. 'They know what's aboard, all right. Since your little indiscretion in front of Governor Wu every no-good on the Yangtze knows. Whether they believe it or not is another matter.'

Ward let a beat pass. 'Anyway, pirates are not our big problem. It's the customs house we have to get by without being squeezed.'

'How much do they try to take?'

'As much as they think they can get away with. There's no such thing as a government salary. These fellers have to buy the right to extract squeeze. If they can't find anything they want aboard they'll impound the boat and ransom it back to the owner.'

'What do you do?'

'I do what anyone who means to make a profit has to do. I sail right on by.'

'And what do they do?'

Ward's laugh was almost scornful. 'What do you think they do? They get piss-angry and give chase. Better get aboard, Doc. We'll need to catch the tide.'

Ward crossed the gangway as Burgevine began shouting in pidgin to the coolies who were carrying great conical baskets of coal on their backs. Immediately Lindley went aboard he felt the pulse of the steamer. He loved the familiar coal and mineral oil taste, the taste of civilization, it was easy to see how to the peasant Chinese these ships shrieked superhuman power . . .

'Lin-li!'

Lindley's thoughts stopped dead. He turned at the head of the gangway, then came back to meet Fei on the quay.

'What is it? What's happened?'

She stared back at him silently. She was dressed in long, black baggy pants and her quilted cotton jacket, and she had a bundle with her.

'What are you doing here?'

'Massa, I come machine boat,' she said.

Annoyance gripped him. She was choosing to behave like a reluctant child – stubborn, disobedient, wilful. He saw Burgevine watching her with interest. Ward too.

'Go home.'

'No go home.'

'We've been through all that. You're not coming.'

'I plentee terrify. This cow chillo father come Macao. Takee back.'

'Fei, stop talking like that. Go back to the house.'

'Mr Shen stay house. Very good.'

He switched to Shanghai dialect, knowing exactly what she was trying to do. 'Speak properly. We agreed you must stay here. It's too dangerous.'

'No! I come with you, Lin-li.'

The two Americans had found her arrival very amusing. Lindley looked around, and said acidly, 'Excuse us, would you?'

'Don't worry, Doc, no need to get all embarrassed. We're all men of the world here. We understand.' Ward grinned and gave an hospitable flourish. 'Tell her she can come along. What do you say?'

Lindley turned, angry now. 'I say no! She's employed to keep my father's house. And that's what she'll do.'

Ward came back down the gangway. 'Hey . . . she's not your slave, Doc. '

'You keep out of this!'

Ward raised his hands like a man showing he was unarmed. It was a conciliatory gesture, but he winked at Burgevine. 'Look . . .'

Burgevine caught on. 'Say, Colonel, is the *Hyson* your vessel or ain't she?'

Ward searched out Lindley's eye. 'I say, the woman can come aboard if she likes – so long as she can cook.'

Lindley's anger smouldered as he watched Ward gesture to Fei. She darted up the gangway and went aboard.

The Yangtze was a vast, glassy river. The name meant 'Son of the Ocean'. Fei had said that it was called that because it was almost as big as the ocean. Here, fifty miles from the mouth, neither bank would have been visible from centre stream, but Ward was not steering for centre stream. He kept the *Hyson* close to the southern shore, never moving off it further than a couple of hundred yards.

The *Hyson*'s engine throbbed with monotonous steadiness. The stern paddle churned, pushing them up against the current. Nothing moved except the birds which flapped across their course. The waters of the Son of the Ocean were heavy with the fertile red earth of China. Clusters of mat hovels clung to the mud at the bank. Lindley felt exhilaration every time they sighted a ma-yang-tzu – one of the great river junks – and felt a certain relief when it slid by without altering course towards them. Yangtze junks were about fifty feet long and ten in the beam, he saw, and manned by enough crew to pull ten or twenty oars a side. Ward said they were armed with a bow-mounted gun, and usually carried another in the stern.

He got up from his position and went aft. A belch of greasy heat hit him as he passed the engine room hatch. Below two Chinese stripped to the waist were shovelling coal into the furnace with practised competence. They were watched by the fat Chinese engineer who polished the glass of a big copper gauge like it was a pagan idol.

Lindley hauled himself up the companionway to the open bridge. Above it the stars and stripes hung at the masthead, stirring a little.

'How far now?' he asked Ward.

'Fifty, maybe sixty miles.'

'One more night aboard, then.'

'Uh-huh.'

The broad expanse of water stretched out to starboard, catching the light like molten lead. To port the bank rolled by, flat and muddy. Amidships the steam engine thumped and astern the paddle beat the brown water into a froth that drained out behind them. Ward cast an eye at the binnacle, absently resettled the pistol across his belly.

What were you doing at the Grand Hotel when first we met? Lindley wanted to ask him. What business did you have with those two sailors? Why does Burgevine call you 'Colonel'? And what's your great business scheme all about?

'I didn't expect we'd stay close by the bank like this.'

'This river's full of shallows and bars, all of them uncharted.'

'If they're uncharted wouldn't it be safer to be out in mid-stream?'

Ward stretched his shoulders until his joints cracked. 'Mid-stream's where pirate junks hang out, waiting for boats like the *Hyson* to run aground. If we don't want to get taken we've got to stick to what Sam knows.'

'What about the customs post?'

'You'll find out about that soon enough.'

Ward turned away, and Lindley moved to the rail. The river slid through the waterlogged land regardless as a serpent. It seemed an abandoned land, a land ruined by some nameless disaster. Where were the thriving millions he had expected? What had created this *desolation*?

Fei came to him with rice and chicken. He shook his head. She turned to Ward, and Lindley saw a momentary suggestion of alarm or dismay in her eyes – he did not know which. It had been there all voyage, despite her determination not to show it.

'Thank you.' Ward took the bowl and chopsticks from her

with a lingering smile. 'Just a moment.' He reached out to her and she allowed him to hook his finger round a stray thread of hair and set it back over her ear. 'That's better.'

When she went below again Lindley's anger boiled dry. He could not stop himself from facing Ward and asking, 'Why don't you leave her alone?'

'Why don't you mind your own business?'

'She is my business.'

'You've got no claim on her.'

'I told you: she's my housekeeper. You shouldn't have asked her aboard. You know you shouldn't.'

'Like I said, she's not your property.'

Ward had a knack of matching incoming aggression exactly. Rage dried Lindley's mouth, tightened his throat. 'What's your bloody game, Ward?'

'You know the answer to that. She's the best-looking woman I've seen in five years, and that's a fact.'

Lindley's finger shot out. 'I'm warning you, Ward. You keep your bloody hands off her. Do you hear me?'

'Or else what are you going to do?'

'Take that bloody pistol out of your belt, and I'll show you.'

Ward's hand moved slowly to the revolver's grip. It was a 100-bore six-shooter, its cylinder engraved with a scene from the Texas war. Its long octagonal barrel was dull as pencil lead. Lindley knew that the bullet it fired was heavy enough to stop a charging bull in its tracks.

Ward cocked the hammer and held it out to where Ningpo Sam stared determinedly ahead.

'Take it!'

The pilot made no move.

'Sam!'

Sam took the Colt. Ward's smile was diamond hard.

'Now what are you going to show me, Doc?'

Lindley's eyes never wavered from Ward's, but then a distant report came from shore, and Ward snapped round, his eyes scanning the horizon. Up ahead a billow of grey smoke was thinning near the ramparts of a mud fort. A shambling collection of huts stood inside, the biggest with a low-pitched roof, thatched with woven mats. There was a jetty and an armed Imperial junk tied up to it.

'Damn!' Ward took the revolver back and shoved it into his belt.

'What is it?'

'The squeeze station.'

Lindley took out a small telescope and focused on the smudge of smoke. Men were waving flags below it. Others were leaping aboard the junk, unshipping long oars and casting off the hawsers. She carried half a dozen gingalls – small cannon-like swivel guns. Ward was looking up at the smoke belching from the *Hyson*'s funnel. 'We'll outrun her! Sam, steer us in. And tell those no-good stokers to get shovelling.' He bellowed. 'Henry!'

Lindley scanned the rampart. It was notched with three gun embrasures, and they were steering a course past it. The *Hyson*'s engine began to sound a more urgent beat. Another blossom of smoke appeared over the ramparts of the mud fort and, a moment later, a furrow of white spray was thrown up from the water just ahead of them.

Burgevine went forward with the deck hand, preparing to work the gun. Sam spun the wheel and the *Hyson* crabbed and heeled, turning in toward the bank. Lindley steadied himself holding one of the wire funnel stays. The engine bumped and cranked and sent vibrations resounding through the iron frame and up into Lindley's guts.

'Why steer directly towards them?' Lindley asked. 'You want them to think we're coming in to be searched?'

Ward laughed. 'That's not the reason.'

'Wouldn't it be better to get far out into mid-stream, out of range?'

'Mud.'

'What do you mean "mud"?'

'Mud. Brown stuff. Why do you think they put the customs post here? The only navigable channel runs right by the bank.'

'Shit!'

'Last time I came past here it was pretty rough. They sent a blizzard of iron our way from that battery over there. I was obliged to bring our thirty-two pounder to bear. Gave them a warning message aimed up high. No point hurting them unless you have to.' He grinned, his teeth very white. 'Most of their shot passed wide – excepting one that cut a funnel stay as I recall.'

Lindley took his hand quickly off the funnel stay. 'What about the junk?'

'They pull fast. They're very shallow and sit light on the water. But see those bamboo sails? Junks only go well before the wind and with the current. Fortunately both are favouring us.'

'She can still block our way.'

'Then I'll ram the son of a bitch!'

Smoke burst from the gingalls as they fired, but the shot passed harmlessly. Ward took the wheel and steamed directly for the junk at full speed. Lindley could see the ferocious faces of the men who crowded the sides, the men straining at the long oars and tiller, and those levelling cumbersome firelocks and waving axes. He heard the insults they hurled, shouts of 'Yang quitzo!' – foreign devil. But as they closed the junk was forced to go about to avoid a collision.

Musket-fire peppered the air as they passed by. Several shots penetrated the *Hyson*'s defensive planks, but the danger was already growing less, and the Imperials seemed to know they had missed their chance.

Ward relinquished the wheel, and grinned. Lindley's anger at him had vanished. It was hard not to like him, and impossible not to admire him in a tight moment. 'I'd say you earned your fee there, Mr Ward. Or should I say "Colonel"?'

'Thank you, Doc. Now, where were we?'

'As I recall I was about to punch the living daylights out of you.'

Ward chuckled. 'Is that a fact?'

'Aye. That is most definitely a fact.'

As dusk bloodshot the sky they moored a little way off shore, putting down a heavy anchor and falling back on it with the current. All night they kept steam up and doused the lights. Lindley slept in one of the two small cabins, and shared the night watch with Burgevine. All watch he sat on the cold, silent, ink-black bridge, Brunswick rifle cradled on his lap, watching the stars disappear behind clouds and wondering what had happened to the man who had stepped off the *Chusan* in Hong Kong.

In the first grey of daylight they worked up abreast the

anchor and shipped it with great difficulty. It came up thick with stinking ooze that fouled the chains and the capstan post.

As the sun gained strength they passed the remains of an immense joss-house, a Buddhist temple, that had been crushed to dust as if by immense forces. They passed close by so that Lindley was able to see at close quarters the incredible destruction that had been wrought. Not one stone was left standing on another. The ancient pagoda had been spread over an acre of ground, and here and there among the tall, rank grass, the mutilated remains of Chinese deities stuck out. All were decapitated. He could not see one statue or one brick or one glazed tile remaining whole among the debris. The building had been shattered by hatred.

'Who would do that?' he asked, awed.

Burgevine grunted. 'Rebels.'

'But it was a temple. No one would do that to a temple.'

'God-worshippers would.'

'Who?'

'God-worshippers. Long-hairs. Chang mao – it's what the Imperials call the rebels.'

Lindley watched the ruins recede, his thoughts haunted by the rebel leader he had seen cut to pieces. He had complete conviction, he told himself. The way he suffered. The way he prayed. 'I didn't realize the Taipings hate Buddhism, but they must. That temple – they didn't just destroy it, they obliterated it. They tried to lay waste the very idea of it.'

Fei served a breakfast of savoury dumplings and glutinous rolls with rice, with a large bowl of scalding hot soup. 'Eat well,' she said, and it seemed to him that she wanted to say more, but then the light went out of her eyes, as it had so often, and she went away again.

What am I going to do with her? he wondered as he ate. I can't let her land with me in Chiang-kiang. She'd be a complete hostage to fortune. And I certainly don't want her to stay aboard the *Hyson*.

He looked up. Ningpo Sam was calling. Ward appeared and climbed quickly up to the bridge, his eyes following the pilot's gaze. Then there was a short discussion.

When Lindley looked to shore he saw ruins, but as they

drifted in what he discovered was a ravaged town. It was a wasteland, completely deserted except for a population of large, black crows. The usual defensive walls had been largely demolished. The usual tumble of buildings inside had been fired, so that everything was levelled.

'Jesus . . .'

Lindley could not stop himself staring at it, so staggering was the scale of the devastation. He thought of the Bible passage he had read back at his father's house, the one that mentioned the beginning of sorrows, as the boat came in close. The pier had been reduced by burning to black pilings. He looked to the empty space beyond, once the heart of a thriving river port. It was carpeted with countless bleached bones.

'Want to go ashore now, Doc?' Ward said. He played with his yellow jade ornament. Fei appeared carrying a food tray. As she passed, Lindley smelled the spicy liquor and experienced a moment of revulsion. Fei did not look to him but concentrated on the tray as she mounted the companionway to the bridge.

'What did you say?'

Ward gestured at the field of bones. 'We're here. This is it. Chiang-kiang.'

The shock passed through him like a wave. 'Chiang-kiang's a town of a hundred thousand people.'

'It used to be.'

With a shock he saw four men standing on the bank watching them. They were dressed in black and strangely turbaned. He looked back to the *Hyson*'s bridge and saw that Fei was offering Ward the breakfast tray. He turned and took it from her, but as he did so, she reached under the tray and pulled the revolver from his belt, cocking the hammer and aiming it expertly at Ward's heart.

'Fei!'

She paid no attention. The scene was frozen like a photograph. The pilot continued to hold the wheel. Ward continued to hold the tray. Fei started to give an order to Ningpo Sam, who turned the wheel, and then Lindley saw Burgevine snap out of it. Two paces away he pulled out his revolver and levelled it.

'No!'

Lindley made a grab for the pistol just as Burgevine fired.

The shot went astray as Burgevine thrust him away. The engine room hatch cover slammed shut nearby. He struggled with Burgevine, got one hand round the big American's throat, the other on his wrist. Another wild shot was squeezed off before the cook swung his cleaver. The heavy blade connected with Burgevine's head and the American went down, the gun spinning into the scuppers at the cook's feet. Lindley realized it would be suicide to make a lunge for it. Burgevine was groaning, holding his head in a bloodied hand. Lindley watched in horror as the cook picked up the revolver and pointed it at the American. When Burgevine staggered back Lindley saw that the cook had not used the sharp of the cleaver on him, but the broad back of the blade.

'Don't move!' Lindley shouted. His fingers were spread out starkly in a desperate effort to make himself understood. 'Henry. Listen to me. He's got a gun on you. He'll kill you if you try to get up. Be quiet now.' Burgevine seemed to hear. He collapsed into a sitting position in the scuppers. Near him the skinny young deck hand had lost all presence of mind. He squared down, trembling like an aspen leaf.

Up on the bridge Ward was laying the tray down on the deck infinitely slowly and raising his hands as he had been told. Fei gave a sharp order to the pilot who steered in closer towards the place she indicated.

Lindley shouted up at her in Shanghainese. 'What are you doing?'

'Tell her to put the gun down,' Ward said, his tone deadly. He was as still as a tiger waiting to spring.

'For Christ's sake, don't do anything stupid,' Lindley shouted. 'Listen to me, Fei! You know what's aboard. You know there's nothing to fight over. Why are you doing this?'

She made no answer, her face set.

The *Hyson* edged closer to the bank. Ward started to spread-eagle himself on the deck while the muzzle of the revolver hovered over him. When he was spread flat Fei directed the gun to a spot just behind his ear and held it there.

The cook motioned Lindley to sit down and raise his hands. He heard a small boat bang alongside. More turbaned men appeared, climbing over the protective planking. The first two carried boarding axes and jumped nimbly down onto the deck. They were dressed in short, red jackets, fitting tight to the body, and wide pants of black silk, bound round the waist with long yellow sashes. Most held short swords, two also held obsolete flintlock pistols.

Lindley's eyes remained on Fei as his hands were bound to the starboard rail. 'Why?' he demanded bitterly. 'Answer me!' But she would not hear him or look at him.

Ward laughed humourlessly, filled with rage. 'Well, what do you think of that? Huh, Doc? The little lady here's played us both like fish, hasn't she? Hasn't she?'

Lindley blazed inside. The betrayal had disgusted him.

At a warning from the cook one of the Taipings began to smash viciously at the hatch cover, until Ward shouted for him to stop. When Fei verified the request, Ward called the engineer and his two men up from below. The crew emerged to be tied by their wrists to the starboard rail. Then Lindley heard the sound of hammering and splintering wood, and the rifles that he had so carefully cleaned on the journey up river were carried on deck.

Hyson dropped down the river a little way with the current. After what seemed to Lindley an age, she was brought in tight to the bank and secured. He watched the Taipings. There were a dozen of them, including three women who were dressed similarly to the men. The men wore long hair plaited into pigtails that were worked with red silk cords. They lifted the cargo of crates on deck and began opening them up with iron bars. As the crate lids were torn up, Lindley saw neat oil paper wrappings. Underneath were brand-new Enfield rifles.

He struggled until the ropes cut into his wrists. Anger made him forget the pain.

'You bitch! You bloody lying, deceiving bitch!'

Beside him Ward laughed again and again, but there was something dark in his voice that made Lindley believe he was going to die.

BOOK II

The ice-bound city waited in a freezing pre-dawn. Throughout Peking, on any open space, but especially around the walls of the Forbidden City, silent regiments of citizens performed the slow ghost dance of the tai-chi in mental and physical preparation for the new day.

Prince Kung shivered as he got out of his palanquin under the huge vermilion walls of the Meridian Gate. Despite his furs the cold was intense. His lips were chapped, his hands sore and locked together inside his sleeves. The bitter air that came out of Mongolia was too dry for human beings to bear. He listened to the din as thousands of eunuchs hawked and spat and gave vent to eerie howls, clearing the unhealthy humours of night from their bodies.

Prince Kung waited, attended now by his elderly servant, Cheng Wei. He damned the inconvenience of the 'special audience' that had been arranged, and damned Yehonala for having prompted it. As he waited darkness began to thin and the planets and stars grew dim. Finally a bloody sun levered itself above the horizon and sent beams of gold across the paved square, until the rows of gilded bosses – nine rows of nine – on each of the huge red gates glinted. Only then were the gates opened and the august procession allowed to move inside.

'Do you remember when my father was sixty-nine years old and fell ill?' he asked Cheng Wei longingly.

'Yes, Highness. That was a sad time.'

'He called his Grand Councillors to him to discuss which prince should train for the succession. That prince was to be allowed to read memorials to the throne and to receive Councillors in audience. I have often wondered why I was not chosen.'

Prince Kung's mind was in turmoil as he thought of his father. The late Emperor's ghost had been terrifying his mind lately. He had been an unbending adherent of tradition, devoted to Confucian virtues and rules. 'Confucius wrote the rules that tell us what we must do for the best,' he said. 'There's a correct way to do everything. Everything is governed by rules. Everyone has his proper station. Confucius gave us the rules to live by. That's why he's the greatest sage of all. No wonder that ever since Confucius died China has tried to build and maintain the ideal state he described.'

'Confucius is the basis of everything, Highness.'

'But were we so busy doing what he told us that no one ever thought about Progress?'

Cheng Wei allowed a moment's silence to pass, then he said, 'Excuse me for speaking, Highness. I am old and useless and full of aches and soon to die. It is my duty to tell you a long-kept secret.'

The Prince turned. 'Only fools disregard the wisdom of aged persons.'

'Highness, perhaps it will help you in coming days to know that the succession was almost settled on your own head.'

The Prince was astounded at the revelation. 'Are you sure?'

'Yes. The valet of the Chief Privy Councillor told me that your father actually chose you, his sixth son, to succeed him. But your father was not sure if he had chosen in accordance with the tao.'

The tao was the 'way' – the correct flow of events. Every human decision, no matter how humble, contributed to the weaving of the future, and the decisions of an Emperor were the most crucial threads of all.

Prince Kung felt his heart beating faster. 'Who can ever really know what is meant to be?'

'The Taoists maintain that with training it is possible to feel the tao, and so gauge the best way forward. His Imperial Majesty was a devout believer in this doctrine. He felt that he must not disregard his fourth son. He was on his deathbed when he called you both before him.'

'I had no idea that was a test.'

'Nor had I at that time, Highness, but, oh, yes, it was certainly a test. Whatever enquiries his Imperial Majesty made you answered in full, with much merit and intelligence.

His Imperial Majesty thought you most worthy to rule the Empire.'

'Then, why was I not chosen?'

'Because of your half-brother's tutor. He knew he was no match for you in the matter of state affairs. There was only one way for him to win. Your half-brother was advised to fall down on the floor as soon as he arrived in the room, to say nothing but remain inconsolably distraught, shedding abundant tears to show his extreme filial piety.'

'And so my father decided in favour of Hsien-feng? On the grounds that he was full of that virtue which the ancient sages called the most admirable?'

Prince Kung felt the huge knot inside his chest growing tighter and tighter. Hsien-feng is a fool, he thought savagely. Since he succeeded to the Dragon Throne, he has become, without doubt, the most decadent and inept ruler in the history of the dynasty. Seeing that, how can I continue to value traditional wisdom?

He imagined himself bursting into a run and leaping over one of the white marble balustrades, tearing his hat and ceremonial chao fu robe and shouting at the top of his lungs to dispel evil humours from his body, to dispel evil humours from the whole of the Forbidden City!

On the far side of the Hall of Supreme Harmony Yehonala also waited. Her tiny dog, Sea Otter, pushed his flat pug face out of her sleeve, his liquid eyes begging love from her as usual. She enfolded him again, inwardly imploring Kuan Ti, the god of war and justice, to watch over her lover. She longed to see Jung-lu, even though it was by her manipulation that he had been sent into the Far West to put down a band of Mongol bandits. Please send him back to me whole, she prayed. Six months in the desert will free his mind from all the foolishness and frustrations that have accumulated during his time in the capital. In six months he will see my position and his own with greater clarity.

She surveyed the gathering assembly anxiously. Today's special visitor had been arranged at her prompting. She had given An Te-hai a great many taels of silver to make his visit possible, and this morning she had offered prayers to her personal goddess, Kuan Yin, to ensure success.

She watched Hsien-feng's ethereal gaze wander over the gathering as the visitor was announced.

'Tseng Kuo-fan, Commander-in-Chief Imperial Forces Central China, is received in audience.'

Instead of a figure arrayed in splendid ceremonial armour the General appeared in a simple blue soldier's robe. A stocky man in his late forties, he carried himself with immense dignity. Yehonala knew he was a Han Chinese of poor but very venerable family, originating in the land-locked southern province of Hunan. He had been engaged in a death-struggle against the rebels for seven years, fighting with bitter strength against an enemy who had laid waste half of China.

The General crossed the threshold and approached the throne. A eunuch led him and showed him the correct distance from the throne to kneel. The procedure was originally a precaution against sudden attack, but was now just another absurd fossil of formality. The General surrendered his hat to a eunuch. Despite the cold, moisture glistened on the sun-dyed skin of his shaved head and neck as he prostrated himself in full kow-tow before Hsien-feng. It was done with such reverence that Yehonala's heart was seized with admiration.

Tseng is Han Chinese, she thought, a brilliant general and the only man who has been able to check the Taipings so far. He is singlehandedly keeping our Manchu Dynasty in power. Surely he appreciates that, and yet he allows no sign of resentment to show in his manner. His personal strength must be immense. He understands the true power of submission as described by Confucius. I pray that he continues to maintain dutiful respect for the robe of Imperial yellow, for surely it must be impossible for him to respect the man who wears it.

'Imperial Majesty, I come to make report to you of the state of affairs in the South . . .'

The Emperor nodded and the General began his rehearsed speech.

'I come, Sire, with grave warning of two threats that now face your Celestial Realm. The first is the growing insolence of the "Outer Barbarians". The second is the rebellion in the South by those who call themselves Taipings. Sire, it is vital—'

'What is this man saying?' Hsien-feng said. 'Tell him to speak up. Who can understand his southern accent?'

The General bowed his head in submission and began his address again, this time more loudly. When he had outlined the problem as simply as he could, he bowed his head and said, 'It is my belief, Sire, that the Celestial Realm cannot win against both these forces at the same time.'

There was a gasp from those who watched and listened. To suggest such a thing was tantamount to treason. Shocked murmuring began.

'Why do you say this?' Hsien-feng asked, horror in his eyes. 'Is it to shame me?'

'No, Sire. Only to forewarn you.'

'Is not a general a rod? An instrument of punishment?'

Yehonala watched the Emperor look about himself. He was greatly discomfited, and wanting his pipe. When confused he has a way of making utterances so vapid they are taken by the sycophants who surround him as deeply philosophical, she thought with disgust. But Prince Kung said that even as a boy his mind was a waving hand, never a fist.

The General broke courtly protocol to continue his appeal. 'Imperial Majesty, I advise that the Outer Barbarians be given—'

'Outer Barbarians!' Hsien-feng repeated, trotting out the lessons of his youth. 'Outer Barbarians are of no significance to the Middle Kingdom. They are mere traders, attracted by tea and silk, which goods they purchase in special sea ports set aside for the purpose. This has been the customary way. This is the law.'

'Imperial Majesty, they choose no longer to abide by your law.'

Hsien-feng looked about himself once again as if something did not make sense. 'Then they must be chastised. Surely a general knows how to do this?'

A bead of cold sweat from the General's temple ran down to his chin. 'Sire, these Outer Barbarians are more powerful today than ever they were. Their incursions are increasing. Because they worship Shang-ti—'

Hsien-feng fidgeted. 'Shang-ti, Shang-ti! All you Southerners know is Shang-ti!'

The General remained silent as the Emperor's words echoed away. Then with exceptional courage he forced himself to say, 'Imperial Majesty, the worship of Shang-ti has in Barbarian minds become a poison with which they have infected the Taiping rebels. This gives their soldiery great strength. In the year the Yellow River changed its course, the Taipings marched out of the Far South and took the great city of Nanking as their capital. In the autumn of the third year of Your Majesty's auspicious ten-thousand-year reign it will be recalled that they began a march on Peking, a march that almost succeeded.'

Hsien-feng does not recall that march, Yehonala thought, because he does not know about it. He has never been interested enough to ask about it, and nobody has had the courage to tell him.

'These rebels could not have succeeded, or they would be here now,' the Emperor said, looking to his Grand Councillors. They found amusement in his remark.

'Sire, many scholars believe the Taipings were able to march their army three thousand li through five provinces because of their fanatical belief in Shang-ti. However, it is my own belief that—'

Hsien-feng made a dismissive gesture. 'Their erroneous worship of Shang-ti does not bring them success. You will invite them to surrender.'

The General allowed the silence to hang over him once more, then he said, 'Sire, they will not obey such a command. And there is no known way to compel them – without retaking Nanking.'

Yehonala watched General Tseng's performance with relief. He had gone even further than she had dared to hope. It was vital he came here in person, she thought. Without that he couldn't have got so much as a string of copper cash, and the retaking of Nanking will be a fantastically expensive operation. When the Taipings took Nanking their treasury amounted to eighteen million taels – an incredible amount. At the time of Hsien-feng's accession our own Imperial coffers contained a mere eight million, and now we have less than three. It will take an Imperial decree ordering General Tseng to raise whatever sum he believes necessary by borrowing if we are to win against the rebels. But will the decree be written now that Su-shun heads the Board of Revenue?

She saw Hsien-feng glance at Su-shun. There was muttering

as he whispered with messenger eunuchs who departed from the hall, then the Emperor stood and withdrew. A spokesman stepped forward. 'General Tseng, these matters concerning the safety of the Empire must be deliberated by his Imperial Majesty's councillors. You will be notified of any decision. Dismissed!'

She watched the General crawl backwards from the throne, raise himself to his knees, bow deeply, then regain his feet to retire with appropriate respect.

Those present took their leave, exactly observing the rules of rank and precedence. Outside Prince Kung was filing down the crowded steps with the rest of the Grand Councillors when he heard An Te-hai call the General by name.

'Tseng Kuo-fan! Tseng Kuo-fan!'

The General stopped and turned, his face still grave as granite. An grinned at him, one hand behind his back, holding something.

'Tseng Kuo-fan! Are you forgetting something!'

The General stared back, mystified by the capering little eunuch. An's voice was wheedling and loud enough to command an audience. It soared above the commotion.

'Tseng Kuo-fan! Where can you be going inside my city dressed like that?'

The face-destroying remark struck home. The General stiffened, an intense burst of anger detonated inside him, but it remained almost wholly contained. He turned and began to leave.

'Tseng Kuo-fan! Stop! You are improperly dressed!'

The General stopped again, and turned, this time very slowly. 'Please explain what are you talking about?' he said icily.

'Tseng Kuo-fan! Your head is bare.'

The realization that he had forgotten to collect his hat mortified the General. He raised a hand halfway to his head, then let it drop, his dignity in tatters now.

'Tseng Kuo-fan you left this behind.'

An's head bobbed with amusement. He produced the General's hat as if he were a stage magician and held it out. The General swallowed his pride and took three steps forward, but just as his hand went out An snatched the hat away.

'It is customary to offer cumsha to Imperial eunuchs for services rendered.'

The General made an involuntary grab for the hat, but An danced lightly away from him. 'No, no, Tseng Kuo-fan. No soldier brawling! Remember where you are. This is not some southern army camp. This is the Imperial City, and I am its guardian.' An clicked his tongue theatrically. The audience of Councillors and eunuchs looked on, delighted by his performance. 'General, you have broken our laws of etiquette. Now you must buy back your hat.'

The General's face was set with fury and embarrassment. 'Give it to me,' he demanded.

'I will. For one thousand taels!'

The General stared, quivering with rage, then he seemed to realize his own impotence. He turned and strode for the Meridian Gate, his two young ensigns following in attendance.

'Five hundred taels!' An's voice called out.

The General's pace did not falter.

'Two hundred, then!' An called, playing the disappointed merchant. 'You can't expect to pay less than two hundred taels for a fine quality hat like this!' He fluffed the tassels with his fingers, preened the two long peacock tail plumes, then peered at the hat closely, finally wrinkling his nose. 'Oh, perhaps not. This hat is quite cheaply made.'

He dropped the hat and strolled away. Prince Kung watched as a young eunuch picked it up and scurried after his master.

'Oh, but that was a very bad mistake.'

Prince Kung stiffened as he heard the oil-smooth voice murmur close by his ear. Su-shun had come up behind him unnoticed, and the uninvited presence so close made his skin crawl.

The new President of the Board of Revenue bowed his head shallowly in mocking greeting. 'General Tseng won't forget an insult like that. Never in ten thousand years.'

'What does it matter what the General forgets? An Te-hai knows he is quite safe here.'

Su-shun's eyes searched him. 'Many years ago I saw a little boy poking a stick at a caged tiger. The tiger snarled, of course, but the little boy kept poking the stick through the bars of the cage and wouldn't stop. All the while the tiger grew angrier and angrier and snarled louder and louder, but it could do nothing to prevent the poking. The tiger became exhausted by its own fury. Do you know what happened then?'

Prince Kung began to walk away. 'No.'

'Eventually the tiger's owner came back and saw what the little boy had done to the spirit of his expensive animal.' Su-shun laughed. 'And then the child received the severest of beatings.'

The Prince turned and inclined his head with false piety. 'Those who depart from the Harmonious Way, evil things befall.'

Su-shun grunted. 'We ought to get rid of him, you and I.'

Prince Kung's words remained polite in form, but they were suddenly sharp edged, 'A man with your reputation, Su-shun? Troubling himself over a damaged worm? You surprise me.'

'Ah, if my reputation is for anything, it is for employing cruelty.'

'Wrong. Your reputation is for enjoying cruelty.'

'A most interesting philosophical point.' Su-shun bowed fractionally at the Prince's retreating figure. 'We must debate it sometime.'

Lindley closed the door as the clock began to chime midnight.

'Happy New Year, Dr Lindley,' Shen said.

Happy New Year, he thought. A new day. A new year. A new decade. Things can only get better . . .

What had hurt him most was Fei's attitude, her refusal to speak to him, or even to look at him. There had been no goodbye, no explanation at all. She had just done her work and left. Coldly. Ruthlessly. And for ever.

He still felt betrayed and cheated, but he was far more angry with himself. All the way back down the Yangtze he had burned with humiliation.

The efficient way the Taipings had taken off the cargo into a flotilla of punt-like sampans had been amazing to watch. One of them had hammered soft iron nails into the vents of the *Hyson*'s guns to prevent them being fired. Another had blown off steam, leaving them powerless. Their leader had ordered the last of his people off the boat then drawn his sword and approached the young deckhand, speaking softly to him before cutting through his left wrist binding to release him. He told him to wait until they had rowed clear before untying the others. Ward had clamoured to be released as soon as the rebels shoved off. The youth had fumbled with the rope tightly knotted around his own right wrist, then went searching for a knife. By the time they were free and had got up steam again the rebel sampans had vanished.

No one aboard said anything for a long time. Ward watched the river bank in silence while the engineer tried to tap out the gun vents and restore their weapons to working order. Lindley stewed, wanting to tell Ward what a fool he was to have encouraged Fei to come aboard against his will. He said nothing because he himself had been duped even more.

Finally, Ward said, 'You should have let Henry shoot the bitch.'

'Nobody had to die,' he said.

'No?' Ward's laugh was bitter. 'Because of you twenty-four hundred modern rifles are now in rebel hands. How many people do you think are going to die because of that?'

The downstream trip had been swift. They had passed the squeeze station before its garrison realized they were coming, and as they left the mud fort behind Ward had asked, 'What do you know about rifles, Doc?'

'Not much.'

'How do you think they got inside those crates?'

He had been forced to admit it. 'I let the girl arrange the warehousing. She could have switched them at any time.'

'Great.'

Lindley thought about his first sight of Fei, how she must have targeted him and followed him around Hong Kong, how she must have been steering the whole project even then. But how could she have known I would be there? How could she have known I would agree to smuggle her aboard the *Chusan*? So much seems to have been merest chance. But it wasn't. And the implications are huge.

After a while he asked, 'What sort of guns were they?'

Ward grunted. 'Rifles. Short Enfields – five-seven-seven calibre, thirty-three-inch barrels, by the look of them. I didn't see if the rifling was three-groove or five, but my guess is they were recent Royal Navy issue. I counted forty-eight per crate. Twenty-four hundred, all told.'

'I suppose they're better than anything the Imperials have.'

'Far better. Accurate up to nine hundred yards. Muzzle velocity a thousand feet per second. Which makes them as deadly as any weapon in the world. With modern weapons the Taipings will be able to break the Imperialist siege of Nanking.' Ward cast him a significant glance. 'You know what that means? War.'

'Is that what happened to Chiang-kiang?' he asked, still haunted by the satanic litter of human bones.

'What do you think?'

'Was it the Taipings or the Imperials?'

'What's it matter? Dead is dead.'

'What do you think happened to my father?'

Ward shrugged. 'Maybe he went to Nanking.'

'What makes you say that?'

'Just a guess. He's a Christian minister. The Taipings are Christians. Nanking's their stronghold.'

He looked at Ward with incredulity. 'The Taipings are Christian?'

'Didn't I tell you that?'

Another piece of the puzzle fell into place as he remembered Fei asking him if he were Christian. 'If you were sure a cause was right, would you fight for it?' That's something else she had asked him. And, 'Are you prepared to die for it?' He damned himself for not having read the signs. In hindsight they were glaring. He said, 'I thought you said Nanking was under siege.'

'It is, but loosely. It's on the Yangtze, and it's impossible to maintain a blockade on this river with junks. Also, the Chung Wang – he's the best of the Taiping generals – has got a large field army roaming the country west of Nanking.'

'Why do you think they let us go?'

'Because they got what they wanted.'

'They could have had the *Hyson* and her big guns too. She's a prize catch.'

'Sure. But they can't afford to upset Westerners too much, not if they hope to court Shanghai trade interests – which they do. What I don't understand, Doc, is just exactly where you fit into all this.'

Does Ward really think I knew about those rifles? Lindley wondered now, feeling again the American's parting hostility. Maybe he does.

Shen asked, 'You want go Bund? Watch firework?'

Lindley felt a pang of despair as he imagined his father's precious Bibles being torn up and rolled into tubes and filled with gunpowder. 'I don't feel much like welcoming in the New Year. And it's not our way.'

'Chinese New Year different,' Shen said. 'Most happy festival. Family time. Chinese calendar like moon. Chinese New Year coming many weeks yet.'

'What about the Taipings? Which New Year do they celebrate?'

Shen looked at him strangely, then said, 'Both.'

'Both? That's absurd – or remarkably convenient.'

'T'ien Wang – Heavenly King – he Taiping leader. Born ten day, twelve month, eighteen year of Chia-ch'ing Emperor.'

'And that happens to be January the first, I suppose?'

'Yes!'

Lindley savoured a whisky nightcap, then turned in. As he lay alone in the darkness he listened to the cracks of exploding rockets half a mile away over the British Concession. Half a mile in the other direction the Chinese City slumbered in darkness. He thought about Ward and the mystery of his secret business enterprise. First he thought of the money he still owed him – five hundred taels. In addition he had agreed half the cost of replacing two Colt revolvers and a rack of twelve muskets. He was due to come by tomorrow afternoon to collect his money ... But then, as Lindley drowsed, a suspicion came to him that made him sit upright.

'Of course!' he said aloud. 'Ward's been in league with Fei and the Taipings all along!'

That would make sense. It was Ward who invited Fei aboard the *Hyson*, wasn't it? I don't know much about rifles, but Ward certainly does. No wonder he was at pains to show me how barbaric the Imperials were. I'll lay you a pound to a penny that his secret business enterprise is rebel gun-running! And they've used me as their stooge!

Oh, God! He wiped his mouth, his mind spinning in the darkness. Ward's been procuring weapons for the Taipings, and Fei is his connection! The two of them worked out a way to fleece me. All those glances I saw passing between them – yes! They knew one another all along.

Then an even more appalling thought hit him.

But that can't be right because Fei picked me up in Hong Kong. Which means she must have been sent there knowing about the cargo. She must have been expecting it. Which means . . . it must have been rifles even then. He stared into empty space, his mouth dry. Which means I was used as a courier. There never were any Bibles. They must have had people buy the rifles in England and crate them for shipping. Jesus Christ – they must have forced my father to write to me and tell me they were Bibles. No wonder the letter warned me to not to discuss the contents with anyone.

Lindley got out of bed. 'What do you know about my father, Mr Ward?' he asked the darkness, but his only answer were the distant explosions on the Bund.

Frederick T. Ward looked at the high wall surrounding the traditional Chinese mansion. His whole body was jangling with expectation as he stepped down from his sedan chair. I didn't plan on coming here again so soon, he thought, but those rifles have changed everything.

The high wall was topped with green glazed tiles. The gate was stout, locked against the outside. Like all traditional Chinese houses Yang Fang's mansion turned its back on the world. It was built with security in mind.

Yang Fang might seem westernized, but underneath he was very Chinese. His house was also a yamen – an office. All of Taki bank's most important deals were struck there. Taki was Shanghai's foremost finance house, and Yang Fang was its founder. He had walked out of Chekiang province with nothing twenty years ago to escape the famine. A sixth sense had led him to the doors of Jardine, Matheson & Co., Shanghai's largest Western merchant house, where he had quickly risen to become comprador, or native agent. His unique skill in dealing with Westerners had allowed him to gather the seed of a vast fortune.

Twenty years later he not only headed Taki bank, he was the pivot of half a dozen Chinese-Western front organizations. He was also director of the Committee of Patriotic Chinese Merchants, the group that met at intervals to decide how best to handle the Taipings so far as trade is concerned. Yang's business depended on Western trade, but also on keeping the Imperial authorities sweet. Without permissions bought from City Governor Wu and Provincial Governor Hsueh, Taki bank would die.

Ward tugged a bell pull and servants in red livery and green waist sashes swung open the gate. When he entered the courtyard he was met by a pretty young girl in her late teens. She whispered a coy greeting as she admitted him. He followed her, struck by the aura of disquiet that seemed to surround her. Who is she? he wondered. And why's she so unhappy?

The girl bowed Ward into the reception room, then melted away. His thoughts followed her, until he caught himself. She's broken your concentration, he thought. Get a hold of yourself. What happens here today could make you a rich man if you don't foul it up.

The room was sparsely furnished, the decor an unsettled mix of East and West. Everything was of the best quality. Three large stylized landscape paintings dominated, and under them three upholstered couches. Governor Wu sat on the middle one. Ward's heart sank, but he tried not to show his disappointment. Yang received him smilingly, and offered him a seat.

'Thank you.' Ward turned to Wu, nodding a greeting in halting but adequate Shanghainese. 'Mr Magistrate.'

'Unfortunately His Excellency Hsueh Huan, the Provincial Governor, cannot attend as previously arranged,' Wu said, pronouncing the name 'Shway-hwan'. 'He hopes you will accept his sincere apologies, and has asked this humble servant to pass them on to you.'

Damn! Ward thought. They've gotten me marked down as unimportant already. That makes it an uphill struggle from the start. Was it a faint recommendation from Yang, or did Wu decide? Either way it's a slight, but I must not treat it as such openly.

'Naturally I accept His Excellency's apologies,' he said with cordiality. 'He must be a very busy man. However, I'm confident that what passes here today will be of interest to him at a later date.'

How much does Hsueh know about the Enfield rifles? Ward wondered. Maybe that's why he's not here. Jesus, I wish I'd never clapped eyes on Harry Lindley. The bastard knew damned well what was in those crates.

Yang ordered tea. It was brought in by the inconsolable girl. When Yang acknowledged her, Ward realized she could only be his daughter. She's no slave, he thought. My information is that Yang Fang is a dutiful family man. He has two sons and several daughters, all married now except one. So this girl must be Chang-mei – God help her. She's the one my spy called Yang's 'bad luck daughter'.

Wu seemed ill at ease. The secrecy of the meeting had meant that his customary cloud of attendants were absent. He made the minimum number of pleasantries before getting to the point. 'Mr Yang tells me you wish to discuss a particular matter.'

'Mr Yang is correct. I would like to offer a solution to the Taiping threat.'

Wu and Yang exchanged glances. Both appeared startled by the incredible directness of Ward's reply. Whoa, steady, Ward warned himself, realizing his mistake. Mention of the word 'Taiping' forces them to recognize that a civil war is in progress. No mandarin has officially been allowed to speak to Westerners about events in the interior. Wu's skittish, so speak more obliquely.

He turned to Yang. 'Sir, Taki bank supports the Bureau for the Suppression of River Piracy and the Homeless Refugee Fund and so many other public-spirited institutions. Might it not perhaps be time to consider the trade of the Yangtze Valley in a new way?'

'What new way?' Wu asked.

'It is now possible, I believe, to ensure continuity of trade at Shanghai for the foreseeable future at minimum cost.'

Wu gave nothing away. 'There is no threat to trade here. Neither to tea, nor to silk.'

'Perhaps not today, but what would be the consequences of an interruption of trade in the future?'

'That might be inconvenient,' Yang mused.

It would be absolutely disastrous for you, and you know it, Ward thought. And Mr Wu here would be dead meat. The British are the dominant power here, and they'd not hesitate to sail their gunboats up the river. The last time they did it was three years ago at Canton. Governor Yeh of Kwantung was put aboard HMS *Inflexible* and hauled off to

Calcutta after being disowned by Peking. He'll never see China again.

Ward spread his hands. 'By working together it might just be possible to foresee difficulties and find solutions to even hypothetical problems.'

Yang grinned encouragingly. 'As in the case of the river pirates where we have managed to reduce the problem significantly.'

Wu nodded, but not in a way that signalled acceptance of the point. He knew the piracy problem had not gotten smaller. Taki had merely set up a protection racket and extended it to the vessels of their most valuable clients.

Ward said, 'Mr Magistrate, if a trade problem was to arise it would need to be rectified swiftly. This would require a force capable rapidly of securing certain key strategic centres.'

Wu seemed to find the idea absurd. 'The Imperial army would be more than capable of imposing order in the countryside, whatever circumstance arose.'

'Undoubtedly.' Ward thought of the poorly trained, badly armed, and appallingly led men raised from the local peasantry who ran in terror at the first sound of gunfire. 'Imperial forces could win the day in the end. But aren't we agreed that swift rectification would be necessary?'

Wu watched him wordlessly.

'Suppose – hypothetically – that someone were to recruit a modern, Western-style force.' Ward put his hands together. 'A Foreign Arms Corps that could operate alongside regular Imperial Green Standard forces. A force trained in the latest methods. Mobile. Well-armed. Unstoppable. Then, Mr Magistrate, there would be a means of keeping the arteries of trade open whatever happened.'

Wu remained motionless, his face set. 'What you say is true. But it is also out of the question. The Emperor does not permit mercenary troops to operate within the Chinese Empire – no matter what.'

Ward sat back in his seat, but his eyes remained on Wu's. 'Not . . . officially.'

'No, Mr Ward. Not at all.'

'Perhaps Provincial Governor Hsueh would take a different view.'

'Who can say?' Wu shifted, his attitude cool. 'We have

been speaking hypothetically. There is no problem with trade at Shanghai. And there is no need for a Foreign Arms Corps. And now, I regret that I have pressing matters.'

Yang stepped in, bringing the discussion to an end gracefully. 'Thank you for the honour of being allowed to entertain you, Mr Wu.'

Wu rose. 'On the contrary, Mr Yang. It is I who am honoured by the invitation to visit your magnificent home. It was pleasant to meet you, Mr Ward.'

'And a pleasure to meet you too, sir.' Ward watched the pantomime of leave-taking, the ceremonial protests and regrets, and wondered at the wholly negative reception his proposal had received. Wu had shown him a stone wall, disappointing his hopes more completely than he had thought possible.

Ward's eyes followed the infinitely sad girl who accompanied the departing guest to the door. She waited forlornly, and when the door closed she vanished again.

'The young lady must be your daughter,' Ward said as Yang returned.

The banker switched to very proficient English, 'Please forgive her. Her name is Chang-mei. She is my youngest.'

'She's very . . . quiet.'

'Oh, yes. That is because she is broken-hearted.'

He felt surprise at Yang's words. 'I'm . . . sorry to hear that.'

'Yes, just nineteen years old – and blighted.'

'Blighted? What do you mean?'

'You know that in Chinese tradition all marriages are arranged many years in advance. But Chang-mei's fiancé died before they could marry.'

Ward's tone showed his sympathy. 'Her fiancé's death might account for her sadness, but why do you say she's blighted?'

Yang Fang's eyebrows lifted. 'Because she is cursed with very bad luck now. Like a house with bad feng-shui. No man will ever marry a girl like that.'

'But that's absurd. She's quite lovely.'

Yang's joviality broke into open laughter. 'Beauty is in the eye of the beholder. That is one of your most famous sayings. But what beholder can find beauty in a bad luck woman who will bring the roof of his house down around his ears?'

Ward shook his head slowly. He realized that he was sailing onto dangerous shoals, and changed tack. 'Looks like Mr Wu was not convinced. He was pretty negative.'

'On the contrary. He will consider what you said very carefully.'

'What about Governor Hsueh? Why wasn't he here?'

'That's perfectly normal. No insult was intended. Your proposal will be referred to him. That's all.'

'Our proposal, Mr Yang. We're partners, remember?'

'Of course.'

Yang's face was open and attractive. He showed no arrogance. His mannerisms were those of a man who was eager to please. He invited trust with every gesture. Ward saw how Yang's face had made him many friends and great personal wealth, and he warned himself against believing. He thought again of Lindley and the rifles, and saw a possible way to turn the situation to his advantage.

'You have to understand, Mr Yang, I have a hundred men ready to sign. Today. They'll be the core around which I can forge the Governor his own private army. But if I don't get a training camp set up soon they'll evaporate and we'll have to start over.'

Yang tossed the matter aside lightly. 'Keep paying the retainer. Things will come good in time.'

'Mr Yang, I don't have time. You don't have time.'

'Why do say that?'

'Because, according to my information, the Coolie King is stirring up a storm. The Taipings are gathering themselves to move. There are three hundred thousand of them in Nanking. If their armies bust out they'll spill out right across the whole Yangtze Valley. It'll be ten years before the Imperials will be able to bottle them up again.'

'Rumours.'

'No, Mr Yang. Information.'

'Who can say what is in the T'ien Wang's mind. He is insane.'

'Even more reason to move. He possesses the means to kill trade at Shanghai stone dead. My spies tell me he's losing patience. Our men need training. Discipline is vital, and that can't be instilled in them overnight. We really don't have a moment to lose.'

Yang smiled enigmatically. 'China has been here for a long time. Impatience is unnecessary. Let me tell you some things about your enemy – the man you call the "Coolie King". His millions of followers call him T'ien Wang, which means "Heavenly King". His real name is Hung Hsiu-ch'uan. He is not Han Chinese like myself, he is of the Hung clan of the Hakka people. He was born forty-five years ago in a poor country village near Canton in the Far South, the brightest of several sons of the village headman. In our system a competitive examination for the sheng-yuan degree takes place every year in each province to find those men suitable to enter government service as mandarins. When Hung came of age his father put him forward, but each year he was entered he failed to gain a pass.'

Ward nodded. 'I guess his father didn't pay enough squeeze, huh?'

'Certainly. But with each failure Hung saw his dream slip further away. Instead of becoming a source of pride to his family he became a source of shame. It was after his third examination failure that Hung chanced to receive a tract written in Chinese extolling the virtues of Christianity. On his return to his village he read the message that it contained, and it drove him insane.'

'That's impossible.'

Yang shook his head. 'Not for Chinese people. Whether you believe it or not, there is magic power in words. That power changes people. In Hung's case it infected his brain with madness. It made him fall down in a fit that lasted many days, and during that time he saw amazing visions. He went up to the thirty-third Heaven and was received by Shang-ti, the Emperor of Heaven, and also by Shang-ti's son, Jesus Christ. Together Hung and Jesus travelled to the borders of Heaven, and slew the devils who live there, and when they returned Shang-ti said, "Hung Hsiu-ch'uan, now you must know the truth: you are my son, and Jesus is your Elder Brother. It is time for you to return to Earth and destroy all the evils that are there."'

Yang paused, gauging Ward's fascinated reaction, then he went on. 'When Hung came out of his fit he began to write of his mission. One by one he gathered a small group of disciples, just as his Elder Brother had once done. They in turn went out among the Common People and gained other converts to their cause.'

'What made them join him?'

'The power of his message. They followed him in their hundreds. He promised uneducated peasants their own patch of land. He promised them fairness. He promised them life after death. Within a few years he had hundreds of thousands of followers. A few years later and he had millions. When a powerful Imperial force was sent to crush him he defeated it. After that, Hung marched on the Yangtze Valley's rich rice-growing lands. He captured city after city, including Nanking – and established his capital there.'

'He sounds like a class-one lunatic,' Ward said.

'Oh, yes. And a most dangerous one. I doubt if any madman in the history of the world has killed so many people. By now millions have died. Millions more will follow.'

Ward listened to the resignation in Yang's voice and he felt a pulse of disrespect. Thinking for yourself is hard, he told himself. That's why so many people prefer to follow. But I don't follow. I never once followed.

As Yang spoke he noted Chang-mei ghosting from room to room, and he wondered at the magic of words and the power of belief. What do you follow, bad luck woman, he asked her silently. You're calling doom upon yourself by believing as you do. Why make your misery a self-fulfilling prophecy? What about the pursuit of happiness? Did you never think about that as an idea? When he left Yang Fang's yamen she showed him out. He wanted to speak to her, but saw no possible point of contact. He offered her a kindly smile and she acknowledged it remotely. Her eyes held tremendous pain.

As the chair was lifted and bore him away, he could not dispel those eyes from his mind. It's more than pain, he thought. It's more than her coming to terms with having to live for the rest of her days in isolation, with no husband and no children, with the housemaid-like status of a dependent youngest daughter within her father's house. What I saw in her was guilt. She really believes that stuff about her being to blame for her fiancé's death.

The chair entered a market area and wove in and out of

the thousands of jostling people who packed the street. People of all ages were buying and selling. Old men were clustered under a row of trees from which they had hung bamboo cages, each containing a small agitated bird. Counters were spread with all kinds of strange vegetables, women squatted haggling over crates of fowls or basins filled with live fish, dirty-faced porters were labouring along under vast loads, or propped aimlessly in corners smoking. But then he saw something that sent a shock through him.

'Son of a bitch!' he muttered and leapt out of the chair into a doorway.

The bearers staggered and a flurry of angry words came from those around, but then normality closed up again. Ward hardly noticed the commotion. His eyes were following the tall peasant woman who was moving among the crowd no more than twenty paces away.

That's her, he thought exultantly. That's the cow chillo bitch who made a fool out of me!

He waited until she had gone past then pulled the lead bearer close to him and pointed the girl out discreetly. 'Follow that woman. Find out where she goes. Everywhere until nightfall. Savvy? Then come to me.'

.He promised the bearer five hundred copper cash – a week's wages for a labourer – and watched him depart eagerly.

It's about time I paid Harry Lindley a visit myself, he thought, his blood boiling up. He still owes me five hundred silver taels and replacements for the weapons his friends stole. If he's shipping more Enfields I want to know about it. I should have seen through the pair of them far sooner. All that garbage about his father being a missionary and him having taken the girl in as a housekeeper . . . Next time I won't be so gentle with either of them.

Yehonala sat at her private desk reviewing the latest Imperial memorials to have issued from the Forbidden City. Since the Emperor had given permission she had begun to read all the decrees and rescripts issued under his seal, and to look at as many of the other communications of his government as she could manage. She had begun to understand the ferocity of the storm that was gathering over the Empire.

And the more she had understood the more terrifying the picture had become.

The room was dominated by a huge bed with a teak canopy from which curtains of blue silk hung. The curtains were embroidered with crab-apple blossoms, reminding her that the spring had arrived. Beside the bed was a small, teak stool only a hand's width in height and upholstered in yellow silk.

She looked round to where a eunuch had flung himself to the floor. He was new – very young and still below the thirtieth class. 'Your Imperial Highness,' he said with self-conscious awe. 'The Prince Kung has arrived.'

She went out to meet him. 'Prince Kung, what a very great honour you do me by coming here so urgently.' She clapped her hands. 'Tea!'

He cut her greeting short. 'You said this was an important matter.'

'It is. I've been spending a great deal of time at the Hall of Records, and what I've found out requires immediate discussion.'

'Go on.'

'A year and a half ago, Imperial negotiators Kuei and Hua signed a disastrous treaty at Tientsin giving the Outer Barbarians the right to present ambassadors at the Celestial Court.'

'Correct. It was unavoidable. And signed under duress.'

'It was disastrous. These Barbarian ambassadors have given notice that they will refuse to kowtow before the Emperor, which can only mean they believe their own barbarous lands to be equal to China.'

'It's utterly preposterous,' he said. 'but they do believe this. I've never seen an Outer Barbarian, of course, but it's said they're all vile and bad-mannered sub-humans, huge and hairy, with red faces and ugly noses. That such smelly, uncultured sea-traders could even think in terms of equality with civilized people is completely monstrous.'

She pursed her lips. 'That we acceded to Barbarian demands is even more monstrous. It amounts to a national disaster. My husband's advisors, it seems, have consistently used the rebellion in the South as their excuse for giving way before the Barbarians. If I had known the clauses to which Hsien-feng was putting his signature chop I would have counselled him properly.'

'Are you accusing the Grand Council of inefficiency?'

'A five-year-old child could have predicted the disaster that would result – that has now come to pass. Read this.'

She passed to him the reports she had read of the battle that had taken place six months ago in Chih-li district. This was not the Far South or Shanghai, but North China, the very mouth of the Pei-ho river. The Outer Barbarians had sent their ambassadors by boat and landed on the part of the coast closest to the capital, but then they had been stopped from entering the Pei-ho and proceeding to Peking. The twin forts at Taku had turned them back, firing cannons at them and killing many. It had thrown the Outer Barbarians into a frenzy of threats and demands.

'Were you aware of this incident?' she asked.

'Of course.'

'But – don't you see the danger? They will be back. The hearts of these Barbarians are bloody with revenge.'

His tone remained superior. 'You have too much confidence in provincial reports, Yehonala. Local officials magnify their own importance all the time. No one has any way of verifying what they say, and which Councillor could allow himself to be disturbed by news of every little event that touches the harmony of the Empire? A Councillor who did that would drown in a tide of memorials.'

She narrowed her eyes at his scoffing. 'Prince Kung, you should know that my studies at the Hall of Records have not been in vain. That place is full of lies!'

'What do you mean?'

'The easiest way for governors to deal with a problem is to sidestep it. If a city is threatened by rebels the governor does not think to oppose force with force. It is far simpler to bribe rebels to move on to the next city. After they leave, the city governor can tell the provincial governor that his army has driven the rebels away. What provincial governor, other than an imbecile, would want to investigate such a claim? How much better for him simply to embellish the figures and pass on the report to Peking.'

Yehonala watched the tea arrive. She saw the Prince's chin jut and his defences rise further. 'The Council is quite able to interpret provincial memorials. You forget there are severe sanctions against provincial governors who behave improperly.'

'Severe sanctions against failure make it impossible for provincial governors to report defeats. The vastness of the Empire means that no effective control can be exercised from the centre. But while Peking neglects to check the truth of a provincial governor's report, so long shall that provincial governor feel able to tell lies.'

'And if we did check?' Prince Kung demanded. 'If it was found that a victory had been falsely claimed, what then? Then the governor's head would have to fall and a new, inexperienced governor be installed, by which time most rebellions would have blown themselves out in any case.'

Yehonala nodded, her point neatly made. 'This is certainly not the case with the Taipings. They are not a passing cloud, but a winter that may never end.'

'If you have nothing more urgent to tell me than that,' the Prince said, rising, 'I'll bid you good night.'

She watched him leave and returned to her papers. I still don't know what lies behind the jade carving Hsien-feng gave to me, she thought. If Prince Kung suggested it as an overture his manner just now has shown that he is not seeking an alliance of equals. It's entirely possible he was seeking only to get back at Little An, whom he hates. I wish with all my heart that this tiresome struggle could cease. But it cannot. There is no alternative but to scheme and to fight at least as well as the rest if I mean to survive. And I have come a long way.

She recalled the humiliation she had endured on Hsien-feng's accession. An Imperial Decree had been issued that all eligible Manchu women must attend the Imperial Household Office for selection to the Emperor's harem. Yehonala was among the sixty who were presented for scrutiny by the critical eye of the previous Emperor's widow. 'Run, run, run,' the Empress Mother had shouted, making them complete the circuit of a large courtyard in front of a gaggle of eunuchs in order to make sure their perspiration was normal. More tests followed, some severe and others intimate. Then the young Emperor himself had inspected the finalists from afar, but it was the Empress Mother who had examined them and made the choice.

I hope you can hear me, Old Bitch, she thought now, still

hating Hsien-feng's dead stepmother with undimmed intensity. You were wrong about me. I climbed to the top despite you. While you were alive I was just another of the twenty-eight Imperial concubines, and of the four ranks you saw fit to place me in the third. We were all no more than your servants, but now your bones are cold as stone whereas I am supreme. I can't express the satisfaction I felt when you died and your son officially raised my rank in honour of your passing.

She started at a sudden noise in her doorway. The new eunuch had returned.

He looked up at her pleadingly. 'Your Imperial Highness, I bring a letter.'

She noticed he was sweating and fearful. She hesitated, her own senses suddenly alert, but there seemed to be no sense of threat about him. The letter was probably a petition that he had agreed to present directly to her in exchange for a large sum of cumsha. It was a perilous thing to do. One word to An Te-hai would mean a severe whipping followed by banishment.

He began to kowtow furiously. 'Imperial Highness, I beg you to accept.'

'I hope they paid you well,' she said, her fear turning now to anger, 'because you're taking a very great risk. Give it to me.'

It was probably from some provincial petitioner, a minor matter that could be dealt with in seconds. She felt a certain foreboding as it passed into her hands. Letters sometimes contained poison that seeped into the fingers. She decided to open it immediately, broke the seal and looked first at the all-important signature. It was unfamiliar.

'Who is this?'

'Lady, I am informed that the sender is Wu Hsu, Taotai of Shanghai.'

Wu Hsu was a rare and striking two-character name – both characters carried the meaning 'nothingness', together they were intended to give the impression of extreme humility and correct self-effacement, but Yehonala felt immediately that there was something sinister there. She looked up. 'Shanghai? How did it come here?'

'A messenger sought me out. He begged me to bring it

immediately and directly to your Highness' attention. He told me it was of huge importance.'

'Huge importance to whom? Not to me.' She sighed. 'All eunuchs ever think about is cumsha.'

'Lady, my family is poor, my fate unfortunate . . .'

'Oh, stop whining!' Her feelings of foreboding intensified. She examined the letter closely. It was not a simple petition after all.

She began to read, and the more she read the more interested she became. The letter was couched as a report praising the good management of Kiangsu province by the incumbent futai, or governor, Hsueh Huan. Many literary references were made to the the the Four Books and the Five Classics, but in reality the letter was both a complaint and a warning.

My guess is that Wu's a jealous man, she thought. Probably dissatisfied with his status of taotai. Certainly ambitious. Reading beneath the surface he probably considers himself worthy to rise beyond his present station. And he's definitely implying that his superior, the Governor of Kiangsu province, has been up to no good. I must find out more.

'This requires a reply. Send my secretary.'

'Immediately, Lady Yehonala.' The eunuch got to his feet. 'Wait!'

She allowed her mind to focus on the eerie revulsion that coiled and swirled in her belly, and realized that her intuition was screaming at her. It was the tao, or more exactly a disturbance in its smooth currents, that she was feeling. It was as if something dangerous lay ahead in the flow of events, something that would need to be steered around.

She tipped the young eunuch with ten taels and dismissed him. It bothered her that she recognized him, and it did not escape her that his fear seemed nevertheless to conceal a measure of slyness.

An made his way towards the Western Palace, six eunuchs entrained at his back. He watched the eunuch of the thirty-fourth class, Yu Shih-tsan, leave the Western Palace and scuttle away down the alley that led to the Imperial Gardens. What was your business here today? he thought, his suspicions aroused. You were dismissed the post of ward to the heir nearly six months ago, so why were you here today? He made a mental note to investigate Yu's movements, and went on. When he came to the crossroads he halted, astonished to see Prince Kung's retinue. He got down on his knees, knowing the palanquin would pass by, but it did not.

'Skeleton Face!' the Prince shouted. 'Despicable crow! You're a hell-damned, stupid, cockless fool!'

He began to kowtow furiously as the Prince got down, feeling the rage boiling inside the other's body. 'May this day and all days dawn auspiciously for you, Imperial Highness.'

'Shut your foul mouth, cretin! And get up!'

He saw the paleness of the Prince's face, and delighted in his anger. By making his obsequies flamboyant he rendered Prince Kung the minimum acknowledgement possible, turning the other's fury white hot.

'Get up, I said!'

'If I have displeased you in any way—'

'Get up! Or I will order your head off immediately!'

'The Imperial Highness must do whatever seems most fitting – as long as it is in his power so to do.'

An grovelled in body, but inside he was laughing. Eat filth, he was thinking. You and all your turtle shit brothers, you're nothing more than ignorant coolies for all your position. One day I'll rob face from you as I robbed face from that thick-necked Southern general. And you won't be able to do anything more about it than he could.

'By all the gods, you'll die for what you did!'

'May this slave's head be struck off and buried in a separate grave if this slave has offended a Prince of the Blood.'

Fire flashed in the Prince's eyes. 'How dare you jeopardize important policy because of cumsha? How dare you?'

'Imperial Highness, as chamberlain of the household this slave is responsible for six thousand subordinates – everyone from craftsmen and clothiers to garden sweepers, from actors to those who maintain the Imperial buildings, from the lamas of the eunuch's Buddhist temple to the drudges who dispose of the Imperial night soil. By time-honoured tradition matters of cumsha are entirely my preserve.'

'She agrees with me. She will destroy you because of what

you did. Get ready to feel your head bouncing off the cobbles, An Te-hai, because your time has come!'

'Imperial Highness.' He presented a perfect figure of pious acceptance as Prince Kung's retinue moved off, but then he dabbed his lips with a paper tissue. You're right, Prince Kung, she's angry with me – very angry with me. But my head's still here on these shoulders, as it'll always be here on these shoulders, because I know something that you don't. Something that makes me absolutely invulnerable. Ha!'

As he passed on a tall eunuch was slow to make obeisance. An Te-hai paused his procession and approached the culprit.

'You! Stand up!'

When the eunuch obeyed An slapped him across the face as hard as he could. Then, with his other hand, slapped him again, across the other cheek. The eunuch almost toppled back, but he kept his feet and his downcast gaze resumed. His mouth began to bleed.

'What do you say?'

'Thank you, Master An.'

'You know your crime! No next time!'

An turned away and swept on, leaving the offender standing forlornly.

'One must have discipline,' he told his entourage as he walked. 'By tradition a Chief Eunuch punishes at will, but you see how I am touched by the spirit of justice? I am merciful by nature, therefore I make known before all what is the scale of punishment for those who fail in their duty. The portents say we are entering difficult times. In future, those who leave their post without permission, or who offend in any way, will be beaten. Those who offend a second time will be beaten severely – once to distress the flesh, then once again before healing is complete. Three-time offenders will have the cangue put around their necks for sixty days.'

All who heard feared the cangue. It was a thick wooden disk that closed around the neck, and was designed to humiliate. It was tantalizingly just wide enough to prevent the wearer's hands from reaching his mouth. Without seeking help he could neither feed himself nor scratch the maddening itch of head lice for two months.

An considered the dangerous leniency of his system. 'I did

think that a fourth offence should bring banishment for life,' he said 'Offenders sent away to work in desert wastes that are parched in summer and frozen in winter, but perhaps this would prove too costly to administer. Perhaps I should neaten the rule, and make it simple decapitation, as is the case with all serious crimes, such as theft. Come along! Come along! We must not linger.'

Yehonala tried to calm herself as An appeared before her. She sipped fragrant tea and felt the swirling currents of the tao carrying her headlong into danger. The letter lay on the table beside her.

I knew the Barbarians would not rest, she thought. Revenge is strong in them. They can sense our weakness and they will persist with their unreasonable demands until we are made to submit to them. Such behaviour is in the nature of Barbarians.

'Lady?'

'Ah, Little An. I've called you here because I require your opinion.' She handed him the letter. 'Look at this.'

An took it greedily and scanned the signature. 'May I ask where this came from?'

'Shanghai. Read it and give me your opinion.'

He did as he was told. According to Wu's report Hsueh Huan, Governor of Kiangsu, was raising what he called an anti-piracy force near Shanghai. In reality it was a secret mercenary army composed of heavily armed Barbarians. An looked up. He shrugged, but his eyes were gleaming. 'A matter of little concern in a place that is far away. The coasts of the South are said to be swarming with Barbarians of all kinds.'

She took his answer with dismay. 'Is that all?'

'May I know how you came by this?'

'No, you may not. Forget about cumsha for once, and tell me what do you make of the information.'

An blinked as if a door had been slammed in his face. He looked at the letter again, 'Let me see . . . Barbarians are of various clans: British, French, American, and there may be others . . . City Governor Wu says there are already a thousand of them prowling Shanghai . . . He says they are led by a chief called General Ward, an American, and reputedly a famous conqueror among his own people . . .'

'I must know what they want here.'

'Who can say what Barbarians want? They are red-faced demons. Wherever they go they are said to destroy harmonious government and dig up ancestral graves.'

'Is that so?' she asked, revolted.

'Oh, yes. It's well known. They're disgusting creatures who like to eat the meat and bones of the dead. Certainly we must assume they're armed with devil guns and all the hellish apparatus that Barbarian minds are naturally inclined to invent. I don't know if it's true, but I've heard that a single foreigner carrying a devil gun is capable of killing ten thousand of us.'

Yehonala's long nail protectors closed elegantly around her porcelain tea cup. She put it to her lips and sipped at the pale, fragrant liquid. 'What do you think Hsueh Huan could want with such a terrible force?'

An peered at the letter again. 'Wu mentions he has traced funds passing to something called the Bureau for the Suppression of River Piracy. Ostensibly its role is to counter Yangtze river pirates.'

'An Te-hai, you and I both know that such a force of armed Barbarians could be used to make Hsueh the most successful warlord China has ever seen, a power dominating the South, able to operate without reference to Peking. Shanghai is fast becoming the hub around which China is turning. Hsueh Huan seems to be unaware of this.'

'Whereas . . .' An trod with conspicuous care. 'Now you are aware of it, you will be able to use this army of Barbarians for your own ends.'

She stared at him coolly, her appraisal of him complete. 'Absolutely not. If once we allowed Barbarian soldiers inside the Middle Kingdom we would never be able to expel them again. They would not rest until they had completely obliterated us. This so-called anti-piracy force must be disbanded immediately.'

An pursed his lips. 'Whatever you think best, Lady. You decide policy, not I. But I ask again, how did this letter reach you?'

'And I reply again, I won't tell you that. You are dismissed.'

He looked back at her for a lingering moment, so that she was unsure if he would obey her or not. But then he bowed and left. An knows he can destroy me, she thought suddenly. What if he's turning against me?

She told an attendant. 'Go to the Hall of Records, Imperial Archive, and tell the scholars to select all memorials submitted to the Throne by the Taotai of Shanghai during the past five years. I want them brought to me here as soon as possible.'

'I am an American citizen, not a British subject.'

Ward stared hard at the man who faced him across the gas-lit saloon bar of the Grand Hotel. Captain Charles Strickland was a tall, upright ex-army officer, flax-haired with iron-grey eyes full of condescension. He worked for the British Consul.

'I'm aware of what you are, Mr Ward.'

'So what gives the British Consul's lackey the right to tell me what to do?'

'It's quite simple. You'll heed the advice we're giving, or your own Consul Smith will deal with you.'

It was part of the American Consul's job, Ward knew, to act as Marshal for the American community. He had the power of arrest. But he's in no condition to do anything. Billy Smith is unwell, overworked and homesick for Buffalo, New York. He gets raging headaches from swallowing too much quinine for his malaria. Half the time he doesn't know what day of the week it is. What's more, he doesn't have a jail-house.

'Sure. Billy Smith'll lock me up. Now, if you'll excu—'

Strickland put out a hand to stop him. 'Consul Smith is permitted to borrow our jail when the need arises. The next time you so much as pass the time of day with a British sailor or soldier, Ward, the need will most definitely arise.'

'I'm an American!'

'We'll worry about the paperwork afterwards. A long time afterwards. Is that clear?'

'Captain Strickland, why don't you just get out of my way?' He brushed past and made for the back room where a dozen more potential recruits waited.

Matters were growing urgent. Two weeks ago a small Taiping expeditionary force had broken out from Nanking and had penetrated to within forty miles of Shanghai. The two exploratory trips he had made alone into the war zone by sampan had shown him there had been tremendous slaughter. He had entered a maze of canals one night and moored near a village taken the week before by the Taipings. Vast numbers of dead bodies had been floating in the canals. For two or three hundred yards he had had to push his boat through a solid raft of decomposing bodies. Many had been killed by the Taipings, but such was the terror whipped up among the country people by the mandarins in an effort to stiffen resistance that most of the dead would have been suicides.

Ward crossed the hotel lobby and on the way he was given an envelope by the telegraph boy. He dropped a coin onto the silver tray and opened the letter, reading it with concealed satisfaction.

Burgevine met him at the door. 'Strickland again?'

'Uh-huh.'

'He can't do nothing.'

'Maybe he can.'

It was true. This was the second time the British Consul had warned him off. The last thing he wants is an American sticking his nose into British colonial plans, he thought. Britain was by far the richest and most powerful nation in the world, a tremendous manufacturing powerhouse with a huge overseas empire spanning the globe. Britain possessed a gigantic modern navy more than twice the size of all other navies in the world put together. One thing was certain, Consul Meadows held all the power in Shanghai.

'The British can make life hard for us if they choose, Henry.'

'What are you going to do?'

'Ignore them.'

Burgevine grinned. The wound he had taken from the meat cleaver was no more than an angry pink line down his face now. He had refused Ward's suggestion aboard the *Hyson* that he ask Lindley to sew it up. 'I don't trust doctoring. Besides, I want to remember him for what he done.'

Ward took up his parade-ground baton and slapped it into his palm. 'Lindley still owes me five hundred taels. It's about time I paid him a visit.'

'I'll visit him if you like.'

'No, Henry. This is between me and him. And anyway, there's another piece of business that has to go down first.'

He gave a discreet wave to Annie Phillips. Her estranged husband was Eden Phillips, a big, bluff man, the richest and most powerful independent trader in Shanghai. He headed the Shanghai Trade Association, and had never been able to understand why his wife had turned herself into a whore.

She's a rare one, a strange one, Ward thought. So sweet-looking. So delicate and pale, with that fine-stranded blonde hair and that pretty, girlish smile, but she's totally depraved underneath.

Eden Phillips had publicly disowned her, though she said he kept telling her he loved her. She said that what he really loved was possessing things, that his true and only love was his business, and where did that leave her? Whatever Eden said or did would not stop her. She had a lethal taste for freedom.

'I heard something the other night you might find very interesting,' she said quietly, coming over to him.

At a small signal from Ward Burgevine nodded and melted away.

'That man gives me the shivers,' she said.

'Henry? He won't do you any harm.'

The first time he saw Annie he had been fascinated by the shape of her face. There was something deeply vulnerable in her manner and those eyes of maddest blue were an enigma. He had smiled at her, not knowing who she was, and to his satisfaction she had started to come on to him. And when he was well and truly hooked she had reeled him in. He had been genuinely surprised when she had said, 'I have to ask for a little consideration. You do understand, don't you?'

'Consideration? You mean you want me to pay for it?'

She had been faintly indignant. 'I have to pay for this room, don't I? A girl has to get by. Eden gives me nothing.'

He had laughed. 'That doesn't surprise me. You won't do a damned thing he says.'

'I never would,' she had smiled wryly. 'And now I'm free to do what I like, aren't I?'

Ward had got up and left her, his desire for her vanished. But her desire for him had only grown stronger.

Annie put her mouth close to his ear now. 'One of my friends told me something I think you ought to know.'

'What kind of "friend"?'

'An undersecretary at the British Consulate. He told me a

big army has landed up in Hong Kong. Ten thousand British and Indian troops, and seven thousand French.'

'What?' he said, marvelling. 'That's the entire strength of the US army!'

'And there's more. The diplomats in charge are Lord Elgin and Baron Gros. Elgin is a Scottish lord. The elder brother of the man whose ship the Chinese fired on at Taku last year.'

'Thanks.' He pulled one of Yang Fang's ten-dollar bills from his wallet and folded it lengthwise before inserting it into her blouse.

'You know you don't have to do that.' She smiled, delighted by the consideration. 'I told you before – for you there's no charge.'

'A girl has to pay her way. Remember?'

He patted her rump as she turned to depart, then left the Grand Hotel's brightly lit lobby.

Thoughts of Lindley's pretty Chinese accomplice ran through his mind. He had had her followed, but she had not gone anywhere near Lindley's place. The place she lived was a mean house in one of the poorest riverside districts near the Chinese City, a house that sheltered at least a dozen rough-looking coolies. 'All secret Taiping. Damn sure.' That had been Ningpo Sam's opinion.

She's a careful one, he thought. But not careful enough. And not smart enough to get out of the bind I've got her in right now.

He came to a meeting hall a hundred yards along the Bund from the Grand Hotel and looked in on the roomful of human trash. Every day a few more were recruited and a few others disappeared. So it went, and so it would go – two steps forward and one step back – until a permanent camp could be established out of town.

Still, he thought with gnawing impatience, at least Yang Fang's paying up promptly, and Wu's finally mentioned a plot of land about fifty li south-west of the city.

He left the meeting hall and took a chair to the far side of Soochow Creek where a rice warehouse belonging to Taki stood. When he reached the door he tapped out three sets of triple knocks with his baton and was admitted. Inside was darkness. He could smell the river. The rail he touched as he climbed the stair was covered in fine starch dust. At the top there was a curtain that screened off a long, empty floor lit by a single oil lamp flame. It flickered as the silhouettes surrounding it gambled with muted excitement. A few yards away a blindfolded woman sat on a chair. She had been tied to it.

Ward pulled off her blindfold. 'What are you doing in Shanghai?'

She defied him with a furious silence.

'That was a clever manoeuvre you pulled off up river.' He lifted her chin with the tip of his baton. 'You fooled me, missee. Then you robbed me. I didn't like that.'

She jerked her head away. 'Ai ya! You don't suffer any loss. We could have taken your steamer. We could have killed you. But we let you go.'

'Your people took my property – a dozen of my guns. They threatened my life, assaulted my associate and the men who work for me. It was your doing.'

'So what? Why do you come to China? You don't belong here.'

'I think I'll hand you over to the taotai.'

He saw a glaze of horror pass over her face, but then she spat at him.

He wiped his cheek patiently. 'You seem to know pretty well what he'll do to you. Now, I want to know what you're doing in Shanghai. And you know what? You're going to tell me.'

Fei felt the terror eat into her like acid. It was only two hours ago that she had been bundled off the street and brought to this place. At first she thought she had been taken by the taotai's thugs and began to prepare herself for the inevitable, but when no robed mandarin appeared she had dared to hope. Now that same hope had vanished again, undermining her as it did so.

'See, I need to know where I can get hold of more of those beautiful Enfield rifles.'

She continued to stare fixedly at the patterns in the rice flour that dusted the floor.

How could she say she had been sent to spy on Ward's preparations? How could she tell him that even now a gigantic Anglo-French army was coming to overwhelm Peking and that its victory would cause the downfall of the hated Manchu dynasty? Soon the Taipings would be victorious. Whatever happened.

May Shang-ti, Lord God of Heaven, help the martyrs of the glorious Taiping cause!

The slogan she shouted in her mind gave her solace, but still the fear of what was about to happen ate into her. It bit deeper when he knelt, brushed a strand of hair back from her face, smiled and said, 'You're going to have to tell me sooner or later. You know that, don't you?'

British and French forces had been arriving from Hong Kong all week, so that now the river was crammed with shipping and the Bund crowded with personnel.

Drink was flowing liberally at the British Consulate as Lindley watched the formal reception move towards its climax. He still had not been able to work out why he had been invited here, or by whom. His letter to the Consul had been sent weeks ago and had not even received a reply. An orchestra was playing. Lord Elgin, balding, stout and avuncular, had arrived and was holding court under the chandeliers, surrounded by dozens of younger men. The rest of the gathering was mostly traders and their wives and naval captains and cavalry majors in splendid uniforms.

Lindley looked around. So far he had not been able to put his enquiries to the Consul. Instead he had been impertinently questioned by an aide called Strickland, had talked with a crashing bore, a trader by the name of Eden Phillips, and after ridding himself of that man's company he had fallen into conversation with a dour captain of the Royal Engineers who had spoken about the intended march on Peking with relish.

'We'll sail from Shanghai, destroy the Taku forts and secure Tientsin. Then we'll march on the Chinese capital. And that, my dear fellow, will be the end of the business.'

'Aren't you giving the game away, Captain Gordon?' he asked, appalled at the man's words.

'It doesn't matter if I am. We're going to Peking, and there's nothing the heathens can do to prevent us. God is on our side, you see.'

'Yes,' he had muttered, embarrassed. 'Of course. Would you excuse me?'

He moved away again, thinking again of Fei as he had last seen her, brisk and pitiless and stone-faced, and the humiliation still burned enough to bring a flush to his own. He thought of Ward too. I'll fix that bastard. Somehow I'll find a way to get even with him, but I have to be careful – I may just need him. He had decided for the moment to spend some of the money subscribed in Scotland to build the Ebenezer Mission. A simple surgery seemed like a good idea. The Chinese city was swollen to bursting with refugees now, and disease was rife. He had made an application to Governor Wu, but it had not succeeded. Now he knew why. Wu's mandarins were active on the streets, spreading hatred. He had seen wall posters all over the place calling on the people strenuously to resist God-worshipping. He had read one of the official proclamations:

'Let the people beware! Christianity and other religions based on it use magic to ensnare converts and drive them mad, to make them smash their ancestral tablets and violate shrines. They boil the corpses of their priests to extract the ointment used in baptism. They use the flesh of new-born babies and the eyes and hearts of the dead for medicines, for alchemy, and even for photography. Their success at alchemy accounts for the speed of machine boats and the hellish accuracy of their guns. They gather ill-gotten riches especially to seduce Chinese converts. These foreigners drink the menstrual blood of women, hence their pungent and horrid smell. Their priests act as spies for their country . . .'

Lindley had torn it down, but Shen had said, 'Mandarin say: death if Chinese person even listen to foreigner.' When he wrote again to Governor Wu he was told there had been a well-subscribed petition to the magistrates not to allow it.

Lindley looked behind him now, and saw Captain Strickland standing with a group who were watching couples whirling in a Viennese waltz. He noticed Lindley and beckoned to him.

'May I introduce H. B. Loch? He's a fellow Scot. Mr Loch, Harry Lindley.'

A seated man, sensitive and copper-haired, stood up and shook hands with a surprisingly firm grip. 'How do you do.'

'How do you do.' Lindley smiled. 'Are you with Lord Elgin's party?'

'I'm his lordship's private secretary. And you? A trader in teas or silks, I suppose.'

'Neither. A humble medical man, I'm afraid.'

'Why . . . that's a relief, at least.'

Lindley accepted the remark with humour, surprised at the immediate rapport he felt with the stranger. 'I understand his lordship's been sent out to supervise the opening of diplomatic relations with China – whether they like it or not.'

Loch grinned. 'Aye. You've been talking with our Captain Gordon. Unstoppable, is he not?'

'His Christianity certainly seems to be of a very – shall we say – muscular kind. '

Loch's eyes were restless and watchful. His sandy colouring made his ice blue irises even more pronounced. Lindley saw Elgin pass a summons. 'Excuse me. Duty calls. It was good to meet you Doctor. Perhaps we'll meet again.'

'He's a charming fellow,' Strickland said.

'Yes.' There was something faintly supercilious about Strickland's manner that irritated Lindley as much as Loch's personality agreed with him.

'You wouldn't think he'd served in the Crimea, would you? He was with Skinner's Horse in India, too. But old H.B.'ll have his work cut out for him while he's here.'

'Why do you say that, Captain?'

'It's obvious. He speaks very little Chinese.'

'I don't see how he can be his lordship's secretary under the circum . . .' Lindley looked to Strickland suddenly. 'Just a minute – do you know why I was invited here?'

Strickland's face gave no clue. 'Consul Meadows would like to tell you that himself. Though I imagine you can guess. Let's go and find him, shall we?'

Lindley followed, seeing a little way from Elgin a tall, bearded man with an imposing physical presence and an energetic manner, the man whom Strickland had identified as Thomas Meadows. He was in conversation with a thin-faced man who Strickland said was William Smith, the American Consul. Lindley watched Meadows' way of standing too close when in conversation. It seemed deliberate, an attempt to put the person he was speaking to at some kind of disadvantage. As soon as Smith moved away Strickland steered him in.

Lindley took Meadows' hand. 'I'm delighted to meet you at last, sir.'

'And I you, Dr Lindley. I you.' Meadows allowed a crisp, appraising silence, then said, 'I have it that you're an excellent Chinese speaker.'

Lindley smiled circumspectly. 'I can read and write quite well. I've learned to speak a very little Shanghainese. I seem to have a wooden ear where their tones are concerned. Listen, I was wondering if—'

The Consul dismissed the reply instantly, his eyes were like steel. 'But you have good Mandarin.'

'My tutor in London was a Mandarin speaker, and so was a gentleman I conversed with on the passage out. I believe he was in the government service, so perhaps—'

'Ah, our Mr Gilbert.'

Lindley was surprised. 'Yes, indeed. Do you know him?'

'It's my business to know everything that happens in Shanghai, Doctor. Who comes, who goes. What they get up to.'

Lindley detected a dangerous undercurrent to the man's words. 'You're implying something,' he said smoothly, 'but, for the life of me I can't understand what it is.'

Meadows' smile vanished. 'You've already made one mistake too many, Dr Lindley.'

'Have I indeed?'

'Frederick Townsend Ward.' Meadows paused, watching him, then said, 'I see the name is familiar to you. An American freebooter. A filibuster of the worst kind. We don't like him. We don't like him at all.'

Lindley wondered at the warning.

'You say in your letter that you want me to intercede with Provincial Governor Hsueh Huan. You want permission to travel to Nanking. Have you any idea what you're asking?'

'As I explained to you, I came to Shanghai to meet my father.'

'Ah, yes. The elusive Reverend Lindley.' Meadows smiled tightly. 'Do you by any chance know the Chinese name for gunpowder?'

'They call it "big strength powder".'

'That's right. Here religion is gunpowder of the very biggest strength.'

'Mr Meadows, I need to go to Nanking.'

'I shouldn't bother asking a mandarin for permission.'

'Why not?'

'They're not empowered to give it.' Meadows braced his shoulders, his hands clasped behind his back.

'The only people who can permit that are the Peking bureaucracy.'

'Then, what do you suggest I do?'

'Maybe we can ask a favour for you. You know the Taipings will triumph if foreign powers don't interfere. The Manchu might just as well try to blow the sun out of the sky as quench this flame that their folly and tyranny have set blazing.'

Lindley said nothing, but he watched the tall man's eyes study him.

'So you know, Doctor, that the highest honour the Chinese Emperor can confer on a subject is permission to prostrate himself before the Dragon Throne? Oh, yes. It's supposed to be a ceremonial of the greatest magnificence. And vastly difficult to obtain. It was accorded a little while ago to General Tseng Kuo-fan, Commander-in-Chief, Imperial Forces, Central China.'

'I don't follow.'

'Dr Lindley, Tseng Kuo-fan has had to withdraw his forces. News came to me not two hours ago of great Taiping celebrations in Nanking. The Imperial siege is well and truly broken. The Taipings' main field army has burst through the blockade, and food, ammunition and supplies have started pouring into the city. The Imperial army, you see, has had to be pulled north – in anticipation of our own little invasion.'

Lindley rapidly tried to work out the consequences. 'I don't see why this should affect me,' he said uneasily.

'From now on you must take greater care. And at this particular time finding your father is the very last thing you should be trying to do.'

Lindley let his irritation show. 'Look, don't try to patronize me. I have a right and a duty to try to find out what happened to my father. He came here to do good, to save the people. For twenty years his dream was to open a mission house in the Old City, a place of charity – a surgery, a hospice, an orphanage – good God, man, what's wrong with any of that? And what good is a bloody treaty if no one abides by it? You should be trying to help me, not fobbing me off.'

Meadows left a cooling moment, then said. 'China's a very hard lady to understand, Doctor. She's a vast cesspool of humanity. And none of her teeming millions has any idea about morality such as we might understand it.'

'Aye, I've heard all that before. "Life's cheap in the East", "People who believe in reincarnation don't care about dying." Well, let me tell you, I think that's just bloody nonsense. The Chinese are no more spiritual or worldly than we are. Underneath all that mumbo jumbo they're just the same as us.'

Meadows drew breath. 'But it's the mumbo jumbo that's the problem, you see. The first year that I arrived here an epidemic broke out. An order of Roman Catholic nuns opened an orphanage near the French Concession. No Chinese came, so they offered money for orphans. After that they were brought in by the dozen. They amazed the Chinese by offering more money for children who were sickly – and so likely to die before they could be baptized, one supposes.'

Lindley compressed his lips. 'Aye, well. That was just silly of them.'

'Ah, I can see you're way ahead of me, Doctor. You already know what I'm going to say, and you're quite right. Of course rumours began to spread of monstrous magic being practised on helpless babes. As a result the mandarins questioned the convent's Chinese cook. They tortured the poor soul into a "confession" actually. Then a mob gathered at the cemetery and started digging up babies' corpses. When the mandarins demanded to search the convent the mob pushed their way in and burned the place down. Then they started on the cathedral nearby. A dozen of the Little Sisters of Mercy were herded naked through the streets, then cut to pieces. A dozen other foreigners, including a couple of priests, were killed too. So you see, Doctor, I'm not just thinking of your safety when I say that you must take greater care. It doesn't take much here to spark a very sizeable holocaust.'

Lindley said quietly. 'I should like to find my father. I'm sure you'd want to do the same if you were in my position.'

Meadows gave no ground. 'Doctor, you are provoking great unrest in the Chinese City by your insistence. I think you should know that travelling to Nanking is quite out of the question for you.'

Lindley tried to hide his disappointment and also his determination. 'Thank you for your advice,' he said evenly. 'I see I'll have to seek elsewhere for help.'

He was about to disengage himself from Meadows' company, when the Consul said, 'Maybe I shall help you . . . if you'll agree to help me.'

His suspicions prickled. 'In what possible way could I help you?'

'There's only a handful of Britons in Shanghai who can read and write Chinese and speak Mandarin. How would you like to become Lord Elgin's official translator?'

The young eunuch was led forward to the punishment post in a disused secondary courtyard of the old Palace of Abstinence.

'What's happening?' he said shakily as eunuchs spread-eagled him against the square timber post. They made no reply as they chained his hands wide on the cross-piece and secured his feet to ringbolts set into the ground on each side.

'No! No! Master An, please tell them it's a mistake. Please tell them to stop!'

An watched in silence as Yu burbled in terror.

'Master An, what am I supposed to have done wrong?'

When An spoke his voice was low, thick with anticipation and suppressed delight. 'I think you know what you've done, Yu Shih-tsan.'

'Master An, I don't know! Tell me – what is my crime?'

'I fear . . .' An paused, looking Yu up and down. 'I fear that what you've done is to have forgotten the meaning of loyalty and respect to your superiors.'

'I have never been disrespectful or disloyal to my superiors. Never! I promise.'

'Oh, I think you have.'

Yu's hands flexed. His eyes were swimming in his head. He shut them tight as An produced the yellow bag and withdrew one of the birch rods.

'What are you going to do to me?'

An smiled, enjoying the other's blurting, white-faced fear

as he flexed the rod experimentally. 'You must take punishment.'

'Punishment for what, Master An? I am crimeless! Please tell me what you are going to do to me!'

An gestured that Yu's robe be removed. One of the eunuchs cut through the collar and tore the fabric down to the waist. Then he cut through Yu's belt so that his beads and waist ornaments fell to the cobbles. The skirt of the robe tore easily to the hem, then that was cut through so that the robe parted.

An strolled around the post, then put his mouth close to Yu's ear. 'Do you know, I have been ordered to whip you to death.'

An savoured the stink of panic rising from his victim. Yu Shih-tsan groaned, then his voice grew desperate, full of sick pleading. 'Please don't whip me, Master An. I'll tell you anything. Anything at all.'

'There's nothing I want to hear from you. The command is to hear only your screams. And then your silence.'

Yu Shih-tsan's knees buckled.

An nodded. 'Wake him up. He's ready now.'

Golden afternoon rays slanted over the roofs as a bucket of cold urine was thrown over Yu. His ivory skin was delicate like a woman's. The whole of Yu's back, his buttocks and the backs of his quaking legs dripped. They were still striped with the faint marks of the switch, marks sustained during his last flogging, six months ago. He awoke into the nightmare.

'Promise me my jar, Master An!' he raved, sobbing. 'Please promise me my jar . . .'

The eunuch with the knife cut away the arms of Yu's blue robe, so that it fell away. An saw the obscene remains of Yu's manhood, a stump no bigger than the last joint of his thumb, through which he was urinating involuntarily. Beneath was a scar on the place where his adolescent testicles had been removed six years before. Those pieces of black, withered flesh, An knew, were carefully preserved in Yu's quarters, sealed in their jar. Like all eunuchs he had had to buy them back from the family of hereditary eunuchmakers who had cut them off. Once a year they were presented to An at the Ceremony of Inspection, when prayers were recited by the lama of the eunuch temple and

145

dire warnings read to the gathering that those who wished to be reborn whole must be buried whole in the eunuchs' cemetery outside the city wall.

An came very close. 'Why should you have your jar, Yu Shih-tsan, when you tried to cheat me?'

Yu's eyes opened with utter horror. 'Cheat you, Master An? Never!'

'You know that I am due my share of all cumsha. Yet you did not render it to me.'

'When?' The word was a shriek.

'When you tried to fly above my head. You passed on a letter to Her Imperial Highness, the Empress of the Western Palace, and you accepted a reply. All this you did, yet you did not pay me a single copper cash of my dues.'

Yu wailed. 'I did not mean to cheat you, Master An. I was sworn to tell no one about the letters. How could I keep my word and still pay you?'

Te-hai sighed deeply. 'I see your dilemma. But what would happen if I allowed every maggot in my city to go behind my back on secret errands of their own? The correct course would have been to confide in me.'

'Please forgive me, Master An!'

'I think you know it's far too late for that.' An made to turn away, but then pretended to have second thoughts. 'Unless . . . you might feel disposed to do me one small favour.'

'Anything, Master An! Please forgive me!'

An nodded genially. 'How much were you paid?'

'A hundred taels.'

'A hundred taels? Greedy maggot!'

'Have it all, Master An! Have everything!' The young eunuch was sobbing. 'Have the Barbarian books . . .'

An looked up very slowly. 'Did you say "Barbarian books"?'

Yu's lips writhed and he swallowed drily. His breathing was shallow and fast, coming in gasps as he hoped and hoped. 'Master An, I beg to tell you that I was meant to give them to the Lady Yehonala, but I was too scared to deliver them. They are hidden in my quarters.'

An despatched two eunuchs to conduct the search, then he beamed at Yu Shih-tsan. 'Now do you see what I mean by loyalty and respect?'

146

Yu's eyes rolled in his head, but he managed to whisper, 'Yes, Master An.'

'Excellent! Perfect loyalty, and abundant respect. Don't you feel a great sense of relief now that you have put down your burden of lies? You see how easy life becomes when you give yourself over to correct thoughts?'

He walked to the barred gate and murmured to a guard eunuch. 'Is the Lady Yehonala still closeted with Prince Kung?'

The guard eunuch made a distinctive wave to a builder's coolie who squatted on the roof ridge of a nearby hall. He stared hard over his shoulder then returned the wave.

'Yes. Master An. She remains with the Prince.'

Yehonala and I are natural allies, he thought, satisfied with the day's events. But she spends far too much time talking with Prince Kung. How long can I tolerate sharing a political camp with that man? He's an ambitious running dog who hates all eunuchs and wishes he was Emperor. I know he'd turn on Yehonala if ever they succeeded in vanquishing Su-shun. Certainly, he will try to destroy me at the first opportunity. Therefore, why should I help advance his cause? Perhaps I'll create a rift between them, and use it to obliterate them both.

A sudden thought struck him. Su-shun would certainly accept me as an ally if I was able to bring with me control of a secret force of Barbarians.

As he left the compound one of the guard eunuchs asked about Yu Shih-tsan.

'Strangle him.'

An started out for the gate once again, but looked back at the punishment post briefly. 'No. Don't strangle him.'

The sun was an hour above the eastern horizon, and the dew was already lifting from the roofs of the Forbidden City when Yehonala emerged from her sleeping quarters. She endured her dressers' attentions and privately teased out the mystery of the unexplained silence: there had been no more letters from City Governor Wu Hsu for almost three months, and she sensed a powerful tao warning in it.

Since the great floods Imperial messengers riding fresh horses in relays took five days to reach Shanghai, and five more to return. The longer this silence goes on, she thought, the more I believe the Shanghai Foreign Arms Corps does not exist and has never existed, that it's a hoax devised by Su-shun to goad me into injudicious action against him. On the other hand, what if some mishap has befallen Wu? There are a hundred explanations, and it's impossible to choose between them.

'How is the Lady Niuhuru?' she asked An Te-hai.

He brought out the coral earrings he had helped her to select.

'I have not seen her Imperial Highness this week, Lady Yehonala.'

'Ah, summer . . .' she breathed. 'It was summer when Niuhuru and I first entered the Forbidden City. I remember looking across the moat and seeing the velvety leaves and pink chalices of lotuses floating on the water. Dragonflies were darting among them. Free. So very free.' She sighed. 'The Lady Niuhuru is so beautiful.'

'That is very true. But . . . is there not a difference between beauty and attractiveness?'

'A charming idea.'

'Excuse me, Lady Yehonala, but it is said that attractiveness always outlives beauty. The Empress of the Eastern Palace is no longer young. Her cosmetician tells me that fine lines are appearing in her face every day.'

Yehonala nodded. 'She did not look her normal radiant self when she came to the last audience.'

'Ah! That is because her earrings were jade. Jade reflects a happy mood. It is associated with youth and laughter. If one who is tired or unhappy wears jade then the jade itself becomes lacklustre. This in turn brings out her lines. When last I saw her the Empress Niuhuru's skin looked exactly like a piece of dry wood, not nearly as attractive as your own.'

Yehonala smiled at the exaggeration and An's flattery. She admired her flawless complexion in the pair of French looking glasses. Her face was the picture of classical beauty – highly-arched eyebrows, small nose and rosebud lips. She lifted the second looking-glass and angled it at the first so she could check her profile, then she tried the coral earrings. Her jewellery collection was huge and stored in a special strong-room. Her jade collection alone was beyond price. Three hundred chests stood on shelves lining the walls. Some contained neatly catalogued trays of pearls and jade, others displayed coral or gold or ivory, others still, some of the most attractive she thought, held items of little actual value, being made of kingfisher's feathers or butterfly wings. There were no diamonds or emeralds or rubies, such as were prized in the southern vassal states of Burma, Siam and Annam. It's truly perplexing what strange things the semi-barbarous races of the earth are apt to consider desirable, she thought. How much less are we able to fathom the minds of real Barbarians?

What did Little An think of my regal image yesterday? she wondered. After I tumbled vigorously with Jung-lu among the furs for two hours I must have looked far from Imperial. But my lover's yang energies have re-invigorated me. It was good to welcome him home.

The soldier's spell of duty in the Gobi Desert had done him good. She had been right about having him posted far away for a while. He had ridden almost to the place where the sun sets, and the fresh air seemed to have erased the more dangerous notions from his mind. She recalled snuggling against Jung-lu's great chest, listening to him recount the thrilling mission he had led to destroy the Mongol bandits.

'If your Imperial Highness would turn her head a little toward the light,' An said.

Yehonala complied and smiled now inwardly as she recalled how Jung-lu's tales about the clever tricks he had used to trap bandits had given her the vital idea about how to deal with An Te-hai. Yang energy, being male and active, required yin energy, female and passive, to neutralize it. Eunuchs were neither male nor female, and therefore very hard to deal with.

'You must ensure that my complexion does not clash with my gown,' she told the make-up eunuch who arrived.

The make-up eunuch dusted her cheek bones with a soft brush. 'This powder is a mixture of rice powder and the very best white lead, Lady.'

'We must be very particular about our appearance,' she said. 'Today we must put on a face for the sake of the nation.'

'Everything is of the very best, Lady.'

Today's gathering was important. A 'picnic' in the Summer Palace. The Emperor would be present, and so would

Prince Kung. For the last three days Little An had been unusually attentive and obedient. He's up to something, she thought, and decided to gamble everything on her plan to bind him more firmly to her.

A messenger eunuch appeared at the threshold and waited for permission to enter.

She roused herself. 'Approach!'

The eunuch prostrated himself. 'The papers you requested from the Hall of Records, your Imperial Highness.'

She opened the sealed scroll and began to read. The scholars who kept the Imperial records so meticulously had finally transferred the documents and located the latest information she had requested. All the questions she had asked had been answered – sums of money had been sent by Su-shun to a Shanghai banker named Yang Fang. It seemed suddenly to Yehonala as if the puzzle was coming together. But why would Su-shun be transferring funds to the South? There must be an explanation.

The make-up eunuch was packing away the cosmetics, and neatly arranging items on a lacquer tray. She examined herself in the mirror, and suddenly doubted if she was looking at her own reflection.

She put fingertips to her chin. 'Sometimes, Little An, I don't know who I am at all. What am I? What have I become? How is it that the little girl from Pewter Street must now change her appearance for reasons of state?'

'You are the Lady Yehonala, Empress of the Western Palace and mother of the heir.'

'Am I? Perhaps I should have been born a man.'

'Oh, no, Lady! Don't say that!'

She sighed. An hour from now she would be in audience with her husband. 'It's hard when a man cannot live up to his responsibilities. Weak men are no good to the world.'

There was a pause, then An said, 'I have heard it said that many great people are given to wondering who they really are. Once the great sage, Chuang-tzu, dreamed he was a butterfly. In the dream he didn't know he was Chuang-tzu. But then he woke up and there he was: Chuang-tzu just as always!'

Yehonala smiled, touched by his solicitous words. 'In that case, perhaps this is a dream. And I will wake up soon.'

'Ah! But that would not bring peace of mind.'

She turned to him, 'Why do you say that?'

'Because when Chuang-tzu woke up he didn't know if he was Chuang-tzu who had dreamed he was a butterfly, or a butterfly who was dreaming he was Chuang-tzu.'

Prince Kung broke wind as he lay prostrate on the massage table. Something was interfering with his digestion, and caused him flatulence and a dull pain in his belly.

The early breakfast of sweet eel cutlets in oil and thick noodle soup had been exquisitely prepared and extremely costly but it had not had the effect he had hoped, that of charming his fellow Princes of the Blood towards a more reasonable point of view. Like eels they had once again wriggled out of his grasp.

He forced himself to relax and allow the fingers of the masseur to sink into his flesh. He watched Prince Cheng and regretted the fiercely independent streak the man possessed. His title, Cheng, meant 'sedate', but his character was wholly stubborn. They had talked for months now, without an alliance coming together against Su-shun.

Now more hot water was ladled over Prince Cheng's head. Prince Kung knew that when the man opened his eyes he must be faced with the essential question.

'I believe the time has finally come for you to choose sides.'

Prince Cheng took the ladle from the body servant and brandished it playfully. 'Are you threatening me?'

'No. Merely warning you of the coming storm. And proposing that you take cover while you may.'

'I've said it before. I don't see any storm coming.'

'Then open your eyes to what's happening. The Court is splitting inexorably into two camps. Those who are prepared to allow Su-shun to control them, and those who are not. In which camp will you dwell?'

Prince Cheng grinned like a porcelain Buddha. 'Equally you might have said that the Court is split between those who are prepared to allow Yehonala to control them, and those who are not.'

'Our enemy – your enemy and mine – is Su-shun.'

'I'm still waiting to be convinced of that. Until my spies bring me word of a large potential gain I see no reason to realign myself.'

Prince Kung recalled his talk with Su-shun two days ago. The man's eyes had been yellow with rice wine and his manner full of extravagant ambition. 'Don't the Sages teach us that dynasties are established by men of noble virtue and great force of character? That succeeding generations deteriorate, until some Emperor is reached who combines debauchery with cruelty and only works for evil in his ruling of the state? This way comes ruin.'

He had been shocked. 'You dare speak of the Imperial line thus?'

'I merely repeat what the Sages have observed.' Su-shun had smiled. 'I have more interests in more provinces than you can presently imagine, so I counsel you to be very careful.'

Yes, he thought now. He's the most dangerous man in the world. He wants to be the next Emperor of China. He's already disposed of Po Chun. He's secretly in favour of starving the Southern army of funds so that the Taiping rebellion will rumble along for ever and continue to enrich him. I must be careful not to make myself into too prominent an enemy of his – not until I'm certain I can destroy him.

Prince Cheng dressed and thanked his host for a pleasant morning. Then he departed, his retinue following.

After his guest had left Prince Kung felt the pain in his belly crescendo. Should I have told him about how it was my idea to put Jung-lu forward as nominee for head of the Imperial Bodyguard? As soon as Yehonala heard about that she made sure he was sent away to the Gobi. Why? Could it be they are lovers, as the spy reports don't quite manage to say? Rumours are rife, though there's never been any proof offered as yet.

He considered the spy who regularly fed him reports about Yehonala's doings. The last report a month ago had seemed to be far from promising at first, just some routine report about a letter arriving from a City Governor in the South, but now that piece of information had changed his entire strategy. He had subjected the spy to close questioning. 'Did you see what happened?'

'Immediately she read it she tore the letter into tiny, tiny bits and scattered them around her.'

'Why did she do that? It must be a secret.'

'Maybe it was a secret, Highness. On the other hand that's her favourite way of disposing of any written advice that displeases her.'

'Displeases her? What happened to the fragments?'

The spy had looked up at him stupidly. 'I don't know, Highness. I suppose the wind must have dispersed them.'

'Go back and find them all!'

'But Highness. They are worthless. Impossible to read.'

'Give them to the embroiderers of Ten Thousand Years Hill. They have a good eye for pattern. Tell them you want all the pieces glued together in the proper sequence. Also they are illiterate, so they will not understand what they have done. Go!'

Prince Kung thought of the letter that had been recovered. Its astonishing contents had told of a secret army of Barbarians being brought together in the South. It made him think of a black cloud suddenly blotting out the sun.

'With your permission, Lord, I'll tell you a story of ancient times.' The masseur's voice grew faraway as his thumbs circled the blockages he had located. 'Think, if you will, of the time before memory, when the Ming ruled China and we Manchu lived on the far side of the Great Wall and were ourselves thought of as Barbarians. Then it was that the Manchu chieftain, Nurhachi, conceived a very clever idea. He knew that while there is no limit to how gently a big axe may be used, there is certainly a limit to how deep a small axe will bite. Therefore, he wished for the sake of protection to unite the various clans of Manchuria into one single axe, with himself wielding it.

'In those days, however, there was great resistance to the idea of clan unity, and no one opposed unity more than Buyang, the chieftain of the Yehe clan.

'When war came the Yehe suffered appalling slaughter at Nurhachi's hands. Hardly a male clansman was able to escape with his life. As he lay dying Buyang vowed: "Even if a single woman is left of all my people, I charge her with the duty of avenging us of Nurhachi's butchers."

'This caused the Manchu rulers to make a specific law that no Yehe woman should be allowed into the palace of Mukden for any purpose. Few remember this ruling today. As her name implies Yehonala is of Yehe descent.'

Prince Kung broke wind again as he felt the last of the

blockages dissolve and the chi suffuse him. The pain in his gut vanished. Yes, he thought, suddenly elated. Perhaps it will be possible to trawl the Imperial Archives and see if that law has ever been repealed. If not, it might provide a means of excluding Yehonala from the Forbidden City, and from all future contact with His Imperial Majesty. Perhaps that would deflect Su-shun's vendetta against me. Perhaps there is a way to dismount this tiger after all.

The night was hot and uncomfortably humid, so that the Forbidden City was more oppressive than ever. Despite the thickness of the air Yehonala's attendant maids and servants were fully alert, not daring to lift their eyes. The Empress had been visibly on edge all day.

There was the rustle of robes outside the door, and An Te-hai's slight form appeared. The flaring oil lamps cast a jaundiced light on his shaved skull. The atmosphere in the chamber solidified as soon as he crossed the threshold. The face of the Chief Eunuch was unreadable as he kowtowed formally.

'Approach.' Yehonala's voice was curt. Fear and rage warred in her as she noted the self-control An Te-hai was exerting. She knew absolutely that he had been planning to betray her. That was why she had summoned him.

'I want your advice on a difficult matter.'

'Certainly, Lady Yehonala. What is it?'

'A matter of communication with the South. As you know, I received a letter from City Governor Wu Hsu. I have received no more. This puzzles me.'

'A letter like this?' He produced a paper from his sleeve.

She took it, immediately verifying the broken seal, then comparing the chop marks with those on the previous letter she had received. They were identical.

'Where did you get this?'

'I won't tell you that.' An's face was as inexpressive as a stone. 'It's enough for you to know that it came into my possession some time ago.'

'You dared interfere with a communication addressed to me?' she said, battling to keep her tone even. 'You dared do that?'

'My intention in doing so was to protect you, Lady.'

'Protect me? From what?'

'Entrapment. Plots against you.'

She stared at him, knowing it was a lie. He had kept the letter from her to use for his own ends. She compared the brush-strokes of the third letter. All three were unmistakably made by the same hand, and the Imperial Archives had confirmed that it was City Governor Wu Hsu's.

'Did you interrogate Yu Shih-tsan?' she said, pushing the exchange into new realms. 'If you did he appears remarkably unharmed.'

'He told the whole truth without my having to harm him – which was fortunate, because I needed him.'

She forced herself not to look at the letter. 'He lied to me. He swore that no more letters had come from City Governor Wu Hsu.'

'That's correct. He lied because I told him to lie.'

She tried to control the anger seething inside her. She could not stop herself glancing down at the letter.

'Why don't you read it?' An said. 'I think you'll find it most . . . interesting.'

'They could still be forgeries,' she said, looking at the broken seal. 'This is Wu's calligraphy, but what if he's being paid, or otherwise coerced?'

To her surprise there was comparatively little about Provincial Governor Hsueh Huan and the mercenary army. This time City Governor Wu was reporting that a huge Barbarian devil fleet had arrived at Shanghai, where the intentions of its leaders had been made loudly public: they were going to land a devil army at Taku and then march on Peking.

'You withheld something as urgent as this?' she said disbelievingly. 'Are you insane?'

'I'm very sane, Lady. You told me you knew it would happen. You said you knew that the Outer Barbarians would not rest until the insult they received at Taku was avenged. You said that they would return in force. There will be nothing subtle about their approach because they're going to try to intimidate us. Therefore there's no urgency.'

'Why didn't you take the letter to Su-shun?'

'Because the gods told me not to desert you.'

She thanked Kuan Yin, her guardian goddess, for giving her the foresight to use An's superstitious streak against him. She had known that he went regularly to a fortune-teller near the Fu Cheng gate to have his future cast. The payment of a small bribe had ensured that the fortune-teller would reveal that An's future was 'bound to the orchid.' Since her own name had once been Lan Kuei – the Little Orchid – An would instantly realize the significance of the reading. To make sure, on his return, she had worn one of the orchid gowns especially made for her, a design no one else in the Forbidden City was allowed to wear.

She said, 'You know I've been advised to have you killed, Little An?'

A raw laugh escaped him. 'You couldn't have me killed Lady. If you did that the truth about you would come out.'

'Nevertheless I've been thinking about it a lot recently. There's been a catastrophic breakdown in trust between us. You've wavered very badly in your loyalty.'

A familiar look of chastened humility stole over him. 'At least I'm admitting it now. And apologizing.'

'Yes. And I'm accepting your apology. And warning you: no more mistakes, An Te-hai. No more mistakes.'

'Anyway, I couldn't take this letter to Su-shun,' he volunteered, his lips pursing. 'Su-shun already knows about the mercenary army in the South.'

She felt the fear seize her. 'What?'

'He already knows. Because he's funding it.'

'How?'

'Through the Governor of Kiangsu. Hsueh Huan is Su-shun's servant. His underling, City Governor Wu, wrote to you only because he's hoping for his superior's downfall. Wu wants to be promoted from the city governorship of Shanghai to the provincial governorship of Kiangsu province, in Hsueh's place.'

'What would you do if you were me?'

'I would try to find some way to arrange it so that Governor Wu replaces Hsueh Huan as overlord of Kiangsu. In this way Su-shun's power there will be destroyed.'

After he had gone some of the wild desperation left her. She picked up Tsai-ch'un's white rabbit toy. He had been in the care of his nursemaids since the Hour of the Rooster. For a long while she sat still, stroking the toy, wanting nothing more than to cuddle the heir to her. His little life and the motherly love she felt for him were the only fixed and certain things in her life.

Su-shun's become too powerful, she thought. It's time to start fighting or we will all die!

Immediately the newborn resolution began to lift her mood. She raised her teacup to her lips in a private toast. But the tea had already gone cold.

The water gardens of the Yuan Ming Yuan – the Summer Palace – basked under a remorseless sun. Azaleas and peonies bloomed riotously between the waters, but rain clouds were beginning to appear in the eastern sky.

Yehonala enjoyed walking here: this was where Tsai-ch'un had been born. Whereas the Forbidden City is a citadel, she thought, vast, mysterious and labyrinthine, the Yuan Ming Yuan is a place of relaxation. It's always such a relief to come here. Last time was early spring when it was still drab, but now nature has worked a miracle and the whole park is a place of amazing beauty.

Below the hillock, the lake known as the Sea of Blessings glistened in brilliant sunshine. From time to time a fish would send widening circles across its surface. She set off towards it, the maid Wen hurrying after her.

'What are you thinking?' Yehonala asked.

'Only that I hope it doesn't rain and spoil his Imperial Majesty's day.'

'It wouldn't spoil my day,' she said. 'I enjoy walking here when it rains.'

'I have seen you visiting gardens in the rain often, Lady,' Wen said cautiously. 'Many times I have seen you picking flowers and gourds in the part of the Forbidden City called The Deep Recesses Among the Plane Trees. You went without an umbrella, while we in your retinue huddled patiently in the cloisters, waiting for you.'

'I never mind rain. It comes as such a relief after the dryness of winter and the dust that blows out of the Gobi. Rain is gentle and brings life. I believe it is very yin.'

They came to the Garden of Eternal Spring and Yehonala looked up at an exotic facade of European stone columns, wondering again at the strange Barbarian minds who had conceived it. They were very yang. A hundred years ago the fantastically powerful emperor, Ch'ien-lung, had brought in Barbarian architects of the Jesuit tribe to add novelty to one of his five pleasure parks. The palaces here were repositories, treasure houses of enormous richness in which Imperial gifts and items that had been presented as tribute were now stored. It was a collection of incalculable value – the concentrated wealth of the world's greatest empire.

She turned her mind away from beauty and instead began to survey the political landscape: Prince Kung wearing his blue travelling robe and General Sang conversing together near the aviary, Su-shun's retinue encamped around the belvedere, the Princes Cheng and Yi nearby, the one leading the other in the direction of the flower garden maze, Mu Yin, Secretary of the Board of War, hovering with other Grand Councillors . . . in a moment they'll be swarming like wasps, she thought with satisfaction. None of them knows that I have any idea about the Outer Barbarian army that's coming to attack us. But they soon will.

Hsien-feng himself was walking the lake's edge with the heir, holding his hand. Nursemaids and eunuchs hovered anxiously nearby. The boy was reluctant, uneasy, as if sensing something. The Emperor was pale and gaunt and unsteady on his feet. He kept scratching at his neck. He had not noticed her arrival, and she decided not to approach him. Instead she glanced at Prince Kung. It was urgent that she speak with him, but vital also that she was not seen to approach him directly. She saw the Lady Niuhuru shaded by a parasol, and set off to greet her.

Niuhuru was an elegant woman. Her smile was beautiful, but her heart far too open. She was wearing jade earrings.

'Yehonala, how good it is to see you again. What a beautiful gown.'

'Thank you, but it is not as lovely as yours. The red and white crane pattern is delightful. And what exquisite earrings.'

'Do you really think so?'

'Of course. They are so smooth and perfect. Little An tells me he is always suspicious of carved jade. He says that carving is there to hide imperfections. There is not a flaw in yours anywhere.'

'Yehonala, you make me feel so happy. How I enjoy your company. We really must take tea together again soon.'

'That would be so nice.'

'Yes.'

'Isn't this wonderful?' She breathed deeply. 'How fragrant

now the flowers are in bloom. Perhaps it would be enjoyable to stroll in this direction?'

She steered Niuhuru along until they were within earshot of Prince Kung. He was holding forth to General Sang and Mu Yin, displaying his superior learning, toying with the Mongol general's ignorance, and testing him with quotes. A dangerous game, because Sang Ko-lin-sen commanded the Peking garrison. Also Su-shun was watching, and he would certainly try to make capital out of any opportunity that arose.

Prince Kung had not noticed Yehonala's approach. He was saying, ' . . . but, General, Sun Tzu told us that the art of war is of vital importance to the state, that war is not necessarily a road either to safety or to ruin.'

She turned to Niuhuru, 'Talk of war seems so out of place in this tranquil garden.'

Niuhuru laughed lightly and Prince Kung turned, acknowledging them.

Sang Ko-lin-sen was stocky and unimaginative, but also a fanatically loyal servant of the Emperor. It was his task to protect the Forbidden City and crush any hint of sedition in the capital or the surrounding province of Chih-li. He said, 'Lady Yehonala. Lady Niuhuru. How can the tranquility of these gardens suffer when two such perfect flowers are in bloom?'

'So many flowers are trodden down by war,' Yehonala said archly. 'I hope the clouds of war are not gathering over our heads.'

Prince Kung was quick to intervene. 'The General and I were discussing the Classics. Specifically that written by Sun Tzu, the title of which is 'The Art of War.' Naturally, we—'

'Required reading for soldiers,' she said, quickly interrupting. 'And all Princes of the Blood.'

She noticed her 'wasps' beginning to swarm, drawn irresistibly by the sight of two Empresses, a Prince of the Blood and the commander of the Imperial bodyguard talking together.

'It seems to me that maintaining large and useless garrisons in all our provincial cities causes the people to be impoverished,' she said, keeping her innocent expression. 'Surely so many so-called troops on the payroll causes prices to go up, and high prices cause the people's substance to be drained away.'

She saw Prince Kung recognize she had been quoting from Sun Tzu, and he was prickled by it. Sang had been thrown into complete confusion. He stared back stonily. Women, no matter what their rank, never made comments about war, or how to conduct it.

'So, tell me, General Sang. Is war coming?'

'Lady, who can predict such a thing? Those decisions are made by Emperors. But consider the scorpion. When he is happy a feeling of affection wells up within him. But when angry his poisoned sting is brought into play. That is the natural law that governs his being.'

She put her hands together daintily. 'Sun Tzu also said, "There is no instance of a country having benefited from prolonged warfare."'

'But Sun Tzu also said that all warfare is based on deception.'

The astonishing remark had been spoken by Su-shun. He had approached stealthily and now looked from face to face as he came up with Prince Cheng and Mu Yin. 'Please excuse us for interrupting a private conversation.'

Prince Kung said coldly, 'What we were discussing was not private in the least.'

Yehonala's gaze switched to Prince Cheng. 'Sun Tzu also said, "If your opponent is of evil temper, seek to irritate him. If he is vain, pretend to be weak so that he grows arrogant."'

Prince Cheng roared his amusement. 'Your knowledge of the Classics does you credit, Lady.'

The Emperor approached and they all turned to him like sunflowers. Close to, his skin was like old parchment, his eyes horribly bloodshot.

'Did I hear raised voices?'

Yehonala's own voice was breathy now. 'Please excuse us, Imperial Majesty. We did not intend to create disharmony in this beautiful place. Su-shun was just talking about . . . war.'

'War?'

Prince Kung carefully avoided Su-shun's eye. 'The feeling is that perhaps your Imperial Majesty might like to dictate a decree to the effect that henceforth, there will be no circumstance under which an Outer Barbarian may be permitted to enter the interior of China.'

Su-shun's reply was a measured rumble. 'This goes against the treaty his Imperial Majesty's ministers have already signed at Tientsin.'

'But not yet ratified.' Prince Kung said. 'We all know that the Treaty of Tientsin was imposed by force. At present we are only bound by the provisions of the previous Treaty of Nanking. By that agreement we must allow Outer Barbarians to travel one day's journey from any of the five Treaty Ports of Canton, Ningpo, Foochow, Amoy and Shanghai. And those who break that law may be expelled.'

'I repeat: the Treaty of Nanking is obsolete,' Su-shun insisted. 'It has been superseded by the new Tientsin Treaty.'

'And I repeat: that treaty has not yet been ratified!'

'A mere formality.'

The cords stuck out on Prince Kung's neck. 'Since that treaty was signed under compulsion, we have a right to consider it null and void.'

Hsien-feng glanced helplessly at Yehonala, and she seized her chance. 'I've looked at the new treaty, Sire, and it seems to me that the issues are quite clear. Prince Kung is quite correct: if we ratify the treaty, we lose everything. By the new treaty we would be forced to open ten more Treaty Ports, and to declare that China was not the centre of the world. We would forever after have to allow foreign envoys to live in our capital, and treat foreign nations as diplomatic equals. There would be no necessity for them to kowtow before you as a sign of submission. In this way the Dragon Throne would be diminished.'

Hsien-feng turned to Su-shun. 'Is all this true?'

'Majesty, the Lady Yehonala has allowed herself to be confused by technicalities. The proposed additional Treaty Ports are all obscure southern towns, places of no importance – with the exception of Nanking and Hankow, which are cities both presently located in rebel-held territory. And what does it matter if Outer Barbarian envoys come to Peking? All along the dynasty has courted the ambassadors of vassal states, Mongols, Tibetans, Annamese, and the envoy of both the Dalai and Panchen Lamas.'

'But they all kowtow before the Dragon Throne,' Prince Kung said.

Su-shun spread his arms. 'Outer Barbarians have inexplicable ways. Certainly they share a superstitious aversion to this normal way of showing respect. The Barbarians of the Flowery Flag Country, for example, will only kneel before gods and women.' Ships from the flowery flag country showed flags striped in red and white, with a blue square in the top corner on which many little white flowers were sewn.

'They kneel before gods and women?' Hsien-feng said, taken with the novelty of the idea. 'How extraordinary!'

'However,' Prince Kung said, 'Su-shun has so far failed to mention the most important part of the new Treaty. It gives free access to the interior to Barbarian religious advocates. These black clothed devils desire to walk the Empire from end to end, spouting repugnant ideas and rousing the Common People to acts of rebellion against you.'

'Majesty, I urge you not to listen to your half-brother. He has become quite hysterical lately.'

Yehonala saw Hsien-feng look to her, and understood that she had no choice now but to support Prince Kung and oppose Su-shun openly. 'It would be a noble and glorious thing, and highly pleasing to the sacred gods and to your ancestors, Sire, if you prevented the Common People from listening to the sacrilegious talk of the black-robed liars.'

Su-shun looked to his brother, Prince Yi, who said, 'Majesty, the Treaty of Tientsin has been agreed. We cannot, without extreme loss of face, go back on it now.'

'Order the exclusion of all Outer Barbarians, Sire.' Yehonala pleaded. 'If not from all of China, then certainly from those areas adjoining the territory of the Taiping rebels. And most especially foreigners must be forbidden to go anywhere near Nanking.'

When Lindley entered Meadows' office, the Consul was at his desk, bearded and bearlike. Captain Strickland was present. The office was heavily furnished and lined with hundreds of books and the place reeked of good cigars.

Meadows, he had found out, possessed an unparalleled knowledge of China. He had studied Chinese in Munich before arriving in Canton nearly twenty years ago. He rose as Lindley came forward, and ushered him to a seat. 'I suppose you think I should offer you my hearty congratulations,' Meadows said as he sat down again.

Lindley returned Meadows' stare, ignoring Strickland. 'Congratulations? What about?'

'About this.' Meadows held up a piece of paper as if it offended him. 'You've proved me wrong. You've got permission to go up river after all.'

Lindley took the paper and read it. The calligraphy showed that it was composed by Provincial Governor Hsueh Huan.

'All you have to do now is decide what you're going to do about it.'

Lindley looked sharply up. 'What do you think I'm going to do? I'm going to charter a river boat right away.'

'If you recall, I asked you last time we met if you'd agree to be Lord Elgin's interpreter. You said you'd think it over.'

'I have thought it over. The answer's no.'

'You'd be doing a great service to your Queen and country.'

'Oh, aye? No deal.'

'I might tell you that that permission you're holding has not been granted through any official intercession by the Consulate. On the contrary.' Meadows acknowledged a knock and the door opened. H. B. Loch appeared, carrying a stack of papers which he put down heavily on Meadows' desk.

'Been told the good news, then, Harry?' he said cheerily.

'Aye.' Suspicions writhed in Lindley's mind. 'Just now.'

'So, we'll be working together after all, eh?'

'What are you talking about?'

Loch's perplexity showed and Lindley's suspicions climaxed. He looked angrily to Meadows. 'Now, you listen to me! I'm bloody well going up the river Yangtze! And that's that!'

Meadows' voice was placating. 'As I was trying to explain to you, I want you to know that I made no contact with Hsueh Huan on your behalf.'

'So? What does that matter? A permission's a permission.'

'You'll note that the Provincial Governor neglects to extend his personal protection to you. Without that – well, it's an advertisement to every pirate and kidnapper and murderer in the Empire to fall on you.'

'I don't believe that for a minute!'

A burly figure of medium height pushed through the half open door. He was bald, bulldog-faced and he wore shirt-sleeves and waistcoat. Strickland got to his feet before being casually signalled to sit down again. The newcomer was Lord Elgin.

'Ah, Mr Lindley,' he said pleasantly, searching the desk. 'I'm very pleased to have you aboard. Consul Meadows tells me that Englishmen who've mastered Mandarin Chinese are as rare as unicorns. Keep up the good work.'

'Scotsmen. And it's Dr Lindley, as a matter of fact.'

Elgin looked to him again momentarily. 'Of course. Of course. Capital. A fellow Scot. Capital.'

'I don't know what Mr Consul Meadows has told you, your lordship, but I'm not going anywhere.'

Elgin rifled through the papers on Meadows' desk, selected some, nodded distractedly and left without another word.

'What the hell's going on?'

Meadows sighed. 'You understand that I have the power to deport you from the Concession – if I decide to.'

Lindley was outraged. 'On what grounds?'

'Any grounds I decide. There are plenty for me to choose from – jeopardizing trade, conspiring with undesirables, creating a menace to the inhabitants of the Concession, fomenting riot among the Chinese . . . need I go on?'

'This is blackmail!'

Meadows smiled blithely. 'Yes. Wicked, isn't it?'

'I won't comply. To hell with you!' He stood up.

Strickland rose too, and edged protectively towards the door. 'Of course you will. You're a British subject, Harry, and your country needs you.'

Meadows said evenly, 'Her Majesty's government requests and requires you to act as interpreter on his Lordship's mission. Sorry, old man.'

'Go to hell!'

'Come along, Lindley.' Loch said. 'See sense. We're here in China for just one thing: trade. Anything – or anyone – jeopardizing that has to be sorted out. We don't want individuals raising the political temperature in Shanghai, and you've been antagonizing the mandarins in the worst possible way. You'll go north with Lord Elgin's party as interpreter. The matter's agreed.'

'Deport me! I bloody dare you!' He put both hands on Meadows' desk and leaned over. 'Because when I get home your name will be all over *The Times*. You can't go around doing just what you like to private individuals. Who the hell do you think you are?'

Meadows turned to Loch, unperturbed. 'Be so good as to fetch in Mr Bowlby, would you please?'

Loch departed.

'Who the hell is Mr Bowlby?'

Meadows ignored the question. 'What I've said goes very largely for your Mr Ward too. He's interfering. He may think he's immune just because he's not a British subject, but if he defies me I'll show him who really runs Shanghai. And that's a promise you can carry back to him.'

'He's not my Mr Ward. I don't give a damn what happens to him. If you ask me, Ward's in league with the rebels. He's a bloody gunrunner who wants his own private army. He can go to hell too!'

Strickland and Meadows exchanged meaningful glances. Then Meadows said, 'Did you say gunrunner? To whom?'

'To the rebels. You must know about that. You know bloody everything! Remember?'

Loch returned with a red-faced man in a tweed coat who Lindley remembered had attended Lord Elgin's reception. Meadows took the man's hand briefly. 'May I introduce Dr Harry Lindley? Mr Thomas Bowlby. You'll both be accompanying his Lordship's mission. Tommy and I go back a long way. He's special correspondent for *The Times*.'

Lindley's eyes narrowed at Meadows. 'You're a bloody bastard. Do you know that?'

'Oh, yes. A bastard doesn't usually get to my age without knowing he is one. And besides, I'm a diplomat. It's my job.'

Lindley marched out of the office without another word. Loch and Bowlby went after him. Meadows turned to Strickland. 'You heard what he said about Ward running guns to the Taipings. I thought you'd warned him.'

'I did.' Concern narrowed Strickland's eyes. 'But it doesn't make any sense. Ward's trying to gather together a pack of desperadoes to fight the Taipings. He'd hardly be wanting to arm them first.'

'He might be. All the better to sell the idea of his Foreign

Arms Corps to the mandarins. You'd better find out what he's up to.'

Strickland closed the door as Loch returned.

Meadows asked, 'How is the good doctor?'

'Spitting blood. But he'll recover.'

'Good.' Meadows looked at Strickland with eyes that were very old. 'I sometimes wonder about this place,' he said. 'Its filth must rub off on a man eventually.'

Strickland stiffened. 'I know what you mean, sir. Johnny Chinaman is a pretty vile creature. Cunning. Deceitful. Wholly given over to crime, gambling and drug taking.'

'I love China,' Meadows said, wishing Strickland was not so stupid. 'I love the Chinese and their culture, their art, their language, their cuisine . . . everything. But, by God, I can't begin to say how much I loathe and despise their filthy Manchu government. It's no way to administer a quarter of the world's population: a semi-divine Emperor, all powerful yet sickly and personally degenerate, closeted in the Forbidden City with two Empresses, one almost a fool, the other anything but a fool. Their heir fourteen years away from majority. Their isolation guarded by an elite army, commanded by fanatical Mongol generals. All access controlled by a vain and fickle Chief Eunuch, jealous of his privileges. All government carried on by a civil service of Byzantine inefficiency, headed by mediaeval mystic scholars, and interfered with by an aristocracy of Princes of the Blood whose factions vie constantly with one another. How can a monstrosity like that possibly take its place in the modern world? It's utterly impossible.'

Strickland's face mottled. 'We ought to ban half those thieving coolies from entering the Concession. As far as I can see, sir, Johnny Chinaman's got absolutely no moral fibre.'

Meadows laughed quietly. 'Shall I tell you something about "Johnny Chinaman", Captain? You've never been out of the Concession, so you can't be expected to know, but you can take it from me that all across the Chinese Empire the wretched people witness scenes of death and torture every day of their lives. Two centuries of Manchu overlordship has made the horror of it quite invisible to them. They are not naturally a callous people, but the ceaseless persecution of their own government has degraded them. They're branded with the shaven-head, which is a mark of slavery. Their human spirit is deliberately smashed up by a system of grinding tyranny. Their lives, their property, everything, is at the mercy of the most ruthless, grasping officials on the planet. And there's not even any appeal to justice. The judges rule only according to the size of the bribe they receive. "Cut the rebel into a thousand pieces," that's their remedy. They torture to death anyone they choose with impunity, they decapitate on suspicion, kill in a hundred cruel ways. And they do all this quite deliberately in order to terrorize their population and thereby make them easier to rule. So, is it any surprise if the ordinary Chinese sometimes seems cunning and deceitful to us?'

'They don't understand Christian ethics, and what's more they don't see why they should try,' Strickland said.

Meadows saw that his words had washed over the man, hardly touching him. He went to stand by the window. 'Since we founded Hong Kong the Chinese have been able to talk freely with "Outer Barbarians". I used to hope they'd learn about our laws and our government. I wanted them to become more and more dissatisfied, until they revolted. I used to think: one day the Chinese people will rise up and do away with it all, and the sun will shine again. But look what's happened? How many tens of millions of Chinese have died out there?' He paused at the unanswerable question, his eyes on the far bank of the river. 'It's all because of us – you know that, don't you? All our fault.'

'I don't see how you can say that, sir.'

'Don't you?' Meadows sat down at his broad mahogany desk and brought out a small poster that had come to him from the Chinese city. It said simply, in Chinese,

JOHN 6:47
Verily, verily, I say unto you, He that believeth on me hath everlasting life.

'One thing's for certain,' he said grimly. 'The Taiping leader, the T'ien Wang, has a great deal to answer for. And so has the Reverend Lindley.'

Fei saw the refugees flooding toward the West Gate of Shanghai's Old City and plunged in among them. A sickness

167

of fear was gripping her stomach. She still felt dazed at the tremendous news that had broken.

Events were moving with ferocious speed now. Since the T'ien Wang had ordered the break out from Nanking, Taiping arms had succeeded magnificently. The advance of the Chung Wang's army along the Yangtze was going better than anyone could have hoped. And had it not been for those incredible victories she would not have been given such an honour.

The interview with the American had yielded unexpected fruit. She had dreaded being turned over to the Governor's men, because that would have meant certain death, but Ward had only wanted to know where he could buy rifles like the ones that had been taken inland. What had really surprised her was that Ward imagined Lindley to be her secret associate.

Why tell him the truth? she thought. But maybe I should have. Lin-li will be in danger now because of me, and that's not something I ever wanted. She saw she was allowing her emotional guard to drop, and warned herself strictly. 'The purpose of remembering is as self-criticism,' she told herself, quoting from her lessons. 'A Taiping solider must recall his or her faults, so they may be corrected. This is the wisdom of the T'ien Wang, the all-wise.'

Thoughts of how she had several times come close to failure made her feel shame. She directed her mind to her first meeting with Lindley and the detailed instructions she had received about his arrival.

She had been ordered to go to Hong Kong and to wait there until the *Chusan* came with the rifles stowed aboard. She was to locate Lindley as soon as he came ashore and shadow him until he left. Nanking thought that rumours about the incoming consignment of guns had reached the ears of the mandarins, but no one knew the extent of their information. They were right to send me to protect the unwitting courier during his stay in Hong Kong. How strange to think that my main task was to deflect any attempt to kill him, yet he knew nothing of this.

Perhaps it's permitted to feel some satisfaction for rescuing the operation and bringing it to a successful end, she thought earnestly. But it's still a sin to be prideful of one's own efforts. Everything that a Taiping does must be selfless and wholly directed towards the building of the Heavenly Kingdom of Great Peace. All else is self-indulgence . . .

The American had been another unexpected turn. Nanking expected us to move the consignment up from Shanghai by river junk, she thought. But once Ward came into the picture what better way was there to get the rifles past the customs post? Why do I upset every plan? Something seems to interfere with the tao whenever I exert my will just lately. I am such a failure. Also, my discipline is appalling. The truth is, I am a worthless person in the sight of God, with no right to call myself Taiping. How can my father have entrusted me with so important a duty?

Thoughts of Lindley caused her to blush. Why did I act like that? What magic spell could have happened between us during our few days together? Whatever it was, it made me feel something I've never felt before. We are in need of a modern steamer almost as much as we are in need of modern rifles. So why did I persuade our people to let Ward and his boat go? I did it because I didn't want Lin-li to be shot.

She thought back to the robbery, and how afterwards she had helped take the precious cargo of rifles on to Nanking. There she had sought out Lin-li's illustrious father and begged him to write a letter ordering his son to stay in Shanghai, to wait for him patiently – however long that took. To her astonishment he had granted her request, and the letter was in the pocket of her coat, next to her heart.

Our Taiping victory is coming, she thought now, exultantly. Perhaps Lin-li will see that now there is no need to go to Nanking, because Nanking is coming to him! So! The American wants Enfield rifles too. He offered me money. How could he imagine that I would betray the Heavenly Kingdom of Great Peace simply to make money for myself? Does he think I don't know what he is planning?

'You'll tell me where to find more Enfield rifles or I'll give you to the taotai,' Ward had told her.

So she had assured him that she could get more Enfields. Then she had given guarantees good enough for him to release her – guarantees that involved Harry Lindley.

Since then, with her own security compromised at the old Taiping house, she had been forced to find a new base of operations. It had not been difficult. There were many

Taiping sympathizers in the city now, and so many new-comers that strange faces were nothing new in any part of the town. Orders from the Heavenly Capital had become contradictory. First she had been recalled to Nanking then, just as she was about to quit Shanghai, a countermand had been issued, telling her to stand by for important information: she was to be briefed for a vital mission. Now that briefing had been delivered, and she had not been able to believe her ears.

I am not worthy, she thought. Truly I am not. But I will do my best to carry out my orders properly this time. If I can help bring forward by one single breath the moment when this filthy Manchurian dynasty comes crashing down my life will not have been spent in vain.

She swam against the tide of wretched humanity filling the road, and pity made her damn the country mandarins for the lies they told against the Taipings. Barefoot peasants dressed in rags and carrying all they owned on their backs, women, children and old folk, had been terrified here, so that now they dogged all the routes they hoped led to safety. The walled city had long ago reached bursting point. Hundreds of thousands had already fled to escape the fighting, and more were coming in every day. These latest arrivals would soon swamp the city's diminishing capacity to feed them. They were camping in huge numbers, in crude shelters pitched on every scrap of wasteland that surrounded the city. Hundreds of thousands, filling the streams and canals they drew water from with their own filth.

As she walked sore-covered beggars called to her pathetically. From their way of speaking she knew they had come from the land around Hangchow. She saw in their faces only exhaustion and hopelessness, empty eyes, toothless mouths crying for food. It was heartbreaking, so she turned her thoughts away yet again, avoiding also her own secret desperation.

She carried on along the bank of the Huang-pu, then turned north towards the foreign concessions. She pushed against dense crowds as she came to cross the bridge over Soochow Creek. Many handbills had been scattered along the way, trampled underfoot and sullied with mud, but their Chinese message had been read, and the promise made.

JOHN 5:24
Verily, verily, I say unto you,
He that heareth my Word,
and believeth on Him that sent me,
hath everlasting Life,
and shall not come into Condemnation;
but is passed from Death unto Life.

A thrill passed through her. With the Chung Wang at
their head our troops are truly invincible, she told herself.
First Soochow, and then Hangchow. Now our glorious army
has occupied Sung-chiang, only sixty li away. The Final
Victory is at hand! Soon we'll take Shanghai, and then we'll
have a port, which means we can communicate with the
outside world. After that the whole of the South will fall
under Taiping control and the T'ien Wang will be able, at
last, to proclaim the true Heavenly Kingdom of Great Peace!

Three days ago she had sent her report about Ward to
Nanking. Spying was a dangerous game near Sung-chiang.
Her man in Ward's camp close to that city had disappeared
a week ago, and no one in the rest of the network knew for
sure what had happened to him. Even so, the report he had
given her days before, and which she had passed on to her
Nanking courier, had contained vital information. It was
now confirmed that General Ward had received a shipment
of silver bullion. The spy's estimate was 50,000 taels. And it
had come from the banker Yang Fang.

Other significant shipments had followed, and in the last
week alone more than twenty covered barges had been seen
navigating the Huang-pu and the system of canals that
converged on the village of Kuang-fu-lin. Tons and tons of
gunpowder, she thought. Boxes of ammunition. And guns.
Almost certainly modern guns. How much easier must it be
for Ward to get supplies than it is for us. There have been
rumours of Minié rifles turning up in Shanghai, Prussian
needle guns stacked on the wharfs at Hong Kong, hundreds
of percussion-cap muskets, vastly more lethal than the obsolete flintlocks and matchlocks that most of our troops possess. There's increased night activity in Ward's stockade.
Recruitment in the British Concession is increasing too, with
all kinds of evil-looking foreigners arriving at a public hall
on the Bund. Ward was definitely present with a small

number of men when imperialist troops attacked Chia-ting and T'ai-ts'ang villages. I believe he is going to launch a major attack soon. If I was him I would storm the most strategic town in the area. And if I was Governor Wu I would order my new weapon to move against Sung-chiang.

With a free hand I could have found out how to intercept all those supplies, she thought. I could have sabotaged his plans and hindered his preparations to the greater glory of the Heavenly Kingdom but instead the Heavenly King himself has honoured me with a far more important mission.

It was a dazzling sign of respect that she had been shown. The last courier to have come from Nanking had delivered a message carrying the personal chop-mark of the T'ien Wang himself. But the responsibility of the task he had given her was awesome. The courier had made the sign of the cross and saluted her formally before he had left. 'Your father told me to inform his daughter that mighty God is with her. He said, this is a mission that can only be given to one who can be trusted absolutely.'

That's true, she thought now, pride and fear mingling nauseously inside her. Because this mission is inescapably a suicide mission.

Ward felt the joy of the moment spoiled by doubts. He sat in the bows of the flat-bottomed boat as it was poled silently through a moonless night towards the walls of Sung-chiang. A heavy Colt Dragoon pistol was holstered at his side and a Sharps buffalo rifle lay on the thwarts beside him. A dozen other figures were crouched at his back, and a dozen other boats followed. The attack was now no more than thirty minutes away and the tension was showing itself in bravado and nervous laughter.

They aren't ready, he thought. I told Governor Wu: they aren't damned-well trained up to this kind of work yet. They don't have the discipline yet to conquer their own fear.

'Will you take a little courage, Colonel?'

Henry Burgevine wore two bandoleers of shells crossed over his jacket. He passed a bottle forward.

'No thanks.'

'Jesus, this place stinks like the devil's ass-hole.' Burgevine took another slug and passed the bottle back the way it had come.

'Tell them to go easy on that stuff,' Ward whispered. 'And keep the noise down. We don't want to wake the whole district.'

The hubbub subsided, but as the boats moved along the reed-choked canal it began to grow again. He knew the men were feeling their fear now. There were at least a dozen nationalities – Americans, English, Irish, Scots, Prussians, French, Italians, Swiss, Greeks . . . So far they had learned how to march and fire modern guns, and they had showed they could follow orders on a parade ground. They were each armed to the teeth, but Ward knew he had made a mistake listening to Governor Wu.

He watched the ramparts of Sung-chiang loom larger and struggled to overcome his suspicions. Governor Wu had told him, 'You have cost us much money. It is now time for you to show your worth.'

'Sir, we need a little longer to prepare. And I need to buy more equipment.'

But Wu had insisted. 'We pay – now you fight!'

And so Ward had agreed to lead the Foreign Arms Corps out in support of the Imperial Green Standard troops under General Li. The General had ousted the few long-hair skirmishers who had taken control of the villages of Chia-ting and T'ai-ts'ang, and Ward's men had returned to camp after the two easy victories in a mood of swaggering boastfulness. Only Ward seemed to remember that his men had seen none of the fighting. A few days after the Green Standard's own garrison town had fallen to a unit of the main Taiping army. The Chinese regulars had fled in disarray.

The boat passed through another patch of bad air, raising comments from the men. The stench of the canals in this area was indescribable.

'Here's to pig shit and good luck,' Burgevine grumbled, swigging again at the liquor bottle.

We'd better have good luck tonight, Ward thought. Without it we'll catch hell, and that's a fact.

Sung-chiang was only twenty miles from Shanghai, and the taking of it – if they could take it – would break every one of Sun Tzu's sacred rules of warfare. They had not brought siege equipment, because they did not possess any. Just one ladder, and no artillery. The waterlogged land did not allow trenches or mines because all diggings filled with water before the spade could leave the hole. He had not been allowed time to carry out adequate reconnaissance. He had only learned yesterday what their objective was going to be. The only advantage left to them was surprise.

As the boat nudged the shore Ward jumped out, and crouched in the reeds that hid his force from the town walls. Burgevine shoved a peg into the wet earth and tethered the boat as the others stumbled onto the bank. Behind, the other boats were disembarking too. He heard a bottle smash and an oath go up.

'Keep it quiet,' Ward hissed, going among them. He could smell the stink of liquor rise off them. The tall grass shimmered and rustled as they fell amongst it. Ward's eye passed along Sung-chiang's ancient walls. They were stone, twenty feet high and a mile long on each side. At the centre of each side was a gate, with stout timber doors. Exposed causeways bridged a wide, silted moat, and could be raked with fire. The plan depended on a small number of men swimming the moat, scaling the wall and opening the gate for the rest who were waiting to rush the causeway as soon as its covering fire could be interrupted.

'Advance party ready?' Ward asked in a whisper.

The men had wrapped their rifles in sailcloth and water-proofed the chambers of their revolvers by packing them with grease. There were to be two parties of five. He would lead the first over the wall, then Burgevine's party would shift the ladder to the other side of the gate and scale the walls from there. He called them off, 'Blake?'

'Here.'

'Wellman?'

'Here.'

'Rifel?'

'Ja.'

'Not so loud! Brossard? Eisner? Andersen ... Where's Andersen? You there – go find Andersen! Quinlan? Forrest?'

Forrest appeared with another man. They were dragging a dead man between them.

'What the hell happened to him?'

'Never got out of the boat, Colonel. Son of a bitch is starfish drunk.'

They released Andersen, who fell heavily onto his face. He groaned. Someone started laughing.

'Shut that man up!' Ward whispered hoarsely. He stared around in the gloom. 'I need another volunteer.'

Burgevine's gritty voice rumbled, 'Come on, boys! Two hundred dollars! What's the matter with you?'

Ward heard a cynical comment. He ignored it, tried to check his watch but couldn't make out the hands against the dial. They were going to have to be across the moat by moonrise. The moat was many dozens of yards wide and of unknown depth.

'Mr Forrest, you're in charge of the main body. Keep a look out for us. As soon as you see the second party, put the ladder in place. Get going. Whatever happens make sure you're all within sprinting distance of the foot of those gates when we open them.'

'Yes, sir!'

They slid the scaling ladder forward and ran crouching, rifles slung, through the tall grass. Three times before they reached the moat they encountered unexpected boggy cuts into which they sank knee-deep. The noise of their feet churning and sucking in the mud sounded dangerously loud. The smell they stirred up was sickening.

'Satan's shit! Why's it stink so evil?' a voice asked. It was Quinlan.

Ward said nothing. He knew that some of the richest men in China ran night soil empires, franchises that collected every last scrap of town dung to sell on to farmers to manure their fields. Also the Chinese lived mainly on pigs, and the slurry of ten thousand pigsties discharged into every canal. The filth had been collecting here for thirty centuries.

Another voice said, 'How deep is it, Colonel?'

'There's no way of knowing. Most of the watercourses are silted up. They're badly maintained, so with luck we'll be able to wade across.'

'With luck?'

'Come on, boys. It's time to earn our bread.'

He slid into the water. It was thick and stagnant and came up to his waist. A light mist curled on the surface. He felt the water penetrate his pants and suddenly rob his skin of body heat.

'By Jesus, my fucking scrotum,' he heard Quinlan mutter, and a man beside him giggled.

Ward waded on. The bottom slime was ankle-deep. The

others followed, gasping and cursing softly, defenceless as they held their guns up out of the water and pushed the floating ladder out beyond the protection of the reeds.

What the hell am I doing here? he asked himself. This is not how it's supposed to be. War's supposed to be glorious. Well, I guess you always wanted to put yourself to the test, and this is where it's got you. You'll soon know what the all-conquering Taipings are like in a real fight.

Fifty yards ahead the earthworks towered indistinctly against the lighter sky. The water reached to Ward's chest now as they approached the middle of the moat. The surface was covered in stinking scum, and he wondered if anything deadly lived in the blackness. There was a species of crocodile that lived on the Yangtze, but he had never seen one. He began to pray that the water would get no deeper. Then, incredibly, a bright flash illuminated the walls like lightning. A split second later the report of a musket shattered the silence.

Ward stared through blinded eyes, the horror seizing him. The men pushing the ladder froze. When they looked to him he had already realized that the shot had come from behind – from his own men.

'Back!' he hissed, turning. 'Back! Quickly!'

He heard shouts coming from Sung-chiang. Sentries on the walls began to call challenges into the night. Their feet pounded along the walkways. Ward felt as if he was trapped in a nightmare. Time began to run slow. Pushing back to shore was like wading through molasses. The others let go the ladder. They dropped their weapons and began to swim for it.

'Keep wading!' he called out to them, knowing their splashing would attract fire.

The first shots peppered the water around him. Muzzle flashes lit the oily water and reed-fringed shore. The reverberating gunfire was followed by shouting and the barking of dogs, then another volley spattered around them.

Ward continued to push the scaling ladder unflinchingly as the musket balls threw up plumes of water close by him. If they have just one Enfield rifle up there, I'm a dead man, he thought, setting his mind against the terror. Now surprise is lost why aren't Forrest's men putting up covering fire for us? God damn you, man, what's the matter with you?

As the lead swimmer crashed into the reeds and began to haul himself up onto the bank, an answering fire came at last from his own men. Burgevine turned in the shallow water, then plunged back to help him. 'Come on, Colonel. Leave the fucking ladder!' he shouted, but then helped Ward haul it out and carry it away. All the others, except Quinlan, had not even tried to help. Ahead a hail of gunfire had begun to blaze into the night from a line maybe fifty yards away. Shot was singing close overhead.

'For Christ's sake!' Ward roared at them, his temper breaking at last. 'What the hell are you doing? Cease fire! D'you hear me? You're just wasting ammunition! Cease fire!'

Rage surged through him, rage fuelled by shame. The attack was turning into an unqualified disaster. His unstoppable army had shown itself to be a bunch of circus clowns. When news of what had happened reached Shanghai he would become a laughing stock.

'Where are those sons of bitches?' he shouted, meaning the men who had run for it. 'Jesus Christ!'

When they got close he saw Forrest running among them throwing their rifles out of their hands and shouting for them to cease fire.

'What happened?' Ward demanded, shaking.

'Some bastard fired,' Quinlan muttered.

'Which man?'

Forrest's face was a mask. 'Colonel, I didn't see.'

'Forrest! Which man?'

'I don't know!'

Ward strode along the line, roaring at them, 'Which man? Which man fired?'

There was silence as he put his fury in one face after another, demanding to know who it was who had almost caused his death. Then he drew his Colt and cocked the hammer.

'So help me, God, I'll blast the lot of you if you don't tell me who it was fired that shot!' He grabbed the nearest man and lifted him off his feet.

'I don't know, Colonel! It wasn't me. I seen nothing!'

He put the weapon to the man's forehead, saw the whites of his eyes huge. A terrible moment passed. The man was gagging on his own fear. It seemed that after all he was telling the truth. Some of Ward's anger left him. He threw the man down and strode away towards the boats.

Burgevine watched him go then turned to Forrest. 'Come on, Ed. Let's get these boys out of here.'

BOOK III

Imperial guardsmen had surrounded the central pavilion of Ten Thousand Years Hill. They were stationed every three paces along the steep pathways that snaked toward the summit, lighting the way with flares. The south side of the gigantic artificial mound was a magical garden, set with flowering trees and fantastically shaped rocks imported from all parts of the Empire. Deer wandered among the outcrops. Birds chorused in the dawn. What better place than this, Prince Kung thought, to view a summer sunrise?

The approach had been arduous, the steps slicked with a heavy dew, so that the half-naked palanquin bearers panted and steamed now as they waited. A hundred maids and eunuchs hovered in attendance as the awesome figure of Hsien-feng got down from his palanquin in the last moments before the world turned into light.

The Emperor, otherworldly as a lobster in his finery and just as ponderous, crossed the three paces from his palanquin to a throne that had been placed in the dead centre of the pavilion. Eunuchs of the Person steadied him as he sat. His headdress shivered and the long cones that protected his fingernails glittered like daggers as his robes were arranged about him. A line of Chief Secretaries and Grand Councillors waited and watched as his pale face surveyed the mist-wrapped city below.

'Why do the Common People flee our capital in this seventh moon of the "Keng Shen" year?' he asked, his voice small like a child's.

Su-shun took it upon himself to answer. 'Imperial Majesty, there is no cause for concern. The Common People are merely spreading hearsay one to another.'

'What hearsay?'

'They are frightened for no reason, Imperial Majesty.

179

Periodically the Common People will whip themselves into a panic, but their panic soon subsides by itself.'

Prince Kung monitored the conversation closely. Hsien-feng had been sucking the opium pipe all night. The time to attempt explanations was past, but it was still possible to use the audience to rip at Su-shun.

'What the President of the Board of Revenue says is not quite true,' Prince Kung said.

Hsien-feng turned fractionally. 'Why do you say that?'

'The people are hungry, Sire. They are saying that a fire-breathing dragon has appeared at the mouth of the Peiho river and gobbled up all their food.'

'A fire-breathing dragon? Can that be true? How I would love to see such a marvel.'

He flashed Su-shun a dagger glance. 'That is what the Common People imagine when they see a Barbarian iron ship, Sire.'

Hsien-feng's eyelids drooped. He murmured, 'How can it be that iron floats on water? Iron ships must be evil things, inspired by devils and driven by magic.' He opened his eyes again slowly, his mind benumbed. 'Even so, the Common People must not leave Peking.'

Prince Kung bowed his head, knowing there was no way to prevent the bleeding away of the population from either the Inner or the Outer cities. Naturally Peking is in panic, he thought. Because this fire-breathing dragon wants to kill. When the British first tried to force their envoy past the Taku Forts our guns caused them to retire. Now they've sent a prideful ultimatum demanding an apology, just as Yehon-ala predicted they would. But that's not all. They've claimed a huge payment for the damage done to their dignity. They have also demanded that we ratify the Treaty of Tientsin. If we do not comply immediately they say they will land troops and march on Peking.

Now Prince Kung showed his frustration. 'This matter is urgent, Sire. A Barbarian army is coming to force open our door. Once that door is opened I believe it will never be possible to close it again.'

'Perhaps we will not be able to defend ourselves even though the Son of Heaven orders it?' Su-shun said. 'We must negotiate.'

'Sire, we must throw our entire force at that Barbarian army and destroy it.'

Hsien-feng's nail-protectors glinted. 'What if their magical weapons should prove too ingenious?'

'Well said, Majesty,' Su-shun said smoothly. 'We must delay them with words.'

Prince Kung turned on him. 'What does the President of the Board of Revenue know about Outer Barbarians? We must oppose them utterly. We should rather die than swallow a pail of leeches. Don't you see that's what they are? We will be sucked dry from the inside.'

'With respect, Majesty, none of us wants Outer Barbarians here. We differ only in our view as to which is the best means of preventing it. Should we try to fight? Or should we rely on persuasion?' He turned to Mu Yin. 'Prince Kung doesn't want us to try to come to terms with the Barbarians. But why is that? Perhaps because he thinks he knows best how to rule the Empire better than the Son of Heaven?'

'Sire, I oppose Su-shun's plan because the payment the Barbarians have demanded is more than our treasury contains. Silver will have to be borrowed. Silver from Su-shun's own private fortune. And that will further establish his power over you!'

The silence that followed the outburst was intense. Su-shun let it linger, then struck back. 'Isn't the truth that the Lady Yehonala has filled your head with lies against me?'

Prince Kung turned to his half-brother in direct appeal. 'The Lady Yehonala is convinced that if ever the Middle Kingdom was stupid enough to accept "equal nation status" with a Barbarian tribe the Common People and the leaders of all tributary states would regard that as absolute proof that the Emperor had lost the Mandate of Heaven. She believes that in those circumstances the dynasty would certainly fall.'

'Not so,' Su-shun said. 'Dealing with the Barbarians on their own terms is a good idea. It will lead to more trade. Trade is all they want anyway.'

'Therefore more squeeze, and further enrichment for you and those you control!' Prince Kung felt his hatred of the President of the Board of Revenue flame brilliantly. 'Sire, make no mistake: if Barbarians come before the Dragon Throne and refuse to kowtow you will be forced to abdicate.'

Prince Kung saw that the Emperor had ceased listening and he disengaged. The sun rose up, blistering the eastern horizon, ready to burn off the heavy dew. Today, he thought, it is going to be unbearably hot.

As the heat of the morning continued to mount huge clouds sealed in the sky. Beihai Lake became a shimmering mass of lotuses, a profusion of leaves and gorgeous pink chalices, now fully opened to the day. Dragonflies as startlingly coloured as the silk threads of her gown darted across the surface as five flat-bottomed gondolas stood on the water. In one of them the heir and the two Empresses sat amid the perfume of the newly opened buds, accompanied by twenty maids and eunuchs. They had just witnessed a miracle.

Niuhuru said, 'It's glorious to see the lotus flowers open. Even the fish are happy today. Look how they make circles of silver.'

Yehonala noticed two rare white blossoms among the pink. She turned to An Te-hai. 'Little An, tell the boatman to take up his pole and steer us to the white blossoms. Before we take breakfast I will place them in the vase on Kuan Yin's altar.'

Niuhuru breathed the lotus perfume. 'You are right, Yehonala. Only the Goddess of Compassion should have such rare beauty as this for an offering.'

Suddenly the green carpet close to the boat exploded. A near-naked man burst upwards and thrashed through the water until he was only a spear-length away. He gasped, dived and resurfaced, then horrifyingly he hauled himself up across the prow of the boat. A long, curved knife was in his hand, and he began bellowing and started to hack frenziedly at those near him.

For a moment no one else moved. Then Yehonala grabbed the heir and pushed him down, falling across him and throwing up her arms to protect herself. The knife flashed, and she heard the tear of silk and flesh. Someone groaned. She saw An Te-hai watching, still paralyzed in the prow of the boat. Then a dozen arrows flew from the guard boats that flanked them. The attacker collapsed, transfixed and writhing in agony beside his victims.

Yehonala hugged her son, and he clung to her, under-standing nothing. Maids and eunuchs began screaming.

Shouts came from the guard boats. She heard An Te-hai's high-pitched voice yelling. 'Don't kill him! Don't kill him!' Then one of the guard boats slammed across them and three White Banner guards leapt in, sending bloody water swilling in the bottom of the gondola. They smothered the attacker, pinning him down. Then Jung-lu pushed his way through to her. His eyes were blood-red. 'Tsai-ch'un! Where is he? Is he hurt?'

Yehonala grasped Jung-lu's sleeve, wanting to pull herself to him. Then shock began to beat through her, making her shake. 'Get away! The heir is unharmed.'

'Show him to me!'

'Get away from him!'

She stared at the unreal scene. Niuhuru was vomiting. All around was whimpering hysteria. Maids, some wounded and some untouched, turned white faces up at Jung-lu as he stepped to the centre of the drifting boat and stood over the attacker. He thrust the guards aside and hauled up the arrow-pierced torso by a shaft bedded deep in its breastbone.

He knew a corpse when he saw one. All spirit was gone from it, and he let it fall. 'Heads will roll for this!' he shouted, his anger boundless as his eyes sought the men whose duty it had been to check the lake before the Empress and the heir arrived.

Yehonala heard the strain in Jung-lu's voice and knew that he understood perfectly. The assassination may have failed, but it had succeeded in baring his own neck for the sword.

The procession of servants and eunuchs wound through the Forbidden City, heading for the audience being held in the Hall of Heavenly Purity.

Yehonala spoke to Jung-lu through the curtains of her palanquin as he walked beside it. 'Who was he?'

'A gardener. A man addicted to gambling and playing wei-chi. We found a hollowed-out cane floating in the water. We think he used it to breathe. My guards checked the lake thoroughly. The assassin must have remained submerged for a very long time.'

Her jangling nerves threw into her mind a picture of the tormented slaves who had been forced under the ice of Kunming Lake so long ago. 'Who put him up to it?'

'No one knows.'

'Someone does.'

'My people are trying to discover the whereabouts of his family.'

'It may already be too late. Don't leave my side today.'

'I won't.' She heard the assurance in his voice, incredible under the circumstances.

'There will be a clamour for your head today. I will resist it.'

'Will you be able to?'

'Yes. For the moment.'

'I would rather die like a warrior than submit like a dog.'

'Nothing is settled. This city is no longer the domain of Heaven. The dragon that lies under Ten Thousand Years Hill has begun to stir. Use your people to find out about those who are behind the would-be assassin.'

An Te-hai, she thought. I will question him later about who was responsible for suggesting Jung-lu be attached to the Imperial Bodyguard. Also I must speak with Prince Kung as soon as possible.

As the head of her retinue approached the Gate of Heavenly Purity she heard a commotion. She looked out of the palanquin and saw with sudden stomach-freezing dread that the doors had not swung open for her. She motioned to Jung-lu to take charge.

He drew his sword and hammered on the great scarlet doors with his sword hilt. When no one appeared, he strode to one of the great man-sized bronze urns that stood nearby and began striking it like a gong.

The doors were opened just wide enough for one man to stand in the gap. Yehonala dismounted her palanquin and approached him. He was a captain of the Imperial guard. At his back was a column of White Banner troops, filling the thoroughfare inside. She said, 'Why is the gate shut?'

'Because, your Imperial Highness, the Grand Council is in session.'

'I know. I am invited to attend. Stand aside.'

'On the contrary, your Imperial Highness. I have express orders that you are not to be admitted.'

'Orders from whom?'

'His Imperial Majesty, the Son of Heaven.'

'The Emperor? That can't be!'

'These orders are written in the vermilion, your Imperial Highness.'

'It cannot be!' The earth fell away beneath her. 'Let me see!'

The guard captain had anticipated the demand and produced his copy, handing it over. 'You will see that everything is in order, your Imperial Highness.'

She took the paper with trembling fingers, her mind racing. 'What is this nonsense? A new law excluding women of the Yehe clan from audiences? But that's ridiculous!'

'Apparently, it is an ancient law, your Imperial Highness.'

'But I am the Empress of the Western Palace. The mother of the heir. I have never been excluded in the past.'

'The law is the law. I am only doing my duty.'

She imposed discipline on herself. 'Yes. Of course.'

The guard captain withdrew. She tried to stay him, but still the tall doors slammed shut. She stared at them for a moment, her anger contained by a mind-filling fear. The array of fist-sized golden studs – nine rows of nine – glowered down, mocking her.

What are they doing in there? her mind screamed. Without access to my husband or to the Council chamber how can I fight my enemies? Is this the palace coup I've dreaded for so long? Has Su-shun made his move today? Is Prince Kung able to hold them? Are we all already as good as dead?

There, before the Gate of Heavenly Purity, before the gaze of her entire waiting retinue, she closed her eyes and fought to drain herself of emotion, to blank her mind and so allow herself to feel the subtle currents of the tao.

There is still hope, she thought, courage rising in her. The Barbarians are coming. The Emperor must stay, or he must flee. Which will he do? That is the only question now. Feel the tao and believe you will see the way! Dimly she became aware of a voice shouting.

'Master An! Master An!' The young eunuch caught his breath as if he had just run all the way from the main gate. He prostrated himself, and directed his excited words to An. 'Master An, the news is wonderful!'

An turned, his face ashen. 'What? What did you say?'

The young eunuch stared, suddenly aware that he had burst in on a moment of incredible tension. 'Black Jade,' he said, his voice tailing off. 'Black Jade has just given birth!'

'Black Jade?' An said, as if waking from a dream. 'Who is Black Jade?'

Despite her shock, Yehonala saw that An was genuinely at a loss. She also saw the way Jung-lu looked murderously at the young eunuch, suspecting trickery.

'Little An,' she said, redoubling her efforts to recover her composure. 'Black Jade is one of my favourite bitches.'

'Wha—?' An turned on the young eunuch, his eyes full of unreasoning fury. 'You will be whipped for this outrage!'

Yehonala lifted her fan, stopping him in his tracks. 'You know I've always liked dogs, Master An. You know that I always visit the Imperial kennels whenever I can obtain His Imperial Majesty's permission. This servant did well to bring news promptly.' She turned to the young eunuch. 'How many puppies?'

'Four, Imperial Highness!'

'Since we are already entrained we will go there now. An Te-hai, assemble a retinue appropriate to travel to the Summer Palace.'

Inside the Hall of Heavenly Purity the audience was in session. A dozen Grand Councillors were in attendance. Prince Kung was fighting a desperate rear-guard action to keep himself and his policies alive.

'Imperial Majesty, it is our belief that you should consider reopening the Imperial hunting lodge at Jehol,' Su-shun said.

Jehol was a hill resort five hundred li north-east of Peking. It lay far beyond the Great Wall, in Manchuria. In the glory days of the Manchu line the emperors had spent their summers there, hunting and sporting far away from the capital's oppressive heat. But forty years ago Hsien-feng's forebear, the Chia-ch'ing Emperor, had been killed there, and since that time all the palaces and temples of Jehol had stood empty.

Prince Kung had anticipated Su-shun's move and parried it. 'Don't forget, Sire, that it was at Jehol where our most revered grandfather was blasted to death by a bolt of lightning. The place is haunted by evil spectres. Our father would never go there.'

'We also believe Jehol to be an inauspicious place,' Hsien-feng murmured.

One of the Princes of the Blood lent his support to Su-shun. 'This would be an excellent opportunity for his Imperial Majesty to renew links with his dynastic homeland. And there are the benefits of taking pure country air.'

'Let us not forget the approach of the Barbarian army,' another prince said.

The Emperor shifted his weight. He seemed barely able to sit upright, like a man groggy with drink. 'But I don't like Jehol.'

'Majesty, the local people are our own Manchu cousins, the descendants of our own illustrious ancestors. And besides, the Imperial establishment is very well fortified.' Su-shun smiled.

Prince Kung said. 'Sire, what fortress could be greater than that of Peking?'

'And let us not forget that a Barbarian army is marching on Peking,' the Prince of the Blood who had spoken earlier said. 'They say it is a most . . . *fearsome* army.'

Hsien-feng's eyes slid to the prince. 'Have we not been insulted enough?' he asked irritably. 'Have we not been treated with contempt enough? Now the dragon will stand up. And those who have come to despoil us will return where they properly belong, to their own lands, and leave us in peace.'

The Prince of the Blood looked about helplessly. Then the Censor, Tang Yuan-chun, upright and incorruptible, spoke. 'Sire, there is a saying that a really good sword remains in its scabbard. If these Barbarian weapons are as powerful as everyone says they are, perhaps they will not use them.'

'Who knows what will happen with Barbarians?' Su-shun said, roughly dismissing the Censor's opinion. 'From what I hear they think about the world in a completely different way to us. Why risk it? It's best to withdraw. Isn't that so, Wu-chia?'

The Forbidden City's chief Taoist priest bowed his head. 'Everything will come out right if people will only do nothing and instead tune their minds to the tao.'

Hsien-feng turned listlessly to face Lo-han, the Buddhist abbot. 'And what do you say?'

'I say it is better to stop short than to fill to the brim. Over-sharpen the blade, and the edge will soon become blunt. Amass a store of gold and jade, and no one can

187

protect it. Claim wealth and titles, and disaster will follow. Retire when the work is done. This is the Way of Heaven.'

The Emperor was in torment. He shouted, 'But-what-shall-l-do?'

The howl rang in the rafters, then silence congealed again. The Censor said, 'Your father, whose reign name was "Glory of Great Principle", never lost faith in the wisdom of the great sages. Confucius taught that everyone – everyone, including Emperors – must learn what role he is expected to play in society and live accordingly.'

'But do I stay? Or do I go? Which?' Hsien-feng looked around as if he was seeing the chamber for the first time. 'Where is Yehonala?'

Su-shun flashed a glance at Prince Kung who said, 'She is not here, Majesty.'

'Not here?'

'The law says that women of Yehe blood may not attend the Emperor.'

There was another appalled silence in which the Emperor seemed to collapse inside himself, but then he stared defiantly. 'I don't care about the law. I don't care what Confucius said. I don't respect any of it. I wipe my backside on it!'

Prince Kung's disdain was ice cold. He's talking like a foul, drunken peasant, he thought. But he's not a foul, drunken peasant, he's the Emperor of China, and Su-shun has done this to him.

Su-shun said, 'Look how this unseemly dispute has upset you, Majesty. Why not let it be known that the Court will remove north for a brief while? Then we can all call this tiresome audience to a close.'

Hsien-feng tossed his head, determined now to be fickle. 'I said I don't like Jehol. Do we not possess the wisdom of Sun Tzu? Our brave soldiers will fight the Barbarians, and they will wither away like autumn leaves. Respect this!'

With that Hsien-feng gave the signal to be helped to his feet. He staggered up, surrounded by Eunuchs of the Person and left the hall.

Su-shun's face wore a half-smile. He said, 'He'll go. Maybe not today, but he'll go. You can be sure of that.'

The Prince could not resist a formal declaration of war. 'You are a very stupid man, Su-shun.'

'Yes. And you're an isolated man. And a scared man too. Aren't you?'

Then Su-shun smiled again, and was gone.

Two hundred eunuchs and Bordered Blue Banner guards and ladies in waiting were in the retinue that left the Gate of Military Genius and crossed the moat bridge. It was the biggest retinue that could be assembled. The kennels were on the north-eastern side of Ten Thousand Years Hill, and as the procession passed the south-eastern corner of the precinct Yehonala called them to halt.

The palanquin creaked to the ground, and she led Tsai-ch'un out by the hand. The shock of having the doors of the Council Chamber shut in her face had not yet left her system. Echoes of fear still beat through her, but anger was slowly replacing the hollowness, and a hunger for vengeance against those who had tried to murder her son was burning up in her heart. She knelt beside him and made him look up at a carob tree as the entire retinue gathered around them.

'Look there, my son!' she told him, but really telling them all. 'This is the tree from which Ch'ung-chen, the last emperor of the Ming dynasty, hanged himself over two hundred years ago. No dynasty in history has a better right to rule than ours. We Manchu had no intention of taking over when China was left in chaos at the end of Ch'ung-chen's reign. It would have been the easiest thing in the world for Manchu armies to have overrun Peking then, but they were never ordered to do so. We did not destroy the Ming as many liars try to assert. No! Peking was invaded by the Chinese bandit Li Tzu-ch'eng, and that's the reason Ch'ung-chen hanged himself.

'According to the histories the last Ming Emperor came by the same route we have taken today. He came with a small escort of horsemen and was met here by a eunuch who said that for an Emperor to run away was more shameful than death, so the Emperor returned to the Forbidden City. There he told his wife, the Empress, to strangle herself and his three sons to commit suicide. Then he came back to the place where his cowardice had been recognized and corrected. He took off his boots and hat and hanged himself.

When the eunuch saw the body swinging from this tree he was satisfied and committed suicide also.

'After that, Warlord Li ravaged the city without mercy, until in desperation the Pekingese asked us – us, the Manchu – to drive him away. And we responded. The Chinese came out to welcome us into their ransacked city. They invited us to rule, for they could no longer rule themselves. So it was that we killed the Warlord Li and exterminated the rest of those violent bandits who scourged the land.

'My son, the Chinese invited us here. They praised us when we made a study of their sacred rituals. We Manchu rule China by right, and anyone who says that we should go back beyond the Wall again speaks treason!'

She took her son up in her arms and climbed back into the palanquin, ordering the procession to move off again. Su-shun would soon learn about her speech. He would know that she had stated her position unmistakably in public, that despite his efforts to prevent her, the Lady Yehonala had found a way of advocating that Hsien-feng should stay and fight.

When they came to the kennels she called An Te-hai to her and said, 'Today I discovered two white lotus blooms growing on Beihai Lake. It was my order that they be placed upon the altar of the Goddess of Mercy, Kuan Yin.'

'I'll see to it personally, Lady,' An said, still awed by the passion of her speech.

'No. I want them placed upon the altar of Kuan Ti.'

'Kuan Ti? The God of War?'

'The God of War,' she echoed. 'And also the God of Justice.'

Fei looked along Yan'an Street, her heart beating loud in her head. In a moment she would see the great, white frontage of the European-style house – those tall windows, so open to the street now that the opium boards had been taken down, the garden free for public inspection, the wide entrance hall into which she had once climbed through the window.

He had been so angry with her that day. He had truly cared for her.

I've tried to tell myself that I slept with him only for the sake of my Taiping duty, she thought remorsefully. I wanted to believe I was binding him close to me the better to control him for our cause.

But that was never the case, and God has not let me believe such a self-made lie. The truth is I wanted Lin-li for myself, and I gave in to my own selfish desire. I always wondered what foreigners meant by 'falling in love', and that made my discipline crumble so that I jeopardized everything.

She thought back to Nanking and the way she had gone on knees, elbows and forehead before Lin-li's illustrious father, pressing the five parts of her body to the floor like a peasant prostrating before an emperor. She had begged him and begged him to order his son to stay in Shanghai, and not to waste his life needlessly.

It is the least I could do for him, she thought, taking the letter from her pocket. The spectre of pain and death that haunted her made her turn her face away. Shame burned in her, and she knew she could not endure seeing his eyes reprove her.

Instead she knelt, seeing his face only in her mind's eye. 'I'm sorry Lin-li,' she said softly, putting her hands together. 'Please forgive me. As God is my witness, I hope with all my heart that we'll be able to meet again one day in heaven.'

She took the silk ribbon tie from the letter, slid it under the door and then turned away, tears in her eyes. As she made her way back towards Chin-ling Road she felt leaden in spirit. On the corner sullen porters loitered, squatting by the gutters, or resting by carts that were loaded high with sacks. They watched her with superior, knowing glances. Perhaps they remembered her from before, when she—

Suddenly hands seized her and pushed her to the ground. A knee was pressed into her back, making her gasp with pain. Fear exploded inside her. There were three men holding her down. One of them, she knew, had been loitering on the corner, but he was no idle porter. He searched her and found her knife.

They bound her arms then pulled her up. Pain lanced through her shoulders and she grimaced. Passers-by glanced her way but did nothing. All Chinese had learned to ignore summary arrests, to look straight past the salutary beheadings that splashed the street corners with blood from time to time. Fei knew that neither shouting nor struggling would do any good. Her captors were pleased to have found her and they were taking no chances. As they pulled her along half her mind was blind with terror, the other half popping with rage at her own stupidity. She had had to visit Lindley's house, there was no question of that – even if it risked jeopardizing her mission. But once again she had allowed private feelings to blind her. She had underestimated the size of the risk, let herself believe that they would not see her, or if they saw her, that they would not recognize her.

Your mission! she screamed to herself. You've ruined your mission! Failed before you even began!

Of course the governor's men were watching Lindley's house night and day. And of course this had nothing to do with her being recognized. They would have arrested any Chinese who visited. How could she have imagined otherwise?

Ward lay in the perfumed bed, drowsing, A hundred thoughts weltered in his mind like the distant sound of battle, just below his threshold of consciousness. All else was warmth and comfort.

Annie Phillips was seated at the window, combing out her long hair, her back towards him. She was naked and for a while the curve of her body fascinated Ward's half-lidded eyes. He twitched awake, and sat up.

'What are you doing here?'

She turned to him. 'I just got up.'

He thought back, desperately trying to recall the previous evening, crawling with disgust: Annie was a prostitute, it was worse than if she had been his sister. Then he remembered. He had been full of rage over the fiasco at Sung-chiang and when that had blown itself out he had felt drained, physically and emotionally. He had come back to the Grand Hotel and had gotten drunk. He thought he had gone to bed alone. Annie must have climbed in beside him.

'Nothing happened,' she said as if reading his mind. 'I was tired and wanted to be near somebody. And I missed you.'

'Missed me?' His head pulsed with pain. 'Annie, since when did you ever want for male company?'

She faced him brazenly, bare-breasted, hair fluffed with static. 'All right, I'm a slut. But a slut needs her friends more than most.'

'You're crazy, you know that? What you're doing is going to get you killed.'

She laughed privately. 'That's great, coming from you.'

'A bullet's quick. You know what syphilis does to people? There's no cure for it, you know.'

'We're all dead in the long run. Did you mean what you said about leaving Shanghai?'

He massaged the stiffness from his neck. He saw that his gold-plated .41 calibre Derringer lay on the bedside table. 'Me? Leaving Shanghai? What gave you that dumb idea?'

'Last night you said you'd thought about going back to the States. That a war was brewing up there.'

'Last night I was drunk. Get out of here, will you?'

She came to him and tried to reach out for him, but he took her by the wrists and pushed her away.

'Get dressed,' he said, aware of how curt he sounded now, but not caring. 'Get dressed and go.'

She did as she was told. Silently. Without demur or accusation. When she had gone he stretched and felt the weariness in his limbs. Defeat hurt. It was like an illness. It felt like defeat to be back in the Grand Hotel after the training camp. He had almost died for nothing at Sung-chiang. He had told the Governor it was going to end in disaster. The Corps was not ready.

He looked at the sheets where Annie had been sleeping and felt a thrill of disgust. He had seen syphilitic sailors dying in ports all over the world, and the disease had always terrified him. He went to the washstand and took out his shaving equipment, then called down for hot water.

In the mirror his face looked drawn. Maybe it is time to go back to the States, he thought. There'll be blood and glory enough back home if I'm reading the signs right. They may have turned me down at West Point. But I'll show them. I'll show them all . . .

On his last visit to Yang Fang's house he had promised the banker that he knew where to get cannons. He had the name of an opium trader jotted in his little blue book, a man who said he might be able to supply muzzle-loading field guns – British. Ex-Crimea. Up to a dozen six pounders, and maybe even some twelves. That would be a miracle but, strangely, it was the rifles that were proving most difficult to find. He had thought he would be able to buy them in from the United States.

'Albert, how about a reduction on quantity?'

His contact, Albert L. Freeman, had shrugged. 'Discount? Sorry. It's a sellers' market right now. And it depends what you mean by quantity. Five thousand? Ten thousand?'

'Let's say five hundred.'

'Not possible. I can probably get you flintlocks.'

Albert, I need up-to-date percussion locks – Sharps rifles and Colt revolvers. What the hell's going on back home?'

'More than you realize. The country's on the point of breaking up.'

Looks like I'll have to go see Harry Lindley again after all, he decided. The hot water arrived. He positioned himself in front of the mirror, clipped his moustache and goatee and stropped his razor, whipped up some soap in the shaving jug and inspected his jaw in the washstand mirror. He had known that Lindley and the Taiping girl were working together, but what he had learned from her about Lindley's father had been sensational. That piece of information alone had convinced him he could afford to let her go.

While he was shaving Burgevine knocked on the door. 'Thought I'd show you this, Colonel.' Burgevine handed over a copy of Shanghai's English language weekly. It carried a lurid report of the events at Sung-chiang.

'. . . and now those miserable drunkards have all deserted their erstwhile commander, the self-styled Colonel Ward, and left the Concession. We may hope that Ward himself shall soon decide to do the same.'

Ward folded the paper and put it down.

'Isn't that a son of a bitch, Colonel?'

'What do you expect, Henry? The *Herald*'s editor is nothing but a mouthpiece for Meadows. He wants you and me run out of town. He said he'd do it, and now he's working up to it. Sung-chiang just gave him his big opportunity.'

'Sons of bitches. The English think they run the whole world.'

'It may have escaped you, Henry, but the fact is they do.'

'The way those traders are talking . . .' Burgevine whistled. 'They're mad as hell that we're still in business.'

'What strength are we up to now?' Ward made a mental

note to write the total in his ever-present account book. He had discharged everyone from the payroll and only rehired those men who had shown some kind of courage or initiative under fire.

'Twenty-five.'

'Twenty-five. That's good.'

Burgevine lingered. 'Colonel, is that Chinese honcho still paying us out?'

'Yang Fang? Yes, he is.'

'You sure he ain't gonna pull out on us?'

'Henry, will you let me worry about business? If there's any change in the financial arrangements I'll make sure you're the first to know.'

'Sure.'

Burgevine left. When Ward had finished shaving he dressed, then went down and called up a chair. Twenty minutes later he was looking up at the white house on Yan'an Street. He knocked, waited, then knocked again. It was the second time he had tried the place, and neither of his letters asking for a meeting with Lindley had been answered. The time had come to use the explosive information about Lindley's father that Fei had let slip. When the door opened he saw Lindley's housekeeper, Shen.

''Where massa Lin-li?' Ward asked.

'No massa. Lin-li gone long time.'

He looked at the sullen servant penetratingly. 'Where gone?'

'Far way. Never mind.'

The man tried to close the door on him, but Ward pushed forward and grabbed him suddenly by the froggings of his shirt. 'Hey! Where Lin-li go?'

'River. River.'

'Where?'

'With army. With navy. All same, never mind.'

'Army and navy? What're you talking about?'

'Don' know. All same, never mind.'

Ward let the man go. Army? Navy? It made some kind of sense. Lindley's language skills were at a premium. Maybe Meadows had commandeered him to get him out of Shanghai. If that were so he would be sailing north with Lord Elgin's diplomatic party. The idea galvanized him, and he wondered if their vessel had left the Huang-pu yet.

He took a small boat back up to the Concession but then decided to stroll along the Bund. The city felt strange. There was an uneasy buzz in the air. Fear that the port should have been left so exposed at a time when the Taipings are still threatening to march east. The river was almost empty. Only one small British gun boat lay at anchor now. The big warships had gone.

In the past few days he had heard several traders repeat the rumour that the Taipings' objective was Shanghai itself. There could be no truth in it – it just didn't make sense, but the fact that people believed it made his own job harder. Their uneasiness had become focused on the fight at Sung-chiang, a focus magnified by the rantings of the *North China Herald*. He slackened his pace deliberately, knowing he was being followed.

He turned down a filthy back alley, steaming with cook-pots and washing and screeching women, and the clacking of mah-jong tiles, searched by a hundred mistrustful eyes. He walked on by, counting the yards. A medicine store stuck out into the alley like a protruding tooth. A group of men watched him sullenly from ten or fifteen paces away like scavengers watching a dying beast. He heard the footsteps gaining on him and he tensed, ready to whirl on his attacker at the most effective moment.

'Su nombre es Coronel Ward? Hableme en mi idioma si usted entiende.'

Astonishingly the voice had asked Ward to speak in Spanish if he understood the language. He turned to see a well-built young man, in his early twenties, oriental, but not a Chinese.

'Si, comprendo.' I understand.

'They told me you had fought in Mexico. And also in Nicaragua.'

'Whoever they are, they're right.' He watched the man closely, ready for any move. 'And who might you be, friend?'

'My name is Vincente. Vincente Macanaya.'

'Well, Mr Macanaya,' he said, without relaxing his state of alertness. 'What can I do for you?'

'I am from Manila. Me and my Filipinos – we want to fight for you.'

Careful, he thought. Maybe this is a crude attempt to

entrap me. The Philippines were a colonial possession of Spain, but Spanish interests in China were minimal.

'What does the Spanish Consul think about your ambitions?'

Macanaya's grin broadened. 'I don't know, señor. I didn't ask him.'

Ward took a calling card from his vest pocket and held it out between two fingers. When the Filipino took it, Ward raised his fingers to the man's head as if they were a pistol, and made as if to fire. 'Sure you want to fight for me? It could be very dangerous.'

The man looked back steadily and grinned. He drew a machete from the back of his belt and spun it up into the air, catching it deftly by the handle as it fell before pushing it back into its hidden sheath. 'If it's very dangerous, then I'm sure.'

'Tomorrow, then.'

'Si. Mañana.'

He watched the Filipino go on his way. So far his recruits had been American or European – white men – because that was what Yang Fang wanted, but there were a good many Filipino seamen in Shanghai. Everyone had learned to respect their reputation for hard work and toughness – and their sobriety.

As he walked on Ward pondered the way the British employed their Indian troops. They had brought to China Sikhs and Punjabis and Baluchis – all excellent soldiers. He recalled stories he had heard of the way various Indian races had fought with extreme bravery alongside the British during the recent uprising of the sepoys against the rule of the East India Company.

'My men were faultless in the retaking of Delhi,' he had heard one English captain boast. 'That was real warfare.'

'Which regiment?' Ward had asked, wondering how many of these 'faultless' fighters could be persuaded to leave their present employment.

'The men of whom I am speaking, sir, and from whom I am now sadly parted,' the officer had said with pride and regret, 'are the Gurkhas.'

He had been puzzled. 'They don't sound very British.'

'My dear fellow, they're not. The Gurkhas are Nepalese – little men who come from the high Himalayas, the tallest mountains in the world. They look to be half-Indian and half-Chinese, but whatever their origins they are absolutely peerless warriors. And in the recapture of Delhi, in which I myself had the good fortune to take part, they proved themselves to friend and foe alike.'

Yes, Ward mused. Why not? It makes obvious sense. Manilamen would make perfect mercenaries. And Chinese soldiers can be disciplined to fight too. I can't understand why I didn't think of it before.

He looked at the lone British naval ship riding at her moorings. She was waiting to take Lord Elgin's diplomatic retinue north. Ward clenched his fist, suddenly filled with new purpose, and began to walk back towards Soochow Creek and his riverboat.

Governor Wu took the message from the boy and decided to bring the unsatisfactory meeting with the banker to an end. 'Mr Yang, I cannot adequately express my disappointment. So much money has been poured into this banquet, but still you tell me no food is cooked.'

'You must decide, of course, your Excellency. But I beg you to give Mr Ward one more chance. After all, what alternative do we have?'

'A hollow dumpling looks better than it tastes, Mr Yang . . . And now, unfortunately an aspect of administration requires my urgent attention. You will please excuse me.'

Wu made the dismissal intentionally curt – it was important that Yang Fang understood how much loss of face the affair at Sung-chiang had already cost.

After Yang had left, Wu followed the boy outside. His men had put the Taiping spy in the part of the yamen beyond the kitchen and banqueting room, at the far end of the second courtyard. There was a store room with hooks in the rafters and a stone floor that drained to a hole in the centre. This was where four times a year pigs were brought to be slaughtered and hung. Between festivals it served as an interrogation room. Two men in official robes were waiting outside.

'Did she speak with him?' Wu asked the eighth-grade mandarin who had brought the girl in.

'No, Excellency. For some reason she approached the house, made obeisance at the door, then left again.'

'Did she deliver anything?'

'I don't think so, Excellency.'

Wu nodded. 'Good. The less foreigners and rebels infect one another the better. There will certainly be much useful information to be extracted from her.'

They had dumped her in a corner, tied and gagged. A short bamboo pole ran under her knees and across the crooks of her elbows, so she was trussed into a ball. She was surprisingly youthful and unblemished, beautiful even, though she lacked bound feet. But defiance radiated from her, and so Wu felt a physical stirring of anticipation.

'Take the gag off,' he said, his voice thickening. 'Who are you? Why are you in Shanghai? And why did you go to see the foreigner?'

She said nothing.

Wu looked accusingly at his man and struck him a heavy blow across the mouth. 'You told me she was ready! She's not ready! Put the gag back on her and hang her up for three hours. Then cut off both her ears and ask her the questions again. If she still says nothing, cut off her nose. When she wants to speak send word to me and I will come again.'

He left and began to walk slowly back to the front of the yamen, at the same time savouring the muffled sounds of terror he was leaving behind.

When Lindley reached the *Hyson* he was boiling with anger. Meadows' attempt to blackmail him had only hardened his resolve to go to Nanking and to find his father by any means possible. Now, the sight of Ward's riverboat sitting idle in Soochow Creek stoked his temper to melting point.

He threw down the empty half-bottle of Scotch onto the granite kerb. The sound of the bottle breaking surprised Ningpo Sam, who was eating. Lindley strode across the gangplank, uninvited.

'Where's Ward?'

Sam stopped chewing and stared back wordlessly.

'Where's Ward?' Lindley repeated, his temper on the edge of eruption. He grabbed the river pilot with both hands and lifted him up. 'I want Ward. You'll take me to him. I have some unfinished business to settle with that bastard!'

'You can settle it here and now, if you've a mind.' Lindley

turned. Ward was at the bulkhead, standing with his feet apart, negligently wiping his hands on an oily rag. It was an incitement Lindley could not resist. He felt his chest tighten with overwhelming anger. 'You're a thieving gunrunner, Ward, and I mean to have your boat for what you've done to me.'

Ward smiled. 'Over my dead body you will, Doc.'

'That can be arranged!'

'Come on, then!'

Lindley leapt for him. Ward staggered back as the bigger man made contact with him. As they struggled face to face the Colt revolver in Ward's belt fell to the deck. Lindley locked his left hand on Ward's throat and connected a swinging punch with the side of the American's head. The blow struck bone and sent a shock of pain right up Lindley's arm, then he felt two hands grab him from behind and pull him back.

Lindley crashed down on Sam who yelped in pain, but Lindley hardly heard it. There was a monster loose in his chest now. It took no notice of either pain or reason. It thundered with strength and a lust to be avenged. It made Lindley lift Sam bodily and dump him over the side, then renew his attack on the American.

Stunned for the moment by the huge right-hander, Ward was down and making for his revolver. Lindley's foot scythed it away, so that it went spinning into the iron scuppers, but the kick unbalanced him and Ward seized his other leg and heaved, bringing him down hard to the deck.

'Scotch sonofabitch! Get the hell off of my vessel!'

'I'll kill you Ward, you hear me?'

Ward stood over him and began raining blows onto his head and face. Lindley screamed back incoherently and a great wave of primitive instinct fountained up, filling him with fighting power. He threw the American off then charged him, slamming into him and throwing him against the bulkhead. The impact seemed to glaze Ward's eyes for a split second, long enough for Lindley to line up a pile-driver. But when the punch came, Ward doubled up and Lindley's fist smashed into the bulkhead.

Lindley felt the pain in his hand, but heedlessly, so consumed was he with fury now. Ward buried a jabbing blow in his guts, then followed through with an uppercut that threw him back. Ward came on relentlessly now, picking his target, swinging punches from left and right, until Lindley was driven hard up against the starboard rail. He would not go down, but neither would Ward stop punching, until Lindley roared, grabbed him by the ears and butted him hard in the face.

The American's nose exploded in blood and Lindley tore loose. He went on the offensive again, and when Ward backed off he picked up a deck mop and swung it wildly in an arc, catching Ward's ear and throwing him down over a hatch cover. Lindley dived on him, his hands forcing the wooden mop handle across Ward's neck. When the wood snapped a jagged end swept across Lindley's face, just missing his eye, and as he stumbled Ward managed to get his knee up under his opponent's body and turn him over.

The throw sent Lindley sliding forward toward the anchor cable. He rolled, taking most of the fall on his back, but his outstretched right arm overturned a pail of water, so that when Ward followed up with a kick to his ribs the American slipped on the wet deck and landed hard.

They struggled together like madmen now, neither getting the better of the other, both breathing hard. They wallowed in water and blood, hampered by torn clothing, threshing, tearing at one another. Ward's bleeding nose had streaked him red. Lindley's whole face was numb and lump hard. For a few minutes more the blows landed then, with arms too aching to punch, they fell to wrestling one another into a groaning, exhausted deadlock.

When they pulled apart again the monster had gone from both of them. Up on the quay a group of young Chinese boys, none of them older than eight, were watching them with absorbed interest.

'Bugger off!' Lindley bellowed at them, and they fled.

For a while he and Ward sat on opposite sides of the deck, bleeding and gasping for air, neither one with the strength to attack the other.

'Sonofabitch!' Ward said eventually, spitting blood and wiping his mouth. 'What do you want coming down here anyway?'

Lindley felt his left eye closing up. 'Don't try to deny it—' Lindley croaked. 'You're a gunrunning bastard. You set me and my father up. What have you done with him, Ward?'

'Boy! You take the cake, Doc! You really do!' Ward tried to get up but sat back down again. 'See, I know you and the Taiping woman are in cahoots!'

'Cahoots? With her?'

'She told me!'

'You mean the woman you insisted come along with us upriver?' Lindley pulled his shirt back over his shoulder and rolled forward. The pain in his ribs was making itself felt now.

Ward looked at his bleeding knuckles. 'I mean the woman you were living with!'

Lindley examined his good jacket. It was ruined – torn to shreds and covered in blood. 'Bastard!'

Ward rolled over into the scuppers and recovered his revolver. He wagged it at Lindley. 'Hey you! Get off of my boat!'

'Go to hell, Mr Ward. Go to hell and burn, why don't you?'

'I guess you didn't think I knew she was back in Shanghai! Well I do.'

Lindley stared, feeling groggy, not caring about the revolver. 'What?'

'I said, I know she's here.'

Despite the unspent drink still inside him mistrust surged through Lindley as he watched Ward's eyes searching his own. 'Where?'

'You're trying to tell me you don't know?'

'Where is she?'

'I tracked her to a Taiping house near the Old City.' Ward stopped. He shoved the revolver back in his belt and began to stand. 'You really don't know do you?'

'You'd better start making sense, and quick, Ward, before I start on you again, revolver or no revolver.'

Ward laughed wearily. 'Hey – maybe we owe each other an apology. See, I kinda thought the two of you were working together.'

'Oh, for God's sake!'

'She's the number one Taiping spy in Shanghai, Doc. It all fitted.'

Lindley felt the information sink in like ice. Suddenly he knew that Ward was telling the truth – he had never been Fei's accomplice.

Ward shook his head as if to clear it. 'I had her followed, and then I had a little talk with her. What she said was she'd fix it with you to get me a thousand of those Enfields.'

'And you *believed* her?'

Ward's shrug showed he was making a hard admission. 'I gambled. I was pretty sure she'd keep the bargain. What was I supposed to think?'

'You really know the Chinese, don't you? You're such a smart man.'

Ward smouldered. 'So I made a mistake. All right?'

'You certainly did.'

'Well, you can rest assured I won't do it again. And just to show there's no hard feelings, you can forget about the five hundred taels you owe me. I don't want to see your Scotch hide ever again. Now get off my boat.'

'Ward, I need to find her.'

Ward laughed again. 'Well, I hope you get to her before the mandarins do.'

Ningpo Sam came along the quayside. He was dripping and armed now with a machete. When he came aboard he was intending to use it, but Ward intercepted him and asked him to go below. Sam thought about it for a second, but then he saw the Colt was safely back in Ward's belt, and he grudgingly did as he was told.

'Ward, you've got to help me.'

The American wiped the blood from his nose. 'You've got the strangest way of asking favours.'

'At least tell me where you found her.'

'Maybe I will,' he said. 'In return for something from you.'

'What do you want?'

Ward's eyes narrowed. 'You know that.'

'I already told you I can't get you Enfields.'

'No, but maybe you can persuade Meadows.'

'You're out of your mind.'

'Persuade him not to throw me out of China.'

Lindley balked. The request seemed impossible. 'I'll speak to him, but I can't promise anything.'

'Make it a condition of your going north with the expedition.'

'I'm not going north with the expedition. I'm going to Nanking. I came to China to find my father and that's what I'm going to do.'

'It's your funeral – and it will be. You won't get five miles.'

'I have to try.'

'That's plain stubborn. If you take my advice, you'll do as Meadows wants. You've got no choice anyhow. Nobody is going to take you up to Nanking. Not me, not anybody.' Ward made an open-handed gesture. 'You know, Doc, Meadows has got me all wrong.'

'Sure. If you're not running guns, what's your real game? Opium?'

Ward spat over the side. 'I'll tell you: I'm getting a . . . force together.'

'A what?'

'A military force. A foreign arms corps.'

'You mean mercenaries? A private army?'

'Yes. Meadows thinks I'm crimping Royal Navy personnel, but most of my boys come off of American merchant ships. I'm just exploiting a legal loophole. Under American maritime law, if a seaman is discharged in a foreign port the ship's master has to give him three months' pay.'

'Fair enough.'

'—but nothing if the man deserts.'

'So?'

'So it's a well-meaning law that doesn't work in practice. Because if you beat a man enough, he'll desert – and then you don't have to pay him anything. Catch my drift?'

'So ships' masters force troublesome men to desert?'

'Exactly. Some of the guys who reach Shanghai look worse than we do. They've had a hell of a time. Either that, or the officers get the men drunk in town then sail without them. Ward inclined his head. 'What did Meadows offer you if you went on the Peking expedition?'

'He promised to help me find my father when it's finished.'

'Yeah, I'll bet he did.'

'What do you mean by that?'

'Meadows already knows exactly where your pa is.' Ward's brown eyes pierced Lindley and once more he knew he was hearing the truth. 'That Taiping woman of yours let slip something else you might find very interesting. Your pa was the man who first introduced the Taiping founder to Christianity.'

Suddenly the deck of the *Hyson* became unsteady. 'What did you say?'

'Yeah,' Ward laughed mirthlessly. 'Fifty million dead so far, and it's all down to your pa. Quite a thought that, isn't it? No wonder Meadows wants you out of town.'

The executioner's sword flashed in the sun as it was brought down on the rebel woman's neck. Blood fountained and her head bounced on the cobbles, then rolled into the gutter. The moment of justice had been accomplished.

At his desk Governor Wu nodded once to his secretary, and re-inked his chop before taking the placard which read.

CONCERNING REBEL SPIES
SHIH FEI-CH'IEN

Lest it be thought that rebel vagabonds presently
at large in the vicinity of Shanghai shall affect
to the contrary the good governance of the Empire,
or that persons lacking the necessary qualities of
humility and obedience shall be tolerated in our
midst, look upon the evidence I hereby present to
the contrary.

RESPECT THIS!

Wu Hsu
Taotai
Shanghai

'Make sure the head adorns a spike for at least seven days,' he told the secretary as he handed the placard back approvingly. 'Take steps to have the head violently defaced before it is exhibited as a street ornament. The woman was quite pretty, but rebel heads must serve the worthy purpose of striking fear into rebel hearts, not of exciting pity.'

He thought of his hurried meeting with Yang Fang. The banker had told him, 'The woman is Shih Fei-ch'ien, daughter of Shih Wen-kuang, the Taiping leader known among the rebels as the "Kao Wang" or "High King". This traitor is responsible for the day-to-day running of the rebel government in Nanking. His daughter directs the Taiping spy ring in Shanghai. She is very important. Very knowledgeable. Very trusted.'

After that he had wanted to torture her immediately, but Yang Fang had said, 'It might be a mistake to harm her.'

'Why?'

'That would incur the wrath of her father, so that when Shanghai falls you will be an especial target of the rebels.'

'I must find out what she knows.'

'I can already tell you that. The foreigner Ward says that the woman was sent to Shanghai to monitor the arrival of the foreign forces and to spy on his camp at Kuang-fu-lin. But he has recently caught another spy who confessed that he had been sent to take over from her.'

'Oh? Why?'

'The woman has been given orders to go north to Peking.'

'Peking?'

'Yes. One can only guess the reason, but Ward believes she may have been chosen to deliver some kind of ultimatum to the Imperial government regarding Shanghai. Perhaps a peace treaty that will leave Nanking in their hands, and Shanghai in ours.'

Wu smiled at the memory. He had had the woman brought before him and untied. He had seen for himself that she was tall and had unbound feet. Without doubt this woman is racially a Manchu, he had thought. So perhaps she really is Shih Fei-ch'ien, the daughter of the so called 'Kao Wang', whom I know to be a Manchu traitor expelled from Peking twenty years ago.

'Is your father the Kao Wang?' he had whispered to her. The name meant 'High King'.

She had said nothing, but he had seen the answer in her eyes. So, he thought, revelling in the discovery. She is the daughter of the number one Taiping administrator. There's no doubt about her identity, or her mission. What other woman would have been given so vital a political task?

Wu stood up, pleased with himself. The body being dragged away to the cart was leaving a trail of blood. He had not been sure if he should execute her. But it seemed to be in his interests that a Taiping ultimatum should reach Peking, and that his opponents should think Shih Fei-ch'ien was dead. That was why he had secretly let her go, and had put another woman to death in her place.

*

Fei entered the Forbidden City by a side portal of the Western Flower Gate. As the tall doors banged shut the sound echoed down the tunnel that burrowed through the huge rampart wall into the infamous lair.

At her side was the solemn eunuch in a blue working robe who had met her at the moat gate. His face was maggot pale, and he walked with a limp. Just one more of the small lives that had been twisted and broken by the Imperial monster, she thought, feeling fearful yet determined.

The eunuch had not greeted her, just instructed her to follow, and now he led her through the tunnel wordlessly. The foreigners will never smash through these walls, no matter what guns they have, she thought, her mind focused on the blinding brightness ahead.

She emerged into the brilliant sunshine, and shaded her eyes against the glare. Then she was led down a servants' thoroughfare of dowdy workshops, and between two of them she caught sight of a vast space opening beyond. The whole of the courtyard was paved with cobbles, in every direction terraces of white marble rose up, fenced with the same stone, and above everything impressive crimson halls and galleries, shaded by huge yellow roofs. Despite herself she was impressed by its magnificence.

'Don't look that way. That's not for you.'

She averted her eyes instantly. 'Please excuse me, sir.'

'Don't call me "sir". Wait here and don't move.'

The eunuch vanished, leaving her to stand alone.

So this is the lair of the dragon, she thought, feeling the inviolate, brooding power. We're coming for you, yellow monster! The Heavenly King will strike you through the heart and obliterate you for ever. One day soon we will sweep you away and this place will become a great school where ten thousand smiling children will read the Book and set their minds on the building of the true Kingdom of Heavenly Peace.

The Peking agent who had received her yesterday was her father's younger brother. He had lived in Peking under an assumed name for twenty years. It must have been hard, she thought, knowing that in China to be without a name was to be without a family, and that was almost like being without a life. He told her that everything was prepared, that he had bribed the Chief Eunuch with an enormous sum to have her taken on as a maid, saying she was the daughter of a country cousin who wished to show his loyalty to the Son of Heaven. Such a thing, she knew, was not unusual.

An older eunuch with an odd-shaped head appeared and looked her over.

'Girl! Come with me.'

'Yes, sir.'

He spun on her, his face grotesque. 'You do not call me "sir"! That word mocks me. My name is Master Huang.'

'I didn't mean to—'

'Speak only when spoken to! Were you born to coolies?'

He led her to a small, enclosed courtyard. She saw there were many faces watching her from the windows that surrounded it.

'Take off your clothes and put them there.'

She hesitated, horrified.

'Obey quickly, or you will be beaten! We have no use for outside clothes here. You are not permitted to bring anything into the Forbidden City. Here you will wear apparel that displays your rank.'

Her fingers fumbled with the ties of her surcoat. She shrugged it off, folded it and laid it on the bench behind her, then she took off her slippers and put them neatly together under the bench.

'Quickly! No need for modesty here. There's no privacy in the sleeping barracks. Those clothes will be burned. Your old life means nothing here.'

She loosed the drawstring of her pantaloons and they fell to the ground. She stepped out of them and began obediently to unbutton her long shirt. She saw another eunuch appear with a yoke across his shoulder. He set down two pails of water with a sponge floating in one of them.

Her shirt fell away and she was naked. The old eunuch approached her. He lifted her feet and checked soles and the spaces between the toes. Then he began searching through her hair and scalp minutely. After a while he stepped back and began to discuss her with another eunuch who had appeared. They seemed to agree on something, then the second eunuch left.

'Put your hands above your head.'

She obeyed, conscious of the faces at the windows and

the way her breasts rose, feeling the burning humiliation of the search.

'Open your mouth. I want to look under your tongue.'

He put a finger into her mouth and felt the spaces between her teeth and cheeks.

'Now bend forward and part your legs. Wider!'

The intimacy of the procedure was abhorrent to her. She had not been prepared for anything like this. To escape it she set her mind on the briefing she had received last night at her uncle's little shop on Drum Tower Lane. She had spent the evening learning about the disaster that had overwhelmed the family. 'Your father's banishment destroyed us all. Your grandmother still believes he died at Black Dragon River. I never had the will to tell her the truth. And now she's too weak to hear it.'

There was a half-finished coffin standing on trestles in the courtyard. Her grandmother knew she was dying. The smell of approaching death made her chamber cloying. Fei sat beside her throughout the Hour of the Dog, seeing at times her own face in the old lady's wizened features, and at other times the skull beneath her skin.

'Your father – my number one son – died in disgrace, child. I loved him best, and he grew up to be the most honourable of men. But it was because of his honour that he destroyed our family. The shock of his arrest killed my husband. We lost everything we had. And now we live here in misery and shame in this tiny house, living under a false name because the people we once were are no more.'

'It is good to know that you loved your first-born son,' she said, showing her grandmother as much well-mannered consideration as she could. It hurt to deceive the old lady. 'It's good for me to hear that my father was an honourable man.'

'He was honourable and talented, child, but he was also very stupid. It is always unwise to disagree with emperors, and he never understood that. We were important people then. Aristocrats. I was a lady-in-waiting for seven years. But nobody got away with mocking the Tao-kuang emperor. Not even your father. Now we live here under false names, like fugitives, because our true selves are not permitted to come within a thousand li of the capital. My son worries about my dying, but I don't. We are already ghosts, and have been for many years.'

Fei had wanted to ask her grandmother about the Court. 'I was told that the great Tao-kuang Emperor never saw any of the Common People who were his subjects.'

The old lady started, as if shocked at her naivety. 'Never. No Emperor ever does that.'

'I wonder why not.'

'It's impossible,' her uncle said. 'No commoner is ever permitted to look upon the Emperor. That is the law. Whenever His Imperial Majesty passes along a highway it is always deserted. Every street in the city is emptied ahead of an Imperial procession.'

'Don't the Common People make tiny holes in their paper windows and watch anyway? Just to satisfy their curiosity?' She asked. 'I would.'

The old lady chuckled and some of her severity had vanished. 'Oh, but your father surely lives on in you, child! Losing your head is a high price to pay for one glimpse of the Imperial yellow. And anyway, no one could see His Imperial Majesty, or any of the Court. They ride in closed palanquins. Actually, when I rode in them I used to pull my curtains aside to look out, but never enough to allow myself to be seen, or else I would have been severely criticized.'

Fei's mind came reluctantly back to the present. She endured the search, fortified by the knowledge that this was only half reality, that none of these vile eunuchs could know she was not an obedient victim of the Imperial system but a dangerous Taiping officer sent here to help liberate them and to smash their despicable traditions once and for all.

'Do you have any questions?' the eunuch asked, washing his fingers.

'Master Huang, why did you punish me when I've only just arrived?' she asked in a small voice, playing her part well.

'This is not punishment. It is a search. Such a search is necessary. You would be surprised at what some people try to smuggle in here.'

You call it a search, but you are really only trying to impress authority through humiliation, she thought defiantly. There's no search thorough enough to reveal what

210

I've brought into your citadel, because it's here inside my head, a message and an ultimatum that is going to blow your old world apart.

She imagined herself delivering the ultimatum: 'I am sent by the T'ien Wang, the Heavenly King, in token of the sincerity of His message. Leave Nanking to the Taipings, or we will march on Shanghai and occupy it while your armies are busy dealing with the foreigners in the North.'

Then we will move on Peking itself, she thought. And Shanghai is the key, for once we possess a port we will be able to talk to the outside world. We will convince our brother Christians in Europe and America of the righteousness of our struggle. We will be unstoppable.

'Master Huang, in the Forbidden City must I always avert my eyes from noble personages?' she asked.

'The question does not arise. You will not see any noble personages.'

'But why, Master Huang? Is the Imperial family not here?'

'Enough questions, impertinent girl!'

She fell silent, her eyes obediently downcast, but her mind raced, wondering how she could rectify the mistake. Where are the Imperials? she thought. Could it be they've already left Peking? Or perhaps they're at the Summer Palace. If so, how to get there?

'Now scrub yourself.'

She complied. As she washed her limbs she saw a eunuch of obviously high rank, wearing a brown and blue robe emblazoned with the character for longevity, come into the small courtyard. Huang behaved fawningly towards him. The newcomer's eyes appraised her, then he nodded and left. She thought she had caught the word 'virginity'.

At length the pails were emptied over her. Then a towel was given to her. She dried herself, combed back her wet hair and began to put on the modest cotton clothes of a scullery maid.

'You will work at the Western Kitchens for the time being. Follow me.'

For the time being, she thought. What does that mean? And what were they saying about me?

The heat mounted over the Summer Palace as dragons writhed in the upper airs. On the Isle of the Phoenix and the Unicorn a lone pavilion baked beneath a thunder filled sky.

Within, Yehonala clung to Jung-lu's muscular body as he roared and thrust into her with the mindless urgency of approaching climax. Tomorrow he must go to war. She would not see him again soon. She might not see him again – ever.

She clung on, tighter, wanting to lose herself, but she could not allow herself to be as heedless as her lover was in the peaks of pleasure, because as that amazing moment came for him and his body went into spasm, she always had to make him withdraw so that his seed did not enter her and spoil everything. It could never be like it had been once, when her aim had been to make a baby as quickly as possible. This must be an endless and unendurable torture for him.

Now she felt his body tensing. Heard his animal noises intensify. His fingernails digging into her. He was readying. She moaned at the imminence, feeling different. This was not as normal. The times were not as normal. Tomorrow he was leaving with General Seng's army to face the Barbarians, to face death.

Abruptly she felt him start to spurt inside her, and she knew she had left her escape too late.

'No!' She cried. 'No! Get off me! Get off! Stop!'

But this time he did not stop. The thrusting went on and on. And though she struggled he held her and there was no remedy. When he pulled away he was drained. He had raped her.

In the quiet that followed she looked at him. 'You are dog shit,' she said, insulting him as she had never insulted him before. 'Dog shit!'

He took it, as he had never taken an insult from her before. Silently. Accepting blame. He knew exactly what he had done because it had been deliberate.

'What does it matter?' he said. 'Tomorrow the world will lie shattered in ten thousand pieces.'

He dressed in silence and left without a farewell. No departure could have been pleasant given his orders, but this was certainly not how it should have been. She lay alone regretting her terrible pride, knowing that if he were to die she would never forgive herself.

Tears came to her eyes, but there was no way to call him back.

The troops of Colonel Ward's private army lay on the beaten ground, unable to raise themselves even to their elbows. Two hundred men, mostly Chinese and Filipinos, sweated and gasped for air, tortured by cramp and burning under a blazing sun.

Ward's face had healed now, and the memory of the fight with Lindley had begun to give him a curious satisfaction. It felt good to reach a state of mutual respect with another man, however that state was achieved.

He detected a faint smell in the air. When the breeze blew from the west there was always a fetid taint to it. Unimaginable killing was going on inland, and the smell, he knew, was the unmistakable reek of death.

He watched his troops recovering for a few moments more, then put on his French field cap and tucked his silver-tipped baton under his arm, and walked along the line of ten gleaming British field guns – two twelve pounders and eight six pounders. They had just been raced up and over a ten-foot-high dirt bank and across a twenty-foot-wide ditch, back and forth, again and again, until the men could no longer stand up.

'Power,' he shouted, bringing them immediately to heedfulness. Translators spoke his words simultaneously in Chinese and Spanish. 'Power . . . and mobility. Now you truly understand what these are.' He took his baton out from under his arm and pointed to his left. 'This cannon is a twelve pounder. It fires an iron ball weighing twelve pounds. It has a brass barrel six and a half feet long. Total weight three thousand three hundred pounds. This is power.' He pointed right. 'And this is a six pounder. Barrel length five feet exactly, total weight seven hundred fifty pounds. This is mobility. You men have performed well this morning. This afternoon you will do it over again. That's all.'

He turned on his heel, retracing his steps to the stockade perimeter. The Kuang-fu-lin compound was alive with activity. Previously it had housed a garrison of Imperial troops. Two accommodation blocks had been added on each side of the parade ground and the original quarters extended, along with a secure arsenal, stables, three kitchens and an officers' mess. There was a medical office, and a Dr MacGowan had already been hired to staff it. Ward's own commander's hut had been built in the centre, and flew a faded green flag blazoned with the Chinese character 'Hua', which was as close as the Chinese language could come to his name.

He discovered from one of his recruits that the British had set Indian and Malay rates of pay for Chinese labourers to work as baggage coolies: one pound ten shillings sterling – about seven dollars fifty American – a month, plus two uniforms and daily rations. Incredibly generous, but even so they had not been able to recruit adequately, and each time the British increased the rate the fewer Chinese came forward, until at nearly two pounds – ten dollars – a month, not a single Chinese offered himself.

'Why?' he had asked Yang Fang. 'Two pounds sterling is a fortune to a Chinese labourer, more per month than he can usually make in a year. Something must be making them scared to sign on. What? Or should I say "Who?"'

Yang Fang smiled but said nothing.

'Wu's behind it, isn't he? What game's he playing at?'

'No, it's not His Excellency the taotai's fault. The coolies will not come forward because they are scared.'

'Coolies are never afraid of hard work. Chinese peasants work like demons.'

'Ah, you're thinking like a Westerner again,' Yang Fang had cautioned him. 'Chinese peasants believe that to gain such riches they will be at least required to perform suicide attacks on the enemy.'

Ward thought about that, then he grinned with understanding.

'Let this be a lesson to you, Colonel Ward.'

'Oh, it will be, Mr Yang. It will be.'

A week or two later Yang had asked him, 'Why did you ask me about the executed spy?'

'Because I spent a little time on a river boat with her once.'

Yang nodded judiciously, seeming to know more than he was prepared to say. 'Did you find her attractive?'

Ward did not expect that question, but he fielded it openly. 'Yes. I did.'

'Only . . .' Yang's voice hovered crucially over the word. 'You know, some Westerners don't enjoy Oriental women. I hear that some Western men don't respect Chinese girls and call them "monkeys".'

'Well, then they're fools.'

Yang looked him up and down strangely, then he said. 'Colonel, you should give more thought to how you dress now you are in command of an army.'

After that Ward had given more thought to several matters he had previously ignored. No people on earth respect a suit of clothes more than the Chinese, he had thought. It makes sense. They've had sumptuary laws for centuries, and so they're easy to awe with splendour. In their minds the worth of a man is fixed absolutely by rank, and his rank is shown by what he wears. That's why the Manchu impose the pig-tail and plain dress on the mass of their subjects, and why the Taipings refuse it and dress in flamboyant colours instead. Yes, Yang's right. If I'm to have my own Chinese I ought to give them something special to hang their thoughts on.

A week ago he had put on new knee boots and a well-tailored coat. It was cut in the style of Prince Albert to just above the knee, with a neat rounded collar and falling fashionably open from the top button. Yang Fang had approved, and called his daughter in to see it.

Yang liked my idea of disciplined Chinese troops, Ward mused now. You bet. Whereas once he was paying fifty dollars American per month for difficult drunken scum, now he's paying next to nothing for men who never touch liquor and who do exactly as they're told.

The recruits were making excellent progress. This morning he had watched eighty Filipinos working through rifle practice. They were fast learners, and Vincente Macanaya had turned out to be a natural leader. Everyone except Burgevine liked him and called him by his first name, regardless of rank. Ward walked over, pleased he had decided to sign the man. 'Hearing is forgetting and seeing is remembering,' he said. 'But doing is understanding. By the way, I'm making you my aide-de-camp with immediate effect.'

Vincente took the unexpected promotion modestly. 'Any reason for that, Coronel?'

'If your men perform as well under fire as they've done in camp, we'll have the Taipings licked inside of six months.'

The Filipino showed a row of even, white teeth. 'Thank you, Coronel.'

'I want you to select a personal guard of twenty men for me. Issue them with Sharps repeating carbines. Tell them they'll wear a special dark green uniform.'

'Yes, sir!'

Ward walked back towards his office in determined mood. News of Vincente's promotion was going to be hard for Burgevine to take. Over the past week or so many petty jealousies had started to fester. Keeping ahead of the bigger threats to the Foreign Arms Corps had meant that he had not been able to pay much attention to the smaller ones. Now too many stupid rivalries were reaching a head. And there was no time for stupid rivalries – Sung-chiang had to be taken.

This time he was going to do it properly. He had gone alone into Taiping-held territory, exploring the fringes of the war after dark, creeping up on Sung-chiang from different directions, making notes and thoroughly surveying the moat, the ancient walls and the gun batteries the rebels had installed to defend it. He had gathered one vital piece of tactical information among the night mists, but then he had made a horrifying discovery.

At night especially, the stinking earth gave up its foul odours, and the stench of mankind's bloodiest war hung over the waterlogged land. More than once he had stumbled into death pits where incredible numbers of bodies had been loaded down into stretches of shallow water. As he staggered through long grasses, lost and seeking higher ground, the oily pools had belched foul gases at him, and in places the reeking mounds of rag-clothed corpses had stood taller than he himself. As far as his eye could see the victims of a vast genocide were rotting away in thousands of mass graves located all over the countryside.

Alone and cold and stumbling in the loathsome fog he had muttered against the blasphemy of what had been perpetrated by the so-called God-worshippers, and tried to multiply out the death count in his mind. It was said that Sung-chiang had gotten away lightly, compared with many of the other once-populous cities of the Yangtze valley. There were dozens upon dozens of cities with more than a hundred thousand dead in this province alone, in this latest campaign alone. Such was the bleeding weal of the Taiping scourge when it passed across the land.

After that night he had preferred to spend his evenings in Shanghai, either meeting with Yang Fang, or doing business with his suppliers, dodging Captain Strickland, and giving the slip to Meadows' other people. He had also been at pains to avoid Eden Phillips and the powerful Shanghai Traders Association. Ward had bought drinks for Eden Phillips' estranged wife on more than one occasion in the past month. Annie Phillips had been dazzled by his new way of dressing when she saw him climb the steps of the Grand Hotel. She had always been attracted by his aura of power. Since he started dressing to emphasize his character she had been especially attentive. In the past week she had searched him out twice, sending her Chinese maid out to Kuang-fu-lin to pass on pieces of information. Two evenings ago she had come along the opulent passageway to his rooms on the second floor of the Grand Hotel, dressed only in a thin silk robe.

'I'm worried for you,' she had told him when he had opened the door to her. 'The Traders Association have just had a meeting. They're really gunning for you now.'

'Nothing new about that,' he said. Her perfume was sickening to him. Her body warmth was noticeable as she squeezed past him into the room.

'Eden's friends think you're going to bring the Chung Wang's army down on Shanghai. Consul Meadows agrees with them. They don't want you to fight the Taipings for fear that the flow of tea and silk will dry up. I saved this from yesterday's *Herald*.'

He took a clipping from her and read it. Then he screwed it up and tossed it away. It was more uninformed scaremongering.

'They're trying to stir up the whole Concession against me.'

'Aren't you afraid?' Annie asked, engaging him with a fierce concern.

'Why should I be afraid?' he said. 'Nobody knows what the Heavenly King wants for Shanghai. Since the Chung Wang took Soochow he hasn't shown the slightest interest in attacking east. His troops haven't come within twenty miles of here.'

217

'But they could. And easily. Isn't that true? Everyone says you're provoking the Chung Wang to attack us. They say we'll be overrun, and if we are it'll be your fault.'

He betrayed no emotion. He had surmised the real reason the Taipings had not directed their massive field army against Shanghai yet – they were still waiting for Peking's answer to their ultimatum. 'You shouldn't pay too much attention to those men friends of yours. Or to what you might read in the *North China Herald*.'

'They say we're all going to die.'

'I told you: don't dwell on it. You'll just upset yourself.'

She had smiled up at him then, her expression turning suddenly wanton. 'You act brave, but you're a man who fears what he doesn't understand, aren't you?'

He stepped away from her, his nerves sparking, and looked out of the window towards the north-west. 'Annie, the fact is I'm giving the Chung Wang a good excuse to stay put. It's my guess he's enjoying his time in Soochow. If I was in his shoes the last thing I'd want is to take on Shanghai and maybe have to go back to Nanking with my tail between my legs to renew my bowing and scraping to the Great Leader.'

She came and put her hands around him and her cheek on his back. 'They say the T'ien Wang belongs in a madhouse.'

He turned, a hard look in his eye. She shrugged her robe off, revealing her nakedness, and he saw that amazingly she had shaved off her pubic hair. The sight sent a pang through his lower belly, and he felt a powerful impulse to seize her and throw her back on the bed as she wanted. Instead he said tightly, 'What the hell have you done to yourself?'

She followed his eyes and smiled. 'Most of my clients like it like that. Don't you?'

A sudden revulsion overcame him. She was beautiful, but she was almost certainly diseased.

'Cover yourself.'

'I want you to make love to me.'

He snatched up her robe and threw it at her. 'There's plenty of men who'll do that.'

'Why don't men ever understand? Having sex is not the same as making love.'

He shook his head like it was too difficult to explain. 'Annie, get out of here.'

She did as she was told, but lingeringly. She had a natural insolence about her that he found compelling despite himself.

To hell with what crazy Annie wants, he thought now. To hell with Eden and Meadows and Wu and all of them. Like Annie says, none of us is on this earth for long.

His thoughts turned to the Taiping girl's last ordeal. I ought to write and tell the Doc. He deserves to know what happened to her. Seemed to me he was in love with her. And anyway, I owe him for keeping Meadows off my back. I haven't heard any more from Strickland for a while.

He reached his office and saw Forrest and Burgevine waiting for him. They stopped talking when he entered.

'You've got an invitation to meet with the American Consul tonight,' Forrest said. 'It came by messenger this morning. Will you go?'

'No.' He sat down and put his boots up on his desk.

Forrest shot a quick glance at Burgevine. 'Colonel, he's our government's senior representative in China. Don't you think—'

'He's a drunken disgrace to the flag. What's more he's in the British Consul's grip. And he'd sure as hell sign a paper for my arrest if Meadows leaned on him. I'm not walking into any trap.'

Burgevine said, 'Maybe you better make an old tarheel like me commander instead.'

'You better smile when you say things like that, Henry.'

Burgevine did smile, but his eyes were dead. 'I'm serious, Colonel. On paper, I mean. It's a hell of an idea.'

'It better be good, Henry.'

'I been thinking, Colonel. It stands to reason that come this November, if things go like everyone says, no American Consul is gonna be able to touch me.'

Irritation flared inside him. 'Henry, what the fuck are you talking about?'

'Didn't you hear? South Carolina's gonna secede from the Union if Abraham Lincoln gets to be President. If South Carolina goes, North Carolina will, too. All the South'll go. It looks like we're soon gonna be from two separate countries, you and me.'

'I told you before: leave home politics out of it.'

'Just trying to think ahead.'

He felt his anger rising. 'Henry, don't think! Just follow orders!'

Forrest took his leave diplomatically, but Burgevine waited like a man with something more on his mind. Ward knew his words had cut, and that Burgevine would have to come back at him.

'I guess you saw Annie Phillips in Shanghai.'

Ward said in a low voice, 'Maybe I did. So what?'

'Just I heard some powerful stories about her.'

'How about you shut your mouth about Annie Phillips?'

Burgevine lightened his tone a little. 'I know you like to take her to your bed from time to time, so I was wondering—'

'What I do in private is none of your goddamned business!'

'Whatever you say, Colonel.' Burgevine rubbed a hand over his stubble. The noise of troops doubling time across the parade ground to Spanish commands came in through the open window. 'Think I'll go over and kick that damned Flippo's ass.'

'That damned Flippo's name is Vincente. And a man of his rank doesn't need his ass kicked by anyone, especially you, Henry.'

'What do you mean his rank?'

'I made him up to ADC in place of McMahon.'

'Why?'

'Because I decided to. And I sure ain't looking for a debate about it with you.'

Burgevine took his hat off the stand and left, leaving the door open.

Ward studied the door for a few seconds, then brought his feet off the desk, went over and closed the door with delicate care. When he sat down again he took the little blue account book from his breast pocket and wrote up several entries from memory. As he reached the last of them Forrest came in and asked how business had gone in Shanghai.

'Fine,' he said.

Forrest watched Ward put the account book back into his jacket pocket, and said, 'What about Taki bank, Colonel? I'd like to know when I can expect to pay the men out. They want silver dollars. Spanish mint. It's what they respect.'

'Don't worry, the bullion's all arranged. Mr Yang's been working hard to win over the mandarins again. I believe I know just how to do that.'

'Colonel?'

'Another operation against Sung-chiang, this time coordinated with Imperial troops of the Green Standard under General Li.'

'Did Governor Wu approve a joint operation?' Forrest asked.

'Let's just say it met with a non-committal reception from Wu – which around here means it's under serious consideration.'

Forrest nodded thoughtfully. 'I guess so. Yang Fang's the key to everything, isn't he?'

'He sure as hell holds the purse-strings. And he's really putting his money where his mouth is this time.'

'Oh?'

Ward met his eye. 'The moment we take Sung-chiang the Corps gets a bonus of seventy-five thousand taels of silver.'

Forrest whistled. 'That's a hundred twenty thousand American.'

'Yang's been living off the opium racket for twenty years. He's richer than God.'

Ward thought suddenly of Yang's daughter, Chang-mei. On his visits to Yang's home he had begun to notice her more and more. The last time he visited she had served tea, and even exchanged a few coy words with him. Come to think of it, he mused, Yang left her alone with me twice – which I thought at the time was an unprecedented sign of trust. Afterwards he started asking me questions about what I thought of her predicament, as if I was a member of his family.

Forrest said, 'So, when does Mr Yang want the attack to go ahead?'

'I don't care what Mr Yang wants. This time I'm not going to let him or anyone else set our schedule. The impatience of others can cost a man his life.'

'Is it wise to attack Sung-chiang again?'

'The Corps can take it,' Ward told him, looking up. 'This time we're going to kick down the front door.'

*

Vincente Macanaya gestured silently to his men. They slid their scaling ladders forward into tall grass and the stinking darkness swallowed them noiselessly. A few yards away a broad moat, fed by the five major canals that converged on Sung-chiang, lay covered by vapours. On the walls above, Ward knew, unseen sentries were patrolling, and on the towers of old masonry that flanked the stout timber East Gate there was a battery of heavy iron guns.

This time Ward had hand-picked the men for the assault and had briefed them thoroughly. Kuang-fu-lin was surrounded by too many hostile eyes, so Forrest was left behind at the training camp with orders to be liberal with drink and to keep the less able officers noisily amused. Meanwhile his picked men were to creep out of the stockade in small groups and under cover of darkness, then rendezvous at the canal.

By eight o'clock he had quietly embarked a force of one hundred and twenty aboard the *Hyson*. The guns were already stowed, their carriages dismantled for transport. They steamed along the Ching-p'u canal for an hour, then they stopped in a misty reach and Ward went ashore with Vincente, Burgevine and the main gun-party, allowing the steamer to go on. After crossing a neck of land they came to the small boats that were waiting for them.

Now it was eleven o'clock and all was ready. Ahead the East Gate rose like a spectre out of a sea of dense white mist. Ward broke out two of the precious signal flares and gave one to each of two green-uniformed Filipinos, then he dismissed them and hunkered down with Burgevine and Vincente. He said in a low voice, 'We made good time. Too good. I can't have everybody waiting here, something's bound to go wrong. I'm going to advance the attack one hour. Is that clear?'

Both men nodded, and Ward sent a messenger with the information to General Li's holding point. Ten thousand of his Green Standard troops were, even now, secretly marching to the position half a mile away.

'Why did you choose the East Gate when there's a battery on it, Colonel?' Burgevine asked. 'Those gates look to be made out of giant railroad ties. There must be easier ways to get in.'

'There are. Along the west side. But I found out one very

important piece of tactical information when I visited here at night. The west side catches the last rays of the sun, so all the water fowl roost down there. We'd wake them up and lose our surprise.'

Burgevine took the information in silence.

'Remember,' he said. 'Military plans never survive a meeting with the enemy – the Taipings haven't heard our plans, so they can't be expected to follow them. That's why I'm here – to think it up as we go along. And it's your job to make sure I get what I call for when I call for it. Any questions?'

There were none. Vincente crept away to check on his men, vanishing into the sound-killing fog. Ward punched Burgevine in the shoulder. 'Give it your best shot, Henry. Let's make it work this time.'

'See you later, Colonel.'

For a moment Ward was alone. He squeezed his silver-tipped baton. He carried no other weapon. Suddenly he was aware of the currents of energy circulating inside him. There were feelings in his chest and belly, like worry or fear or exhilaration – powerful, like the feelings that swarmed up inside a man who stood too close to the edge of a cliff. Maybe it takes danger to make those currents, he thought. Maybe they come whenever a man's destiny is about to fork. Jesus Christ, this is living!

He remembered what Chang-mei had told him when he had joked with her and told her about his hopes for the future. In Yang Fang's yamen he had drunk tea and modestly made small of his courage which she had politely said must be very great.

'Perhaps you can learn to feel the flow,' she had said, seeming to him as delicate as a flower.

Her words had surprised him. She had been so contained, so reticent, so forlorn. On previous occasions she had never ventured so much.

'Feel the flow? Of what?'

'Of the tao.'

'Ah,' he had nodded thoughtfully. 'I've heard Chinese people speak of it, but it was never explained to me.'

'The tao cannot be explained. But it is possible to feel the tao inside you.'

'How?'

'By looking within. The tao can show you which way you must go.'

'That sounds like a useful skill.' He had smiled, knowing he had to be gentle with her.

'First you must learn how to feel it.'

'Can you feel it?'

She had hesitated, and a fearful look had come into her eyes, and he knew she had been reminded of how deeply her life had been damaged.

'No. I cannot feel the tao. Not any more.'

He had wanted to cut away from the subject, to turn aside without pursuing, but instead he asked, 'Why can't you feel the tao now?'

And she had met his eye directly for the first time, and made her dreadful admission. 'Because my spirit is dead inside me. I am a bad luck woman.'

Ward roused himself from the mordant horror of that moment and brought his mind back to the present. The air was still and fetid, and he thought of the waterlogged graves he had stumbled into on the west side of the city. Thousands of emaciated bodies were there, most of them women and children. Were they killed by Taipings or by Imperials? And why should innocent inhabitants be massacred each time a town changed hands? Was that another immutable Chinese tradition?

Ward had seen the Chinese way of besieging a city. Huge numbers of Imperial troops girded up their loins, tucked up the bottoms of their pyjamas, wound their pigtails around their shaved heads and advanced in broad daylight. They made a terrible display of huge flags, roaring gongs, bamboo shields painted with hideous faces, and an amazing waste of gunpowder. He had visited one of the towns on the Grand Canal near Soochow. He had watched the Imperials move forward with terrific, cloud-rending yells only to establish themselves safely out of cannon-range of the walls. But no attack had been pressed home. They never attacked, instead they sealed off the doomed town with an immense series of earth-works and stockades, and waited until the defenders starved to death. It was infinitely patient, and infinitely horrifying.

But Sung-chiang's an oyster, he thought grimly. We're

going to prise open the shell, so that Li can come right in and cut out the meat.

He saw a large figure materialize from the fog. It was Burgevine.

'That you, Colonel?'

'Here. Trouble?'

'It's those goddamned no-good Chinese sons of bitches you hired.'

'What about them?'

'They're sat down on the road crying their slanty little eyes out.'

'Crying?' Ward drew an incredulous breath. 'It's your job to stop them crying. I'm not paying good wages to men who aren't prepared to fight!'

'What the hell do you want me to do?' Burgevine's tone was that of a wronged man. 'Like I said before, they're cowards. No-good coolies. All afraid to die like men.'

Ward met his eye. 'Mister, we're all afraid to die, but a soldier's got to be a soldier. You better impress that upon those boys real quick!'

He tracked back to the roadway and found Vincente with the Chinese troops. They were squatting on their heels sobbing quietly.

'What the hell's the matter with them? They were fine back on the boat.'

'These boys do not lack courage, Coronel,' Vincente said. 'They're not afraid. They will risk death as bravely as any soldier.'

'Then what in God's name are they crying for?' Ward asked, his exasperation boiling over.

'Because they can feel some ghosts.'

'What?'

'They are sorry for their ancestors' sake. They are young, and so have done nothing yet to repay their parents and forebears for the life they have been given. This makes them feel guilt before the spirits of the dead in case they should die tonight.'

'You mean they'll still fight?'

Vincente shrugged, trying to bridge the gulf of understanding. 'Of course. To the death. Why else would they be trying to settle their affairs?'

Ward gestured with his baton. 'Henry, you heard that?

225

Just move them out on time. Get the guns in place. Vincente, we've got work to do. Let's get this vessel under weigh!'

Just before eleven o'clock the guns opened up, firing almost simultaneously at short range. The heavy timbers of the East Gate were banded in iron, but they shattered like pine laths under the impact of six- and twelve-pound iron balls. Before the smoke from the volley cleared twenty men surged up out of the fog-filled moat, screaming like demons, and followed Vincente into the breach.

Ward led another ten over the causeway after them, but when he burst through the shattered gates he saw a heart-crushing sight: a second, inner pair of gates, just as strong as those outside. Musket fire flashed down from the walls that overlooked them, filling the narrow space between the inner and outer gates with incredible noise.

'Coronel! What'll we do?'

We're done for, he thought desperately. I've led them into a death trap. If the rebels are able to turn just one of their cannon on us we're finished.

His men began to return fire to the figures who had appeared on the walls above. Vincente shouted orders and the scaling ladders began to rise, despite the muzzle flashes that speared from the darkness above. But he saw that the tactic would not succeed, and as the rain of death increased over his men, the survivors dropped their ladders and ran for the meagre cover afforded by the outer gatehouse.

'We've got to blow those gates!' Ward shouted, knowing that Burgevine couldn't fire the big guns again while his men were crowding the gateway. Nor could he ask his men to abandon cover and retreat back across the causeway.

'Come back with me!'

'Madre! Not across the causeway, Coronel. It's suicide! The men—'

'Tell them to make a stand here. We need to hold the outer gatehouse. Tell them we'll be back!'

He ran for it, and Vincente ran after him. For fifty yards all across the causeway they were exposed to heavy enfilading fire. Taiping musketeers crowded along the length of the walls to left and right. Flashes lit the darkness. Shots thudded into the ground around them and sparked off the stone kerb at their side.

'What's gone wrong?' Burgevine shouted.

'Powder,' Ward yelled back. 'Inner gates! We got to blow them!'

The artillery were charged from twenty-pound kegs stored in spark-proof lockers near the guns. Ward flung them open and grabbed up a keg under each arm. Vincente did likewise, following him back up the causeway.

As they approached the moat, one of the Taiping cannon on top of the gatehouse fired. A tongue of blinding flame blasted out over their heads and pulverized the ground they had just crossed. The world disappeared in choking smoke. Ward dived through the maze of reduced timber and brick-work and found the gatehouse niche. Vincente was hauled in after, then Burgevine slammed into the breach with two more kegs. As he reached the niche he punched the air, his bull face alight with the triumph of being alive.

Shots continued to rain down in the killing space outside, plus stones and debris and anything else the rebels could find to throw at them. Ward saw a dozen bodies lying in the open, a couple of them still moving. Six of the men who had been holding the gatehouse wore dark green uniforms. At Ward's order they stepped up with their powerful Sharps repeaters, and began to give a hail of rapid covering fire. At least two were shot, but their fire drove the defenders back just long enough for Ward and Vincente to jam five of the kegs up against the bottom of the inner gates, and for Ward to break open the last of the kegs, trailing a fuse from it as he ran.

He skidded back into the partial safety of the gatehouse, a whirlwind of stones and shot following in after him. His tunic was torn and his shoulder was bleeding.

'Damn!'

'What's the matter?' Burgevine asked.

'Powder trail ran out short,' he said, thinking of the flare in his pocket. 'There's better than a thousand Taiping defenders inside that gate, and they couldn't be more roused if they were hornets stirred up with a smoking stick. I hope to God old General Li's ready to come up in support. It's been twenty minutes since the first shot.'

The plan they had agreed was straightforward. The Green Banner's ten thousand troops were to hold formation behind a slight rise almost two li to the east. They were to be ready to march from the first sound of attack, and to advance the moment the Foreign Arms Corps secured the East Gate. A flare was to be the General's signal to move up. Ward carried one in his pocket, but two more had been issued to the two best-trusted men of his bodyguard, to be fired in the event that he was killed.

'What now?' Burgevine said.

Vincente took out a Manila cheroot and began to light it, an unconcerned look on his face.

'Are you crazy?' Burgevine shouted at him.

The Filipino grinned, 'I think, señor, I must be.' Then he scrambled out to a sudden volley of musketry and tried to touch the cheroot to the powder trail.

Ward crouched in the flashing darkness. Sweat streamed from him and he breathed heavily. He looked to Burgevine. Then a stupefying concussion hit and the blast roared by them and a shower of dislodged masonry clattered all around them.

Ward's ears hummed. He shook his head to clear it. There was coughing and wailing from outside. He tried to look out, but the dust-laden air was impenetrable. As the murk began to settle, the noise of musketry peppered the silence and began to rise to a crescendo again. He crawled to the corner of the gatehouse and saw Vincente huddled in the open, half buried in debris, his arms tight round his head.

He dashed out and dragged him to cover. He was bloodied and dazed, but he seemed not to have been shot through.

'The gates!' Burgevine shouted, his arms swimming dust out of the air. 'Look! They ain't there no more!'

Ward suddenly realized the urgency of the situation. He screamed at the men to follow him towards the inner gateway and glory. And they did.

Lindley was still in shock as he watched from the rail of the gunboat *Coromandel*. Plumes of smoke rose above the huge compacted earth ramparts that flanked the Pei-ho River. The great lashed bamboo booms that had barred the river mouth had been cut away now, and a flotilla of foreign ships had already begun moving up toward the city of Tientsin, the port that served Peking.

He found it hard to believe he was looking at the Taku forts. His resolve not to come here could not have been stronger, but what Ward had said after their fight had made him reconsider his options. After that he had returned home and found the letter in his father's handwriting. It had been brought by hand from Nanking. And only one person could have brought it.

Fei had made his decision easy. That night, as he had bathed his cuts and bruises, there had been no question in his mind about what he must do. He would do as his father asked and stay in Shanghai – but only so that he could look for her. The letter proved she was not lost to him. So he would find her. Then she would help him find his father and discover the truth.

But the following day Meadows had destroyed him. He had visited with a poster taken from the Chinese city. 'You'll be interested to see this,' Meadows had said. 'That Taiping gunrunner who deceived you into going upriver aboard Ward's boat has finally got her reward.'

The effect of the execution notice had been to throw him into a state of shock. Suddenly nothing made sense any more. If Fei was dead, then what did it all mean? More than anything else it made him want to leave Shanghai. A bare hour before sailing Meadows had persuaded him into boarding the *Coromandel*, and once aboard the numbness and black thoughts had begun to overwhelm him.

The bulk of the British and Indian forces had already gone ashore at Talienwan to establish the bridgehead. At the same time the French had disembarked at Pehtang, setting up lines of bell tents, so that when seen through Loch's collapsible telescope the two camps had resembled a couple of small towns. Then the armies had landed their artillery, supplies and horses, easily fighting off attacks by the Manchu cavalry who came down in large numbers to harass them, but who soon learned to respect the deadly range and accuracy of rifled arms.

After a week of preparation the two armies had advanced across the swampy flats to converge on the landward sides of the strongholds known as the Taku forts. Loch told Lindley sombrely, 'These were the forts that fired on Lord Elgin's brother twelve months ago, and which proved such a hindrance to his lordship a year before that. I trust we'll see a different outcome this time.'

'I trust we will,' Lindley had said darkly. 'I sincerely hope they have the good sense to give in.'

'But I think they will not. Their eyes see only Outer Barbarians marching on their capital city. They do not yet perceive the inevitable march of history, the path down which all nations must eventually march.'

Lindley shrugged. 'I have the strangest feeling that the Chinese are really only sleepwalking. They're living in a pipe-dream where they're the masters and everybody else counts for nothing. But the world isn't like that any more.'

Yesterday Generals Grant and de Montauban had attacked the rear of the inner northern fort that guarded the river passage to Peking. The Chinese were proud of the Taku forts and imagined them to be invulnerable. An artillery bombardment had started the advance, then lines of uniformed infantry had fixed bayonets and swarmed over the maze of canals and moats that protected the fort, launching an irresistible assault on the walls.

Lindley noticed Elgin watching silently from the rail a few yards away as the ramparts of the devastated Taku forts slid by. The Armstrong guns had blasted the first fort's heavy wooden gates to kindling. The great blockhouse standing on a truncated pyramid in the centre was smudged by smoke now, and it was flying both the Union flag and the Tricolour. It was surrounded by countless sharpened wooden stakes and littered with the bodies of thousands of Chinese. Reports had come in of some four hundred allied dead. General Grant had announced that he would be making recommendations for six of the new Victoria Cross medals to be awarded. Signor Beato, an Italian artist, had brought with him equipment to make photographs of the victory. He was now ashore exposing plates among the dead.

Thoughts of Fei still weltered through Lindley's mind. The tender moments they had shared, their joys and their intimacies and what might have been, circled in his consciousness like leaves trapped in an eddy. But those bright flashes were consumed by the terrifying darkness of the way her life must have ended.

'There was no need for any of this,' Elgin told Loch as a heavy summer rain began to fall. 'The Manchu must by now realize they are merely delaying the inevitable.'

'His lordship is not a contented man,' Loch said as soon

as Elgin moved out of earshot. 'The French believe he's planning to back the Taipings officially. Baron Gros suspects we want to install them at Peking in place of the Manchu.'

Lindley stared at him. 'Is it true? Has his lordship been told to back the Taipings?'

'No.' Loch looked away and lowered his voice. 'His orders merely instruct him to act at his discretion. His only instruction was to annex the peninsula of the nine dragons – Kowloon – that's the Chinese mainland directly opposite Hong Kong island.'

'Then, why wasn't it annexed?'

Loch smiled. 'Because, in the event, annexation wasn't necessary. Our troops were able to camp at Kowloon without any bother.'

Lindley grunted. 'I suppose they just seized the place without any thought to the legal owners.'

'You've become a cynical man, Doctor. The truth is that his lordship arranged to rent the land from the Governor of Canton at a rate of a hundred and sixty pounds a year. It was all quite amicably concluded.'

Lindley gave a short laugh. 'You mean to say the Governor of Canton played willing host to a foreign army bent on marching on his own capital?'

'That's right.'

'H. B., that's the equivalent of the mayor of Edinburgh renting out the foreshore at Leith to a Chinese army so they might find it more convenient to march on London.'

'Aye, well, that's a good idea too.' Loch smiled again, impishly, trying to raise his spirits. 'You see, the North and the South don't get along in China nearly as well as we've learned to do in Great Britain. Mind you, it took several wars and a great deal of patience with our neighbours to make it so. Reconciling the two ends of a country is a major political undertaking. It generally takes time. And it's never a pretty sight when a country falls apart.'

The remark made him think of the worsening news from the United States, and that made him remember Ward again. What the man had said had stunned him: 'Fifty million dead so far, and it's all down to your pa . . .'

He had demanded to know what Ward meant.

'C'mon, Doc. Your father was a young missionary at

Canton when Hung Hsiu-ch'uan failed his mandarin examinations. You can't tell me you never wondered about that.'

'What are you saying?'

While he tended Ward's wounds, the American had explained how Hung Hsiu-ch'uan had been an ordinary clerk from Canton who had suffered a mental breakdown and a series of sweating fits. At about the same time he had chanced to read some Christian tracts, after which Hung had written his own tracts, perverting the Scriptures, and feeding the gullible hill people of his native district with his own twisted version of Christianity. Hung had called his writings the 'New Testament', while the actual New Testament was renamed the 'Former Testament'. The Trinity was refigured as Shang-ti, Christ and Hung himself, while his followers were required to undergo a strange baptism, a ritual designed to sever their future from their past, in which each man or woman was obliged to confess their evils to Shang-ti by writing down every sin they had ever committed. The confessions were then burned in a cleansing flame, and as the smoke rose to Heaven so their blemishes were supposedly forgiven, and their souls became Taiping souls . . .

'That in itself was enough to gain him a powerful grip on their minds,' Ward had said. 'But what brought the peasants flocking to his cause was much more material. The political doctrine Hung always preached is one of freedom. Freedom from the tight confines of Confucianism. Freedom from corrupt local officials. Freedom from greedy landlords. Those who choose to become Taipings pay no taxes, they have protection, and they have land of their own. And now he's offering them everlasting life too.'

He had listened in silence, stiffly resistant to what the American had told him. 'Maybe all those things are what the people of China deserve.'

'But what has he given them in reality? Only poverty, enslavement and death.' Ward had sighed and shrugged unhappily. 'I'm sorry, Doc, but it was your father who wrote that Christian pamphlet. The one that put all those crazy, twisted ideas into Hung's mind in the first place.'

Lindley looked out now as the downpour increased, making muddy pools on the corpse-blighted land. The red earth of China was once again soaked with unnecessary blood.

'Hell,' he said, feeling the blackness within. 'Nor am I out of it.'

Yehonala waited in the Imperial garden, concealed from casual view by a tumbled breastwork of rock. All around, among the trees and flower beds were curious, twisted lavas that had been brought to the capital from far away, rocks that were weathered and patterned so they fed the poetic imagination. Here ferns and mosses had been artfully arranged so the display gave the impression of a miniature landscape. It made anyone who sat among them feel like a giant.

An Te-hai had told her about the Emperor's habit of slipping his guard and visiting this place at the Hour of the Horse. Shortly after the drumbeats marking the change of the hour she heard Hsien-feng coming.

When he saw her in his island of peace he recoiled, as if from an apparition. There was genuine fear in his eyes.

'What are you doing here?'

'Yi-chu,' she said softly, using his princely name. 'Have you lost all faith in me?'

'Yehe woman, are you here to murder me?'

'Why do you look at me that way?' she asked.

'I no longer know you.'

'Is that why you caused me to be excluded from all councils? Is this the way you have chosen to reward the mother of your son?'

His eyes remained on her. 'Before the Prince Yi rode out to chastise the Barbarians he told me about a curse concerning Yehe women. That a Yehe woman will cut the blood line of Nurhachi.'

She released his eyes, knowing she must win him with motherly reassurance and obligation. 'The Prince Yi is mistaken. There was never any such curse. The chieftain, Buyang's, death-bed utterances were of revenge against Nurhachi, it is true, but they were not a curse. You must see that an ancient law written at Mukden over two hundred years ago is being used by those who are jealous of me to keep me away from you.'

He lowered himself gingerly onto the marble bench. 'Sushun told me you were trying to poison me against him.'

Hsien-feng's spinelessness revolted her, but she maintained

her outward show. 'The opposite is true. Su-shun is a danger-ous parasite, but you do not yet see that.'

'I can trust no one.'

She maintained her appeal to his sense of duty. 'In what light do you regard your people? In what light the shrines of your ancestors and the altars of the tutelary gods? Will you cast away the inheritance of your ancestors like a broken shoe? If you did that, what would history say of the Hsien-feng Emperor for a thousand generations to come?'

Hsien-feng lost his composure. 'All is contradiction! I am pulled this way and that, until I am pulled in pieces! How can I know the truth of what people say to me?'

'Sometimes not even the Emperor of Heaven can divine the true hearts of men.'

He looked up, his hand clenching. 'Yehonala, there is no one I can trust! No one!'

She deliberately softened her attitude again. 'It is foolish to trust everyone, but it is impossible to live if you trust no one at all. Therefore you must make a choice.'

He hung his head. 'Please ... do not talk to me of the world outside. Here I come to be alone. This is my little land of peace. I could not bear it if this too was taken from me.'

She stared at him unmoved, knowing the very immobility of her expression was giving away her innermost feelings. Deep in his heart he knows that I merely pity him, she thought.

'Yehonala, please help me.'

'Let me remind you of the story of the fox. How, long ago, the fox had nine tails. Each of those nine tails was a vice which made him bad: drunkenness, recklessness, dis-honesty, bad temper, desire for vengeance, gluttony, greed, violence and the desire to keep bad company. Eventually, so much evil made the Emperor of Heaven angry, and he said: "You must lose one of your tails. Choose." But the fox enjoyed all his tails and would not choose, so the Emperor of Heaven seized the tail of drunkenness and cut it off. The fox's drunkenness stopped, but his other vices continued, and so the Emperor of Heaven cut off another tail, and then another and then another, until only one tail remained, which was his desire to keep bad company. This was the most dangerous vice of them all, and explains why to this day the fox is hated universally by all right thinking people.

Do not listen to Su-shun. Refuse the company of Prince Yi and Prince Cheng. Do not send Prince Yi and Mu Yin to do your bidding, but rather choose to fight the Barbarians yourself. Ride forth from the Forbidden City at the head of your army and all the Common People will instantly love you.'

He would not look at her, but continued to sit on the bench, staring at the pathway gravel.

'No one has ever loved me.'

He said it so forlornly that she almost lost her own strength of purpose.

'Tell me this,' she said. 'Did you ever love me?'

His tone was that of a victim. His perverse spirit was feeding on self-pity. 'I have always loved you. Right from the first moment I saw you.'

'Then, why will you not trust me?'

'I cannot.'

'Yi-chu, if you have ever loved me, seize the reins of power in your right hand. They already belong to you! Stay here in Peking and fight!'

'I cannot.'

'Then, at least cancel the prohibition on me.'

'I cannot.'

'You must. Or you will be reborn a tapeworm for all the evil you have done by your inaction.'

She whirled and left him, seeing that further talk now would be useless.

Elgin announced the dinner at the final stalling of talks. 'Unless an undertaking is received from the Chinese capital by midnight tomorrow night, this expedition will quit Tientsin and begin the overland march to Peking. Since Admiral Hope and Mr Bowlby of *The Times* are the only persons present who are not Scots, perhaps they will do us the honour of accepting some good Caledonian hospitality.'

All through the meal Lindley picked at his plate, unable to think through the implications of what Ward had said about his father. The question about what to do when the expedition ended plagued him.

The smoke from Elgin's cigar reached him, and he brought his attention back to the present just in time to hear Grant say in confidence to Elgin, 'The Admiral's vessels should remain here in strength. Your lordship's safety in Peking will be far better guaranteed if Tientsin remains under the guns of British warships.'

'Aye, I'm inclined to agree with you, though I wish it were otherwise.'

Loch said, 'Your lordship, the Tientsin Chinese say that Peking is in an absolute uproar of funk. Do you think they're sensing that their Emperor is about to flee now that negotiations have broken down?'

Elgin continued to sip at his whisky. 'I've told you before, Mr Loch, we were not negotiating. Agreements have already been reached. They were reached two years ago, and at this very place. Two days ago I told the Chinese Her Britannic Majesty would have her ambassador at Peking. Therefore, come what may, there will be a British ambassador at Peking. And there's an end to it. A letter has been despatched to their capital to that effect.'

The Admiral grunted. 'Damn it, though, my Lord, if this isn't the most extraordinary way to deliver a letter!'

'They should thank their lucky stars that's all we're here to do. Heaven help them if we'd had conquest in mind. What do you say to that, Doctor?'

The ship's bell signalled midnight. Elgin's interest in his views made Lindley squirm. He said, 'I say we should not be giving them opium.'

Elgin balked at the remark. 'Come, come. The Chinese were smoking opium centuries before the first Westerner ever came this way.'

'Opium is addictive! It enslaves the mind!'

'Aye, Dr Lindley, and so does power and so does religion and so does love and self-righteousness and a thousand other things.'

Lindley rose and put down his napkin. 'Gentlemen, you'll please excuse me.'

The volcano inside him continued to erupt as he stared out over the rail at the slumbering city of Tientsin.

After a while he heard a hatch open and the faint smell of cigar smoke tainted the sweetness of the night air. Frogs were calling in the darkness. Elgin tucked a thumb into his dinner jacket. 'It's both a wonderful and a terrible thing to be here on the other side of the world, is it not?'

He hung his head, not knowing how to reply.

'By God, Lindley, it's nights like this I really miss my wife.'

He thought again of Fei, and the pain was almost too much to bear. After a while he said, 'My lord, I should like to apologize for what I said at table. I haven't been myself lately. My behaviour was unforgivable.'

'Maybe,' Elgin said. 'But maybe not so bad for a man who's been commandeered against his will and pushed onto an expedition of which he doesn't approve.'

'I came of my own free will.'

'A surprising change of heart for a man who came to China only to find his father . . .'

'You know about that?'

'Aye. Consul Meadows told me what he thought I should know.' Elgin flicked ash into the Pei-ho's inky waters. 'Lindley, you know that your ability to speak Chinese makes you the master of the present situation, don't you?'

Coming from anyone else it would have seemed like flattery, but he saw that Elgin was speaking from conviction. 'I suppose so.'

'Lindley, you have my word that if you see this expedition through, when this whole nightmare's over I'll do my best to see the road to Nanking smoothed for you.'

He felt the man's unsolicited kindness add to his burden; he had been drunk five minutes ago, but now he was sober. 'My lord – you've tried to ease my mind,' he said. 'And I thank you for taking the time.'

Elgin nodded. 'One day you'll come to learn that politicians and diplomats rarely have to deal with conflict between good and evil. Our task is solely contending with evils big and small, and trying hard to choose the lesser of them.'

The empty courtyard was still grey in the dawn light. An swept out patterns in the air in the slow-motion dance of the tai-chi. He had been to his fortune-teller, and in that dim, oil-lit room, hung about with talismans and the arcane instruments of the diviner's art, he had asked about the likely futures he faced.

'We all travel from our pasts into our futures along a road beset by many crossroads. When you come to such a junction you must feel the tao moving within you, and sense the correct way forward. This advice is better than any reading I can make for you. Practise your tai-chi. This will help focus your mind inwardly. Then you will start to feel the currents of the tao and so discover which way you must head. Only then can I help you to read the signs.'

'I want you to make a reading now.'

The fortune-teller had hesitated, but then he had offered the box and An put his hand inside, believing absolutely. His fingers felt the hundreds of papers each printed with a hidden word. The paper he had withdrawn contained the character 'tsu' – soldier.

'Originally, this character was a picture of a soldier's tunic. It came to mean soldier. The meaning is that you must behave dutifully. Like a soldier. But tsu also means "pawn" – as in a chess game. This indicates that you are not presently in control of your own actions. That they are being controlled for you by another.'

'Who?' he had asked. But the fortune-teller had lowered his eyes mutely, showing that that was a question that could be answered only by the client himself.

An opened his eyes and composed himself. It was time to attend the Empress of the Western Palace, and in this good fortune seemed genuinely to have smiled.

Yehonala's meeting yesterday with the Emperor had spawned two unexpected consequences. The first was that Hsien-feng had issued a public proclamation, but instead of announcing his departure on a hunting trip as many had predicted, he merely wrote:

'We learn that the Barbarians continue to press upon our capital. Their demands were all complied with, yet they insist upon presenting to us in person their barbarous documents of credentials, and demand that General Sang shall withdraw his troops from Chang-chia-wan. Such insolence as this makes further parley impossible. General Sang has gained one great victory already, and now his forces are holding the enemy in check at Pa-li-ch'iao.'

The second unexpected consequence was that the Emperor had summoned An to him and ordered that a beautiful gift be selected for Yehonala.

Immediately An had suspected the Emperor's displeasure, but when Hsien-feng had made it clear that he would pay the cumsha himself, he had breathed a sigh of relief.

The junior eunuch who had been ordered to fetch the kitchen maid stepped forward.

An sighed doubtfully. Look at her, he thought. I really ought to present her to Su-shun. He would delight in receiving such a willowy creature, and such a gift might help me should the future turn out badly for me and, besides, I did take the bribe.

'Come along,' he said, collecting her.

He went directly to the Western Palace, where Yehonala received him immediately. She was still in her sleeping pyjamas. Imperial dragons were embroidered into lavender silk on front and back, while the sleeves and legs were decorated with peonies.

'Lady Yehonala,' he said in his best formal voice, 'This humble slave has been instructed by His Imperial Majesty to select an addition to your retinue. Knowing your delight in beauty the Son of Heaven requested particularly that I select appropriately.'

Yehonala paid no attention as the girl came forward. Her mind was on much weightier matters.

'Kowtow to your mistress,' An prompted. 'This girl is new to us. She is still untrained in essential etiquette but I believe—'

'Look at this.' Yehonala walked past the prostrate maid, offering An a paper. 'It has just been issued.'

She watched his eyes carefully as An began to read, but he appeared to be as surprised as she had been herself. He said, 'Can this be correct? The Imperial Hunting Lodge at Jehol is to be reopened and staffed, pending a possible "autumn tour of inspection"?'

'Su-shun knows that retiring the Court to Jehol will bring him closer to Hsien-feng. Within the Forbidden City, it is not always easy for an official or even for a Prince of the Blood to approach the Son of Heaven, but Jehol is an informal setting. The rules will be more relaxed in a hunting lodge nestling among the northern hills.'

'But ... this goes against the proclamation issued last night, Lady. You and I both know that the departure of the Court to Jehol would be a disaster for you. Surely General Sang's victory over the Barbarians has—'

'Last night's proclamation was merely an attempt to calm the city in readiness for this announcement. You can be

239

sure there has been no victory and no holding of the Barbarian army.'

'But the Emperor's gift to you surely means—'

'Gift?' Yehonala snorted. 'She's probably a spy. Now take this message to Prince Kung. Do it in person. I require a reply. Now, I'm going to bathe.'

Fei remained in the kowtow position, silent, listening, as the Chief Eunuch humbled himself and left. Her heart knocked against her ribs as she lay on the floor, hearing the anger of the Empress filling the room. Everything had happened so quickly, and she had not gotten over the arrival of the Chief Eunuch's runner in the kitchens, let alone being presented to the Empress of the Western Palace.

When the Empress had used the word 'spy' it had made her blood freeze. She had readied herself to jump up and shout the Taiping ultimatum, but then caution made her look inward, and she had decided it would be better to see how matters lay. You've come so far she thought now. It's best to be sure. One more day will not affect anything.

The Empress collected her retinue of six eunuchs and four maids and led them briskly to her bathing room. She inspected it carefully. Then two of the eunuchs carried in a pail of steaming water while two more brought two large silver basins and the others carried in dozens of freshly-laundered towels. When she sat on a low stool the eunuchs departed. The towels for her arms and upper body were put out in readiness. They were white with a yellow border, with pairs of yellow dragons embroidered on them.

The most senior of the maids told Fei, 'My name is Wen. I am to train you. For the moment, stand there. Observe what happens, and do nothing.'

Fei watched in amazement as the serving maids all took their places – one behind Yehonala, one in front, and the others standing on each side. They worked together, dipping towels into hot water, wringing them dry and soaping them, then applying them to arms and body, as all the while the Empress issued instructions and gave opinions.

So this is how they live, Fei thought, smelling the heavy freshness of flowers permeate the air. Everywhere I look there are huge sprays of chrysanthemums standing in ornate vases, expensive screens and wall hangings portraying birds and animals in lacquer and mother-of-pearl. Even the tiniest details of these rooms are finished in scarlet and gold or minutely carved expensive woods. Incredible opulence while millions starve. How can she be at such leisure at a time like this?

Fei's time in the kitchens had been grinding drudgery. She had found that the kitchen maids were already grouped into closed alliances into which it was impossible to gain entry, except by months or years of grovelling subservience. As the latest arrival she had been given the hardest and dirtiest jobs. She had fetched and carried and scrubbed, but it had not mattered because all the while her mind had pondered the gigantic question of how she could break away from her duties and get close enough to one of the Grand Councillors to successfully deliver the vital ultimatum.

Time was passing. It was essential to deliver the message at the most effective moment – while the foreign army was pressing hard on Peking, and while the momentum of events in the South was continuing to build. Her orders did not specify which of the princes ought to be approached. She had been told to select the member of the ruling elite who in her opinion was most likely to act on the ultimatum. Her uncle had given her the titles of the Forbidden City's principal political figures – a bewildering multitude of censors, grand councillors, generals, presidents of boards and ministers, of whom Su-shun, the Princes Yi, Cheng and Kung, and the bolder of the two Empresses seemed to be important. But since gaining entry there had been no way to observe any of them, let alone make a choice.

She watched as the indulgent ritual continued. As soon as the Empress's skin was fully soaped four more towels were dipped in water and used to rinse her, then four more to dry her before honeysuckle lotion was rubbed into her skin. The Empress was never completely naked in front of servants: she put on the top half of her silken pyjamas again before removing her pantaloons. Then a fresh silver basin was filled and placed before her. She stood in it, and the maids began to soap and rinse and dry and apply lotion all over again, this time to her legs and lower body, working with practised skill.

While her maids busied themselves Yehonala's mind calculated how to counter the threat posed by the Jehol announcement. Fortunately, she thought, it's a contingency

I've already anticipated. Prince Kung and I had to call in several valuable debts but we've organized a crucial memorial to the throne, and it's a document to which every available influential chop left in Peking has been applied. It remains only to be dated and presented.

She recalled its outrageously outspoken conclusion:

' . . . thus His Imperial Majesty cannot be spared for long from the Forbidden City where he has so many duties to perform. Therefore we humble servants beg that he will give over his plan and not be swayed by alien influences.'

It's a demonstration of our power, she thought. But is it sufficient? Or must we truly declare war?

Her toilet completed, she left the bathing room, but instead of going direct to her wardrobe, she dismissed her maids, including the new girl – the present was proof at least that Hsien-feng had not abandoned her.

The moment has come to take a step that is beyond all etiquette, she told herself. A step that is irrevocable, that will set loose a torrent of consequences. She went to her writing desk and sat down. Inking her brush with stolen Imperial vermilion, she poised it to write a letter in the name of the Son of Heaven. It's time to put a price on Barbarian heads, and to tell the generals to execute captives.

What have you become? a distant voice inside her asked as she began to write. Where did you learn to write sentences of death?

But this time there was no reply.

Lindley tore down the poster angrily. 'Look!' he shouted, thrusting it toward the mounted men assembled in the deserted, fire-blackened village. A heavy dew had fallen overnight, but even so a haze hung over the village and the stench of burned grain was heavy on the air. They were a mile from the town of T'ung-chow, and no more than ten miles from Peking. 'What more proof do you need? We must get back to camp immediately.'

'What is it?' Loch asked. He was flanked by Bowlby and de Normann of Elgin's staff. They had ridden here through fields of ripe millet that stretched to the banks of the Pei-ho River to make final arrangements for a meeting with senior mandarins.

Lindley shook the paper. 'It's an Imperial decree – a decree composed by the Emperor himself.'

'What does it say?' Bowlby asked. He sounded frightened.

'It says: "I command all my subjects to hunt down the foreigners like savage beasts. Let the villages be abandoned as these wretches draw near. Let all provisions be destroyed which they might secure. In this manner their accursed race will perish of hunger like fish in a dried-up pond. Respect this!" Gentlemen, I warn you, we are now in the greatest danger.'

'But you said you'd been invited here to talk,' Bowlby said accusingly. 'You said Imperial negotiators were waiting to receive us at T'ung-chow.'

'That's what was arranged.'

All the way as the army had advanced along the Pei-ho the Chinese Commissioners had continued to urge them to turn back. Letters were presented daily. Prince Yi and Mu Yin, President of the Board of War, arrived to continue where Kuei-liang had left off. Lindley had agreed with them that the allied army would wait outside T'ung-chow while Lord Elgin and Baron Gros rode on to Peking, each with a ceremonial escort of 1,000 cavalrymen. Prince Yi, a tall, dignified man with an intelligent face, had said it would be impossible for Lord Elgin to meet personally with the Emperor, and Lindley, mindful of their sensitivities, had decided not to labour the point.

Lindley turned now at the sound of hooves. A hundred yards away a column of horsemen were cantering forward. As they came up he recognized Colonel Walker by the rolled black umbrella he always carried. With him was Thompson of the Commissariat and an escort of six King's Dragoons and twenty Sikhs of Fane's Regiment of Horse.

'Good morning,' Walker called amiably. 'Weather's a little on the warm side, what?' Walker's studied complacency was at odds with the musket-ball hole in his helmet.

'Look at this,' Lindley told him, handing over the proclamation and explaining its message.

'Thought as much from their disposition. We're on reconnaissance. Johnny Enemy appears to have gathered in rather large numbers. It seems he's keen to have us leave T'ung-chow.'

Thompson, dapper, punctilious, stabbed a finger at the

horizon. 'We've seen squadrons of Manchu cavalry roaming about. They daren't come near our main battalions, but I daresay they're quite capable of surprising and annihilating small groups.'

Walker turned in his saddle and surveyed the flat land. 'There's a bridge across the Peking canal at Pa-li-ch'iao. He'll want to hold that.'

'They're making a stand? Here?' Bowlby asked, his anxiety audible now.

Lindley climbed back onto his Indian pony. 'I don't think so,' he told Walker, seeing everything with sudden clarity. 'Look at the land around here. Flat as a fluke – fields of tall crops separated by ditches. You could hide an army in there. They're not making a stand, they're outflanking us, enveloping our column as it advances.'

Walker's eyes roamed the land as he deliberated. 'You might have something there. In any case someone ought to warn General Grant that he might be walking into a trap.'

Lindley turned. 'H.B., weren't you in Skinner's Horse in India?'

'I was adjutant.'

'Will you go?'

Loch shrugged. 'Of course, but . . . what about you?'

'I suggest you take two of Colonel Walker's Sikhs with you if he's agreeable.' He turned back to Walker, who nodded. 'Ride like the wind, H.B., and you'll have half a chance of getting through.'

'I said, what about you?'

'H.B., you're wasting time.' He leaned over and slapped the hindquarters of Loch's horse to send it on its way. Then he said to Walker. 'If you could spare me two more men I'd be most obliged.'

'What for?'

'Someone has to ride to T'ung-chow and see if the Commissioners can be persuaded to stop this bloody madness before it turns into a slaughter.'

'You can't do that!' Thompson said.

'Someone has to.'

'But they'll take you!'

'Can anyone else speak Mandarin?'

Walker waved the proclamation. 'What about this? It sounds like they'd kill you on sight.'

244

'I don't think so. And a lot more will be killed if I don't risk it.'

'Two volunteers!' Walker laughed like a grindstone. 'Come on, you glory-seekers. Who wants to die?'

One of the Sikhs nudged his horse forward. 'Jawalla Singh.'

Not to be outdone one of the dragoons presented himself also. 'Lieutenant Anderson.'

Lindley acknowledged their bravery with a nod of his head. 'You're both maniacs, but I'm very glad of it.'

Captain de Normann and Bowlby volunteered to ride with him.

'No. You'd better stay with the column.'

'I'm sorry, Dr Lindley,' de Normann said, 'but that won't be possible. I'm so poorly mounted I'd slow the Colonel's reconnaissance down. Perhaps fatally.'

'Do you know what you're saying?' Lindley asked, touched by the man's courage. 'What about you, Mr Bowlby?'

Bowlby blinked with barely dominated fear. 'I'm a newspaper correspondent. It's my job to be in the thick of it. And anyway, if we're to be captured I'd prefer to be in the company of a Chinese speaker. That's logical, isn't it?'

'Very well.' Lindley took out a large handkerchief and tied it to the Sikh's lance top. 'Mandarins have recognized the white flag in previous dealings. Let's hope they do so now.'

Lindley waved farewell to Walker and Thompson, and kicked his horse along the track that led to T'ung-chow. He pulled up when he saw the extent of the Chinese advance. Thousands of troops had come up overnight to meet the expedition. Their grey columns were now issuing from T'ung-chow, crossing bridges and shuffling forward into position. Now the morning dew had vanished and clouds of dust were beginning to rise over the places where cavalry were being marshalled. The bright sun glittered on their weapons and the cries of the military mandarins grew loud as Lindley reached their lines.

He rode up and called down to one of them. 'I come under a flag of truce. I bear important news for Prince Yi. Please tell me where I may find him?'

A junior mandarin stared up, astonished that a party of Barbarians had appeared among them.

'The Prince Yi is in T'ung-chow,' he said.

The thud of distant artillery rolled across the plain, and the soldiers nearby began to stir menacingly. There were angry shouts, sudden hostility, and men began to close around the mounted party, their spears outstretched. The mandarin turned on them with extraordinary ferocity and drove them back into formation, then he turned once more with complete formality to Lindley. 'Please. I invite you to follow me.'

'No, no. We must go to T'ung-chow,' Lindley told him. 'This matter is extremely urgent.'

'First we must go to my commanding officer.'

'Who is your commanding officer?'

'Please follow me. You will have safe conduct.'

Lindley considered, then dismounted.

'Hey, what about us?' Bowlby asked anxiously.

'We'd better keep together,' Lindley told him, but as the others began to dismount the mandarin shook his head.

'Only you are to come.'

'They must all come with me,' Lindley said.

'No. Only you. Others must wait here.'

The situation rested on a knife-edge. Lindley saw that he was in no position to argue, so he nodded, told the others to wait, and allowed himself to be led in the direction of T'ung-chow.

They crossed a stinking moat and passed inside the town's walls. When they reached a traditional walled compound guarded by elite banner troops four heavily-armed men broke off to flank him. He was taken to the outer courtyard and made to wait under guard as the mandarin hurried to the interior gate.

The courtyard was bright and already hot. Lindley craned his neck, trying to see where the mandarin had gone. Several minutes passed and he wiped the sweat from his face. The tension mounted unbearably. 'I have an urgent message for the commander of the army,' he told the guards, but they showed no reaction. When he took a step toward the inner compound they seized him and held him. He struggled until one of them drew a sword and thrust its point at his belly.

'I understand!' He shouted, a surge of fear flooding through him. 'I understand.'

Another age passed, then a burly silhouette in studded

war-gear appeared in the shade. A knot of other officers surrounded him, but Lindley realized with dismay who had been summoned. The moment he came into view the guards tried to force Lindley to his knees. Again he resisted, staggering against their strength.

'What are you doing?' he demanded determinedly. 'How dare you? I'm an official messenger empowered by Lord Elgin to treat with—'

The burly man stepped forward, and Lindley recognized him as Sang Ko-lin-sen, the Chinese commander-in-chief who had attended silently during the last two negotiation sessions at Tientsin.

'Kowtow!'

Lindley's legs were roughly kicked out from under him. He landed on the side of his head, and was hauled upright and held. His jacket was wrestled off him and his shirt torn open.

'Kneel before the General!' the mandarin shouted, his previous hesitancy replaced by officially-sanctioned hatred.

Lindley felt his numb lip start to ring with pain. He pressed the tip of his tongue to his teeth to check if any were broken and spat blood onto the cobbles. 'I am empowered by Lord Elgin to treat with Prince—'

Immediately the mandarin came forward and slapped him as hard as he could across the face. 'How dare you spit in the presence of an Imperial general? Open his mouth! You will learn manners!'

The guards forced open Lindley's mouth and the mandarin grabbed up a handful of dirt and thrust it in, choking him.

'Now bind him!'

He coughed, but dared not spit out the dirt. His nostrils flared as he gulped in air. Then he felt his arms pulled behind him and the cords pulled tight on his wrists. Sweat drenched him. Out of the corner of his eye he saw a mandarin ransacking his jacket pockets. He saw the glint of silver as a locket with his mother's picture in it was taken out and examined. The mandarin tried unsuccessfully to open it, then put it to his ear before discarding it.

Dear God please help me, he prayed, remembering the executions he had seen. They think nothing of killing captives. Maintain your dignity. The more dignified you are the better. All the while he looked at Sang Ko-lin-sen, the man British troops had cheerfully renamed 'Sam Collinson'. The absurdity of it gave him a kind of strength.

There was movement at the gate, and another figure was led in and forced down. Lindley's attempt at a glance sideways was answered with a blow to the kidneys by his guard, but he had already seen enough to cause his hopes to plunge. It was H.B. Loch.

'They've taken us all—' Loch said before the wind was knocked out of him.

Sang walked around them menacingly as Loch was beaten to the ground and his arms tied. 'I know who you are. You are assistant to the Barbarian leader. And you – ' he jabbed a finger at Lindley. ' – you are the voice of his arrogance! You are the worm who tries repeatedly to humiliate the Son of Heaven. You are the worm who attempts to speak familiarly with Grand Councillors of the Celestial Empire!'

Lindley stared ahead woodenly, mouth open, his face smeared, blood and mud dripping from his chin. Sang motioned for his mouth to be cleared.

'Now you will go out and order your army to retreat. The other prisoner will stay here.'

'May it please your Excellency,' he said tightly, not daring to listen to H.B. Loch's laboured breathing, and knowing that an ill-chosen word could easily kill them both. 'But such an order is not in my power.'

Sang screamed. 'You will order it! You will order it, or you will die!'

Ward stared at the patterns of light that played across the ceiling. The baroque plasterwork of his Grand Hotel suite was every bit as intricate and expensive as any hotel in Boston or New York, and just as Western. He closed his eyes, shifting again on the crumpled blankets. He had blown out the lamp two hours ago. The ache in his arm had grown in the darkness. It had put out fingers of pain, so that now his whole shoulder hurt down as far his elbow and halfway across his chest.

He was profoundly tired and needed sleep, but could not find it here. No air came in through the open window. Down below, the Bund was seething with ceaseless midnight traffic, and his mind kept turning over the fighting at Sung-chiang and a web of business matters – gun purchases, investments Yang had suggested, the bonus that was supposed to be coming. And every now and again his mind would turn to the sad, pretty face of Yang Fang's tragic daughter, or to Annie Phillips' smooth, white body.

The night of the attack he had burst through the wreck of Sung-chiang's inner gate, mad with the need to get to the batteries that commanded the causeway. His instinct to go into battle armed only with a baton had been exactly correct – it had proved to be the best weapon of all. An unarmed man can lead in a way that's free and pure. He uses all his time to think, and not to worry about himself. For what enemy would make a target of an unarmed man when the rest have guns that can kill? And who would refuse to follow such a leader?

He had felt a powerful euphoria when he found the flight of stone steps that led to the ramparts. He led the charge up them. At close quarters Colt revolvers were the perfect weapons. Burgevine had killed with two fists, and the Manilamen fought with guns in one hand and machetes in the other. They overran the tower in seconds, cutting down the Taiping gun crews, and pitching them over the walls.

Once the cannon were taken the rest of the Corps were signalled across the causeway, and the seizure of the East Gate tower gave him a vantage point that commanded a long stretch of the city walls. He sat down and savoured the victory, feeling for the magnesium flare that would bring the Imperial forces down on the town, but then he noticed the ragged hole in his black tunic and the blood soaking him, and he marvelled that it was his own.

He was astonished to find himself shot. It had been painless. Pain was something the human mind was capable of setting aside. His mind had been too busy to register that he had been hit, proving that pain could not get into a mind whose gates were shut tight against it.

He told Burgevine, 'Lead's a poison. Leave the shot in there and the wound'll fester and rot. It has to be fished out. Will you fix it for me, Henry?'

Burgevine's face puckered. 'I don't know nothing about doctoring.'

'You don't need to. You just find the bullet and fish it.'

'What with – my fingers?'

Burgevine's hands were filthy, his fingers short and thick. He recalled the luxury of Harry Lindley's black Gladstone bag – all the little bottles and clean steel instruments inside. But Harry Lindley was a thousand miles away. Doc Mac-Gowan could see to it later.

'You got gun pliers, haven't you?'

He took off his coat and shirt and Burgevine brought him the pliers and he burned the ends in a little heap of flared up gunpowder.

'I learned that trick back in Sonora,' he told Burgevine.

'What's it for?'

'To stop the pus turning bad later.'

Then Burgevine poked the pliers into the wound while Ward watched black blood welling and running down his arm in trickles and dripping from his elbow. It had not hurt until some time after one of Vincente's men bandaged him up. Then it had started to burn, and he had known that his mind was relaxing and letting the pain be recognized.

'Do you want to keep this?' Burgevine had asked, a sticky lead ball in his palm.

'I will if it'll bring me luck.'

'Here's something that oughta,' Burgevine said, holding up the signal flare.

When the flare soared up and burst, it sent a lurid light ten thousand times as bright as Venus over the squalid rooftops of Sung-chiang. The glare persisted for several seconds, inviting a hail of bullets, and Ward and his men crouched in inadequate cover while the Taipings sniped at them. He willed General Li to advance, then after ten minutes he ordered another flare sent up, but still the Green Standard did not show themselves.

'The bastard isn't coming,' Burgevine said.

'He'll come,' Ward said through gritted teeth. Inside he seethed, thinking the entire attack had been betrayed. Ten minutes later he ordered their last flare launched skyward.

After that the Taiping sniping fire built up and up. Inaccurate but waspish, and effective in a cumulative way. Around three o'clock the moon began to rise. Burgevine went to relieve himself and was winged by a ricochet. His anger was vocal as he threatened to rush the section of wall where he thought the sniper lay.

'Stay right there, Henry! There's seventy-five thousand

taels riding on tonight. There's nothing we won't be able to achieve once we get a-hold of silver like that.'

'Let's just go give those sons of bitches hell!'

'I told you to stay put!'

As the minutes passed into hours, and the hours greyed into a sluggish dawn, the Foreign Arms Corps fought on, exchanging dogged fire with more than a thousand Taiping defenders. Burgevine spat blood all night, calling General Li every filthy name known to man, but Ward refused to budge. They held the gatehouse until full daylight turned the world real again. And only after General Li had satisfied himself that a Taiping column was falling back westward away from the city had the Green Standard moved forward.

Complete self-belief can achieve anything, Ward told himself, willing a victory over himself in the darkness. A commander must have self-belief. Total. Complete. Perfect. A man who has perfect self-belief can conquer the whole world. He can walk without fear. He knows that bullets cannot harm him. He feels himself to be immortal – like a god. He can silence pain . . .

He heard a noise outside. A floorboard creaking under thick carpet. Automatically he listened for a door opening and closing, but there was nothing. He turned in the bed again, threw off the covers, then a soft knock at the door froze him. He had learned during his time with William Walker's private army in Sonora that it was wise always to leave his pants and gun where he could find them in a hurry. This time, he knew, no gun would be necessary. It's only Annie, finished with her commerce and wanting conversation.

The knock came again, still soft, but louder this time. At the third knock he got out of bed, irritated. He threw on a silk robe and opened the door.

'Ah? Colonel. How gratifying to find you in residence tonight.'

Ward's heart sank. It was Strickland with four uniformed Sikhs behind him. The British Consul's lackey wore a malign smile, and his fist was closed around a revolver.

'What do you want, Strickland? Come to shoot me?'

'I wouldn't hesitate. I wonder if you'd care to come along with me for a little chat with Consul Meadows.'

'Why don't you go to hell?'

'You can't say I didn't give you fair warning. Get dressed. You're under arrest.'

There was nothing for it. They walked him under guard to the British Consulate. Meadows was waiting for him in a room that smelled of cigar smoke.

'I'm requiring you to disband the Corps,' he said without preamble.

'And who the hell are you to "require" an American citizen to do anything?'

'The attack on Sung-chiang – sixty-two foreign subjects dead, another hundred wounded, three British among them. That makes it my business.'

'They weren't British. They were Americans. New York immigrants. I have their sworn affidavits.'

'They were British. One of them has a wife and children in Deptford. You enticed them and others from active service in Her Majesty's armed forces.'

'You can't prove that.'

'I don't have to. Your men looted a quantity of silver when Sung-chiang was taken. With it you've bought artillery from a man who works for H. Fogg & Co., and deposited the rest of your blood-money with Jardine-Matheson. Need I go on?'

'What happens at Sung-chiang has got nothing to do with you. And neither have any of my business transactions.'

Meadows began to turn over a silver letter-opener in his fingers. 'Your men handed over Taiping prisoners to Imperial Chinese officials in Sung-chiang. More than a thousand rebels were ritually disembowelled and beheaded. What do you say to that?'

'It's a lie.'

'Ward, I'm not going to allow you to jeopardize British trade – not you, nor anyone. You've already been told that I don't care two pins about diplomatic niceties. Governor Wu might think you're a hero, but I think you're a dangerous filibuster who's bringing the Taipings down on our heads.'

Ward felt a stab of anger. 'I've got news for you, Mr Meadows. The Taipings have a hundred thousand men sitting out there. If they want to come here they'll come here. All I'm doing is showing them they can't expect to come here without a fight. If they get a bloody nose they might think twice before trying.'

'How much did Yang Fang pay you for opening up Sung-chiang for the Green Standard?'

Ward laughed scornfully.

Meadows' face hardened. 'I want you out of here. Do you understand?'

'Sure. Like you wanted Harry Lindley out of here. But the difference is you've no right to push me around.'

'I may not have the right, but I certainly have a mandate and the power to carry it through. And I have a duty too, to the business community here in Shanghai.'

'You want to know about business, Meadows? We have a deal. Lindley went with Elgin as interpreter in return for your promise to keep your hands off me.'

'Lindley had already agreed to go. I told him that when he tried to plead your case.' Meadows folded his arms. 'How much do you want?'

Ward laughed at the absurdity. 'You're trying to buy me off?'

'How much? To abandon Sung-chiang and leave China for ever: name a figure.'

'It may surprise you, Meadows, but I didn't come here just to make money.'

'Then why did you come? For the danger? For glory? To be in command? Is that what you want? Go home, then. Enlist. You could easily get a commission.'

'That's not it, either.'

'Your own country is falling apart. Go home and fight.'

'America can get by without me.'

Meadows let a moment pass in silence, then he said, 'You like to come across as a hard-shelled businessman, Mr Ward, but I know what you really are underneath all that talk. You're a bright-eyed idealist.' He made the word sound dirty. 'And do you know the trouble with idealists? They're arrogant. They always think they know what's wrong with the world and what it ought to become. And the most arrogant idealists of all think they know how to make it happen. In that way, you're just like the T'ien Wang, aren't you? What you really want is to change China.'

Ward damned Meadows' cynicism and also his perceptiveness. 'Maybe I do think the way things are done over here could use some improvement. The people live worse than pigs, most of them. They're slaughtered and starved in their

253

tens of millions, while we all sit here on their coast, sucking for all we're worth like piglets on a sow's belly. And that's just how they see us.'

'And is that how you see us?'

Ward snorted. 'What's happening a hundred miles up that river is the bloodiest war in all history. More people have died in this rebellion than in all European wars that ever happened added together. And no one is doing any damned thing to stop it.'

'It's not our place to get involved.'

'Isn't it?'

'What do you want here?' Meadows put down the silver letter-opener. 'Democracy? The Chinese simply do not believe that a hundred million men are wiser than one. According to Confucius there's only one right way for China to be run properly.'

'Is that a goddamned fact?'

Meadows' face clouded. 'I want you and your band of merry men out of Sung-chiang, Mr Ward. You've got three days.'

Lindley and Loch had been joined by two dozen other men. He glimpsed Bowlby, de Normann and Jawalla Singh. There were about a dozen other Sikhs, some dragoons, and several Frenchmen, including a Catholic priest and a man who kept protesting that he was a scientist until he was beaten unconscious. Then General Sang ordered them all whipped to Pa-li-ch'iao, where another general lined them up near the strategic canal bridge and threatened them with beheading if the Barbarian army should advance another step.

Lindley knelt, listening to the booming artillery. In his bloody-minded way he willed the allied army to keep advancing. What Meadows had told him about Fei having died a heroine's death gave him the strength now to defy the Imperial will. Even when General Sheng-pao ordered him dragged to a tent where writing materials were laid out he mutely refused. The General raged at him and struck him down, his life under an ultimatum of death. 'You will write to your impudent master, and tell him to halt his advance at once!'

'I respectfully ask your Excellency to tell me,' he said, his mouth foul with the taste of blood and bile, but sweet with

254

irony, 'what else can my lord Elgin do but continue his regrettable advance? You must agree that for him to halt his army now and lose everything for the sake of a few worthless hostages would be stupid.'

'You will write, rebel. Or you will die!'

'Excuse me, but even though I am to die, I am not a rebel for I never was your master's vassal. You must go to him and tell him I will not write.'

'Then you will die! All of you!'

'If you kill us all then you will have no hostages. Surrender to me, while there is time. There is nothing you can do to stop the advance.'

Sheng-pao's dignity was shattered by the suggestion. His reaction was that of a thwarted child. He lashed out at those around him, then stamped away. Lindley's arrogance was punished. After hurried consultations with senior mandarins, Captain Brabazon was hauled forward to the middle of the bridge and beheaded, then the French priest quickly afterwards.

'Now you will write! Tell them they must go away!'

He refused again, though the others watched with terror in their eyes. Then he and Loch were pulled away, thrown into a cart and driven at speed to Peking. The ride, ten miles over bone-hard, rutted roads, battered them. They were taken to the Board of Corrections, there to await the decision on their lives.

Throughout the first day they saw a dozen others brought in. They were assembled in kneeling rows in the heat of the courtyard, deprived of water and kept in silence. Their hands were bound behind their backs, and the bonds wetted whenever they gave in to the pain and cried out. When each night fell they were dispersed to four separate prisons. They were loaded with chains and shackled to the wall, confined with Chinese criminals who behaved with every consideration towards them.

That first night Lindley found a way to speak with Lieutenant Anderson without calling down the screaming rage of the guards, and so managed to piece together some of what had happened at Pa-li-ch'iao. 'The battle stormed all the rest of the day,' Anderson whispered with difficulty. 'It was a glorious sight . . . our four thousand-strong army marching on thirty thousand Chinese . . . and still carrying all before them. As you prophesied, General Sheng-pao was unable to stop our advance . . . he was horribly wounded and after that he ordered more executions.'

Just before French bayonets forced the bridge, the heads of Englishmen, Sikhs and Frenchmen alike were kicked into the canal, their mutilated bodies dumped over the parapets. The display of savagery had only driven the allies to a more certain victory.

Now, on the fourth day, the prison of the Board of Corrections was already sweltering in ninety degrees of heat and stank of human excrement. The groans of the captives had wearied with every nightfall, but the nightmare had begun afresh with every blistering dawn. Lindley followed the guard unsteadily. His stubbled jaw clenched as he tried to concentrate on walking straight. His thirst raged. His body was covered in cuts and bruises where he had been beaten. But worst of all his hands were still tied behind his back. They felt like two lumps of nerveless meat now, and he knew they must be swollen and black like those of the others, even though he had managed to loosen the rope a little.

He towered above his three guards as they manoeuvred him with their spear shafts. He knew it would be foolish to try to say or do anything as they led him out of the building and across a parched grey courtyard. The far corner was already brilliantly lit by the sun, so that the brightness hurt his eyes. When he reached the middle they forced him to his knees and pulled him about until he was in the correct kneeling position once again. He was sure he could not remain conscious through another eight hours of this torment.

All the prisons of the Board of Corrections were infested with flesh maggots. Last night Lieutenant Anderson's screams had not subsided, no matter how much the guards beat him. No blood had entered Bowlby's hands for three days, and the correspondent's fingers had blown up like black sausages. A madness had overcome Anderson when he saw the worms crawling inside Bowlby's hands. His frantic efforts to break free from his bonds had alarmed the guards so much that they had clubbed him to death. Lindley had listened, and it had taken a special kind of strength to endure Anderson's shrieks, knowing he himself had caused them by cruelly robbing General Sheng-pao of face.

No! he told himself, hardening his mind against the weakness of guilt. They would have done this anyway. They think of us as rebels. And that means they will kill us as rebels. Tied hands have always been their prescription for rebels awaiting execution.

His body jolted suddenly. He had felt himself slipping again. Flies buzzed around him. He tried to will his fingers to move, but this time they would not. He knew that his mind's only real refuge was the professional detachment he had always practised. All physicians learned the trick of looking at a cadaver on an anatomy table without seeing the person. In the same way he tried to distance himself from his own body. He told himself it was simply a machine of flesh. The key was concentration: not to try to blot out the pain, but to convince himself not to mind that it hurt.

Yesterday he had distracted himself with challenges, recalling the names of all the two hundred and six bones of the human skeleton, putting them into alphabetical order, then in the order of their articulation, and back again. Today he made a start on the muscles of the head and face, but he lost his place time and again, and wondered now how long it was possible to stand against the delirium that was creeping upon him.

'Lin-li!'

It was Fei's voice.

He opened his eyes, and was surprised to find he could not focus them.

There were grey-robed men moving about, then he felt hands grip his arms, hauling him up and trying to make him stand on legs that had lost all feeling. They dragged him away, somewhere shady, somewhere cool. When the bonds were cut from his wrists the pain that had been dammed up for so long flooded his whole body and he called out. Then everything was swallowed up in darkness.

After a while Lindley became aware of the pain again. It burned him like hot coals, handfuls of pain, pain that was deep and throbbing and eventually unbearable. Then, slowly, it began to vanish.

He opened his eyes in heaven. There was a gloriously blue

sky, and surrounding him were soaring columns, white and fluted like those of a Greek temple. Thoughts of Elgin's father and the Parthenon's statues and the Taiping leader's bizarre visions knitted together confusingly in his mind. A flowering vine with huge, blue trumpet blossoms scented the air powerfully nearby. There were weeping trees and bird song and a peaceful lake unstirred by any breeze.

But if this is heaven it must be a Chinese heaven, he thought, because there on that island in the lake is a pagoda and an arched bridge.

For a moment he fancied himself transported to the world of a willow pattern plate, but then an old man in black appeared in his vision and held his face expertly, regarding him closely like a piece of fine porcelain, then started sticking fine needles into his cheeks and neck.

As Lindley's mind cleared his eyes took in the scene more clearly. He saw guards posted at a distance. A mandarin was present. His robes were dark blue, and of fine silk.

'Your name is Lin-li?' the mandarin asked.

He tried to speak, but could not.

'Give him water.'

Lindley gagged at the bottle, tasting the ointment that had been applied to his chapped lips.

'My name is Heng-chi. I am an Imperial Commissioner.'

'Where am I?'

'You are in the Yuan Ming Yuan.' The Garden of Perfect Brightness.

'The . . . Summer Palace?' He struggled to sit up, but the Chinese doctor steadied him. 'Where are the others?'

Heng-chi loomed over him, a fleshy, but careworn man whose mouth twisted as he spoke. 'You will write to the Elgin. You will tell him to put aside all his demands.'

'How many days have I been here?'

'You will write to the Elgin. If you do this, you will be sent to live at the Temple of the North Star. If you do not, you will go back to prison.'

Lindley made a tremendous effort to marshal the hideous memories that haunted his mind. It's coming back now, he thought. The kneeling in rows . . . the beatings . . . the screaming mandarins . . . the thirst . . . maggots crawling in wrists . . . that hellish night when Anderson died. What about Bowlby? And the Sikhs? And the French? But most of all what about H.B.?

'If I agree to write a letter, you must allow the other prisoners to go to the Temple of the North Star too,' he murmured.

'You cannot make conditions. If you do not write, you will die. This is Prince Kung's order.'

'It is a humble request,' he said. He forced himself to consider Elgin's position. There must have been some kind of exchange of letters by now, he told himself. I hope he hasn't made our release into a condition. If he shows weakness now they'll never let us go.

'You will write.'

What should I tell him? he wondered. His own life is probably hanging by a silk thread. I must find out more information. He said, 'When will I be able to speak directly with Prince Kung?'

Heng-chi stiffened, affronted. His anger increased. 'I am his Imperial Highness's intermediary! You will write!'

Yes, he thought, slipping back toward unconsciousness. You're frightened. Your lords have told you what they expect from you. They've warned you not to fail them. You only know cruelty, and that in the end makes you powerless.

He coughed, jerking awake suddenly. A water bowl was being held to his lips. The Chinese doctor began sticking needles into the joints of his arms and hands. He flexed his right hand weakly. His eyes watered as he felt the intense stinging of pins-and-needles. Then incredible pain flowed up both arms, crucifying him. Nevertheless, as the pain crescendoed, to his astonishment he began to feel his fingertips again. Heng-chi swam back into vision again.

'Excuse me.' Lindley panted, his body still shuddering. 'My question about the other captives is a very practical one.'

'Explain.'

'Before any negotiation can begin I must assure Lord Elgin that all prisoners of war have been treated according to international law.'

Heng-chi erupted. 'The Empire of China takes no account of Barbarian laws!'

'You call us Barbarians, but is this the way civilized men treat prisoners of war?'

'It is a soldier's business to face death. War must be taken seriously. Men who allow themselves to be captured are cowards who deserve to die.'

'We are not all soldiers. We were kidnapped while showing a flag of truce.'

'Rebels must always be dealt with severely. This is the law.'

'We are not rebels. China is not the whole world, merely a conquered and backward country that must now begin to learn civilized ways.'

'China has been civilized for three thousand years.'

'Civilized people do not approve of torture. They realize it is degrading to those who inflict it. Civilized people know that it is better to do unto others as you would be done by yourself.'

'Vile Christian dogma!'

'No, simply good sense. And until the Manchu learn this lesson they will remain a worthless people, a childish people barbarous, cruel and weak.'

Heng-chi stared back, realizing his own impotence. A vein throbbed visibly in his forehead. He said. 'You will . . . please . . . write to the Elgin.'

He heard Heng-chi pronounce the word as if his mouth was stuffed with dirt. He was suffering pain in humbling himself so far before a Barbarian captive, and Lindley knew he must reward his effort. 'Mr Commissioner, I will do as you request, but Mr Loch is Lord Elgin's private secretary. Any letter from me must be countersigned by him. Without his signature it would not be taken as genuine.'

'I will seek permission for the man, Loch, to be brought. Then you will write – in Chinese and in English.'

Why Chinese and English? he wondered, his mind's focus going soft again. Is it a test, to see if I will try to deceive them? What have you learned from Heng-chi already? You know that he is obliged to refer to a higher authority. Who? Prince Kung. You know that Heng-chi knows that Loch is alive. You know they have someone who they can trust to read English . . . The pain rose again, and then the weariness that always followed. For a moment he drifted on the edge of unconsciousness. Concentrate! he ordered, and breathed deep. Think! What is it you need to ask him? What is it you need to know?

'Mr Commissioner . . . what are your demands?'

'I will dictate at the appropriate time. You will write what I tell you.'

The oppressive heat of early afternoon had passed away now, and a pleasant cool had come to the main courtyard of the Western Palace. When the music stopped Fei could hear birds disputing in distant eaves, and the sounds of their careless freedom broke her heart.

The Empress had been at her writing desk since noon, so Fei and the other maids were excused usual duties. They sat at ease on cushions under a plum tree, listening to two musicians. The old men who played the hsiao and the di tze – the big flute and the little flute – had been ordered to wait upon them. They had played a soft accompaniment as Wen recited the 'eight precious poems'. As the recital finished, Wen looked to her, hoping to find a response, however faint, in the new girl's face, but Fei's mind was far away.

I should have gone right up and knocked on his door that day in Shanghai, she thought, meaning Lindley. I should have given him the message from his father personally. How can I be sure he is safe? Instead I turned away, and that's the mistake for which I was punished.

The hour drum sent dull thuds echoing from the walls. Fei looked up at the wasp-spotted leaves of the fruit trees, and felt suddenly fearful. The seasons were turning, and she would never again smell those chill, misty nights as winter came. Like the wasps and the autumn leaves, she must soon disappear back into the earth for ever.

As they rose to move indoors and resume their duties Wen murmured to her, 'I think you are too moody a person for the Empress's retinue. Perhaps you will not be happy here after all.'

She put a remorseful expression on her face. 'Oh! Please excuse my inattention, Elder Sister. This palace is very awesome at first. It takes more than a little getting used to.'

'Some girls are never able to do so.'

Being in the Empress's retinue was vital. 'Please, Elder Sister. It is only my anxiety to do well that makes me seem moody. I realize the honour the Imperial family has done me in allowing me to serve here.' She added an extra tone of fawning to her voice. 'The favour Master An has done my family in accepting me could never be repaid.'

Wen saw the implication that lay under the remark and softened her tone. 'Just remember in future: this is no place for a girl who sulks.'

You jealous little she-goat, she thought. If you knew what the truth was about me you'd die. I'm an unexploded bomb sitting among you, and I'm not going to let you jeopardize my mission. She said, 'If Elder Sister would only give me a little more time to adjust.'

Wen gathered her skirts about her. 'I wonder if there will be time for that. Now, go and attend Her Imperial Highness.'

She moved to obey, keeping her true thoughts hidden. When she came inside she saw the Empress was still seated at her writing desk. Papers surrounded her; dozens were scattered about on the floor. Fei kowtowed unobtrusively as she had been taught to do, and assumed a kneeling position close to the Empress but not close enough to distract her.

As the Empress moved from court to court within the Forbidden City her maids moved with her, always kneeling nearby in silence with eyes downcast. She, as the most junior attendant, did nothing. Her duty was merely to be fragrant and to learn.

As she waited on the Empress, Fei watched and waited with calculation in her heart. It's time to focus my mind, she told herself. Time to become once more a Taiping, to remember discipline and leave aside all self-indulgent thoughts. It's not as I first supposed. Things are far from tranquil and the great factions are in furious dispute. Who should I approach?

After kneeling for an hour Fei's knees began to ache. Finally the Empress sat back and stretched. 'Take all these waste papers and burn them,' she said, rising. 'Then give these seven letters to my messenger. This one is to his Imperial Highness Prince P'u Lun. Say that it is especially urgent. And remind Wen that tomorrow we must pay our annual respects to the silkworms.'

Fei obeyed. She gathered up the papers and shuffled them together. Then Wen came in and directed her out into the courtyard and to the rear of an outbuilding where a kettle simmered perpetually over a charcoal brazier. One at a time she began to feed the papers into the fire, watching the flames lick up brightly as each was consumed.

When the Emperor arrived at the Hall of Supreme Harmony his Councillors were already assembled. They fell immediately into the kowtow and began to call off their names as if reminding the Son of Heaven of their continued loyalty. But Hsien-feng seemed like a blind man. He blundered among his ministers and the hundreds of eunuchs who also kowtowed as he passed through their ranks on his way to mount the steps of the Dragon Throne.

As was customary Su-shun waited for permission to speak, but the expression on his face was grave. When the Emperor nodded, he said, 'I have news that contradicts that received yesterday from General Sang, Majesty. This report says that the Barbarians have destroyed his army at Pa-li-ch'iao, and that their leader defies all attempt at reason.'

There was a pause in which no sound was heard. Then the Emperor's sheathed nails clattered on the arm rests of the elevated throne, breaking the spell. 'Where are the Barbarians now?'

'They are marching on the city, Sire. They will be here this time tomorrow.'

Hsien-feng's reedy voice wailed at them. 'Who is at fault for this? Must Barbarians always be at war with us? We do not understand why they must always be fighting and killing our people. Why are they fighting?'

Su-shun tried an appeal. 'Your Majesty, war should not concern the Son of Heaven.'

Hsien-feng paid no attention, he turned to Prince Kung. 'General Seng said my armies outnumbered the enemy five to one, and yet Su-shun says they are beaten. How is this possible? You advised the Court to stay and my army to fight.'

'To fight. Yes, Sire. To fight, and not to run away.'

Su-shun levelled an accusing finger at his enemy. 'As I warned, the Prince has followed the custom of trying to delude His Imperial Majesty! He tries to do so still.'

Prince Kung shook with anger. 'Sire, the Barbarians have reached the capital, but how will they get inside? The walls of Peking are strong!'

'But how can you know if our walls are strong enough?'

Hsien-feng's question was born of fear, but it was unanswerable. Su-shun understood its importance well enough. So did the ministers, who knelt silent and motionless, waiting for his reply.

'Sire, they have fewer than twenty thousand troops. We know their commanders lack courage for they trifle endlessly over the lives of captives. If you would have tranquillity in your heart then stay in your capital. Such Barbarians as these cannot succeed!'

Su-shun said with heavy irony, 'Prince Kung suggests that your Imperial Majesty remains at peace in his heart. That we should all simply remain here, and nothing will happen to us. Now you may see the strength of our strategy and the weakness of Prince Kung's. If our advice fails then little is lost. If your Imperial Majesty travels unnecessarily to Jehol, then the Court has merely made an inconvenient trip. However, if Prince Kung's advice is followed and proves to be wrong, your Imperial Majesty will have been exposed to the greatest danger.'

High above the argument Hsien-feng's ashen features became wraith-like. He sat in ghastly silence, his eyes unblinking, staring at nothingness, so that all in the Hall of Supreme Harmony waited, wondering at what the Son of Heaven could be thinking. For a long time he did not speak. His hands lay motionless in his lap, his face immobile. Then he said: 'You are both right. The Son of Heaven must inspect his palaces and worship at long-neglected ancestral tablets. Peking no longer pleases me. Therefore the Court will remove to Jehol. Those of you who would come with me I command to come with me. Those who would stay I command to stay here with Prince Kung. He shall remain to defend Peking in my place.'

Looking neither to right nor left, Hsien-feng descended the throne steps and started back toward his private residence. Prince Kung stared after him, noting that he moved quicker than he had been seen to move for a long time. But Hsien-feng was old. Years older, ages older, than he had been yesterday.

The Temple of the North Star stood to the north of the walled city of Peking. Its compound was secure and its interior comfortably appointed. The Confucian priests had abandoned it, but Lindley could not discover if they had left because of the approach of the allied army, or because Commissioner Heng-chi had requisitioned their building.

Now they had set up a game of wei-ch'i – 'the surrounding game' – and a board between them was half-filled with black and white counters. Both he and Loch were wearing grey mandarins' robes that were far too small. Their own clothes had been taken away, along with all their personal possessions. During their separation Loch's personality had altered as much as his hands. His engaging smile had vanished. Even his voice had changed. He seemed to feel personally betrayed by events. Last night Lindley had slept badly, his peace disturbed by the dozens of devil statues ranged around them. One of the statues was stark-eyed. It reminded him of the Reverend Alfred Chapman, the zealous preacher with whom he had shared the long voyage to China.

'I asked Heng-chi why so many Chinese idols were represented as demons,' Lindley said, trying to make light of it.

'Why?' Loch murmured.

'Because nice gods can't do us any harm, but the devils have it in their power to make life painful, so it's important that a man bows and scrapes to them.'

Loch found no humour in the remark, and Lindley sighed softly. After a while he said, 'Your move.'

Loch's hands were crabbed and bruised, but he was able to place the black wei-ch'i counters down on the board. He made a move that did him no credit.

'An astonishingly clever game, don't you think? Simple to improvise. Much easier to learn than chess, and yet so fiendishly difficult to master. I learned it . . .' He thought of Fei. '. . . from a Chinese friend.'

He played a stone. A little later Loch's hand came forward and trembled over the board. He persisted for a moment, studying the maze of interlocking patterns of black and white counters, then sat back. He sought Lindley's eye and said, 'What right have we to come here? Why can't we just leave the heathens well alone?'

'A little while ago I would have been asking you that question.'

On arrival at the temple the Chinese had struck off their chains and served them an absurd banquet, an overwhelming meal of sixteen courses. Their shrunken stomachs had rebelled against the lavishness of it, but their minds had rebelled more. Nauseated, they had not eaten any of it, but had bathed and slept instead.

'It seems as if they're trying to make amends,' he told Loch this morning.

'As if starving a man for four days could be set right by offering him a feast,' Loch had muttered bitterly. He too had watched his fellow prisoners suffer and die in misery. 'What about our comrades. Harry? What about them? While we sit here being treated like . . .'

He looked at Loch's hands now, knowing the man would never be the same again, knowing that he blamed him. I did what I had to do, he thought dourly. And what I did was for the best. The situation is changing by the hour. Soon they'll either kill us or free us.

'Your move,' he told Loch again.

'Heng-chi will be back soon,' Loch said, as if reading his mind. 'Will you do what he wants?'

'I'm certainly going to ask for some more fashionable clothes to be sent out to us.'

His levity clashed jarringly with Loch's sudden earnestness. 'I want to know, Harry. Are you going to do as Heng-chi wants and write the note?'

'Yes, I am. Your move.'

Loch stared at him for a moment then stood up suddenly and threw over the board. 'My move? My bloody move? Damn you, Harry Lindley! Why didn't you say so right at the beginning? At Pa-li-ch'iao?'

He kept his voice level. 'Because things were different at Pa-li-ch'iao.'

'What about Jai Singh? And de Normann? And Brabazon? And the Abbe, de Luc? And the rest? I saw five men die around me! Look at my hands, Harry!'

He watched without expression as Loch collapsed and began to sob.

'Can you hold a pencil?' he asked. Loch did not reply so he made his voice commanding. 'Mr Loch, I want you to tell me: can-you-hold-a-pencil?'

Loch recovered himself. 'I . . . I suppose so.'

'Good.' He paused, until Loch looked to him again. 'Now,

I hear you were in India with his lordship. How's your Hindustani?'

'Adequate.'

'Can you write in Urdu script?'

'Some.'

'I want you to sign your name on the letter I write to his lordship. If you do it exactly as I tell you, I think we may be able to help our friends. And if we're very lucky, we might be able to get out of here alive.' He righted the table and set the board up again, sweeping up the counters that Loch had scattered. 'Now, let's start again, shall we?'

Fei's fingers twined anxiously inside her sleeves as the procession came to a halt outside the grand temple. The silk house was close by. This was the place where the silk workers revered the spirit of the girl who first discovered silk.

Eunuch runners went ahead of them, shouting, 'Li-la!', giving warning of their arrival. The Empress was greeted by the director, a grinning elderly man, surrounded by younger assistants. They lined up to receive the Empress so she could make an offering to Fu-hsi, the First Sovereign and God of Happiness, the deity who watched over silkworms. But Fei knew as she waited in the late afternoon sunshine that there was a more important reason for the visit.

The Empress had decided on a tour of the Imperial cocoon sheds, because Prince P'u Lun, a scholarly and retiring member of the Imperial family, maintained a mansion nearby. An invitation to stop and take tea with him on the way back would underscore his sympathy for her position, and give him a chance to indicate the support of the members of the Hanlin Academy, China's premier house of learning.

'Silkworms are the strength of China,' the Empress announced as they prepared for the visit. 'The more we have the richer we become. It's time for our moths to lay their eggs, therefore we must inspect them.'

In the fading light the streets near the Temple of Silk Making were silent and eerie. As usual, the thoroughfares of the Inner City had been cleared for the Empress's procession, so it was impossible for Fei to judge the mood or number of inhabitants who remained in the capital. Since yesterday it had become even harder to concentrate on her mission. Her beleaguered mind went back to the moment she had stopped feeding the Empress's discarded papers into the fire. She had jumped back suddenly to throw a half-burned page to the ground and stamp it out. The list contained the surname 'Lin-li'.

It can't be, she thought, denying, not wanting to believe. What's in a name? A dozen common surnames account for half the people in China. Maybe it's the same with foreigners. There must be many Westerners called Lin-li in China. But still she had read the half-burned paper over, and still her heart had turned stone heavy when her fingers traced the Christian name. It was listed as 'Hao-li'. Origin: Shanghai. Occupation: physician and translator to the Barbarian Chief. He had been taken prisoner near T'ung-chow – and his execution had been confirmed.

So, Lin-li, she thought now, her discipline in ruins. It seems we're both going to die – both of us will be eaten up by the five-clawed yellow dragon, after all. Of course there is nothing to be done about that, but will it not be fateful if our souls arrive at the St Peter Gate together? Doubtless that venerable angel will accuse me of treachery in this life, but I will be able to tell the truth at last and show myself to be a martyr to the true religion. Perhaps then there will be forgiveness and we will enter the City of Heaven together . . .

Her thoughts were severed by shouting that came from the enclosure outside. One of the director's young assistants ran into the hatchery, his silhouette stark in the doorway. He was breathless and distressed. 'Soldiers!' he shouted, 'Soldiers on the road! Coming here!' Then he remembered himself and threw himself to the ground before the astonished director. Everyone stared at him uncertainly, then looked to one another.

The Empress gasped. 'What kind of soldiers?' she demanded. 'Do you mean Barbarians?'

'No, Imperial Highness. Horse soldiers. Manchu.'

It's a trap, Fei thought. Look how furious the Empress is to have been caught out so badly by events. Prince P'u Lun has betrayed her!

'Which banner?' the Empress shouted at the prostrate man. 'Speak!'

'Imperial Highness – they are the Bordered Blue!'

'The Bordered Blue? Are you certain?'

'Imperial Highness – in this light it is hard to tell.'

The sound of hooves thundering into the enclosure outside made them turn. Many of the girls sank to their knees. They were too frightened to run. The doors slammed open and through them strode a heavily-armed figure. He was war-torn and his right sleeve was soaked with blood.

Fei saw the Empress's fear dissolve into relief when she recognized the warrior.

'Jung-lu,' she said, barely recovering her composure. 'You are intruding on us.'

'I beg to be forgiven, Imperial Highness,' he replied formally, approaching and pushing his fur-trimmed steel helm back on his brow as he knelt. 'But the war goes badly. I've ridden hard from the Summer Palace. I must speak with Your Imperial Highness urgently.'

'Speak now.'

Jung-lu cast a suspicious glance at the entourage then launched into a tortured explanation. 'Imperial Highness, the Barbarians are marching on the city. The power of their weapons is beyond imagination – at Pa-li-ch'iao they were able to destroy whole squadrons of our cavalry at incredible distance. They cannot be stopped.'

The Empress stared at his bloodied sleeve. 'Your arm . . .'

He flexed his hand in dismissal. 'Nothing, Imperial Highness. Better men than I died proudly in their saddles today.'

'You said you've come from the Summer Palace?'

'The Emperor is there. News of the defeat has spurred panic among the people of the Court.' He lowered his voice. 'I believe the Emperor is preparing to leave.'

Fei heard the dismay in his voice. For this soldier it was as if the axis of the earth had sheared and everything had gone spinning off into darkness.

'Preparing to leave?' The Empress gathered herself. 'Where is the heir? He should be at his lessons in the Forbidden City! I must get to him! Ride ahead, Jung-lu! Ride ahead and find him!'

Yehonala's departure from the building was the signal that sent the silk workers running.

'The worms! The worms!' Fei heard the director shouting hopelessly in the dying light as she ran after the Empress's palanquin. 'What about the worms?'

*

269

It was after dark and the guards had left the Barbarians alone so they might dress themselves. Lindley tried to ignore the sense of unease he felt surrounded by the strange symbolism of Buddhism – the coiling dragons, the clouds and ocean waves, the conch shells, Buddha statues sitting in lines, enigmatic brass goblins all as self-satisfied as magnates.

Loch put on his trousers and struggled to button the fly, while Lindley laced his boots for him.

'Are you sure there was nothing? No message of any kind?' he asked again.

'I'm absolutely sure,' Loch told him.

Lindley glanced about the sparsely furnished room. The table was set with their wei-ch'i board on which patterns of black and white stones sketched out a half-finished game. Beside it was a heap of captured stones and two of Loch's embroidered handkerchiefs.

He went through his own pockets again, convinced that a note must have been hidden. He had done what Heng-chi wanted in writing out the list of demands, but when Loch had added his 'signature' at the bottom of the paper it had taken the form of a note, written in Indian Urdu script, telling Elgin that the letter had been forced out of them. It had also begged Elgin to send news.

Lindley held his spare shirt up to the light. 'His lordship must have sent something. Maybe it's sewn into a lining somewhere. What about your handkerchiefs?'

'What handkerchiefs?'

'There on the table.'

Loch followed his glance. 'I thought they were yours.'

Their eyes met.

'You know, the Chinese can never be made to understand the purpose of these,' Lindley said, picking up the top one. 'They're amazed at our habit of treasuring blasts of nasal phlegm on cloth squares and hiding them about our persons.'

'I suppose civilized people snort directly onto the street.'

'So they believe.'

Lindley fetched a candle and examined the stitching. 'H.B., tell me. Can you read this?'

Loch bent over and then looked up. 'Good God, Harry. It says the Emperor's gone to the Summer Palace!'

Lindley began to think it through. 'He's going to run.'

'But surely that means we can get a settlement now,' Loch said fervently. 'His lordship will be able to present himself before the Dragon Throne without kowtowing. The fact that the Emperor won't actually be sitting on it at the time won't matter.'

'What else does it say?'

Loch's blackened forefinger traced more of the tiny Urdu words. 'Sang Ko-lin-sen's defeated army has retired to the north of the city . . . his lordship's still waiting at T'ung-chow for siege guns to arrive . . .'

'So that's the delay. Peking's city walls must be fifty feet thick. They're not earthworks like at Taku, they're solid stone. What else?'

'The Chinese are worried that our army will enter the Forbidden City and begin looting if they open the gates . . . Prince Kung refers to us as "guests" . . . many Chinese officials have abandoned their posts . . . eighty-six thousand troops are roaming wild in the streets of the Chinese City, without orders and without pay . . . Prince Kung is nominally in command of an empty citadel with orders to resist and a number of advisers who are divided as to whether this is possible.'

'Heng-chi must know about the siege guns coming,' Lindley said exultantly. 'Imagine what must be happening in the city – confusion and disagreement, utter dismay and panic at the Emperor's departure.'

Loch's eyes implored him. 'Will they kill us now?'

'No, no. Of course not.' He wiped his face. 'Prince Kung's just playing for time. Did you feel the chill in the air this morning? Summer's drawing to an end, and the autumn here is very short. When the winds start to blow out of Siberia in a few days' time the temperature will begin to plunge. Peking's winters are cruel – far too cold for our army to weather under canvas.'

Loch's eyes went back to the message. 'See, here . . . It looks as if his Lordship agrees with you. It says that the bombardment is scheduled to begin the day after tomorrow.'

'So he's calling Prince Kung's bluff. Is that all there is?'

Loch nodded. He went back to trying to do up his trousers. He contained his frustration with the buttons as best he could, but after a short while he said, 'Harry – I'm sorry to have to ask. I'm shaking like a leaf.'

Lindley went over to finish the job. As he knelt down an echo in the passageway outside turned his stomach over. His fear had never gone away entirely, no matter how much he fought it down or tried to joke. The door swung open and one of their guards, the one they had nicknamed 'Jimmy Long-face', stepped in and came suddenly to attention. A moment later Commissioner Heng-chi appeared. He was followed by a porter who carried in a large cloth-wrapped box.

Heng-chi's studied the half-played game on the wei-ch'i board and nodded appraisingly. He almost seems affronted to find us still here, Lindley thought, regarding the man's flat, humourless face.

'I have come to return your property to you,' he said, indicating the box. Lindley thought that sounded ominous. He opened the box and took out his locket. He pressed the hidden catch that sprung it open, then looked briefly at the tea-brown photographic image of his mother, before closing it again. He pressed it to his lips before putting it away.

'Thank you, Mr Commissioner.'

Heng-chi watched gravely as Lindley pocketed his other effects. When the box was empty an attendant produced paper, ink-blocks and brushes, and Lindley knew it immediately as a bad sign. He struggled to master his inner feelings as Heng-chi said, 'I have been instructed to inform you of the decision to reject your leader's demands.'

He heard Loch utter a despairing oath.

Heng-chi went on stonily. 'It has been decided that the first shot fired against the walls of Peking is to be the signal for your execution.'

Lindley felt the news resound through him like a physical shock. He knew that in this scholar-led society paper and writing materials were traditionally provided to those deemed worthy to record their last thoughts on the eve of execution. It was a kind of honour.

Heng-chi offered a small paper packet tied up with fancy silk tape. 'The Prince Kung makes you a present. It is special Imperial tea. Very costly. Very rare.'

Lindley took the packet from his jailer, aware for the first time how vast the gulf was that lay between them. With difficulty he said, 'Please thank his Imperial Highness, and assure him we will drink it soon.'

Heng-chi bowed and withdrew. The door banged shut with a sound like the booming of artillery. The tall candles shivered, and they were alone again in the demon-filled night.

Ward took a chair from Shanghai's Grand Hotel to Yang Fang's yamen. He was received graciously, took breakfast, then got down to business. First they discussed investments and how money could be doubled in the government salt monopoly, then Ward outlined the plan to attack Ch'ing-p'u tonight.

Yang listened but with the distracted politeness of a man who has already delegated a task to a capable subordinate. Yang ordered more tea brought and then, after his solemn daughter had disappeared again, he steered the conversation round point by point to domestic matters and a reminiscence of his wedding.

Yang said, 'We do not think of "love" as you do. Ideas of romance are quite strange to us. Here, there is duty and blood. One must consider the question of heirs. Do you think a people who regard so highly their ancestors would neglect the continuation of blood lines?'

'You make it sound like a business transaction.'

'Here we treat it with equivalent seriousness.'

'What if the girl's unwilling?'

Yang was patient. 'Naturally, the girl is assumed to be willing.'

'So a girl must always be dutiful to her father's wishes? Whatever the circumstances?'

'Of course.'

'And so when he wants her to marry, she must obey?'

'We must not forget the duty that a father has towards his daughter, which is to be wise and compassionate. He must see that his daughter is married to a man whom she will find acceptable.'

'And if their opinions happen to differ?'

'She has a right of refusal.'

'In theory.'

Yang smiled. 'It is true that in practice few girls challenge the wisdom of their own father.'

Ward glanced fleetingly at Chang-mei as she flitted past at the end of a long corridor. 'What I'm getting at is . . . what if they find out they're not right for one another?'

'This situation is always anticipated. Before marriage a matchmaker is called to consult horoscopes, to see if bride and groom are well-suited.'

'Horoscopes? You mean like sending in the feng-shui man when you plan to buy a property – to check for proper aspect and all?'

Yang smiled approvingly. 'Something like that.'

Ward could not believe what he was hearing. They must have ice-cold hearts, he thought. But just think for a moment. Doesn't what Yang say make some kind of twisted sense? Isn't our way of choosing partners full of jeopardy as he says?

He asked, 'What if a girl's still not happy when she marries? Despite the horoscopes?'

'Then she will be unhappy. But by not showing her unhappiness she will be doing her filial duty. And by doing her filial duty happiness will come to her in the end.'

'And what about the man? What if he finds his wife . . . unappealing?'

Yang laughed. 'I don't know why Westerners always confuse separate things. You have only one God, but it seems obvious to any Chinese that there must be a huge god – Shang-ti, who created the universe – and many other small gods who watch over each place and each person's doings. So it is with sex: a man marries a wife for propriety and for giving him a son to be his heir, he keeps concubines for pleasure and bearing offspring to take into the family or to sell, as he pleases.'

'Did you say "sell"? Sell his own children?'

Yang chuckled. 'Often there are too many babies. Some must go.'

Ward scratched his cheek, nonplussed. 'How many concubines is a man allowed?'

'A man may have as many concubines as he can afford. The more accomplished ones can be quite expensive. Chang-mei's mother cost me three thousand taels, her sister was even more expensive, but then she was a trained entertainer.'

Ward shook his head, not wanting to embarrass Yang

Fang by an open show of disgust. He switched the conversation back to business, then left for Sung-chiang. All the way back he thought about the extraordinary conversation and wondered what reason Yang Fang could have had to begin it.

There was no guard on the East Gate when he arrived back at Sung-chiang. He called Burgevine over to him and walked with him towards the square. When he saw the headless bodies he felt a surge of anger.

'Get them out of here,' he growled. 'I want proper burials.'

'Proper burials, Colonel? But our boys—'

'You heard what I said!'

He had decided to make Sung-chiang his headquarters. Imperial forces had withdrawn over the past few days. They had looted the city meticulously. The Taipings had left six thousand taels of silver and several hundred pounds of gunpowder. The Green Standard had taken everything. Now they had gone, and the town was in the hands of local mandarins.

'What happened?'

'Old scores, I guess,' Burgevine said.

He entered the East Gate. Labourers were working on the blasted masonry. 'You've got to learn how to keep control when I'm not here, Henry.'

'They were Taipings.'

'They were prisoners!'

'Yeah, their prisoners.' Burgevine shrugged. 'What am I supposed to do, start an argument with the local mandarins? If they want to kill rebel prisoners, what the hell does it matter?'

'I don't allow it,' he told Burgevine patiently as they came to his yamen. 'When the Taipings overrun a city they kill any man who refuses to cut off his pigtail. When the Imperials re-take the place they behead any man without one. You see?'

'Sure. They figure them as rebel sympathizers.'

'Right. But the fact is they're just innocent peasants who'll lean any way the wind blows. I won't have them slaughtered on a junior mandarin's whim. Not in my town.'

Burgevine murmured, 'Your town?'

Ward's anger snapped. 'My town! That's what I said!'

'Jesus, what's the matter with you, Colonel?'

One of his Filipino bodyguards appeared, a Chinese woman with him. It was Annie Phillips' maid. He took the note from the woman, read it, folded it and tucked it inside his jacket as Burgevine watched. 'Give the girl a dollar and see she gets safe back to Shanghai,' he murmured to one of his lieutenants.

Burgevine's eyes followed her as she went, but he said nothing. When he left, Ward sighed and threw his head back, an ache behind his eyes.

When he reached the impressive yamen he had chosen as his residence Forrest was waiting for him. He seemed to want to ask something, but then changed his mind.

'You ought to watch out for Henry,' Forrest said amiably.

'Oh, yeah? And why's that?'

'He says he thinks you're going soft.'

'When I want you to start telling tales on my second-in-command, I'll ask you. And if I want his opinion about me, I'll ask him. Got that?'

Forrest looked stung for a second, but then he quickly hid his feelings. 'Sorry.'

Ward rubbed a hand over his face. 'What do you want, anyway?'

'We had a lot of visitors in the last couple of days. A hundred or more men came out to volunteer. Europeans from Shanghai. Eager as hell, the lot of them. They said the stories going around town were that we found a hoard of Taiping silver here. They're queueing up to join now.'

'That's Meadows and his damned rumour machine. Some infernal story he's been putting round has backfired on him.'

He took Annie's note from his vest pocket and looked at it. She had heard loose talk about foreigners signing on to fight as mercenaries with the Taipings, but she didn't know where. Momentarily, he wondered if it might be Ch'ing-p'u, and if Strickland was involved in recruiting them. It's too late now, he thought. The attack goes ahead tonight as planned.

'What did you tell these visitors?'

'I took their names and sent them back to Shanghai. Said we'd be in touch if we wanted to use them.'

Ward nodded. 'Good. I want all the gates but one closed, and the East Gate manned continuously from now on. Issue papers to our people, which I'll countersign. No other Europeans are to be allowed in. Chinese can come and go as they please. Has the medical station been fixed up yet?'

'Not quite.' Forrest rubbed his chin. 'Our Dr MacGowan's got an unquenchable thirst. I hope I never get an ailment when he's around. The Chinese are terrified of him. Some of the mandarins have criticized the torture tools he keeps in that black bag of his. They've told the people he's an evil wizard.'

'He's the best we can do. I wish to God Lindley had signed on with us.'

Forrest lingered. 'Colonel, has the bonus come through yet?'

'I'll discuss money with you later.' Ward did not look at him. 'That's all. Send Vincente in, will you?'

'From now on,' he told Vincente Macanaya, 'you're in charge of talking to the local mandarins whenever I'm not here.'

'Coronel, I don't know if I can deal with—'

'The trick in handling mandarins is never to tell them "no". Agree to everything.'

'And if I'm wrong?'

He smiled a flat smile. 'Don't be. Vincente, it's a matter of handling "face". You understand it, Henry doesn't.'

He heard the city drummers beating the Hour of the Horse, and checked his watch – 11 am. The attack on Ch'ing-p'u would begin at the Hour of the Tiger – sixteen hours from now. He stirred himself; there was a lot still to do.

Ch'ing-p'u was located twelve miles to the north-west, a square city like Sung-chiang, walled and moated and at the meeting of a canal network. There were only three gates, of which those facing east and west were most easily defended. The Corps would therefore attack the main South Gate. Surprise would be hard to achieve, so a furious all-out assault would have to be mounted – three hundred men in officered platoons of ten would rush the walls. As before, ten thousand Green Standard troops would await his signal, then move on the South Gate once the way had been opened.

General Li had given no reason for withholding support at Sung-chiang, and Ward had not demanded one. In a land where a commander-in-chief's powers are absolute, he thought, there's no point in going through a pantomime of explanations, especially when we both understand the truth already.

Ward paraded the men at noon, checked the ammunition and other purchases, then assembled his officers and went over the plan again. After that he told Vincente to dress some of the Chinese troops in civilian clothes and send them over to find out what they could from the Green Standard. The rest of the afternoon was filled with last-minute preparations, and only when all was ready and darkness began to fall did he return to his yamen. He sat alone in his chair, giving himself over to a few moments of meditation, recalling what he had been told about the tao. He tried to feel for the flow as Yang's daughter had described it, but what did a man do to feel it?

'Massa? My wantchee come.'

Ward's unquiet eyes opened suddenly and roamed the darkened office. He nodded brusquely and his servant crept in to light the lamps. When the man had gone Ward's glance fell on a chair. There was a book there, a battered volume of Shakespeare he had brought with him from home. He had always meant to read it in the slack times of a soldier's life. Somehow there had never been times slack enough.

He picked it up and looked into it, turning the dusty pages idly, opening it at random, looking at the strange old-fashioned words. The play was called *Julius Caesar*, the character Brutus was speaking:

We have tried the utmost of our friends. Our legions are brim-full, our cause is ripe. The enemy increaseth every day. We, at the height, are ready to decline . . .

Its aptness caught his interest. The language seemed to him like that of the Bible. He knew that some folk set great store by what they found when opening a Bible at random. He began to read the passage out loud.

There is a tide in the affairs of men, which, taken at the flood, leads on to fortune. Omitted, all the voyage of their life is bound in shallows and in miseries. On such a full sea are we now afloat, and we must take the current when it serves. Or lose our ventures.

'I guess that's the tao,' he said in wonderment. 'That's what he's talking about.'

He snapped the book shut and leapt out of the chair, suddenly filled with urgency. Three paces and he was at the door. He flung it open and shouted, 'Vincente! Henry! Get over here! It's time we moved out!'

They floated the guns up to Ch'ing-p'u on canal barges. There was excellent discipline and precise timing. Everyone knew what to do and did it exactly according to Ward's plan.

Vincente came to him as the first attack got into place. 'The men you sent to the Green Standard just arrived back. They found out something: the Taipings have sent their best strategist to defend Ch'ing-p'u.'

'How many defenders are there?'

'They said ten thousand.'

'That's just an expression in Chinese meaning "a whole lot". Do they know for sure how many?'

'They just said ten thousand. The rumour is they're the Taipings' best soldiers.'

A last-minute reinforcement? he wondered, but then put the thought out of his mind and ordered the scaling ladders forward.

There was no moon. Everything was in pitch blackness. They crossed the moat and pushed a dozen ladders up against the walls. Amazingly no alarm was raised as Ward led them silently up the rungs. He reached the top and glanced from side to side, and waved his baton to urge them forward in silence. The night was dark, but still it was wildly better than he could have hoped that not a single look-out had seen them.

They climbed up onto the open rampart, pausing warily, others following until fifty men had got up onto the walls. But as Ward led them to find the steps a snake of blue flame surged out in the darkness below and burst into crackling brilliance. A trench of fire twenty feet below swept along the wall illuminating them perfectly. Ward saw with utter dismay the heavily barricaded steps and realized it was an ambush.

'Get back!' he shouted desperately. 'It's a trap! It's—'

His words were cut off by a deafening volley. They're

Enfields, he thought, recognizing the reports of rifles. We're all dead if we don't get off this wall.

Bullets were hailing into them, hundreds of small arms blasting them from beyond the blinding light. There was screaming and yelling all around him. He felt a heavy punch connect with his side. The blow whirled him and he went down. This time he knew he had been hit by a bullet. A second went through his calf, a third entered his thigh. Even so, he regained his feet. A dozen men lay dead or dying on the exposed wall as he frantically tried to get the rest of his assault party back over the battlement. Another bullet winged him in the chest as he held ground until the last of his men had got onto the ladder. Then he saw one of his own Chinese running towards him, hands waving, his face screwed into a grimace. He seemed to be trying to shout a warning, but as Ward turned he saw another Chinese Corpsman near him, rifle levelled, a flash, and an instant later a horrifying blow smashed into the side of his head, and everything dissolved into blackness.

When he came to his senses a moment later he found himself in hell. He choked, coughing up a mouthful of blood. Bright flames were dancing all around him. Blood was pouring from his face and his mouth was numb. He saw the man who had been running towards him lying inert in a dark, spreading pool. Then Vincente's arms were under his own. He tried to speak, but could not. Somehow Vincente lifted his body and dumped him onto the head of a ladder, and somehow he remained there long enough to be manhandled down and away from the walls.

As at Sung-chiang Burgevine had been detailed to lead the second attack wave. He had come forward to the edge of the moat to open a covering fire. Defenders had sprung up on the South Gate tower and were picking off the fleeing attackers as they re-crossed the moat.

Ward struggled furiously as they laid him on the ground. I'm all right! I'm all right! his mind kept shouting.

The Chinese around him stared wide-eyed at his injury. He called for paper, making signs in the air, and started to write out orders. In response the Corps rallied and regrouped. The six pounders were run forward and opened up a damaging fire on the South Gate at close range. They blew in the big timbers and shattered the stonework that supported them, filling the air with smoke that partly screened them.

Ward passed a scribbled note to Burgevine.

HOW MANY DEAD?

'Half,' Burgevine told him as he ran up, panting. 'Colonel, we got to get out of here.'

'The Colonel's dying,' he heard someone say nearby.

The hell I'm dying, he thought angrily. He reeled, put a hand to his chin and felt his shattered jawbone grind as he tried again to speak. His tongue probed. All the big teeth along his lower left jaw were loose or missing, and there was a ragged hole through his right cheek where the bullet had made its exit. But his lungs were not filling as he had feared, and the hits he had taken in the leg were nothing at all. The bullets had gone right through him, and he was hardly bleeding from any of his wounds.

He looked around, fought the horror and fought the fatigue, took up his pencil and wrote another order, calling the second attack to go in as planned.

'Colonel, the Taipings are fixing to sally out after us,' Burgevine shouted. 'We've got to get out of here now.'

He grew violent, slashing with his baton, spitting curses at Burgevine. Orders were being shouted, but they were the wrong orders, and instead of attacking, his men began to draw off towards the boats. He regained his feet, tried to set things back on track, but many hands seized him and carried him away.

How did the Taipings know what we were going to do? he thought furiously as they bundled him into a sedan chair. Blood was pouring from his face now, dripping onto the crumpled paper as he tried to write. His fingers still gripped the bloodied pencil, but the sedan was jogging along now, making it impossible for him to make his wishes known.

He thought of the Chinese soldier on the top of the wall. The man's screwed up face and urgent gestures. He tried to warn me and that's why he died . . . warn me of what? What happened up there?

You were shot by one of your own.

His mind recoiled away from the thought. Half my army dead and me shot to hell! I led my boys straight into an ambush. No wonder he shot you . . .

He felt a coldness coming upon him, and the blackness yawning at the edges of his vision, threatening to swallow him. As it did so he seethed with anger. No! Not yet! I must know who it was. Who betrayed me! Who did this to me? I was set up. That's it! They tried to murder me! By God, I'll find the one responsible! I'll kill him! If I live out this day I promise you, dear God, I'll kill the bastard who tried to murder me!

Fei saw the lone horseman as they came in sight of the Forbidden City. It was Jung-lu, riding back like a whirlwind.

'The school room is empty and the heir is gone!'

The Empress was aghast. 'Are you sure? Where?'

'Yehonala, the Forbidden City is now an empty shell. The ramparts are still manned, but the gate keepers at the Gate of Military Prowess say they have orders not to prevent anyone leaving. I saw many eunuchs fleeing towards the Summer Palace with armfuls of valuables. The Emperor has appointed the Prince Kung as caretaker.'

'Where is he?' Yehonala demanded.

'In hiding inside the Forbidden City. He tried his best to persuade the Son of Heaven to stay and was left in charge of Peking himself.'

Yehonala's anger foamed up. 'Where's that dung-maggot, An Te-hai? He should have warned me an hour ago!'

'At the Summer Palace. That's where Tsai-ch'un must have been taken.'

'Go on ahead. Find my son, Jung-lu! Find him!'

'Do not worry.' His eyes blazed. 'I will!'

As Fei watched him gallop away the Empress climbed back inside her palanquin. The bearers and as many guards as could lend their strength lifted the car and began to carry it at a jog into the semi-darkness of the Summer Palace road.

As the maids scurried after their mistress, Fei's mind began recalculating desperately. You've left it too late, she thought. You've waited and waited, and now matters have moved on down another road. What to do? Think! Does this really change things? And if so, how?

If the Emperor is running away beyond the Wall that will surely be the end of the Manchu. That will be the end of Emperors and mandarins, and the whole ancient system. The foreigners will take charge in Peking, but they are too clever to want to be left in charge. China would be far too costly a place for a foreign power to govern. They would far rather place the nation in the hands of a puppet ruler, one whom they can easily control. But who will they choose?

Yes, of course! How foolish of me not to have realized it sooner. The boy!

They continued along the starlit road, until Fei saw a haze of light appear on the northern horizon. Soon afterwards they came in sight of the walled gardens of the Summer Palace. The road beside the main gate was a mass of palanquins, covered carts and clamouring people. Many held up lanterns, others were loaded with the Emperor's priceless possessions.

Fei saw only servants and eunuchs. The Common People, she knew, were too terrified to watch, let alone approach. She followed close behind Yehonala's litter, as the mass of squabbling eunuchs gave way before the Bordered Blue banner troops who forced a way through. The Empress of the Western Palace headed for the centre of the human morass where Hsien-feng's huge palanquin tossed like a boat on a troubled sea. The Empress's face was set and pale with rage. She was shouting the name of the heir all the way to the Imperial palanquin. She fought her way up onto it, ignoring Hsien-feng's body servants, and tore aside the curtains.

'Where is he?'

Fei gasped at the sight. The Son of Heaven was not inside, just a scared and sickly coolie dressed in finery and wearing long nail-sheaths and employed, she imagined, to decoy the entourage long enough for the Emperor to make good his escape. The coolie flinched back wordlessly.

'Where is he?' Yehonala shouted, undaunted. 'Where is my son?'

'Yehonala, we must escape! The Barbarians are coming!' the coolie shouted.

'Coward! Turtle-dung coward! Your ancestors have disowned you! Where is Tsai-ch'un? What have you done with him?'

Suddenly, with an incredible shock, Fei realized that this coolie was the Emperor after all. It seemed impossible. The lantern light was lurid, the air flavoured with violence. All around her the men of the Bordered Blue were rushing from palanquin to palanquin, opening curtains and inspecting occupants. They were looking for the heir, but in so doing they discovered many greedy eunuchs hiding piles of treasure. Fighting broke out as the men of other banners tried to stop them, then a warrior of fearsome size shouted out, and Yehonala was called to the litter of the Empress of the Eastern Palace.

Niuhuru shielded the boy as the curtains were pulled aside. 'Yehonala! You've come at last! Your son's quite safe! I promise you he's come to no harm!'

'Give him to me, child thief!'

Yehonala wrenched the boy away, gripping him to her in one breathless motion. Then she turned, the heir tight in her arms, and started running back with him towards her own palanquin.

An imperious man in travelling attire blocked her way. There were Bordered Red guards at his back. 'Where are you going, Empress?'

'Nowhere! You're the ones who're running away! You're filth, Su-shun! You and your family are all filth, back to the hundredth generation!'

'His Imperial Majesty, the Emperor, is obliged by law to hunt in the autumn. He has ordered his Court to Jehol. He has decided the heir is old enough to come too.'

Yehonala's eyes glowed. 'Tsai-ch'un's staying with me! We're both staying here!'

Hsien-feng called down from his palanquin. 'The Barbarians are coming! We must all go! Leave everything! I order it!'

The jostling crowd drew back in fear as Jung-lu launched out his sword, ready to rush at Su-shun, but Yehonala, clutching the heir to her, screamed at him to be still. Immediately two dozen swords – Bordered Red and Bordered Blue – sang from their scabbards, and the soldiers faced each other across the beaten earth of the roadway.

Fei saw there was no way out of the stand-off. The Bordered Blue were outnumbered three to one, and the slightest move by either side would trigger a deluge of blood. Yehonala had to give in. She flung herself forward and down, occupying the middle ground on her knees, imploring. 'Please, mistress! The child! Think of the child! He will die!'

It was a small distraction, but it bought enough time to

cause the soldiers to remember themselves, and to bring the Empress back to her senses.

'We will do as his Imperial Majesty orders,' Yehonala said, her eyes coals. 'Jung-lu, return to the Forbidden City and report to the Prince Kung for your orders.'

Jung-lu stood motionless, his sword arm itching to strike.

'Do as I say!'

Without another word Yehonala turned and carried the heir to her palanquin and climbed inside. With a tremendous effort Jung-lu tore himself away and called his men after him. Su-shun nodded to his Bordered Red guards and they flanked the palanquin as it began its journey north.

As the crowd of eunuchs surged around her, Fei got to her feet and rejoined the Empress's entourage.

The maid, Wen, came to her and said, 'The Empress thanks you.'

'Please don't consider me,' she replied with false humility, her heart still hammering. 'I simply did my duty.'

Lindley placed down the white wei-ch'i stone near the northern corner of the board, his opening move of this seventh game of the night. So far he had deliberately lost them all.

As Jimmy Long-face began to blow out the candles, Lindley's eyes adjusted to the grey dawn light. He rubbed the soreness from the small of his back and stretched. There had been a slight frost and the temple was cold and dry and dusty. The relentlessly smiling idols glinted dully around them, as if mocking the unreasoning stubbornness of Barbarians. Heng-chi had sat with them almost the whole of the night, conversing, drinking Imperial tea and watching them play. It had been the longest night of his life.

Now the smell of tallow smoke was acrid on the air. Lindley had thought often about the moment when the last of the candles would be blown out. He had helped Loch write his last letter, then he had written his own – to his father. He had addressed it to Colonel Ward, asking him to pass it on if ever such a thing became possible. After the writing materials had been taken away there had passed an uneasy hour during which Loch had knelt in the corner, his wiry frame hunched, his hands pathetically clasped, as he whispered prayers to his God. He had noted Heng-chi's inquisitive eye, and his deduction that the two prisoners must be of different tribes, since the one prayed while the other did not. Do I believe in God? he asked himself, knowing already deep inside what the answer was. Strange that it takes an experience like this to give everything crystal clarity.

The sound of distant thunder jolted them. Lindley glanced up at Loch's face and saw it was stark with fear. Heng-chi avoided their eye as he got up. 'Please excuse me,' he said, and went to the door.

'Maybe it was thunder,' Loch said.

'It was gunfire.'

'Oh, God . . .'

An age passed before Heng-chi returned. When he did his face was granite hard. 'You must go now.'

'Where to?' Lindley asked. His heart beat painfully against his ribs. His hands felt suddenly cold. He did not move. 'Where are we going?'

Heng-chi gave a curt order to the guards. They entered the room menacingly.

Lindley saw there was no alternative. He lifted his head and led the way outside. Loch followed. The inner court was cold and still. Bronze sand-filled urns stood to each side of the steps, wisps of incense rising up from them. The elephant-grey cobbles were gritty underfoot. Lindley found himself fighting to breathe. The dry, bitter air of Peking caught in his throat and he coughed.

Ahead there was a circular exit – a moon gate – but dead in the centre of it now the globe of the sun rested, a gorgeous orange ball newly risen above the horizon and still wreathed in morning purple.

They were led through the moon gate. Outside a covered cart waited, its two wheels each as tall as a man. It was escorted by a dozen mounted white-banner troops. Lindley endured the wait, alive to every sound, every inflection in the voices around him.

'Where are they taking us?' Loch asked miserably.

He saw the cart was like the one that had brought him here. It had belonged to the Prison of the Board of Corrections. 'I don't know.' Then they were thrust forward. The interior of the cart was filthy and stank. They were pushed in, and said nothing to one another as the backboard was hitched up and the cart began to rumble away.

The moment they were in darkness Loch let go and began weeping like a child. Lindley made no move to comfort him, but got to his feet and pressed his eye to a gap in the side slats. He could see nothing but a small patch of sky occasionally obscured by eaves or the top of a wall.

'For God's sake, shut up,' he hissed.

Loch's whimpers died away in gulps. 'I'm sorry,' he said. 'I'm sorry . . . I . . .'

'I said, shut up, damn you! I'm trying to listen out.'

The cart's iron-shod wheels grated over the road surface – sometimes cobbles, he thought, more often compacted earth. The way was pot-holed, but straight. Everything remained deathly silent, except for the creaking of the cart and the clattering hooves of their escort.

After a few minutes studying the cast of shadows Lindley told Loch, 'I think we're going east. If I'm right we should soon pass under one of the gates in the city wall.'

Loch began praying miserably now. Something about the abjectness of his state both touched Lindley's sympathy and at the same time revolted him. More minutes went by, and then the patch of sky disappeared. The cart came to a halt and they sat in complete silence, straining to listen. He fought the urge to react to it, knowing that they must have re-entered the prison.

When he heard the sound of iron bolts being run back and huge timber doors being swung open, it confirmed the worst. Something snapped inside him, filling him with tremendous strength. He tore off one of the ribs of the cart with his bare hands and began to rub the end of it against an iron fitting, sharpening it.

They began to roll forward again, yard after yard, but the journey was timeless for Lindley. When it stopped he leapt to the backboard and braced himself to fight and die. But when the cart was opened Lindley was blinded by low glaring sunshine. A chill wind swept across the plain from the east. As his vision cleared he saw familiar white campaign tents set up all around and men in red uniforms waiting. He saw another cart being opened. A French officer, four French troopers and a Sikh, climbing down but unable to stand. Then he saw more carts and a line of a dozen or more roughly-made timber coffins.

An army surgeon came forward solicitously, but Lindley pushed the man aside. 'I'm all right,' he said. 'I must see Elgin.'

Major Charles Gordon of the Royal Engineers knelt by the baroque facade of the Hall of Audience and joined the final fuse to the explosive charges that had already been placed in the foundations.

The smell of burning was in his nostrils. He heard distant shouts, sounds coming to him from the men of Sir John Michel's First Division as they ranged the grounds of the Summer Palace, seeking their own targets in the vast pleasure park. The looting so far had been prodigious. The French had arrived first and begun the orgy, stealing ornaments of solid gold and silver, jade, furs, pearls and intricate enamels. One of the two hundred palaces in the park displayed a huge assortment of gold clocks from Europe, another housed two ornate carriages manufactured in London over half a century ago. So easy had been the pickings that such ordinary items as porcelain, silks and bronzes had been left to the very few Chinese who had dared venture over the unguarded perimeter wall to join in the ransacking. Gordon arrived to the spectacle of men of the 44th and 67th Regiments throwing down items of incredible value whenever they came upon still more precious loot.

By God, he thought, if they had been my men, they would not have run riot like that. I would have shot them dead first. And they know it.

But it had not been the private soldiers who had most disgraced the Queen's Colours. Who could blame them when their officers were behaving in the same way? Three Dragoon Guard officers broke into the Emperor's apartments and swept open the canopy of his bed to find his hat laid out for him and his opium pipe waiting to be used. They took what they could, before emerging to see the spectacle of a dozen foot soldiers, drunk with joy, half of them dressed in richly embroidered robes of Imperial yellow, dancing over the bridge after their sergeant. Somewhere else in the Summer Palace a group of Indian troops located a chamber stacked with gold ingots and barricaded themselves in. There had been nothing like it since the sack of Rome.

Last night, when Generals Grant and de Montauban had finally managed to restore order, there had been a half-hearted attempt at sharing out booty according to rank. Everyone in the army was to receive something, except the commanders and their immediate staffs.

Gordon thought guiltily of the forty-eight pounds he had been allotted, and wondered again if he should turn it down. He stood up and wiped the perspiration from his forehead, then called his men out of the palace and counted them off. They lined up and sang out their names promptly, standing well clear of the fuse.

Just as well Lord Elgin ordered the destruction, he confided to his God. It's right to avenge the killings and the torture, but this will also cover up and make what has been an out-of-control ransacking seem as if it was planned all along. I'd much rather not be here, for who can revel in destruction of this sort?

He looked back as his men began to march away. Plumes of heavy smoke were rising from the many wooden structures that had already been put to the torch. His eyes went to the far horizon. As he bent to light the fuse he saw that the northern hills were brilliant with snow.

BOOK IV

The Empress of the Western Palace watched her breath coiling in the dim light as she waited for the door to be opened by the new maid. Candles guttered blood red in the freezing air of the open verandah. They were Manchu candles, as big as a man's forearm, encased in lanterns with windows made from buffalo horn. They gave a greasy odour to the air as they burned, and the light they cast was disquieting.

'What are you thinking?' she asked, turning to the new maid.

The girl hesitated. 'Nothing, Mistress.'

'Oh, don't be so sullen! The atmosphere here is bad enough without maids sulking. Look at you, deliberately ruining a pretty face.'

'I apologize, Mistress.'

'Stupid girl! Maybe it would have been better if you had not intervened outside the Summer Palace. Maybe it would have been better if Jung-lu's sword had slashed them all down, and we had been killed also. Call An Te-hai.'

'Very good, Mistress.'

There are evil ghosts stalking these lodges, Yehonala thought. She felt the loss of her little dog, Sea Otter. His warmth and liquid eyes would have lifted her spirits now. He would have been such a comfort on the journey. The Imperial caravan had fled north and east across the plains, moving into hard land along a road that weaved between the smooth-shouldered hills of the Yan Shan. On the third day they had seen the Great Wall snaking over steep hills, a project so astounding that it seemed to Yehonala beyond the powers of mortal men. Two days after that snow had fallen, and a week later the Valley of the Lions had opened before them, welcoming them with a blast of icy breath.

The great hunting park at Jehol was protected by a small

replica of the Great Wall. Within its compass were dozens of pagodas and pavilions and lodges, much like those in Peking's Summer Palace, White hills were ranged about the park, and a dozen huge lamaist monasteries were visible beyond the northern perimeter, and the sight of their austere ramparts made Yehonala feel the remoteness of the place. She saw deer sheltering forlornly under stark trees, and Hot Spring Lake steaming despite a crust of ice. But Jehol was an abandoned palace. The Imperial family had quit when the Chia-ch'ing Emperor was struck by lightning. In the forty years that followed, the staff had grown old and few and their habits more like those of owners than servants. The gardens were barren now, the pleasure palaces rotting, the pavilions home to vermin, full of spiders' webs and dust.

I'm no more than a prisoner here, she thought bitterly as she watched the sulking maid return and resume her position. I'm a prisoner in a frozen wilderness, not allowed to see my son, not allowed to approach my husband. Hsienfeng is dying; I can sense it. How clever of my enemies to have separated me from my allies. Prince Kung is in Peking, Jung-lu also, I accused Niuhuru of trying to steal the heir from me, and she has not forgiven me for that. Only An Tehai is here. And that only because the law says Imperial eunuchs may not, on pain of death, stray more than a hundred li from the Emperor's person. Unfortunately, I can no longer trust Little An after his betrayal.

When the Chief Eunuch arrived she faced him with overwhelming anger.

'Vile turtle! You deserted me at the crucial moment!'

An recognized the extent of her anger and grovelled. 'I sent messages to you, Lady. You were not to be found anywhere.'

'You knew exactly where I was! I should have done as Jung-lu suggested, An Te-hai. I should have had you snuffed out!'

'But you must not do that, Lady,' he said, fearful but also sly. 'When I am the only dependable friend you have.'

'Dependable? I told you I was going to visit the Temple of Silk Making! I told you I had arranged a meeting with Prince P'u Lun!'

An cowered before her. 'Lady, please excuse my poor

memory. I do not recall you giving me any information about the Temple of Silk Making.'

'I wrote to you! You cannot deny it!'

'Ah, wrote . . . Letters often go astray.'

'Don't wriggle like a snake!' She searched his face then, looking for a clue. 'Are you telling me the truth? You did not receive my note?'

'It is the absolute truth, Lady. What advantage would it have brought me to disobey?'

'That's the trouble with you: I can never tell what you're thinking! Now get out!'

When An Te-hai left she flashed a glance at her silent companion. 'Disobedient girl! Didn't I tell you not to sulk? If you won't do as you're told you can get out!'

The girl said nothing. Did nothing.

'Did you hear me?'

The girl's eyes rifled slowly to impale her. 'Don't talk to me like that, you Imperial bitch, or I'll cut your throat.'

Yehonala thought she must have experienced a trick of the mind. Often in the Forbidden City she had wished that someone would just once have the courage to contradict her, but she felt the hatred now like a blow to the face. No one had ever spoken to her like that before. The shock turned to fear as she saw a knife appear from her maid's sleeve.

'Don't make a noise. Not a sound, or I'll cut your liver out.'

The voice was fierce, but also calm and compelling. She flinched back as the maid came to stand over her.

'Ready yourself to hear my words, Empress.'

'Who are you?' she whispered, her mouth drying.

'A messenger.'

'If you harm me, my guards will torture you.'

'You cannot threaten me. I am already dead.'

The eerie words thrust loathing through her. 'Who sent you?'

'I am here to deliver an ultimatum from the T'ien Wang.'

Yehonala gasped. 'The Heavenly King? Then – you're Taiping!'

'Yes, I'm Taiping. I'm instructed to warn the Manchurian usurpers not to attempt to renew their siege of Nanking. General Tseng must withdraw his forces from the Yangtze

293

valley. You must leave Nanking to us, or we'll march on Shanghai.'

'Shanghai?' Her voice was an echo. Such a move was unthinkable. Shanghai would represent a huge escalation in the war, a reason for Outer Barbarians to come flooding into Central China.

The terrifying whisper went on, 'While your troops are busy dancing with the foreigners who occupy your capital, Taiping armies will sweep down on China's greatest sea port.'

'The Barbarians will not let you,' Yehonala said, recovering her wits. Her eyes remained fixed on the evil blade. 'They are traders. They will never allow Shanghai to be occupied. They worship trade like a god. Anything that—'

'Listen to me! The foreigners will have no choice. Our irresistible forces will enter Shanghai, then we will make a deal with them. When we promise to open all of the South to trade they will accept us. Every tael of tea and silk revenue we take from you we will use to strengthen ourselves. We will make a separate kingdom of the South. All this will befall if General Tseng is not recalled immediately.'

'Why were you told to bring your message to me?' Yehonala asked.

'Because you are the mother of the heir.'

Yehonala looked at the girl and felt hysteria begin to grip her. She started to laugh, but the laugh stuttered into nothingness. 'I have no power. You might as well be talking to a gardener!'

'You can inform your ally, Prince Kung, who holds executive power in Peking. Let him act. This message I bring from the T'ien Wang. That is all.'

The girl's face was tortured now. She had done her duty and was drained. Yehonala looked again at the knife, and managed to compose herself enough to ask, 'Do you plan to hold me at knife-point for ever?'

'I am but a messenger. I have delivered my message. Therefore my task is accomplished.' Her voice was barely audible as she said, 'There is one more thing. You must tell Prince Kung that he must not execute the foreign captives or it will be the worse for him.'

Yehonala watched as the knife quavered in the air, but

the girl did not drop it. Suddenly Yehonala realized what the knife's intended target was.

'No! It's too late,' Yehonala snapped. 'I signed the order for the Barbarian executions. They are already dead.'

The girl drew herself back from the edge. 'No. I burned your letters.'

She watched the girl close her eyes and her mouth begin to move in prayer. Then the knife struck. As it did so, Yehonala made a grab for the girl's wrist. She screamed and began to fight with wiry strength and a powerful resolve to die. The struggle seemed to go on for a long time, two wills battling against one another, but suddenly the room was full of flickering light and grey-robed eunuchs and then the struggle ended.

The ice on the ornamental lakes was as deep as a man was tall. Fei had slept well. The comfortable, heated bed ledges that were built over chimney flues stayed warm all night. Her own was strewn with hard cushions and piled with quilts of lightest duck down.

She awoke at first light to a day that she had never counted on seeing to find eunuchs watching her closely. At first she could not understand, then the memory of the night's events came back to her like a breaking wave.

She was given a little breakfast of sweet rolls and bean paste and tea. Then she dressed and was brought before the Empress, who ordered the room cleared.

As soon as they were alone the Empress said, 'I should have you tortured for what you did.'

'Do. I told you, I'm already dead.'

'No. You've changed. I can see life in your eyes.' The Empress paused, waiting for a reply, but Fei offered none. 'And you're a fool to have let yourself be used as worthless and expendable.'

'I've seen more than you could begin to imagine.'

'I wonder what kind of bad magic casts so strong a spell of self destruction over a person's mind? You would gladly have died to deliver a message.' The Empress sounded intrigued.

'This is the example of Jesus Christ. He also died to deliver a message.'

'Oh, of course. Your Taiping religion is taken from the

Barbarians. Little wonder then that you behave like a mad woman. Your head is full of eastern ideas and western ideas all mixed up. Naturally you are confused.'

'Ours is the one true religion. We worship the one true God.'

'So say all worshippers. Is it true you believe the gods of China are just so many plaster figures to be smashed by soldiers?'

'They are all worthless idols that grip the minds of the people! One day you will feel the T'ien Wang's power, and understand that the Brother of Jesus Christ has come to save China!'

'Your beliefs are your own concern. They don't interest me. What does interest me is how you came to me, and why? Remember, there is still a chance that we may be able to use one another to mutual advantage. Do not jeopardize that possibility.'

'I will answer no questions.'

'As you wish.' The Empress regarded her for a long moment, then said, 'An Te-hai tells me that it was he who arranged for you to enter the Forbidden City.' The Empress paused again, but again she made no reply. 'He says he was planning to give you to Su-shun as a plaything, but then he received a thousand taels in cumsha to find you "a more genteel position".'

The Empress sipped tea, waiting. Still Fei said nothing.

'The man who introduced you was a shop owner of Drum Tower Lane. An says he is of Manchu blood.'

Fei tried to give nothing more away, but a huge weight had lifted from her with the delivery of the ultimatum. Coming so close to death had been a liberation that had put everything into sharp perspective. Maybe you should help this Imperial whore as much as you can, she thought. She has spared your life – saved it, in truth. You owe her something.

'You're correct,' Fei said with pride. 'My father was once a Manchu lord, banished it's true, but a Manchu lord nevertheless.'

'Then a measure of respect is due to you.' The Empress said it smoothly, but Fei was not sure if she was being sincere, ironic, or had noted her pride and was saying it just to trick her. The Empress added, 'So – your father was packed off to Hei Lung Kiang, was he?'

The name meant 'Black Dragon River'. It was the place all officials banished by the dynasty were sent.

'Yes,' Fei said, her resentment burning bright. 'Even as a young man he recognized the corruption of your dynasty. He bravely fought to overthrow it.'

'It's strange, because rebellion is the greatest of all crimes, and the most severe punishment is public decapitation. Next is the silken cord that accompanies the order to commit suicide. Both these punishments are applied to offenders who plot against the Dragon Throne – so there must have been good reason why your father was shown clemency.'

Fei's rancour put words into her mouth. 'Do you call what my father suffered "clemency"? It was decreed that he strip the insignia of rank from his own person in public – his official robes, the button from his hat, even his peacock feather. All his lands and property and money were confiscated. He was banished from the capital for ever. It was decreed that his descendants would never again hold offices of profit or trust.'

'But he might have lost his head.'

'To an honourable man loss of face is worse than death. If not for his heroic journey to the South my father would have been forced to live a dishonoured life – fingers pointed at him, his name scorned by all, living in poverty, feeding only on bitterness and disgrace, and suffering in the knowledge that all his family had suffered because of him.'

'Who is the shop owner of Drum Tower Lane?' the Empress asked. 'You won't tell me? No matter. Then let me ask you about the Barbarian captives instead. Why must Prince Kung not execute them?'

Fei knew she was trapped. This woman was incredibly shrewd.

'Our spies in the foreigners' camp have told us that if Prince Kung does not release all the captives, they will order Peking to be destroyed,' she said, knowing her lie was weak.

'What interest do you have in these captives?'

This time Fei made no answer. She tried to hide her alarm.

Then the Empress burst into abrupt laughter. 'It doesn't matter, because they're all dead, whether you burned my letters or not. And in retaliation the Barbarians have destroyed not Peking but the Summer Palace.'

Fei felt despair closing in on her. She said a silent prayer for Lindley.

'Unfortunately, that wanton destruction has proved to be the final nail in the coffin of the Son of Heaven. The news has distressed him beyond all recovery. And when he dies, I will be swept away also.'

'Not if you do as the T'ien Wang requires. Give us Nanking and the Yangtze valley. Our armies will withdraw from Shanghai. And your Southern armies can liberate Peking from the foreigners. Old China will be partitioned into two New Chinas.'

'I told you: I am powerless to make such an agreement.'

'But your ally, Prince Kung, is not. He is ruling.'

'Perhaps I could persuade him . . .' The Empress fell into a thoughtful silence. After a while she said, 'At present I have no secure means of communicating with Peking. You must take my letter to Prince Kung yourself, and return with his reply.'

It was the Hour of the Dragon, still early morning, and the sun had not yet driven the mists from the courts of the Forbidden City. The French Tricolour and Union flag had flown together over the Meridian Gate for a full month, but now they were gone, and both Lord Elgin and Baron Gros had gone with them.

Why did I agree to stay? Lindley wondered. Was it simply vanity after all? Did Elgin flatter me by telling me there was nobody else who could remain behind and deliver diplomatic letters to the Dragon Throne? No. The truth is I just don't want to go to Nanking. After what Ward said about my father, I don't want to find him any more.

When he looked up he saw Prince Kung's eunuch secretary staring at him with mistrust. He followed the man inside the gloomy hall. The Court had changed to winter dress and Prince Kung's yellow dragon robe was trimmed with black fur. He was solemnly enthroned, and grave-faced councillors flanked him on either side. Lindley's physician's eye noted again how many of the seemingly aged Manchu nobles who had stayed behind when the court fled were not aged at all. They carried the disfigurements of inbreeding and infant ill health – one side of the face totally different from the other, or a strange squint, or four or five teeth run together in one piece like a bone, or a big scar in the forehead, or a beard of six long, stout bristles, or a set of eagle's claws instead of nails. Many were deeply pock-marked, and together they presented a cretinous and grossly unhealthy appearance.

Lindley watched bleakly as the Russian ambassador left the Hall of Preservation of Harmony. The sound of his spurred boots on ice-coloured marble seemed somehow tri-umphant. As Ignatieff passed him on the steps his nod of acknowledgement was smug. He had come here to carve a slice of China for the Tsar. A year ago the Russians had annexed Manchuria's east coast and the strategic port of Hai-shen-wei, renaming it Vladivostok – 'eastern pos-session'. Now they were using the Anglo-French victory to extract confirmation that the territory would remain Russian for ever.

Lindley came to stand at the prescribed distance before the elfin figure of the Prince and bowed. 'Your Imperial Highness, I come first to convey the best wishes of my own government, and to ask what the government of China has decided regarding the Russian Treaty.'

A representative came forward and called out, 'His Imperial Highness informs you: "You lack proper decorum and this matter is none of your business."' Then, after a barely audible word from the Prince, he added in the same sing-song, 'It is also his Imperial Highness's pleasure that you should know the treaty of which you speak is now ratified.'

Up on the raised platform the Prince Kung was growing more and more irritable as he watched the rankless foreigner stumble through a catalogue of meaningless complaints. 'What's the matter with him?' he said to his Chief Advisor. 'Why does he bite off his words like that?'

'It is remarkable that a Barbarian speaks intelligibly at all, your Imperial Highness.' The Chief Advisor was an effete man, but usually perceptive.

'Do you think they intend some kind of insult by choos-ing him to remain as their spokesman? They must be. Did you say he's one of those we imprisoned then released?'

'That is so, your Imperial Highness. Ex-commissioner

Heng-chi let him go before the order for his execution could arrive.'

Kung nodded slowly, understanding at last why Heng-chi had strangled himself. 'I have heard it claimed, that this one is a medical doctor.'

'No one has been able to discover how far this claim may be true, Imperial Highness, but I have read that Barbarian medicine men are little better than the shaman medicine men of the Mongol tribes. They know nothing of acupuncture, nor even how to prepare herbs properly. Their progress in the health-giving arts is supposed to be confined to a sort of crude knife butchery. It is in their nature to cut, you see. And it is whispered that to become initiated as a Barbarian witch doctor a candidate must chop a dead body into thousands of pieces and put each piece in its own separate eunuch jar. A sort of proof of wickedness.'

'How disgusting!'

'Absolutely, Imperial Highness.'

He watched the Barbarian emissary conclude, bow again in unsatisfactory fashion and withdraw. The moment he did so, a Court runner came to his station behind the throne and whispered that there was urgent news from Jehol.

'When?' he asked, thrills running through his mind. What if Su-shun has triumphed? he thought. What if Yehonala is dead? I have Peking but what should I do with it?

'Imperial Highness, the courier has only just arrived.'

'I will receive him in private quarters.'

When he arrived in the secluded courtyard he was surprised to find four Bordered Blue banner guards encircling a kneeling peasant, their razor-sharp pole blades held at the man's throat. He looked like a bundle of rags crusted with dried mud.

As in the days of the Great Khan Imperial couriers travelled the Jehol road with no coin on their persons. They wore silver hawks on their caps as their sign of office, and belts hung with bells so that the Common People and bandits alike were forewarned of their coming. Everyone in China knew that to interfere with an Imperial messenger, even to refuse him food or shelter, would bring down all the ferocity of Heaven upon them. But these were strange times, times when a disguise would serve better than an advertisement.

The 'courier' looked up and Prince Kung saw with surprise that she was a woman. Her face was filthy. She wore a Mongol-style fur hat with ear-flaps pulled down and a padded jacket. She was covered in mud but her eyes burned.

Astonishingly she tried to rise and said, 'Prince Kung!'

The guards growled at her in alarm and postured around her as if she was a dangerous wild animal.

'Who are you? How do you know me?'

'I come from Jehol.' She went to unfasten her coat and the guards reacted again. 'Why don't you call off these monkeys?' she demanded.

He gestured them back a pace, and took the sealed packet she offered. It was a letter from Yehonala. He read it gravely, then looked at the messenger for a long moment. Then he called for his Chief Household Attendant. When the man came running, he said, 'Prepare quarters for this woman. Bathe and dress her, and give her something to eat. I'll speak with her at the next hour drum.'

When the Hour of the Snake was beaten she was brought in. He received her coolly, then when he was sure, he dismissed the attendants and guards to stand out of earshot. The latter – two senior men responsible for Prince Kung's life – looked involuntarily to one another before remembering themselves. But then they knelt briefly and retired.

Fei waited, feeling the warmth of the bath water still invigorating her flesh. It was so good to be clean and to wear fresh clothes again after a journey of such hardship. It had taken two weeks for her to cross the Yan Shan mountains, trudging through snow and sleet from village to village to beg morsels of food like the widow she had pretended to be. Now she regarded the Prince's squint with loathing. She knew his reputation from her uncle: 'He's haughty, and a clever dealer in false emotions. Like a wily child he cries tears from his right eye, but looks with his left to see what effect it has on those who see it.'

'There can never be dialogue with rebels,' the Prince said, his tone harsh.

'We Taiping are not rebels. Our movement is a popular rising – Chinese fighting against the Manchurian occupation.'

His face opened in amazement at being contradicted. He

shot out a finger. 'The Taiping are rebels, defying properly constituted authority!'

'Whatever you call us, negotiation is better than fighting.'

'Only those who fear they are losing would say that.'

'Only those who fear the truth refuse to talk.'

She saw how uncomfortable he was with her and knew how to use that to her advantage. She changed her tone. 'Because others have refused to face reality China has lost so much. If they had agreed to talk with the foreigners as you did, things would have gone so much better.'

'Incredible effrontery! Address me properly. And how dare you attempt to advise a Prince of the Blood?'

She put on an impish expression. 'Because I know far more about foreigners than you do. I've learned how to get what I want from them, whereas you have not.' She folded her arms – a colossal impudence. 'Perhaps you could invite me to sit down?'

His crescent moon face was aghast, but he gestured her to a chair, glad that he had dismissed the servants and guards.

'Perhaps some tea also?'

He called for tea.

'First you should know,' she said, 'that the continent of Europe is unlike Asia. In Europe there was never one single dominant nation that was able to treat all the others as vassal states as China does. In Europe a nation might blossom supreme for perhaps a single century, then it fades and makes way for a different flower. So far, every one of them has had its turn. This is why, over the centuries, the European foreigners have evolved a most effective system of diplomacy.'

'Our age-old system suits our situation,' Prince Kung said stiffly. 'We treat neigbouring lands as vassal states because that is what they are.'

'Excuse me, but that is no longer true. Consider how much better it would be if there were official channels through which my master, the T'ien Wang, and your government could discuss what must be.'

She saw the Prince watching her with his turned eye. He scowled, but she knew that his fear was beginning to vanish. He too wants a new way, she thought. And he knows the time has come.

*

302

Lindley nodded at the jolly-faced eunuch, and began to make small-talk in Mandarin. The technical books some of the Royal Engineers had left had been eagerly seized and read by members of the Chinese Academy, and this man was full of wonder.

As for himself Lindley was intrigued at the physical effects that castration had brought to the eunuch's body. Voice and hair were most affected, but so was the tone of the skin, the distribution of fat on limbs and torso, and something unique that showed in all their faces, especially the flesh around their eyes.

Since arriving in Peking he had learned to his surprise that castration was the only surgical procedure known to classical Chinese medicine. Eunuch castrations were either performed by specialists who first scalded the flesh and then took off the penis and testicles with one cut of a sickle-shaped razor, or by tying off with a ligature and allowing gangrene morbidity to wither the organs. A Chinese doctor had told him, 'Tradition says that a hundred days is enough for a eunuch to recover – if he does not, he dies.'

Lindley roused himself from the memory and said in Mandarin, 'Please forgive me. You were saying?'

'I come to your legation house to say: good news comes south from the Imperial hunting lodge.'

'Good news?'

'His Imperial Majesty the Son of Heaven has expressed regret at the breach of friendly relations that once happened between our two countries. He has decided to concede the right of having permanent ambassadors reside within his capital.'

'Oh, this is good news indeed.'

'However the Prince Kung regrets that without the Seal of Legally Sanctioned Authority no document that transfers funds from the Board of Treasury can be recognized. This is an Imperial prerogative. This tea is most excellent, by the way.'

'Thank you. It is my duty to remind the Prince that, according to the convention signed on the twenty-fourth day of the last moon, China agreed to pay eight million taels in indemnities, this being the estimated cost of the war.'

The eunuch showed a row of long teeth. 'It is said that

according to the foreign system of thought, war is like gambling.'

'I don't understand.'

'Loser pays, ah?'

As he smiled he watched the eunuch savouring his cup. 'The tea is oolong – from Formosa.'

'Ah, Taiwan! China's island province. Excellent, excellent! Rest assured, our government will pay the damages some time.'

'The Treaty does specify fixed instalments.'

'An unavoidable delay, never mind. Of course, British subjects will now come to trade at Tientsin?'

'That was stated in the Treaty too.'

'Excellent! To be welcomed. And many Chinese people will be welcomed into British Colonies?'

'So the Treaty says.'

'For what purpose please are these excess peasants required?'

Lindley shrugged. 'To live and to work.'

The eunuch's smile congealed momentarily on his face. 'Excellent! Chinese people work very hard!'

'Yes, we know.'

'Making British Queen very rich lady. Ha! Ha!'

'Ha. Ha.'

'Making very many railway through Barbarian lands.'

'Ha. Ha.'

'One day can have transatlantic telegraph cable in China also?'

'One day.'

Lindley sipped his tea, glad there was whisky in it. He was counting the days to the ambassador's arrival. China was no place for him any more. He made up his mind to go home.

The eunuch leaned forward and made a confidential gesture. 'The Prince Kung does not want any missionary to be killed, nor any merchant defrauded. Modern government must be easy and good-natured. He believes that things always right themselves in the end. And you know, he likes you very much.'

Lindley took the hint gratefully. 'I'm honoured. And . . . please tell him that I like him too.'

'Perhaps you can meet with him privately?'

'I should very much like to meet with the Prince privately.'

'Excellent! Excellent! Perhaps you can advise him on the setting up of a bureau.'

'A bureau?'

'A Board of Government – specially convened for dealing with the world outside.'

'A foreign office?' He grinned, for the first time sensing that a huge step forward had been made. 'Why, that's a capital idea! A foreign office. Oh, yes. That would help a great deal.'

The eunuch's eyes gleamed with satisfaction. 'Excellent! It shall be called the Bureau for the Mutually Acceptable Chastisement of Wayward Foreigners.'

The tall foreigner was standing with his back to her when Fei saw him. There was no doubt in her mind who he was. The only uncertainty was whether he was real or imaginary.

In the moment between her seeing him and his turning around she felt a powerful urge to run, but before she could move his eyes had locked on her. As they did so all expression fell from his face. She knew that she too must be a picture of astonishment, because both her hands were pressed to her mouth.

He half stretched out his arms and took a step toward her, but she froze as if he was a dangerous animal, and he halted.

'Fei-ch'ien?' he whispered. There was neither love nor hatred in his voice. He said her name as if she was a ghost. She felt tears coming, confusion churning inside her. 'Fei-ch'ien? Is it you?'

'Lin-li . . .'

His name broke the spell and they fell into one another's embrace. For a few seconds she clung to him and he to her. Her mind was whirling and she found she still could not take her hands away from his face.

'How long have you been here? What are you doing in Peking? Fei-ch'ien – is it really you? I was told you were dead.'

Suddenly his eyes were urgent. 'Do they know you're here?' he whispered. 'Do they know what you are? Fei, speak to me. Say something. I thought you were dead.'

'I . . . I . . . Lin-li, I didn't expect. Please,' she said. 'We must not be seen like this.'

They entered a vacant courtyard, an old palace apartment used now as a storeroom. He led her to the stone curb of a well and held her in his arms for a long time.

When I read the message from my father, Fei, I knew it must have been you. I knew you were thinking of me. Why didn't you wait for me? Why did you run away?'

'I could not wait for you. I could not neglect my duty.'

'Fei, just five minutes would have been enough. I needed to see you.'

'Ten thousand years would not have been enough,' she said, her eyes filling with tears. 'Lin-li, I was so scared for you. When I was last here in the Forbidden City I read your execution order. It was written out in red, sealed and ready to send.'

'Consul Meadows showed me a poster that named you as a rebel spy. I thought you were dead, Fei.'

She told him how the Governor had released her, how she had come into the Forbidden City, how she had burned the order for his beheading the day before the Emperor had fled. As he listened he marvelled that an inexplicable force seemed to be leaving its mark in their lives. Perhaps that's what the Chinese call the tao, he thought.

The well's hinged wooden cover was attached by a chain to a pivoting wooden beam and counter balance. Lindley pulled on the beam and the heavy lid lifted up. Twenty feet below a queasy disc of light reflected their two heads. He seized her and kissed her, and they embraced beside the well for what seemed a very long time.

'I love you, Fei. I want you to know that.'

He took a large silver coin from his waistcoat pocket and threw it down the well. She looked at him, surprised that he had thrown money away deliberately.

'It's our custom,' he said. 'We drop coins into wells.'

'Why do you do that?'

'In the hope that a wish will come true, of course.'

'Shall I try?'

'Yes. You must.'

He gave her a coin and watched it splash, loving her delight.

'Can you guess what I wished for?' she asked.

He put a finger to her lips. 'Whatever it is, you must not tell me.'

She was suddenly disappointed. 'No?'

'No. If you do, it will never come true.'

'Then it will be my secret.'

She grinned back at him, her face blemishless, her teeth regular and very white, and the moment was perfect. Above the deserted courtyard the sky was china blue and cloudless and somewhere over the wall there were songbirds hanging in cages in the trees. But then the high, red walls of the Forbidden City began to press in on them.

'I must go now,' she told him, a steely dullness appearing in her eyes.

'Not now, Fei. Surely?'

'I must return to Jehol today. I am to take a message.'

'To Jehol?' It was as if a plug had been pulled from him and his lifeblood was draining away. 'Why?'

'I cannot tell you any more.' She turned away. 'But I must go back there today. The journey is hard, and it's important that I reach the first way-station before night falls.'

He could not engage her eye. 'You won't be safe. Stay here with me. Your job's done. Someone else can take the message back.'

'I cannot . . .'

'Why? Just stay here. Marry me. Be my wife.'

'I cannot.'

'Why not? Don't you want to? If you do, then just do it!'

She lowered her head. 'You once told me that we are responsible for making our own destiny – our own heavens and our own hells. If you are right then the future of China rests on what I do next.' Her eyes rose to meet his own. 'You know what I want. But you must also know that what I must do is my duty.'

'As a Taiping?' he said, his voice suddenly a cutting edge.

'Yes. As a Taiping.'

'What have they done to you, Fei? Don't you understand? I love you.'

'I don't yet know what love is, Lin-li. One day I hope that—'

'Fei! It's me you're talking to!'

She stared back, almost defiant now. 'I am a soldier. And the Taiping nation is at war.'

'That's nothing but a bloody slogan and you know it! There's only one sane choice between love and war. You must make it.'

'I have already made it. I must do my duty.'

He looked at her incredulously, loving her, but hating the power that had enthralled her mind. 'To hell with your duty!'

A tremor ran through her. She closed her eyes. 'A deal is very close. Please wait for me.'

'Why? So you can betray me again? Like you did last time? Fei, you must change your mind. You're a rebel. You're less than nothing to these people. They'll kill you as soon as look at you.'

She did not answer him, instead she pulled away. He watched her turn and start to leave, but then she looked back.

'Until again,' she said, and the sadness of it tore his heart open.

After a moment, standing in the empty courtyard, he said, 'Until again . . .'

But it sounded hollow in his ears. Like the echo of coins in a wishing well.

Ward stepped ashore at Shanghai, old anger boiling up in him once more. The scars on his cheek and chin were barely visible now after so many months' convalescence. He wore a hat and an anonymous brown jacket with a Japanese silk lining, and his hands were thrust deep down in his pockets against the cold rain as he looked both ways up and down the Bund. Something in his manner warned off the chair bearers who normally flocked to solicit any Westerner they saw on the roadside. Finally, satisfied at what he had seen, he merged into the noisy throng.

Despite his unannounced arrival, he knew, dozens of eyes would have noted his coming, and that even before he appeared at the Grand Hotel word would have reached the ears of every important man in the city.

It should have been a pleasure to be back in the most enticing port in Asia, but blood red revenge was blotting out any pleasure there might have been. For two weeks following the fiasco at Ching-p'u he had tried to set his affairs on an even keel, both in Sung-chiang and in Shanghai. Despite

his shattered jaw he had bought two more eighteen pounders and a dozen smaller field guns, and had signed on a
number of experienced Europeans. In that time he had
endured the not-so-tender mercies of Dr Daniel J. Mac-
Gowan and two other so-called physicians, but despite bathing his wounds in whisky six times a day his jawbone had
refused to knit.

Vincente Macanaya had pointed out to him that a coroner
had to be sober to give orders. Henry Burgevine had told
him that it was time to let a real doctor take a look at his
face, but he could find no real doctors in Shanghai: there
were none within five hundred miles. Finally the pain and
the swelling had got so bad that he had let Edward Forrest
and Yang Fang persuade him that Sung-chiang could continue for a while without him, and he had sailed for Hong
Kong.

That lie had been for Consul Meadows' benefit. Ten miles
out he had switched ships and taken a steamer to Nagasaki,
and, half-mad with pain, had found an American naval
surgeon who had set his jaw and dressed his other wounds
in a way that stood half a chance of healing.

For weeks, as he lay recovering, his mind festered with
black thoughts. He replayed the events of that disastrous
August night at Ching-p'u over and over in his mind, and
decided that the five wounds he had picked up could not all
have been accidental.

Someone was most definitely trying to murder me, he
thought now, as he went up the steps of the Grand Hotel.
And I know exactly who it was.

The lobby of the Grand Hotel was busy. He looked
around. Finally, sure that the man he was looking for was
not there, he sent a boy to Sung-chiang with a message for
Vincente Macanaya to meet him. Then he ordered beer,
took out his little blue accounts book and sat down to wait.

There were many British and French uniforms in evidence
in the lobby. There had been plenty of them on the Bund
too – mainly men of the 44th Foot Regiment and some
French marines, all back from Peking. The letters that had
reached him in Nagasaki had spoken of British deserters
applying to join the Corps in greater numbers every day.
And they were needed too. Governor Wu had authorized
the recruitment of another thousand Chinese, plus the

establishment of two hundred Western officers. The letters also mentioned that units of the Taiping field army had moved into the protection zone that had been declared for thirty miles around Shanghai.

While Ward had been in Japan the Taipings had advanced towards the European Concessions with just three thousand veterans. Their column had tried to approach, but a heavy fire had been opened on them by the residents and ships' crews from behind a line of hastily erected barricades. For five days the Taipings had waited on the perimeter, then an outraged message from their chief had been sent, addressed to the Western consuls:

'I am the Chung Wang, military commander of the Heavenly Kingdom. I have come to Shanghai to make a trade treaty with my Christian brothers. I have not come to fight with you. Verily this would be like the members of a family fighting among themselves.'

But no answer had been sent back to them. After that the Taipings had withdrawn from Shanghai, and within a few days the vast horde had marched westward, back toward Nanking, ready to engage Imperialist armies in the interior. Even so, a great many Taiping troops had been left behind to consolidate territory that had been overrun, to garrison the cities and towns they had taken. Now almost all of Kiangsu province was under Taiping occupation.

Yang Fang had finished his letter by saying that Lord Elgin had detached a force from the northern campaign and sent it down to Shanghai. Looks like it's been here some time, Ward thought grimly. Meadows is probably panicking about another attack. And if he's panicking it's an even bet he'll start trying to make life difficult for me again – which won't be hard for him now with all this spare manpower around. Well, to hell with him! And to hell with Strickland too. Let them do their worst.

Ward looked around the lobby with a deadly eye, but the man he was looking for was not there. He went up to his suite, saw that his trunk had not arrived yet. He passed Annie Phillips's door on the way back, hesitated outside and listened to the silence for a moment, then decided to return to the lobby.

The sky outside had turned a sickly yellow and there were

lurid flashes every now and then. As he passed the desk, someone called to him by name. He went over and picked up a letter. It was tattered and dirty, but it was addressed to him. It turned out to be from Harry Lindley. He had no idea how it had reached him, but instead of rising his spirits fell as he read on. It was grisly: Lindley's last letter, written before his execution. It contained a smaller, sealed letter intended to be forwarded to his father, should such a thing ever be possible.

As he looked up from the letter something about the lobby made him uneasy. The big, moustachioed manager had gone, and a new, skinny-faced one had taken his place. Even at the best of times there was a feeling of false gaiety about the people who dined and drank in the Grand Hotel. Now they seemed falser than usual. What was it about them? Irritability? Expectation? Foreboding?

Men were gathered in twos and threes, talking in hushed voices, coming in out of the rain. Pointing out items in the *Herald* and the *Daily Shipping List* to one another. There was an impatient queue at the messenger desk. In the window seats people craned their necks to watch what was happening on the Bund. Everyone was watchful, their eyes searching those who arrived, briefly but in detail.

Hurry-up-and-wait, he thought, his mood darkening further. That's the state of mind in Shanghai now. They all feel trapped. Forrest was right when he wrote me that the city's in real fear of a Taiping attack. Meadows' damned newspaper's got them all in a bubbling funk. They think doom's coming this way. For God's sake, where's Vincente?

He called a waiter and had him bring a copy of the *Herald*. Habit made him look over the back page first – weather reports, and a column-inch discussing a faint comet that had been growing brighter in the southern sky. That'll mean trouble, he thought. The Chinese think comets herald disaster. When he turned the paper over he read that Frederick Bruce, Lord Elgin's younger brother, had arrived in town. He wondered what diplomatic feeding had brought in so important a shark. Then a leading article on the front page caught his eye.

We have said many times that the steps taken by the taotai, Wu Hsu, and other Imperial authorities in employing

311

Western filibusters was ill-advised. This policy has definitely misfired on them. Their experiment at Sung-chiang seems to have ended in large numbers of the most lawless European ruffians being recruited by the Taipings themselves. It seems that now the Chung Wang's men are to be taught a career of violence and depredation in the interior of the country, beyond our control . . .

He flung the paper to the floor. Lies and damned lies! he thought. This whole rag might as well have been written by Meadows himself!

He took out his little blue book and started jotting in it again, but suddenly looked up to see three large strangers converging on him. He got to his feet, but two of them seized him before he had even straightened up. He slipped neatly out of his silk-lined jacket, shoved one assailant away and swung for the other. But as he did so a gut-rupturing fist was driven hard into his belly, and as he doubled up another heavy blow jarred into his side.

He heard women's screams, a tea service smashing to the floor. People scattered. He almost went down, but as they lifted him up a sudden strength surged inside him and he flung off the man on his right. This time he twisted round and delivered an elbow to the other's head. The man keeled over like a felled tree, and Ward spun again, lifting his boot into the second assailant's groin. Instinctively Ward planted his feet and raised his arm to protect himself from the chair that came flying at his head from the third. He caught the chair effortlessly and placed it on the floor undamaged.

'C'mon, sailor, what are you waiting for?' he invited.

The last man hesitated, but then a foolhardy courage overcame him and he charged at Ward. Ward moved fluidly with the man's momentum and seized his arm, wheeling him into a tall, gilt-framed mirror. The impact was stunning and shards of glass rained off the wall.

A half-circle of waiters and other hotel employees stood uncertain as to how to react. Each waited for others to move. Ward shrugged at the remains of the mirror, brushed off his jacket, and put it over his arm. He swept back his hair, then said expansively, 'Sorry about the interruption, folks. Come on, boys, I'll pay for the mirror. Why don't you get these sad excuses out of here. And champagne for everyone in the house.'

But no one moved, and no one warned him as a blow crashed into the back of his neck. The next he knew he was struggling on the floor amid the broken glass, with a hand holding every part of him. They pulled him out of the lobby and threw him down the steps of the hotel and into the mud.

'And don't come back!'

His hat rolled down after him. Then his accounts book. He recovered it, carefully cleaned off the dirt, and prepared to shake out his jacket.

'I'm going to teach you the lesson of your life, you bastard!'

Ward raised his head to see Eden Phillips standing in the pouring rain. He was a big man, bearded and barrel-chested, and he was shaking with fury. He carried a bull whip in his right hand and a Bowie knife in the other.

'I was on my way to see you, Phillips. Looks like you've saved me the trouble.'

'Shut your filthy mouth, Ward!'

Ward sized his man up. 'Why don't you shut it for me? Let's see if you've got any guts man to man.'

The taunt enraged Phillips further. He sent the whip slashing through the air. It cracked in Ward's face, missing him by a fraction.

Ward recoiled, surprised at the other's adeptness. 'Son of a bitch!'

'I'm going to kill you, Ward! Do you hear me?'

Phillips's three thugs burst out through the hotel entrance, and flanked the steps.

'Don't touch him!' Phillips screamed. 'He's mine!'

'Is that a fact? You're a real man, Phillips! A real man!'

He tried to dodge as Phillips laid the whip on him again. This time it curled wickedly round and bit into his shoulder. That whip was lethal and Phillips knew exactly how to use it. As it landed Ward made a grab, but it snaked away again before his fingers could close. He turned his jacket tighter round his left arm, his eyes never moving from the man who had paid for him to be shot down at Ching-p'u.

'Try again, big man!'

Phillips shrieked, 'I'm going to cut you to pieces!'

313

Ward tried a lunge, but the whip drove him back. He lunged again. The next crack almost took his eye out. Again the whip was pulled out of reach too quickly for him to grab it. A shaft of fear lanced through Ward. He knew that if he didn't think of something soon the trader would make good his promise.

The next crack cut into Ward's back and side. Blood seeped through his wet shirt. He groaned, but the intensity of the pain stung him into a desperate attack, and as the whip came at him again he threw himself straight onto Phillips's knife hand. The bigger man was taken off balance, and crashed back against the railing, his wrist snapping in sudden agony.

Phillips's men made a move, but Ward already had the edge of the Bowie knife hard up against Phillips's bearded throat. Ward fixed them with a stare. They understood and backed away, not realizing he was going to slaughter Phillips like a pig whatever they did.

'Why did you do it?' Ward demanded, his voice ice cold. 'Why did you pay to have me shot down? I want to know. Was it Meadows? If it was I'll kill him too! You tell me, you son of a bitch, or I'll cut your windpipe out right now, God damn you!'

The rain coursed over them, splashed up the mud. Beyond all reason, Phillips began to struggle and thrash violently, but Ward held him helpless. The man's voice, strangled by rage and fear, gasped incoherently. 'Bastard! She may – be a whore – but she's still – my wife!'

Ward's hand tightened further on the knife. It was a foot long and razor sharp. 'I never touched your filthy wife! She's a whore! I never touch whores, do you hear me?'

'Maybe not you – but you gave her – gave her to your boys – like meat – like meat to a pack of dogs! You did that, you bastard!'

He sawed at Phillips's neck until the fight left the man. 'What are you talking about, you son of a bitch?'

'Your man Burgevine – brought a dozen men with him – they damn near killed her!'

Burgevine! he thought incredulously. What had he done? 'When?'

'You know when, you bastard! Three days ago!'

'If you're lying to me—' Ward's fury began to abate, but

314

then he thought of something that made no sense. 'If it was only three days ago why did you try to have me killed at Ching-p'u?'

'I surely wanted you to die at Ching-p'u, you bastard, but I didn't do anything to make it happen. I only wish I'd thought of the idea!'

'Where's Annie now?'

When Phillips made no answer Ward dug the knife into his throat so that it drew blood.

'I said, where is she?'

'Where she can be looked after. Aboard one of my ships. Where no more of your animals can get their filthy hands on her.'

'That's good.' The knife glittered in his hand. 'You should have taken care of that a long time ago.'

Phillips struggled again. 'You'd better kill me now, Ward, because if you don't I'll shift heaven and earth to make you pay for what you did to her.'

'Didn't you hear me? I never touched her. Never once. I'll swear that to you here and now. I never sanctioned any of my men to go near her. And if I find any who did, then I'll punish them. You better believe I will. Now get up.'

He pulled Phillips to his feet, pulling back on his hair, so that his head was thrown back. Phillips's men – seamen from one of the man's fleet of merchant clippers he supposed – continued to menace him, but they did not dare make any move.

'If you believe what I say, you'll call them off.'

Phillips said nothing. The Bowie knife was hard at his throat. His wet hair was bunched in Ward's fist. A trickle of blood was washing down from his throat, staining his shirt.

'Come on, Phillips! Tell them!'

Phillips gasped, struggled with himself, then said, 'Let him alone.'

'Do you really believe I had nothing to do with what happened to Annie?'

'Yes.'

'Do you swear to that?'

'Yes. I swear.'

'A trader's word is his bond. And that's good enough for me.' Ward stared unflinchingly at the seamen, then he released Phillips's hair and brought the knife slowly away.

With a sharp jerk of his arm he slammed it into the wood of a nearby railing post, turned and headed towards the crowd of onlookers. They parted before him as he strode away down the Bund in the direction of Soochow Creek.

Ice was still in his veins when Ward stepped off the boat at Sung-chiang. All the way down the Huang-pu and along the canal that led to his town the whip weals burned and seared in his flesh, but his cool mind kept its grip.

His mind teemed with unanswered questions. If it wasn't Eden Phillips then who? Strickland? Meadows? Governor Wu? Yang? Which of them wants me dead the most? But Henry said it was Phillips . . .

During his last days in Japan he had heard fresh news from home with every American vessel that put in. Republican Abraham Lincoln had won the election to become America's sixteenth President, South Carolina had seceded from the Union. Then Mississippi, along with Florida, Alabama, Georgia, Louisiana and Texas. Then the news came that the breakaway states had united to form what they called the Confederacy – but Lincoln had declared it illegal. The latest rumours said that both halves of the nation, North and South, were mobilizing for war.

The recollection reminded him of the crack Burgevine had made about being put in charge of the Corps, because if the South seceded he would no longer be under the US Consul's jurisdiction.

He sure got his wish, Ward thought as he reached the gates of Sung-chiang. The Chinese sentry who guarded it stared at him as if he had come back from the dead. He passed the checkpoint unquestioned, leaving whispers of astonishment in his trail. The street he had ordered well-kept was now untidy. He heard no drilling, saw no uniformed presence, no signs of discipline. To left and right along the main east-west street he saw European faces – Corpsmen all right, but men he did not recognize. They were sitting around, a pair playing backgammon, others openly drinking. They nudged one another as he passed. Their eyes followed him. One called. 'Hey, you!' after him. 'You got business here?'

He ignored the shout. The flagstaff on the command post was bare. His green and red personal standard had been taken down. He reached his yamen and went inside. Burgevine gawped at him.

'Colonel . . . when did you get back in town? Your face sure is looking a whole lot—'

Ward grabbed him with both fists and hauled him out of his seat.

'Whaaa—'

Burgevine's protest stopped as a hook from Ward's right fist sent him reeling across the room. He put his hand to his mouth, looked at the bloody tooth in it and said in amazement, 'What the hell was that for?'

'Get up!'

Burgevine was still stunned as Ward picked him up again and punched him to the floor again.

The third time he was lifted up he started to struggle. Ward punched him down again mercilessly and lay about him until his face was a mass of blood. When he stopped, Burgevine was screaming at him.

'What'd I do? What'd I do?'

'It's not what you did, Henry, it's what you didn't do.'

Burgevine tried to get to his feet, but Ward slammed him down again. As he rolled squalidly on the floor Ward picked up his Colt Navy. Six copper caps shone in the drum. He checked the chambers and weighed the revolver in his hand with businesslike deliberation. He felt just fine.

'What was it I didn't do?' Burgevine howled.

'Henry, you didn't learn the first rule.' Ward shoved the Colt into Burgevine's face. 'Outside!'

Burgevine flinched as Ward lifted him. 'What you gonna do with that?'

'This is a pistol, Henry. I'm going to assemble the Corps on parade and ask my officers a few questions about Mrs Annie Phillips. If I hear answers I don't like, I'm going to haul you out front and kill you with it.'

As he left the office, Forrest's voice trailed after him. 'Hey, Colonel! Colonel!' Ward stopped long enough for Forrest to come up, a paper in his hand. 'Colonel, am I glad to see you back. You've got to see what the taotai just sent over. Jesus Christ, what's happ—'

Ward took the paper from him, his knuckles cut and bloody. 'What is it?'

'. . . a proclamation. It's from the Chung Wang. Hundreds

of these have been posted in the Chinese city this morning
– uh, Colonel, are you all right?'

Ward read the poster.

How is it that you Shanghai people alone withstand all
reason, and still listen to demon mandarins who do you
nothing but injury?

Your offences compel me to set troops in motion for your
extermination. I advise you that an egg cannot oppose a
stone. Make up your minds speedily, therefore, and submit
yourselves. I shall establish my will as firm as a mountain,
and my commands shall be as flowing water. My soldiers
are coming. Don't try to tell them that I gave you no
warning!

'Who's in command of British forces in Shanghai?' Ward
asked, his mind calculating hard.

'Admiral Hope.' Forrest's eye flicked to the ugly, bleeding
wounds on Burgevine's face. 'Colonel, what are you going
to do?'

'I'm going to take care of a little domestic business here.
Then I'm going to pay a social call on Yang Fang. If the
Chung Wang's army is coming back, I ought to be asking
him for more guns and men.'

Fei watched over the Empress as she slept. Shafts of pale
moonlight projected a pattern from the eaves, spilling complex shadows across the floor. A big black bed dominated
the centre of the room, and in the corner niche a slender
vase displayed flowers before the sublime figure of the goddess, Kuan Yin. There was always a small lamp burning in
this room, and always a maid on duty. One maid would
kneel inside her chamber, keeping silent vigil – two attended
when the night was moonless.

Fei tried to keep herself alert through the longest hour of
the night. She had to continue her routine duties so the
pretence of her being a maid could be kept up. The others
had been told she had tried to commit suicide because of
homesickness, and that Yehonala had allowed her to run
back to Peking for one last night with her lover. And they
believed it because they had been ordered to believe it.

It's ironic, she thought, because that lie is so close to the actual truth.

On her return Yehonala had taken the message from her, verified Prince Kung's personal chop – his signature was inscribed 'No Hidden Heart' – and checked that the letter had not been tampered with. She opened the seals, her eyes flickering down the finely brushed columns of code until at last she looked up, her lips closed together in concern.

'Is it bad news?' Fei had asked.

'What concern is it of yours?'

She had not allowed that. 'Since I have troubled to bring it here to you, and not to leave you to your fate as I might have done, I believe I've earned your confidence.'

'Have you? And have you also earned Prince Kung's confidence?' Yehonala's words had been loaded with meaning.

'He agreed that the T'ien Wang's demands must be met as soon as normal government can be resumed.'

Fei watched the sleeping Empress now, and tried not to think of Lindley. True love and unswerving loyalty to the cause could not live in the same heart. Therefore it was no use thinking of a man she would probably never see again.

Outside, a night bird stirred. She heard guards carrying pole blades pass along the high perimeter wall of the Imperial park. Companies of men walked the circuit of twenty li constantly, always keeping sight of one another. They were jittery because of the comet that hung overhead, warning of disaster, even though tonight its evil veils were drowned in moonbeams. More men guarded the enclosure of the Empress' residence, though none was allowed inside. On warm summer nights such as this, Yehonala's household eunuchs slept like guard dogs on her verandahs, lying in her doorways and propped in the corridors and corners of her apartments.

Yehonala groaned softly and turned over. Fei looked at her and felt a grim sense of satisfaction. Much had changed since her visit to Peking. Everyone had waited out the winter like fish at the bottom of a frozen lake. The tensions in the Imperial hunting lodge had been immense. Despite Yehonala's predictions Hsien-feng's emaciated body had survived both the snows of winter and the mists of spring. He had lingered on incredibly, his mind drifting in drugged painlessness while his wheezing, sore-covered body rotted away to a yellow skeleton.

Fei shifted her position fractionally. Outside there was no wind. The room was silent and filled with the sickening, heavy scent of lilacs. Several times she had heard rats moving in the fabric of the building. The bed was laid with three thick mattresses. The coverlets were brilliantly embroidered. Yehonala's cheek showed pale above – she always slept on her side, curled like a baby in the womb. Then Fei looked again at that cheek and saw the shadow.

At first she thought it was a trick of the light, but then she saw a highlight glistening in the moonbeam and realized it was real. Gossamer, and a fleck of black floating in the air – as if by magic – above the Empress's head! She stared, inclining her head to see better. It was a black needle, but it wasn't floating, it was attached to a fine thread, a thread that was almost invisible, and no coarser than a human hair.

As she watched in amazement the needle dropped a hand's-breadth then stopped, as if it was a spider descending from above. Automatically she looked to the ceiling. There was nothing there to see.

Again the needle dropped a little. Now it was just a hand's breadth above Yehonala's ear.

Fei froze. Anxiety began to beat through her as, mesmerized, she watched the needle drop a third time. Then a tiny black spot appeared on the ceiling, became two, then three. More spots began to descend in a line, following one another slowly down the invisible thread.

Suddenly Fei understood what was happening and sprang up. She threw a pillow over Yehonala's head, then lunged for her hand to drag her out of the bed. As she did so a shower of black ink drops spattered the pillow. She screamed and grabbed the flower vase up out of its niche and flung it through the window, shattering the peace.

'Help! Help me!'

Within seconds the bedchamber was full of startled eunuchs, several of them armed with brooms and bronze doorstops and whatever else had come to hand. They surrounded Yehonala's gasping form and pulled Fei away from her roughly, holding her down.

'What is it?' Yehonala demanded, her eyes huge.

'Up there!' she shouted, pointing at the ceiling. 'Assassin!'

'Where?'' One of the eunuchs demanded. He was white-faced, astounded by her madness, fearing evil spirits had repossessed the maid who had once tried to kill herself. 'Where? There's no one there! You're dreaming.'

'In the space above! Quickly! Call the guards. Have the building surrounded.'

Two of the eunuchs fled. The rest stared up at the blank ceiling anxiously, half crouching. The maids stood, petrified, with their hands clamped over their mouths. They had all come too quickly out of sleep, and drew back as Yehonala got to her feet. 'What's the matter with you?' she demanded, furious now.

'Don't go near the bed,' Fei warned. Eunuchs still pinned her, gripped her hard. 'Don't ˙ touch the pillow. It's poisoned!'

'Poisoned?'

'Let me go. I'll show you.'

Yehonala gave a half-nod and the eunuchs released her. She came forward and searched. 'Look at those spots. That's venom. And there! See the thread? A strand of silk, weighted by a needle. And see the tiny pin hole in the ceiling?'

The Empress marvelled at the barely visible needle, swinging now like a pendulum. 'It was pushed through the hole and lowered to just above your ear, lady. Then black drops started to run down it.'

Yehonala's expression became thunderous. 'Fetch the captain of the guard! I want the assassin captured alive! He must be brought before me. Me – no one else.'

Fei was suddenly mindful of her status before them all. She knelt. 'He was trying to drip poison into your Imperial Highness's ear. I saw it. I swear!'

Yehonala examined the bed. 'Burn the pillow. Have the thread cut down and saved in a box. Be careful. Make sure no one touches it. I've heard stories of the poisons that hired assassins use. They're distilled from spider venom and rare medicine plants. Some are so powerful that a single drop in contact with human skin can kill.'

Horror blanched the faces of those who watched. One of the maids fainted. Outside, the courtyard was alive with the sound of running men. Lanterns were being lit and swung up to the eaves, orders were being shouted, eunuchs swarming. Guards arrived and thrust spears and pole blades up into the ceiling, cutting a hole through which one of them climbed up into the dark space above.

For a long time the scene was chaotic and Fei was not surprised when the captain of the guard returned and flung himself down in front of Yehonala to report that the would-be assassin could not be found.

The Empresses of the Eastern and Western Palaces walked together beside Silver Lake, their peach-coloured parasols raised against the fierce sun. When they came to the source of the warm spring they saw fish thrashing in expectation of being fed. Yehonala took dough balls from the gardeners, and the two Empresses wandered onto the wooden bridge a little removed from their retinues. There they stood idly for several moments, smiling and speaking in low voices.

'Isn't the park beautiful in August?' Niuhuru said, gazing up at the wooded hills with their well-sited pagodas.

Yehonala detected longing in her companion's voice and decided it was time to put the crucial proposition to her. 'The beauty is extraordinary, but is it not all so very . . . artificial?'

The remark unsettled Niuhuru. The park was landscaped according to well established rules, laid out according to immutable tradition. To criticize its artificiality was to question that tradition and the teaching of the sages responsible for it. Niuhuru laughed lightly, turning the handle of her parasol, but making no answer.

Yehonala inclined her head. 'Since we've been here almost the whole year round, we've had opportunity to sample all of the thirty-six scenic views recommended by the K'ang-hsi Emperor in each of the four seasons – yet still my heart yearns for Peking.'

She glanced at Niuhuru again, gauging her.

Niuhuru sighed. 'I sometimes think it would be nice to return to the old times. How terrible to think they are gone for ever.'

'Why do you say that?'

Niuhuru drew breath, showing surprise. 'Don't you know? Su-shun says that our capital has been completely overrun by red-faced Barbarians. Everything is polluted or destroyed. This is surely the cause of our husband's illness.'

Yehonala burned at the lie. She rebuked herself for not having approached Niuhuru sooner. 'I think you will find that Su-shun is . . . mistaken about Peking.'

'You mean there is hope that we can return some day?'

Yehonala threw another dough ball into the water and watched the fish compete to devour it. 'The Prince Kung has written to me, assuring me all is now quite well in the capital. The Barbarian army has gone away at last. The Common People have returned and the streets are full of wedding processions.'

Niuhuru's face filled with delight. 'Oh, but that's wonderful!'

'It's true that the Summer Palace was destroyed, but everything else remains just as it was.'

'This wonderful news could make our husband's spirit vigorous once more. Perhaps he will decide to return now.'

Yehonala hesitated. 'That would be marvellous. But . . .'

Niuhuru's face clouded again. 'But?'

'I don't think our husband's illness is quite as Su-shun describes it. The doctors believe he is not strong enough – may never again be strong enough to accomplish a difficult journey such as the one to Peking.'

'Oh, please, don't say that. Bad thoughts cause bad outcomes. Isn't that true?'

She saw that Niuhuru was closing her mind, trying to shut out the evil. She had allowed the meaning of Peking's many weddings to pass her by. People were marrying because weddings would be forbidden during the twenty-seven months of Imperial mourning that would follow the death of an Emperor. That was the invariable custom.

'Of course I don't like to imagine anything bad,' she said, throwing another dough ball into the water. 'But the time may be coming when we might have to start to consider certain difficult ideas. Such as what might happen after ten thousand years have passed.'

A wave of discomfort passed through Niuhuru as she heard the phrase that referred obliquely to the Emperor's death. She tightened her grip on her parasol handle, and said breathily, 'Tsai-ch'un is heir.'

'Everyone has naturally assumed that Tsai-ch'un will succeed, but I understand that our husband has made no written will. Nor has there been any official decree stating explicitly that Tsai-ch'un is to be his heir.'

'But . . . it's obvious to everyone.'

'What is obvious to everyone now may not seem so obvious to certain parties in the future.'

Yehonala threw another dough ball and the fish once more threshed in frenzy. Ripples were spreading across the lake, shaking the reflections of palaces and pagodas alike. Yehonala spoke cautiously, feeling for the way to proceed. 'I must remind you that while my child may be the Emperor's only son, under our law the succession may pass to any male of the Imperial bloodline who is able to perform the Rites.'

'Tsai-ch'un is a wonderful child,' Niuhuru said neutrally.

'Of course, as his mother, I agree. But he is only five years old. Which means that, even if he is accepted as heir, there must be a regency. A Board of Regents will be formed to advise my son in matters of policy.'

'Then all will be well.'

Yehonala held her course. 'But only if the regents chosen are wise. If Su-shun and his friends seek to control the Emperor while he is alive, will they not seek to be regents after his death?'

The crudeness of the question overwhelmed Niuhuru and she recoiled. 'I'm certain a wise decision will be made in the end. We must hope that everything will turn out for the best. Look at the fish. How happy they are.'

'It seems to me that we are like these fish,' she said, a bleak warning note in her voice now. 'We live only if we are nourished by the gods. We die if Heaven disapproves of us and stops nourishing us. That is why we must make a well ordered world, not simply wish one could happen. We must be regents ourselves, Niuhuru.'

Niuhuru was mortified by the idea. She said, 'What will be, will be. Fate cannot be influenced.'

'That's just an idea designed to enslave the minds of peasants. Its purpose is only to prevent rebellion. Fate is something to be spun like silk and woven as we wish.'

'How? No one can see into the future.'

'Astronomers can.'

All summer the omen of doom had lingered in the skies. Week after week the pagodas nestling in the valley of the

Lions had been overawed by the gigantic portent that out-shone the stars – a comet, more brilliant than any in living memory, shining like a huge sword near T'ien-niu, the constellation of the Heavenly Girl. The Imperial astrono-mers in Peking whose task it was to question the Heavens had been warned by Prince Kung to swear that this was a magnificent omen, one that surely heralded the Emperor's return. But here in Jehol Hsien-feng had refused to believe in a recovery, and his fearful mind had interpreted the comet only as a Heavenly Headsman's sword hacking at his neck.

'I, too, can see into the future,' Yehonala said. 'And you – you have access to our husband, access that is presently denied me. Don't you see that together – and only together – will we be able to weave a coronation robe for Tsai-ch'un? If you love the child as you claim then promise to speak to Hsien-feng about him.'

Niuhuru looked away. 'Surely it would be a crime to disturb the tranquillity of the Emperor's mind when he is suffering such an unpleasant illness. Perhaps he will be well again by the time his thirtieth birthday celebrations have begun.'

No, Yehonala thought, he won't be well, but he might be dead. She sighed. 'Niuhuru, a wicked man is in control of the Emperor's mind. Because of this I have not been invited to the birthday celebrations.'

Niuhuru turned back to her, speechless.

'Yes, of course it's a monstrous insult, but what can I do? I'm being treated like an autumn fan!'

Niuhuru understood the literary reference well. Two thou-sand years ago the Lady Pan Chieh Yu had been loved by a Son of Heaven, but then forgotten, put aside as the heat of the Emperor's passion had cooled.

Niuhuru lowered her eyes. 'Perhaps it was unwise for you to have criticized the Son of Heaven as you did.'

Yehonala softened her voice. 'Whatever the case, it is no longer possible for me to approach our husband to ask him to write a will in favour of Tsai-ch'un. Therefore you must do it.'

'I am just a woman. I cannot meddle in politics.'

'Niuhuru, please listen to me. Our husband must issue a decree that makes his son the official heir – a decree that leaves no room for doubt. More than that, he must name you and I as regents. If you do not persuade him to do this, Su-shun will take the Dragon Throne for himself. Undoubtedly, that would be the end of us. You would die, and I would die, and my darling boy would be murdered in his bed. Do you understand?'

The nakedness of Yehonala's words appalled Niuhuru so much that she tried to shut them from her mind.

'I think it's time to go now,' she said, hurrying away.

'Please think hard about what I've said,' Yehonala called after her. 'Perhaps we can walk again together another day.'

'Perhaps.'

Yes, think very hard, Yehonala told her counterpart silently as the Empress of the Eastern Palace tottered away across the arch of the wooden bridge towards her servant retinue. Let the vision of my words invade your gentle dreams and turn them into nightmares. Then maybe – maybe – we can both survive.

Fei walked the Iris Path, looking across the waters to where the Imperial birthday picnic was being held. The Iris Path was a narrow, raised walk modelled on the famous Su Causeway in Hangchow. It snaked across Silver Lake and connected the Isle of Moonlight and Murmuring Streams with the lake shore.

Banners stirred lazily in the breeze. Yellow silken barriers formed an enclosure that was filled with formal lines of hundreds of eunuchs and functionaries. Behind was a giant yurt – a squat, Mongolian-style tent of the kind Genghis Khan had once used. This one was decorated in Imperial yellow, and erected, Fei realized, in imitation of the practices of the great Ch'ing Emperors. She saw the Emperor, sitting motionless in his seat, an old, old man of thirty years. He was flanked by youthful pages holding ceremonial fans made from peacock tail-feathers. Imperial musicians in red robes played their ancient instruments. Near the Emperor she noted the lilac robe of Niuhuru and the easily recognized figure of Su-shun. She also saw the tiny form of the heir, standing obediently with his nursemaid some distance away, among the retinue of Su-shun's wife.

On the seventh day of the seventh moon Yehonala had despatched a secret courier to Prince Kung, informing him of the critical condition of his half-brother. She had urged him to send a second detachment of the Bordered Blue as soon as he could. Her pointed exclusion from the birthday celebrations had also demanded action.

This morning Yehonala had taken up station in the Tower of the Mist and Rain, and turned it into a theatre. She had put on a devastating white robe and had sat on the upper balcony of the Tower in clear view of the Imperial party. There she had watched over the initial festivities, in mystery and seclusion, like the disembodied spirit of a betrayed wife and mother. She had implied reproach by her presence and righteousness by her straight-backed meditation posture. White was the colour of mourning. She had not moved a muscle for four hours, but as the festivities climaxed, at the exact moment when the Emperor's palanquin arrived, she withdrew with vast dignity, utterly stealing his thunder.

Fei watched the Emperor now from the Isle of Green Lotus. She had been told to watch and to report, and to pay special attention to how much favour was shown to the heir. The time had come for Hsien-feng to officiate. Eunuchs of the person moved to each elbow. He rose, took several faltering steps, but then collapsed to the ground. Fei watched in alarm as watchful courtiers began to crowd around the Emperor's body. An attempt was made to lift him upright, but he seemed to be unconscious, and he was quickly carried inside the yurt. Then the Imperial palanquin was brought up close.

'He's dying,' Fei mouthed. Her mind raced over the possibilities. I must go to Yehonala's apartments to warn her. But by the time I get there she'll have heard. What about the heir?

Her eyes searched for the boy. He had been instantly surrounded by guards, and she spotted him now being hurried out of the Imperial enclosure. She began to run back along the Iris Path and Cloud Causeway as if chased by dogs.

They'll take Hsien-feng to his quarters, she thought, frantically trying to decide what to do. Doctors will be brought. If he's found to be dying, then all the Princes of the Blood will come and surround him. There'll be an obscene display of power greed as the scavengers climb over one another to get to his carcass. I must find An Te-hai.

When she arrived at the Imperial apartments the whole complex was overrun by panic-stricken eunuchs and courtiers. Access was not difficult to obtain for one who had learned palace ways. Mistakes were ferociously punished. Everyone wanted to avoid responsibility, including the guards. So rigid were their procedures that none of them dared show personal initiative.

She was stopped twice inside the walled complex, but then allowed to pass after pleading breathlessly, 'Urgent message for Master An!'

When she found An Te-hai he was grey faced. He was giving orders in a reception area next to the Emperor's bedchamber. He had already located the heir and the boy's retinue of nurses and was shepherding them together. Half a dozen guards stood by, not sure what to do. Maids stared at one another anxiously. As she joined them they recognized her immediately as one of Yehonala's following.

'Does the boy's mother know yet?' the chief nursemaid asked in a terrified whisper.

'Yes,' Fei lied. 'She's on her way here.'

'She won't get in. These are Red Banner guards.'

Fei saw the boy look up, scared. Then An Te-hai noticed her, and a surge of fear flowed through her too. The Chief Eunuch remonstrated with the guards, but his attempt lacked conviction. He's not going to do anything, her intuition screamed at her. He's going to wait here and do nothing!

'Where's the Emperor?' she whispered.

'Next door.' The nursemaid's face was anguished. 'I heard him calling for his son as they brought him past me. It was terrible! His voice was so small.'

Fei knew she could be cut to pieces for what she was about to do. She swept up the boy and darted past the Chief Eunuch and the distracted guards, carrying him straight in to Hsien-feng's presence. Four eunuchs leapt forward but hesitated when they saw the heir, not daring to lay hands on him.

Fei was aware of Su-shun and the princes that surrounded the Emperor's bedside. They turned to look, but she threw herself on the floor.

'Imperial Majesty, your son and heir, Tsai-ch'un!'

Hsien-feng had been barely conscious, but the arrival of

his son stirred him from his stupor. His face was bloodless against the coverlets of Imperial yellow, and he grinned like a death's-head when he saw the frightened child. At first the heir did not move. He had sensed the importance of the moment and was on the point of bursting into tears. When Hsien-feng reached out a skeletal hand terror lit the boy's face.

'My son, be happy,' the Emperor said, 'for today you will climb the steps of my throne.'

Lindley sat on the stone bench, enjoying the warmth of the summer sun as he waited for Prince Kung to appear. A host of climbing plants were blooming in the walled Imperial rock garden, perfuming the rain-washed air. Birds were hopping about on the grotesque rocks and chirruping in the branches of the cypress trees, while gardener-eunuchs quietly hoed the flower beds.

'You seem thoughtful, Dr Lindley.'

He looked up suddenly to see the slight figure in plain black silk. 'Oh ... excuse me, your Highness. Good afternoon.'

'Good afternoon. I hope I didn't interrupt your thoughts.'

'Not at all.'

'I hope you are quite well.'

'Very well, thank you.' He replied with meticulous formality, knowing better than to mistake a greeting formula for an actual enquiry into his state of health. 'And you?'

'Also very well.' After a pause the Prince sat down on the bench.

'How is your chest?'

'Dreadful. Some wheezing. Maybe a little worse today than yesterday. But these summer illnesses are never severe. The worst are always in the autumn. It's the dust. It comes out of the Gobi whenever there's a west wind and it blocks the passage of chi within the body. That desert is the source of all plagues, and all evils. Genghis Khan came out of it.'

The Prince fell silent. He watched a pair of eunuchs passing through the garden some distance away, chattering loudly. 'It's quite remarkable how nobody notices me when I go about in my plain jacket.'

Lindley smiled. 'Of course. You have forbidden the eunuchs to announce you, except in ceremonial situations.

Everyone knows you wish to be in disguise, and naturally they respect that.'

The Prince laughed. 'You are very wise. What was the English maxim you told me? "One must not judge a book by its cover."'

'Correct. It is a very common mistake with us.'

Prince Kung nodded in appreciation. 'And with us too.' He hawked and spat neatly over the back of the bench. 'How is Mr Bruce? In good health, I hope?'

'Very well, your Highness. And he is delighted to hear you have agreed to put China on a proper diplomatic footing with the world. He says, if he can be of any assistance in this . . .'

'Yes, yes.'

Lindley decided he could afford to guide the Prince a little further. 'Now there are steam ships and the telegraph and railways the world is shrinking. You know that Japan also has had a policy of seclusion. It has been Western policy to open Japan to trade, and to promote cultural relations.'

'That is a mistake,' the Prince said definitely. 'According to the Classics the Japanese are a wicked people. Ferocious islanders. It is a bad idea to force the Japanese out of their lair against their will. Sleeping dragons should not be disturbed.'

'Just as it is a mistake for China to come into the world?'

'On this point I remain . . . undecided.'

'But it is the modern world, your Highness, and China should be a part of it.'

'Yes, yes.' The Prince considered for a moment then said, 'Concerning a certain foreigner you will know. I wish for personal advice about his character.'

Lindley smiled at the mistake. 'The world is a larger place than you imagine, Highness. Not all foreigners know one another.'

The Prince absorbed the information thoughtfully, then said. 'Perhaps not. After all, this man is of the Flowery Flag Country. Even so, he is a famous warlord in his own country, I think. And since he came to China he has been involved in some wonderful adventures in our city of Shanghai.'

Lindley shifted uneasily. 'Is his name by any chance, Colonel Ward?'

'Ah!' The Prince clapped his hands together. 'Then, you do know him?'

Lindley smiled wryly. 'Yes, your Highness. I must admit that I do.'

'I knew it! Tell me. Is he an honourable man?'

Lindley thought back to the day he and Ward had fought to a standstill on the deck of the *Hyson*, and he nodded without hesitation. 'Colonel Ward is many things, your Highness. But, yes, I would say that he is a very honourable man.'

The Prince nodded slowly. After a moment he sighed and slapped his robed thighs lightly in satisfaction. Then he took off his hat and to Lindley's amazement snapped the huge pearl from it. 'Your advice to us is of great benefit, Dr Lindley. You shall have this, my pearl, as reward.'

Lindley took the priceless object, overwhelmed as much by his impulsiveness as by his generosity. 'You are too kind. But . . . I cannot possibly accept it.'

Prince Kung stared at him, nonplussed. 'You are a physician. Do you not know that pearls contain the light of the moon? They are rich stores of the yang principle, essential for health.'

Lindley took the pearl between finger and thumb. 'That's too much to swallow.'

'No, no. It must be pulverized. It is recorded in the Classics that he who swallows gold will live as long as gold, and he who swallows pearls will live as long as pearls. A physician should know this.'

'But would it not be a shame to waste such a beautiful pearl?' His heart was burning to ask the Prince a wholly different favour. At night, between going to bed and falling asleep, he had imagined himself riding the lonely track over the Yan Shan mountains, but he had known that that was an impossible fantasy – the Emperor had gone to Jehol expressly to avoid Barbarians. There was no point in even raising the subject.

'You know, it is unheard of for anyone to refuse a gift from a Prince of the Blood. And why did you say "waste"? Did your master not burn down the Imperial Summer Palace just to show how foreigners prize health above riches?'

Lindley felt disinclined to offer explanations. Instead he said, 'No offence was meant, your Highness. I believe the pearl is better left whole simply because I do not know enough about your system of medicine to use it effectively.'

He had learned something of how the Chinese regarded the body. Everything was based on the idea of yin and yang. Yin was female: dark, passive and of the Earth. Yang was male: light, active and of Heaven. The human body was supposed to be made from a mixture of 'the five elements' – earth, water, fire, wood and metal – each controlled by one of the five planets, and each linked to one of the five states of the air, and the five directions, and the five odours, and the five tastes, and the five tones and the five animals, and the five colours. They believed that each of the five greater organs and the five lesser organs required the correct balance of yin and yang to function properly. It was complete nonsense.

'I am not a physician,' Prince Kung told him, 'but in China all educated men know the main principles of medicine. In most cases, any lack or excess of yin or yang principle may be righted by certain herbs. The five great organs – heart, lungs, kidneys, liver and spleen – are reservoirs of yin and yang, and the five lesser organs – stomach, bladder, small intestine, large intestine and gallbladder – are responsible for voiding them from the body.'

'How very interesting, your Highness.' He tried hard to show polite curiosity.

'The liver, for example, is associated with wood and the planet Jupiter, also with green and the number eight.'

'That sounds like ideas once believed in Europe.' Lindley meant astrology and alchemy.

'According to the Classics the body also contains three hundred and sixty-five bones and three hundred and sixty-five joints.'

'One for each day of the year, I take it?'

'Yes, yes. Then there are the channels that carry blood and air and regulate the twelve pulses, also the twelve channels that carry chi.'

'Chi?'

'The life essence. And of course tears are secreted by the liver, and saliva from the heart and kidneys . . .'

Lindley remained polite. 'A most interesting view of anatomy.'

The Prince was disgusted. 'Anatomy? No, Dr Lindley. Not

in China. The mutilation of corpses is repugnant to religious thinking. It is prohibited by law.'

'Even for the purposes of scientific dissection?'

'The law cannot make exceptions.'

'Then how do you know what structures are to be found inside the human body?'

'We have the writings of Master Wang. Sixty years ago Wang Ch'in-jen happened to be visiting a plague region and chanced to see wild dogs scratching up some shallow graves and eating the bodies of children. Wisely he made descriptive notes . . .'

It will accomplish nothing to be rude to the Prince's face, Lindley thought, hardly listening. But how I wish these meetings could have been otherwise. Mr Ward was right: everything the Chinese believe is absurd mediaeval nonsense. They cling to faulty old ideas as if they're universal truths. Because they rejected the idea of progress they're just going round and round in circles, stuck fast in the Middle Ages, and ten thousand miles away from any real truths. And what's worse, they're unable to accept they may be wrong, even when the products of our 'system of thought' steam up their rivers and open fire on them.

Lindley thought again of Fei. Throughout the spring the memory of their miraculous meeting had warmed and chilled him. Warmed him because he loved her, chilled him because he saw that the terrifying force emanating from Nanking had enslaved her will. He remembered the strange look in her eyes when she had spoken of her mission. It was the same as the steely blankness that possessed her that final day aboard Ward's boat. He waited for the Prince to pause, then said, 'Highness, please grant me permission to leave your capital.'

'Leave?' There was genuine regret in the Prince's voice. 'Last time we met you expressed an earnest wish to stay longer.'

'That was before Mr Bruce came. I believe he has now asked permission for me to travel to Nanking.'

The name of the city worked like a bad odour on the Prince. 'Unfortunately that city is experiencing temporary administrative difficulties. It is not an appropriate place for foreigners.'

'Perhaps. But my father is there, and I must go to him.'

'Your father?' The Prince looked side-long, almost as if suspecting a trick. 'I was not informed of this.'

'No.' He lowered his head, disposing quickly of the explanation. 'My father came to China many years ago. He is a Christian missionary.'

The Prince was unable to conceal his surprise. 'Nanking is no place for foreigners,' he said again.

Lindley decided to take an immense gamble. 'Do you remember a messenger who came from Jehol in the winter? A woman?'

The Prince was instantly on his guard. 'Imperial messengers are always men.'

'She was not an Imperial messenger, even though she brought you information from the Empress in Jehol.'

The Prince's face darkened. 'What do you know about that?'

'Very little in fact. And I care even less. I'm merely interested in the woman who carried the message. You see, she's a close friend. I need to know if she's safe.'

'A friend? A friend?' The Prince was growing more agitated. The gardener-eunuchs began to melt away from their flower beds. 'What is this friendship?'

Lindley saw the situation slipping away from him. 'The woman's name is Shih Fei-ch'ien. We are lovers.'

The Prince's eyes registered shock, then fear flared, driving out all geniality. 'Lovers? Do you know that this woman is a Taiping? A rebel?'

'Yes. But she's only a messenger, quite unimportant. I wish to marry her. One day. When the war is over.'

'She is not unimportant. She is their chief negotiator.'

Guards appeared at the gate of the Imperial gardens. They hovered uncertainly. Lindley felt despair at what was happening. 'With respect, Highness, that's not so. Changing circumstances have made her—'

'Do not contradict! This woman's father is a well-known criminal. Now he is the Taiping prime minister, but before that he was a minister here. He is treacherous. He joined the rebels after he was banished. Twenty years ago he committed many evil crimes.'

Now Lindley was horrified. 'Crimes?'

'The charges against this traitor have been very many.'

The Prince watched him for a reaction, then said, 'He was caught visiting ordinary restaurants.'

Lindley's mind could not comprehend what he had heard. 'Did you say restaurants?'

'Nobody can understand how a man of good family, with high social connections, and the full trust of the Son of Heaven could do what this man has done. It is incredible. Who can believe that any man could do things like this if his mind was right and his heart was in the middle?'

Lindley glanced again to the doorway. The knot of guards had grown, and they were clearly anxious now at the raised voice of the Prince. 'But . . . what's wrong with eating in restaurants?' Lindley asked. 'I'm sorry, I don't understand what you're saying.'

'Such a thing is utterly forbidden! No official of high rank may visit a restaurant! Restaurants are for the Common People only!'

'Please excuse my ignorance of your customs.'

'This is the man who is father to the woman who calls herself Shih Fei-ch'ien. He is a very wicked man!'

A runner entered the garden, and Prince Kung turned on the man, enraged by the intrusion. 'I ordered no disturbances!'

The runner grovelled, knocking his head to the ground with furious diligence. When he raised his face it was a grotesque mask of pain. His eyes were red and full of tears. Lindley was shocked.

'Grand Councillors report a great calamity!' the messenger blurted.

'What calamity? Speak!'

The runner burst into tears then collapsed to the ground, sobbing uncontrollably.

'Shut up! Shut up, or you will be beaten!'

As the Prince walked out of earshot, Lindley looked out over the yellow-tiled roofs and his eyes drank in the mild, faultless blue of the vault of heaven. Why are you doing this to me? he asked Infinity. I never wanted to get involved with pulling this vast mediaeval monstrosity out of the Dark Ages. It's nothing to do with me. I'm just an ordinary man who came here to find his father. Will the Court ever return to a capital contaminated by Barbarians? And if it does will Fei return with it?

He felt inside his jacket and took out a tattered letter. It was the one Ward had sent. It stated that Fei had been beheaded as a rebel spy. If he was wrong about that, he thought, closing his eyes, maybe he's wrong about my father too. If Fei comes back from the north alive, then maybe we can both go to Nanking. With Prince Kung's permission who could stop us? I'll ask Bruce to make British cooperation in the coming trade negotiations dependent on it. Surely Bruce will stand by his brother's promises. Surely the Prince will do as Bruce asks. I'll . . .

He opened his eyes, and the dream vanished in a blaze of unanswered questions.

The Prince was returning. His usual nervous tension had almost gotten out of control. 'Please accept my apologies,' he said shakily. 'But I must now attend to affairs of state.'

'Your Highness . . . you are unwell,' Lindley said, standing. 'Please, sit down for a moment.'

'Thank you for your concern, but you must excuse me.'

The Prince's quick hands moved distractedly, and his face twitched, then he said, 'I have just been told that ten thousand years have passed. My brother, the Son of Heaven, has gone to join our ancestors.'

The alarm came in the dead of the night, waking Ward instantly. He shouted for his servants, then damned them when they tried to light the lamps. Outside he heard men running, and shouts. It had to be an attack.

His first thought was that he had been betrayed. He had planned a raid to clear the rebels out of the strategic town of Kao-ch'iao, near the mouth of the Huang-pu river, and the plan was close to completion, but then he realized that the men in the street below were his own green-uniformed elite. He had put his Filipino bodyguard on special alert since returning. Now they shadowed him everywhere and closed protectively around his yamen at the first sign of danger.

When Vincente Macanaya reached him he was already dressed and armed. 'What the hell's happening?' he demanded.

'British uniforms, Coronel!'

'Where?'

'East Gate.'

He felt a shaft of anger. 'It's got to be Meadows' doing. Close the gate! Don't let the bastards in.'

'They're already in. They've brought a mandarin – and official papers.'

'Goddamn! Get up to the safe house and warn the boys. They know the drill.'

'But what about—'

'Just do as I told you! The safe house. Move!'

The safe house was where his British and American officers were quartered, a place separate from the other nationalities, a place from which they could make a quick getaway. The upper storey concealed a comfortable barracks for fifty men, proof in part against casual prying, but not wholly secret.

Ward cursed. He had suspected for a long time there would be a raid. All kinds of escape drills and signals had been worked out. As Vincente left the yamen he went out and shouted after him. 'Where's Henry?'

'He's trying to stall the British.'

'What about Ed?' he said, meaning Forrest. 'Did he get away yet?'

'I don't know . . .'

Ward wiped his mouth and glanced toward the North Gate then up at the moon. The curfew-stricken streets were empty of townspeople. The moon was full. From its position he estimated the time at around three a.m., maybe three-thirty. A fifth of the silver Yang Fang had paid over for the taking of Sung-chiang was lodged in his strong room, as was all the thousands of taels gifted to the Corps by Taki bank when the Taipings had marched on Shanghai. It was all operational money – for paying wages and buying supplies and munitions. He resisted the temptation to stay near it, and set off instead for the safe house.

He knew he had judged Burgevine right the day he had given him a beating. That night, with Burgevine's face like a carved beetroot and his eyes narrowed down to slits, Ward had sold him back his life. The price of it had been the names of the men who had made Annie Phillips bleed. The next day, not wanting to trust his prisoners to British justice, he had personally taken them on a short riverboat trip and turned them over to plead their case to one of Eden Phillips's ship crews. Not one of them had come back to Sung-chiang.

I was right about Annie, too, he thought. What happened hasn't changed her. Within six weeks she was back at the Grand Hotel, degrading herself again. Deep in his mind he knew it was Annie Phillips's determination to do as she pleased that both attracted and repelled him. She would do what she wanted, no matter what, and he admired that – but he despised what her wilfulness made her into.

The safe house was at the northern end of Sung-chiang's main north-south meridian, a wide boulevard that split the city into two equal halves. Ward saw a body of uniformed men following an officer along the street. The officer was Strickland, and he seemed to know where he was going. Ward ducked into a doorway, then crept along the crumbling brick wall before turning into a long, narrow alley. Dogs penned up in the walled courtyards of houses barked as he ran by. A hundred yards further north and the alley opened out onto a broad street, but before he could reach it they saw him.

No shots were fired, but he heard shouts and the clatter of boots. He easily reached the safe house before Strickland and went up the stairs, through the barracks, relieved to find that all his British officers had got away safely. He stared around, panting, then heard noises outside and went up into the eaves, pulling the ladder up after him.

He closed the trapdoor, locked it and manoeuvred a heavy barrel over it. Then he swore at having got himself cornered, but he had needed to know if Forrest and the others had escaped. He lay quietly, listening to his heart in the absolute darkness. He put his eye to a gap in the eaves and saw Burgevine almost directly below, standing four-square in the doorway.

Strickland faced him, a detachment of fifty Royal Marines at his back. They looked as if they meant business. Three unhappy local mandarins were in tow.

'Stand aside. I have orders to find British deserters.'

'Sure, you do,' Burgevine said evenly. 'Whether they're here or not.'

Strickland's exasperation was plain. 'They're here, and I'm going to find them. And when I do I'm going to arrest them. I'll arrest the American crimps who enticed them here too, just like this consular warrant says I will. You included, Mr Burgevine.'

'Is that an accusation?'

'Don't be clever with me. This authority is countersigned by the United States Consul.'

Strickland tried to force a way past, but Burgevine stood his ground. 'No you don't. This here is private property.'

'I said stand aside.'

'And I told you there ain't no British in Sung-chiang. The only foreigners you'll find in this town are subjects of the Spanish crown, and me – a citizen of the state of North Carolina, CSA. And I don't think we have ourselves a consul in town yet.'

Ward felt a burn of joy at Burgevine's well-rehearsed performance. Strickland was almost dancing with fury as he pushed past and entered the building. Ward heard the boots of the marines clattering on the floor planks as they searched the ground floor, then the sound of them climbing up the stairs to the barracks floor. Ward remained absolutely still as the smell of burning lamp oil filtered up to him. Then he heard a kicked beer bottle roll, the rattle of unwashed crockery, silence, then one of the marines shouted down to summon Strickland.

'Knives and forks, sir.' An English accent.

'Well done, corporal.' Another silence then, 'Well, Mr Burgevine?'

'Well, what?' He heard the half-mocking tone in Burgevine's voice. 'No law against Chinamen learning how to eat proper, is there?'

'There must have been fifty Europeans here. Where's Ward?'

'I don't know what you're talking about.'

'Sergeant, take this place apart.'

'Sir.'

For several minutes Ward heard the sound of furniture being moved, crates of stores rifled and examined. Then Strickland's voice said. 'What's up there?'

Ward gritted his teeth. There was no way out from under the heavy, grey tile roof. More furniture was being scraped across the floor and piled up down below, then a rifle butt was slammed repeatedly into the trap door until the nails holding the closing bolts pulled free. A shaft of lamplight cut into the gloom. Two marines heaved the barrel aside, and as it rolled away they climbed up warily into the roof space. A third followed with the lamp.

Strickland's head appeared. 'Well, well, well,' he said with savage glee.

Ward smiled back at him. 'Captain, I wish I could tell you I was pleased to see you again, but that would be a lie.'

'Never mind about that, Mr Ward. I'm more than pleased enough for the both of us.'

The smell of incense filled the Valley of the Lions, blotting out the scent of the last remaining flowers of summer. Gone were the reds and golds of joy. White, the colour of mourning, was everywhere. On the death of the Hsien-feng Emperor all flags had been furled, all decorations taken down or covered. All the usual pastimes had been cancelled. There could be no music, no picnics, no laughing. Boating on Silver Lake was no longer allowed. Anything pleasurable was prohibited as disrespectful, even conversation was hushed for fear of disturbing the late Emperor's most profound sleep.

Fei watched from a distance as ally and enemy alike filed past the coffin and bowed politely to the Emperor's widows. The writing of the closing Annals of the Reign and the reading of Hsien-feng's valedictory Decree had been staged with faultless attention to detail. But all the while, Fei knew, Yehonala was in the greatest danger.

Court dress had changed overnight. All the gorgeous summer robes and headgear had gone. Now heads were unshaved and everyone except monks and priests had put on plain white. Chanting bonzes – the maroon-robed priests of Jehol's surrounding monasteries – mouthed a continuous dirge. There were endless demonstrations of formal grief but, in death as in life, a lethal struggle continued to rage around the person of the Son of Heaven.

'So they've done it,' the Empress whispered to the Chief Eunuch as they left the gathering.

An said, 'Yes. Su-shun's brother, Prince Yi, is now calling himself President of the Board of Regents. He has issued this valedictory Decree.'

'Let me see it.'

Yehonala's outrage mounted as she read. 'The Decree praises Hsien-feng's reign and goes on to announce Tsai-ch'un as Emperor, but it violates correct form with every line. By appointing himself head of the Board of Regents, Prince Yi has raised himself to a position only ever occupied before by elder brothers or uncles of a boy-emperor. He's taken the title "Chien Kuo", to concentrate all power in his own hands. Most importantly, there's no reference to either Niuhuru or myself.'

'No, Lady.'

'They're trying to freeze us both to death,' she said hollowly.

An's lips pursed. 'The next step is the Decree announcing your death.'

A wave of fear passed through Yehonala. 'You don't need to remind me of that!'

'On the contrary. I do.'

An Te-hai offered his mistress a second paper, and she took it in nerveless fingers, her face barely controlled now. Yehonala forced herself to read the paper aloud: 'and by the order of the Board of Regents the Yi Concubine is hereby sentenced to death'.

An took the paper from her. 'It is only a copy, Lady. It has not yet been issued. My spies say that Su-shun will claim that His Imperial Majesty gave the order as his last act.'

'Who will believe that?' Yehonala hissed. 'My husband wouldn't have done that! He wouldn't!'

'Everyone will believe it, Lady,' An said. 'Everyone. That's why I listened to your new maid when she told me there is one certain way to change everything.'

Fei thought of the Emperor's remains, lying in the extravagant pavilion of lacquer and gold and silk. Was his soul at peace now? Could such a soul ever gain entry to Heaven through the Pearl Gates? Or would it burn in the fires of hell? Certainly, the Hsien-feng Emperor's life had been a hell on earth. Suddenly, after being certain for so long, she could not decide what was the likely destination for the Son of Heaven's immortal soul.

The Empress arrived at her private apartments in a foul temper. She swept past her maids and snapped at their bowing figures, 'I do not wish to be disturbed tonight.' A moment later the maid who usually sat with her shot out of the hall and the door slammed shut behind her.

Fei waited in the greyness of dusk until An called her to

follow. He made his way through deserted halls and court-yards to a building she could not name. The gate was recessed and barred, guarded by two Imperial bronze lions. A side building nearby had been left unlocked. They hid, watching.

Fei's heartbeats filled her ears. 'Why are we waiting?'

An's voice was reedy in the way that only a eunuch's was. 'For the changing of the guard just before dawn. After that it will be easy. The garrison commander here is Yehonala's ally. He has been heavily bribed. The guards themselves will have to die lingeringly, of course, but they know their families have already been sent into the South and will be provided for up to the third generation by the gift they took with them.'

It was a surprising admission, and so shocking to hear this all-powerful master of the household speaking to her openly of his methods.

'Haa,' he whispered gloatingly, seeing her surprise. 'I know who you are, Shih Fei-ch'ien. I know why you suggested this excellent theft. I know everything about you.'

'And I know about you,' she said archly, but feeling panic knotting her insides. 'I don't know why you have decided to do this for the Empress. You, who thinks only of his own neck? Can't you see the way the wind is blowing?'

He cackled softly, then said, 'Remember the silkworms? They live only to spin the silken thread. They do nothing else but eat mulberry leaves. There is nothing for them in this life except mulberry leaves. That is why I am fond of those worms. They are like me, and I am like them. There is nothing in this life for me except the Forbidden City. I may live only if there is an Emperor. And that Emperor must be Tsai-ch'un.'

Fei thought she heard the regret of lost possibilities in his words. His voice was like cracked leather. In the indistinct light she saw shrivelled flesh, skin drawn tight across his skull so she saw all the bones of his face. She was sorry for the life his father had chosen for him.

'Yehonala does not believe in my loyalty,' he said, 'but I have always been loyal to her. Always. She has come a long way because of me. She was nothing. Nothing.'

'They say that even the highest pagodas arise from the ground.'

342

'True,' An said. He smirked in an ugly way, monstrous for a moment. Then she saw his face grow human again. 'Who but me would have thought the lost little girl who was the Yi concubine would climb to such a stomach-churning height? We have climbed together, she and I. Climbed, not through ambition, but through fear. We had to climb to survive. To fall from power in Peking means to step down from a throne and into a grave.'

'How did she do it?'

An grunted. 'By craft.'

'Craft?'

An's head seemed to her perfectly balanced on his scrawny neck. 'Yehonala gave herself to Jung-lu.'

Fei breathed out in genuine awe. No words formed themselves in her breath.

'She said she wanted to please him and make him forget for a while that he was a soldier.' An paused, triumphant, his expression suddenly far away. 'For a long time they played a vigorous game of "love crazed butterfly and wild bee", until at last he lay back. "I could not have enjoyed you more, even if I was the Emperor," he said to her. I'll always remember that. '

'You really watched them? Listened to them?'

'Yes. I've never told anyone before.' He turned to her, his eyes still sparkling like those of a true connoisseur of intrigue. 'It was exactly nine months after that that the heir was born.'

For a moment she could not grasp his meaning, then with a sudden intake of breath she realized the immense significance of his words. The shock thrilled through her and An enjoyed her confusion, seeing her start and the way she raised her hand to her mouth.

'It's true,' he said. 'Oh, yes.' Then his sigh quavered. 'Quite, quite, quite true.'

She looked away as her mind raced over the implications. So! The new Emperor, only son, a cuckoo chick after all. What about Yehonala? Was that her intention all along? Yes, of course. It must have been. She's a woman whose head rules what she does, not her heart nor her honeypot. It would not have been a sudden passion. No wonder Prince Kung gave me an escort of Bordered Blue guards to return here. One of them must have been Jung-lu. Did Yehonala order that he be sent? Does she still love him?

Her mind froze. Why did An tell me about it?

She stole an infinitely careful glance at the eunuch. He was sitting with his back against the wall, his knees drawn up and his head hanging down. People give up their secrets on their deathbeds, she thought. Maybe An believes he's going to die at Jehol. I saw him cowering and shivering the night the thunder crashed. He's famous for believing in many superstitions.

But then another thought came to her, like the sound of a stone dropped into a deep well: maybe it's my death he believes in. He could have me killed any time he wants . . .

It was a terrible thought – not because she was scared of death, but because she still had a job to finish. She heard noises and tensed. A double column of men were approaching – twenty of them, in war gear and carrying pole blades, coming down to visit the gate. They halted, then two men stepped out from niches inside the portal to be replaced by two fresh men from the column.

As soon as the soldiers left, An led her out of the side building, past the bronze lions and up the steps. He unlocked the door and they slipped through. As arranged, neither guard did anything to stop them, but instead stared as sightless as statues, remaining at attention on their platforms. A shiver ran down Fei's back. The inner court was deserted. The sky seemed much lighter now. The day was dawning quickly. Fei felt exposed as they crossed the marble cobbles, and climbed another tier of white marble steps. Once inside An produced a big iron key and opened the door. Inside the aromatic smell of nanmu wood made the air resinous. All around, like magic amulets, were laid in their places the vital instruments of the state.

The Imperial seals were carved from priceless jade. They were big as melons. Each stood on its own lacquer platform, and was covered with cloth-of-gold. An Te-hai went from one to the next throwing off the covers in search of the Seal of Legally Sanctioned Authority.

'This is the one,' he said at last.

She approached, ran her hands over the handle. Its smooth surface was cold. She tried to lift it. It was massive and heavy and inert, just as she had always imagined it to be. This was the magic imprint that turned Manchu whims into Imperial decrees, the stone that stamped in blood the decrees that regulated all China . . .

She thought again of the moment when Hsien-feng had pronounced his son heir. As soon as could be arranged Su-shun's wife had said it was harmful for the boy to remain by his father's bedside. She had hurried him from the Imperial death chamber and the doors had been barred.

The future of the Empire depends on Su-shun's claims over what occurred in that locked room, Fei thought. Prince Kung has commanded the scholars at the Imperial Archives to search out precedents for the regency, and told the experts in dynastic law to bring the weight of their opinions to bear. Yehonala has tried to rehearse the arguments and drum them into Niuhuru, but all will be in vain if we fail tonight.

The Empress of the Western Palace was bathing when An Te-hai arrived.

'Imperial Highness, listen to this!' he called out. He opened out the newly-issued document and related it breathlessly. He had brought the paper immediately it had been posted and now began to quote from it. ' "It is the first order of this Board of Regents that the reign title shall be Ch'i-hsiang – Good Omen Happiness . . ." But hear this! ". . . also both the Empresses of the Eastern and Western Palaces shall be raised to the rank of Empress Dowager, the former bearing the honorific title "Tz'u-An" – Motherly and Tranquil – and the latter "Tz'u-hsi" – Motherly and Auspicious . . ." '

'You know the rule, An Te-hai,' Yehonala told him, her voice stern. 'I am never to be troubled while I am bathing. Never.'

An's excitement drained away with the rebuke. 'Ten thousand apologies, Imperial Highness.'

He withdrew, and began pacing the verandah outside, his excitement building again unbearably until finally she deigned to receive him.

He watched her read the Board's decision, a look of stony indifference on her face. She considered carefully, and then said, 'The Lady Niuhuru and I will both be pleased to use the title Empress Dowager, since this is in accordance with

345

time-honoured precedent. However, we make plain that we reject the choice of reign title for our son, since we do not recognize the authority of this so-called Board of Regents.'

'But, Lady . . . will not such disobedience enrage them?'

'Yes,' she said, the hint of a smile on her lips as she prepared to leave her apartments. 'I hope it does. Never forget that the threat from any enemy is at its greatest when concessions are being offered.'

Autumn sunshine slanted through the trees, dappling the courtyard of the Hall of Frugality and Sincerity as she approached the steps. Within, the Board of Regents had convened for the first time. Everyone of importance in Jehol was gathered there – except the two Empresses. Yehonala knew she must now fight for her life.

Both sides of the hall were occupied by seated Court officials dressed in mourning white. Three fifths of them, she knew, were hostile to her, the remainder were silent. The seven usurpers were seated on a raised dais, Su-shun at the centre, flanked by his brother and other Princes of the Blood. All wore self-satisfied expressions like Buddhas. She noted their dismay as she appeared, and knew in that moment how madly her enemies itched to annihilate her.

She had waited until the meeting was almost at an end. This would be a sudden and unexpected entrance. She had already calculated that the hall would not be guarded against her. She had told An Te-hai as much yesterday, when he had delivered the invitation to attend. 'These so-called Regents would like nothing better than for me to appear before them, because in so doing I would recognize their authority and thereby give face to their position. Reply that I am presently indisposed. And the Lady Niuhuru had better be indisposed too.'

She bowed low, holding her breath to a count of three, knowing that the least departure from strict formal politeness could be turned into an excuse for impeachment. She knew that her only protection lay in her perfect knowledge of Court procedure.

'Please excuse me for insisting on my prerogatives,' she said with apparent humility. 'But an important complaint has just been received from the capital and this seems a convenient moment to present it.'

346

As she hoped the news that she had been in touch with Peking since the Emperor's death shook them. Su-shun, vastly wary, was bound to ask, 'By what right do you claim to be heard here?'

Yehonala absorbed the attention of a hundred pairs of eyes, performing brilliantly. Her voice was wounded and small. 'As Empress Dowager – and officially recognized by all here as such – in that capacity I am obliged to act as channel for a serious grievance. It is my duty to pass this matter on at the first opportunity.'

'What is the nature of this complaint?' Su-shun asked.

'On the eleventh day of the eighth moon, you issued a Memorial—'

'Please excuse me, Lady!' Su-shun rapped out the words. 'That to which you refer was an Imperial Decree. It was issued by the Board of Regents, of which I am President.'

'Ah! You will please pardon me for pointing out what must surely be quite obvious, but is it not true that Imperial Decrees invariably bear the Seal of Legally Sanctioned Authority?' She gave a tiny shrug. 'The paper you issued, Su-shun, did not bear that seal. Surely, therefore, it was a Memorial only.'

'That seal cannot be located at present. Special arrangements have been put in place.'

Yehonala raised her eyebrows, still keeping her form of words correct and her delivery humble. 'Ah – special arrangements. Sadly, one has not heard of "special arrangements" before. We mortal people are as flowers. We are born and then we die and are born again. Only the Rites endure for ever. Our entire civilization is governed by this principle. All truth and all wisdom spring from it. It is certainly true that the Rites cannot be altered without error.'

There was a mumble of assent. Some of it, she knew, genuinely heartfelt.

'Truth is that which is accepted as truth,' Su-shun replied, anxious to keep the initiative. 'Wisdom is the adapting of the world to appearances, whereas error is when we take the world only for what it is.'

Yehonala raised her voice, her tone still venom-sweet. 'In the capital respected authorities are asking what confidence may be had in the ability of seven black crows to preserve

347

the realm in difficult times when they cannot guard one of their own eggs?'

The word-bomb exploded. All outward show was stifled, but Yehonala saw that her insult had struck deep. The 'eggs' were the official seals of state that An Te-hai had removed from their resting places.

Su-shun's anger rose, but he mastered it. 'The Empress should know how easy it is sometimes for an egg to be taken from a nest.'

'Perhaps the Prince has not heard what is today loudly whispered in the capital?'

A ripple of unease passed through the awe-struck assembly. Yehonala knew she had reached the limit of her licence with the threat. Her appearance here, cool, fearless and self-possessed, in the hottest part of the crucible that wanted to melt her down, was winning her respect even among enemies. She raised her voice a little more. 'The Censor Tang Yuan-chun has ruled that the Lady Niuhuru and I be appointed Co-Regents immediately. He, and all of Peking, are curious to know the grounds on which you base your claim.'

Su-shun's face was a deadly mask. 'Incontrovertible grounds: the last wishes of His Imperial Majesty, the Hsien-feng Emperor.'

'In that case, Su-shun, perhaps you would permit me to inform the Censors that you take as your warrant of authority an unwitnessed – but not so far as I know undisputed – death-bed utterance of the late Emperor, my husband?'

'Do you deny His Imperial Majesty's last wishes?'

'Unfortunately, as Su-shun knows, I was physically prevented from approaching my husband's bedside at the time he is alleged to have made his final remarks. Therefore I have no means of confirming or denying them.'

'You were excluded by His Imperial Majesty's own order.'

Yehonala met her enemy's eye, still adhering to correct form as she allowed an injured silence to unfold. Then she said, 'It is certainly true that I was excluded from His Imperial Majesty's presence, though by whose order no independent person can say. It is also true that my infant son has been removed from his mother's love at the order of unknown persons. This unnatural and intolerable state cannot now be allowed to continue.'

Su-shun made a quiet aside to his elder brother, the Prince Yi, who said, 'At today's proceedings it has been agreed that, whereas the Yi Concubine was denied contact with the Heir Apparent during the latter days of the Hsien-feng reign, it is deemed consistent that she should also be denied contact with the new Emperor at the present time.'

'I beg the Prince's pardon, of course, but I must repeat: documents issued by this Board do not bear the Seal of Legally Sanctioned Authority. Therefore the proclamation announcing this meeting is void. These proceedings are irregular.' Yehonala's voice took on a querulous note. 'Su-shun and his colleagues have adopted an insolent tone towards the Empress of the Eastern Palace and I. They have forgotten the reverence due to our rank.'

'We, Lady, are the Board of Regents,' Su-shun said.

'According to you, Su-shun, my husband established a Board of Regents to guide the Empire until my son is old enough to perform the Rites. Strange that you, your elder brother and your closest allies have all been included – though none of pure Aisin Gioro blood. Strange that all were with the Emperor at the time of his death – to the deliberate exclusion of all others. Strange also that no mention was made of Prince Kung, whom my husband thought fit to act in his stead in the capital during the emergency, and who has managed affairs with extraordinary adeptness since.'

Su-shun's gaze was malevolent. 'Fortunately, the Hsien-feng Emperor's wishes were written down for all to see.'

'If this unsealed document is to be believed, all the Emperor's dear brothers have been forgotten. As has the Empress of the Eastern Palace who bore him his first child. And myself, the Imperial mother.'

'Are you saying that you dispute the document?' Su-shun demanded.

'No. Only its authenticity. Why should anyone believe it? Since it is not in my husband's hand.'

'It was not written in the Emperor's own hand because the Son of Heaven was incapacitated at the time. The Decree was dictated. It bears the Imperial chop.'

'Please correct me if I have misunderstood anything, but according to our law an Imperial decree is only an Imperial Decree when the Seal of Legally Sanctioned Authority has been applied to it. Until then it remains an ordinary piece of paper. Therefore the seven so-called regents are not regents, and before any legislation can be enacted we must discuss who should be appointed to that position.'

'The question has already been settled!'

'Not to my satisfaction. Nor to Prince Kung's. He is a natural choice to sit on the Board of Regents, by virtue of the reasons already given. These apply equally to Niuhuru, whose rank of Empress Consort gives her automatic right.'

Su-shun snapped his trap shut. 'Lady, there are two precedents for convening a Board of Regents, those of the Shun-chih and K'ang-hsi reigns. You will find that we have applied them scrupulously.'

Yehonala knew that this was the one flaw in her argument. Empresses had been denied a share in Imperial power in both previous regencies. She said, 'In his most recent private letter to me, Prince Kung says, that according to the Censor, Tang Yuan-chun, the creation of a Board of Regents is, I quote, "an inauspicious act".' The knife drove home. A stir of discomfort passed round the chamber. It was a crucial moment to announce the backing of the magistrates. She twisted the knife. 'Su-shun will understand that the so-called Board is regarded as non-legitimate by the legal authorities in Peking.'

All eyes were on Su-shun as he made to answer. 'Nevertheless, Lady, this Board is sanctioned by precedent. It will continue.'

'Excuse me for insisting, but I am bound to repeat: it has been ruled inauspicious. Vastly so.' Yehonala looked around the hall, her eye passing along the rows of officials. 'Those here assembled would do well to remember that all K'ang-hsi's regents were eventually either sent into exile or presented with the silken cord.'

Su-shun's patience snapped. He stood up, quivering with rage. 'Madam, have you quite finished?'

Yehonala met Su-shun's eye for the last time. She bowed low to him, punctilious to the end. 'Please excuse me for taking up so much of your time, however one final matter requires clarification: It is my undisputed right as Dowager Empress and wife-in-mourning to know if anyone here present has plans to interfere with the auspicious date on which my husband's body must depart for Peking.'

'The late Emperor's funeral procession will depart for the capital as arranged – on the second day of the ninth moon.'

Yehonala smiled inwardly as she took her leave. The tao was in spate inside her, and Su-shun knew he had been outmanoeuvred.

Two marines guarded the bottom of the gangway of Her Majesty's Ship *Urgent*. The duty officer on deck was roused by their stamping challenge to the worried junior mandarin who approached the ship. Behind, on the quay, a mandarin of magistrate rank was stepping from an ornately painted and tasseled chair, guarded by an escort of spear-carrying troops.

The duty officer sent below for Meadows, who appeared on deck almost immediately. As soon as he recognized the visitor, he put on his hat, straightened his jacket and started down the gangway.

One of the junior mandarins stepped forward and announced in sing-song English his customary rubric. 'Tremble and submit! His Excellency the Taotai of Shanghai comes!'

'Your Excellency,' the Englishman said politely but without concession. 'My name is Thomas Taylor Meadows, Consul for Her Majesty's Government in Shanghai. May I perhaps enquire the purpose of your visit?'

Wu Hsu spoke through an interpreter. 'It has been represented to me that you have imprisoned a subject of the Son of Heaven aboard this vessel.'

Meadows recognized the man as one who worked for Yang Fang. He carried several papers that looked like legal documents. Meadows managed a taut smile. 'Sir, you have my absolute assurance that there are no Chinese aboard this ship.'

'Yes, yes. The man's name is Colonel Hua.'

'I assure you, no such man is aboard this vessel.'

'You may know him as "Ward". I am informed that he was kidnapped out of Chinese territory by British soldiers.'

'Kidnapped, sir?' Meadows made a show of puzzlement. In reality he was vastly wary. 'Mr Ward is an American.'

'You must tell me if he is aboard this ship.'

'Yes, he is aboard.' Meadows inclined his head an inch. 'But, as I say, he is an American.'

'Not so. Colonel Hua has revoked his American citizenship, as these papers clearly testify. He has become a naturalized subject of the Son of Heaven. Therefore I must now investigate the matter.'

Meadows took the papers slowly and looked them over. Two things are absolutely certain, he thought. The taotai is not coming aboard this ship. And Ward is not leaving it. Papers or no papers.

'This is frightfully interesting. But these papers must be—' Meadows was going to say 'forgeries', but he managed to bite back the word. 'These papers must be – properly authenticated by a legally qualified person.'

Wu's words snapped back at him. 'I must see Colonel Hua now!'

'I'm afraid that is not possible, sir.'

'I insist! Have him brought immediately!'

The taotai's Green Standard guards were armed with pole blades and heavy swords. Several carried side arms – old fashioned, but lethal at close quarters. Meadows' face began to flush as he addressed the taotai. 'Should it eventually prove to be the case that this Colonel Hua is indeed a Chinese subject, we will then release him into your custody. Until that time he will remain here. And be advised, sir, that if and when he is released to you, we shall demand that he be put out of the Concession for good.'

Until now Wu Hsu's expression had remained bland and his voice fierce, but now his eyes opened with feigned surprise. 'Why would you ask this of me?'

'For suborning British military and naval personnel, and recruiting them to a private army based at Sung-chiang. As we have seen today, this man is a menace to international relations. Who knows what trouble he will cause in the end if he is allowed to go unpunished? We must all ask ourselves: is one man worth a war?'

As the interpreter conveyed the threat Meadows took a half-pace back. He watched, gratified, as the taotai changed tack away from danger.

'You will see that these papers are passed to Colonel Hua, and await further instructions.'

'As Your Excellency pleases.' Meadows bowed solemnly.

Governor Wu returned to his chair and was transported away. Meadows watched the retinue out of sight and saw the marine guards relax visibly as he went back up *Urgent's* gangway. At the bulwark he nodded to the deck officer who was holstering his revolver. Below decks a dozen marines were ready at the foot of the companionway with rifles. He stood them down, and went aft to the spacious captain's day room where Ward was confined under guard.

The cabin was well appointed – a canvas-covered deck painted in diamonds to look like a black and white marble floor, Indian rugs, a writing desk and a leather chair. An ultra-modern photographic portrait of Queen Victoria took pride of place on the bulkhead. The cabin contained all the furniture a commander on the China station could want to recreate an English drawing room on the far side of the world. Only a pair of huge black sixty-eight-pound Armstrong breech-loading cannon roped up to the big, square ports intruded on the illusion.

'You may be interested to know that your backer has just tried and failed to take you off,' Meadows said as he prowled the day room, papers in hand.

Ward laced his hands behind his head and stretched. 'Is that a fact?'

'I sent him packing. And if he comes back I'll send him packing again.' Meadows paused, but then he said, 'You might also be interested to know that we recovered silver bullion amounting to four thousand pounds sterling from Sung-chiang.'

'Recovered? Stole it, you mean.' Privately he was surprised. Forrest must have got half of the payroll away at least.

'Where did you loot it from, Ward? Did you do a deal with the Green Standard? Did you torture it out of the peasants or did they?'

Ward pierced him with a hard look. 'I don't know why you don't just shoot me, and have done with it.'

Meadows grunted. 'That's always been one of my options.'

'Yes,' Ward said, saving the vendetta up undiminished. 'Like you tried to do at Ch'ing-p'u. You can't have me killed now, not when all of Shanghai knows I'm in your tender care. Why didn't you kill me in Sung-chiang, right there where Strickland found me? There were no witnesses. It would have been easy. You blew your best chance, Meadows. You know that, don't you?'

The Englishman looked at him thoughtfully. 'You're a very strange fellow, Mr Ward. I can't work you out.'

'That's good. If you could understand me I'd start worrying.'

Meadows went to stand beside one of the big guns. 'If it's any consolation, it looks as though your little private army would have been put out of business even if we hadn't caught hold of you. Admiral Hope has sailed up to Nanking to seek assurances that no Taiping field army will ever again move on Shanghai, and that henceforth trade will not be hindered on the Great River by rebel actions.'

'That won't stop the war.'

'It's a civil war. It's not up to us to stop it.'

'Don't you think someone has the right? The duty? Great Britain is by far the world's most powerful nation, by far the richest too. You have a responsibility.'

'Where did you say you were born, Mr Ward?'

Ward laughed shallowly. 'You know, Meadows. I don't believe I did say.'

'Just a friendly enquiry. No harm in telling me that is there?'

'Sure, sure.'

Meadows saw the manoeuvre would get nowhere and slapped the papers down onto a mahogany side table. 'Well, these – forgeries – doubtless provided by Taki bank, and delivered to you by your amiable friend Governor Wu – purport to show that you're a Chinaman.'

Ward shrugged. 'Maybe I am.'

'You claim that you were last employed by Mexico, that you used to be a citizen of the United States, but are not now?'

'I sure as hell am no Englishman.'

Meadows looked him up and down and said, 'That is most definitely the case. Anyway, it doesn't matter what you are. Because at noon tomorrow *Urgent* will be under steam, and you'll be on the first leg of a journey to beautiful New South Wales.'

After he had gone, Ward went to the lamp and turned the wick up. He examined the papers minutely. A moment later he found what he was looking for. The characters embedded in the chop marks were not Chinese. There was a stylized representation of a sampan and four little bell shapes in the middle.

Satisfied, he turned the lamp down and pocketed the papers. Then he went back to his seat, laced his fingers behind his head again, and smiled back at the austere portrait of Britain's Queen.

A few hours later, at two in the morning, four bells were rung on the *Urgent*'s deck. Ward ran a finger round the inside of his collar and said to Strickland, 'Mind if we get a little air in here?'

Strickland shifted in his armchair and said in clipped tones. 'What's the matter, Ward? The smell of rope getting to you?'

'Sorry to disappoint you, Strickland, but your boss isn't fixing to lynch me. In fact, he's promised me a vacation in Australia.' He stood up, stepped to the cannon port and opened it. The sound of the Huang-pu's ink-black waters lapping against the hull came up from twenty feet below.

'I don't think it's a holiday Mr Meadows has in mind for you down there.'

Ward eyed the sixty-eight-pounder, calculating. Then he strolled past Strickland. His Webley Longspur revolver had not left his hand since he arrived to sit guard. Outside the cabin door two Royal Marines stood to attention, and the mess tables of the *Urgent*'s 200-strong crew stretched out along the flush-deck beyond filled with men whiling away the late hours.

'I told you, Strickland. I'm not going to do any deals . . .' Ward started to say, but then he snapped around and ran back across the cabin. Before Strickland knew what was happening Ward dived, launched himself along the cannon's polished barrel and out through the port.

There was a moment of blind falling, then the water hit and cold blackness closed around him. He knifed down, kicking out and pulling deeper. He knew that even now as the bubbles roared in his ears Strickland would be aiming his revolver into the dark. He pulled again, and again, until the craving in his lungs forced him up.

When he broke the surface the *Urgent*'s huge black hull loomed up, her masts ghostly above. Strickland's head was at the port. Two blinding flashes showed as he fired off wild shots to raise the alarm. Ward struck out toward the *Urgent*'s stern to narrow Strickland's angle. The man's shouts were furious.

Ward swam about twenty yards and looked back. So far so good, he thought. But there were figures already at the ship's rail. Orders were being shouted and ratings were readying the divots to swing a cutter outboard. Soon the *Urgent* would strike up a searchlight. Because of the threat of piracy a signal lamp was always available to the duty officer. Ward knew that the *Urgent* would be making to the shore station now, and that the Bund would swarm with personnel long before he could reach it.

The Huang-pu shore opposite the Bund was a mass of stinking mud flats, swept by treacherous estuary currents. In the dark, and on a strongly ebbing tide, he would be taken out to sea if he tried to reach it. Ahead two of Eden Phillips' sleek clippers were moored in centre stream, mocking him, while behind him the first of the *Urgent*'s three cutters was already touching water. They were fast row boats with a well drilled crew of eight. Once the piercing beam of the search-light located him they would bear down on him with inescapable speed.

Ward trod water momentarily. That was four bells I heard, he told himself. So where in damnation is Henry?

The chop mark he had looked for earlier on the papers Governor Wu had delivered were decorated with four bell shapes in the centre and a sampan underneath. The design had told him all he needed to know. Four bells was two hours after the start of a sea watch. The position of the bells in the centre of the chop meant the middle watch, which fixed the time at two o'clock in the morning. The sampan indicated his means of escape.

The thought entered his mind that he had been set up, but then he saw the sampan grey and silent in the dark, the single oarsman braced on the stern board. He swam towards it.

I hope to hell you know what you're doing, Henry, he thought. Those cutters have three times the speed of a sampan.

'Hey!' He called. 'Over here!'

'Coronel?'

It was Vincente. He bent down and hauled him inboard, got him under the rush mat cover.

'Vincente, you better tell that oarsman to row like he never rowed before. They're launching cutters.'

'Don't worry, Coronel, we got a surprise for them.'

A change of clothing and his Colt Dragoon revolver were waiting for him. There was time, he decided. If he made it to shore, a man in dry clothes might avoid being picked up by the patrols. He pulled off his water filled boots and stripped, pausing only to check the little blue accounts book in his inside pocket. Its cover was wet, but the precious pages inside were intact.

'Where's Henry?' he asked.

'Back at Sung-chiang.'

He looked up to see a sampan cut across their bow. He crawled forward and looked out. The Huang-pu was alive with shadows – dozens of sampans, all identical to his own, had come out of Soochow Creek and were zig-zagging all over the place.

'Well, I'll be damned! They're like a flock of birds!'

Vincente grinned back. 'You can blame this plan on Mr Yang.'

'It was Yang Fang's idea?'

'He is a very clever man.'

Ward stayed under cover as the *Urgent*'s searchlight blazed into the darkness. Its beam passed briefly over them, then went on to pick out other craft. He watched as the first cutter put out from the *Urgent*'s side and he was still watching as it overhauled the first of the bewildering flotilla of decoys. In the confusion that followed six of them were stopped and searched, but none of them contained an American.

Fei could hear the wind stripping the first yellow leaves from the trees. The day was cold, and the Valley of Lions was turning bleak under an iron-grey sky. Hsien-feng's bier was almost finished.

She had kept careful watch every day as the carpenters laboured from sunrise to sunset until a yellow cube, curtained with silk and roofed with golden fish scales, was completed. A mystical number of bearers had been selected, and each day they underwent training with a replica of the

Imperial catafalque. Four lines each of thirty men took the huge crimson support poles on their right shoulders, shuffling the weight forward for three steps, then stopping for three gong beats before setting off again.

Fei looked up to see the Empress. She followed dutifully behind as she approached the captain of the guard.

'Soldier, how far is it to the capital?'

The captain bowed low. 'Four hundred and fifty li, Imperial Highness.'

'And how many li will the Emperor's bier be able to travel in one day?'

'Halts have been planned every forty-five li, Imperial Highness.'

As soon as she was sure they were not overheard Fei indicated the bearers practising with the empty catafalque in the square, and asked, 'Why do you look there as if for salvation?'

'That is my husband's bier,' Yehonala said. 'He always feared coming to Jehol. He always said it was a bad luck place for his blood-line. He was right. But I see good omens attending his return to Peking.'

'Why do you say that? Your enemies retain control over both the late Emperor's body and your son. Why are you so sure of yourself?'

Yehonala's eyes followed the empty bier. 'Look at them learning how to carry an Emperor to his rest. See the brightness of the gold and how the yellow veils billow out in the wind. Isn't that a glorious sight?'

'I see no glory in riches filched from the rice-bowls of the poor. It is a meaningless dance of fools.'

The Empress's laugh surprised her. 'Do you know that the Rites even specify how the Emperor's body must be transported? On exactly this kind of specially constructed bier. It must be shuffled forward three steps at a time by one hundred and twenty pall-bearers. Golden sand must be strewn before it, so that a highway of Imperial yellow is created.'

'A ridiculous superstition.'

'But what delights me is that on the journey the bier must be accompanied by my enemies. Hsien-feng's embalmed remains will travel in cumbersome state, and all the so-called regents will be forced to travel alongside it.'

Shocked, Fei turned suddenly to face the Empress. 'But surely you also must travel with it?'

'Not at all.'

'But . . .'

Yehonala's lips pursed, a mannerism she had picked up from her Chief Eunuch. 'Niuhuru and I are not regents. We are widows. The Rites demand that we travel ahead of the funeral procession. We and the new Emperor must arrive in the capital before the late Emperor's body. It is our duty to prepare a reception for him at the An-ting Gate.'

Fei felt the vastness of what had just been said. For a while as they continued to watch the pall-bearers training it seemed almost as if Yehonala's self-confidence might be justified after all. Overhead a ray of sunshine burst from the clouds. But moments later it began to rain.

The steady downpour continued for a week. Water spilled noisily from the huge glistening roofs and formed pools in the corners of the courtyards. Summer turned to autumn in just seven days.

On the second day of the ninth moon, Hsien-feng's elaborate golden bier left the bad luck palaces of Jehol. The Son of Heaven departed, preceded by a mounted guard, flanked by gong-beaters and succeeded by the white palanquins of seven Regents and those of a thousand other courtly officials. A gaggle of wailing eunuchs and chanting lamaists followed after as the procession passed through the Gate of All Virtue, and began the climb out of the Valley of Lions, heading south and west towards the Great Wall, and China proper.

In the Yan Shan the brown hills met a grey sky. In rain-drenched passes avalanches of mud and stones turned the road to a bog of churned filth in which the rain-filled footprints and hoof marks of the boy-Emperor's passing could still be seen.

The banners of the Empress's escort fluttered blood-red now at the head of their column. Yehonala closed her tiny viewing slit, tired of staring out at swirling cloud and a sleet-blasted land. The swaying rhythm lulled her. She nestled inside the shuttered palanquin, wishing she could have her son inside with her. But protocol made that impossible now that he had become Emperor.

She thought of the insincere enquiries the Board of Regents had sent forward each day asking after her son's health and comfort. She knew they were meant to unsettle her and to show her that she had not escaped their reach, but she was always careful to return polite replies to which her own chop and that of Niuhuru were applied equally. These replies did not forget to ask after the progress of their late husband's bier.

'This time send a present of twelve hundred taels to be shared among the pall-bearers,' she had told An Te-hai this morning. 'Every step they take is making me stronger.'

She thought of the tiny robe of Imperial yellow that was being made, the little blue satin collar studded with pearls that would be Tsai-ch'un's coronation robe. How small he was. Too small to be a god, but god he must now become.

The latest coded messages that had come through from Prince Kung had renewed her hopes. The news from the South was growing more brilliant every day, with General Tseng inching his armies back into a strangling grip on rebel-held territories. The Taipings still had a dangerous field army at large, but the freedom with which it was able to roam the land was being limited at every turn. Already it had been drawn away from Kiangsu province, and the threat to Shanghai had thereby been lessened.

Governor Wu had written again, but this time the request was strange. It begged her support in an outrageous request. He wants me to intercede with Prince Kung, to help persuade him to allow an Outer Barbarian to be given the status of subject of the Celestial Empire.

'This man comes from the Flowery Flag Country far across the ocean, but he has shown himself to be a loyal and ferocious fighter. His trained band of warriors has already proved itself in the task of freeing the countryside around Shanghai of stubborn rebel garrisons that cannot be dislodged in any other way. These good works would be greatly helped by the mark of Peking's favour.'

Yehonala searched her memory, trying to recall a precedent. Certainly ordinary Barbarians – Koreans, Mongols, Tibetans, Annamese – had been made subjects from time to time, whenever necessity dictated, but never, so far as she knew, an Outer Barbarian. And which one was the Flowery Flag Country?

Governor Wu has a fertile mind, she thought, but how can I be sure what such a seed would grow into? On the other hand, anything that keeps the rebels away from Shanghai is to my advantage. Perhaps I will ask that this 'Hua' be made into an honorary Chinese, if Prince Kung agrees.

She secured the viewing slit and settled back comfortably. What happens in the South is crucial to my survival. I must keep the Taiping agent ignorant of events until we reach Peking. Then I will have to make a decision what to do about her.

She thought again of the stolen Seal of Legally Sanctioned Authority, almost feeling the power of its presence in the secret compartment under her seat. Its theft had been a master stroke. She closed her eyes and listened to the rain pattering once again on the top of the palanquin. Mixed in with it she heard the sound of her ancestral voices. They were prophesying victory.

Jung-lu's eyes slitted as he watched the swaying bier descend haltingly into Long Cloud Pass. He saw the palanquins of the Regents following into the defile and his whole being seethed with the desire to fall on Su-shun and wipe him out.

What if I ordered it tonight? he thought, nursing his hatred. My horsemen are hand picked. They're all Gobi Desert veterans; all have survived the devil guns of the Outer Barbarians. They would follow me even if it meant the lingering death, even if it meant committing treason . . . He had been working out his plan for the last three days as the rain turned colder and the roads grew steadily more difficult. That his troops had been accorded the honour of escorting the rotting remains of Hsien-feng had preyed on his mind. It had certainly been done for a reason.

There had been no way to refuse the duty, nor had he been able to talk with Yehonala before her departure. He had watched a squadron of the Red Banner leave with her and had felt a shifting disquiet in his stomach. It was foolish to ignore inner feelings like that.

He imagined massacring them all, beheading the Regents one after another on the edge of the precipice, then ordering the catafalque pushed over to follow the tumbling heads. Blood and mud, mingling on the road, he thought, just like it was when we caught the bandits in the Gobi. It's been far too long since my sword tasted meat.

He watched the curtains of the Imperial bier straining and flapping in the gale. If my son is now Emperor, that means I am the father of the Son of Heaven. This is unnatural, a situation that cannot be. Perhaps I cannot be. Perhaps, in the eyes of the judges of hell I am already guilty. How we twist up the fabric of existence when we lie and deceive and cheat. One day Heaven will make everything smooth once again.

The gong-beats started up again. The procession began to move. The sand-spreaders went ahead, casting their pure golden handfuls uselessly into the morass. The costly sand was trodden into the dirt. This weather's a sure sign of Heaven's scorn, Jung-lu told the coffin silently. A recognition of your failures. Heaven says you were never an Emperor, Hsien-feng. You were a mistake. By the gods, I say you were not even a man.

They rounded the last bend as the daylight died. Before them now, at the foot of the valley, the halting place was ready. Streamers fluttered over an encampment of mat-shed palaces built around an ornate central stage. He saw the kitchens where fires glowed and wisps of steam twisted up from huge pans of noodle soup and bean porridge. He searched out the windbreak and fodder that waited for his horses. Hundreds of mats had been placed along the roadside to protect white mourning robes. An awning sheltered the carpets on which the Regents would kneel.

When the bier came level with the central stage, everyone except the bearers assumed their ceremonial positions and began to kowtow. They remained in low kowtow until the bier was placed under the shelter. Jung-lu stayed watchful. He spoke to no one as he settled his horse and ate his meal of pork and pai-ts'ai cabbage, and warmed his hands by a basin of hot cinders. His men knew better than to approach him when he was in reflective mood. All except one. The trooper was a man well-known to him, ambitious and clever. He would have considered carefully before braving his captain's displeasure.

He whispered, 'It's only a rumour, honourable sir. But perhaps you should hear it.'

Jung-lu continued to pick his teeth. 'Go on.'

'The reason our duty was switched at the last moment was not so we could have the honour of escorting the Imperial bier, but so that the Red Banner could ride with the Dowager Empresses.'

'I know.'

The man's face stayed earnest. 'I heard the garrison commander the day we departed Jehol. The order came from the Chien Kuo's own lips . . .'

When the trooper crept away Jung-lu continued to listen. The rain was pelting against the matting of the shed. Outside eunuchs were noisily fetching and carrying between the kitchens and the place where the Regents were dining. A messenger came to him with a sealed letter. He opened it, read it, then lit it on a lantern candle. He watched as the chop of Ching-shou, one of the Regents, was consumed.

Jung-lu picked up his cup. His tea was almost cold, but he finished it in a single swallow. Then he looked to his men and to where aisles of saddles and helms were lined up in the gloom. He drew his sword from its scabbard, rested it in his lap and began to whet it slowly.

Across the sea of sanded mud, lanterns illuminated the entrance of the Regents' sleeping quarters. Jung-lu watched the comings and goings unsmilingly.

'Red meat,' he murmured.

Fei trudged on, following the road in failing light, wondering when they would reach the next camp and put an end to the ordeal. She was hungry and close to exhaustion. Since daybreak she had been staggering blindly forward. Her fingers were numb with cold. She clutched her jacket to her throat, but the cotton fabric was drenched.

At the head of the column, the Red Banner escort abandoned all pretence of ceremony. They dismounted, picking their way forward, leading their horses into the murk. The ground is falling away now, she thought, dimly sensing the gradient of the road and the shape of the hills that opened into the next valley. The camp for which they were heading was supposed to be near a hamlet called Ku-pei K'ou, but so far they had seen no sign of its lights.

The hawk-faced captain of the Red Banner rode back, spattering the line of eunuchs with mud as he passed.

Yehonala spoke through the viewing slit of her palanquin. 'Why have we stopped?'

'Imperial Highness. A gully has opened across our path.'

'Gully? How big a gully?'

'The road bed is washed out. It's wider than a running man could jump. Impossible to lead palanquins across.'

Fei heard some of the eunuchs start grumbling about omens. It was late afternoon, and the light was dying.

'I recommend we go back, Imperial Highness.'

Yehonala was adamant. 'The Rites demand that we go on.'

'But, Imperial Highness, come and see. We cannot do anything about it.'

'Cannot? What do you mean? Captain, you must do your utmost.'

Fei watched the Empress Dowager argue stubbornly, as if she feared the approach of Hsien-feng's bier more than she feared braving the gully and pressing on in darkness.

'The only answer,' Yehonala said, 'is a log-and-dirt bridge.'

The captain of the Red Banner moved uncertainly. 'Imperial Highness, this upland is barren. There are no trees.'

'There were trees in the last valley, I smelled them.'

The captain ordered a forage party back to the same valley which they had toiled out of an hour before. The village had an orchard. While the Red Banner captain was away Tsai-ch'un started crying. Guards moved to his palanquin, but Yehonala defied protocol and pushed through them furiously, saying, 'Listen to the Emperor call for me! Which one of you would defy his will?'

By the time a grove of suitable timber could be found and felled and brought up, darkness had almost set in completely.

'Oh, I wish this journey was over and we were already in Peking,' one of Yehonala's maids said as they prepared to pass over the bridge.

'It's said there are many desperate bandits in the Yan Shan,' another said.

'They would have to be mad as well as desperate to think of doing banditry on a night like this.'

The road twisted and turned and began to descend steeply now. It went down and down, and the cold air lost its bite. There were trees here. The ground was treacherous under foot, rocky and slimy with fallen leaves. The six identical white palanquins showed dim and ghostly as they took the bends, emphasizing the danger in Fei's mind. One palanquin carried Yehonala, one Niuhuru, another was intended for the boy-Emperor. The rest were decoys, carrying only baggage.

It's all right for you, Lady Empress, Fei thought. You're being carried in a warm, dry palanquin, resting at your ease while we labour through all this disgusting muck.

Then, fifty paces ahead, she saw the lanterns shiver and go out and the white palanquin of the Empress of the Western Palace lurch into the trees.

Yehonala came awake in the swaying darkness, an aching fear welling up inside her once more. The dead weight of her sleeping son pressing against her right side had shut off the feeling in her thigh and arm, but she did not shift. He may be Emperor of China now, she thought caressing him tenderly, but he's still my baby boy. He has been denied mother-love for far too long.

It was impossible to know the hour, or how long she had been sleeping. She listened, her ears sensitive in the darkness. Rain was still crackling on the roof, the bearers' grunts were still muffled, but then other sounds came from the distance that alarmed her – shrill shouts and orders passing, then the sound of men rushing by urgently.

The bearers staggered and faltered under the poles. Then the palanquin dropped to the ground. She clutched Tsai-ch'un to her, set his unconscious form among the furs, moving away from him to open the viewing slit.

Outside the lanterns had been doused. There were a dozen mounted guards drawn up nearby, fearsome indistinct grey forms, wrapped in draggled furs. They stood beside their horses, swords drawn. Then she heard rapping on the palanquin and a breathless voice. 'Imperial Highness! Please come outside!'

It was the Taiping girl.

Rain spangled cold on her face as Yehonala opened the door. 'Who ordered the column to stop?'

The girl's face pleaded urgently. 'Please, there may be danger. You must not be recognized. Come this way.'

Yehonala's heart began to beat fast. She lifted Tsai-ch'un out of the palanquin. Then the girl threw a dark cloak around her shoulders, and she enfolded her son, hurrying him away, off the road. There was the sound of tumbling water nearby. The tree trunks and branches around them were clothed with strange, bearded growths. A green smell hung in the air, full of autumn decay.

'Where's the guard?'

'Lady, look!'

Back up the road, high above them, there were points of yellow light, swaying, descending, coming closer.

'Bandits!' Yehonala rasped.

Fei heard the horses first – a whinny, then the jangle of gear. Men were picking their way down the twisting roadway, those in the lead carried long poles on which lanterns had been fixed, illuminating the road ahead. Then an order was given and the poles were dropped and the lanterns quickly extinguished. All their commotion went suddenly silent.

Tsai-ch'un had woken up and was crouching in the rain. His mother clasped him to her. They watched as the guard captain backed by a trio of Red Banner guards rode forward, ready to bar the road. Fei saw their hands on their sword-hilts, heard the guard captain's challenge. It was gruff with authority intended to overawe. He shouted into the empty night, but no answer came back. When he shouted again Fei heard the taint of fear in his voice. Then she felt a hand close around her mouth and pull her down.

The man in the mandarin's dress uniform tried to put his worries out of his mind as the final ceremonies of the wedding began. By the end of today I'll be a legally married man, he told himself. You've surely come a long way from Salem, Massachusetts. And that's a fact.

The night he had escaped from the British warship he had been smuggled straight to Yang Fang's house. The banker had spoken seriously with him. 'It is very important that His Excellency Wu Hsu does not lose face. So you must agree to become a subject of His Imperial Majesty.'

'Whatever you like,' he had said easily, willing to sign any bureaucrat's paper or mouth any meaningless official oath if it meant he could get back to Sung-chiang before the raid on Kao-ch'iao was due to be launched. 'What do you want me to do?'

'Excellent, excellent!' Yang grinned. 'Now please just get married with my bad luck daughter.'

Within a few days, the most auspicious moment had been calculated by the astrologers, presents exchanged and a handsome dowry agreed. A long series of preliminary betrothal gifts – ducks, piglets, rice cakes, jars of fine wine, outrageously expensive Korean ginseng roots – had begun to arrive at Yang Fang's home.

Now Ward was standing outside his own new house in the French Concession, amid a noisy crowd of servants and family and well-wishers. He had paid extra to have the house finished in time for the wedding so that his bride would not lose face before the guests. He had agreed to wear the clothes and hat of a mandarin of the third rank today for the same reason. A turquoise ball decorated the spire of his hat, a tiger was embroidered across his chest, showing his military rank of colonel. The only addition to official robes required for the marriage ceremony was a crimson sash draped over his right shoulder and tied at the waist. Yang Fang told him smilingly that it signified the cloth used to carry a baby.

His acute embarrassment over dressing in mandarin clothes – complete with silk boots, tasselled hat and peacock feather – had now begun to wear off. Despite huge pressure from Yang Fang he had refused point blank to have his hair shaved and braided. He cast a serious glance at his Corpsmen. Vincente Macanaya, smiling broadly, had come with a dozen men of his green-uniformed elite to form a guard of honour. Since the attempt on their leader's life they never left his side. Three other officers were present, but Henry Burgevine was not one of them. He was cursing and swilling liquor back in Sung-chiang, trying to dull the pain of a serious wound he had taken a few days ago.

The curtained bridal sedan arrived. Ward stepped forward and tapped with his fan on the sedan's post. Chang-mei climbed down, and he saw that her dress was breathtaking – an embroidered skirt under a long crimson silk jacket with a very elaborate collar. Hidden under her skirt were tiny crimson slippers of embroidered cloth. A crimson veil covered her head and face. Red was the colour that ensured good luck.

'The hung kua – the wedding jacket and skirt – are always

richly decorated,' Chang-mei had explained to him. 'It is very important that they show the characters for long life and double happiness, and also the dragon and the phoenix.'

'Why the dragon and phoenix?' he asked. 'I thought they were reserved for the Emperor and Empress?'

'Confucius said that on a wedding day it is important to signify obedience to the will of the Imperial family. It is a custom that goes back to the Yuan dynasty. If you are to be Chinese, you must be obedient to the Son of Heaven.'

Luck and good planning had so far extended to leading the Corps to two highly significant victories, the first at Kao-ch'iao on the Pu-tung peninsula, a town guarding the mouth of the Huang-pu river. It had had no walls, but a formidable network of trenches and earth works had been set around it by the garrison of 10,000 Taipings. The Foreign Arms Corps had taken the town with the loss of only a handful of men. After that Governor Hsueh had listed him as a fourth-rank mandarin.

Last week the Corps had stormed an even bigger concentration of Taipings. The city of Hsia-t'ang stood on the Huang-pu, just where the river turned north, and about twenty miles from Shanghai. It was walled and its approaches had been massively fortified with ditches and barricades manned by a garrison of six thousand Taipings. Ward had led an attack on the city, personally killed two high-ranking Taiping officers and seized their battle standard. In recognition of this triumph Hsueh Huan had promoted him to the third rank, swapping his dark blue button for one of light blue. He had also sanctioned the increase of the Corps to two thousand Chinese.

But not all was well. Henry Burgevine had been shot through the pelvis, and the Taipings who had escaped Hsia-t'ang were now trying to link up with a much larger force from Ch'ing-p'u. They're massing their strength in a last bid to crush the Green Standard, he thought. There's the biggest battle of all coming. Both armies are manoeuvring even now as we sit around grinning. Unless I do something to save it General Li's army will be stamped into the ground and obliterated.

Should I save the Green Standard?

Or should I let it perish, and General Li with it?

The elaborate wedding ceremonial had already taken up two precious days. Yesterday, after shedding tears and making obeisance to Chang-mei's ancestors, the hair had been removed from around her forehead in the ceremony of 'hoi-min' – 'opening the face'. Today, the whole morning had been taken up preparing his bride's dress and make-up. A rule said that she must wear an even number of garments to signify the female yin principle. He had had to provide two pieces in white, two in black, and over-clothes of red. He himself had had to put on an odd – yang, and therefore male – number of garments.

He approached his bride now, for once setting aside all other thoughts. As he lifted the red veil there was applause. Then a burst of firecrackers filled the air with noise and smoke. Chang-mei's face was meticulously made-up, beautiful in its fragile solemnity. Her now revealed headdress was of silver, gilded and decorated with strings of pearls and kingfisher feathers. She looked away from him demurely, filled with the joy of a day she had been sure could never dawn for her. He was deeply pleased for her.

For a brief while thoughts of the coming battle had left his mind, but now he was reminded of his duty by a volley fired into the air. The dozen men of his ever-present Filipino bodyguard reloaded their rifles with impressive precision and coordination and fired again.

The approving crowd, swelled by curious passers-by, pressed forward around the Ward house, and now the ceremony of the bride's arrival reached its climax. The next ritual to be observed was to purify Chang-mei. She was lifted onto the back of a female servant who carried her over a small, symbolic charcoal fire. Another servant held a basket of rice over her head, and over that a third servant, the oldest of the three, held a parasol to shield the bride from bad luck and the curses of demons.

Ward conducted his bride inside, but she hesitated momentarily, and he did not understand why.

He asked Yang Fang, 'Am I . . . doing something wrong?'

'Not to worry, son-in-law. It is not your fault that you have no ancestral rolls, nor any altar in your home at which my daughter can worship. At this time it is customary for a bride to kowtow to her husband's parents and bring them tea. However, since this is impossible I have suggested that we go direct to the wedding feast.'

Chang-mei changed her shoes to symbolize her passing into a new family, then they moved into the dining room where tea and cakes awaited them. Ward noticed that as he prepared to sit Chang-mei tugged at his robe, trying to pull a piece of it under her as she took her place.

'What are you doing?' he asked, perplexed.

Those who watched laughed uproariously, and Yang Fang told him too late that he had made a big mistake. 'Oh! You should not have let my daughter do that,' he said. 'This means you will now become a husband who is a slave to his wife's slightest wishes.'

He grinned. 'That sure was a mistake. Why didn't you warn me?'

She smiled, and for the first time he saw her teeth were as white as the pearls that shivered on her headdress. Their eyes met, and he too felt unexpectedly consumed by the joy of the occasion. He wanted to kiss her, but he knew that a simple kiss would be an outrageous breach of Chinese public manners.

Instead he just looked at her, and she looked back at him, swathed in the crimson of good fortune. When he smiled she seemed to him for the first time free from the dreadful shadow that had blighted her life. No longer was she Yang Fang's bad luck daughter, she was an important mandarin's wife.

Ward lay with his wife in the warm afterglow of the moment. Night had fallen over Sung-chiang, and the curfew's silence shrouded the town. He turned over in his mind his final plans for the battle that lay ahead. A force of rebels had escaped from the destruction of Hsiao-t'ang. They had fled north and joined up with a much larger Taiping force from Ch'ing-p'u. General Li had sent the Green Standard against them, but in a bloody slaughter near Ssu-ching the Imperials had been surrounded and butchered. The Taipings from Ch'ing-pu were veterans who outmatched the Green Standard in every way, and Ward knew that tomorrow, unless the Corps intervened, General Li's army would be obliterated.

That's why I've asked Governor Wu for funds to increase

the Corps to four thousand men, he thought. And every victory will bring another request from me, so that one day I'll have an army of twenty-five thousand disciplined men equipped with modern weapons, and then there won't be a force in China that can rival it.

He turned over. Chang-mei's naked body was soft and golden beside him in the lamplight. He had taken her virginity as gently as he could, but she had not enjoyed it. She had not responded to his caresses, but had lain there like a log of wood. As she pulled her robe about her he slid his hand inside it and stroked her side and then her breast. She made no acknowledgement, showed no pleasure, but still she permitted his hand to roam freely. He stopped.

'I must get up soon,' he said. 'I'm sorry. It's not much of a honeymoon for you.'

'I will implore my ancestors to bring my honoured husband a great victory.'

Her hair was held up with a single jade pin. He noticed that it was carved with the figure of an old man. 'That's cute. What is it?'

'A medal of Taoism, master,' she said meekly. 'Taoism is very good. Certain Taoists can live for ever.'

'What?' He laughed at her. 'Chang-mei, nobody lives for ever.'

'Of course you are right, master.' She said automatically and then looked away as if chastened. 'I am very foolish.'

He put a hand to her face, suddenly solicitous. 'No, Chang-mei, you're not foolish.'

'I am not foolish, master,' she murmured.

'How many times have I told you, I don't want you to call me "master"?' She saw annoyance in his face, but for some reason he made his voice deliberately kind. 'Look, if you have an opinion then speak out. Don't be afraid. Say what you believe, just like I do. You can think what you like and say what you like. Do you understand?'

'Yes. Thank you, master.'

He shook his head and uneasiness surged through her. He must be hugely displeased with so spoiled and so stupid a wife, she thought, hating herself. How can my wise father have done this cruel thing to so great a Barbarian general? As for me, it was understandable. I am twenty-one, very difficult to be disposed of, except to a very elderly virgin-seeker. Cursed as I am with evil, there was no alternative. In my case my honoured father was wise, for what use was I but an unwanted expense upon his household, and a festering cause of ill-fortune?

She looked at Ward sadly. It should have been easy to hate him, but the warlord Hua has turned out to be a kind man, and genuinely caring in a way I do not deserve. That is why I must be very careful not to fall in love with him. I must never love him, no matter how much I may want to, because my curse is very deadly, and if once I love him he will die.

She said with a small voice, 'Please tell me again what is required of me.'

'Just remember what I promised.' He told her softly. 'I said we'd have a Chinese wedding, but an American marriage. That means we're both allowed to have opinions. What I think is my opinion. And what you think is your opinion. Now . . . my opinion is that nobody lives for ever. What is your opinion?'

'Nobody lives for ever.'

'No, no,' he said, exasperated. 'Your opinion. Your opinion!'

She said nothing, paralyzed, wanting to please him so far as it was possible, but not knowing how. She saw him smile a terrible false smile, his patience strained to the limit.

'Look . . . your opinion is that some people do live for ever. So . . . just say that.'

'Some people do live for ever.'

He nodded with satisfaction, and laughed. 'You see? That wasn't so hard was it?'

'Not hard.'

'But it's still a ridiculous opinion.'

She echoed his laugh, but privately was appalled at his inside-out way of thinking. How can I obey him if his command is to oppose him? How can a wife support her husband if she must always disagree with his views? How can a woman please a man if he will not tell her what is required of her? I will never understand him, she told herself. Never.

*

The next day Ward spent the morning at Sung-chiang, then just before noon he set off for Shanghai. He went by river-boat, then by chair into the French Concession, flanked by his ever-present bodyguard. First he visited his town house and looked it over. Chang-mei had told him she did not want to live there, no matter how grand he made it. She wanted, she said, to live with her 'good husband' in Sung-chiang. He wandered the neat, freshly-painted, newly-fur-nished rooms for a while, inspected the line of house ser-vants and then left, going as arranged to the reception at Provincial Governor Hsueh Huan's yamen in the Chinese city.

The Governor took tea with him and privately congratu-lated him on his victory at Ssu-ching, before publicly prais-ing him to a packed yard of mandarins for 'cooperating with' General Li's army so successfully. Li was present, and so was Wu Hsu, and they both played their parts in the charade without a flicker of embarrassment.

Everyone knows that I saved Li's army from annihilation, he thought silently as the crowd applauded his exploits. Everyone here understands that without my Corps there would be no Green Standard in Kiangsu, and that Li Hung-chang's head would be decorating the walls of Ssu-ching. And more than half of you know how much Wu Hsu and General Li hunger for the Governorship of Kiangsu province and hate Hseuh Huan.

Recognition of what had really happened at Ssu-ching had come that morning when the genial Hsueh had approved his application to increase the Corps' strength to four thousand disciplined Chinese.

Now Hsueh bowed in welcome. 'His Imperial Majesty is pleased to announce the promotion of Colonel Hua to the official rank of brigadier-general. He sends this coat as a token.'

Ward came forward to accept the commission. The yellow jacket was richly made, embroidered silk with a round collar in turquoise and wide sleeves.

'The Son of Heaven does his unworthy servant undue honour,' he said. A thousand curious eyes watched him make the customary kowtow of thanks. He touched his head to the floor at Hsueh Huan's feet three times.

'Also, by Imperial command, what has previously been

called the Foreign Arms Corps shall from this time forward be known as "Chang-sheng-chun". This is a title of great honour.'

Ward bowed as he accepted. The assembly of gowned and hatted officials dutifully showed their appreciation of his good grace.

'Chang-sheng-chun'. The phrase, he knew, meant 'Ever-victorious Army'. It doesn't matter to me what the Corps is called, but names are extremely significant to the Chinese. They believe that a person's given name must please the ear when spoken and caress the eye when written, but above all it must be auspicious. According to the Classics the name a man's parents give him will affect his fortune all his life. He will grow into his name, and others will have expectations of him because of it. There's even a Chinese maxim that says, 'A tiger leaves its skin after death, but a man leaves only his name.' So Hsueh Huan is right: it is a great honour.

'"Chang-sheng-chun" is a name already famous in Chinese history,' Hsueh told him afterwards as Ward prepared to depart for Sung-chiang. 'A Chinese army was once led by a foreigner centuries ago, during the Sung dynasty. This army, too, met with unstoppable success.'

He took the commemorative scroll as he climbed into his chair. 'I am deeply honoured, Your Excellency.'

'An interesting note accompanied these robes,' Hsueh Huan told him. 'It tells that a friend of yours was instrumental in persuading Prince Kung that you are an honourable man.'

'A friend?'

'His name is Dr Lindley. I am told he is part of the British legation in Peking.' Hsueh Huan's eyes creased as his avuncular smile spread. 'Also there is granted citizenship and third mandarin rank to Mr Burgevine. I hope his health recovers quickly.'

Hsueh Huan turned away, and Ward looked up in surprise. 'To Henry? Why?'

Hsueh turned back slowly, his bland expression not faltering. 'He has been injured in His Imperial Majesty's service. This award is a mark of the Son of Heaven's gratitude for your colleague's exceptional loyalty.'

A high honour like this just for being wounded? Ward

thought on his guard. It doesn't add up. What's the real reason?

He said, 'Unfortunately I fear there may be a problem with that.'

'A problem? Why?'

'Mr Burgevine comes from a province where the inhabitants absolutely refuse the kowtow. To them it is an abhorrent gesture, worse than nakedness.'

Hsueh gave no ground. 'I am sure this difficulty can be surmounted.'

'Perhaps. But unfortunately . . .'

'Unfortunately?'

'Unfortunately, he may feel deeply unworthy and may be unable to accept the award unless he is furnished with a more detailed explanation as to why he has been thus richly honoured.'

Hsueh saw that Ward had cornered him, and he capitulated. 'Perhaps the war in your own country will end suddenly – as everyone hopes and expects.'

The answer puzzled him. 'What if it does?'

'I am advised that in such circumstances the question of citizenship and consular powers will arise once more.'

'Why is that important? Mr Burgevine has no need to enter the foreign Concessions, neither to acquire weapons, nor to negotiate with the trade interests there. That's my prerogative.'

'Quite so.' Hsueh hesitated delicately, then said, 'But if on some occasion you fail to survive, then the Corps would require a new commander. How much better it would be if there were no complications over nationality. Shall we be caught unprepared when this is a matter that can be solved beforehand?'

Ward nodded to show he had understood the point, but he did not show his approval. Henry's behind this, he thought, a shaft of suspicion knifing through him. What if he hasn't forgiven me for what I did to him? What if he's gone behind my back? What if he's worked out a deal with the Governor? What if, all along, he was the one who . . .

He blanked the thought savagely, and said, 'I thank the Son of Heaven on my second-in-command's behalf. Please assure His Imperial Majesty that Mr Burgevine is making a swift and complete recovery from his injuries, and that when he is well again he will be in a position to consider with a clear mind the honour contemplated for him.'

Ward left the Governor's yamen deep in thought. He ordered the chair-bearers to take him on to the British Concession. He thanked God he had made his peace with Harry Lindley after that bloody fight aboard the *Hyson*, but he also speculated on how Hsueh Huan might have been advised on the consequences of American politics, and his mind would not quit on Henry Burgevine. One thing's for sure, he told himself, finally breaking away from his suspicions. The war's roaring to white heat and there's urgent business to be done. I must get more weapons right away. But how? And where?

Throughout the busy winter months he had followed the news that arrived from home, by letter and by newspaper. His father had written that the army of the new Confederacy had fought and won a bloody battle in Virginia, just twenty-five miles from the nation's capital at Washington, DC. A few days ago a New York newspaper had reached him, proclaiming a terrible calamity. He had read that the Confederates had lost two thousand men, the Union nearer three, and he had tried hard not to make comparisons with the immense losses sustained so far in the Chung Wang's eastern campaign alone. Already the Chinese rebellion had cost tens of millions of lives. What if it happens like that in the US, he thought, appalled. There's always an ocean of blood when a nation begins to break up, and with today's weapons killing is a cinch.

He crossed the Bund and found the offices of Eden Phillips. He sent in his card, and was admitted immediately. The office was appointed with green leather sofas and adorned by prints of biblical scenes. The place smelled dry and clean and businesslike. Phillips was behind a huge, empty desk, stiff and grim faced. He dismissed his two compradors as Ward entered.

'I'd be obliged if you'd get to the point,' he said as the door closed. 'I don't believe in wasting time.'

'I didn't think you'd see me at all.'

Phillips bridled. 'I'll tell you straight, Mr Ward, I don't like you.'

'I don't think much of you either, but I'm here on business, not pleasure.'

Phillips's chin jutted. 'I make it a rule never to refuse a business meeting to any man of his word.'

'You believe that of me, after all that's been said?'

'The first lesson of business is to judge a man by his actions, not by his promises or by tittle-tattle. I forgot that once, to my detriment. I brought a false accusation against you, and that was wrong of me. Now do as I ask, and get to the point.'

'All right. To call this a business meeting would not be exactly accurate. I want you to answer a question.'

Phillips sucked his teeth, then said, 'Ask it.'

'Do you know who tried to have me killed at Ch'ing-p'u?'

'No, I don't.'

'But you would have known if it had been Meadows, or Strickland, or someone connected with the Shanghai Trade Association?'

'That I would. I can tell you for certain it was neither of the gentlemen you've named, nor any member of the Association, nor indeed any British subject.'

'Thank you for your honesty, Mr Phillips.'

'You're welcome, Mr Ward. I now consider my moral debt to you fully and fairly discharged. You'll not be welcome to come here again under any circumstances – unless of course you propose bona fide business. Good day to you.'

Ward nodded and left. The Bund was bustling as he headed for the British Consulate. He sent up a request to see Meadows and waited. A few minutes later the sentry admitted him, and he was led up to the first floor.

'Come to gloat, have you?' the Consul asked as he entered the man's office.

'As a matter of fact I've got a proposition for you.'

Meadows' sour expression hardened. 'A proposition? You've got incredible nerve. Do you know that?'

'Until today I believed it was you who ordered my assassination, or I'd have come to you for help sooner.'

'Assassination?' Meadows absorbed the idea with a laugh. 'That's a very grand word. Do you think we'd have gone to all the trouble of arresting you and trying to ship you out if I'd been prepared to have you killed?'

Ward ignored Meadows' question, keen only to tell the man what he had come to tell him. 'Since February there have been six battles within thirty miles of this port, all fought with great loss to the rebels. I never deployed more than twelve hundred men, the rebels always fielded between five and twenty thousand. Before I came along the rebels always had the beating of Imperial troops, but not now. Not with my Corps to spearhead them.'

'The point being?'

'The point being that you can't maintain so called British neutrality with this state of affairs. You can't walk your favourite tightrope between the Taipings and the Imperialists any longer. Face it, Meadows, your kind of hypocrisy is now out of date.'

Meadows eyes were rapier sharp. 'What do you want, Ward? Your own army? Or do you want your own kingdom now? Do you want to be lord of Kiangsu? Is that it? Or do you want even more than that?'

'I told you before: I want to finish this war. I want to put an end to it. For good.'

'For . . . good?'

'You heard me.'

Meadows spread his hands, unable to understand. 'Why?'

Ward's eye locked with Meadows' own. 'Because I can.'

Meadows watched him for a long time, still not sure, but knowing there was respect where once there had been none.

'Then why don't you finish the war, instead of sitting here talking to me?'

Ward readied to tick off the points on his fingers. 'One: I have the manpower to do the job, and with every victory I'll get more. Two: I know how to discipline the Chinese and make excellent troops out of them. Three: I know how to reduce walled fortifications, drive out occupying forces and hold ground. Hell, you've seen me do it a dozen times, Meadows. You know I can do it again and again.'

'But?'

'But I want to do it quicker. I want to finish this war as quickly as it can be finished. And for that I need modern river steamers, ten thousand rifles and fifty pieces of breech-loading artillery.'

'Ten thousand?' Meadows mused. 'Do you mean that? Or is it just an expression you've picked up from your new compatriots?'

'I mean ten thousand.'

'So go to your usual suppliers.'

'The United States is at war, and that war is getting hotter with every month that goes by. They need every gun they can turn out. Those that do reach the Chinese coast are grabbed by your conniving Customs men. That's why I want to buy arms from Great Britain.'

Meadows laughed, fascinated by the incredible effrontery. 'Why should we give you arms?'

'Because the British government has finally made up its mind about who it wants in power in Peking.'

'How do you know that?'

'Never mind how I know. The French knew all along that you were prepared to install the Taipings at Peking. You would have done it too, if the Chung Wang had gone ahead and taken Shanghai. But he didn't send his full force here when he was able to do so. Why? Because he thought we would welcome him into the port with open arms, as fellow Christians, as brothers with a common purpose of destroying idolatry and superstition and driving out the tyrant. But the Hsien-feng Emperor ran off to die and left Prince Kung in control, and you figured you could work with him better.'

He watched Meadows' eyes and knew that he was right in all particulars.

'I see I've underestimated you, Mr Ward.'

He became aware of the distant hum of human enterprise down on the Bund. He felt suddenly as if some cosmic cogwheel had moved round a little.

'That sounded like a painful admission, Mr Meadows.'

Meadows put his hands together and touched them to his lips. 'So – what do you want me to do?'

'Arrange an immediate meeting between myself and Admiral Hope and his French equivalent. Also invite Shanghai's key traders. They want this war finished as fast as possible, and so do you now. Believe me, Mr Meadows, no one's better placed to finish the Taipings than me – if you'll let me.'

Harry Lindley paced the floor restlessly as he listened to the tall, elegant, sallow-faced man in the armchair. The legation house had been one of the princely mansions, but was now fitted out with modern Western furniture brought in from Calcutta.

The man who faced Lindley was Frederick Bruce, British

ambassador to the Chinese Empire. He was Lord Elgin's younger brother, and as unlike him in appearance and manner as it was possible to be. Since his arrival in Peking he had honoured all Elgin's promises. So far he had submitted a formal application for Lindley to travel in the interior, and he had sent his people to find out what they could about Fei's father.

'It seems the charges laid against Shih Wen-kuang were more serious than you at first imagined,' Bruce told him, indicating a document copied from the Hall of Records. 'The man was accused of stealing public funds, taking gifts intended for the throne, extorting money from a number of powerful merchants, forcibly selecting concubines, allowing his servants to beat an aged beggar who had dared to cross the street ahead of his cavalcade . . .'

Lindley said, deflatedly, 'He sounds like a complete villain.'

Bruce nodded. 'As for the crime of visiting restaurants, he appears to have been found guilty of that too.'

'What does it mean?'

'Not at all what it seems. My advisor says that Shih annoyed the Tao-kuang Emperor. So diversion charges were trumped up against him.'

'Diversion? What's that?'

'It's the duty of all provincial mandarins to look out for anything of surpassing beauty or value in their area and to offer it as a gift to the Throne. No one is allowed to take it from its container on its journey or to delay its arrival. Diverting contributions intended for the Imperial treasure store is a crime.'

'So this whole list of accusations is just a formula designed to blacken a man's name?'

'And they made him out to be an abuser of women and old folk for good measure.'

'Quite.'

'So what was Shih's real crime?'

Bruce's voice was underscored by the sound of the drum tower beating the Hour of the Monkey. 'Nobody seems to know that. Or if they do they won't tell my people. It must have been serious, and it must have involved members of the Imperial household, but beyond that I can't probe. This is the official record of his verdict. You must make of it what you will.'

Lindley took the paper and read it.

'It is decreed that the criminal, Shih Wen-kuang, shall strip the insignia of rank from his person and the button from his cap, and he shall tear away the peacock feather. All lands, property and money shall be confiscated and rendered as tribute to the Dragon Throne. Furthermore, he shall be banished from the Court and exiled to Black Dragon River for ever. His relatives and descendants to the third generation shall all be likewise impoverished and banished and may never again hold offices of profit or trust in our government.'

Strong stuff. Lindley said, 'What would be the punishment if an exiled man returned to the capital?'

Bruce clicked his tongue. 'That would be defiance of an Imperial Decree.'

'Meaning?'

'Decapitation, of course.'

'And his relatives?'

'The same.'

'Under all circumstances?'

'As I said, this verdict has the power of an Imperial decree. Since the Tao-kuang Emperor is dead he cannot amend it. And for anyone else, even one of his successors, to do so would show disrespect to an ancestor.'

Why are you unable to settle this afternoon? he asked himself after Bruce left, patience at its absolute limit. There's no special cause for anxiety, is there? At least, no more than yesterday, or the day before, or the day before that. All Peking is in a ferment, and it will stay that way until the new Emperor arrives . . .

For days his mind had been spiralling in on the same painful target. If Fei's still alive she'll arrive with the Imperial retinue. But what then? How will the Imperials treat her? It's not unknown for them to cut off the head of a messenger and return it to the sender to show they've rejected an unwelcome message. How will they treat a woman who's the daughter of a traitor and a rebel chief to boot? I can't even plead on her behalf.

There had been no more informal conversations with

Prince Kung since that tumultuous day in the Imperial gardens when news of the Hsien-feng Emperor's death arrived. The Prince had written, begging forgiveness that unfortunately his time was now wholly taken up with preparations for the Emperor's return and the settling of the succession, but Lindley knew it was not the truth. He had come to know the man well enough to realize he was embarrassed and avoiding difficult explanations. He knew about Fei, and no permission to travel to Nanking had been issued.

'If you want something doing around here,' he muttered grimly, 'you've got to do it yourself.'

'Massa Lin-li!'

He turned, hearing the legation's Hong Kong Chinese housekeeper banging excitedly through the doors into the entrance hall. 'What is it, A-choi?'

The entire household appeared, a dozen faces ready to drink in the news. 'Massa, massa! Emprah come! Ai ye! This one piecee Manchu coming big-time! Plenty big fuss and all!'

'Where?'

A-choi's eyes shone. 'Nor'-ees gate!'

Lindley felt something snap inside him.

'Fetch me a horse, A-choi.'

'Horse?'

'Yes, you know ... mah!' He picked up Bruce's cavalry crop and slapped the arm of a sofa. 'A horse! Mah!'

A-choi looked at him with astonishment. 'You want horse? Where I get horse?'

'Mr Bruce's horse, you imbecile!'

He opened a drawer and checked the chambers of two heavy revolvers – a Webley 48-gauge and a Tranter double-trigger revolver. Both were powerful modern six-shooters.

He looked up to see A-choi hovering, horrified. 'Massa, what for you need horse this time? Nobody allowed to go street when Emprah come.'

'Just bring me the bloody horse, A-choi!'

Fei marched beside the white palanquins as the wall towers of the capital came in sight in the far distance. The road here was dry and dusty, the land around cultivated but deserted. Everyone had fled to hide their faces. The procession had lengthened as stragglers failed to keep up and the pace at the head of the column was kept up relentlessly. She recalled the horrifying night just before they had reached Kou-pei K'ou when she had thought everything was lost. Her hand had searched for her dagger hilt, the Empress had squeezed her son to her. They had been dressed in white mourning robes and, unable to hide, they had prepared to die by a mountain stream.

Strange, Fei thought, that they did not seem to be the Dowager Empress and the Son of Heaven in that moment. They were simply a mother and a five year-old child. Because of the noise of the rain and water rushing in a stream nearby I could not hear the soldiers coming towards us, but the Empress must have sensed them, because she picked up her little boy and ran out onto the road.

The horsemen had caught Yehonala almost immediately, but they were the guardsmen of her own clan and when they saw who she was they fell down before her.

The bodyguard captain, Jung-lu, had knelt in the pouring rain. 'I was ready to kill the Regents,' he told his mistress. 'But then I recieved a message from one of them that Su-shun had staked everything on an ambush. You were to be killed by "bandits" at Kou-pei K'ou. Forgive me for acting without orders, Lady, but I decided it was more important to protect the Emperor than to kill traitors.'

Su-shun's ambush never came. With the escort swelled to three times its original size and the benefit of surprise stolen away an attack had become impossible. At Kou-pei K'ou the road had started to come down from the mountains. The weather had cleared, and then their progress had been set at a furious pace.

Fei watched now as a Court runner was guided to Yehonala's palanquin by one of the escort. The runner threw himself down in the dust, then, as the palanquin passed he handed up a sealed letter.

It must come from Prince Kung, Fei thought, seeing the runner's livery colours.

Yehonala read the letter, her eyes flashing like jet, then she ordered, 'We must push on faster to the An-ting Gate. Bring three teams of fresh bearers. The Emperor and I, and the Empress of the Eastern Palace will leave the rest of the retinue behind. Tell Jung-lu and the Bordered Blue to escort me. I want every available soldier.'

Guards turned to obey. Concern gripped Fei as the Empress's palanquin bearers began to jog forward.

She sensed that to be separated from Yehonala at this crucial time would set her at a disadvantage. She ran to the Chief Eunuch's palanquin. An Te-hai had been watching what was happening and reaching the same conclusion. He ordered his own bearers to follow, but four men of the Bordered Blue pulled their horses across the road and slowed them to a walk, allowing the Empress to draw away.

'What about us, Master An?' she asked discreetly.

An shot her a deadly glance. 'We are ordered to follow.'

As the Empress's palanquin disappeared into the distance she prayed again for the success of her holy duty. A huge prize was at stake: peace, and the official recognition of a Taiping state in the South. If the events of the next twelve hours moved in her favour, half of China would become Christian.

The land outside Peking's walls was flat and open, tilled fields that would normally have been heavily peopled by peasants. Nothing stirred, but then a movement caught her eye. It was a horseman, galloping towards them. The horse was large and powerful and the rider kicked it forward furiously. As he approached the head of the column the four leading horses of the Bordered Blue detached to interrupt him. He swerved, and then she saw it was Lindley.

He talked with the guard, but the riders would not let him come closer. She could see his face as he negotiated, see his agitation, and the way he looked for her. When he saw her he shouted.

'Fei! It's me! Hey! Fei-ch'ien!'

The soldiers screened him from her. She saw their uncertainty – their only experience of Europeans was the mauling they had taken at the hands of the foreign army, and they did not know the present situation inside the walls of the capital. An Te-hai's eyes were wide. He shrank back, struck dumb with fear at the strangely garbed barbarian.

Fei gasped. Everything had suddenly become hideous. She wanted to shout to Lindley, tell him to go away, and not to interfere at this most critical time, but she could not. He shouted her name again, then kicked his horse forward, trying now to force a way through. The column came to a halt. It seemed for a moment that the guard were going to let him through, but then An Te-hai's palanquin sagged as two terrified porters abandoned their load. The Chief Eunuch began to yell, and one of the Bordered Blue brought his lance to the advance and another nocked an arrow to his bow.

'No!' Fei shouted.

Lindley tried to argue with them. His face was reddening, and the soldiers were stirred up like hornets now. An Te-hai's panic communicated itself to the others. All around Fei maids were screaming. The sight of this European confirmed every story they had ever been told.

'Get out of my way, God damn you!' Lindley shouted at the lancer. 'Fei! Come here!'

She stumbled forward, hoping to calm the soldiers, but their horses were moving dangerously, their hooves stamping the earth. Then one of the guards reached for Lindley's reins and another jabbed his lance up towards his face. Lindley grabbed the lance, directed its tip under his arm and kicked his horse forward. It was impossible to pull it from the soldier's grip, or the soldier from his saddle, but for a moment they struggled, Lindley's big mount wheeling about like a river junk among pirate boats. Then the lance shaft snapped and in almost the same moment the bowman loosed his arrow.

At short range he could not miss. The arrow seemed to pass straight through Lindley's chest, but the archer had drawn his mark on the foreigner's strangely-shaped jacket and the arrow had flown harmlessly through an outstretched flap. Fei watched with horror as Lindley flung down the broken lance, pulled a pistol and shot it into the air.

Instantly, maids and eunuchs ran crouching for the roadside ditch. The two Bordered Blue riders closest to Lindley drew their swords, but circled away. The bowman began fitting another arrow to his bow. When she saw it, Fei screamed and ran forward. Lindley fired off a second shot and the bowman's horse reared. Then Fei felt herself swept up by Lindley's arm and the big horse galloping free.

*

Yehonala looked up at the huge vermilion ramparts of the Wu Men – the Meridian Gate – and prepared to leave behind her loyal escort. Every time in the past that she had seen these looming, blood-stained walls, she had felt only dread and foreboding. This time it was different. She felt the flow of the tao and took courage. I am no longer merely the Emperor's second wife, she thought, valuing her new official prestige. I am the Emperor's mother.

Even so, as she stepped down from the white palanquin she found it impossible not to stare up at those lethal battlements that enclosed the main entrance of the Forbidden City on three sides, or to notice the fearsome Imperial guards who flanked the gates. She could not help wondering what dangers waited for her inside.

Behind her a precious load, as heavy as jade and wrapped in a protective cloth, was transferred into a small, open palanquin. She climbed in beside it and was for the first time carried into the Forbidden City through the portal reserved for persons of Imperial blood.

The bearers carried her smoothly over the second of the five marble bridges that spanned Golden Water – another honour. Heavily-armed elite guards were ranged along the many marble terraces and to each side of the internal gates. Favoured doors opened like magic before her. Her heart beat savagely. It had been a long time since she had felt the tao flowing so strongly in her favour, and it was unnerving. Isn't it true that good fortune follows bad and vice-versa? she thought. Like yin and yang they are twisted together. You must take care to keep proper rhythm when the music of the cosmos plays for you.

A white marble dragon snout projecting from the corner of the lowest stone rail showed its teeth in an enigmatic smile that reminded her of Su-shun. When the palanquin came to rest she got out outside a plain side building.

Nearby a dozen men had gathered in secret conclave. Prince Kung welcomed her as she appeared. Inside she saw ranged together Prince Ch'un of the Blood, allies Wen-Hsiang and Kuei-Liang of the new Grand Council, General Shen-pao and the Censor Tang Yuan-chun. When she entered, they stood up.

'The Emperor's bier will arrive in Peking in three days' time,' she announced. 'With it will come seven traitors who have dared represent themselves as a Council of Regents. You all know what must be done.'

The officials looked to her, then to Prince Kung. His approval never wavered. All of them understood perfectly.

Prince Kung said. 'Did you bring it with you?'

'Yes.'

'Where is it?'

'I have it safe. We cannot fail while the power of the law is in our hands.'

Prince Kung nodded, thoughtfully. Then the Imperial party moved outside to take their places in the Hall of Supreme Harmony. On the way they were joined by the Empress of the Eastern Palace, and together they made their entrance.

Everything had been minutely orchestrated by Prince Kung. The usual rituals were performed and correct obeisance made. It was all done in such a way that the two Empresses' ranks were formally established. One aspect was stressed: no doubt was to be left in the minds of those standing respectfully in the Great Hall concerning the precise degree of respect that must in future be accorded to the Emperor's mother.

When it was time for Yehonala to speak she addressed them with shocking directness.

'The Annals of the Hsien-feng Reign will clearly show that the displeasure of Heaven fell upon this Empire. This was when Prince Yi was Chief Advisor, and when Su-shun's clique began exerting undue influence over His Imperial Majesty. This clique failed to conclude peace negotiations with the Outer Barbarians, then tried to avoid responsibility by treacherously arresting the Barbarian emissaries – an act which led directly to the burning down of our Summer Palace. Because of these circumstances the Hsien-feng Emperor was forced, greatly against his will, to abandon his capital. Be not deceived! This clique is now planning to destroy those of you with whom Su-shun has no understanding.' She paused, looking each in turn in the eye. 'Therefore, for your own sakes, every loyal officer of the Empire should consider how best to secure his position, and take care over what will be his own entry in the Book of History presently being written.'

*

Lindley struggled to subdue his captive as she fought to get free.

'God help me, woman, I'll knock you cold if you don't stop fighting me!'

Fei's hair cascaded wildly as she tried to throw herself off the horse, but he held her firm across the saddle and all her flailing was useless.

The Tientsin road was normally thronging with people, but not today. News of the boy-Emperor's return to the capital had sent everyone scurrying back to their houses. Even the mandarins had taken refuge in their yamens.

Once the horse had galloped clear of danger Lindley reined in and dismounted. There was blood on his jacket, and a ragged tear where the arrow had grazed his ribs. Even so, when Fei faced him she was furious, her eyes glassy with tears. 'How dare you interfere? How dare you?' she demanded.

'Fei, you're not thinking straight.'

'Why, Lin-li?' Her face twisted in anger. 'Don't you understand what you've done? You kidnapped me like a . . . like a stupid animal!'

He smouldered at her incredible ingratitude, then shot out a finger and snarled back, 'I just saved your bloody life, madam! Don't you understand?'

She marched away from him. 'I must do my duty!'

He ran after her and grabbed her. 'You've done your duty! You've gone far beyond it. How many times must I tell you? It was never your duty to die needlessly.'

'I am prepared to die.'

'And Yehonala will happily oblige you.' He pulled out the copy of her father's punishment warrant. 'Read this. The moment she takes power – and she will – you'll cease to be useful to her. You would have lost your head. Her excuse is right here.'

'I knew Yehonala for many months. You never even spoke to her.'

'I know Prince Kung though. And the way the Forbidden City works. There's not a chance Yehonala would have honoured any of her promises.'

Her fury was unabated. 'By what right do you make decisions for me?'

'What else could I do? You wouldn't have come along by persuasion. I knew that.'

'By what right?'

'Fei . . . I love you.'

'Love? What right is that? I don't need your stupid love. I don't want it.'

That cut him more than anything else she could have said.

'Fei, that's not true.'

'Very true, pig-dung bastard!'

He let her go, and a long silence stretched out before he said. 'Fei, I've had a taste of their torture cells. I wasn't prepared for you to die at their hands. Power corrupts. Always. I thought you knew that. Why can't you look to the future instead of the past? We're going to Nanking together. Just as we dreamed, but never thought could happen. Just as we wished when we threw our coins in the well.'

She took off her slipper and threw it at him. It passed inches from his head. 'Don't talk politics with me. You're only good for one thing!'

He grabbed her again. 'God help me, woman . . .'

'Because of you I'm returning empty-handed,' she said as he loomed over her. 'I could have won half of China for Our Lord. So much for your water-well fairy!'

'Because of me you're returning at all, you ungrateful little baggage.'

'I'm not returning. I'm going back to Peking!'

He put his face in hers. 'Listen! We can do this the hard way or the easy way, but you are going to Tientsin. Now get on the horse!'

She did as she was told, he knew, only because there was no practical alternative. The road stayed clear until dusk, when a light traffic appeared for an hour or so before the curfew. Peasants and townsfolk looked up at them with curious but unafraid eyes. So much out of the ordinary had happened in the past year that they were beyond astonishment. They passed the place where Lindley had been arrested, and crossed the bridge where the beheadings had taken place. A pain speared him when he thought of those who would never return, and he was glad to have the revolver in his pocket.

Fei clung to him as they rode through the night. 'What

389

you don't know,' she told him, more calm now, 'is that the Lady Yehonala's title is now Tz'u-hsi. It means "Motherly and Auspicious". She has become Dowager Empress. She has made promises to me. Promises about ending the war.'

'Fei, things are very different in the South now. There's been some fierce fighting.'

'Has Shanghai fallen to us yet?'

'No, and it never will.' He told her what he knew about the vast Imperialist armies assembled by General Tseng, and how they had been engaging Taiping troops all along the Yangtze valley, 'Things have changed, Fei. And they'll change a lot more, if I'm any judge.'

A little later she said, 'I never wanted to betray you, Lin-li. You must believe that.'

He felt a cloud pass across his soul. 'I do.'

'I was entrusted with a holy duty.'

'And I was in the way of it.'

'I do love you, Lin-li.'

'And I love you.'

'But there is still duty.'

Later, as they were approaching Tientsin, he asked her about his father. She said, 'Lin-li, your father has been our immortal founder's first and foremost spiritual guide.'

'Mr Ward told me that your Heavenly King first learned about Christianity from my father in Canton. At first I didn't know whether to believe him or not. Why didn't you tell me what you knew sooner?'

'There was never a right moment.'

He let it go at that, then after a while he asked, 'What did you wish at the wishing well?'

'Only to be with you again.'

'Nothing about your duty?'

'No,' she told him. 'That's God's work. How could a fairy in a well do anything about that?'

He drew a deep breath, weary of her contradictions. 'I want you to tell me about my father.'

'In the T'ien Wang's young days He read a tract called Ch'uan-shih Liang Yeh – "Good News to Exhort the Age". It was written out by Liang A-fa, who was one of your father's converts. Later our Heavenly King sought out your father in Canton, and then in Hong Kong, so much did he thirst for

Christian knowledge. Your father has been our guiding light. It was he who organized the rifles for us.'

Lindley felt his weariness deepen. 'Why couldn't you tell me?'

'Because I couldn't afford to trust you.'

'Not even after we made love?'

'If you had known maybe you would have been unable to keep the secret from your face. Maybe you would have been taken by Governor Wu's men and tortured. I didn't want that.'

'I wish you had trusted me.'

'Trust is often dangerous. Of course, I wanted to come to your house to tell you everything and to beg your forgiveness, but when I did so I was caught.'

'That was when you brought the letter from my father?'

'Yes.'

Lindley nodded thoughtfully. Then he said, 'I still don't understand why Wu let you go.'

'Because he wanted me to carry my message to Peking. He believes that General Tseng wants to place his own nominee as Governor of Kiangsu. With every month the war continues General Tseng's power is growing. Peace was Governor Wu's only hope of promotion.'

'Fei, I want you to promise you won't ever betray me again.'

'I won't. Ever.'

'Do you mean that? To the centre of your heart?'

'Yes.'

They rode to the river as the dawn began to break splendidly and full in the east. Lindley went aboard the first large British-flagged ship he saw. The captain was not pleased to be roused from his bunk so early, but he only had to look once at Prince Kung's giant pearl to agree to the stranger's request for passage to Shanghai.

The great roofed guard-tower that stood over Peking's open An-ting Gate swallowed a road that had been screened off on both sides for more than a mile. The fence was yellow cotton, too high to be looked over. Inside the gate, the sand-strewn square was cordoned by a line of guards carrying pole blades, and beyond them thousands of monks in maroon robes and yellow horn-shaped helmets

391

sat cross-legged in rows, murmuring over the sacred lamaist scriptures spread in their laps. Hundreds of senior mandarins in mourning white surrounded the square itself. To one side a platform had been raised under an awning, and three empty thrones set there. The atmosphere was tense with expectation.

In sight now, like an approaching army, was Hsien-feng's last Imperial procession, a great host of thousands, and almost at the head the yellow bier, curtains shimmering, the pagoda roof of golden scales glittering in the sun. The steady announcement of gongs grew louder. Three beats, then a pause, then three more, and so on, unending. The lines of robed and hatted bearers carrying Hsien-feng's catafalque swayed in time to the baleful beat. They passed into the shadow of the great grey tower of the An-ting Men, and so entered the Manchu City.

Prince Kung and the two Empresses appeared. Each came forward and Prince Kung and Niuhuru went to occupy the gilded side thrones that waited for them. Yehonala lifted her son onto her knee, and sat on the central dragon throne. The boy wore the appropriate robes and hat of the Son of Heaven, only in miniature.

The first of many dozens of palanquins was turning the corner and progressing toward the centre of a square surrounded by screens and armed men. Every mandarin and eunuch who could be found had been dressed in white to swell the reception. The site and the narrow route to it had been carefully chosen to be too small to allow the bier's following cavalry escort to enter.

When rank upon rank of Court officials rose in silence to their feet the tension in the air was immense. Then the bier came to a halt, and everyone dropped simultaneously into the most respectful of kowtows.

From her position in the very eye of the ceremonial, Yehonala waited, her dress and make-up perfect, her son moving restlessly on her lap.

'Hush now, Tsai-ch'un,' she whispered, her lips barely moving. 'If you're a good boy now, later we'll go and play with Mr White Rabbit.'

Tsai-ch'un grinned. 'I like Mr White Rabbit.'

'Be a good boy, then. Sit up straight and listen to what mummy says.'

The bier came to rest. She watched Prince Kung step forward to offer obeisance, knowing that the future was poised on a razor's edge. Two more of Hsien-feng's half brothers and the Grand Secretaries Kuei-Liang and Chou Tsu-p'ei had been delegated to receive the Regents. She breathed again as they fell dutifully into position as arranged. It seemed that the iron trap was closing around Su-shun exactly according to plan, but much had still to happen faultlessly before it could sever his head.

The Regents got down from their palanquins and came forward. Su-shun approached the platform now, his face hard and unflinching. There was silence as Prince Kung gave the required formal thanks to him for having brought the late Emperor home to his capital, then it was Yehonala's turn to speak.

'The Ch'i-hsiang Emperor wishes to say this: we are grateful to you and your colleagues, Su-shun, for the services you have rendered as guardians of our father's coffin. However, Prince Kung has now performed the Rites that have renewed the Mandate of Heaven for our dynasty. In recognition of this fact, from this day forward our reign title shall be T'ung-chih – "Return to Order". Su-shun, you are hereby formally relieved of all duties.'

Su-shun made no move, but launched into a prepared speech, his powerful voice full of Confucian authority. 'Only the Chien Kuo and the legally-appointed Board of Regents speaks for His Imperial Majesty. Until he is grown to adulthood no one has the power to remove or interfere with the . . .'

But no one was listening. All heads were turned toward the throne. On his mother's knee, the Emperor fidgeted. He leaned his head back and looked at the sky. A loud yawn escaped him.

'. . . the Board legally appointed by the late Emperor, and in accordance with his will, which he made known . . .'

Su-shun's voice faltered. The line of Regents looked around, their faces drained. Officers of the Imperial Guard came forward and indicated that Su-shun must go with them. He hesitated. His eyes flicked from face to face, seeing blank expressions where he had counted on support. He seemed suddenly nauseated by the impossibility of escape.

He raised his voice again, but it had lost its resonance. 'By what right do you presume to make this request? By what right?'

There was no answer.

At a signal, Su-shun was physically seized. He did not struggle. His dignity was acknowledged personally by Prince Kung, and the guards were ordered to release him. He walked from the square, flanked by guards. Prince Yi, Prince Cheng and the other Regents followed.

Yehonala spoke again, her own voice echoing like a flute in the silence. 'The following Decree, the first of the T'ung-chih reign, bears the imprint of the Seal of Legally Sanctioned Authority:

"Last year the coasts of our Empire were disturbed and our capital put in danger. These misfortunes, we know, are due to those princes and ministers who took it upon themselves to advise our late father. Su-shun and his colleagues failed to establish peace. Then they tried to escape responsibility by treacherously arresting foreigners, an act which led to the burning down of our Summer Palace. In consequence, the Emperor, our father, was forced, wholly against his will, to leave his capital.

'Subsequently His Imperial Majesty's health suffered severely from the cold climate of Jehol and from his arduous labours and anxiety, so that he died. When we heard of this our sorrow was as a burning fire! When we consider how wickedly deceitful has been the conduct of Su-shun and his colleagues, we say that the whole Empire must unite in their condemnation.

'Undoubtedly they took advantage of our extreme youth and of the Empresses' lack of experience in statecraft. They have tried to make fools of us. But how could they hope to make fools of the whole Empire?

'Leniency on our part would be an offence to the memory of our departed father and an insult to the Chinese people, therefore it is our intention to punish them. Su-shun, the Prince Yi and the Prince Cheng are hereby removed from their posts. Ching Shou, Mu Yin, Kuang Tu-han and Chiao Yu-ying are also removed from the Grand Council. Let Prince Kung, in consultation with the Grand Secretaries, the Six Boards and the Nine Ministries, consider and report to us the proper punishment which is to be inflicted upon them. Regarding the manner in which the Empresses shall administer the Government as Regents, let this also be discussed and a Memorial submitted so that future procedure may be decided." '

BOOK V

Lindley watched Fei as the Yangtze waters slid by, limitlessly pleased that he had abandoned all reason in Peking. He had kidnapped her because there had been no other way to get through to her. Still, he had laid hold of a wildcat, and in doing so he had risked losing her. Even now he was not wholly sure she had forgiven him.

When they had reached Shanghai Consul Meadows had met them and arranged secret accommodation aboard the *Taikoo*, a British flagged clipper anchored in the middle of the Huang-pu into which they transferred in the middle of the night.

'It's not very comfortable,' Meadows had said, 'but it's the only place you can be sure Governor Wu's spies won't find you.'

Heavy fighting up-country had delayed the *Taikoo*. She was one of Eden Phillips's hulls, waiting to take aboard a cargo of silk. They stayed aboard her until Meadows came to them again and said it might be possible finally to get a steamer through to Nanking.

'By the way, the boat and the dozen or so heavily-armed Filipinos who appear to be on board it come courtesy of your American friend.'

'You mean Colonel Ward?' Lindley asked, surprised.

'You're behind the times. He's calling himself "General" these days.'

'How did you persuade him to lend me his boat?'

'I didn't. When he heard you were back he offered it. It's a little thank you for the military mandarin rank you procured for him.'

Lindley laughed. 'But . . . I did nothing of the sort.'

Meadows' eyebrows arched. 'Lindley, of course you did. According to the Provincial Governor of Kiangsu you recommended Ward's character to Prince Kung. That kind of thing counts for a lot here.'

Lindley mused. 'So, Ward got a suit of mandarin robes . . .'

'Yes, and he got married in them too.'

Lindley was astonished. 'Good God! Who did he marry?'

'Yang Fang's daughter. The Chinese like to keep business matters in the family, and Yang Fang is no exception. What surprised me is that Ward actually seems to be quite attached to the girl.'

Lindley laughed at the Consul's extraordinary dryness. 'Well, good for him!'

Fei turned away from the river now and looked to him. Lindley smiled back. The great bend of the Yangtze began to open out ahead. Here the Son of the Ocean was half a mile wide, but narrowing with high ground rising along the south bank. Ningpo Sam steered for the deep channel. Consul Meadows had warned of a blockade of Imperial junks which they would have to run, but he had also said that with the river in spate any blockade would be no match for a steamer like the *Hyson*. The Taipings had lost control of the Lower Yangtze, but the fortress of Chiu-fu-chou still commanded the approaches to Nanking. Once they passed under its guns no Imperial junk would be able to follow them.

'We're almost there,' Fei told him, her eyes shining. 'Do you see Purple Mountain? You'll be surprised at your welcome. Taiping people are always very happy people. Whereas the lowliest Manchu official always receives foreigners with a most insulting hauteur and considers himself degraded by contact, here you will be met by fellow Christians who want only to show brotherly friendship.'

'How about showing a little friendship now?' he asked, putting his arm around her.

She moved away from him uneasily.

'What? Not one little kiss before we arrive?' Since passing the last squeeze station Ward's Filipinos had had nothing to do, and they sat around on the *Hyson*'s deck, their green uniform jackets unbuttoned. Lindley thought their presence might be unsettling Fei. 'Don't worry about them,' he said. 'They're Catholics. They don't mind.'

Fei turned to him earnestly. 'I must tell you that in the

Heavenly Kingdom adultery is looked on as a very serious crime. There must be no more.'

'Adultery? What are you talking about?'

'Adultery is sex unsanctioned by marriage. What we did was adultery. If anyone finds out, we can be punished for it. Even flirting is impossible.'

He felt all the joy go out of him. 'No flirting? What do single people do in the Heavenly Kingdom?'

'Single men are soldiers. And single women are not allowed to exist. Every woman must either be married, or be a member of a family.'

'What if her husband's been killed and she has no family?'

'In that case she is taken into one of the institutions for unprotected females. They are there to educate and protect young girls who lose their natural guardians, or those married women whose husbands are away on public duty. In Nanking there is no prostitution. It is punishable by death.'

He raised his eyebrows. 'Death? Surely you don't go along with that.'

'It is our law.'

For a long time he watched the mountain turning slowly, felt the impending rain. His desire had collapsed for the moment, leaving him with an ill-defined hunger.

'Did I tell you that Mr Ward had married?' he asked her suddenly. 'He's found himself a Chinese bride.'

'Yes.'

'Then why don't we? Now. We're aboard a boat. And Ningpo Sam is captain.'

She met his eye instantly. 'We? Marry?'

'Yes. Why not?'

'I must have my father's permission.'

'Of course, but – do you think he would object?'

'Perhaps not.'

'Only "perhaps not"?'

'In the Heavenly Kingdom we do not marry for love.' She blinked rapidly. 'Nor is it a daughter's place to usurp her father's prerogatives. And you are . . .'

'. . . and I am, after all, an Outer Barbarian.' His smile mocked her. 'I thought you Taipings were meant to be progressive – people who smash the past in order to create a new and better society.'

'Even in the Heavenly Kingdom we are still Chinese. A

Taiping is allowed one wife, and to her he must be regularly married by one of our ministers.'

'That suits me. We'll do it tomorrow.'

'A Taiping may marry only when considered worthy, and after permission has been given.' She looked to him penetratingly. 'Lin-li, the custom of casting off a wife at pleasure, or selling her, or divorcing does not find favour with us. The marriage knot, when once tied, can never be undone.'

'I have no intention of undoing it. I asked you, will you marry me? I didn't say anything about divorce.'

'If and when my father says a marriage is allowable, then we shall be able to marry.'

'Well, tell him I paid a priceless pearl for you. Prince Kung gave it to me. He told me that if I'd ground it up and eaten it instead, it would have caused me to live for ever.'

'He'll think you're a crazy man.'

'I don't care much what he thinks. I want to know what you think. Do you want to marry me?'

She frowned and looked at her lap.

'I'll take that as a "yes", shall I?'

She nodded, and he saw that tell-tale half-pout on her lips. 'Yes. What do you think?'

'Good.'

He fell silent, quietly pleased, but a greater worry remained. He had noticed the changes in her as they neared Nanking. With every mile she had grown quieter, her manner more formal. After long periods in his company her inner self always emerged, but now she was withdrawing again, becoming the dutiful Taiping once more. Part of his mind told him that once she passed inside the walls of the city she would be the Heavenly King's property once again.

His eyes took in the broad sweep of land that lay below Purple Mountain, its summit now wreathed in low white cloud. Then he saw the gigantic grey walls snaking around the hilly contours, and enclosed within them a large and ancient city.

'Oh, now that's truly incredible,' he said, hands on hips at the rail, staring at the vastness. 'Those walls must be forty feet high and all of twenty miles around!'

'Thirty-five miles,' Fei told him. 'They're thirty feet deep at the top, the greatest city walls ever built. They were ordered five hundred years ago by Hung-wu, who was the very first Ming Emperor. The Ming dynasty made their capital here.'

He thought of the way the city walls of Old Shanghai had impressed him on his first arrival, but these walls were ten times as impressive. Each roofed tower flew a huge black triangle of silk as a banner. 'Look at those gatehouses – you could garrison five thousand men in each of them. What kind of stone is that?'

'It's not stone, Lin-li. It's brick. Each one is signed by its maker so that everyone would know who had supplied the best bricks, and who the worst. They were contributed by every village for a hundred li around. There is also a moat.'

'A moat? You mean all the way?'

'Yes. You can't see it from here, but the north-eastern side of the city has a lake that connects with the moat. That lake has islands with walkways between and is very beautiful. There is also a second earth wall outside these main walls. That one runs for two hundred li.'

'Good God! That's seventy miles!' He marvelled at the gigantic scale of the endeavour. Edinburgh Castle, impressive as it was, was a tiny pinprick of a fortress compared to this, as were all the fortresses of Europe.

'I can easily see why the T'ien Wang chose Nanking as his capital. How on earth did he manage to capture it?'

'You must not call this city Nanking any more, Lin-li. "Nanking" means "Southern Capital", just as "Peking" means "Northern Capital". When the T'ien Wang took it as his own he renamed it "T'ienching" – the Heavenly Capital.'

'But I can't understand how he got inside – how anyone could ever get inside – if the people already in possession decided not to allow it.'

'The people welcomed us in. You must remember that when the T'ien Wang marched his army along the Yangtze valley all the discontented people flocked to his banner. They heard his message and knew that salvation and freedom had come at last. When he reached the city our Heavenly King's army numbered three million. The city threw open every one of its seventeen gates in joy.' She smiled, pleased to be able to tell him of the movement's greatest victory.

'But what about the Manchu garrison? I was told there

401

were twenty thousand men here, with their families. What happened to them?'

'They were all killed.'

He turned to her. 'But . . . what happened to their women and children?'

She turned to look at the city and the ominously darkening sky. 'It was said of the enemy that not a root must be left to sprout.'

They were nearing the port now and Lindley saw a vigorous commerce going on along the river bank. Hundreds of porters – both men and women – were unloading small boats with baskets of fish and boxes of vegetables and a hundred other kinds of produce from small craft. All wore long hair, either loose to the shoulder, or bound up in colourful turbans.

Here and there were overseers armed with obsolete matchlocks and steel-tipped bamboo spears. They began to mass as the steamer closed with the quay. Their leader directed the boat to come alongside. Lindley saw they were all dressed in the fashion of the people who had ransacked the *Hyson* – trousers of black silk bound round the waist with sashes, short red jackets and long hair braided with red and black cords wrapped around their heads. Each had a sword thrust into his sash. One or two of them carried pistols. The sight of them unsettled him more than he imagined it would. It unsettled the green-jacketed Filipinos aboard the *Hyson* more, and Ningpo Sam stood in silence on the open bridge, his revolver holstered but visible on his belt and hostility showing in his stance.

The quay was hung with thick mats to prevent boats scraping their sides. As the riverboat touched, men threw securing ropes across the gap to hold her briefly against the current. Lindley saw Fei's excitement heighten as she climbed up onto the stone jetty. There was a brief exchange with the leader of the armed men, then he followed and they began to head for the nearest gate.

Lindley looked back through the milling crowds and waved once to the *Hyson* which was already pulling warily away. Neither Ningpo Sam nor any of the Filipinos on deck returned his wave. He then looked to where a line of people queued at the checkpoint, tattered papers in their hands, but he and Fei were waved through urgently. A dozen armed men were detached as escort. Lindley was urged towards a tunnel-like entrance that burrowed for a hundred paces through the massive gatehouse. As he passed along it he felt an inner coldness seize him.

I'm here at last, he thought, the realization hard and sudden. Here, inside the citadel of Nanking. An hour from now I could be talking with my father. God, if you're there and listening, grant me that.

As they emerged the vista widened. He saw a reception square surrounded by the usual sprawl of houses and stalls, but the usual temples and red-columned mandarin yamen were not there. He supposed they had been pulled down and replaced by other buildings.

'See how Taiping men are released from the shaven head?' Fei said, her smile bright. 'Have we not given the people back their dignity? Is not their noble appearance utterly different to that of the crushed-down people of Manchu-governed cities? They are free Christian souls.'

He looked around and nodded. 'They seem quite well-nourished too, considering the siege. And so many women are at work outdoors. Is that usual?'

'The position of women here is completely different to their position in the Manchu-conquered parts of China. We have abolished female slavery. Here no man may keep concubines. This is Taiping law.'

'That's progress,' he said lightly. 'Admirable.'

Privately he compared her words with what Meadows had told him, that in the Taiping-held territories rigid rules governed everyone's lives, men were made to live separate from their wives and families, and that even minor transgressions were punished by death.

'Land was never redistributed as the T'ien Wang promised it would be,' Meadows had said. 'They just took it from the landlords, then laid it waste. Ownership has been abolished, and everything declared "common property", but the Taipings haven't founded the equality they boast about. Their leaders have banned unsanctioned sex among their followers on pain of death, yet they still maintain large personal harems for themselves. And the harem of the "Brother of Christ" is the largest of them all. He keeps eighty young girls locked up inside his palace.'

Lindley noted the incongruous sight of a huge timber

403

cross standing in the centre of the open area. An empty lectern was set up before it on a platform as if a speech was about to be made, while behind it, dominating the distant ground, there rose rank upon rank of ghostly pale palaces, resplendent with white walls and gilded roofs, a citadel that reminded him of the Forbidden City.

That must be the hall of the living god, he thought, touched with wonder despite himself. The T'ien Wang, the Heavenly King – the man who founded this extraordinary dream. What kind of man is it who is able to inspire millions to such inconceivable sacrifice on his behalf? Can he really be mad and evil as they say he is?

On the journey upstream Fei had told him of the heroic early struggles of the Taiping movement. She told him that the T'ien Wang had once been called simply by the human name, Hung Hsiu-ch'uan.

'The Hung family came from the mountains of the Far South, Lin-li, but Hsiu-ch'uan was taken up into Heaven and charged by God with the task of converting China to Christianity. So powerful were His words when He began to preach that His following soon swelled to many hundreds of thousands. When the Imperials tried to destroy His movement, ten years ago, He proclaimed himself T'ien Wang, and His followers "Taiping T'ien Kuo", which means "the Heavenly Kingdom of Great Peace". After that the Heavenly King put on a robe of Imperial yellow and ordered a march to the north.

'In the months that followed many Imperial armies were sent against us, but they were always destroyed. Every day we drew ever closer to the Yangtze valley, until eventually our armies cut off the great river port of Hankow. We captured it, and also the neighbouring cities of Hanyang and Wuchang. It was at this time that the Heavenly King showed His true purpose. Having fooled the Imperial armies into thinking He was going to march all the way to Peking, He moved instead against Nanking. What could be a better feint than a genuine strike transformed in mid-thrust to a different target?'

Lindley recalled the way her eyes had shone as she had told him. She had been very proud of Taiping achievements, and in awe of the Heavenly King. But what Ward had said, and what both Meadows and Elgin had confirmed about the

Taipings, had been less fulsome in praise of the movement. Fei made no mention of Hung Hsiu-ch'uan's fevered hallucinations, nor of the pirates and Triads who had flocked to his black banner. She had said nothing about how the Taiping army had suffered defeat at Yung-nan on their way to Nanking, nor had she admitted that the heroic Taiping field army that had actually marched on Peking had been cut to pieces on its retreat south.

He walked beside her through the streets, keeping his thoughts to himself, reserving judgement. Whatever Fei thought, and whatever she knew, she was not alone in her beliefs. Nanking appeared to be just what she had predicted: everywhere was ardent toil, and nowhere the pigtail or any other sign of Manchu overlordship. Red and white posters covered many of the walls – biblical quotations in Chinese, and slogans that exhorted the people to greater effort and deeper belief. He did not see a single foreign face, nor a single palanquin. The people seemed as contented with their lot as any in China.

But what about the Manchu garrison that surrendered here in the third year of Hsien-feng? he thought. The one that was slaughtered – man, woman and child, so that 'not a root was left to sprout'? Was that an example of Taiping justice?

When he looked behind he saw a crowd following their escort. There was frank curiosity on the people's faces and no sign of the hostility he had seen in Shanghai's Chinese city. Whenever he caught someone's eye, that person grinned at him, as if greeting a lost brother. They were pleased to see him, and made a sign at him by crossing their two index fingers, clearly hoping he would recognize the crucifix. When he made the sign back at them he heard their delight.

'You see how happy the people are?' Fei said, grinning.

'It's . . . surprising. What do they want?'

'Only to see you. Please forgive them. Most are country people whose families did not live by the coast. They have never seen a non-Chinese. They only know that you are one of our Christian brothers from across the Southern Ocean.'

It started to rain. By now they had come almost to the citadel in which the central palaces stood. They entered a high-walled compound overlooked by a series of grand gold and white buildings. The chattering crowd pushed into the large cobbled space that opened under the golden eaves of the gatehouse. They did not try to follow further.

'Welcome to my father's house,' Fei told him as they passed inside.

He looked up. 'It's . . . really quite something.'

The palaces within were every bit as impressive as those of the Forbidden City. They had been built only a few years before, and on the site once occupied by the Imperial palaces of the Ming dynasty. Their style was still undeniably Chinese, but it was somehow different, as if an altered set of rules had been used in their design. Perhaps it's their whiteness, Lindley thought, but these palaces seem even more celestial than those of Peking.

Fei led him up steps, through a reception room and into a magnificent hall where she was received by a group of awestruck servants. After she had despatched them she turned to Lindley. 'I must go to my father. Please make yourself comfortable. Tea will be brought.'

Yehonala's robes were Imperial yellow, trimmed with sable. She wore a band of large pearls round the coil of her hair, and a flaming pearl stood out on her forehead. This morning she had remained behind the yellow curtain hung at the rear of the Dragon Throne, coaching her son through the delivery of his latest Decree, ordering more troops to be poured into the war against the Taiping rebels.

An Te-hai took the fur mantle from Yehonala's shoulders and handed it carefully to his young assistant to pack away in its paper-lined cedar wood box. Today was the last day of the winter dress code. Tomorrow, whatever the weather, the Forbidden City would dress to greet the spring.

She allowed An to remove the precious flaming pearl from her forehead. It was large and in a setting of seed pearls and coral representing tongues of fire. Just before the winter solstice An had suggested that she should adopt this powerful jewel for official occasions, and she saw the wisdom of the idea immediately. The flaming pearl was an ancient Imperial emblem worked in fabrics and carvings wherever the five-clawed Imperial dragons were to be found. The pearl blazed with fire as a pair of dragons reached out their talons to seize it. 'The flaming pearl symbolizes omnipotence,' An explained to her. 'The dragons fight each other to gain it, but of course they can never attain it.'

All the while as An spoke Yehonala felt the vague disquiet of the tao churning inside her. And later when she went to inspect the Imperial silk dyeing vats, and walked with her son and Niuhuru among the hundreds of racks that held newly-dyed skeins, something about the Chief Eunuch's manner gnawed at her.

All around them the terraces blazed with vibrant colours. Yehonala led the boy-Emperor by the hand while Niuhuru, now entitled 'Joint-Empress Tz'uan' waited in the courtyard.

'Mother, why does the step-mother cry today?' he asked.

'Because she is so pleased. They are tears of joy because we do her honour by inviting her on this visit with us. And because now she is rich, where once she was quite poor. You have given her a title, my son.'

The T'ung-chih Emperor thought for a moment, then said brightly, 'I'm pleased I gave step-mother a title. I'm pleased I have two Regent-mothers.'

'That's right, my son. Two is the best number for Regents.' Yes, indeed, Yehonala thought, and added, 'But those titles only bring mother and stepmother a hundred thousand taels a year each. Fortunately, when your last Decree ordered the digging up of Su-shun's house the soldiers found an underground dungeon filled with millions of ounces of gold and silver.'

The child's eyes brightened. 'Can I see it?'

'Oh, no. It has been put away in safety. It was all stolen in the first place from the Board of Revenue. But don't worry it will not be wasted. Those Imperial confiscations have swelled your coffers and made you very powerful.'

She thought of the way Su-shun had been humbled, and a warm glow of satisfaction spread through her. At the trial the Censor, Tang Yuan-chun, had addressed the dock. 'Of the seven accused, one we find blameless: Ching-shou you are free to leave. All your former rights and privileges are restored.'

How the others stared at him! she thought with relish. Lucky for him he betrayed Su-shun's assassination plans when he did. Prince Yi should never have appointed him to the Board of Regents knowing he's married to one of Prince Kung's sisters.

The verdict had continued: 'Of the six who remain, all are stripped of title and property. Three of you were leaders in conspiracy, three mere followers. Mu Yin, Kuang Tu-han, Chao Yu-ying – you are committed to the prison of the Board of Corrections until further notice.'

Three necks saved by a clever political deal, Yehonala thought: three necks in exchange for support for my cause from their allies and relatives. Within five years their names will be salvaged and their positions reinstated.

The Censor had handed over proceedings to Prince Kung for the verdict on the nobles: 'Prince Yi, Cheng and Su-shun, you have each been found guilty of the second of the Ten Abominations, that of subverting the state. In accordance with the law, therefore, the punishment of dismemberment and the lingering death shall be inflicted upon you. These executions are to be carried out in public, as with common felons.' Su-shun had ground his teeth, fuming with hatred. The Princes had made no sound, but continued to stare at the floor. They had heard the verdict, but it was merely an echo in a world that was now itself unreal.

'In addition, the Memorial of our Imperial Commission recommends that the Princedoms of Yi and Cheng shall be attainted. All Su-shun's offspring are forbidden to hold state office in future. All Su-shun's property is to be confiscated. It is unanimously determined that the law allows of no leniency, but the private law of our dynasty allows discretion where Princes of the Blood are concerned. Therefore, the Princes Yi and Cheng are hereby permitted to proceed immediately to the "Empty Chamber" and their souls are instructed to begin their wanderings beside the Nine Springs.'

'The Nine Springs' was the poetical term for Purgatory. Yehonala recalled the coolness with which Prince Kung had closed the proceedings. I was right, she thought, never – under any circumstances – to give you the Seal of Legally Sanctioned Authority. You're a very wicked fellow at heart. What's more, you've always wanted to be Emperor, and I certainly don't trust you now any more than I did when Hsien-feng was alive.

So finally Su-shun was executed like a common criminal in the Cabbage Market, she thought, pleased with herself. And to add to the bargain I've inherited a most efficient and extensive spy system from my old adversary. How ironic – and yet how like the tao – that such amazing greed should come to nothing in the end . . .

'What shall I spend all that gold and silver on?' the boy-Emperor asked An Te-hai, still mesmerized by the idea of Su-shun's glistening millions.

An bobbed his head indulgently. 'What would you like to spend it on, Imperial Majesty?'

Yehonala put a hand on Tsai-ch'un's arm. 'The building of your father's tomb is very costly and will take two more years. He must be buried in grandeur according to the ancient Rites as soon as the tomb is finished. Don't forget, your father was a very great Emperor.'

The boy darted away to chase a beautiful blue butterfly into the gardens. He ran after it and pounced clumsily every time it settled. After the fifth time he was breathless and toppled over a tree root, grazing his hands. There were tears, and when Yehonala knelt to comfort him he said, 'Look what it made me do!' He picked up a handful of gravel and threw it after the butterfly.

'Bad temper!' Yehonala said firmly, straightening his arms by his side to make him listen. 'It is not permitted for an Emperor to show anger. Anger is an energy that others can always turn and use against you. Next time, if you want to capture a butterfly, send a eunuch to do your bidding. That is the way.'

'I wonder why you said that to His Imperial Majesty?' An Te-hai asked when the boy had wandered away again.

'What do you mean?'

'About Hsien-feng being a very great emperor.'

She looked to him, uneasy again and alerted by his presumption. 'In China, it's never a good idea to speak ill of the dead.'

'This land is so full of ghosts,' he said distantly, his lips pursing.

'Whereas much can be gained by revering those who are past hurting us.'

'And rectifying those who are not past hurting us.'

He said it glancingly but in a deliberate voice, so that Yehonala knew his meaning. He wants me to move against Prince Kung, she thought. How like a child he is. A child who tries to enlist the aid of a parent against another child by telling tales.

She chose the quiet evenness of tone that usually deterred further argument. 'You may be interested to know that I have succeeded in rectifying Prince Kung.'

An's eyes danced. 'Perhaps, but then perhaps not.'

'What else can he do?' she asked impatiently. 'There was a time when he truly believed I would step graciously back from the stage of government once Su-shun's clique was dust and our position secure. He should have known me better than that. I was never going to drift aside like Niuhuru.'

'His behaviour has recently become surly and sulky, like a man who considers himself betrayed. You have not bought him.'

'Betrayed by whom? What more can he reasonably want?' She wondered at this latest development. 'His Imperial Majesty has bestowed many gifts of jade and lacquer on Prince Kung, and other gifts less tangible but of greater worth. He has been appointed "Adviser on the Governing of the Empire". He is Director of the Tsung-li Yamen, and is therefore able to decide many matters which concern both the Outer Barbarians and the prosecution of the war in the South. His nominees Wen-Hsiang and Kuei-Liang have both become Grand Councillors, and two more will follow. He has even been excused the kowtow before the Emperor. Now I'll hear no more of it.'

'But you know what he really wants.'

'An, I said I'll hear no more of it.'

A junior eunuch ran up, prostrated himself and poured out a hasty announcement. 'Imperial Majesty, the Prince Kung comes!'

Prince Kung's face was wrathful. Yehonala saw An Te-hai watching him slyly, slipping his hands out of his sleeves and keeping his eyes down in a semblance of respect.

'Yehonala, I told you that I wanted to be included as Regent. Why have you ignored my wishes?'

'Have I?'

'You've made your opposition known publicly by issuing an Imperial Decree. Why?'

'His Imperial Majesty issues Imperial Decrees,' she said, waiting to see if he would dare unmask the fiction of government whose source was the will of a six-year-old boy. He did not.

'It would be better if His Imperial Majesty felt it was important to honour his uncle.'

'The Son of Heaven feels that the fewer Regents there are the better.'

Her words inflamed him. 'So – just two Empresses alone should take the title? Yourself and another? A lady who is most courtly, but completely under your domination?'

His eyes flashed to the loathed eunuch, and to the thumb-ring of green jade he wore. 'Show me that pang-tze!' he demanded.

Three steps took him across to where An stood. The eunuch remained immobile as his hand was grasped. The pang-tze – an archer's ring, made to be worn on the thumb – was of dark green jade. It was priceless.

'That's my ring! Yehonala promised it to me.'

'Pardon, Lord, but this ring is mine.' An Te-hai, shrivelled and diminutive, looked to her. It was true. She had promised a suite of jade pieces to Prince Kung, then allowed Little An to wheedle the pang-tze from her.

'It's true,' she said. 'I gave the ring to An Te-hai in return for an important service he rendered me. It is a very small thing—'

'Not to me! What is a suite of jade with one piece missing? Dismiss him!' Prince Kung's voice rose. 'Dismiss him now, so we may speak!'

She saw it would be impossible to calm the Prince with An present, so she nodded to An. 'Leave us.'

An slid away, quietly victorious.

He's been useful to me, she thought, watching An go. But now his utility has become far outweighed by his capriciousness. He is too often an embarrassment. Did he really have the Taiping spy murdered, as Su-shun's old spies said? If not, what has he done with her? What a pity there is no way to quietly retire a troublesome eunuch to the provinces. Like all his kind, the law says he must remain within a hundred li of the Emperor's person at all times . . .

'Look at him strutting like a cockerel!' The Prince ground out the words in fury. 'He thinks he's made himself safe from all discipline by his intriguing. I tell you: he is about to be undeceived!'

411

'It's just a ring. You know it's his right to take a cut of all transactions made within the Forbidden City. Think of it as cumsha.'

'Cumsha? On personal gifts sent by you to me?'

'Technically, he has a right.'

'I remember when General Tseng came on his visit to Peking. He was deliberately embarrassed by that maggot. That too was over cumsha. His behaviour then almost destroyed our policy.'

Yes, she thought, marvelling at how Prince Kung's loathing had incited him. You're angry, but you're right. An thinks he's secure because of what he knows. And, like you, he should have realized that I don't permit anyone to hold a sword over my neck for long.

An hurried down the grey hutong looking for the Fu Cheng gate. The fortune-teller's house was locked up, but his banging on the door brought the man's 'daughter' to the door. She let him in, a look of awe on her face, and offered him a seat in an untidy visitor's anteroom, bowing and apologizing all the while for the inadequacy of the furnishings.

'Take this.' An thrust forward a string of silver coins.

The girl disappeared, and An paced the room, listening to the noise of a throat being cleared in the courtyard. Moments later the fortune-teller appeared in a simple over shirt and black slippers that were stamped down at the heels. His hair was mussed from his sick bed and his eyes were caked and there was little of the customary ceremony of greeting he had always lavished on his best client. He carried a pot of hot water in his hand.

'Master An, what brings you to the house of a sick man? Perhaps you will take tea?'

'No time. Listen: you must cast a fortune for me now.'

'Now?'

'Immediately!'

The fortune-teller's oyster eyes appraised him with a new seriousness. 'Of course. Of course. Please come this way.'

He led An to a cold, windowless room in the back of the house to which he had paid many a previous visit. It smelled strongly of lamp-oil and sandalwood incense. The fortune-teller's daughter began lighting lamps and joss sticks from a long waxed taper. She withdrew as the fortune-teller shrugged on his robe and composed himself.

'Honoured sir, what brings you to consult with the tao? Are you troubled by ghosts?'

'No. Why do you say that?'

The fortune-teller wrinkled his nose. 'Too bad. I felt something come into the room with you.'

An felt a blast of fear. 'What could it be?'

'Something is disturbing the tao. Something acting as a lode stone of bad joss. The spirit of an ancestor perhaps?' The fortune-teller sucked his teeth. 'Are you wearing any charms?'

'No.'

'Are you absolutely certa—'

'I said, no!' In the secrecy of his sleeve he screwed off the jade ring and held it clenched in his fist. The fear strained his voice as he said, 'I came here to learn what will come to pass. Are you an idiot?'

The fortune-teller hid his annoyance at the insult. 'First I must ask how things have been since last you consulted with me.'

'I told my most precious secret just as you said I must,' he said, disgusted at the way he had been misused by Heaven. 'Heaven has broken the bargain with me. You said there was no alternative!'

'I warned you, and told you that you must tell your most precious secret – only your most precious,' the fortune-teller leaned forward, his manner assured. 'Or else the best protection from thunderbolts would not work.'

An gaped. 'But I did. I did!'

'And, Master An, as a result you are alive and well. The lightning of Jehol could not harm you.'

'But the woman to whom I told my most precious secret has disappeared!'

The fortune-teller's eyes moved like a pig's in their fleshy pouches. His instructions from Yehonala had been to milk the Chief Eunuch for as much information as he could. He had not counted on Master An choosing to confess to a total stranger. 'What woman is that?'

'Never mind what woman! A servant – someone I thought I was going to be able to silence. But now she's been kidnapped by an Outer Barbarian, and . . . oh!' An rocked nauseously in his chair. 'If that secret gets out I will have no protection from anything. Use your skills. I must know how things will turn out.'

'In what respect? Personal or professional?'

'Didn't you hear me? Everything!'

'As you wish, Master An. As you wish.'

The fortune-teller placed before him a box filled with little squares of paper. On each was written a beautifully brushed character. He shook the box with a negligent gesture that demonstrated practised expertise and pushed it forward. 'Choose.'

An's hands remained in his sleeves. 'Shake them again.'

'Please. Choose.'

'But you always shake them three times. You have always done so before!'

The fortune-teller grunted. 'It doesn't matter. That's just show. Please – choose.'

An stretched out a reluctant hand. His eyes rolled. Then he picked a piece of paper, withdrew it and passed it across.

When the fortune-teller unwrapped the paper and showed it, An gasped.

The character he had chosen was 'nu' – woman.

'What does it mean?'

An air of scholarship settled on the fortune-teller's shoulders. 'As you must know, honoured sir, in the lore of writing, the first character "an" in your name means "peace" or "tranquillity". But it is made up of two other characters. These are pictures of a woman and a roof. Because the ancients were wise one woman under a roof means peace and tranquillity, whereas two women under a roof forms the character for discord, and three women under a roof corresponds to gossip. The character you have chosen is the one meaning 'woman', that is to say, the character for An, minus the roof.'

'But what does it mean?' An said in agony.

'I will not pretend this is a good omen. I think it may be very serious for you.'

'Tell me. Tell me!'

The fortune-teller nodded as if showing how much he wanted to relieve his client's burden but doubting there was any way to do so. 'The choice permits of only one interpretation. This means that you are in danger of decapitation.'

414

An felt his guts clench. He was terrified. 'Ahhh!'

'Do not be alarmed. Nothing is certain. Only – you ought to be extremely careful for the current period.'

'What do you mean "current period"?'

'The tao is like an invisible fluid that permeates everything and extends up into Heaven. Therefore it is affected by the churning of the heavenly bodies, most especially by the sun and the moon. The danger is greatest daily at the Hour of the Monkey, and this will continue for the duration of this year.'

An sat still for a moment, then a feeling of incredible claustrophobia overcame him and he staggered to the door.

The fortune-teller accompanied him back to the ante-room, showing concern at his client's suddenly very sickly complexion.

The awestruck girl reappeared.

'Please sit – daughter, bring Master An tea!'

'No, I must go.'

'Please, just a moment to catch your breath. Master An, the reading does not mean you will necessarily be killed, only that the danger is higher than normal for the duration of this year . . .'

But An was already staggering towards the gate.

Fei stood before the assembled ministers as her father quizzed her about what had happened in Peking and Jehol. She had told him everything, leaving out only the way she had been kidnapped, and taken forcibly out of Peking.

'Therefore I must report, Venerable King,' she said, leaden with shame, 'that despite every effort the ultimatum has finally been rejected, and that my mission was a failure.'

The Kao Wang was dressed informally in black and red cotton Taiping jacket and pantaloons and black canvas slippers. Unlike everyone else his grey hair was cut very short. He had shown no sign of pleasure at seeing his daughter again.

'You chose to deliver the ultimatum to the Yi Concubine,' he said. 'Why did you do that, when she is a notoriously evil woman, a witch who everyone knows held the Hsien-feng Emperor under a spell?'

'For that very reason, Venerable King. I calculated that she

415

and Prince Kung would eventually triumph. I reasoned that only those who took power could possibly be of use to us.'

The Kao Wang shifted uneasily. 'You said the Yi Concubine made verbal promises to you in Jehol, but when she returned to Peking she broke all those promises?'

'Yes, Venerable King.'

'Was there not a time stipulation attached to her promises?'

'Yes, Venerable King. The phrase the Yi Concubine used was "as soon as normal government can be resumed".'

'Why did you allow that? It could mean anything.'

'Please excuse my stupidity, Venerable King, but I was not expecting to negotiate. I was not formally empowered to speak on behalf of our blessed Heavenly King. And, of course, I had no power to hold any of the Imperial persons to their promises.'

Fei felt her father's glance cut into her. He seemed to know that she was using the sin of presumption as a hiding place. He said, 'Why did you leave Peking so soon without a written reply? It was your duty to obtain that reply, or die.'

'Because—' She stumbled, her tone wholly self effacing now. 'Because evasion is always the Yi Concubine's favoured way. I saw there would never be a "yes", and there would never be a "no", only endless delays while the world turned beneath her. Also, as a woman I knew very well when she had changed her mind. I was ready to insist, and to die, but I decided it was more important that this Council be told what had passed.'

The Kao Wang looked at her long and penetratingly. He seemed to her vastly disappointed, and vastly angry with Peking. His unspoken conclusion hung in the air for all to hear before he gave voice to it.

'We have no choice. The T'ien Wang shall make good His promise. Our armies will take Shanghai.'

Lindley looked around the incredible hall and tried to decide what the decor implied about the Taipings' values. The structure was built according to classical Ming architectural rules and opulently decorated and furnished in a traditional style, but almost every interior surface here had been gilded. But among all the decoration nowhere could he see any animal or bird or human figure. There were no depictions of the Confucian ideal here, no images of Taoist Immortals or Buddhist bodhisattvas. There were no images at all.

A meal of fruit, cakes and tea was brought, and he ate, looking up at the wall hangings and further up the huge shadowed space into which a dozen gilded columns disappeared. Could all of this beauty have come from madness and evil? he asked himself, wanting not to believe it. Surely not. Surely there is goodness at the heart of the Taiping philosophy. Surely my father's work has not been in vain.

When he finished eating a young woman came to him with a basin and cloths and fragrant oils. She knelt before him, took off his shoes and began to wash his feet. As she massaged he felt his impatience begin to lift, and he decided to put all thoughts of his father away for the moment. As he relaxed his eyes roamed over the silk paintings that hung on the walls.

The young woman finished washing and drying his feet. She rubbed oil in them silently for a few minutes more before withdrawing. When Lindley heard the beating of the drum tower again and realized that another hour had gone by he put on his shoes and began to pace. Fei's unexpected appearance must have astonished everyone, he thought, especially her father. To find her alive after so long, after she had travelled so far, and on so lethal a mission must have delighted him.

When the sound of the rain lessened he took out his watch and began to wind it. On the other hand, he thought, forcing himself to sit down again, it must have been her father who approved her damned suicide mission in the first place. I wonder how I'll react to him when I meet him?

He cautioned himself. Don't prejudge the High King according to Western standards, he thought. It's meaningless. The Taipings are at war, and Fei is one of their veteran soldiers. Her father was honouring his daughter by giving her a vital mission. Remember that. And remember that what you want more than anything is for this man to accept you as his son-in-law.

Finally, there was an echo at the entrance, and Lindley looked up to see a figure dressed in a flamboyant robe walking towards him. The man was in his mid-forties, tall, with a commander's bearing. On his head was an elaborate golden coronet, bejewelled and tasselled. Long hair came from beneath it, covered his ears and cascaded to his shoulders. His long yellow robe was styled in the fashion of the Ming dynasty, covered in longevity symbols worked in gold and silver. He wore gold embroidered slippers quite different to the black satin boots always worn by the Manchu.

Lindley got to his feet. After so long in the Forbidden City he found it unnerving to be greeted by a man dressed from head to toe in Imperial yellow. What's worse, he thought, it looks like he's put it on especially for my benefit. For a moment he wondered what greeting to offer, but then the man put out a hand and shook Lindley's own firmly and in the Western way.

'Welcome to the Heavenly Capital, Dr Lin-li. My name is Shih Wen-kuang. I am called the Kao Wang.' The name meant 'High King', but the information was passed without self-consciousness.

'I'm pleased to be here at last,' Lindley said, thinking again about the impromptu proposal he had made on the boat. He wondered if Fei had mentioned it.

The Kao Wang's eyes seemed very knowing. He said formally, 'If you will consent for the time being to reside in my humble home you will do me great honour.'

'The honour is entirely that which your kindness bestows,' he answered with equal formality. 'Sir, I would value the opportunity to talk with you about a matter—'

But the other cut in. 'Dr Lin-li, I hope you will excuse me for the present. I have tiresome but urgent business that requires my immediate attention. We will meet again soon. Meanwhile my servants will ready lodgings for you.'

The Kao Wang left as suddenly as he had appeared, leaving Lindley alone and unsure if he had imagined a vision. A few minutes later a servant came and led him to prepared quarters. They were light and spacious and tastefully furnished with magnificently carved rosewood furniture and hangings and antique screens that showed scenes of river life. There were paintings of well-ordered rural landscapes, pictures of farming and fishing, sugar-loaf hills with hermit caves, a gorgeously worked portrait of a golden pheasant and another of a heron. The sight of such ortho- dox treasures hidden away in a private room jangled a

418

warning in his mind, but then he thought, what does it matter if the Kao Wang has rescued fine art from the past? Wouldn't you do the same? And don't European gentlemen keep nude classical sculptures and hang erotic paintings in their private rooms while keeping the strictest propriety in public? Isn't that perfectly allowable?

After he bathed he found his clothes taken away and fresh clothes laid out for him. They were in the Taiping style. There was no mirror in the room and he felt a little embarrassed as he tucked in his waist sash awkwardly and tried to get used to the feel of the loose silk trousers and jerkin. When Fei came to him she put her hand to her mouth, amused at his new appearance.

'Truly you are one of us now, Lin-li! Maybe I will marry you after all!'

'You haven't seen me in my kilt yet.'

She smiled, but her uneasiness struck him. 'We have been granted a great honour.'

'Oh?'

'Tomorrow we will be allowed to dine at my father's table.' She looked up at him. 'For your own sake and mine, Lin-li, I ask you not to mention to my father, or to anyone, how it was that I left Peking.'

'What should I say?'

'Only that you helped me to escape after my mission was completed.'

'Of course.' He took her hand. 'Did you say "we" are going to dine with your father tomorrow? Both you and I?'

'Yes.'

'Then we are truly honoured. I never saw a woman share a table with men in Peking, or anywhere else in China.'

Her eyes slid away from him. 'Lin-li, the Taiping way is not the Imperialist way. Here we are enlightened. We do not practise foot-binding, nor do we tolerate prostitution or opium smoking. We are Christians, just like you.'

Outside there was a rumble of thunder.

When An Te-hai was announced Yehonala refused to admit him.

'Tell him I'm indisposed,' she instructed the door eunuch. 'He is to wait. Instead call for my doctors.' She sat in a chair as maids brought tables and set them to right and left of her and laid thin handkerchiefs over her wrists. All four doctors wore the robes and hats of mandarins of the first rank, their exalted station being necessary to allow them to approach the Empress Dowager's person. They kowtowed first, then knelt two to each side.

The two most senior doctors each put three fingers onto her wrists, feeling through the thin fabric for the twelve pulses, while the other two doctors looked on studiously. They continued for over an hour, their fingers feeling the pulses and their trained minds assessing the thirty qualities that described each pulse and indicated the state of health of the organs.

At last the doctors kowtowed and backed away, going to an ante-room to consider their diagnoses and prescriptions. In an hour she would receive a horrid herbal tea, and she would drink it even though there was nothing wrong with her. What a ridiculous game, she thought. Each of them is as much a charlatan as the others, but so long as they keep frowning with professional solemnity over pulses and so long as none of them betrays the truth they will retain respect and status. When Hsien-feng died all four were disgraced, even though they did nothing to hasten or hinder his death. Still their insignia were stripped away and they were sent to Black Dragon River in formal disgrace until Tsai-ch'un was enthroned.

After further thought she decided it was time to call in the waiting eunuch. 'I am so pleased you have decided to do as I asked,' she said, offering An no smile.

He looked unhappily at the thumb ring as he placed it before her with suffocating humility, utterly unaware that he was sliding into a chasm. He said, 'Of course, one should never think to oppose the will of one's betters. The truth is, I no longer love this ring. It is an object of evil omen. I could feel it distorting the tao whenever I wore it.'

Yehonala had already read the brief report from the bribed fortune-teller near the Fu Cheng gate. It told how yesterday's reading had made a profound impression on the Chief Eunuch, how he had believed in the charade completely. 'But you're pleased that Prince Kung should wear the ring?'

An's head inclined a fraction in a subtly ingratiating way. 'It would not necessarily be of evil omen to anyone else, Imperial Majesty.'

'Perhaps.' She played her nail sheaths delicately over her rope of pearls. 'You know that Prince Kung has renewed his promise to shed your blood, unless you make an apology.'

He swallowed as if his mouth was dust dry. 'Imperial Majesty, help me to protect myself.'

'How?'

'It seems to me that I can only avoid the danger by avoiding a critical period.'

'What period?'

'Until the year's end.'

'If you believe that Prince Kung's wrath will settle in that short a time you are mistaken. His loathing for you is very deep.'

'Doubtless. But it is not his wrath that frightens me. The heavenly signs agree that, for the moment, I must put myself beyond his reach.'

'Then do so.'

'But . . . it is a capital crime for an Imperial eunuch to travel further from Peking than Lu-kou-ch'iao whenever the Emperor is in residence.'

She feigned surprise, tutting. 'Ah, you want to leave the capital?'

'I must remove myself. It is the only safe solution. The present year is critical. I beg you to allow me to make a journey across Black Moat River bridge.'

'I could intercede with His Imperial Majesty on your behalf, but . . .'

'Thank you, Lady! A Decree would solve everything. No one else need know!'

She considered, then sighed dubiously. 'But . . . you would still require a viable pretext to tour.'

'Perhaps—' An's eyes flickered in thought. 'Perhaps I could be sent to collect tribute from the provinces.'

'But, An, you know that each province already has its own tax collector.'

'Ah! All except the newly reconquered territories of the South.'

She tapped her nail sheaths and said wearily, 'This is against my better judgement, but I will ask His Imperial Majesty to do what you ask. However, I warn you: if you are released to travel, be circumspect. And go quietly about the country.'

An thanked her profusely, then begged leave to make immediate preparations. She agreed, and when he had gone she looked at the jade thumb-ring and put an already-prepared letter beside it. Then she called her most reliable personal messenger to her and said, 'Have this ring boxed and wrapped in yellow silk and delivered with this letter to Prince Kung immediately.'

The Kao Wang took up the long chopsticks to serve from the wonderful dishes that had been arriving at the table. He wore a yellow silk tunic tonight, piped in black, with black pantaloons. Without a headdress his long grey-black hair cascaded to his shoulders.

They had talked together in a general way as the tea pot went around the table, then a variety of interesting hors d'oeuvres – goose meat, eel, turtle – were served up. There were no toasts and no alcohol to drink, and as the storm intensified outside the Kao Wang spoke proudly about the city and the achievements of the Chinese people.

'The Ming dynasty explorer, Cheng Ho, constructed two hundred ocean-going junks here in Nanking, each five hundred of your feet in length. He made seven voyages to the South Sea each time in a fleet manned by between ten and twenty thousand men. He ranged as far as the coasts of India and Africa, and all this was done four hundred and thirty years ago, before European explorers even began to go out into the world.'

'It's interesting to think what would have happened had Chinese navigators ever reached the Thames and begun to trade at London,' Lindley said.

'You see how the coming of the Manchu limited us? China has been nothing but a land of slaves since the first year of Shun Chih.' Lindley knew he meant 1644, the year the Manchu took over the Forbidden City. 'My daughter tells me you were lately at Peking, that you were engaged in diplomacy on behalf of your country.'

'It was hardly diplomacy,' Lindley said. 'Officially I was employed as an interpreter.'

Lindley appraised the Kao Wang carefully, seeing the undoubted source of Fei's charm and intelligence, but in him these qualities were overlaid by a hard and dark varnish.

'My daughter says that you were more than an interpreter, that you negotiated with the alien regime.'

He parried. 'Between the departure of Lord Elgin and the arrival of Mr Bruce I did transact some business with the, ah, alien regime – but it was insignificant.'

'You gave advice over the iniquitous Russian treaty, did you not?'

'What Fei has told you is true, Mr Shih. However, the remarks I conveyed about the Russian treaty were made through me simply because I was the only one of my countrymen in Peking during the winter who could speak Mandarin.'

'But you met regularly in an informal way with the former Emperor's half-brother.'

Lindley hesitated. He glanced at Fei, realizing how thoroughly she had briefed her father. She did not meet his eye. He said, 'What passed between Prince Kung and myself were purely personal conversations.'

'Ah, yes, personal meetings. You must have impressed him, because he rewarded your services by giving you an important Manchu heirloom.'

'He gave me a valuable pearl, but that was more to do with my being a physician. His own particular beliefs in the medicinal value of pearl dust were . . . extraordinary.'

'In what way extraordinary?'

'He wanted me to grind the thing up and eat it.' He grinned. 'Can you beat that?'

'You gave advice to Prince Kung on the bringing into being of a bureau for international relations.'

Lindley glanced again at Fei. 'Sir, you're remarkably well informed. The truth is that I hoped to open Prince Kung's mind to the possibility of China taking her proper place among the nations of the world.'

'So you believe, as does your government, that China should continue to be ruled by the alien regime?'

A lurid flash lit the western sky, and Lindley felt another measure of the Kao Wang's amiability evaporate. This time he decided to counter it. 'I don't personally approve of the Manchu regime. However, I never was in any position to influence who rules China. Nor do I expect to be in the future. I'm a physician, and that's all I am.'

'But the British government is able to influence who rules

China. The British and the French have shown how easily they can overwhelm the Manchu. They caused the hated Hsien-feng Emperor to flee. They humbled that usurper and caused him to die of shame. So much is only just and correct retribution against a sinner. But now it seems your government has permitted the usurper's infant son to rule in Peking. Why is this?'

'I can't speak for governments. They're not my concern.' He cast Fei a cautioning glance. 'However, I'd like to ask you something that is of greater concern to me. Your daughter must have told you that I came to China to find my father. I believe he's very well known in Nanking, and I'm wondering why so far tonight you've avoided all mention of him.'

The Kao Wang faced him, and for a lingering moment he said nothing. Fei's eyes were on her plate. Her chopsticks stilled. After a while the Kao Wang said, 'Of course your father is known to me. He is known to us all here in the Heavenly Capital. Among Taipings he is deemed to be as great a man as John the Baptist.'

Lindley's hopes soared. 'Then he is here?'

'Not at present. Your esteemed father regularly visits the towns and villages of the district.'

'Then I'll ride out to see him – with your permission, of course. You understand my anxiety?'

'I'll see that he's informed as soon as possible of your arrival.'

Lindley heard the evasiveness in the Kao Wang's answer, but he assumed a quick smile. 'Thank you. I would appreciate that.'

As the meal progressed Lindley watched Fei, pleased at least that he had raised the subject of his father, but unsatisfied with the answers he had received. Softly, softly, he told himself. Take it slowly. You don't know enough about this place yet to make demands. At least you've established that he's alive and well. They can't hide him from you for much longer.

A messenger came to the door and waited. When the Kao Wang beckoned the messenger approached and knelt, offering up the note. The Kao Wang read it then stood up.

'Please excuse me.'

'Not bad news I hope?'

The Kao Wang did not answer immediately, but then he

said, 'I must attend to an urgent matter. Please continue. I will rejoin you as soon as possible.'

As soon as they were alone, Lindley turned to Fei. 'It seems you've told him just about everything about me. Did you find time to tell him that we've decided to get married?'

She bit her lip. 'Lin-li, I can't ask his permission yet.'

'Fei, why not? I don't see any reason to delay. And I can think of several good reasons to hurry the process.'

He leaned over to kiss her, but she leaned away.

'Please, no.'

'Come to me tonight. Or let me come to you.'

'You cannot.'

'Fei, what's the matter?'

She seemed petrified. 'I told you before. We might be seen.'

'By whom? There's no one here.'

'Servants. Anybody.'

'So what if they do?'

'It's not . . . seemly.'

He recoiled, annoyed. 'Fei, I'm not proposing we do anything other than what we've done many times before. What business is that of anyone else's?'

'Our laws are very strict. No woman may have intercourse outside marriage.'

She made the word sound ugly. He tried to kiss her again, but again she pulled away.

'For God's sake, Fei, I'm only going to kiss you.'

'That would not be appropriate here. And please do not blaspheme in my father's house.'

He lowered his voice. 'How many times have we shared a bed? We're determined to marry, so where's the difficulty? Don't you want me to kiss you?'

Her smile was bittersweet as she engaged his hand. 'Of course I want it, but we can't. We must wait. We must not be caught.'

'You make it sound like some kind of beheading offence.'

She looked at him directly. 'It is a beheading offence.'

He stared back at her, incredulous, but the Kao Wang was returning, and so they both turned to him. His tunic was rain-spotted, and his composure no longer completely intact. 'Dr Lin-li, an unfortunate circumstance has arisen that means I will not be able to finish supper with you. Please forgive my rudeness.'

As soon as he left, Lindley asked Fei, 'What's happening?'

'The news my father received was important.'

'Yes, I could see that. Come on, Fei, you've been on edge all day. What is it?'

She battled with herself. 'You may not know.'

'Do you know?'

'Yes. But I may not tell anyone.'

His anger surged. 'Fei, I've had just about enough of this. Surely you can trust me?'

She shook her head. 'Of course I trust you, Lin-li, but no one else may know. This is the Heavenly Father's personal order.'

'Fei, what's wrong?' He seized her and held her and felt a titanic struggle going on inside her. 'You must tell me what's worrying you. What is happening?'

For a moment he saw her waver, but then she broke away from him. She ran to the door, her hand to her mouth. As she left he caught the words, 'Tomorrow you will know.'

That night he slept badly. The storm woke him and he watched it glittering in the west. 'A storm in the west means bad luck,' the Kao Wang had said at dinner, quoting an old Nanking proverb. That certainly stands to reason, Lindley thought as he lay awake. Heavy rain in the west is bound to swell the Yangtze and send a torrent surging through the I-ching gorge. The Son of the Ocean deluges the lower valley every decade, bringing death to millions. Bad luck they call it. I call it cause and effect.

The next morning Fei greeted him as if nothing had happened. She told him that a public proclamation was to be made in Drum Tower Square and they should go to read it. They went down and were permitted to leave the palace citadel. Outside the square was filled with people. As they pushed forward toward the wall that served as a giant official notice board everyone stared at them. Lindley listened to the chatter around him, but could not make it out, except to know that it was good news. When he came close enough to read the posters over the sea of heads he was surprised.

*The army led by the Chung Wang shall move to punish the
impudent heathens of Shanghai, where the Heavenly Kingdom
of Great Peace shall be proclaimed once again . . .*

The tone of the proclamation was triumphant. He saw Fei's
radiant joy. He heard the people talking excitedly around
him, and he watched their faces as they laughed and passed
the good news around. They were as convinced as Fei was.

Lindley knew that Chung Wang meant 'Loyal Prince'. Fei
had told him that the man was a brilliant general and
commander-in-chief of the main Taiping field army. But
Lindley also knew that no matter how brilliant the general's
tactics, nothing could prevent the annihilation of his army
if he tried to enter the thirty-mile zone of exclusion that
had been declared around Shanghai. British guns would see
to that.

And when the Chung Wang's army is forced away from
Shanghai and the other coastal cities, as it surely will be,
Lindley thought, where will it go? I can see no alternative
but for it to fall back here. And with the blockade tightening
once more around Nanking, how will the people feed themselves and a hundred thousand soldiers too? The city will be
doomed.

Suddenly he heard a commotion and people began running to the western end of the square.

'What's going on?' he asked, but Fei did not know, and
they followed the crowd to see what was exciting everyone.

Guards were dragging in a line of a dozen or so prisoners.
They had been stripped to the waist and their hands were
tied behind their backs. Their faces were swollen and bloody
where they had been beaten about the head. Lindley craned
forward and saw that the prisoners lacked the Manchu
queue, but their hair was not as long as Taiping hair. The
guards were headed by a man carrying an executioner's
sword.

'Who are they?' Lindley asked.

Fei stared hard. 'Not Taipings.'

'Are you sure?' The memory of the Shanghai executions
filled him once more with disgust. 'Prisoners then?'

Fei could not answer. 'I . . . don't know.'

Lindley shoved his way forward through the tightly
packed crowd, Fei following in his wake. 'Lin-li! Stop!'

Anger was pulsing in Lindley's head as he turned. 'Fei, what have these men done wrong?'

She saw his anger and implored him, 'Please, Lin-li, don't try to interfere!'

But he looked back to where the men were being made to kneel and he struggled onward, pushing people out of his way as if they were children. When he reached the iron barrier that kept the crowd back he saw something that made him vault right over it.

One of the men was Ningpo Sam.

'Jesus Christ! It's the men from the *Hyson*!' he shouted. 'They're Ward's Filipinos!'

Fei made a grab for him, but he tore away from her and pushed forward into the open space. The guards tried to intercept him but he had already reached the executioner, who was readying himself beside the first victim.

The burly swordsman turned to face Lindley with astonishment.

'What are you doing to these men?' he demanded, enraged to white heat. At the same time he raised his arm and swiped a powerful back-hand slap across the face of the executioner. The man reeled back, his sword ringing to the paved ground, and Lindley grabbed it up. Instantly a group of four guards reached him, their spears levelled now. Lindley raised the sword ready to cleave the first man who dared to stab at him.

The guards could have killed him, but they hesitated, mesmerized by the huge foreigner who had gone mad. Fei was screaming at them not to touch him. Some of the Filipinos, their features cut and grossly swollen, were trying to rise unsteadily to their feet, forcing the other guards to push them back down again. The crowd was shocked to silence, unable to believe what they were seeing.

When the executioner got to his feet again he pushed his way through the guards and launched himself at Lindley, intent on recovering his sword at all costs. Lindley side-stepped him and slammed the sword hilt into his temple stunning him. The man went down again, but the guards had seen their chance to close with him and they threw down their spears and dived foward.

Lindley's chest was bursting with rage, but the monster that had loosed itself inside him that day aboard the *Hyson* was not in him today. His mind was cool and remote and as he felt the wiry strength of the men who surrounded him he realized they had thrown down their weapons because they believed they must not harm him.

They clung to his arms to secure him, but he raised his voice and bellowed at the crowd. 'Hear me!' They tried to pull him down, but he shouted over them, 'It is the Heavenly King's order that there be no killing today!'

The guards continued to hold him. One managed to get an arm-lock on his neck, and choked him to silence. He saw that the executioner was getting to his hands and knees now, shaking the pain from his head. An official had come forward now that Lindley was safely controlled. He unsheathed a sword as Fei remonstrated with him. When he saw the weapon Lindley bucked and fought, wild with a sudden intent to break free, but the guards renewed their grip on him and subdued him.

The crowd was stirring. The official's fury was mounting, but Fei stepped away from him and shouted something into the crowd. She started to chant her father's name, then several people in the crowd began to follow her lead.

'Kao Wang! Kao Wang!'

Lindley saw the executioner pick up his sword and walk towards the first of the prisoners. Lindley felt himself being throttled. 'No!' he wanted to shout. 'These men are under a flag of truce! They are here only because I wanted to come to Nanking, only because of me. They are under my protection!'

The chanting spread and grew louder.

'Kao Wang! Kao Wang! Kao Wang!'

Lindley fought to breathe. He saw the sword raised and knew that his efforts had been in vain. But in the same moment that the sun glinted on the stationary blade there was a flurry of gunfire. The executioner paused, looked to the official, whose own attention was directed towards the gold-roofed palaces on the far side of the square. There was more gunfire and Lindley saw plumes of smoke where shots had been fired into the air. The chanting died and gave way to sporadic screams, then silence followed. Lindley saw a disturbance at the back of the crowd. It began to part and soon the Kao Wang himself appeared, his way cleared by a cadre of guards each holding Enfield rifles.

When he reached the iron barrier he ducked under it and walked straight to the official, ignoring Fei. Lindley watched the official explain what had happened and direct a brief glance his way. The Kao Wang walked back past his daughter and came to where Lindley had been brought to bay. He examined him in silence for a moment, and when he was sure that Lindley posed no threat, he motioned to the guards who immediately released their grip.

Lindley gasped for air. For a moment the world swam and he feared that he was going to black out. When his vision cleared, the Kao Wang's face showed controlled outrage. He said, 'Why did you do this?'

'These men – must not – be executed.'

'Why not? They are Imperialist fighters. Criminals and enemies, ambushed and captured when their boat halted during last night's storm. They are spies brought here to be lawfully executed.'

'No! They are not spies!'

Lindley saw his contradiction stun the Kao Wang like a physical blow. Somewhere nearby, a kneeling man whimpered, but all else was silence.

'Their uniforms showed them to be killers from General Hua's foreign devil squad.'

'No! These are the same men who brought myself and your daughter here. Their service was a courtesy done us by a friend. They are protected!'

'Protected by whom?'

'By every civilized code! By me! By my word of honour!'

The Kao Wang's control began to dissolve. 'By you? Who are you to say who shall live and who shall die in the Heavenly Capital?'

'I gave my word! If you kill them, you must kill me first.'

The Kao Wang faced him, weighing his fate in the balance. Fei stood silently behind him. He turned and asked her, 'Is this so?'

She knelt to answer him, solemn-faced. 'Venerable King, these are the men who brought us from Shanghai. Their service was a great courtesy done by one friend for another. Word was given that the riverboat would be permitted to return without hindrance.'

The Kao Wang turned back to the official. 'Put these men back aboard their boat and release them,' he said. Then

430

Lindley watched him go back beyond the barrier to where his bodyguard waited.

Ward found the crazy Englishman's punt tethered in a silted reach of the Chia-ting canal. All around rice paddies that had remained untended for two years were overgrown with weeds. As the sun rose the land had begun to steam. Now bright sunlight blazed from a blue sky, making the air close and still. Heavy rain had deluged for several days, but now it had ceased, and the chirring of crickets had become deafening once more among the tall grass stems.

The insect noise modulated as Ward entered the wilderness. He looked back warily and motioned Vincente after him, creeping forward, looking for the man who had gone forward into the combat area without permission. 'Where in hell are you, fool?' Ward said through gritted teeth, hoping his surprise had not been compromised. 'You're holding up my whole goddamned army!'

Moments later he reached the edge of the cover. Beyond a shallow ditch the vegetation had been deliberately burned back for fifty yards from the town moat. The earth was black, covered with carbonized stems. Here and there sooty clumps stood up, some sprouting fresh green shoots. Old grass fringed the pea-green moat like a blond eyelash. Vincente pointed to a spot just below the heavily patrolled walls of the Taiping stronghold. Crouching behind a tuft fifty yards away, and hard against the edge of the moat, was the fool.

'Jesus Christ, who is he? And what's he doing out there?' Ward whispered, wondering how to call the man away.

'He's crazier than you, Coronel.'

Ward searched around in the matted earth for a stone, found one, then lobbed it. It landed close to its target. The man heard it and froze, then he looked up carefully, surveying the edge of the tall grass, and put on a wide-brimmed straw hat.

Ward dared not show himself. Sentries were manning the walls, and there would be lookouts. The artist went back to his drawing, and Ward, fuming now, was about to look for another stone when his quarry packed up and began to stroll back.

None of the sentries seemed to notice him. No shots were fired.

When he came by, Ward pounced on him. 'Are you trying to get yourself killed?'

The man was of medium height. When he took his rice planter's hat off Ward saw that he had brown hair set back from a large forehead, a sandy moustache, and eyes made bluer by a freckly tan. He smiled and thrust out a hand. 'Colonel Ward I'd guess by the accent. How do you do? Captain Gordon, Royal Engineers.'

Ward groaned. 'Is that a fact?'

He had been warned about Gordon. He was another of those strange, unsettling, immensely capable but wayward individualists that Britain seemed to produce every generation. Ward set off back towards the canal.

'Weather seems to have cleared up,' Gordon said absently, following on. 'I understand you're planning a raid here soon.'

'You might say that. We're going to open our artillery barrage in ten minutes. You're in the way of a full-scale assault. What were you doing out there?'

'Mapping and sketching.' Gordon chuckled. 'Luke chapter nineteen, verse forty-three.'

Ward stopped. He put his hands on his hips and inclined his head, grimacing. 'What?'

' "For the days shall come upon thee, that thine enemies shall cast a trench about thee, and compass thee round, and keep thee in on every side." '

'Yeah . . .' He started off again.

Gordon called after him. 'If we're going to fight a war here, it's essential we have first class maps of the place – canals, paths, terrain, fortifications, you know the sort of thing. We can save a great deal of time and energy that way.'

'Royal Engineers, huh? You certainly sound like you're an engineer.'

'Engineering wins wars, Colonel. One day scientific soldiering will be recognized as the only way to fight.'

'Meadows told me you were a man of strongly-held beliefs.'

'I don't forget that the good Lord gave me a mind to think with.'

Their pole-men waited on the bank by the boats. Ward gave orders to bring Gordon's punt in tow and return to the place where the Ever-victorious Army's guns had been drawn up. As they slid along the mud-brown waterway the body of a young child drifted by, bloated by gases. He hardly noticed it, until Vincente said, 'It's a boy.'

For weeks now there had been tiny carcasses floating everywhere in the canal network, but they had always been girl-children.

'Things must be getting bad up country,' he said.

Vincente nodded. 'I heard the Taiping garrison turned cannibal at Anking. They're selling human flesh at eighty cash per catty.'

Ten cents American per pound . . .

Starvation was a harrowing feature of Oriental war that Ward knew he could never harden himself against. The land was so heavily cultivated, supported so many people each of whom were making the most precarious of livings, that when any disturbance occurred the system broke down and millions died. Hopeless bags of bones squatted in the ruins of every shattered village. With no one to beg from but one another they waited patiently to die.

'How are your boys?' Ward asked Vincente, meaning the Filipinos who had returned on the *Hyson*.

'What happened up in Nanking shook them up pretty bad.'

'Yeah. I'll bet.'

'Sam said that Dr Lindley saved their lives.'

'Yeah. I guess that's another one I owe him.'

Ward ducked as the punt passed under a footbridge, and he thanked China's ruthless gods that at least the rain had stopped. The water levels were up as high as he had ever seen them. Twenty miles to the north the Yangtze was in dangerous spate, pelting huge quantities of water and suspended mud towards the ocean. Every few years a vast cataclysm would burst open the banks, engulfing hundreds of square miles, isolating cities, sweeping away low-lying villages and drowning people and livestock in great numbers. War only compounded the danger, because higher ground not devastated by flood water drove those fleeing the inundation into perilous unprotected concentrations. Half the time refugees arrived on high ground to find troops or bandit gangs waiting to dispossess them of whatever grain they had managed to salvage.

Ward thought of Fu-nan, the burned village he had walked through three weeks ago with General Staveley and Admirals Hope and Protet. The Shanghai meetings that Consul Meadows had arranged with senior British and French military officers had been a total success. The bastards were finally forced to take my opinions seriously, he thought, feeling the old frustrations still corroding him. Criminal that it always takes so damned long for men in positions of power to reach obvious conclusions.

He had shown the British and French commanders what was happening – and why. 'Foraging parties of Taipings have visited Fu-nan four times in as many weeks,' he told them. 'They've stripped it bare. Fortunately, on the first three occasions the people weren't molested and the buildings weren't touched.'

'What happened the fourth time?' Admiral Protet asked, humbled at what he stood among.

'The last time the people were obliged to resist by a couple of junior mandarins.'

'What did they do?'

'Exactly as they were told, of course.'

The consequences had been fearful. Fu-nan had been made into a fuming heap of charcoal and black bones, and Staveley had stepped back aboard the *Hyson* and said nothing all the way back to Shanghai. The following day, joint operations were agreed. Three days afterwards General Staveley took a thousand British and Indian troops into the Taiping-held town of Chi-pao. Admiral Hope contributed five hundred marines and sailors of the China Station, Admiral Protet three hundred French marines. The combined force cooperated with the Ever-victorious Army to drive out the rebel garrison of Chi-pao.

Ward had led his Corps from the front, baton in hand. Henry Burgevine had gotten himself strapped up tight and almost blind drunk so he could take part in the attack, but the wound in his guts had still parted again, and Ward had had him rushed back to Shanghai. Burgevine aside, casualties had been slight.

The next day Ward had pursued the survivors of Chi-pao to the stronghold of Wang-chia-ssu, an unwalled but massively

434

fortified town occupied by more than five thousand Taipings. Staveley's Armstrong guns had obliterated the place and Ward had chased the retreating Taipings on again, this time to Lung-chu-an where his fifteen-hundred-strong Corps had engaged eight thousand Taipings in a series of brutal assaults. The town had resisted suicidally and then, twenty-four hours after the first attack, it had fallen.

Within ten days the Ever-victorious Army had crossed east over the Huang-pu River and onto the Pu-tung peninsula. With the swollen river held by armed British steamers the land forces had moved on Chou-p'u and its five thousand Taipings and reduced it to rubble, capturing the whole garrison. Then they had switched again, crossing back over the Huang-pu to clear Nan-hsiang, ten miles to the west of Shanghai. Now it was the turn of Chia-ting.

'Don't worry,' Ward told Gordon as he stepped onto the river bank again. 'It'll all be over by nightfall.'

'Yes,' Gordon said, a strange light in his eye. 'I know.'

Many days had passed since the incident at Nanking's execution ground. Lindley had grown bored with confinement among the palaces, and he had asked to be allowed outside to explore the city. Still his father had not returned to Nanking, still Fei was acting with cool formality towards him.

'You were ill-advised to do as you did at the execution ground,' she told him as they finished breakfast.

He saw that her mouth was tight with disapproval. It irritated him. 'Fei, I did what was right – just as you did.'

She looked away and down. 'You left me no choice.'

'Neither of us had a choice.' He felt a little more of his patience evaporate. 'Let me ask you, should I have let those men die knowing I could prevent it?'

'It was very dangerous.' She got up and looked back to him suddenly, still frowning. 'And you caused my father to lose face.'

His short laugh as he rose from the table was humourless. 'Oh, I'm very sorry about that.'

Fei's effort to control her rising anger was visible. 'Lin-li, I want my father to trust you. It's my hope that he would allow you to carry a message of peace to the British at

435

Shanghai. What are the lives of a dozen men against the thousands who will die if that happens?'

He stared back at her wonderingly. 'A message of peace? What are you talking about? He's ordered Chung Wang's field army against the city.'

'It was my hope that you might have had the opportunity to talk with him about such strategic matters. But for that, there would have to be trust between you.' They left the palace complex and began to walk across Drum Tower Square. The sun was bright in a cloudless sky, and although it was early it was pleasantly warm.

'I know you're under pressure, Fei, and I understand that your father has a great deal on his mind, but I really would like to go out to the place where my father is preaching. You must realize how important this is to me.'

'Please try to be patient, Lin-li.'

He saw how the dilemma pained her, and he relented. 'We Scots are known for being an impetuous people. Can't you do something for me?'

She returned his smile. 'I promise. Tomorrow I will ask permission.'

'Ah, permission . . .' he let the word trail off.

'It's a formality that must be observed. We Chinese are a formal people. In the meantime, let me show you the Heavenly Capital. You will not see happier people in all of China.'

'I hope you're right,' he said, thinking it would not be difficult to improve the misery of the rat-infested, cholera-ridden slums in which most of China's teeming millions huddled.

She led him along a wide boulevard, then the ground became hilly and they began to climb Hsiao Ts'ang Shan, a hill near the western walls. There they found a beautiful pavilion with an ornamental garden maintained around it, a maze of gnarled conifers and flowering shrubs and a terraced rockery that spilled down the slope. The old gardener greeted them cheerily at the gatehouse. When he saw Lindley he smiled toothlessly and showed his Taiping affiliations by reciting the Lord's Prayer in Chinese.

The park was empty. Fei showed him the house of Yuan Mei, one of the city's most famous poets during the previous century, then they went down to a secluded spot and stood together looking out over the panorama of the city. After a while Lindley found himself affected by Fei's closeness and the solitude and he bent his head to kiss her neck. For the first time since they had arrived in the Heavenly Capital she did not move away. Instead she allowed him to go on kissing her, and when he slipped his hand inside her shirt he felt her small, firm breasts and her nipples fully erect.

A tremor passed through her. She closed her eyes, her lips parted and a small noise escaped her. Her desire exactly mirrored his own, and he saw that if he continued she would respond to every taboo advance he made. He knew they could easily risk making love here, but he knew also that Fei would view it in a totally different way. An indecency committed in the Heavenly Capital would weigh heavily on her afterwards. She would regret it, and so he asserted his will and drew away from her, engrossing himself in the views over the city instead.

Signs of demolition were everywhere. And wherever he looked gangs of men and women in broad straw hats were digging.

'The Heavenly City seems to have undergone many changes,' he said blandly, still feeling the discomfort of unsatisfied arousal. 'The arrangement of the buildings in China is not as it is at home.'

'That is because of feng-shui.'

'Is a Taiping allowed to believe in feng-shui?' he asked, gently probing her beliefs.

'All Chinese believe in feng-shui, Lin-li. It says that buildings are exposed to certain fluxes of air and moisture above and below ground. These fluxes affect the fortunes of any place and also of the people who live there. Only the wise placing of walls, trees, ditches and pagodas can favourably alter them.'

'Pagodas . . . yes, my father wrote me a letter about Nanking's marvellous Porcelain Pagoda. It sounded magnificent.'

When Fei made no answer he said, 'It's supposed to be over two hundred and fifty feet tall. It should be visible from here. Which way is it?'

She half-turned away, and he recognized once again the struggle that was going on inside her. She said, 'During the Imperial siege many buildings had to be demolished.'

'Oh, no – you mean to say your blessed soldiers pulled down the Porcelain Pagoda?'

She compressed her lips, then said, 'Lin-li, do not forget the destruction of the Summer Palace.'

'Hey, just a moment. I never condoned that. Besides, the two events are not at all comparable.'

'No, they are not. Before the break out, when Imperial troops were besieging us, three hundred thousand people were trapped here in our capital. In those difficult days cabbages were as precious as pearls. Every last patch of ground was needed for planting. Otherwise we would have starved.'

He nodded, openly conceding her point, but privately he was wondering: how many cabbages is it possible to plant on the site of a pagoda? Then he thought back to the war-blasted joss-house and the shattered pagoda and the carpet of bleached bones he had seen in the ruins of Chiang-kiang. The stench of hellish evil that had surrounded him there was present here too – but it seemed that here only he could detect it.

'I hope Ningpo Sam and the others managed to get back to Shanghai,' he said quietly.

Fei made no comment. After a little while she turned to him and said, 'Lin-li, I have something to bring you cheer. Last night I asked my father about us. I think he has decided to give us his answer soon.'

'He'd better,' was all he said.

Disastrous news of the war had reached Nanking by the time Fei was next admitted to her father's presence. This time she came to him as a humble daughter. At the first – official – interview she had stressed Lindley's importance as much as she could, seeing a chance to obtain for him leave to stay for a little while at least inside the city. Now she knew it was vital to be his advocate once again.

'But foreigners are all given to behaving very strangely from time to time, honoured father,' she told him. 'Please allow me to apologize again for his unusual behaviour.'

'He acted like a madman.'

'However he is not a madman, honoured father. He is very highly regarded by his own people. He knows many

British officials personally, including the Consul at Shanghai, Ambassador Bruce in Peking, and even the Lord Elgin.'

'And by his own admission the Barbarian warlord, General Hua – with whom he actually claims a friendship.'

'He and General Hua do not share the same aims. No one would be better placed to plead our cause – ' she poured tea dutifully ' – if only he could become one of us.'

'Become one of us?'

'I mean if he could join us, honoured father. As a trusted ally.'

'How can he become a trusted ally after what he has done?'

'Honoured father,' she said quietly. 'When I was in Peking, Lin-li gave me a silver coin to throw into a palace well. He told me it was a tradition in Scotland that all wells have fairies who live at the bottom. He said that if I made a wish the fairy would see to it that my wish came true. I wished . . . I wished that he could one day become one of us.'

Her father grunted. 'Do you believe he would fight for us?'

'Absolutely, honoured father.'

'Why?'

'Because he has no respect for the Manchu. He agrees they are barbaric invaders from beyond the Wall who have no right to rule in China. He calls China the greatest slave state in the world, a state that longs to taste freedom.'

'But would he *fight* for us?'

'Honoured father, he has already fought for us. He has provided us with our most effective weapon when he brought the Enfield rifles from England.'

'He did that unwittingly.'

'I still believe he will fight for us.'

'Even after you saw him fight so hard to reprieve our enemies?'

She felt panic rising, knowing her father's ability to look deep inside her. He had used the incident at the execution ground to gauge Lindley. 'He is a man of honour. He freely elected to come here.'

'He came here because it is his duty to obey his father's command to come here.'

'That is not really so, honoured father. Our Christian

439

brothers from across the sea sometimes have a strange way of looking at life. Of course they revere the same gospel as we do, but they often take a different meaning.' She felt her inability to tell him what she meant weigh her down: it would have been easier to explain snow to a man of the Far South. 'Honoured Father, it is true that Lin-li came to China at his father's request, but he has come to the Heavenly Capital from his own individual desire.'

Her father stroked his chin for a long time, studying her. 'Tell me – is he Christian?'

It was a question she had dreaded. 'I don't know, honoured father.'

'You must have noticed.'

'He says . . . he doesn't know if he is Christian or not.'

The creases at her father's temples deepened. 'How can a person not know? That's impossible. If he doesn't know he cannot be Christian.'

'Perhaps he can become Christian.'

'Perhaps.' The Kao Wang considered – she saw thoughts in his eyes, but was unable to guess them. Finally he murmured, 'You have lain with this man too often.'

She was mortified by his words. She had not been expecting them. She felt an excruciating flush come to her face which she could do nothing to control. Her lord and father looked at her with the eyes of a Confucian patriarch. She held her silence, waiting for his displeasure and another peremptory question, but his tone remained even.

'I tried always to raise a dutiful daughter. When the time came to entrust you with tasks on behalf of the Heavenly King I did not hesitate to employ you. When I gave you the task of securing the consignment of rifles I told you to set success above all other considerations. You have done as I commanded. You even spent your virginity on a foreigner. I know how this must have pained you.' He looked at her with a judge's eyes. 'When I sent you to Peking I believed I sent you to your reward.'

The words rushed out of her. 'Honoured father, please forgive me. You have favoured me, whereas I have only shamed you . . .'

'No, Fei-ch'ien. You have done well. Very well. And now I shall think on what shall be your next reward.'

The praise washed over her like scalding water. Inside she

felt filthy with deceit. It's the only time I have ever lied to my father, she thought, appalled at what she had dared to do. And how quickly other lies must multiply to cover the first. How can I confess now that I didn't wait for an answer to the Heavenly King's ultimatum? How can I tell my father that it was Lin-li who prevented me fulfilling my mission? How can I tell him that the favour I asked of the well fairy in Peking was that Lin-li should become one of us – through marriage?

' "And many of them that sleep in the dust of the earth shall awake, some to everlasting life, and some to shame and everlasting contempt"!'

Ward awoke in the early morning to the sound of hectoring words. At first he did not know where he was. His successful operations against the Taipings had been continuous. Day after day he had commanded his troops, helping send the Chung Wang's field army into a disastrous retreat. For the first time in two months he was in his own bed in the yamen at Sung-chiang, and Chang-mei was beside him.

What the hell's going on? he thought, a cold anger growing inside him. He jumped up and went to his window, sweeping aside the split bamboo blinds. Down below was a gathering of townspeople big enough to block the street.

Water dripped from the eaves. A spring rain was still falling – a light, drizzling rain, not enough to drench clothing but enough to spangle everything with dampness. But it had not dampened the curiosity of the crowd. Two hundred eager Chinese stood around in the muddy street, listening as a foreign voice fluted and brayed incredible wonders at them.

Ward saw the curiosity in their faces, the stack of Bibles, the printed tracts being handed out by a boy assistant. The preacher was up on a box, a Bible in his raised hand. A second boy assistant stood behind, holding a big oil-paper umbrella over his head. The preacher's face was gaunt; wire-rimmed spectacles, rain-specked, flashed as he turned. He shook the Bible over the heads of his audience, and when Ward saw all the forced gestures and rhetorical trickery of the religious orator, his temper broke.

Chang-mei watched him wordlessly as he threw on his clothes. He went out into the street and made straight for the speaker. The crowd fell back from him as he marched through them, but the preacher's voice continued.

'. . . but remember that according to Matthew, "every one that hath forsaken houses, or brethren, or sisters, or father, or mother, or wife, or children, or lands, for my name's sake, shall receive an hundredfold, and shall inherit everlasting life"!'

'Hey, you!'

The preacher stopped and turned.

'You! Who gave you permission to come into my city? Get down off of that box!'

'Permission? This is the word of God, sir. I need no perm—'

'You're not reading me right, Pilgrim.' Ward stepped up to the preacher, grabbed him by the jacket and pulled him down. As he was thrust away his hat fell off. His Chinese assistant grabbed up an armful of Bibles and retreated. The crowd were wide-eyed, whispering at the violence done to a religious scholar.

'How did you get in past the gate?'

'I don't know who you are, sir, but my name is the Reverend Alfred Chapman. I am lately come into this district from Hong Kong where I have preached for over two years. I have a paper, signed by—'

'I don't care what paper you've got. You get out of my city. Y'hear me?'

'But, this is Sung-chiang, is it not?'

'Get out of here, I told you!' Ward threw the man's hat at him.

Anger contorted the preacher's face. 'You can't interfere with me. I have a right, an absolute right accorded by treaty, to bring enligh—'

'Shut up and move!'

'The Lord's word cannot be silenced. He cannot – will not be silenced by you, nor by any man!'

Ward pulled his Colt and the preacher blanched, backed away and then broke into a run. 'That's right, skedaddle! And don't come back!'

The Chinese crowd saw Ward's grin as he turned away, a grin he put on for their benefit. He threw back his head and laughed. The amazed horror of those who watched suddenly dissolved, and they started to grin too, and soon the amusement was general, with everyone laughing.

When Ward came back indoors Chang-mei left him alone. He said nothing to her as he went into his office. A little later she sent the maid in to bring him tea. When she went in herself he was quietly tallying in his little blue book. Tallying, always tallying.

Whereas a tree is known by its fruit, so a man is known by his deeds, she reminded herself. But my husband thinks like a man of action, and acts like a man of thought. Why then did he come here? Better to do good deeds near at home than go far away to burn incense.

When he had sipped half his tea she asked, 'What for did you threaten the priest with death?'

He grunted. 'Death? I wasn't going to kill him.'

'Then . . . what for did you teach the Common People to laugh at him?'

'Because I won't let him poison my city with his damned silly ranting.' He smoothed the tab of hair on his chin, and looked up from his book. 'Those ideas of his are . . . dangerous.'

'Don't worry,' she said solicitously, coming round to massage his back. 'He's gone away now.'

'Yeah, but he'll be back – him and others like him. They don't understand how much authority the printed word carries out here. They don't understand the depth of reverence that's bred into the minds of the people. They don't know that in China printing ideas makes them true – beyond question, so they carry the force of law and all the power of life and death. They don't—' He stopped himself. 'Preachers are not to come here. That's my order. Next one that does, I'll have the sonofabitch shot.'

After a breakfast of star-fruit and lychees and mangoes brought up from Hong Kong by steamer, he pulled her to him and made love to her vigorously and with an animal passion. He was not as gentle this time as he had been in the past. She did not complain. She was dutiful, compliant as always, but she would still not open herself to him fully, no matter what he did.

'Did I hurt you?' he asked moodily afterwards.

'No.'

'Then why did you hold back?'

'Did I not please you?'

'No, you held back. You always do. And I always sense it. I want you to let go. Fully.'

She would not look at him.

'Chang-mei, you don't dare forget yourself even for a moment, do you?'

She burst into tears, surprising him with the sobs that shook her whole body.

Immediately he felt like a dog. When he comforted her she poured out a babble of words he could barely follow, but he caught enough to get the gist of it.

'Your father told me all about you being a bad luck woman.' He held her at arm's length and narrowed his eyes at her. 'It's pure nonsense. Look, I married you, didn't I? And I'm still invulnerable, aren't I?'

She averted her eyes, mutely defiant.

'Jesus Christ, why do women always feel everything's their fault? You're blameless, Chang-mei. Why won't you believe that?'

'I dare not love you. I am a bad luck woman. If once I give in, you will die!'

'Will you stop that?' He seized her shoulders. 'That's a nasty, pernicious little superstition and I forbid you to believe it. It'll crush you down if you let it, so stand up to it.'

'Maybe you don't understand.'

'I understand better than you think. It's like the spirits that come and stand around you in the dark. They always vanish with the morning light. You know why? Because they don't really exist.'

'Where is the ancestral shrine in your house?' she asked. 'You don't respect ancestors. You don't even believe about ghosts. Why should they visit you?'

'Ghosts are not ancestors, they're fears. You must dare your fears bravely. Confront them, and they'll lose their power to haunt you. That is an order.'

She covered herself with false meekness. 'This slave will try to do as you say.'

But he easily heard the lie in her voice, and he told her, 'Don't give me that! You must do it. For your own sake.'

'But this is my true belief!'

'I don't care to hear that! If it is you must change it!'

'I cannot,' she whispered, lost. And privately, in her inner-most mind she was thinking: so, after all your efforts, it is worse than you believed even at the beginning – he orders you to speak your mind openly only so your deepest true thoughts can be his to know and to take from you.

Her eyes began to fill with tears again. She said, 'A husband deserves to have a wife who is obedient to him in word and deed, but Barbarians do not care about proper obedience. What you want is obedience in thought, which I can never give to you!'

'Can't you see the prison you're making for yourself? A prison inside your own head? It doesn't have to be that way!'

She attacked like a cat. 'You think that if I alter my belief you will be able to escape your fate!'

'No, no, no . . .' He drew a deep breath. 'This is not for my sake – it's for yours. I want you to have peace of mind.'

'My mind is not having peace . . . You destroy my peace always!'

He saw the recriminations burning behind her eyes now, and it pained him. 'I love you, Chang-mei. And I want you to be able to love me. Properly!'

'Then you must let my beliefs alone!'

'Do as I ask. Please.'

'I . . . cannot.' She dissolved into weeping again, and he watched her for what seemed a long time, aghast at what he had done to her. When he hugged her to him she stiffened.

'Try. Try for me.'

'I cannot. I dare not. I want to love you, husband. But I dare not.'

The happy couple emerged from the Kao Wang's palace just before noon on a blazing summer's day. Fei wore a simple white dress and carried a posy of flowers. Lindley wore formal Taiping robes in black silk with a yellow sash to show his honorary commission into Taiping ranks. An escort of two hundred ceremonially uniformed troops led them and followed behind. As they crossed the crowded square spontaneous cheering began. Tens of thousands had come to see the Kao Wang's daughter marry the foreign doctor whose father was the Heavenly King's own prophet.

A cold resentment was now lodged inside Lindley's mind

445

at the way the Kao Wang had manipulated his requests. His promises about my father have all been empty, he thought. And now things have gone badly for the Chung Wang's field army he's decided to turn our marriage into a public circus to raise morale. He damped down his feelings and crossed the square, walking side by side with Fei towards the great Taiping cathedral. They had come here on each Saturday Sabbath, and each time there had been throngs of worshippers packed into the building, passionate to hear. The first time he attended he asked her, 'Is divine service always so full in the Heavenly Capital?'

'The Sabbath must always be observed, Lin-li.'

'Do you mean attendance is compulsory?'

'Worship is the source of our Taiping spiritual strength. No one would think of missing Sabbath prayer.'

'Does the T'ien Wang ever attend?'

'The T'ien Wang has not shown himself to the people for many years now.'

They entered the cathedral now and took their separate places at the head of the aisle. Lindley was a little surprised to see so many crammed in to witness their marriage. Once again he was struck by the plainness of the church's interior. There was no ornament, just a large, undecorated assembly space, paved with mats, with a simple, raised altar at one end over which hung an unadorned cross. The congregation was segregated – men to the right, women to the left.

The proceedings were straightforward, zealously delivered, and listened to by around two thousand souls. Prayers opened, then 'Jerusalem' was sung in Chinese. Afterwards the minister mounted to a pulpit and began a fervent harangue, demanding that pure Christianity must become the religion of all China, and giving assurances that those who had so far died believing in the brother of Jesus Christ were helping to bring it about, and in consequence they would live for ever.

Lindley looked across at Fei again and forced a smile for her benefit. It's not her fault, he told himself for the hundredth time. She loves you, but she's caught up in the workings of this monstrous machine. Her father's only ever thought of her as an instrument to be sacrificed to Taiping policy. And now he thinks I should do the same. He turned his attention back to the preacher, but felt only irritation at the words. It's plain silly that anyone can believe Christ has a Chinese younger brother, he told the preacher silently. And ludicrous that anyone can ascribe wives to all three persons of the Trinity. Either believe the whole lot, or don't believe any of it at all. I wonder what part my father's played in concocting this ridiculous blasphemy. He looked around, dismayed that his father was not present.

'Please rest assured that your father is in good health,' the Kao Wang had told him a week ago. 'He knows you are here. He is coming to the Heavenly Capital as soon as he can, but has been unavoidably detained.'

'Do you think he'll arrive in time for the wedding?'

'The region administered by us is very large – as large, so I am told, as any European country, and twice as populous. All is being done to bring your honoured father to the capital. Please be patient.'

But his patience had turned first to suspicion and then to anger. The incident at the execution ground had appalled him, and there were many other things in the Heavenly Capital that had begun to worry him. So far as he could see the people were not greatly better or worse off than those who lived in Manchu controlled cities, but here there was the feeling that even the people's minds were controlled. He had tried to make Fei see it, but she could not – or would not. He looked at her now, dutifully respecting a sermon that made no sense at all and was blasphemous by any Christian standard. He wondered at the validity of their marriage, and felt a powerful urge to get up and leave, but he knew that Fei had worked hard to bring them to this state, and there was no alternative but to go along with it.

Up in the pulpit the minister was halfway through a passionate condemnation of graven images. 'Take heed unto yourselves, lest ye forget the covenant of the Lord your God, which he made with you, and make you a graven image, or the likeness of any thing, which the Lord thy God hath forbidden thee. For the Lord thy God is a consuming fire, even a jealous God.'

The minister delivered the verses in portentous Chinese, with fearsome emphasis. Lindley realized for the first time how deeply these ancient laws – backed by the force of divine authority and decorated with the trappings of magic – had laid hold of the minds of these simple country people.

The ideas, he knew, came from the Old Testament, when gods came in many shapes and were ever in competition with one another. It was a time when these many gods were being brought under the sway of the one, invisible God of the Israelites.

'Thou shalt not make unto thee any graven image, or any likeness of any thing that is in heaven above, or that is in the earth beneath, or that is in the water under. Thou shalt not bow down thyself to them, serve them: for I the Lord thy God am a jealous God, visiting the iniquity of the fathers upon the children unto the third and fourth generation of them that hate me.'

That's why the hangings in the public areas of the Kao Wang's palace show no depictions of the world, he thought. No animals, no birds, no fish – and no people. It must be the same as the Muslims who believe in the Old Testament and its laws, and so practise only an art based on geometry and mathematical patterns. But here it goes much further than that – here there's an incitement to search out rival gods and obliterate them.

He thought back to his arrival at Nanking and saw that the seeds of doubt that had been sown in his mind then had now grown tall. Beads of sweat began to spangle his forehead and upper lip. He wiped his mouth. The minister's voice brought him back to the present. The congregation was being told to overthrow altars and break pillars and burn groves with fire and hew down the images of false gods, but then the sermon came to an abrupt end, and he realized that the Kao Wang had entered. An armed retinue followed him. He was in ceremonial dress, grave-faced and imposing. He took up station at his daughter's side, ready to give her away.

The ceremony was a grotesque parody of a Protestant wedding. The exchange of vows took only a few moments, then Fei and he stood together as the preacher blessed the union and the ring that symbolized it in the name of Jesus, His Father and His Brother. There followed no public kiss. Afterwards bride and groom were led away to attend to the record scrolls on which official chop marks had to be placed.

When they emerged into the summer heat it was to the applause of thousands. And there, as Lindley looked up, shading his eyes against the dazzling sun that reflected from the golden roofs of the T'ien Wang's palace, he saw one of the high, blank windows and imagined there a dark figure watching him.

Fei's heart pounded as she lay beside Lindley in the moonlight. She looked at the gold ring shining on her finger and felt the sweat filming her body. The night heat in the palace was relentless. Their lovemaking had been vigorous, but now Lindley was face down and unconscious, utterly spent, and she was alone again.

Doubts plagued her like night insects. Was Yehonala really going to have me executed? Was Lin-li correct after all? Or had 'normal government' resumed, and was an answer coming to me even as I was snatched away?

As she lay in the wash of moonlight she felt her undeserving soul crawl with exhausting contradictions. All through the marriage ceremony she had suffered, knowing in her heart that the T'ien Wang knew all her sins, that she was marked down in the Great Book as unworthy of His Kingdom. God knew everything that happened on earth or in the minds and souls of people. The T'ien Wang was the living God. His all-seeing eye was the eye of God. He must know what she was. Why, then, had he allowed this marriage to take place – if not for a greater reason?

The thought that she must be destined for hell consoled her. She looked at Lindley's naked body, wanting only to rouse him and lose herself in ecstasy again, to have him enter her so she could forget again for a moment her wickedness. But he was asleep, and that at least made her grateful that his brain was stilled and the stream of shocking ideas that came from him had halted.

'You must not criticize the principles of the Heavenly Kingdom,' she had told him.

'On the contrary, a free person must always criticize everything. We Scots do. I note that you're very free with criticisms of the Manchu regime, so you should have no trouble learning what's closer to hand.'

'The Manchu are the enemies of God.'

'Enemies of God? Fei, you're my wife. I'm your husband. We're in private. You don't have to maintain any pretences for me.'

'What pretences?'

He shrugged. 'Strict laws for everyone except the leaders. The keeping of concubines shall mean death, except that the T'ien Wang keeps a harem of eighty girls for himself – you know, pretences like that.'

She was appalled, terrified someone would hear. 'No, Lin-li, those ladies are his wives.'

'He has eighty wives? Get away with you – they're concubines. Pure and simple.'

'Shall I tell you about the first son of the Heavenly King?' she said desperately. 'At the very instant he was born thousands of birds, some as large as ravens and others as small as magpies, appeared and hovered about in the air before settling in the trees around his house.'

He grunted. 'Well, so much for the taut logic of Taiping Christianity.'

'It really happened. How can you explain such a thing?'

'Answer me this: why shouldn't I have a harem?'

'Because you are not a king.'

His irony always threw her off balance. 'Oh, I see. That's a really adequate answer.'

'According to the Bible polygamy was the law of well-beloved Abraham's time, when your own religious rules were framed. My father, too, has many—'

He had cut her off, jabbing a forefinger into his temple. 'You know as well as I do that the T'ien Wang is absolutely bloody insane. He's been out of his mind for years. He keeps a harem of eighty girls and does nothing all day and all night but lie with them and utter screeds of bloody silly gibberish.'

She had turned, white with anger, and marched away. He had laughed after her, amused, careless of the magnitude of his heresy. When she had cooled sufficiently she came back and told him, 'We are all responsible for the furtherance of our Taiping cause. If you speak like this again I will tell my father.'

'Tell him.'

'If I do, you will be . . .' She stopped herself from saying it.

'I will be what? Executed? Oh, yes, the Taiping answer to everything!'

'You will be expelled!'

'The truth is too much for you, isn't it? You can't bear it. Nobody here can.'

She lay open-eyed, remembering, watching the moon sink over the roofs of the T'ien Wang's palace.

What was truth anyway? Weren't the old religions sure there was no truth, that everything was merely an illusion? Wasn't truth simply the illusion that everyone agreed was true?

A tear trickled from her eye. She touched it with her fingertip and put the finger to her lips to taste the salt.

I don't know how long I can keep my mind split in two parts like this.

The country mansion of the former Governor of Yangchow was war-tattered, but unlike the temples and pagodas of the district it had escaped demolition by the Taipings. It stood on high ground two miles from the city walls, enjoying excellent feng-shui, and still showed much of the opulence of former days.

From his seat General Tseng Kuo-fan looked out at the city below, and beyond to where the Grand Canal sparkled as it met the Yangtze. Tseng talked with his younger brother, Tseng Kuo-ch'uan, sipping tea and treasuring the rare opportunity to enjoy a little time with his kinsman.

Kuo-ch'uan, now army commander at Chekiang, was speaking of family times. He asked, 'Do you remember what father said just before he died? And the prophecy he made after his pilgrimage to Nan-yueh?'

Tseng closed his eyes, bringing back the memory. 'He said, "Two pearls shall come together. Their brilliance shall one day illuminate Yangchow."' He chuckled. 'I see: his prophecy has come to pass.'

'Ah, what Heaven ordains . . .' Kuo-ch'uan said, warmed by the memory of their father. 'Will you receive Gordon?' he asked.

Tseng was ready for the question. 'No.'

'Is that because he was one of those who destroyed the Summer Palace?'

'I don't care about that.'

'Then why will you not receive him?'

Tseng shrugged. 'Why should I?'

'Because one day he will carry the baton that General Hua

451

wields. Also he has inspected the circuit of defences at Nanking and believes that a decisive victory can be gained by using the new British siege guns.'

Tseng deliberated, then looked up. 'Chinese methods are what will work best for China. You know, I've already determined the strategy that will succeed against Nanking. The melon is almost ripe and ready to cut.'

'Is it that you mistrust Gordon's intentions?'

'I do not even wish to understand them. He is an Outer Barbarian. For example, it is irrelevant what lies behind his offer to serve us without payment. What is offered for nothing is worth that and no more. This is well known.'

Kuo-ch'uan tapped his fingers. 'Certain of your staff privately believe that Gordon's policy of encouraging surrender would speed the victory and limit the slaughter of our own troops.'

Tseng Kuo-fan's face set hard as granite. 'I know what they are saying, but this is erroneous thinking. There must be adherence to right principles. The Taipings are infected by Western ideas. All of them are possessed by a kind of madness. In this way we are fighting against insanity itself, and whatever policy I decide there will still be fanatical Taiping defiance. Therefore surrender is not to be accepted.'

'No surrender. But . . .' Kuo-ch'uan fell humbly silent, and the silence between them grew huge and uncomfortable.

'Yes, Younger Brother. I know what you're thinking, that such a formidable band of rebels has never been known since ancient times. But remember, my task is not simply the winning of a war, but the complete neutralization of the rebellion. This can only be accomplished by the death of its leaders and all their followers.'

Kuo-ch'uan drew breath at the implications of his brother's words. 'Then your policy will be to drive the Chung Wang back inside Nanking? And then to surround the city with a band of iron?'

'We cannot look into men's hearts. To be absolutely sure of eradicating the Taiping disease there must be an extermination of all human life at Nanking. If we are to protect the traditional order, we can afford to spare no one at all. This is unfortunate, but unavoidable.' He paused and then drew a deep breath that underlined the end of the debate. When he spoke again it was with a smile. 'Do I need to ask what more is troubling you? Or are you so important these days that you no longer confide in your elder brother?'

'You always could see through me,' Kuo-ch'uan said, glorying in his brother's customary perception. 'As a matter of fact there has been news of some strange events in my jurisdiction. And it's unsatisfactory for there to be strange events in a place for which I am responsible.'

The General nodded. He thought of the uneasy rumours, of new mandarins turning up to take control in the reconquered territories, news of high-handed appointments made by Peking, of Imperial posts given directly to outside nominees, without thought as to how properly to reward the men who had been fighting hard to stamp out the Taiping vermin in Kiangsu and along the Yangtze valley.

'What kind of strange events?'

'Several days ago a curious letter came to me from Peking. It was impressed with "No Hidden Heart".'

The General felt instantly on guard. 'Prince Kung's personal chop?'

'Correct. He also sent a jar of special pickle as a present for you. It is most beautifully wrapped and boxed.'

'For me?'

'Yes. He said you would surely delight in it.'

The General's face clouded. 'What does he want?'

'I wondered that. Some kind of favour.' Kuo-ch'uan patted the arm of his chair thoughtfully, as if preparing to broach a difficult question. 'Elder Brother, have you ever heard of such a thing as an Imperial eunuch going about collecting taxes – in the *South*?'

The General started with surprise, then allowed a laugh to escape him. 'A preposterous idea!'

'I agree, but it becomes more preposterous still. It seems that this eunuch travels in state along the Grand Canal on a golden barge, like the Emperor himself.'

'Wh . . . what?'

'Listen to what Prince Kung says: ". . . in violation of the law, this villain has gone on a journey into the South. The Governor of Shantung, Ting Pao-chen, has memorialized me, saying he is shocked by an Imperial eunuch having entered Shantung, usurping the prerogatives of the Son of Heaven by travelling along the canals in gilded barges and under dragon-embroidered canopies of the Imperial yellow. Now An Te-hai is reported to be headed for Yangchow.'

Tseng was mortified. 'An Te-hai? Did you say An Te-hai? Coming to Yangchow?'

'So Prince Kung believes.'

'Has the Emperor given him permission to travel?'

'It seems not. Prince Kung mentions no Decree to that effect. In fact – and this is the interesting part – he says that in an effort to rectify the matter he has taken it up with one of the joint-Regents, and that she has issued a warrant—'

'Which joint-Regent?'

'Empress Dowager Tz'uan.'

'Are you sure it wasn't Tz'u-hsi, the Emperor's mother?'

'Absolutely sure.'

General Tseng leapt to his feet, his face beaming. 'Excellent!'

Kuo-ch'uan stared at him as if he had gone mad. 'Is something wrong, Elder Brother? Have I said something that begs reprimand?'

'Oh, no! On the contrary. On the contrary! What you say fills me with joy. Let us unwrap this pickle jar!'

Lindley left the Kao Wang's palace discreetly for the second time in three days. He was alone and determined to walk about the city as he pleased, or at least to see how far the militiamen would let him go before trying to stop him. On his first walk outside the palace complex the Kao Wang's guards had found him and insisted – tactfully but firmly – on escorting him back. This time, he knew, he must be more careful.

Fei keeps trying to convince me that I've come to paradise, he thought. But so far as I can see everything's stinking in the Heavenly Capital, not least the excuses I've been given concerning my father. He followed the wall of the T'ien Wang's palace, always moving briskly, always avoiding the pinch points where he was most likely to be noticed by the militia. He crossed Drum Tower Square and entered a narrow filth-choked alley, hoping it would emerge close to a small market square he had visited the day before. Instead it turned through a dog-leg and became a dusty pathway, hemmed in by rough mortared brick walls only a little taller than himself. Suddenly he heard the question shouted, 'Who is God?'

He froze, looked around but saw nothing. Then again: 'Who is God?'

It seemed to be coming from the far side of the wall. Part of him wanted to walk on, but he could not. He stayed and listened to the same question put over and again. The voice was coming from a courtyard garden overspread by little trees. He found the gate and opened it a little, then stared in.

Fifty or so adolescents were sitting in rows before a busy little man holding a cane and posing the venomous question. Above the boys, suspended from the tree, a filthy, near-naked man squatted inside a bamboo cage. His hair was long and matted and he was covered in sores. He looked starved and weary and as wretched as any broken-spirited animal. The cage in which he was confined did not allow him to straighten his back or legs. Suddenly, Lindley realized with horror that both the prisoner's hands were missing.

Every time the question was posed the instructor prodded the man with the cane. Eventually the prisoner croaked. 'God is the Creator of Heaven, Earth, and all things.'

'Louder.'

'God is the Creator of Heaven, Earth, and all things.'

'Is God a spirit?'

'How many gods are there?'

'One.'

'But the Manchu worship many gods, what have you to say to that?'

'They are all false, the creations of man's imagination, or dead men promoted to the rank of gods by men.'

'Can men really become gods?'

'No. They have the name, but not the reality.'

'What of "Yu-huang," the god who is so universally and highly honoured by the Manchu nation?'

'He also is a made god, and not a true God.'

'Who is Jesus Christ?'

'The Son of God.'

'Is He God?'

'Yes.'

'Why did He come into the world?'

'He came to save men.'

'How does He save men?'

'He died to redeem them.'

The instructor seemed well satisfied. He nodded proudly and smiled at the assembled youths. Then he turned back to the prisoner. 'Very good. Very good!'

Lindley watched, unable to turn away. He opened the gate revealing himself, all thoughts of further exploration driven from his mind.

'Who's there?' the instructor called, coming forward.

'You,' Lindley said, anger bursting inside him. 'What are you doing to this man?'

'Private study. Private study. Please go away!'

'Who is this man?'

The students gaped up at him. The instructor said, 'This was a Manchu general. He commanded the enemy garrison of this Heavenly Capital when first it was captured.'

'What're you doing to him?' Lindley's eyes were burning and he felt himself losing control. 'Let him out of there!'

The instructor bristled. 'This man is for education purposes.'

Lindley wiped his mouth, the mixture of revulsion and rage nauseating him. 'You're torturing him. Let him out.'

'Not torture. Education. Many years ago this general ordered the beheading of ten thousand Taiping captives. His example is to strengthen us.'

Lindley snatched the cane from the instructor and snapped it. Then he strode to the cage, the students scattering away from him. The stench of human excreta filled his nose as he searched the cage for a catch, but it was a perfect cube and there was no door. With disgust he realized that the cage had been built around the prisoner and could not be opened.

'How long has he been inside?'

'You get out now!'

Lindley launched himself at the instructor and grabbed him. 'I said, how long has he been in there? How long have you been doing this to him?'

The instructor was struck dumb, and Lindley threw him bodily aside. He hunted around the garden for something to use to break open the cage and found a small gardener's hatchet. When he approached the cage again the prisoner panicked and began to writhe. Lindley ignored him and started striking at the lashed joints of the cage, breaking them apart.

The prisoner screamed with every blow as if the bamboo was his own flesh, but Lindley did not stop. He hacked until the cage sagged and the bottom fell away. The prisoner dropped out and fell to the ground. He tried to waddle away, but his movements were froglike and grotesque. After years bent double, Lindley realized, he could no longer uncoil his back or straighten his limbs.

He stared at the man's nightmare efforts, too dazed and horror-stricken to help. Then militiamen came crowding around him, bundling him out of the torture garden and back out into the alley.

An Te-hai's litter was carried into the pretty outer courtyard of the Yangchow Governor's mansion and set down on the cobbles. The half-naked bearers panted, their headbands saturated with sweat. An breathed in the air deeply as he got down. The rich fragrance of late flowers filled the garden. The day was dry and dusty and warm, and his rich robes seemed a little too heavy for this mild weather.

Here in the South flowers last longer, he thought. They bloom so much more easily, they are so much bigger and their colours so much more vivid. It must be a land closer to the sun here in the South.

The Governor's mansion was quite magnificent, built on a hill of tall pine trees. The main gate was approached by a winding flight of steps. A young mandarin of the seventh rank came out to greet him with a bow.

'Please, honoured visitor, my master bids you enter his humble home.'

'Your master is too kind.'

An's gaze passed imperiously over the row of kneeling servants. It was gratifying to be received with the formalities accorded a welcome guest of high rank. Gratifying to know that his reputation had preceded him. One who gathers taxes may always look forward to being agreeably treated, he thought, feeling the piquant hunger he had been cultivating. The invitation to take tea with the Governor was sure to entail an elaborate meal, and an elaborate meal in Kiangsu was best anticipated with an empty belly. The constitution of a eunuch was unlike that of a man. Eunuchs were essentially yin in nature, and whereas a man could regulate his bodily balances by practising 'emission control' a eunuch produced no semen to expel. Therefore it was important not to eat too many yin foods.

How I have enjoyed the South, he thought looking round at the impressive walls. I'll be sorry to return at the end of this moon, but return I must. And at least I'll return enriched.

More servants lined the way from his litter. The outer courtyard opened into the inner by a moon gate – circular, like the full moon. Here were three more steps. He mounted them and saw with delight the large inner court crowded with flowers. A table had been set up at the far end of the court, and three men waited ready to greet him. All rose except these three men. Two of them were wearing the hats of senior mandarins, and lined up behind were many lesser military mandarins.

The formality of the reception was impressive. Troops were arrayed for his inspection – perhaps a hundred. As he was conducted past them he rehearsed compliments and enquiries as to the health of the host and of his family that such unlooked-for formality required. Then he advanced towards the seated trio, expecting them to rise also, but no one moved.

The table was set with papers and ink stone and brush. There was something else too, something no bigger than a rice bowl, but covered with a square of silk. The strangely bareheaded figure in the centre sat with bowed head, his arms folded so that the square chest panel of his robe was hidden from view.

When those arms moved An saw revealed the ch'i fin, the mythical animal that was the insignia of the first military grade. When the bare head was lifted An saw the face of Tseng Kuo-fan, Commander-in-Chief, Imperial Forces, Central China. An felt his belly dissolve and his mind freeze.

'An Te-hai. How delighted I am to see you once more.'

'General Tseng . . .' An was like a sleepwalker who awakes to find himself standing on the lip of a precipice.

'You are quite well, I trust?'

'Very well. Very well.' An tried to cover his shock with a negligent gesture, to tell himself there could be nothing to fear. 'I understood that my invitation came from the

Governor of Yangchow. What are you doing here? You are perhaps here to dine also?'

The General's face betrayed nothing. He ate up An's confusion, then he said, 'An Te-hai, unfortunately there is no longer any possibility for you to dine with the Governor of Yangchow. The reason you have been invited here is to read this newly-arrived Imperial edict.'

He passed a paper to the young mandarin and it was delivered into An's hands. As he read it his composure deserted him. 'What is this?'

'As you see – an edict containing the order for your execution.'

Somewhere a great drum was being beaten, dull reports marking the Hour of the Monkey.

'No!' An shouted. 'No! This is a forgery!'

'No forgery. See – it is properly impressed with Prince Kung's seal.'

'Prince Kung is not a Regent! He has no authority!'

'Ah, but it is also sealed with a Regent's seal – in accordance with the law.'

'Then it must be a mistake! Check with Peking!'

'So sorry, there is no time for checking. The order says "immediate execution".'

'No! You can't do this! This is nonsense!' The terror was raw in his voice as he realized they were not going to listen to him. No matter what he said, no matter what he did, they would remain unimpressed. 'Did you hear what I said?'

General Tseng gestured to his Hunanese swordsman. The executioner strode forward, his chest and arms muscular and swart, his pigtail braided and wound on his shaved head in the manner of a man accustomed to physical labour. An saw that the leather bindings on his sword hilt were sweated-in and worn. The pitted blade had seen great service.

An screamed, 'I am protected! If you harm me the Empress Dowager will stop at nothing to obliterate you! She will destroy you Tseng Kuo-fan! She will destroy you all!'

Tseng's face remained expressionless, his tone bland, 'I doubt that. It is the Empress Dowager who ordered it.'

'That's impossible! It's all a mistake I tell you!'

'No mistake. See – she has sent you a final present.'

Tseng stood up. The gold and silver threads of his

embroidered chest square glistened in the perfect sunshine. He lifted the cloth before him and revealed the 'pickle' jar he had been sent by Prince Kung. Inside were the preserved remains of An Te-hai's virgin manhood.

The eunuch's eyes widened and he shrieked, 'My jar! My jar! – The whore! The filthy, trustless whore! That's my jar!'

Tseng made another gesture and An was seized and stripped. Two hundred pairs of eyes searched his nakedness, eager to see what a eunuch's body would be like.

An struggled again, but the guards forced his head down. An sobbed, 'The Emperor's a bastard! A bastard and a whore's whelp, do you hear! The Son of Heaven's not Hsien-feng's son. The T'ung-chih Emperor is an imposter! An imposterrr!'

Everyone stared, unnerved by the insane blasphemy spouting from the eunuch. He had clearly lost his mind. Tseng shifted uneasily, embarrassed by the disgusting ravings. A man facing execution should behave with decorum and spend, in his last moments, all the dignity remaining to him. But, then, you're not a man, An Te-hai, he thought with revulsion. You're not even whole. You're a disgusting, strutting, filthy little eunuch who has made one mistake too many. 'Gag the prisoner.'

Two troopers bowed, ran forward and used their daggers to tear apart the eunuch's opulent robes.

'Wait!' The General picked up the jar and threw it down onto the cobbles, so that it shattered. 'Use that!'

One of the executioner's assistants stepped forward and bent over the pungent fluid that had splashed the ground. He steeled himself, then obeyed, stuffing the eunuch's mouth until the vile noise was muffled. A strip of robe was tied around the eunuch's mouth before he was forced down into the kowtow once more.

'Please disregard the animal noises you have just heard,' Tseng told the assembled ranks. 'To cleanse your ears allow me to offer you a poem of my own devising:

> 'Hold fame and riches cheap,
> Desire little and keep your heart clean;
> Keep far from illicit gain –
> Demons will fear and gods respect you.

Act with utmost care,
Even unto the last hour of life;
If you fail, Seek the cause in yourself.

Let hand and eye work together,
Join mind and strength to strive;
Exhaust all knowledge, push yourself onward,
Even through the night that follows day.'

As Tseng finished he raised his hand. The executioner took up position and readied himself. Then the General dropped his hand and sat down, scornfully ignoring the proceedings now. He dipped his writing brush in black ink and began to write. He did not look up as the eunuch's head was severed at the first blow and a worthless life gushed out across the cobbles.

Absolute silence settled over the courtyard. When Tseng had finished writing he calmly got up and retrieved the head, tore away the gag and examined the bony face at arm's length until the flickering eyelids ceased to move. Then he jammed the dripping trophy on the spire of a hat-stand, before crowning it jauntily with his own hat. Below he propped his newly-written inscription:

'A hat not forgotten by General Tseng Kuo-fan.'

The officers ranged in front of the house looked to one another and began to appreciate the fine joke their commander was sharing with them. The laughter spread until the courtyard was filled with mirth.

When it died away Tseng said, turning to his men, his face grave once more, 'Soldiers of my command. This rebellion of the God-worshippers has been too costly. It has laid waste twelve provinces, destroyed a hundred cities and reduced half the Empire to famine and disease. This war has been far bloodier than any in the entire history of the world. The T'ung-chih Emperor now requires this state of affairs to be brought to an end. You have heard his will. Return to your regiments, and prepare for days of bitter strength.'

That evening, during the Hour of the Dog, a servant came to General Tseng and announced the arrival of an Imperial messenger from Peking. When he opened the letter he saw that the Empress Dowager Tz'u-hsi's seal was on it. It ordered An Te-hai to be sent back to Peking unmolested, that all previous orders regarding him were to be ignored.

How characteristic of the Yi Concubine, Tseng thought, to ensure that a message such as this deliberately arrives just two hours too late.

Then he laughed again.

'You are as soft as a bean curd,' Chang-mei said, laughing.

'Come here!' Ward called after her,

'No!' She darted for the door, but he caught her and threw her down on the bed and began to strip her. She wriggled and bit his arm and he flipped her over and pushed her head into the silk pillows until she submitted. When he turned her over to face him the laughing stopped and they made love.

As she lay back beside him on the silken spread, something caught her eye; something had flown into the room and was moving on the bed canopy. When she saw what it was she stiffened.

His head turned, and he asked groggily, 'What's the matter?'

'Nothing,' she lied.

It was a butterfly, and everyone knew that the souls of dead wives often came from the grave and appeared to their husbands in the guise of butterflies. Could this butterfly, she wondered, be the soul of her dead once-betrothed?

She pushed the thought away from her. The boy was long dead, and anyway hadn't she and her foreign husband just made love, so what business had a dead boy's ghost in coming here? She reminded herself that the written character for butterfly was the figure of a lover sipping nectar from the calyx of a flower, so maybe the butterfly had come to them as a symbol of joy, to celebrate their joining. That's right, she told herself bravely, your husband has told you to think only thoughts that please you. In this you must obey him.

The fear lifted and she brightened. She put out her finger, delighting when the wonderful creature climbed onto it. She shielded it with her hand, and showed it to him.

The wings trembled as they watched together, their thoughts absorbed in the swirling iridescent patterns that looked so much like a cat's eyes. The butterfly was surely a celestial messenger. What other reason could there be for such an impossible creature?

'The colourful butterfly dances among the flowers; the yellow oriole sings on the willow tree,' she quoted, then suddenly she turned to him. 'I hope I return as a butterfly in my next life.'

Hua took the fragile creature. He smiled at her, and seemed pleased to see her smiling, pleased to see her new-found confidence.

Look how gentle he is, she thought. This naked Barbarian warlord who could not destroy a butterfly, yet whose hands are red with the blood of countless human beings! I am still in awe of you, my husband, but I no longer fear you!

He murmured, 'Fly away, little beauty.'

When he launched the butterfly it flittered briefly through the warm air. Then it was gone from the room and all was summer tranquillity again.

Her eyes drank him in. There were beads of perspiration at his hairline, the crow's feet of cheerfulness at his eyes. His neck was thick as a mooring post and there was hair on his well-muscled limbs, but sometimes his face seemed almost Chinese. She pressed herself against him, loving his coarse maleness, and kissed his scars. And for a moment, she forgot that she must never love him.

Fei lay in the bed trying to block the furious arguments out of her mind. Since seeing the Manchu prisoner in the cage Lindley had changed. Today she had told him of the Manchu's release into death, and that had made him worse.

She saw the look on his face. He was touched in the way non-believers were often touched by news of death. Mixed with the sadness there is much unnecessary fear, she thought. I know now that he does not believe in the Lord Jesus. Nor does he believe in salvation and the promise that he can live for ever if only he will believe. He is not a Christian in his heart. Nor will he ever be.

She felt the reprimand. 'I'm sorry to hurt you, Lin-li, but he was our enemy, and so was his wife, and so was his father-in-law and all his clan. I have no grief for any of them.'

When he spoke again his voice was bitter. 'You know what the truth is? The truth is that your Heavenly King's family weren't rich enough to bribe the examiners, or they were too naive to realize that was what they had to do. So he kept failing. And the third time he failed he collapsed, a sensitive youth pushed over the edge by strain and the shame of having let down his family. The pressure was too much for him. He had a breakdown, a breakdown brought on by rigid Confucian social rules applied to him by people from whom he had every right to expect help. He dreamed that the Supreme God scooped out his insides and filled him with a new set of organs. What he saw were not visions, they were hallucinations influenced by guilt and shame. Don't you see that?'

'You must not speak that way, Lin-li,' she said horrified at his ideas. 'The T'ien-Wang's visions were true experiences. God told him to bring China to a state of grace and he has done so.'

'Don't you see how it must have been? Can't you see how a man's mind would crack when placed under a burden of intolerable shame? Isn't it reasonable to you that his tortured mind would spawn exactly the sort of delusion that it did? One of powerful renewal, one of the old Hung being thrown away, and a different, sinless Hung coming into being?' He paused, staring. He was trying to gauge the effect his words were having on her. 'Fei, in that disturbed state he ran into my father. And that was the very worst thing that could have happened to him.'

'There was no misfortune. Your father was the blessed instrument sent by God for the accomplishment of His plan.'

'How can you say that?'

'Be proud! It was your own father who passed on the Christian message.'

'Christian?' He gave a short, humourless laugh. 'You call this . . . blasphemy . . . *Christian*? What happened in Hung's visions? God gave him a golden sword and told him to fight with the demons, and the next thing you know he's setting himself up as Jesus Christ's younger brother! It's obscene.'

'The T'ien Wang is Jesus Christ's younger brother.'

'No! No, he's not, Fei. He's just another poor deluded bloody soul, like you and I.'

She shook her head, searching his face. 'How can you say he is not Jesus Christ's younger brother?'

He sighed and wiped his face with both hands. 'It's a pity a few more people didn't say that. Repeating a conviction persuasively doesn't make it true. Can't you see that? The fact that an idea makes converts doesn't make it true. Hung Hsiu-ch'uan found plenty of people prepared to believe him because there's always a hunger for miracles.'

When she left him Lindley looked at the narrow verandah that jutted out from the Kao Wang's private apartments, and drank down the last dregs of the whisky he had brought with him from Shanghai. His mind was still a-jingle with thoughts.

'Her father only let us marry because she told him I was some sort of diplomat,' he muttered. 'A man of influence with the British government. The truth is I'm a prisoner here. Another wretch to be dangled in a bamboo cage.'

He saw movement in the darkened space beyond the verandah. The T'ien Wang's harem, he thought, bitter at Taiping hypocrisy. It's a fine palace for a man who hasn't shown himself to his people once in over five years.

When Lindley turned the Kao Wang was standing in the shadows at his back. He wore a simple grey suit and his head was bare. He said, 'Do you know why the Taoists and Confucianists failed China?'

Lindley drank down the last of his flask. 'Why?'

'Because the Taoists believe that goodness springs from the natural world. Confucius believed that human nature was the source of goodness. They do not recognize that the Brother of Jesus is where all good originates. The Psalms tell us: "Surely men of low degree are vanity, and men of high degree are a lie. Put not your trust in princes, nor in the son of man, in whom there is no help."' The Kao Wang shifted. 'Why did the British and French break faith with me?'

'Did they do that?'

'They made guarantees of neutrality, yet now they try everything to destroy us. We worship the same God and the same Saviour. We are one brotherhood. Why did they assist the common enemy, the Manchu idol-worshippers and enemies of our Heavenly Father and Jesus the heavenly Elder Brother? What madness drove foreign soldiers to defend Shanghai, while preventing the Chung Wang, their Christian brother, from capturing it? Why did they side with the evil Manchu in the South when at the same time in the North they were at war with them?'

'Perhaps they know you for what you really are.'

The Kao Wang looked at him with a harrowing intensity. 'We only wish to promote the Bible in China, to destroy all heathen idols and expel the Manchu slave masters. We want to establish one complete and undivided Christian empire, and become brothers with the Christian nations of the West. We want to introduce European science, to buy your manufactures. So why do the British oppose us? Have we ever done them the slightest harm? Have we not always acted in good faith and sublime friendship?'

'They do not believe in your friendship. They know you're as insane as the man you serve.'

'The Heavenly Kingdom will last for ever.'

Loathing and pity reacted together inside Lindley. He cradled his head in his hands, then looked out over the desolate city. 'No. The Heavenly Kingdom's going to die. I've been on British warships and I've seen their guns: the stalemate's broken. The martial mind of the Manchu has finally met with modern weapons and tactics. Imperial forces are going to tighten a choking grip on this hellish domain of yours, and when they do they won't let go.' He gestured towards Drum Tower Square where the wedding crowd had once waited for him. 'Did you hear them all cheering us the day your daughter and I were married? Those people? Your people? Why don't you go out there and tell them what you already know? Tell them there's no escape now. That they're all going to be obliterated.'

The Kao Wang seemed not to hear. 'It is written that there was war in Heaven. Michael and his angels fought against the Dragon. And the Dragon fought with the angels and prevailed not. Neither was their place found any more in Heaven. And the great Dragon was cast out, that old serpent called the Devil, and Satan, which deceiveth the whole world . . . You must go to Shanghai and convince the British of our good intent. They will believe you. They must.'

He heard the words and the chance of freedom they offered. He wanted to seize it, but could not. 'I came here to find my father. If you want my help you must show him to me.'

466

'Perhaps in the fullness of time you will see him. But first you will deliver a letter to the British Consul in Shanghai.'

He turned, his eye following the line of the upper storey of the blank, white wall of the T'ien Wang's palace. 'I think the fullness of time has arrived. I think I know where my father is, where he's been all along.'

Ward left his bodyguard at the wharf on Soochow Creek and walked alone along the Bund. It was ten o'clock, but the sun had already burned away the river mists and the air was warm and odorous. He felt something underfoot, looked down and saw it was a sheet of paper. He picked it up, feeling a great foreboding, knowing why the Chinese believed in the magic of words. The handbill was roughly printed and said in English and Chinese.

> JOHN 6:27
> Labour not for the meat which perisheth,
> but for that meat which endureth unto everlasting life,
> which the Son of man shall give unto you:
> for him hath God the Father sealed.

He screwed the paper into a tight ball and tossed it into the oily waters of the Huang-pu. The tide was coming in, pushing against the river's natural flow, so that the paper floated upstream towards the Chinese city.

He climbed the steps of the Grand Hotel, noting as he did so the split railing post that stood to one side. It had been repainted but the scar remained in the wood where he had once stuck Eden Phillips's Bowie knife. He entered the lobby, seeing with dismay that the place had been newly decorated. He looked around, trying to recognize the old and the familiar, but what had once been was now totally gone. The new furnishings seemed to him tasteless and cheap. When he sat down in one of the plush-covered armchairs it sank under him and a smell of new upholstery came up out of it. The lobby, he saw, was crowded with two hundred patrons, none of them men he knew, or who knew him. They looked through him as no one had looked through him for a long time.

No wonder the old crowd have moved out, he thought. The atmosphere's lost its charge. It's downright stuffy in here.

He was pleased to see Annie appear on the stair. She had already seen him and was looking his way. She beckoned to him. Ordinarily he would have waited for her to come over to him, but this time he got up and went to her.

'Let's go up to my room,' she said as he reached her. He recognized the old note of drama in her voice. 'I've got something to tell you.'

'Some things never change,' he said, following, but the remark was lost on her. As he left the staircase behind and crossed the landing she got out her key and opened her door.

'What's the big secret?'

'Burgevine was here three days ago.'

He stiffened. 'I told him I'd kill him if he bothered you again.'

'No, he didn't bother me.'

'Then why was he here? It wasn't to apologize.'

'No. He met with Eden.'

'What?' He was stunned. 'I don't believe it!'

'It's true.'

Burgevine was still no better than half recovered. He was in constant pain and drinking two bottles of hard liquor a day to kill the agony in his guts. Ward fixed her with a steady eye. 'Why would he want to see your husband? More to the point, what would make Eden agree to see him?'

'Governor Wu.'

'Wu? Why?'

'Shanghai's ready to grow. It's a place that's coming up fast. Eden can smell that, and he wants to acquire land to build warehouses along the river on Pu-tung side, and that's in the Governor's gift.'

'But – meeting Henry?' Ward said, perplexed. 'After what he did to you? I can't believe he'd do that. Eden was prepared to kill to set things straight.'

When Annie turned to the window Ward could see the strain in her face, lines that no powders or paints could hide. 'My husband was only ever interested in business. He never really had time for anything else.'

'Annie you're wrong. He was full of rage for you when you were hurt. He tried to whip me because he thought it was my fault.'

'Full of rage for me . . .' she said wistfully. 'That's not love, though, is it? That's just ownership. That's what men can never understand.'

'He loves you. I saw that.'

'You don't know anything about love either.'

'All I know is Eden got angry when you got hurt. He cares about you. And maybe you don't realize how much you hurt him by doing what you did – what you still do.'

She faced him and he saw it in her eyes that he had touched on a truth. 'Don't I?'

'Maybe you do realize,' he said slowly. 'Maybe that's why you give him the hell you do.'

She laughed shortly, a private amusement that only made sense to her. 'Heaven and hell are here and now. And the irony is that nobody can tell which is which.'

'I can.'

'Well, I never could.' Her smile became a self-mocking smirk. 'But luckily nobody lives for ever.'

'You're crazy. Do you know that?' He said it tenderly. 'I've always thought there's a pure little girl inside of you that none of this . . . sordidness ever touches.'

'If you think that then you're crazier than I am,' she said, no longer looking into his eyes. 'Maybe that's why I've always wanted you.'

'They say you should never go to bed with anyone crazier than yourself.'

'They say a lot of things.'

'Yes.'

After he left Annie he went downstairs, his mind working back and forth over what she had said. His thoughts began to spiral away into fantasies of betrayal. 'No, that's just your suspicious mind,' he murmured aloud, disciplining himself. Henry's just trying to fix a little private business, that's all. Wu might have made a Chinese subject out of him, but Yang must know Henry's no leader. He's got no vision and he's got no plan. And anyway, if Henry ever got to lead the Ever-victorious Army it'd be over my dead body, so there's really no problem, eh?

He stared around the lobby, disliking it now. Then he ordered a whisky for old times' sake. He drank it down in one gulp, cast a last look around the lobby of the Grand

Hotel and decided that some kind of heyday had come to a close.

Lindley saw a shadow cross the polished floor. He had come through the Kao Wang's secret passage into the Heavenly King's palace. His heart hammered, a surge of anticipation drove him on.

'Our father, which art in Heaven,' he muttered under his breath. 'Hallowed be thy name. Thy Kingdom come, thy will be done on Earth as it is in Heaven . . .'

The figure had been tall – a Westerner, skirted in clerical black. He followed, until the corridor widened into an open area nine bays long by five bays wide that was flooded with light. The Great Hall of Jesus was at the top of the palace, high under the golden eaves. Huge columns, perfect cylinders of gilded wood, supported a caisson ceiling where thousands of rafters intersected, all finished with intricate interlocking geometric designs. The polished floor of cedar planks gleamed with white brilliance that slanted in between eaves and battlements.

Lindley followed, unseen on the far side of a row of columns, past a great, golden statue of the Saviour, approaching now the vacant throne of the living god. The man in black stopped, got down on his knees, then went into a full kowtow before a Chinese in flowing yellow robes who lay back on an elaborate couch near the throne.

The Chinese was about fifty years old, balding, with lank grey hair. He wore a streaked white beard and many strings of pearls about his neck. He was fleshy, but his complexion was waxen and his busy eyes were darkly ringed. He seemed restless, animated by unfocused nervous energy. A boy of fourteen or so years stood to one side, shy and self-absorbed. The older man exchanged a few words with the man in black, but then the boy started in fright, and when the older Chinese looked up and saw Lindley he began to howl like a wild animal.

The European spun round, his amazed face riven by deep lines. Long hair straggled over his collar and his face was fallen, but there was no mistaking the shape of his nose and the rise of his forehead, and Lindley knew him beyond all doubt.

'Father . . .' It was no more than a whisper. He felt as if a huge force was impelling him forward. 'Father, after all these years.'

His answer came in Chinese. 'Who art thou? Answer me, demon!'

Lindley's mind crawled with horror. 'Father? Don't you know me?'

'Know thee?' He heard the hysterical fear. 'Thou art a demon! And I cast thee out!'

The boy was clutching his hands to his mouth. The T'ien Wang was coiled tight in his seat, panting as if he wasn't seeing Lindley at all, but some monstrous apparition known only to himself. The terror in those screams made Lindley want to blot them out with his own shouts. He tried to seize the man before him, but was thrust off with maniac strength. 'Leave this holy place!'

The blow delivered to Lindley's chest was huge and unexpected. It threw him back a dozen paces. Anger surged in him as he regained his feet. 'Father! Don't you know me?'

The other seized him in an iron grip, his stare fierce, his voice booming. 'Leave this holy place, I say! Be gone from here!'

Again Lindley felt the raw strength in the other's arms, and was pushed back. 'Father, for God's sake!'

'Blessed are they that do his commandments, that they may have right to the tree of life, and may enter in through the gates into the city. Do as I command! Be gone, blaspheming devil from hell! I exorcise thee!' He swept up a sword that flashed blood red in the dawn light.

Lindley backed away, horrified, but hoping to lure his father towards the door through which he had entered. The sword tore the air with a sound like ripping silk as it was swung about the other's head.

'For without are dogs! And sorcerers! And whoremongers! And murderers! And idolaters! And whosoever loveth and maketh a lie!'

The opulently decorated passageway into which he fell back was darkened. He looked behind him and saw there was no exit. He ran back, looking round for something to grab up and use as a shield, but there was nothing but a large wooden chest too heavy to lift. He tore down painted silk wall hangings as he backed away, throwing them, hoping to buy himself time to retreat, but the sword sliced them apart and the man who wielded it stepped forward over them, grunting with effort, and advancing on him.

Behind Lindley there was only a maze-latticed window. He reached it with seconds to spare and tore at it with his bare hands. Forty feet below he could see a garden of fruit trees. He would have to jump. But the lattice was made of iron and fixed into the wall. The sword sliced closer to him. He put up his hands, knowing that he would have to stake everything on a well-timed rush at his attacker's throat, then the sword halted.

'Harry . . .' A voice full of shattered hopes said. 'I prayed to the Lord that you would never come to this place. Quickly! Come this way!'

Outside, a heavy dew had smothered the pre-dawn. As the bloodied sky streamed overhead father and son moved onto a high balcony of the Heavenly King's palace overlooking Drum Tower Square.

'You must go back. Back the way you came. Do it now. Take your chance and get away from here.'

'No,' he said, looking at the man before him. 'I came to find you.'

'You were never meant to do that, Harry. You were never meant to see me like this. Why did you come here? Why didn't you stay in Shanghai, and return home to your mother, as I prayed you would?'

'Because there is no God, or if there is he's not listening to your prayers. My mother's dead. Will you not listen to what I tell you?'

'Go home. Go home . . .' He turned suddenly and stretched out a hand. 'O Lord, how shall I glorify thy name? For thou only art holy, and all nations shall come and worship before thee.'

Lindley was aghast at the shreds of his father's sanity. He felt hopelessness overwhelm him as he searched his father's face. 'I'm going to stay until I get what I came for. I want you to understand. Do you hear me? You must understand what you've done. And you must make your master understand too.'

'He's mad, Harry. Mad. Didn't you see that?'

'Why did you do it? Why did you go along with it when you saw what the Taipings were becoming. This is genocide.'

'You don't know what it's like here – how easily ideas get

472

twisted.' His father's eyes opened wide. 'You can't know how great was my zeal to convert, Harry. The T'ien Wang promised me he would build eighteen chapels in every city in China. Imagine my dreams of a new Reformation. The glory! The glory!'

'You were tricked by your God.'

The beatific expression vanished in a moment, and a haunted look took its place. 'No, Harry. Blessed is he that readeth, and they that hear the words of the prophecy, for the time is at hand. To the seven churches which are in Asia, Grace be unto you, and peace, from Him which is, and which was, and which is to come! I was seduced by Satan.'

The odour of sour breath revolted him. 'You were seduced by your own greed to win souls! You did all this yourself!'

'He promised to deliver the people out of Egypt. To free them from their Manchu overlords – for it shall come to pass in that day, saith the Lord, that I will break his yoke from off thy neck, and will burst thy bonds, and—'

'Free them to do what?' he demanded. 'To be slaughtered? God knows, the Manchu are bastards, but that imbecile is ten times worse! You cannot think otherwise.'

'It wasn't like that when first he preached. The T'ien Wang's sweet promise was of a Heaven on earth. He was filled with light and music. He wanted only to glorify God in the highest. Verily Nanking has broken the rice-bowls of many.'

'You bloody fool!'

'Hush now, Harry! Not so loud. He mustn't hear us. None of them must know you're here, or they'll cut off your head and mine too. We're just poor sinners, and this is God's judgement on us.'

Lindley seized his father in both fists. 'God's not to blame! It's you! Look at yourself! You're still ministering to that madman, stuck in his sick fairy tale castle. Why do you behave as if you don't know what's happening out there?'

His father's eyes bulged at the heresies. 'You mustn't say that Harry!'

'Why? Because he'll murder me, as he murders everyone who doesn't accept his crazy version of the world? Look what he's done – he's devastated a dozen provinces, swept away age-old ways, forced arbitrary laws on tens of millions of peasants who don't know any better than to abide by them. He's smashed their idols and razed their temples and . . . Don't you see? Their ancestors' graves have been desecrated, their world is entirely smashed up. Millions of families have been driven from the fields and into the ranks of his murdering army . . . I can't begin to describe it to you . . . oh, Jesus Christ!'

Lindley let go of his father and walked away from him, knowing his efforts were useless.

'I'm sorry, Harry. Truly I am.'

'Sorry? How can you be? You're still satisfying the craving for glory of a maniac! What's left here? Fifty million starving peasants and one failed Prophet. And you – with all your despicable excuses. I used to imagine you as a big man – wise and kind and capable. I used to think that if only you'd been there to guide me as a child I'd have grown up a better man. But you're not a big man, you're a small man, aren't you? Weak, cowardly and comfortable in your own lies. And I'm better for not having known you.'

'We all of us need someone to look up to.' His father's eyes strayed back toward the Heavenly King's apartments. 'Which of us wants to grow up, Harry? Peasants are like children. They don't need truth. They follow anything that moves. Do you want to know something, son?'

Lindley saw his father's face light with a sickly smile and he felt a shudder of revulsion. 'What can you possibly tell me that I haven't already worked out for myself?'

'The Heavenly Kingdom will last for ever.'

I've got to get away from here, he thought, his mind suddenly blistering. I'm going out the way I came – and I'm never coming back.

'We'll fight to the death!' Fei shouted as he pulled her up from the bed.

'Do you want to know the truth about your Taiping god?' he snarled. 'He's a filthy little dictator. Insane! A despot!'

'He's our Heavenly King!'

'Heavenly King? He didn't go to Heaven to talk with God any more than I did. He's out of his bloody mind.'

'Don't speak blasphemy!'

'He made it all up, so fools like you would follow him, and knaves like your father would see an advantage in joining him. Look at him, Fei! Your father's a swindling, lying cheat who was thrown out of Peking for stealing. He saw Hung as a ticket back to riches and power, and wasn't he right about that? Just look around you, woman! Look at the luxury. Golden roofs while his people are starving. The self-styled brother of Christ rolling around with eighty young women all senseless on opium, while his personal guard run around executing anyone who dares to break his law. Can't you see what he is? Are you blind? Or weak? Or just stupid?'

'He's my Lord and Saviour.'

'Well, I'm your husband, and I forbid you absolutely to take any more notice of this Taiping rubbish. We're getting out of here now!'

'I won't leave!'

'You'll do as you're bloody well told, and you'll like it! Or I'll put you in a rice sack and carry you out myself!'

But then the blow came down on the back of his head and Lindley's world was suddenly enveloped in blackness.

Yang Fang's litter came by steamer down the Huang-pu, and by shallow draught barge along the Sung-chiang canal. The elevation of a son-in-law to the rank of full general must not go unmarked, and it was time to visit the city General Hua had made his own.

The rebuilt East Gate was dressed by troops of the Ever-victorious Army, and bore the famous green and red standard showing the character 'hua'. The square below was lined with a guard of elite soldiers wearing special green uniforms, each carrying an Enfield rifle. A row of civil mandarins stood respectfully to one side, and behind them a mass of townspeople craned their necks to watch the procession of dignities.

Hua welcomed his honoured father-in-law to his domain with due ceremony. Yang Fang felt both pride and unease at the proceedings. Why does Hua stick to his arrogant promise never again to wear the yellow jacket and the peacock feather that was granted him at such cost? he wondered. Does he forget what I have told him so many times about the power that comes of presenting himself correctly before the people? Is this not then pride on his part? And if so, how can a man who stands so brazen-faced and unafraid before gods and men retain the favour of either?

Yang noted the cart-loads of produce waiting to continue on their journey to Sung-chiang's three markets. The fields for three li around the city were tilled and planted. It was amazing to see the prosperity of the town and the well-being of the people so enhanced. Does this not give the lie then to Hsueh Huan's words? he thought. 'Europeans don't care about us or our country. They come to China with the idea of stealing land and getting rich. European lives are a feverish dream to make money and return home again. They think of nothing else.' Is Hua truly committed to China? Or will he make his golden mountain and go home like all the rest?

They took tea at Hua's yamen, then watched a display of disciplined marching. After Hua had taken the salute he called his lieutenants to him and a party of eight retired to a private apartment behind the yamen's second, inner court.

On the way, Yang was welcomed by his daughter, then introduced to a pretty young boy called Chu-jeng who nervously called him 'grandfather'. He patted the boy's shoulder and gave him his best smile. The boy did not warm to it as thousands had warmed to it before. When he had gone, Yang asked her, 'Has your husband adopted this boy formally?'

'Yes, honoured father.'

'Very good. The Emperor will be pleased that he has turned so far toward civilization. How old is he and where does he come from?'

'Thirteen years. When the Taipings re-took Hangchow he saw his whole family slaughtered. His mother committed suicide rather than be captured and raped. He tried to do as his mother had done, and throw himself down the well, but he says he lacked the courage.'

'How did he get here?'

'The Taipings forced him to march with their army when they began to retreat, but he escaped to the safety of Sung-chiang.'

'How does Hua know the boy is not a spy?'

'He always knows truth from lies, honoured father.'

Yang nodded, pleased with his daughter's dutiful reply, but still wondering about the boy. When he rejoined the main party they were sitting on armchairs and sofas arranged around a long low table of lacquered wood. Yang looked around at them one by one: Majors Cook and Glasgow, both of them subordinate and of no political importance, but there was also Edward Forrest the paymaster, polite, saying little; Vincente Macanaya, leader of the elite Filipinos, an open-faced man, fantastically loyal to Hua; Henry Burgevine, eating sparely, grimacing; and lastly the British guest, Charles Gordon.

That is a very dangerous man, Yang thought, his eyes avoiding Gordon. Oh, yes. A fighting Christian, completely inflexible in his mind. No wonder the British have chosen him to understudy Hua, for they know we will never be able to make a mandarin of this man.

Servants brought green tea and hot towels, then the party moved to the dining room, where a splendid round table stood. Eight places had been set, each with a small plate and bowl. To the left was a small sauce-mixing saucer and porcelain spoon, to the right a drinking bowl. The bowls were plain blue and white, the only concession to festivity being the high quality of the ivory chopsticks. One place, Yang saw, was set with silver chopsticks.

'Please sit here, esteemed father-in-law,' Hua told him, directing him to the seat opposite the door that, according to classic protocol, was the position of honour.

As soon as the long ts'ai – hors d'oeuvres – arrived Hua told them to eat, and began to help his guests to the serving dish. There were many delicacies – steamed shad from the Yangtze, rolls filled with crabs' eggs, broad beans fried in chicken fat and eel and turtle cutlets.

Tales of daring were told over a lavish meal of great and lesser dishes. Yang saw approvingly, a Shanghai speciality, yu fu mien – egg and wheat flour noodles – delicious bear's paw, goose and fried snake. These were interrupted by speeches and toasts of mao t'ai – rice spirit.

Forrest told me he paid three hundred taels to attract the services of an accomplished chef, Yang thought. Hua must have paid more from his own pocket, for this man's skill is extraordinary. This menu conforms perfectly to Confucian ideals, being a delight to the eyes and the nose as well as the tongue. The balance of the five tastes is exact in all his sauces: sour, bitter, sweet, hot and salt are in correctly varied proportion. And the textures of crispness and juiciness alternate in a masterful way with dryness and stickiness. Surely there is a message in this – Hua is showing me that although he has little cultural education himself, he appreciates the importance of buying peerless expertise. I wish I could persuade him to shave his head.

'Here's to my Chinese troops,' Hua said, standing to raise his spirit bowl. 'There are none finer in the Empire.'

There was a murmured echo of 'None finer.'

When Hua sat down he wiped his lips and said, 'I'll never drink a truer toast until my dying day.'

Then Vincente Macanaya sprang to his feet and said, 'Here's to our General! The finest leader in the Empire!'

Yang watched their enthusiasm and pondered. He had noted the intense personal devotion Hua's Chinese troops had showed. He put on his most jovial face and waved his chopsticks toward the East Gate. 'Your men are fearsome and excellent in their duty. Tell us: why do they follow you, Hua?'

Hua smiled his private smile. 'Because, honoured father-in-law, they're frightened by devils.'

'So! You're a devil then?'

'No, I'm no devil. But soldiers are always drawn to men who aren't afraid.'

Everyone took the remark agreeably, and another flask of fine samshoo was served with the soup, and Major Glasgow said he could see no reason why the Ever-victorious Army should not live up to its illustrious name, winning every battle, going on to greater glories until the last Taiping rebel was dead. But then Hua's face changed and he said, 'That won't happen.' And when they looked to him, he told them, 'One of these days I'll fail. I'll fail because I'll have been betrayed. Betrayed by someone close to me. Because that's always the way, isn't it?'

There was a howling silence then, until Hua laughed and poured another round and held up his bowl. 'Here's to our new steamer force – *Cricket*, *Zingan*, *Rose* and *Pao-shun*.'

The others drained their bowls. Yang felt the heady spirit cleanse his mouth. He asked, wanting desperately to forget what had just happened, 'How does your artillery stand now?'

Hua turned to his left. 'Henry?'

'It's good. Aside from our old six and twelve pounders, we've got four thirty-two pounders now.'

478

'Plus eight four-and-a-half-inch howitzers, Henry, and don't forget the two dozen smaller ones,' Forrest added. 'Then there's six eight-inch mortars, and some sixteen-pound Hale rockets.'

'Rockets?' Yang smiled. 'Ah, a Chinese weapon! According to the histories they were used against the Mongols six hundred years ago, when K'ai-feng was besieged.'

'These ones are of British design,' Gordon said, his chin jutting. 'They're quite different.'

Suddenly everything has become easy, Yang thought. Now that British policy has changed all the blocks have magically dissolved. Those arms suppliers who were pleading unavailability are visiting Shanghai especially to do business with Hua. A dozen American-made twelve pounders that were embargoed for months have now appeared, and his river steamer force has come together almost overnight. No wonder Hsueh Huan's seat is glowing red hot, for what victorious army ever wilfully abolishes itself when its task is done? And who would be able to believe that my esteemed son-in-law could be content with an ordinary man's destiny?

Yang realized the company was laughing at something amusing that Major Glasgow had said. It brought his mind back to the present, and he smiled too, though he had missed the joke.

Soon afterwards they retired from the table and took up their places on the sofas and armchairs in the reception room. The drink took its toll on them all, except Burgevine who remained as morose as ever. Spectacular southern fruits were served and reminiscences offered, then Hua made another of his strange remarks.

'Just before the Lung-chu-an siege I overheard two of my boys making a bet about which of them would survive the longest,' he said. 'I remember it struck me as pretty funny.'

Yang showed his surprise. 'Did you say funny?'

'Yes. You see, I wondered how the winner was going to collect.'

They all laughed, and for the shortest of moments Yang believed he saw violence in Hua's eye, as if he knew someone among his officers was playing him false. He had spoken to find the man out. But then Burgevine winced and Forrest put out a hand to him and the opportunity was lost.

Hua said, 'Henry, are you all right?'

'It's nothing – Colonel, I just . . .' Burgevine's face screwed up with pain again and he started panting. Hua got up and called the servants in. There was blood seeping through Burgevine's trousers.

'Help me get him out of here.'

Yang watched them rush Burgevine away. He watched the cool compassion Hua showed to his old friend, and he knew that Hua believed Burgevine to have betrayed him.

Fei had overheard the people's distraught words. The news of yet another defeat had started the whisperers again. The Heavenly Capital was ablaze with hysterical news.

'What are they saying now?' Lindley asked, lying blood-ied, his head cradled in her lap.

'That General Tseng has taken Hangchow.'

He looked up at her. His clothes were flecked with dried blood, his voice cracked with exhaustion. 'I told you – it's hopeless.'

Fei looked down at the man she loved, still wrestling with the impossible choice: should she trust her husband? Even if it meant betraying her father and everything she had ever believed in and fought for?

'My father says it's the fault of the British. Once they decided to abandon plans to supplant the Manchu at Peking they started to give arms and steamers to the Imperials so they could destroy us. Why, Lin-li? Why does Mr Bruce hate us?'

'He doesn't hate you. It's quite simple. He can do business with Prince Kung, but he could never trust a madman.'

The blasphemy tore open her heart once again. 'I will never understand why you and your countrymen refuse to help fellow Christians in our hour of need. Your father was always so anxious for us to become God-worshippers.'

'My father never had the faintest idea what he was creating.'

He reached up to touch the back of his head. The wound, inflicted by the haft of a palace guard's spear, had laid him unconscious. He told Fei, 'If your father still imagines I'm going to speak with the British and save everything, he's a sadly deluded soul.'

She shook her head. 'That's not why he allowed me to see you.'

'Then why? What's the reason this time?'

'The youth you saw in the T'ien Wang's palace is ill with fever. Can you make him well again?'

'Nothing is ever simple in China, is it?' he said accusingly. 'Everything's mixed up with correct form and damned face-saving formulas.'

'What does it matter? You're still alive. My father orders you to work your magic today.'

'Tell your father I don't work magic. Nor do I take orders from him.'

'Stupid, stubborn man!' Her eyes pleaded with him. 'Save the Young T'ien Wang's life and you will be allowed to live. Hung Fu-t'ien is only fourteen. He has known no life outside the palace.'

'I'll treat the lad as well as I can, but on two conditions. First, while I'm in the T'ien Wang's palace I don't want to see my father. If I do I'll stop work immediately. And second, I want permission to start treating ordinary Taipings – whether your father thinks they deserve it or not.'

As soon as the conditions were agreed Lindley went through to the Heavenly King's palace. He examined the Heavenly King's son and found that he had contracted a fever, but that he also showed signs of scurvy. Lindley insisted a cocktail be made of the limes and lemons that grew in the T'ien Wang's private garden. He watched as the boy drank down a pint of juice, and then he left.

The day after Hung Fu-t'ien's fever broke, a dozen food-laden junks ran the Imperial blockade to reach Nanking. Provisions entered the famished city, but the junks only got through because for many miles above Nanking sixty thousand of the Chung Wang's desperate fighters had arrived on the northern bank of the Yangtze.

When the sound of distant gunfire reached Lindley's ears he took Fei up to the walls to see for themselves the vast spectacle of the arrival of the last great Taiping field army. They watched together as the few remaining boats ferried men across. The people began celebrating the miracle, but then the starving soldiery of the Chung Wang's shattered army began to arrive, and the celebrations fell silent.

Lindley saw starving townspeople throw down what meagre food they had gathered only the day before to the first of the Chung Wang's army of withered skeletons to enter the Yi Feng gate.

Tears rolled down Fei's cheeks when she saw the valiant people foregoing their only hope of food for their fighting sons. 'This first regiment are Southern veterans,' she told Lindley. 'They have been Taipings since the very beginning.'

When the Chung Wang himself was received into the city his slight figure surprised Lindley. He was of the same generation as Fei's father, but he was clothed in war gear that he had lived in for many months. Fei gasped when she saw his face.

'His eyes – how sunken, and yet so bright.'

'That's the look of hunger and over-exertion,' Lindley said, listening to the greeting exchanges. 'He's at the limit of endurance, burning pure will-power now.'

'We were cut off by massive forces and driven out from all the towns of the coastal plain,' the Taiping commander told the Kao Wang. 'I ordered a forced march to pull the army out of danger. I wanted to fall back and strengthen our hard-pressed garrisons in the silk districts, but our withdrawal fell apart. Part of my force were separated. Another part, those I sent to take Ningpo, were cut off by foreign gun boats in Hangchow Bay. The Imperials tricked their way into Soochow and murdered a dozen of my key officers there. After that everything was chaos. Most of my men were sure they were going to die. We harvested unripe rice before starting the long march back. It was the only option left to us.'

The Chung Wang was taken inside and Lindley began to take his pulse. The commander moved restlessly as he relived the final days.

'The retreat was nightmarish. The Imperials broke the Yangtze's banks at many places so the country we passed through was turned into a swamp. We were forced to cut through mazes of dense bamboo jungle. Much of the land was impassable except by swimming. Our firearms were useless, our powder ruined. All dry ground was occupied by Imperial troops who harassed us from boats and sniped at us from the walls of the garrison towns. They killed thousands of us as we were herded towards Nanking.'

'When did you eat last?' Lindley asked.

'For nearly a month my army has eaten grass and the green tops of bamboo and the bodies of the dead.' His sinewy body stiffened with urgency. 'Now we're on the north bank of the Yangtze there are not enough boats left here to get my army across. My men are crowding the bank for two miles. I must go.'

The Kao Wang asked. 'What's the gunfire?'

'General Tseng was prepared for our arrival. The Imperials have followed us. They are attacking the batteries and forts that command the river. Chiu-fu-chou is cut off.'

Lindley knew it was the fort that controlled the whole north bank opposite Nanking Creek. He told Fei, 'It's as I warned you. The city's bound to fall.'

'I believe in the Chung Wang's military genius, Lin-li. He is a great man. Chiu-fu-chou mounts many heavy guns. The fortress will stand so long as we have faith.'

'Chinese guns,' Lindley said. 'Unwieldy masses of iron bigger than a British sixty-eight, but having the bore of only a four or six pounder. That won't protect a retreating army.'

They went to the walls and watched as squadrons of Imperial gunboats rowed down to attack the fort. At the narrows the grim, embattled walls towered over a gleaming waterlogged plain. Gun flashes lit the river, dense curling smoke dissolved into thin wreaths as continuous noise ech-oed from the walls. The Chung Wang's army provided an easy target, and the Imperial boats swarmed like carrion birds. The Imperials were drawn to them like wild beasts to the smell of blood, falling upon their prey in countless numbers. They saw that the core of the Chung Wang's ragged army was perishing.

That night Lindley told her he must be allowed to help the casualties as best he could. When reinforcements were thrown into Chiu-fu-chou Fei insisted they go with them. Every boat the Taipings could find was sent to help transport the troops across, but their efforts were in vain. There was no organization among the thousands who were dying in sight of salvation. No move was being made to withdraw the army from the bank, and the passive acceptance of fate among those who waited at the crossing chilled Lindley to the marrow. He watched helplessly as Imperial cannon shot crashed among the living skeletons. Men were so densely packed on the river beaches that there was no avoiding the fire whatever they did, but Lindley recognized no will to escape. Instead the crowd was like a mindless thing that periodically surged forward, so that many of those who stood on the banks were forced by pressure from those behind into the river and swept away by its surging current.

They toiled back inside the Yi Feng gate with the last of the survivors on the day the city was closed for the last time. The tattered beggars who swarmed around him, he knew, had been the elite, the men of Kwangtung and Kwangsi who had won the early victories and established the Taipings as a force able to humble the Imperial government. Now they were just fifteen thousand in number.

That night the Chung Wang was received in the T'ien Wang's palace, but there was no delivering of news, no questions put or plans laid for the future. The Heavenly King – strangely lucid yet utterly unconnected to reality – spoke from his golden throne and told his elect:

'The Most High has issued to me his sacred Decree. God the Father and my Divine Elder Brother have commanded me to descend unto this world of flesh and to become the one true lord of all nations upon earth. What cause have I then for fear? Remain with me, or leave me, as you choose. My inheritance of this Empire, which is even as an iron girdle of defence, will be protected by others if you decline to protect it. I have at my command an angelic host a million strong. How then can these unholy Imperialists enter my city?'

When the Heavenly King withdrew the Chung Wang burst into tears and left the hall.

For three days Lindley laboured without sleep. With Fei's assistance he sutured the ghastly wounds of survivors. He made a hospital of the encampment in Drum Tower Square, passing among the endless rows of casualties as if in a waking dream, cleaning and stitching and binding up as best he could, isolating infection and segregating those with the best and the worst prospects of life, until the pavements around the Yi Feng gate were filled with prostrate forms. Those in charge of the casualties would not allow him a saw with which to amputate gangrenous limbs and so save lives, nor would they permit opium to be given, even to those whose lives were failing in inescapable pain.

Nanking was rightly called the 'Furnace of China'. The

weather was blistering, so hot that the white marble paving stones of Drum Tower Square burned through the worn soles of Fei's cotton pumps. The place was a crucible, thirsty for rain. Work gangs had taken up most of the processional way, continuing the hopeless planting programme. By day women scattered seeds among the dry raked rubble. By night children risked death to creep among the dusty beds, winnowing the gravel a handful at a time in an effort to satisfy their hunger.

When she saw the crowd outside the walls of the T'ien Wang's palace her expectations soared. Proclamations had been posted exhorting the people to eat whatever weeds they could find. Anything green was to be gathered and boiled and eaten. That and faith, the proclamations said, would sustain them just as it had the Israelites.

A rumour fluttered briefly through the streets that the T'ien Wang himself had been seen walking the city walls. That His apparition had ordered the people to have faith and to 'eat the sweet dew'. He had told them that a host of a million angels was at hand, swords unsheathed. Then the T'ien Wang had broken the ropes of pearls hanging about His neck and scattered them as a token and a sign to His starving soldiers. But some said the faithless soldiers had wept then, because they could not eat what He had given them.

Lindley went up with Fei to Hsiao Ts'ang Hill, and she thanked him for his dedication. After all the heresies he had voiced she had believed she could never love him again, but among the horror she had seen the goodness of his spirit and had known that here was a stubborn, gentle, unafraid and good man. She stroked his head, seeing the small healed scars that he had got in his fist fight with the American. He spoke wistfully of that time, as if Ward was a long-lost brother, and their fight had been a mighty celebration. Men were strange like that. Their yang natures made them fierce. Now he was too tired to do anything now but drift.

'Tell me. What was it like?' he asked, his blue eyes staring up into the sky.

'What?'

'The Porcelain Pagoda.'

'I remember there were eight sides,' she told him. 'And nine sets of overhanging eaves. Lanterns and little golden

485

bells hung from each ridge. They made a magical music in the wind.'

'It must have been beautiful.'

'The tower was made of the finest white porcelain. The roofs were green tiles, and on the very top was a golden ball, held up by an iron rod and circled by nine rings. Gold chains hung down to the eaves. The people used to say they were "pearls of good augury". They believed the pagoda ensured the happiness and prosperity of the city.'

When she looked down sleep had taken him, and so she said no more.

The next morning Fei entered the Heavenly King's palace without permission, evading the guards by using the secret entrance from her father's quarters. She went from chamber to chamber, asking servants and the T'ien Wang's wives if they knew where the Reverend Lindley was to be found. They were so amazed to see her that none dared answer.

So she ran on, through the central garden with its grove of fruit trees, up into the main concourse and up more stairs again, past a quiet cloister towards the T'ien Wang's private apartments. She found the Reverend Lindley in the Great Hall of Jesus, in the very top of the palace. He was sitting alone before the steps at the foot of the tall, golden statue of Jesus, the Elder Brother. On each side were two huge bronze urns. They were filled with sand and stuck with dozens of incense sticks that burned in steady vertical columns, tainting the still air with musk. The man she had come to find was reading.

She threw herself down before him, but he did not seem to notice her. He sat cross-legged in the lotus position, the skirts of his black robe spread out around him, his gaze directed into a worn black bible. The sound of the thin paper was crisp as he turned the pages.

When he spoke, she heard his voice echoing in the rafters.

'And the temple was filled with smoke from the glory of God, and from his power; and no man was able to enter into the temple, till the seven plagues of the seven angels were fulfilled. And I heard a great voice out of the temple saying to the seven angels, Go your ways, and pour out the vials of the wrath of God upon the earth . . .'

Fei got to her knees, crawled in front of him, her eyes streaming with tears. 'Please Holy Reverend, listen to me!'

'. . . And the sixth angel poured out his vial upon the great river Euphrates; and the water thereof was dried up, that the way of the kings of the east might be prepared. And I saw three unclean spirits like frogs come out of the mouth of the dragon, and out of the mouth of the beast, and out of the mouth of the false prophet . . .'

'Please listen to me! Your son begs your help!'

But nothing would make him listen to her. His voice was gathering power. He put down his bible. His eyes were opening wider, and he began to rise.

'For they are the spirits of devils, working miracles, which go forth unto the kings of the earth and of the whole world, to gather them to the battle of that great day of God Almighty.' Suddenly he leapt up and shrieked, 'Behold! I come as a thief!'

She clasped her hands together, imploring him, her eyes swimming in tears as she heard the words of the Book of Revelations. 'Please listen to me Holy Reverend. You must help me. Come to your son. Speak with him, I beg you! Save your people!'

But he would not listen. He threw back his head and threw open his arms and called into the rafters.

'. . . and the seventh angel poured out his vial into the air; and there came a great voice out of the temple of heaven, from the throne, saying, It is done. And there were voices, and thunders, and lightnings; and there was a great earthquake, such as was not since men were upon the earth, so mighty an earthquake, and so great. And the great city was divided . . .'

She crawled to him, took the skirts of his robe in her hands, but he pulled away from her. His voice had grown to full power now, his eyes huge, his hands clawing the air.

'. . . and after these things I saw another angel come down from Heaven, having great power; and the earth was lightened with his glory. And he cried mightily with a strong voice, saying, Babylon the great is fallen, is fallen, and is become the habitation of devils, and the hold of every foul spirit, and a cage of every unclean and hateful bird. And the kings of the earth, who have committed fornication and lived deliciously with her, shall bewail her, and lament for her, when they shall see the smoke of her burning, standing afar off for the fear of her torment, saying, Alas, alas that great city Babylon, that mighty city! For in one hour is thy judgement come!'

He paced away past the great gilded statue of Jesus the Elder Brother, stepping out onto the open walkway that surrounded the Great Hall. There under the eaves and beside the stone battlements he gestured out over the Heavenly Capital, and it seemed to Fei that nothing could stop the flow of his words.

'Alas, alas, this great city, that is clothed in fine linen, and purple, and scarlet, and decked with gold, and precious stones and pearls. What city is like unto this great city?'

The brilliant light hurt her eyes. She clung to the base of a pillar, imploring him, watching him as he climbed up onto the great grey bricks of the ramparts, spreading his arms like the wings of an angel, his voice full of rapture. When he stopped speaking she heard the noise of people in the square below, day-to-day noise, but seemingly very far away.

She cried to him, 'Holy Reverend, please come to your son . . .'

He seemed to see her for the first time. She crawled towards him, reaching up from the pool of his shadow. His figure blotted out the sun, and she saw the breeze flying his long hair about his head.

'I saw a great white throne,' he told, an intensely confidential tone in his voice now. 'And I saw Him that sat on it. And I heard a great voice out of Heaven saying, Behold, the tabernacle of God is with men. Alleluia!'

'No!' She shouted, but he turned, and as if treading the first step of a stair that reached up to Heaven, he walked off the ramparts and into the open air.

Forty feet below the street sounds changed. There were shouts and screams as the crowd assembled. Fei began to tremble with shock, then a great panic filled her. She climbed to her feet, blinded by tears, and ran from the Great Hall of Jesus and from the palace of the Heavenly King.

General Ward left for Ningpo by river steamer with all his officers aboard and the two hundred men of his elite body-guard around him. Three more gunboats followed, bringing his main force across the glass-flat waters of Hangchow Bay. A flotilla of British gunboats saluted them as they entered Ningpo Creek.

It was late morning, sun-bright, and the flat land lay under a haze of heat and smoke. Dozens of grey smudges slanted up into the sky from fires burning across the district, unmistakable evidence that a large, rogue Taiping force was roving nearby. As they moved upriver past Yu-yao they saw that much of the land was burnt black. The air was acrid and stung Ward's eyes. All along the river hundreds of peasants hid in the reeds that fringed the bank or clung to flotsam, their hiding places opened to view as the backwash swayed aside the tall fronds.

The Ever-victorious Army landed without incident. They came ashore on the untouched verges of the Yu-yao canal and made camp adjacent to a unit of Royal Marines a little way from the Taiping-occupied town. Immediately Ward went aboard the British gunboat, *Hardy*.

'We have a sticky situation here, sir,' the British lieutenant commander told him. 'It looks like the Taipings've finally given up on Shanghai. We think they're going to try to destroy Ningpo instead.'

'They're concentrating over there in some force.' Ward's eyes scanned the devastated land as he pointed out the enemy with his baton. 'Probably trying to get their hands on the district's rice crop.'

'To do that they'll have to take Ningpo. Mr Meadows' instructions are that we are not to allow the rebels to occupy any treaty port.'

Ward's jaw clenched. 'We'll just have to round them up, force them back out west. What do you think of that idea, Lieutenant?'

'Admiral Hope has given me orders to cooperate fully with you, sir.'

Ward took his leave. As soon as his campaign tent was erected he called his officers to a noonday council of war. When he entered they were all sitting, waiting for him: Major Ashley, his commissary general, Majors Cook and Glasgow, Edward Forrest and Vincente Macanaya, lastly the big, stoop-shouldered figure of Henry Burgevine.

'Are we going for another night attack, Colonel?' Burgevine asked, looking up. He and Vincente Macanaya, of all the officers of the Ever-victorious Army, still addressed their commander as Colonel.

'Night attacking is our business, Henry.'

Burgevine had returned from Shanghai two days ago, his abdominal wall stitched up. He was still limping and in pain, though he hid it as best he could. So far he had refused opium, but Ward had been told that he was still downing two bottles of liquor a day.

'What time we going in?'

'I'm looking to mount the first assault at midnight. The second will be ready to go in at one o'clock.'

'In that case I'd better get some shut-eye.' Burgevine started to lever himself up from the low canvas chair. One of the others tried to help him, but he ignored the offer. 'Got to be in good shape to lead my boys.'

'That won't be necessary.'

Burgevine had already been handed his hat when Ward's words stopped him. 'Not necessary? Why not?'

'Because Vincente's going to lead the second assault.'

'Vincente? But . . . Colonel, I . . .'

'Henry, you're to rest up tonight. That's an order.'

'But I'm fine! Look at me! I'm fine!'

Ward faced him, his gaze like steel. 'I said that's an order. I'm sorry, Henry.'

'Sorry?' Burgevine's red eyes burned with appeal. 'What good's sorry? You can't do this to me. We're partners. We've always been partners, right from the start. If it weren't for me you wouldn't be here. None of you would!' He threw a slashing gesture around the tent.

'Henry, that's enough!'

'You're damned right it's enough! I'm going to lead that second assault tonight come hell or high water!'

'If you don't follow my orders I'll have the provosts put you under arrest.'

Forrest put out a conciliatory hand, but Burgevine threw it off. He grimaced, turned and stumped out into the brilliant sunlight.

Ward watched the glances that passed around, the smiles and shrugs. When he heard the phrase 'Johnny Reb' muttered, anger blazed up inside him. 'I won't have that!' he roared inside the tent, shocking them all. 'Now hear me and hear me good. Henry Burgevine's worth any two of you.

And the only reason I did what I did is to save his life. His loyalty to me is beyond question. Beyond question. Is that clear?'

There was a brittle silence as Ward outlined his plan of attack. No one interrupted him, no one asked any questions, and the meeting broke up within the hour, leaving a bad taste in his mouth. He considered going to make his peace with Burgevine, but decided to let the matter lie, then a report came in from his scouts and the opportunity was gone.

The situation was getting urgent. Taiping foraging parties had been out stripping the grain stores and setting the stubble in the fields ablaze. Ward called his bodyguard together and marched to cut them off. The carbon-black land caught the heat of the afternoon sun and made a furnace of it. Four times they came upon human railroad trains – gangs of over a hundred men, impressed as coolies to porter rice sacks into Hu-shan. Each was guarded by small parties of armed long-hairs who fled as the column approached. But not before Ward saw that these were not men from the Chung Wang's crack units, but starving boys and old men, poorly armed and ill-disciplined. They carried no Enfields, just old flintlocks adequate to terrify peasants but no match for properly disciplined troops.

By nightfall the Ever-victorious Army had moved into positions that sealed off Hu-shan. There they began to intercept and ambush grain gathering parties. Ward went back aboard the *Hardy* to dine with the British lieutenant, but as they finished supper a report came in of an unexpected Taiping attack that had been launched on Ningpo itself. The British riverboats departed immediately to give support to the city, leaving only the *Hardy* on standby. When the boats passed out of sight Ward called his officers to him. Burgevine appeared, but said nothing as he listened to the amended plan of attack. His face was haggard. He seemed to be in shocking pain.

'We'll wait for daylight and break Hu-shan tomorrow morning,' Ward told them. 'Guns on the British steamer will bear on the West Gate, and open fire at half past seven.' He turned to Major Cook. 'As soon as the firing starts I want you to mount a mock assault on the south wall.'

'A mock assault, sir?'

'A diversion. To draw as many defenders as you can over there. Then I'll lead the main attack on the breached West Gate.'

He took three hours' sleep, then got up, and for the rest of the night he attended to final details. He had never fought south of Hangchow Bay before, but the practised efficiency of his men as they readied their equipment made him feel that no matter where they fought they would win. The camps were always different, yet somehow always the same, and the familiarity of the sights and sounds and smells filled him with a peculiar joy to know that he had grown it all from a seed in his mind. Gone were the days when he had to attend to everything himself. Now there was next to nothing for him to do, so he doused the lamps and sat in a chair outside his tent to watch the unhurried preparations and to let his eyes wander along the luminous path of the Milky Way, that mysterious veil of light that split the night sky in two above his head.

Last year's herald of doom, the great comet, had disappeared now. The night was warm and windless. Within the hour the lesser stars had vanished into the dawn, and half an hour after that the brighter stars had gone too, leaving only Venus visible in the east, a brilliant diamond that signalled a bloody sunrise. He thought fondly of his wife, missing her. We're getting along just fine, he thought. Now that she's given up on all those dumb superstitions of hers. I guess she loves me for real now.

He washed and shaved, clipped his moustache and the tab of hair on his chin, then he put on a new neckerchief and went to eat breakfast with his men. Finally he cracked open his watch, saw it was almost time, and walked down to inspect the forward positions.

The morning peace was blown away when *Hardy* opened fire. Thousands of water fowl flew up, momentarily filling the sky with fluttering panic. When the guns stopped Major Cook's men mounted their screaming charge across the scorched land exactly as planned. Ward watched them rushing forward with their ladders, saw the plumes of smoke rising from the defenders' flashing muskets and heard the random music of battle. He went out to join a force of men so confident and so used to that music that they stood at their ease in sight of the enemy and chattered to one

492

another, unconcerned as lethal shot whistled about them. They received him with respect and affection as he went among them. They know, he thought, inspired by the beauty of the moment, that the time is come, and that I am with them.

Ten paces away from the commander-in-chief of the Ever-victorious Army, Vincente Macanaya was kneeling to check his weapons. He stood up, watchful, his guts churning.

I don't feel good, he thought. Something is wrong. I can't say what, but . . . something.

He clicked over the chambers of the revolver one at a time, alarm sparking in his nerves. The blast from the guns of the British steamer had already shattered the fruit trees planted along the canal side. Heavy shot was battering the West Gate, and large pieces of masonry had fallen from both towers. A haze of half-dispersed smoke was obscuring Hu-shan now. Under its cover the first assault would go in. Bodies of men were marching up, dressed in ranks of five. A line of skirmishers were picking their targets among the defences.

When Vincente looked to Ward again it was just in time to see him press a hand to his belly. He seemed to retch, or cough, but it was so sudden and untypical a gesture that a frisson of dread ran through Vincente, and he could not stop himself springing to his commander's side.

He found a reassuring smile on Ward's face, then the impossible words.

'Vincente, it's stupid but . . . I've been hit.'

It seemed like some crazy joke. Vincente could not believe it and, to prove that such a thing could not be, he looked over the front of Ward's coat in vain. But when he looked up to search Ward's face he saw the dismay under his smile. When he looked down again he saw a neat hole and a patch of blood spreading through the black fabric. Ward staggered and despite Vincente's outstretched arms, sat down heavily.

Vincente took Ward's baton, then suddenly half a dozen men were crowding around him in alarm and the expression on Ward's face had turned to one of pain. They opened his coat and saw that it was a monstrous wound. Then a disappointed voice said in Spanish, 'Lead them, Vincente. Lead them to victory for me.' And then they were carrying him away as fast as they could towards the Yu-yao canal, and the British steamer.

For Vincente Macanaya the rest of the battle passed in the time it took to dream a dream. He led the first assault and climbed the walls of Hu-shan and planted the famous green-and-red 'Hua' standard, and it seemed to him that in a heartbeat the city was taken. But it did not feel like victory.

As soon as the breach was secured he headed for the British vessel. It was already getting up steam.

The air down below was hot and close and thick with the smell of engines. In the cramped cabin they guarded their Coronel like treasure. It was as if being allowed to stand close to his cot was to be counted a privileged man, and Vincente knew that this was the way it must be with all great leaders when they died. The thought brought home to him what was happening, and something roared against it inside him.

No. You must not get angry, he reminded himself. Anger is a wind that blows out the lamp of the mind.

He pushed forward in the thick air. 'Coronel . . .'

Ward's face was ashen. His eyes opened. 'Vincente.'

'Coronel . . . Hu-shan is ours. The victory is ours.'

He gave Ward back his baton, but Ward shook his head. 'Keep it, my friend.'

When Ward's eyes closed Vincente stared round in despair. 'Quickly! You must get him to Ningpo. You must find a doctor!'

'No, Vincente. It doesn't matter,' Ward whispered. 'Life's a wonderful deal. The world owes us nothing, and we owe it everything. The only true joy comes from squandering yourself for a good enough reason.'

The Colonel's eyes closed as the pain in his side intensified. He swallowed. 'Vincente – I want you to help me square something.'

'Coronel?'

'Listen: you remember – when I sent your boys to Nanking?'

'Your guard, Coronel?'

Ward mustered his strength to nod. 'Yes. The man who saved their lives is still in that city. I want you to promise me that if you're at Nanking when the city falls that you will look out for him. You know who I mean?'

494

It was Vincente's turn to nod. 'Your friend, the Doctor, Coronel?'

'If you find him – I want you to give him this.'

Ward took from his pocket a small piece of yellow jade on a red cord. Vincente took the item and put it in his pocket.

When Ward's teeth began to chatter Vincente wrapped the blanket closer about him. Then, unable to watch, he went on deck and stared down into the water of the creek, making no sense of the blue moonlight that bounced off the water. Pairs of images came into being briefly, rode the waves then collided and died. Sometime in the night he saw Chang-mei arrive dressed from head to toe in white, her face utterly dead white also, her eyes black and blood red, so that none of the Chinese dared look at her. Then, later, her laughing father came and led her off the steamer, and only when they had gone did he realize it was not Chang-mei he had seen visit, but her bad-luck spirit.

'Where is he?' Burgevine demanded again, shaking him by the shoulder. Vincente came awake to see Burgevine sweating and stinking with the sourness of alcohol.

'Down there. He's dead.'

'No,' Burgevine bellowed like a man in hell. 'No, not the Colonel. Not now!'

As the wail turned to silence Vincente's hands tightened on the rail. He watched Burgevine limp into the cabin, heard the big man's pathetic sobs, and knew that an entire world that was, and an entire world that might have been, had come to an end.

On the morning of the summer solstice a mine was exploded under Nanking's walls. It shook the whole city and tore the heart from its defences. Immediately afterwards Imperial forces made a general assault by land and by water. Eighty thousand men attacked the walls and the fighting for the breach was fierce until the Taiping exploded one of their own arsenals and halted the Imperial advance in a blaze of sacrificial fire. At the same time three thousand gunboats – some sampans carrying only one light gun in the bow, others large junks mounting four or five heavy cannon – began to swarm in the river.

By late afternoon, the Taipings closed the landward breach and when the Hour of the Dog was beaten Lindley received an order to attend wounded men on the stretch of wall that overlooked the river. He saw how smoke hid the attacking boats, making it hard for the defenders to aim at them, but as night fell the gun flashes showed their positions and the Imperial fleet was forced to break off. For over an hour he worked through the beautiful glare of night battle, his world lit by explosions near and far and the brilliant tracks of arrow-headed rockets. From time to time a gunboat would explode, or a huge cloud of smoke would be lit up as if by red lightning, but as he worked the tumult slowly died away, until only the sound of the bamboo signals of lone sentinels creaking and the answering drums of the lookout houses that were perched along the walls could be heard. Gradually even these became fainter and less frequent until they ceased altogether.

A messenger ran up to him bearing credentials. 'Sir, you are required to come immediately to attend Kao Wang.'

Lindley was reluctant to leave his patients. 'Has someone been hurt?'

'You are required to come.'

There must be some way to get out of this city, Lindley thought fiercely as he hurried back to the Kao Wang's palace. But they're watching me like hawks. How can I get Fei's cooperation?

When he arrived he found the palace full of armed men. The Kao Wang came to him personally and insisted he follow. Lindley was conducted through the private door that opened into the adjoining palace. When they came to the Heavenly King's bedchamber, the Kao Wang said, 'You must try to save him.'

Lindley pushed past the slim youth who hovered nearby, and went over to the giant bed. Alone, behind diaphanous yellow veils, the T'ien Wang's doubled form writhed in desperate pain.

'What's happened to him?'

'Poison.'

'What kind of poison?' He looked around, impervious to the strangled groans. 'What kind of poison? What's this?'

He snatched up a goblet that stood nearby, sniffed it, ran a finger around the rim, tasted it gingerly – rice wine, but there was no hint of the bitterness of the more common alkaloid poisons. He noticed a crumpled paper, brushed out in vermilion ink. He looked briefly at it, but it was no poison recipe, just some sort of poem.

When he threw back the drapes what he saw made him reel back in horror. Instead of the blue lips and swollen tongue he expected to find, he saw that the Heavenly King's lips and teeth and tongue and the whole of the inside of his mouth was a churning mass of brilliant gold.

'Good god, man! What have you done to yourself?' When Lindley laid forceful hands on him guards were called in to pull him away.

'Don't you understand me? He'll die! He's swallowed enough gold leaf to strangulate his entire digestive system.'

'You may not touch him.'

'I must get his mouth open, and clear his throat. How can I save him if you won't let me touch him?'

'You may not touch him.'

'When did he do this?' he demanded of the Young T'ien Wang, but the youth just stared, transfixed by the scene.

'If I can't treat him he must be made to vomit it up himself,' Lindley told them, but as he called for salt to mix a vomit-inducing drink he saw it was already too late. Cramps had set in and the gasping of the living god was becoming more raucous. When the emetic was prepared, the T'ien Wang would not touch it.

'Where's my father?' Lindley demanded of the Kao Wang furiously as he was forcibly held. 'Have him brought here, so he can see for himself what his devil work has come to!'

He repeated his request twice more, but the Kao Wang refused him.

Lindley attended the bedside until just after midnight, taking visual pulses from the patient's neck at intervals and enduring the lingering decline. He saw a dozen white-robed women presented to the veiled bed, and a dozen other visitors, including the Chung Wang. All did obeisance with the same strange light in their eyes. Five minutes after finding the last detectable pulse Lindley pronounced the Heavenly King dead. Then an incredible hysteria began to grip those to whom the news was communicated. There was wailing and fervent praying, then terrified body servants came in to crown the corpse with the gold coronet and dress it in yellow silk robes as if there was expectation of a miraculous resurrection.

The shrouds in which the stiffening body was wrapped were also of Imperial yellow, and embroidered with Imperial dragons. Lindley watched the proceedings with detachment. As he prepared to take his leave he took up the death message and looked at it once more. It read:

'I hereby declare to Heaven, Earth and Man that God the Heavenly Father is alone most excellent, who was from the spreading out of the heavens until now the exceeding great creator of all things.'

He handed it to the Kao Wang and murmured, 'Now that he's dead you must arrange a general surrender.'

A gunshot rang out in the cloister, plucking at Lindley's nerves. The second sounded closer. Then a guard staggered into view, howling. At the sight of him the Kao Wang sprang to life, shouting furious orders. All along the passageway outside guards lay on the ground, fallen into the kowtow, their weapons laid before them. Another shot rang out as their captain moved from one to the next, helping them to die.

As the Kao Wang fought for control Lindley feared for him. The guard captain's eyes were filled with madness, but even so the Kao Wang stepped up and struck the man as hard as he could across the face. Then he took the revolver from him, and absolutely forbade further killing. The guard captain prostrated himself at his feet, begging for death, but the Kao Wang walked over him, ignoring his pleas.

'Now you see,' he told Lindley, his whisper raw. 'They believe their choice is death or madness. So it is in all the city. Soon Hung Fu-t'ien will be enthroned – the Young T'ien Wang will lead the Heavenly Kingdom of Great Peace. Until then, this death must remain a secret.'

'Order a surrender, man! Don't you see what you must do?'

'There will be no surrender!'

'Why?' Lindley demanded, futile anger twisting inside him. 'Your Kingdom's dead. It was born with that man and it has died with him. It can't be brought back to life. It's all over now! Over!'

The Kao Wang's eyes burned like coals. 'If the choice is death or madness, the people must continue to believe.'

Lindley found Fei waiting for him in their apartments.

498

Her face was drawn, and the sight of her drained the fight from him. He took her in his arms and held her for many minutes, and it seemed to him that the inner struggle that had warred within her since that first day in Nanking was now stilled.

She began to sob, and when she stopped she confessed to him what she had seen in the T'ien Wang's palace the previous morning.

'He stepped off the walls as if mounting a stair to heaven.'

Lindley made no move and said nothing for a long time. He tried to feel, but there was nothing.

Finally she put her head on his chest, and said, 'Lin-li, I'm scared.'

He held her tight again and all the while the sound of a spade digging out a shallow pit in the T'ien Wang's garden jarred the profound silence. Fei clung to him and he told her, as he knew he must, that her living god was dead.

'I knew he was gone, Lin-li. All Taipings must have felt it too. It was like the stopping of my own heart.'

That night Fei's sleep was troubled. Lindley lay awake throughout the scant hours of darkness as she murmured and flinched beside him. By the time dawn broke at five o'clock in the morning she had found a semblance of rest, but he could not set his mind at peace. The Kao Wang's warning that news of their leader's death must have fearsome consequences on the minds of the people haunted him. He would not leave Fei alone for a second.

'Your true God is not dead,' he assured her. He showed her the T'ien Wang's final message. 'At last your leader understood that God is unknowable, that no man can tell truths about Him, and that anyone who says he can is a liar. We all must feel the true God here, inside our hearts. Each in our own way.'

He got up and went back into the T'ien Wang's palace. As the first grey began to seep across the sky he steeled himself. There was no bird song, no breath of air. No guards were on duty at the Kao Wang's personal entrance. The corpses of three men who had shot themselves in the cloister remained sprawled in messes of dried blood at which cockroaches now clustered. When he reached the palace garden he found a mound of freshly turned earth heaped in the corner. All around the Heavenly King's grave a multitude of young women hung suspended from the lemon trees. In their white robes they seemed to him like ghastly angels trapped between Heaven and Earth.

He took up a pruning hook and, one by one, cut them down. When he came back he found Fei sobbing.

The new moon showed its thinnest crescent in the dusk like a sign, and the next day at dawn the broad arm of the Yangtze running past Nanking Creek began to fill with hundreds of Imperial gunboats. They pulled rapidly downstream, running the gauntlet of the outer forts, and made the forts at the entrance of Nanking Creek their objective. They entered the channel between Tasohea Island and the mainland almost before the alarm was given and attacked the small fort at what British maps called Theodolite Point. Lindley watched as the island was taken and the three large Taiping war-junks that defended the mouth of Nanking Creek were set on fire. The other craft at anchor close by were boarded, plundered then set on fire too. By the end of the assault the Imperialists had captured Lung Potzu Shan – Dragon's Elbow Hill. It was the strategic key to the city.

As he and Fei stood together on the wall his eye traced the line of the Imperial siege works that now surrounded Nanking. He could not help but be impressed at the scale of them. They stretched for miles, with a double line of ditches and one hundred and forty mud forts standing six hundred yards apart, each fort housing at least five hundred men. Inside the starving city and its sham palaces all was quiet. Not a flag was flying there now, and a death-like stillness lay heavy on the air. When a movement did catch Lindley's eye it was just a group of Taiping foragers. He watched as half a dozen daring men were lowered from the wall by a rope to gather lentils outside. The men were ignored by the Imperialists whose stockades were no more than a hundred yards away, and it reminded Lindley of a moment along the river when he had seen deer drinking unmolested close to a mud bank where sated Yangtze crocodiles basked. No one's bothering to kill those men now, he told himself, because they're going to kill all of us soon.

The incident triggered a realization that sent a tremendous thrill of fear through him. All approaches to the city on the south, east and west were secured and the grain roads blocked. No field army existed outside to come to their rescue, except a unit that had been sent to try to capture Ningpo, and another rabble that followed the Shi Wang in distant Szechuan, a force that by now had degenerated into a band of brigands. In the hinterland of Shanghai there were still thousands of rebel garrison troops, but the clever ones among them would shave their heads and try to lose themselves among the population.

'The iron ring has closed,' he said, looking at the spoil heaps on Lung Potzu Shan. 'The encirclement is complete. There's no hope of relief. No possibility of another break out. Somehow we must convince your father and the Chung Wang to arrange a surrender.'

She looked at him wearily. 'There is no alternative but to fight to the death.'

He felt a stab of anger at her continuing rigidity of mind. 'I thought that when the darkness was lifted from your mind you'd begun to see sense.'

She touched him in a conciliatory way. 'Please don't be angry with me, Lin-li. I only meant that the Imperialists will not give up until they have killed us all.'

'Surely there must be reasonable men out there! Their commanders are scholars – educated men. How can they respond to a surrender with anything other than humanity? We only have to break down the barrier of mutual suspicion.'

'Lin-li, they are going to try to kill us all.'

'Fei, for God's sake, there's over a hundred thousand people in Nanking! They can't possibly kill us all!'

'They can. And they will. No matter how long it takes, they will do it. General Tseng dare not shrink from this difficult task. He knows that mercy cannot work.'

'Not a root must be left to sprout . . .' he said bitterly, sinking back into his own thoughts. After a while he said, 'I can't understand why General Tseng hasn't used Western siege guns. Bruce must have made them available to him. Well positioned Armstrong guns would reduce even these walls without the need to undermine them.'

'Mines will work eventually. General Tseng will do it his way. The Chinese way. He is no stranger to patience.'

The spoil heaps showed where the mines were being dug out. He had counted fourteen of them. 'It's inefficient to dig galleries under the walls and pack them with tons of powder. Many army coolies will die in those diggings. Any fool can see it requires infinitely more labour than bringing in a few pieces of modern artillery.'

She left one of her thoughtful pauses. 'Lin-li, don't you see? Efficiency is of no importance. The Imperialists revere authority and fear outside influence. They are fighting to uphold tradition. They will not countenance change. Our Taiping T'ien Kuo was revolutionary change. That's why we were so dangerous to them.'

He knew that she had made up her mind: Nanking was going to fall, and she was preparing to die.

The sun was barely slanting over the walls when Fei was thrown out of bed by the earthquake. As she came awake its grinding power shuddered through the palace, toppling a large decorative vase. She saw a crack open in the ceiling then, after an appalling silence in which she feared the ceiling would collapse on top of her, she heard the noise of masonry falling and roof tiles shattering and servants screaming in the courtyard.

Lindley was gone from the bed, and she shook herself out of her paralysis. She jumped up, ran into the dusty shafts of sunlight, looked up to where a monstrous demon had reared up – a rising cloud filling the sky. The courtyard was full of tile shards. The falling masonry she had heard were dozens of big grey bricks, the same big grey bricks that made up the perimeter wall, all showering back to earth.

'Fei! Where are you?' It was Lindley. 'Come with me!'

She grabbed up a robe to cover her nakedness and ran barefoot after him.

'What is it?'

'They've blown the mine at Lung Potzu Shan! There's a breach seventy paces wide in the wall right where the Imperials were massing for the final assault. The militiamen are sealing the palace citadel. We have to get away from here now.'

She threw off his arm. 'No, we must stay and fight!'

'Fei, they'll be pouring in through the breach. Where do you think they'll head? We have to get out of here!'

He took hold of her, but she fought and twisted. 'Listen to me! There's a tunnel that leads out close by the Taiping

502

Gate. My father and the other leaders have prepared for this moment. We must—'

'What did you say?'

'A unit of one thousand elite troops will force a way through and escape.'

He stared at her. 'They're planning to run off and leave everyone else to die? What despicable cowardice!'

'Not cowardice! They must escort the Young T'ien Wang to safety.' She willed him to understand. 'They intend to ride back to the mountains of the South and begin the movement anew.'

He grabbed her angrily. 'Fei, they won't get five miles! General Tseng has three cavalry divisions out there. They'll ride them down as if they were wild pigs.'

She faced him, her eyes speaking loud, 'They must go. Please believe me, they will kill everyone within the city walls.'

He seized her and shook her. 'If you can still trust anyone after what that madman did to you, you must trust me now!'

She felt him tearing her apart. 'But – my father.'

'You must leave him behind, as I have left mine. Now, will you come, or will you stay?'

His eyes pierced her until she could no longer stand it. She pulled the silk robe about her and followed him from the chamber.

They reached the gates as the palace guards were swinging them closed. Servants were fetching up timber props with which to fortify the middle against attack. The guard captain intercepted Fei and ordered her back but she argued with him while Lindley put himself in the way of the men who were putting the cross bar into position. Fei lied and threatened and got them to open the gates just wide enough for Lindley to squeeze out. He turned as he did so, grabbing her by the wrist, and pulling her to him.

'I'm in no mood for any of your tricks this time,' he told her. 'You're coming with me.'

Lindley used his size and strength to force a way through the crowd of starved and panic-stricken people who had gathered outside the citadel hoping to find safety there. The moment the gates slammed shut behind her Fei felt they had made a great mistake. They were trapped in a world of death and madness. Drum Tower Square was alive with men, women and children running in all directions. There were many bodies lying on the ground. She gagged as an acrid swirl of powder smoke blew over them. It sent shadows over the white walls and reddened the sun. The tremendous underground explosion that had shaken the foundations of the city had vomited thousands of tons of debris into the air, and it had come down everywhere. She saw Lindley staring around, his face grim as he took stock of the hellish scene. A maelstrom of distant musket fire filled the air with an eerie roaring, punctuated by bigger explosions. Lindley seized her hand and began shepherding her away from the square.

'Where are we going?' she demanded.

'When the river floods the wise man seeks high ground.'

'Our special place? Poet's hill?'

All hope left her. She followed him, knowing he had accepted death, that he was leading her to the most beautiful place he could think of to die. It was a mile to Hsiao Ts'ang Shan. The streets through which they struggled were strewn with wall bricks. Tens of thousands had fallen as a deadly rain, acting as a signal to those who had no means of fighting that Armageddon was at hand and that it was time to stand before Shang-ti.

Wherever they went they saw old men slaying grandchildren, husbands killing wives, sisters murdering sisters in any way they could – cutting down with knives, hanging, drowning. In a street of tall houses they ran among the bodies of those who had launched themselves into the air from high balconies. A little further along an ornamental pool was choked with the bodies of babies. They rounded a corner and smelled the stench of lamp oil and saw a family of six or seven huddled in a tight circle, all of them flaming hideously.

The horror drove them on, but they could not outrun it. When they reached the summit they found their favourite plum trees stripped of all leaf as the Heavenly King had ordered, and the lone body of the gardener sitting in a bloody chair, his throat deeply cut. Despite everything Fei saw there was something especially grotesque about the way the gardener's wound gaped and laughed at her. She turned away from the sight. Lindley picked up the knife and looked at it with empty eyes. Then he tossed it to the ground.

Poet's hill afforded a panoramic view of the assault, and Lindley watched it unfold expressionlessly for a few moments, before putting his head in his hands and going to sit alone. Fei continued to look out. She saw how the mine had blasted a huge and indefensible breach in the walls. Tens of thousands of Imperial troops were drawn up in blocks beyond it, waiting to be ordered through. Tens of thousands more were presently clambering in over the crater and rubble heaps. Musket flashes showed where the Taiping defenders were firing into the unstoppable flood. She thought of her father and the Young T'ien Wang and the others who would even now be attempting to flee from the palace. It seemed to her suddenly as if she was seeing through Lindley's wise, foreign eyes. Having looked down on the endless hosts ranged against the city, all escape was shown to be absurd, a desperate last gasp that was doomed to fail. How much better to accept what must be in peace and tranquillity.

All over the city now fires were burning. Black smoke was smudging the sky. On the far side of the city the walls were swarming with people climbing up and throwing themselves down into the moat, so that Chin-kuai creek was filling with bodies. When looking down from a great height a person could feel like a god, wholly remote from all the ant-like killing and dying.

She watched the Imperial advance guard win the fierce hand-to-hand fighting and begin gradually to fan out into the city, but their victory was no longer important. What was happening seemed only to be an inevitable consequence of what had gone before. She felt no urge to fight, only an overwhelming sadness that the story of the Great Kingdom of Heavenly Peace should have turned out in the end to have been a tragedy. It was time to finish it.

When tongues of fire began to lick out from under the gaudy eaves of the T'ien Wang's palace Fei composed herself. She went to stand before Lindley, offering him the bloody knife in both hands. When he roused himself to look at her she said respectfully, 'It is your prerogative as husband to choose how to kill me, but I would prefer you not to cut my throat.'

He did not move. He just stared at her sightlessly.

'But when I'm dead,' she asked quietly. 'Who will kill you?'

He reached out and took the knife from her and laid it carefully on the ground. Then he hugged her to him.

Yehonala sat behind the yellow silk screen listening to Tsai-ch'un fidget and sigh.

The Emperor sat on his over-large throne waiting for his courtiers to rise from the kowtow in the vast twilight of the Hall of Supreme Harmony. When they had done so and all was silence the Emperor's voice fluted among the giant red columns.

'An express courier from Tseng Kuo-fan, travelling six hundred li a day, has just arrived at our capital. It bears the red banner of decisive victory, and a memorial describing the capture of Nanking, the suicide by burning of the rebel leader, the complete destruction of the Taiping host and the capture of two of their leading commanders. Perusal of this Memorial fills us with the deepest joy and gratitude, which all our people will share. The leader of the long-haired rebels, one Hung Hsiu-ch'uan, first raised his standard of revolt in the thirtieth year of Tao-kuang . . .'

Yehonala closed her eyes and let her mind drift as her son's unbroken voice haltingly recounted the Taipings' savage crimes. She thought of An Te-hai, and the vanities that had entrapped him. She considered the rewards she had decided to heap upon Tseng Kuo-fan. Then her mind drifted back to the stories she had been told on her grandfather's knee when she was half Tsai-ch'un's age, the stories that had guided her as surely as destiny's hand.

'Ah, little one, Sun Tzu Wu was a native of the Ch'i State. The thirteen chapters of his *Art of War* brought him to the notice of Ho-lu, King of Wu. Ho-lu said to him, "I have carefully perused your theory of managing soldiers, and I have a question."

'Sun Tzu replied, "Majesty, please ask it."

'Ho-lu said, "Does your theory also hold good when applied to women?"

'Sun Tzu said there was no reason why it should not, so Ho-lu said, "Then, you will not mind if I test your theory in practice."'

Yehonala had listened, rapt, as her grandfather had told her how two hundred ladies had been brought out of the Palace, how Sun Tzu had divided them into two armies, and then selected the King's two most favourite concubines to be put in charge.

'Then Sun Tzu addressed them all thus, "You each have a spear. Do each of you know the difference between front and back, right hand and left hand?" The girls all said that they did. Sun Tzu said, "When I say 'Eyes front', you must look straight ahead. When I say 'Left turn', you must face towards your left hand. When I say 'Right turn', you must face towards your right hand. When I say 'About turn', you must face right round towards your back."

'Again the girls agreed. So, the words of command having been thus explained, Sun Tzu began the drill. To the sound of drums he gave the order, "Right turn", but the girls only burst out laughing.

'Sun Tzu told them, "If words of command are not clear and distinct, if orders are not thoroughly understood, then the general is to blame."

'With that he started drilling them again, and this time he gave the order, "Left turn", whereupon the girls once more began laughing. Sun Tzu said, "If words of command are not clear and distinct, if orders are not thoroughly understood, the general is to blame. But if his orders are clear, and the soldiers nevertheless disobey, then it is the fault of their officers." So saying, he ordered the leaders of the two armies to be beheaded.'

Yehonala remembered the icy thrill that had passed through her at that moment. She had searched her grandfather's face, and seen that he was telling the truth.

'What happened then, grandfather?'

'The king of Wu was watching the scene from the top of a raised pavilion. And when he saw that his favourite concubines were about to be executed he sent down a message that read: "We are now quite satisfied as to our general's ability to handle troops. If we are bereft of these two concubines our meat and drink will lose their savour. It is our wish that they shall not be beheaded."'

Yehonala remembered that she had felt relief then, as if it had been her own neck that had been in jeopardy, but her relief had not lasted long because her grandfather had said,

'Sun Tzu made his reply: "Your majesty told me that you wished to test my theory in practice. Having once received your commission to be the general of your forces, discipline is now a matter for me alone."'

'What happened, grandfather?' she had asked, horrified and already sure what the answer would be.

'Of course, the two leaders were beheaded. And straight away another two were installed in their place. And when this was done the drum was sounded and the drill was begun once more. This time the girls turned right and left, marched ahead and back again, all with perfect accuracy and precision, not venturing to utter a sound. Then Sun Tzu sent a messenger to the King saying: "Your soldiers are now properly drilled and disciplined, and ready for your Majesty's inspection. They can be put to any use that their sovereign may desire. Order them to go through fire and water, and they will not disobey."'

Yehonala sighed, remembering how she had been filled with the great sadness that the world should be so hard a place, but knowing that it was not the prerogative of men to change the nature of the world. That this was the work of the gods . . .

Her mind returned her to the present. Tsai-ch'un was coming to the end of the speech.

'This glorious victory at Nanking is entirely due to the bountiful protection of Heaven, to the ever-present help of our Ancestors, and to the foresight and wisdom of the Empresses Regent, who, by employing and promoting efficient leaders for our armies, have thus secured cooperation of all our forces and the accomplishment of this great achievement whereby the soul of our late father in Heaven must be comforted and the desire of all people fulfilled . . .'

The Emperor's young voice still mouthed Tseng's report.

'After exhuming the so-called Heavenly King's body I beheaded it and burned it on a large bonfire. The blackened skull is now being exhibited in those provinces laid waste by the rebellion.

'I am sending his bogus seals to Peking that they may be deposited in the Imperial Archives Department. They were captured with the prisoner known as the Kao Wang. I cross-examined him minutely. His confession, written out in his own hand, is thirty thousand words long.

'My staff advised that all the Taiping leaders we captured should be sent to Peking in a cage. The foreigner, Gordon, also urged this, but it is my judgement that the high prestige of your Sacred Dynasty needs no such sending of petty rebels as trophies or prisoners of war. After the Kao Wang was put in his cage here, another rebel leader was brought into camp. As soon as he caught sight of the Kao Wang, he went down on his knees and saluted him most respectfully. After that I judged it imperative to behead all leaders, and this sentence has now been carried out.

'The two elder brothers of the "Heavenly King" were men of a cruel and savage nature, who committed many foul and impious crimes. When captured, they were in a dazed state, and could only mumble "God the Father, God the Father." I had them both beheaded. I have duly suspended their heads from long poles, and the sight of them has given great and general satisfaction to the Common People.

'And now, victory being ours, I am led to the reflection that this your Dynasty surpasses all its predecessors in martial glory. Here in Nanking not a single rebel surrendered. Many burned themselves alive rather than be taken. Such things are unparalleled in history, and we feel that the final happy issue is due to the consummate virtue and wisdom of his late Majesty, which alone made victory possible. We, who so unworthily hold your high command, grieve greatly that His Imperial Majesty did not live to see his work crowned with triumph.'

Yehonala looked through the yellow gauze at the expectant assembly. The Court had been called to witness the Decree she had written in her son's name recording the fall of Nanking, and so formally transmute the fluid river of events into the solid rock of history.

The boy-Emperor allowed silence to settle once more, then as the courtiers waited he looked around him as imperiously as he could, until a whisper from behind the yellow screen told him to climb down from the throne.

Tomorrow he would come again to the Hall of Supreme Harmony to deliver another Decree announcing that he would go in person to offer thanksgiving at all Imperial temples and shrines, and to make sacrifice to the deities of the sacred mountains and rivers of the Empire.

That's as it must be, Yehonala thought. As it must ever be.

They stepped ashore at the British Concession in the pouring rain. The Bund was grey and muddy and thronging with traffic.

After being captured on Hsiao Ts'ang Shan, Lindley and Fei had been marched before a senior Imperial officer and interrogated. Lindley had begged Fei not to open her mouth, then he had told them, 'I'm a captured British officer and this lady is my Japanese wife.'

They had been imprisoned and he had expected execution, but a reprieve had come, courtesy of Major Gordon. Even so, it had taken weeks for them to be released and to reach Shanghai.

'You see,' he told her the instant they stepped off the Imperial gunboat. 'You can deny your past if you try.'

'I did not deny.'

'Yes you did. By your silence. And I'm so proud of you.'

'I stayed quiet only because I knew they would kill you, Lin-li.'

'No. I've seen it in your eyes. You no longer believe. You know that I was right all along – that what you believed was wicked madness that seized hold of people's minds. You're free from it now, Fei. We're all free from it. Be glad.'

He pulled a page of one of his father's letters from an inside pocket. It was worn through at the folds, and the rain spattered the paper now, washing away the ink as he read.

'The Almighty Power has seen fit to kindle the glimmering sparks of the first Protestant movement in Asia. It has lighted a torch that may not easily be extinguished. Faint and obscure as that light may burn amid the gloom of persecution, this is what has always marked the dawn of Christianity among heathens. The moment will come soon when that smouldering spark will burst into an all-consuming fire.'

He tossed the paper into the road and watched as the bare feet of Chinese porters trod it into the mud. Then he looked up at the arms above the entrance to the British Consulate.

Meadows admitted him immediately and said without ceremony, 'Still alive, Lindley? You do surprise me.'

'Acerbic as ever, Mr Meadows. You know, I believe you're the most cynical man I've ever met.'

Meadows plucked the dart out and smiled. 'And where's your "Japanese" wife?'

'I asked her to wait outside.'

'How appropriate. Well . . . what can I do for you?'

'We want to know what happened to her father.'

'Ah, yes. The big cheese.' Meadows steepled his fingers, all levity suddenly gone. 'Tz'u-hsi ordered the Kao Wang sent to Peking alive and in a cage, to be exhibited as a warning to the people.'

'Oh, for God's sake . . .'

'Yes, quite. But it seems that General Tseng, realizing the dangers of that course, had him beheaded immediately he completed his written confession.' Meadows looked at the ceiling bleakly. 'From his point of view it was a very prudent thing to do. And a mercy for which your father-in-law was no doubt most grateful.'

'Yes. I suppose you're right.'

'I usually am. By the way, you owe your lives to Major Gordon. He remembered meeting you and was struck by your impressive rudeness. He took command of the Ever-victorious Army when your American friend was shot down.' Meadows looked him up and down. 'One of the Filipinos left this for you. I dare say it means something to you.'

Meadows took from his desk drawer a small yellow jade carving on a blood red cord. Lindley took it.

'Thank you,' he said, with Ward in spirit. 'It does.'

'Well, there it is. Now, if there's nothing else . . .?'

Lindley collected Fei and left the Consulate in silence.

'What did Mr Meadows say?'

'That your father died with dignity. His "confession" was unrepentant.'

She closed her eyes.

Lindley said, 'I'm sorry I called your father a charlatan. I was wrong about that. He was true to his beliefs.'

'Yes.'

'Meadows said it was as merciful a death as your father could have expected.'

'Yes.'

A dousing rain came on as they reached the French

511

Concession. Lindley took Fei's hand as they approached the house Ward had built for his bride. It looked to Lindley very much like the one he had come to on his first day in Shanghai, except that someone had tried to burn this one down.

A blonde-haired woman stood near the gate, bedraggled. They watched as she threw a rose into the fire-blackened doorway.

'Annie? Annie Phillips?' Lindley asked.

As she turned her disturbing green eyes looked into his. 'Hello, Dr Lindley.'

'What . . . happened here?'

'A fire. Just a fire. All burned out now. What are you here for? To gloat?' The sudden bitterness of her words shocked him.

'Gloat? Annie, why do you say that?'

'That's what everyone else comes here to do. They want to see the house of the Great White Mandarin.'

He struggled to overcome her rancour. 'We just came by to pay our respects to his widow.'

For a moment she seemed not to hear, but then she tossed her head and said, 'Well you can't. Chang-mei's dead.'

He supposed she meant that Ward's wife had died in the fire, maybe even that she had started it.

'Was she . . . burned?' he asked.

'No, Dr Lindley. Not burned.'

'Then, how did she die?'

'She just stopped living.'

'Annie, what do you mean?'

She looked up. 'Chang-mei died of a broken heart. Some people do. She was a bad luck woman, you know.'

Lindley felt the depth of Annie's sense of loss and knew there was nothing he could say to comfort her. 'Annie . . . if you need anything . . .'

'Thank you. But no. I don't need charity.' She looked around forlornly, then she seemed to reconnect with the world and she fixed her gaze on him. 'You know his body's lying in an open casket in Sung-chiang. Have you visited it yet?'

He shook his head. 'Not yet. Have you?'

'No. I don't want to see him like that.'

'Like what?'

She gave a small shrug. 'In those mandarin robes. With a tiger on his chest and a clown hat on his head. I'm told the powder and glaze of Chinese embalmers makes a face ghastly to Western eyes.'

'He's at peace now, Annie.'

Ugliness filled her girlish face. 'Peace? He'll never be at peace until the world knows how they murdered him. Betrayed like Our Lord himself, by one of his own.'

'Annie he's a hero. He died in action.'

'No, Dr Lindley! They murdered him!'

He saw how close to the edge she was. 'Why do you say that?'

'Because it's true! The bullet that was taken out of his body was fired from a Sharps rifle. Yes – it was fired from his own side.'

Lindley shook his head slowly, not wanting to believe. 'Who told you that?'

She made a sound that was halfway between a laugh and a sob. 'You think I'm making it up, don't you? You think I'm mad. I'm not, you know.'

'Annie, I don't think you're mad.'

Her eyes swam. 'I loved that man. I really loved him.'

He took a step forward, tried to take her shoulders, but she pulled away from him. 'I know what happened. He always carried a little blue accounts book around with him. It disappeared. Along with seventy thousand taels of silver. And all trace of the money Yang Fang owed him. And Edward Forrest.'

'Forrest?' Fei looked to him. Lindley shook his head again, but this time he believed. Ed Forrest had been the paymaster for the Corps.

'Yes, Forrest. He's the one who killed him. Vincente Macanaya told me that before he went home to Manila.'

Lindley took the news with infinite sadness. It was difficult to accept so ironic a trick of fate, but ten thousand times harder to know that at the core was an act of human greed. He asked, 'Annie, what will you do? Have you spoken to Eden?'

The name of her husband seemed to awaken Annie's streak of stubborn self-reliance. She wiped the rain from her cheek with a quick hand. 'My life's my own, Dr Lindley. For what it's worth. As long as I can keep myself I'm as happy as a flower. What about you?'

'We thought . . . Hong Kong.' He shrugged. 'It's where we met, and where our worlds meet.'

'Well, good luck to you both. I have to go now.'

She turned, and they watched her go, alone, her boots crunching over the wet cinders of the road. They waited for a few minutes more, sheltering in the burned shell of the house. Inside Lindley saw a strewn mass of broken porcelain – the figures of the eight Immortals. He bent down and picked up the fire-blackened head of Lu Tung-pin, the warrior. He showed it to Fei wordlessly, then tossed it back where he had found it. When the rain stopped they left for the Bund, and did not dare look back.

HISTORICAL NOTE

Our story ends with a departure, just as it began with an arrival, but real lives go on when stories end. Here are a few of them . . .

YEHONALA
Forever after known by the title Tz'u-hsi, Yehonala maintained her place as Dowager Empress of China through many crises and into old age. Throughout her reign she continued her policy of keeping out the Barbarians, and ensured the Manchu dynasty survived into the twentieth century. The 'Queen Victoria of China' died in 1908, after a life in almost all respects more prodigious than her British equivalent.

TSAI-CH'UN
Little Tsai-ch'un's short life turned out to be every bit as strait-jacketed by tradition and ritual as Yehonala had foreseen. He lived the arid existence of a child emperor and never attained full manhood, falling victim to the smallpox in his nineteenth year. For every one of those years he was dominated by his mother.

PRINCE KUNG
The Prince continued at the heart of Chinese politics, manoeuvring step for step with Tz'u-hsi for over twenty years before finally being thrown down. He went into forced retirement in 1884, but was hastily summoned back into public life after his predictions about the 'terrible ferocious islanders' came to fruit when the Japanese invaded China in 1894. His recall was all too late to prevent defeat, and he died of a fever in 1898.

HAI-LUNG

For those wondering about the fate of Yehonala's sleeve dog, Sea Otter, history records that one of the treasures removed from the Summer Palace was a wandering Pekingese dog. The British officer who took him away christened him 'Lootie' and, on returning to England, presented him to Queen Victoria.

His portrait was painted by F. W. Keyl, a pupil of Landseer. Perhaps Sea Otter was always destined to be an Empress's dog.

*

GORDON

After the rebellion ended Charles George Gordon returned to England, famous as 'Chinese Gordon'. Never comfortable with public adulation he spent the following decade carrying through the British government's policy of stamping out the abhorrent East African slave trade. A much-travelled career of what we would now call 'shuttle diplomacy' ensued.

Chinese Gordon is better known to us today as 'Gordon of Khartoum' after the African city where he died, a spear thrust through his heart, in 1885.

FREDERICK TOWNSEND WARD

F. T. Ward died on the 22nd September, 1862. His body was returned to Sung-chiang, where it was interred after the Chinese fashion, dressed in the uniform in which he was married.

Fifteen years afterwards, a wall was set around his tomb and a hall built to honour the memory of 'General Hua'. Incense was burned daily at his shrine for almost a century. Finally, during China's Cultural Revolution, the site was levelled and the garden of remembrance paved over.

Those interested enough to look for it will find a modest granite memorial to Ward still standing in a churchyard in the town of Salem, Massachusetts, and some of his worldly possessions in the Peabody and Essex museum in Salem's East India Square.

*

THE TAIPINGS

Most of those who had pledged themselves to die for the T'ien Wang fulfilled their promise to him.

Of those who did not, tens of thousands found their way to Singapore and to the British Crown Colony of Hong Kong, to begin new lives in a new community safe from the unanswerable questions of Imperial mandarins.

Other former Taipings fled far overseas, many of them to the United States, where thousands took work laying the railroads and helping to build the new cities of the Far West.